The Involuntary Human

David Gerrold

NESFA Press

Post Office Box 809
Framingham, MA 01701
www.nesfa.org/press
2007

FIRST EDITION, February 2007

ISBN-10: 1-886778-68-X (trade)
ISBN-10: 1-886778-69-8 (slipcased)
ISBN-13: 978-1-886778-68-9 (trade)
ISBN-13: 978-1-886778-69-6 (slipcased)

The Involuntary Human was printed in a limited hardcover
edition of 1000 copies, of which the first ten were slipcased,
signed by the author and artist, and lettered A–J, the next 165
were slipcased, signed by the author and artist, and numbered
1–165 and the remaining 825 copies were numbered 166–990.

This is book ___487___

Publication History

"The Truth About David Gerrold" by Spider Robinson first appears in this volume.

"Author's Rebuttal" by David Gerrold first appears in this volume.

"Interlude #1: Selections from *The Quote-Book of Solomon Short*" first appears in this volume.

"Interlude #2" through "Interlude #6" are excerpts from a privately printed chapbook, *The Quote-Book of Solomon Short* (2002), some quotations from which were used in the first four books of the series, *The War Against the Chtorr,* David Gerrold's "epic seven-book trilogy about an ecological infestation of the Earth..."

"The Martian Child" first appeared in *The Magazine of Fantasy & Science Fiction*, September 1994

"Pickled Mongoose" is an excerpt from *The Martian Child* (Forge Books, 2002)

"Blood and Fire" is an unproduced *Star Trek: The Next Generation* script that appears for the first time in this volume.

"A Shaggy Dog Story" first appeared in *Rod Serling's The Twilight Zone Magazine*, May/June 1986

"The Strange Death of Orson Welles" first appears in this volume.

"It Needs Salt" is an excerpt from the planned, but not yet formally scheduled, *A Time for Treason*, Book Six of *The War Against the Chtorr,* David Gerrold's "epic seven-book trilogy about..."

"The Satanic Limericks #1" and "The Satanic Limericks #2" first appear in this volume.

"...And Eight Rabid Pigs" first appeared in *Night Screams*, ed. by Ed Gorman & Martin H. Greenberg (Roc, 1996)

3

"The Baby Cooper Dollar Bill" is an excerpt from *A Day for Damnation* (Timescape, 1984), Book Two of *The War Against the Chtorr,* David Gerrold's "epic seven-book trilogy about..."

"Digging in Gehenna" first appeared in *Men Writing Science Fiction as Women,* ed. by Mike Resnick (DAW, 2003)

"King Kong: Behind the Scenes" first appeared in *King Kong Is Back! An Unauthorized Look at One Humongous Ape!,* ed. by David Brin (BenBella Books, November 2005)

"King Kong: The Unanswered Questions" first appeared in a slightly different form in *Kong Unbound: The Cultural Impact, Pop Mythos, and Scientific Plausibility of a Cinematic Legend,* ed. by Karen Haber (Simon & Schuster, November 2005) It was revised for this volume.

"The Kennedy Enterprise" first appeared in *Alternate Kennedys,* ed. by Mike Resnick (Tor Books, 1992)

"Chester" first appeared in *The Magazine of Fantasy & Science Fiction,* June 2005

Chess with a Dragon was first published in 1987 by Walker & Company in a modified form. The author's original version appears for the first time in this volume.

"The Green Man" first appeared in *The Peddler and the Cloud,* ed. by Scott Badger (Five Badgers Press, December 2000)

"The Diamond Sky" first appeared in *Hal's Worlds: Stories and Essays in Memory of Hal Clement,* ed. by Shane Tourtellotte (Wildside Press, October 2005)

"Riding Janis" first appeared in *Stars,* ed. by Janis Ian & Mike Resnick (DAW, 2003)

"Dancer in the Dark" first appeared in *The Magazine of Fantasy & Science Fiction,* April 1994

"thirteen o'clock" first appeared in *The Magazine of Fantasy & Science Fiction,* February 2006

Contents

For Tony and Suford Lewis, with love.

The Involuntary Human

The Truth About David Gerrold

By Spider Robinson

FOR DECADES NOW, David and I have had a tradition of writing gag intros for one another, for convention program books or collections like this one, typically consisting of the kinds of jokes one hears told at a roast, made even more virulent by a high pun content, and avoiding as far as possible any slightest taint of truth. But after all these years it has finally dawned on me that comedy is hard work, and that it's amazing how much mature wisdom resembles being too tired.

So, for lack of anything else to do, I guess I'll just tell you the truth for once:

David Gerrold is one of the reasons I do what I do. Why I started in the first place, and why I keep on doing it now that I know better.

Because he continually reminds me *why* I'm doing it. Every time I start to feel I'm wasting my time annoying a keyboard, and am tempted to reconsider a life of crime, he and a bare handful of others keep reminding me what a holy chore, an amazing privilege, and a stone gas it is to be a science fiction writer. That's why one of the most important characters in *Variable Star* by Robert A. Heinlein and Spider Robinson is named Solomon Short.

Like Crosby, Stills, Nash and Young, David is a Sixties Survivor Entering His Sixties who has not just survived but flourished, kept getting higher, kept evolving, kept growing. I'm about the same age as he is, and I wish I could say the same. He still believes, still walks the walk, still claps for Tink—with more grace and style than ever. He's *still* getting better with each story, each book. He's been having one hell of a lot of fun since Day One, and he ain't done yet; evidence indicates he's just getting started.

Like most of the world, I noticed David Gerrold right away. Mr. Scott's final pun at the end of the *Star Trek* episode "The Trouble With Tribbles," David's first sale, made me shout with pleasure. And there were some even more breathtaking puns in his first novel, *The Flying Sorcerers*. (How many were his, and how many can be blamed on co-author Larry Niven? Quick story. In Larry's own solo novel *Ringworld Engineers*, the villain is a Puppeteer named The Hindmost. I spent the whole book waiting for some character to exclaim, "The devil take the hindmost!", and when it failed to happen, I wrote Larry, congratulating him on his enormous restraint. He wrote back, "Spider, it never occurred to me.") I figured if David could get away with puns as unconscionable as the protagonist's name, there was room in the business for someone like me.

But it was equally clear right from the start that he was far more than just a funnyman. The Tribble script was *not* a shaggy-alien story; its humor arose not from situation but from its *characters*—and the author's fondness for them was almost palpable. The same with *Flying Sorcerers*: it wasn't just funnier than a typical Niven novel, it was more *empathic*, more compassionate toward its clueless characters, human and alien alike. (Please don't take any of this as any kind of knock on Larry: he has unique strengths of his own that nobody in the business past or present can match, deserves his dozens of Hugos and Nebulas, and is one of my all-time favorite authors.)

I missed *The Space Skimmer* because I was living in a shack on the shore of the Bay of Fundy at the time, way too busy nursing the garden, turning tall trees into firewood and chopping through a foot of ice for water for morning coffee to get a whole lot of reading done by kerosene lamplight. But I had surfaced again by 1977, and *Moonstar Odyssey* hit me like a bolt of lightning. I'd known this Gerrold guy was good, sure—but I'd had no idea he was Sturgeon-good, Pangborn-good, one of those whose characters become instant old friends.

I was *Galaxy*'s resident book reviewer by then, and I gave that book one of the strongest raves I ever printed. But that just didn't feel like enough. I sent him a letter, whose exact content is long gone from my leaky memory, but the gist of it must have been something like, "I am one of you. You are one of me. Glad you're there, brother." And he wrote back something along the lines of, "I know. We're going to be good friends for a long time."

And so it has come to pass. Thirty years later, we are still good friends. Despite the puns. And an irritating tendency to write trilogies of at least five volumes. And to still win Hugos and Nebulas. And get big movie sales. And drive the coolest car in North America. And tell better dialect jokes than I do.

Come to think of it, the hell with the bastard. Let him write his own furshlugginer intro: I'm out of here.

All right, all right—one Gerrold pun first. *One.*

By great good fortune, the very first time I ever entered Disneyland, my guides were the two people who love that place more than anyone since Walt died: Herb Varley and David Gerrold. It was a totally pleasant day, one of the happiest in my well-stocked memory.

Until we boarded the jungle boat ride at Adventureland, and David started to get steamed.

It's hard not to enjoy robot hippos squirting water at you, and audio-animatronic cannibals menacing you with spears. But the boat's captain kept up a running barrage of attempted humor over loudspeakers throughout the voyage. His jokes were abominable, but what really drove David crazy was the grossly substandard quality of the man's puns. They dishonored the artform. To his credit, David managed to grit his teeth and remain silent for the entire trip.

But as we all prepared to disembark, he leaned over and murmured to me and Herb, "Now, Luke, you will get to see the *dock* side of the farce."

Disneyland didn't even throw us out, once Herb and I explained *why* we had pushed him into the water.

*   *   *

[HBO LOGO]

[music:] "Woke Up This Mornin'," by Alabama 3

THE ALTOS

[SINGER:]

Woke up this mornin'
Wrote himself a pun
David Gerrold been committin' that crime since
Harlie was one...

He adopted a Martian child who
Learned to fly
Born under a good sign with a
Hugo in his eye

[CHORUS:]

Woke up this mornin'
Wrote himself a pun

[SINGER:]

Woke up this mornin'
Readers gettin' sore
Takes him a long damn time to
Mind the Chtorr

He was taken to Heaven but found it
Felt like court
Old Jehovah was pissed that he called
Solomon short…

Got a Jagger-sized basket when he
Starts to dance
No it isn't a codpiece—that's a
Tribble in his pants

[CHORUS:]

David
Woke up this mornin'…
Went right back to sleep
Went right back to sleep
Went right back to sleep

—Tottering-on-the-Brink,
9 September 2006

Author's Rebuttal

To put it in fannish terms, it's time to wrap myself in the cloak of darkness, wield the axe of contrition ("when I hit you with it, you're going to be very very sorry"), lift up my shield of virtue (Hah!) and toss the ring of truth into the volcano—lest I be tempted to put it on one more time and actually say what's really on my mind, and get myself into a lot more trouble than the last time I thought I could get away with it.

Ohell, what can it hurt? I'll just do it until I need glasses.

See, where this started—Tony and Suford Lewis asked me to be the Guest of Honor for Boskone 2007. Putting aside the fact that I've only been waiting for this invitation for 37 years, I said yes. Boskone is one of the most prestigious of all science fiction conventions, it really is an *honor* to be invited as a guest.

Please don't tell the folks who run Philcon, or the folks who run Loscon that I said this, but honest—the fans in Boston seem to be the most intelligent in the world. They don't just collect books, they actually *read* them. Even better than that, they seem to understand what they're reading—and when they approach an author, even if it's only for an autograph, they have the good sense to kneel deferentially, present a box of dark chocolate (Dove or Godiva preferred) and then (three cheers for Boston!) ask an intelligent question that demonstrates a profound awareness of the philosophical dilemma the author has so carefully crafted in the volume in question. What self-respecting author (or even an author with no self-respect, for that matter) could resist?

So, okay, I have yet to attend a convention that will host the one event I have been requesting for the last 37 years of guest-of-honor invitations—nude wrestling with redheads (any gender, I'm not picky) in chocolate sauce. I'm even willing to supply the chocolate sauce. *But no!* Not a single convention has recognized the enormous entertainment value this would have, not to mention making an old man happy by granting his last dying wish. (Okay, I'm not that old, yet, but I'm not above a little shameless pandering to the latent Jewish guilt of whatever fan is gullible enough to fall for it.) And I do want to go on record that the continued denial of this simple request does represent some kind of discrimination—after all, Joe Haldeman got a bathtub full of lime Jell-O at a long-remembered and now legendary Boskone. All I want is a legend of my own. Is that too much to ask? Never mind.

I attended my first Boskone in February of 1969, or maybe it was 1970, I don't remember much of that time clearly—nobody does really, it was the cusp between the sixties and the seventies—but it was one of those seminal events that expanded the event horizon of my sense of wonder. It was a warm, friendly, exciting experience where I actually got to sit and chat with an enormous number of people I'd been admiring since pre-adolescence—folks like Isaac Asimov, Hal Clement, Fred Pohl (who I admire enormously, despite the fact he *never* bought a story of mine while he was editor of Galaxy), Lester del Rey, Betty and Ian Ballantine, Ben Bova, Harry Harrison, and Anne McCaffrey, to name-drop a few. I also got to hang out with a lot of new friends like Larry Niven, Rick Sternbach, Russell Seitz, and the aforementioned Tony and Suford Lewis. It *is* true. You never forget your first kiss, your first time, your first sale, or your first Boskone.

I remember it vividly. Several of us were sprawled across bed, chair, and couch of someone's room party, creating group limericks…

> *The view from the seventeenth floor*
> *is awfully hard to ignore.*
> > *The Suicide Club*
> > *has come up from the pub*
> *to produce a free-fall Ruddigore.* *

> **(This one was wrought by committee,*
> *Stealing credit would really be shitty,*
> > *so thank Russell Seitz,*
> > *who provided delights*
> *when he wrote the last line of the ditty.)*

Someday, I promise—unless someone stops me, either by an act of extreme violence or by offering me large sums of cash not to—I will publish my own book of limericks. Really. As soon as I can find a publisher willing to take the risk. I'm not kidding. For some reason, nobody wants to publish a volume called *The Satanic Limericks.* Publishers, sheesh.

But it was also at that party that I began picking some brains. (Sternbach's was the one in the middle.) I mentioned that I had been thinking about how to invade the Earth—and despite several sharply pointed remarks that it wasn't worth the bother, there's no intelligent life there—I began speculating aloud about how to do it without the investment in a lot of technology. I postulated a biological infestation. Send seeds. If the soil is fertile, add water and wait a hundred years. In the space of a feverish hour or two, several of the best minds in pre-Star Wars fandom collaborated on the invention of the proto-Chtorran ecology, much of which was eventually incorporated into my seven-book trilogy...etc. Never mind, that's another novel.

But that's one of the reasons I love Boskone. It gave me a mission— to write an epic tale so fucking big and all-consuming that it would eat up the rest of my life and keep me from having all the other great adventures I had planned, like sail around the world on a tramp steamer, be quality control in a Hong Kong whorehouse (I did get to Hong Kong eventually, but I couldn't find the whorehouse), take a coast-to-coast bicycle trip, learn to be an *est*-trainer and transform the quality of other people's lives, wrestle nude with redheads in chocolate sauce, backpack across Europe with a guitar and a typewriter, learn to play the guitar so I can backpack across Europe with a guitar and a typewriter, join an all-gay desert commune in Arizona and grow my own food while wearing nothing but a loincloth and a beatific attitude, have an illicit love affair with Candice Bergen, star in a revival production of *Oh Dad, Poor Dad, Momma's Hung You in the Closet and I'm Feeling So Sad*, and adopt a small child and teach him about the wonders of sci-fi. (He wasn't interested, honest! He thought girls were more fun than tribbles and light-sabres. Mea culpa. My biggest failure. I've tried to understand his chosen life style, but...never mind.)

The point is, I could have had a life. A real life. I coulda been a film director if I hadn't attended that Boskone. I coulda remade *Them!* Instead, I have an unfinished seven-book trilogy...that generates an inordinate amount of angry email from readers who have decided in their own heads that I am somehow personally obligated to them to turn out each new volume on a predictable schedule, and that my failure (refusal) to do so is a deliberate affront to each of them individually. (I will say nothing further about the manners of readers. They're paying my mortgage.)

At subsequent Boskones, I met Spider and Jeanne Robinson. I fell in love immediately with Jeanne. Who wouldn't? Beautiful, talented, enlightened, and wise. Plus, a smile to die for. Spider, on the other hand...well, let me put it this way. Someone who can wring three variations out of one breathtakingly awful pun in the space of two minutes—"So we put

out thorazine-laden bread for the seabirds, we left no tern unstoned."
"We visited the George Hamilton tanning competition. The motto was
'No stern left untoned.'" "If you get up to Vancouver, come and visit us.
Just follow the road to the sign that says 'no left turn unstoned.'"—is
probably a man you should only approach with a torch and a pitchfork,
preferably with a mob of similarly armed villagers.

In the years that followed, I returned annually to Boskone, as part of
my regular migratory pattern. (Certain sociology students have postulated that this was somehow related to my breeding habits, but I digress.
Pay no attention to what that man is doing behind the curtain. If you're
genuinely interested in *my* mating behaviors, you should worry about
the paucity of your imagination. If you're really that desperate for entertainment, feel free to speculate and start whatever rumors you wish. Or
call Mike Resnick and let *him* start a few rumors. Just let me know and
I'll invent sixteen other rumors to keep them company. The only thing
worse than being gossiped about is *not* being gossiped about. I'll give
you the list of names to start with. Just don't ask about me and Candice
Bergen. Please.)

But back to Boskone. Good beer, good friends, intelligent and literate
readers. Yes. My ideal science fiction convention. Even better, someone
else is paying for my transportation, room, and meals. What could be
better than that? Why, this book, of course—a book that celebrates some
of the better stories I've written in my career.

Which brings me peripatetically back to Spider Robinson.

See, once I started planning this book with the Boskone committee,
I allowed myself the delightful fantasy that whoever wrote the introduction would take this collection seriously enough to say some really nice
things about my fevered history at the keyboard. Perhaps the chosen
person would write something like, "Gerrold writes the most passionate characters in science fiction, they live and breathe and bleed more
than most real people." Or perhaps he or she would write, "Gerrold's
insight into the human condition is matched only by his outrageous
sense of humor." Or maybe, the key sentence might be, "Gerrold is
a literary-Zelig. Science fiction hasn't seen a stylist this limber since
Heinlein discorporated."

I admit it, it was a fantasy—a little bit of shameless wallowing in
accolade. But it was an understandable fantasy, because after all, this *is*
Boskone, and as I said above, Boskone is one of the best conventions
in the world, probably in a three-way tie with Philcon and Loscon. So
I was living in hope that somewhere at the beginning of this volume,
there would be some genuinely respectful acknowledgment of (at least)
the ambition underlying the work.

Then they asked Spider Robinson to write the introduction.

And me without a torch or pitchfork. Drat.

But surprise—Spider has written much nicer things about me than I probably deserve and he's said all of them with far more wit and grace than I could have hoped for. And for all of that, I should be enormously grateful. And I would be, except—

—Spider is a liar.

No, I mean it.

He lied about what happened at Disneyland. And if he lied about what happened at Disneyland, then why should you believe him when he says I'm a nice guy and a good storyteller?

Here's what *really* happened at Disneyland.

It was 1984, a year that had its good moments and its bad moments—the best of the good moments being the birth of the little boy who would eventually become my son, although I wouldn't know that until 1992—but at the time, a World Science Fiction Convention across the street from Disneyland seemed like a pretty good moment.

Because neither Spider nor Jeanne had ever been to the Magic Kingdom, we planned a marvelous day-long outing for them. I forget how many people were in the group—somewhere between six and two dozen, so there are witnesses, just none who will come forward today and corroborate the facts, so you'll have to take my word for it; but Spider was just like a big kid having his first day at Disneyland—well, yes, he *was* a big kid having his first day at Disneyland—and our first stop, *of course*, had to be the Jungle Boat Cruise in Adventureland.

Yes, I know, some of you reading this are thinking—"No, no, no. Space Mountain is the first ride." Or "Pirates of the Caribbean." Or even the horrible little children ride, deliberately tucked away at the farthest corner of Fantasyland so it's out of sight and mind, except for completists and masochists and unwary innocents who might be operating under the delusion that this particular insulin-deficient nightmare is a necessary experience in the smorgasbord of life.

But if you're thinking any of those thoughts, you don't understand Spider. Or the Jungle Boat Cruise. See, the Jungle Boat Cruise is this open-air boat with a real-live guide who pretends to steer the boat while reciting terrible—I mean, really stinkaroo—*puns* about the robotic animals in the water and on the shore. If you had Spider Robinson in tow, where would you take him first? Right. That's what we did.

The Jungle Boat Cruise. Stop. Close your eyes. Imagine the experience. Right. Open your eyes. Resume reading.

Spider got off the boat with the most astonished expression I have ever seen on a human face. I can remember his expression vividly. I have seen the same amazed expression on the face of a shaggy puppy looking at the very first spare-rib bone he's ever seen in his life—is all that for *me?*

Spider looked at me, his eyes shining with tears of envy. "They get to do that *all day long?*" (And get paid for it too?!!)

I replied, without any hesitation at all, "Of course. They've been seduced by the dock side of the farce."

Spider's eyes went wider. Much wider. In horrified shock, I think, but it could have been jealousy too. "How did you do that?" he asked with noticeable incredulity.

"It's easy," I replied. "The shortest distance between two puns is a straight line."

Spider has no one to blame but himself. He's the one who handed me the straight line.

It took three people to pry Spider's fingers loose from my throat. I still have the scars and I'll be happy to send photographs to anyone sending a self-addressed stamped envelope and a couple hundred bucks so I can buy myself some dark chocolate. Nobody got pushed into the water that day, but yes, Disneyland security did step in, and no, they did not throw Spider out of the park—but after he told them what I had said, they took away my Goofy hat and two plainclothes mice shadowed our group for the rest of the day.

I think it's also worth noting that Spider grabbed both of those puns and immediately stuck them into his very next Callahan's book—and then took the full credit for them! Shameless, just shameless. First he steals my wit, now he lies about the circumstances of the theft.

In the grand scheme of things, where more important questions—like how many elephants can be thrown into a black hole and how many will come out and what the elephants might think of the experience—can trigger the kind of uproar among physicists not seen since Schrödinger was charged with cruelty to animals, a pair o' docksical puns are hardly worth serious comment. Really. But I ask you, in all seriousness—now that you know that Spider Robinson has lied about a (mostly) harmless event (that incidentally resulted in my name and photo being posted at all the ticket booths of the Magic Kingdom), can you *really* trust anything else Spider Robinson has said about me?

I advise you to regard his introduction, even his words of praise, with a large grain of assault. I know I certainly intend to.

Never mind, the important thing is this: Thank you for buying this book. Enjoy yourself and make up your own mind.

—David Gerrold, *writing from The Rose Flower Palace of Intimate Massage (for Gentlemen Only), Hong Kong*

Interlude #1

Selections from *The Quote-Book of Solomon Short*

Citings of Solomon Short have occurred throughout the world. On the Isle of Lesbos, he was identified as a thespian; on Crete, he was apprehended as a cretin; and on the Isle of Man, he was arrested as a female impersonator. Not to mention the Isle of Wight, where he was accused of stealing his muse from a black person. Here is the latest selection:

"There's nothing wrong with growing older…but where does it lead?"

"There's no such thing as a great lover. They only come in pairs."

"There are two things you cannot give a cat. One is a pill. The other is an opinion. No, make that three things you can't give a cat. The third is an enema."

"Most knowledge is only a more accurate definition of your own ignorance."

"The law of conservation of stupidity means that every time one stupid person leaves the room, another one has to enter. This way, the amount of stupidity in any given location remains constant. Unless it increases."

"A quote is what you use when you don't have anything of your own to say."

"Inaction is the weakest form of action."

"A bird in the hand is dinner."

"Piss happens too."

"There will always be death and taxes; however, death doesn't get worse every year."

"Complaining about the way someone else says their prayers demonstrates a remarkable failure of one's own faith."

"There's an enormous difference between going through the motions and producing results. Those who don't understand that have no control over results, no power to produce them, and they are terrified by those who consistently do produce them."

"Change is most necessary when change is impossible."

"A person with experience is never at the mercy of a person with a mere opinion."

"Ignorant people are entitled to pity. Until they open their mouths. Then they're fair targets."

"All those who believe in psychokinesis raise my hand."

"Notice that they are not called 'God-worshipping people', they are called 'God-fearing people'. So why are churches called 'houses of worship' instead of 'houses of fear?'"

"Tis far, far better to be pissed off than pissed on. But those are not the only options."

"How come God only appoints some people and not others? Why doesn't God just appoint all of us and be done with it?"

"I try to go into every subject from the standpoint that I am incorrect… it saves time…"

"*Maturity* is the polite word for *exhaustion*."

"The Roman Empire died from an overdose of taxes, lawyers, and Christians. But we're much too smart to make that mistake again."

"Yes, Mother Nature is a bitch. But she's not *your* bitch."

"Hypocrisy is the attempt to look good while soiling your diaper."

"I've always felt that you shouldn't criticize a man, though, until you've walked a mile in his shoes. That way, when you do criticize him, you're a mile away. And you've got his shoes."

"Terriers are doorbells, nothing else."

"You have the right to free speech. You do not have the right to an audience."

"The devil doesn't deserve due process, but we give it to him anyway because we're not the devil."

"Any given society is like a mule. First you gotta hit it upside the head with a big ol' two-by-four. Sometimes you get the mule's attention, and sometimes you get a really pissed-off mule."

"Rudeness is what weak and stupid people use instead of real power."

"A man's speech should exceed his grasp, or what's a metaphor?"

"I retire all grudges after seven months. Mostly because I'm too old to dig another grave."

"The status quo is always the enemy."

"I'm not worried about puberty. I had it once. Once you've had it, you can't get it again."

"Ignorance is bliss? It ought to be painful!"

"There's not a lot to know about computers. One and zero. If you need greater precision than that, then the states are one, zero, and I don't care."

"The obvious isn't always obvious."

"Great minds often think alike. But then, so do mediocre minds."

"The best you're going to get out of some people is bovine exhaust. But even that is preferable to bovine indifference. At least it indicates an intention to participate."

"The best education is usually self-inflicted."

"No weapon is humane. They all hurt when you get hit."

"All that is necessary for the triumph of evil is for good people to click the remote control."

"Children don't have faults. They have personalities."

"The law presumes you are innocent until proven broke."

"Information is like hydrogen. It leaks and it explodes. Any attempt to contain it is doomed to fail."

"The silliest thing in the world to argue over is the right way to say your prayers. The second silliest thing to argue about is the right way to have sex."

"Age doesn't bring wisdom. It brings exhaustion. The young can't tell the difference."

"The only constant in the universe is change, and even that isn't a constant."

"The problem with just 'saying stuff' is that after a while the stuff you say becomes the stuff you are."

"Reviewers are crab lice on the good fuck of literature."

"The willing suspension of disbelief is necessary for good storytelling and good sex."

"Actually, people get more outraged about money than they do about sex. That's because more people have money than have sex…"

"You can fool all of the people some of the time and some of the people all of the time, but if you don't take your foot out of your mouth when you shoot yourself in it, nobody's going to be fooled."

"Education is not exalting, it's humbling."

"If it weren't for excuses, most people would have nothing to say."

"The moving finger writes, moves on, and having writ,
Oft reveals the owner of the hand to be a raving twit."

"The first place to look for evil is in the mirror."

"Sexual identity is not incidental. It can be marvelously inventive. Ask anyone who's ever worked in an emergency room how inventive sexual identity can be."

"There are two types of people. Those who need closure.

Before I adopted him, before I met him, before I even knew for sure that I would have a son, I knew he would transform my life. Indeed, that was the whole point of the adoption—to create two transformations: his and mine. (Of course, I only figured that out afterward.)

Somewhere in there, in the middle of all that planning, that little gnawing voice that chews at the back of my skull, acerbically pointed out, "You realize, of course, that this is going to have an effect on your writing..."

"Yes," I replied. "What's your point?"

The Martian Child

TOWARD THE END OF THE MEETING, the caseworker remarked, "Oh—and one more thing. Dennis thinks he's a Martian."

"I beg your pardon?" I wasn't certain I had heard her correctly. I had papers scattered all over the meeting room table—thick piles of stapled incident reports, manila-foldered psychiatric evaluations, Xeroxed clinical diagnoses, scribbled caseworker histories, typed abuse reports, bound trial transcripts, and my own crabbed notes as well: Hyperactivity. Fetal Alcohol Syndrome. Emotional Abuse. Physical Abuse. Conners Rating Scale. Apgars. I had no idea there was so much to know about children. For a moment, I was actually looking for the folder labeled Martian.

"He thinks he's a Martian," Ms. Bright repeated. She was a small woman, very proper and polite. "He told his group home parents that he's not like the other children—he's from Mars—so he shouldn't be expected to act like an Earthling all the time."

"Well, that's okay," I said, a little too quickly. "Some of my best friends are Martians. He'll fit right in. As long as he doesn't eat the tribbles or tease the feral Chtorran."

By the narrow expressions on their faces, I could tell that the caseworkers weren't amused. For a moment, my heart sank. Maybe I'd said the wrong thing. Maybe I was being too facile with my answers.

—The hardest thing about adoption is that *you have to ask someone to trust you with a child.*

23

That means that you have to be willing to let them scrutinize your entire life, everything: your financial standing, your medical history, your home and belongings, your upbringing, your personality, your motivations, your arrest record, your IQ, and even your sex life. It means that *every* self-esteem issue you have ever had will come bubbling right to the surface like last night's beans in this morning's bath tub.

Whatever you're most insecure about, that's what the whole adoption process will feel like it's focused on. For me, it was that terrible familiar feeling of being *second* best—of not being good enough to play with the big kids, or get the job, or win the award, or whatever was at stake. Even though the point of this interview was simply to see if Dennis and I would be a good match, I felt as if I was being judged again. What if I wasn't good enough this time?

I tried again. I began slowly. "Y'know, you all keep telling me all the bad news—you don't even know if this kid is capable of forming a deep attachment—it feels as if you're trying to talk me out of this match." I stopped myself before I said too much. I was suddenly angry and I didn't know why. These people were only doing their job.

And then it hit me. That was it—these people were *only* doing their job.

At that moment, I realized that there wasn't anyone in the room who had the kind of commitment to Dennis that I did, and I hadn't even met him yet. To them, he was only another case to handle. To me, he was...the possibility of a family. It wasn't fair to unload my frustration on these tired, overworked, underpaid women. They cared. It just wasn't the same kind of caring. I swallowed my anger.

"Listen," I said, sitting forward, placing my hands calmly and deliberately on the table. "After everything this poor little guy has been through, if he wants to think he's a Martian—I'm not going to argue with him. Actually, I think it's charming. It's evidence of his resilience. It's probably the most rational explanation he can come up with for his irrational situation. He probably feels alienated, abandoned, different, *alone*. At least, this gives him a reason for it. It lets him put a story around his situation so he can cope with it. Maybe it's the wrong explanation, but it's the only one he's got. We'd be stupid to try to take it away from him."

And after I'd said that, I couldn't help but add another thought as well. "I know a lot of people who hide out in fantasy because reality is too hard to cope with. Fantasy is my business. The only difference is that I write it down and make the rest of the world pay for the privilege of sharing the delusion. Fantasy isn't about escape; it's a survival mechanism. It's a way to deal with things that are so much bigger than you are. So I think fantasy is special, something to be cherished and protected because it's a very fragile thing and without it, we're so defenseless, we're paralyzed.

"I know what this boy is feeling because *I've been there*. Not the same circumstances, thank God—but I know this much, if he's surrounded by adults who can't understand what he really needs, he'll never have that chance to connect that everyone keeps talking about." For the first time I looked directly into their eyes as if they had to live up to *my* standards. "Excuse me for being presumptuous—but he's got to be with someone who'll tell him that it's all right for him to be a Martian. Let him be a Martian for as long as he needs."

"Yes. Thank you," the supervisor said abruptly. "I think that's everything we need to cover. We'll be getting back to you shortly."

My heart sank at her words. She hadn't acknowledged a word of what I'd said. I was certain she'd dismissed it totally. I gathered up all my papers. We exchanged pleasantries and handshakes, and I wore my company smile all the way to the elevator. I didn't say a word, neither did my sister. We both waited until we were in the car and headed back toward the Hollywood Freeway. She drove, guiding the big car through traffic as effortlessly as only a Los Angeles real estate agent can manage.

"I blew it," I said. "Didn't I? I got too…full of myself again."

"Honey, I think you were fine." She patted my hand.

"They're not going to make the match," I said. "It would be a single parent adoption. They're not going to do it. First they choose married couples, Ward and June. Then they choose single women, Murphy Brown. Then, only if there's no one else who'll take the kid, will they consider a single man. I'm at the bottom of the list. I'll never get this kid. I'll never get any kid. My own caseworker told me not to get my hopes up. There are two other families interested. This was just a formality, this interview. I know it. Just so they could prove they'd considered more than one match." I felt the frustration building up inside my chest like a balloon full of hurt. "But this is the kid for me, Alice, I know it. I don't know how I know it, but I do."

I'd first seen Dennis's picture three weeks earlier; a little square of colors that suggested a smile in flight.

I'd gone to the National Conference of the Adoptive Families of America at the Los Angeles Airport Hilton. There were six panels per hour, six hours a day, two days, Saturday and Sunday. I picked the panels that I thought would be most useful to me in finding and raising a child and ordered tapes—over two dozen—of the sessions I couldn't attend in person. I'd had no idea there were so many different issues to be dealt with in adoptions. I soaked it up like a sponge, listening eagerly to the advice of adoptive parents, their grown children, clinical psychologists, advocates, social workers, and adoption resource professionals.

But my *real* reason for attending was to find *the child*.

I'd already been approved. I'd spent more than a year filling out forms and submitting to interviews. But approval doesn't mean you get a child. It only means that your name is in the hat. Matching is done to meet the child's needs first. Fair enough—but terribly frustrating.

Eventually, I ended up in the conference's equivalent of a dealer's room. Rows of tables and heart-tugging displays. Books of all kinds for sale. Organizations. Agencies. Children in Eastern Europe. Children in Latin America. Asian children. Children with special needs. Photo-listings, like real-estate albums. Turn the pages, look at the eyes, the smiles, the needs. "Johnny was abandoned by his mother at age three. He is hyperactive, starts fires, and has been cruel to small animals. He will need extensive therapy..." "Janie, age nine, is severely retarded. She was sexually abused by her stepfather, she will need round-the-clock care..." "Michael suffers from severe epilepsy..." "Linda *needs*..." "Danny *needs*..." "Michael *needs*..." So many *needs*. So much hurt. It was overwhelming.

Why were so many of the children in the books "special needs" children? Retarded. Hyperactive. Abused. Had they been abandoned because they weren't perfect, or were these the leftovers after all the good children were selected? The part that disturbed me the most was that I could understand the emotions involved. I wanted a child, not a case. And some of the descriptions in the book did seem pretty intimidating. Were these the only kind of children available?

Maybe it was selfish, but I found myself turning the pages looking for a child who represented an easy answer. Did I really want another set of *needs* in my life—a single man who's old enough to be considered middle-aged and ought to be thinking seriously about retirement plans?

This was the most important question of all. "Why do you want to adopt a child?" And it was a question I couldn't answer. I couldn't find the words. It seemed that there was something I couldn't write down.

The motivational questionnaire had been a brick wall that sat on my desk for a week. It took me thirty pages of single-spaced printout just to get my thoughts organized. I could tell great stories about what I thought a family should be, but I couldn't really answer the question why *I* wanted a son. Not right away.

The three o'clock in the morning truth of it was a very nasty and selfish piece of business.

I didn't want to die alone. I didn't want to be left unremembered.

All those books and TV scripts...they were nothing. They used up trees. They were exercises in excess. They made other people rich. They were useless to me. They filled up shelves. They impressed the impressionable. But they didn't prove me a real person. They didn't validate my life as one worth living. In fact, they were about as valuable as the vice-presidency of the United States.

What I *really* wanted was to make a difference. I wanted someone to know that there was a real person behind all those words. A dad.

I would lie awake, staring into the darkness, trying to imagine it, what it would be like, how I would handle the various situations that might come up, how I would deal with the day-to-day business of daddying. I gamed out scenarios and tried to figure out how to handle difficult situations.

In my mind, I was always kind and generous, compassionate and wise. My fantasy child was innocent and joyous, full of love and wide-eyed wonder, and grateful to be in my home. He was an invisible presence, living inside my soul, defying reality to catch up. I wondered where he was now, and how and when I would finally meet him—and if the reality of parenting would be as wonderful as the dream.

—But it was all fantasyland. The books were proof of that. These children had histories, brutal, tragic, and heart-rending.

I wandered on to the next table. One of the social workers from the Los Angeles County Department of Children's Services had a photo book with her. I introduced myself, told her I'd been approved—but not matched. Could I look through the book? Yes, of course, she said. I turned the pages slowly, studying the innocent faces, looking for one who could be my son. All the pictures were of black children, and the county wasn't doing trans-racial adoptions anymore. Too controversial. The black social workers had taken a stand against it—I could see their point—but how many of these children would not find homes now?

Tucked away like an afterthought on the very last page was a photo of the only white child in the book. My glance slid across the picture quickly, I was already starting to close the album—and then as the impact of what I'd seen hit me, I froze in mid-action, almost slamming the book flat again.

The boy was riding a bicycle on a sunny tree-lined sidewalk; he was caught in the act of shouting or laughing at whoever was holding the camera. His blond hair was wild in the wind of his passage, his eyes shone like stars behind his glasses, his expression was raucous and exuberant.

I couldn't take my eyes off the picture. A cold wave of certainty came rolling up my spine like a blast of fire and ice. It was a feeling of *recognition*. This was *him*—the child who'd taken up permanent residence in my imagination! I could almost hear him yelling, "Hi, Daddy!"

"Tell me about this child," I said, a little too quickly. The social worker was already looking at me oddly. I could understand it. My voice sounded odd to me too. I tried to explain. "Tell me. Do you ever get people looking at a picture and telling you that this is the one?"

"All the time," she replied. Her face softened into an understanding smile.

His name was Dennis. He'd just turned eight. She'd just put his picture in the book this morning. And yes, she'd have the boy's caseworker get in touch with my caseworker. But…she cautioned…remember that there might be other families interested too. And remember, the department matches from the child's side.

I didn't hear any of that. I heard the words, but not the cautions.

I pushed hard and they set up a meeting to see if the match would work. But they cautioned me ahead of time—"this might not be the child you're looking for. He's classified as 'hard-to-place.' He's hyperactive and he's been emotionally abused and he may have fetal alcohol effects and he's been in eight foster homes, he's never had a family of his own…"

I didn't hear a word of it. I simply refused to listen. The boy in the picture had grabbed my heart so completely that I'd suddenly expanded all my definitions of what I was willing to accept.

I posted messages on CompuServe asking for information and advice on adoption, on attention deficit hyperactivity disorder, on emotional abuse recovery, on everything I could think of—what were this child's chances of becoming an independent adult? I called the Adoption Warm Line and was referred to parents who'd been through it. I hit the bookstores and the libraries. I called my cousin, the doctor, and he faxed me twenty pages of reports. And I came into the meeting so well-papered and full of theories and good intentions that I must have looked the perfect jerk.

And now…it was over.

I leaned my head against the passenger side window of my sister's car and moaned. "Dammit. I'm so *tired* of being pregnant. Thirteen months is long enough for any man! I've got the baby blues so bad, I can't even go to the supermarket anymore. I find myself watching other people with their children and the tears start welling up in my eyes. I keep thinking 'Where's *mine?*'"

My sister understood. She had four children of her own, none of whom had ended up in jail; so she had to have done something right. "Listen to me, David. Maybe this little boy isn't right for you—"

"Of course he's right for me. He's a Martian."

She ignored the interruption. "And if he isn't right, there'll be another child who is. I promise you. And you said it yourself that you didn't know if you could handle all the problems he'd be bringing with him."

"I know—it's just that…I feel like—I don't know what I feel like. This is worse than anything I've ever been through. All this wanting and not having. Sometimes I'm afraid it's not going to happen at all."

Alice pulled the car over to the curb and turned off the engine. "Okay, it's my turn," she said. "Stop beating yourself up. You are the smartest one in the whole family—but sometimes you can be awfully stupid. You are going to be a terrific father to some very lucky little boy. Your caseworker knows that. All of those social workers in that meeting saw your commitment and dedication. All that research you did—when you asked about the Apgar numbers and the Conners scale, when you handed them that report on hyperactivity, which even they didn't know about—you *impressed* them."

I shook my head. "Research is easy. You post a note on CompuServe, wait two days, and then download your e-mail."

"It's not the research," Alice said. "It's the fact that you did it. That demonstrates your willingness to find out what the child needs so you can provide it."

"I wish I could believe you," I said.

She looked deeply at me. "What's the matter?"

"What if I'm really *not* good enough?" I said. "*That's* what I'm worried about—I can't shake that feeling."

"Oh, that—" she said, lightly. "*That's* normal. That's the proof that you're going to do okay. It's only those parents who don't worry who need to."

"Oh," I said. And then we both started laughing.

She hugged me then. "You'll do fine. Now let's go home and call Mom before she busts a kidney from the suspense."

Two centuries later, although the calendar insisted otherwise, Ms. Bright called me. "We've made a decision. If you're still interested in Dennis, we'd like to arrange a meeting—" I don't remember a lot of what she said after that; most of it was details about how we would proceed; but I remember what she said at the end. "I want to tell you the two things that helped us make the decision. First, all that research you did shows that you're committed to Dennis's needs. That's very important in any adoption, but especially in this one. The other thing was what you said at the end of the meeting—about understanding his need to be a Martian. We were really touched by your empathy for his situation. We think that's a quality that Dennis is going to need very much in any family he's placed in. That's why we decided to try you first."

I thanked her profusely; at least, I think I did; I was suddenly having trouble seeing, and the box of tissues had gone empty.

* * *

I met Dennis three days later, at the Johnson Group Home in Culver City. He was one of six children living at the facility; four boys, two girls. Because the caseworkers didn't want him to know that he was being *auditioned*, I would be introduced as a friend of the group home parents.

The child who came home from school was a sullen little zombie, going through the motions of life. He walked in the door, walked past me with no sign of recognition, and headed straight to his room. I said, "Hi." He grunted something that could have been "H'lo" and kept on going. For a moment, I felt somehow cheated. I recognized him, why hadn't he recognized me? And then I had to remind myself with a grin that I was the grownup, not him. But, after a bit, he came out from his retreat and asked me to play electric hockey.

For the first few minutes, he was totally intent on the game. I didn't exist to him. Then I remembered an exercise from one of my communications courses—about simply *being with* another person. I stopped trying so hard to do it right, and instead just focused my attention on Dennis, letting it be all right with me for him to be exactly the way he was.

And yet, I couldn't turn off the analytical part of my mind. After reading all those reports, and hearing all the opinions of the caseworkers, I couldn't help but watch for evidence. I couldn't see it. None of it. All I could see was a child. And then that thing happened that always happens to an adult who is willing to play with a child. I rediscovered my own childhood again. I got involved in the game, and very shortly I was smiling and laughing when he did, returning the same delight and approval at every audacious play. And that's when it happened. He began to realize that there was a real human being on the opposite side of the game board. Something sparked. He started reacting to me instead of to the puck. I could feel the sense of connection almost as a physical presence.

Then, abruptly, it was time for him to do his chores. We loaded up the wagon with the cans from the recycling bin and walked them over to the nearby park. We talked about stuff. He talked, I listened. Sometimes I asked questions, sometimes he did. On the way back, he insisted that I pull the wagon so he could ride in it. By now, he was glowing. He was the boy in the photograph.

When we got back to the group home, however, the other children had arrived home from school and were already playing together in the back yard. As soon as he saw them, Dennis broke away from me and ran to the back of the yard. He flung himself into the corner of a large old couch and curled up in a ball. He was as apart from the other children—indeed the whole world—as it was possible to get.

What had suddenly triggered his unhappiness? Was it the thought that now that there were other children to play with, I would reject him? Did he have to reject me first? Or was there something else going on? From inside the house, I watched him as he sat alone. He was a very unhappy little boy. And he had stopped glowing. At that moment, I knew I couldn't leave him here. Whatever other problems he might have, my commitment was bigger. Or so I believed.

The group home parents invited me to stay to dinner with the children. I hadn't planned on it, but all the children insisted that I stay, so I did, specifically making a point of sitting next to Dennis. He didn't talk at all, he was subdued, as if he was afraid of losing something that he wanted very much—or maybe that was only my perception. He ate quietly and timidly. But then Tony, one of the more excitable children, suddenly piped up, "Do you know what Dennis said?"

Tony was sitting directly across from me. He had that look of malicious mischief common to children who are about to betray a confidence. "What?" I asked, with a queasy foreboding.

"Dennis said he wishes you were his dad." Even without looking, I could see that beside me, Dennis was cringing, readying himself for the inevitable politely worded rejection.

Instead, I turned to Dennis, focusing all my attention on him, and said, "Wow, what a great wish. Thank you!" There was more I wanted to add, but I couldn't. Not yet. The "game plan" required me to be Dennis's "special friend" for at least six weeks before I made any kind of commitment to him. He couldn't know that I had the same wish he did. I felt cheated at not being able to add, "So do I." But I understood the rationale, and I would follow it.

"Better watch out," Tony said. "He might make it a Martian wish, and then you'll *have* to."

At the time, I didn't understand what Tony had meant. So I forgot about it.

*   *   *

The next time I heard about Martians happened thirteen months later.

I was in Arizona, at a party at Jeff Duntemann's sprawling house. Jeff is a two-time Hugo nominee who gave up science fiction to write books about computer programming. Apparently, it was far more profitable than science fiction; now he was publishing his own magazine, *PC-Techniques*. I write a regular column for the magazine, an off-the-wall mix of code and mutated zen. It was the standing joke that my contribution to the magazine was the "Martian perspective."

I was sitting on the patio, watching Dennis splash enthusiastically across the pool. He was doing cannonballs into the deep end. A year ago, I couldn't pry him loose from the steps in the shallow end; he wouldn't even let me teach him how to dog-paddle—now he was an apprentice fish. He spent more time swimming across the bottom of the water than the top.

A year ago, he'd been a waif—capable of joy, the picture proved that— but more often sad, uncertain, alienated, and angry. A year ago, he'd told his caseworker, "I don't think God listens to my prayers. I prayed for a dad and nothing happened." On the day he moved in, I asked his caseworker to remind him of that conversation and then tell him that sometimes it takes God a little while to make a miracle happen.

A miracle—according to my friend Randy MacNamara—is something that wouldn't have happened anyway. Now, after the fact, after the first giddy days of panic and joy, after the days of bottomless fears, after the tantrums and the testing, after a thousand and one peanut butter and jellyfish sandwiches, I understood what he meant. And more. A miracle takes real commitment. It never happens by accident. I'd had other miracles happen in my life—one which I'd written about, one which I may never write about—but this one was the best. I had the proof of it framed on my wall.

One afternoon I'd opened Dennis's lunch kit to see how much he'd eaten and found the note I'd packed that morning. It said, "Please eat your whole lunch today! I love you! Daddy." On the other side, written in a childish scrawl was Dennis's reply: *"I love you to. you are very specil to me. I realy think your the best. I love you very much dady I never loved eneyone more than you. I never new anyone nicer than you."* At the bottom, he'd drawn three hearts and put the word "dady" in the biggest of them.

So the miracle was complete. Dennis *could* form a deep attachment. And he could express it. And all I had to do was sit and glow and realize that despite all my doubts and all my mistakes, I was getting the important part of the job done right. I had passed from wannabe to gonnabe to finding-how-to-be to simply be-ing. I was glowing as brightly as the warm Arizona evening. Pink clouds were striped across the darkening twilight sky.

I didn't know anyone else at the party besides Jeff and Carol—and the world-famous Mr. Byte who was in the kitchen begging scraps he wasn't supposed to have. But that was all right. I was content just to sit and watch my son enjoying himself. And then I heard the word "Martian" in back of me, and without moving, my attention swiveled 180 degrees.

Four of the wives were sitting together—it was that kind of party; the programmers were talking code, the wives were talking children. I didn't know enough about either subject, I still felt like a dabbler in both fields, so I made the best kind of listener. One of the women was saying. "No, it's true. Since she was old enough to talk she's insisted that she's a Martian. Her mother has never been able to convince her otherwise. She asked her, 'How do you explain that I remember going to the hospital and giving birth to you?' and she said, 'I was implanted in your tummy.' She's twelve now and she still believes it. She has a whole story, an explanation for everything. She says UFOs are implanting Martian babies all the time."

The other women laughed gently. I found myself smiling to myself and watching Dennis. Remembering for the first time in a long while what he'd once told his caseworker—that he was a Martian too. Interesting coincidence.

Then, one of the others said, "We had a boy in my daughter's school who wore a T-shirt to school almost every day that said, 'I am a Martian.' He took a lot of teasing about it. The principal tried to make him stop wearing it, but he refused. All the kids thought he was crazy."

"That was probably the only way he could get the attention he needed."

"Well," said the fourth voice, "it's a common childhood fantasy—that the child is really a changeling or an orphan and that you're not her real mother. Adding Mars to it is just a way to take advantage of the information in the real world to make it more believable."

I didn't hear any more of that conversation; we were interrupted by Carol announcing that dessert was served; but a seed of inquiry had been planted. If nothing else, I thought it might make an interesting story. If only I could figure out an ending for it. Let's see, a man adopts a little boy and then discovers that the child is a Martian.

Hm. But what's the hook?

Horror story? Too easy. Too obvious—the Martian children are going to murder us in our beds. Besides, Richard Matheson could do it better, if he hadn't already. John Wyndham already had. A hidden invasion? The Martians will take us over without our ever knowing? Fred Brown had beaten me to it by four decades. His story had even ended up as an episode on Hitchcock. Maybe something tender and gentle instead? Parenting a starlost orphan? That would be the hardest to write—and Zenna Henderson had already written it several times over. Sturgeon was another one who could handle that angle. I wished I could pick up the phone and call him. He would have had the most interesting insight for the ending, but the connect charges would have been horrendous. I could call Harlan, of course, but he'd probably bitch at me for interrupting him during *Jeopardy*. Besides, I didn't think he would take this question seriously. "Harlan, listen—I think my son's a Martian, and I'm trying to write it up as a story…" "Yeah, right, David. Have you had your medication checked recently?"

I made a mental note to think about it later. Maybe my subconscious would think about it during the drive home. Maybe I'd stumble across an ending by accident. I really couldn't do anything at all without an ending in mind. It's easy to start a story, but if you don't know the ending, you don't know what you're writing toward and after a while the story goes adrift, the energy fails, and you've got one more thing to be frustrated about. I had a file cabinet full of unfinished stories to prove that this was not the best way to generate pay copy.

*　　*　　*

The next day…we were slicing across the desolate red desert, seemingly suspended between the blazing sky and the shimmering road, not talking about anything, just listening to a tape of Van Dyke Parks and sipping sodas from the cooler. The tape came to an end and the white noise of the wind rushed in to envelop us. Convertibles are fun, but they aren't quiet.

Abruptly, I remembered last night's conversation.

"Hey," I asked. "Are you a Martian?"

"What?"

"Are you a Martian?" I repeated.

"Why do you ask that?"

"Ah, obviously you're a Jewish Martian. You answer a question with a question."

"Who told you I was a Martian?"

"Kathy did. Before I met you, we had a meeting. She told me all about you. She said that you told her you were a Martian. Do you remember telling her that?"

"Yes."

"Are you still a Martian?"

"Yes," he said.

"Oh," I said. "Do you want to tell me about it?"

"Okay," he said. "I was made on Mars. I was a tadpole. Then I was brought to Earth in a UFO and implanted in my Mommy's tummy. She didn't know. Then I was borned."

"Ahh," I said. "That's how I thought it happened. Is that all?"

"Uh-huh."

"Why did the Martians send you here?"

"So I could be a Earth-boy."

"Oh."

"Can we go to Round Table Pizza for dinner?" he asked, abruptly changing the subject as if it was the most natural thing to do.

"Do Martians like pizza?"

"Yes!" he said excitedly. Then he pointed his fingers at me like a funny kind of ray gun. Most children would have pointed the top two fingers to make a pretend gun, but Dennis pointed his index and little fingers, his thumb stood straight up for the trigger. "If you don't take me out for pizza tonight, I'll have to disneygrade you."

"Ouch, that sounds painful. I definitely do not want to be disneygraded. Then I'd have to stand in the dark and sing that awful song forever while boatloads of Japanese tourists take pictures of me. But we're not going tonight. Maybe tomorrow, if you have a good day at school."

"No, tonight! " He pointed his fingers menacingly—both hands now—and for a moment I wondered what would happen if he pressed his thumbs forward. Would I be turned into a giant three-fingered mouse?

"If you disneygrade me," I said, "for sure you won't get any pizza."

"Okay," he said. Then he closed up both weapons, first one hand, then the other. First the little finger of his left hand, then the index finger; then the little finger of his right hand, then the index finger. Each time he made a soft clicking sound with his mouth. Finally he folded his thumbs down—and abruptly he had hands again.

Later, I tried to do the same thing myself. A human can do it, but it's like the Vulcan salute. It takes practice.

*   *   *

I have a pinched nerve in my back. If I do my twisting exercises a couple of times a week, and if I take frequent breaks from the keyboard, and if I remember to put myself into the spa every couple days and let the bubbles boil up around me, then I can keep myself functioning pretty much like a normal person. It's a fair trade. Usually I wait until after dinner to sit in the spa. After the sun sets is a perfect time for a little skinny-dipping.

Several days after the Phoenix trip, Dennis and I were alone in the pool. The pool has a blue filter over the light, the spa has a red one; when the bubbles are on, it looks a little like a hot lava bath. Sometimes we talk about nothing important, sometimes we just sit silently letting the bubbles massage our skins, sometimes we stare up into the sky and watch for meteors; once we'd seen a bright red starpoint streak across the sky like a bullet.

But tonight, as he splashed in the bubbles, I found myself studying the way the light shaped his features. I'm not an expert on the development of children's skulls, but abruptly I was struck by the odd proportions of his forehead and eyes.

Before I'd adopted him, I'd been given copies of various doctor's reports. One doctor, who was supposed to be looking for fetal alcohol effects, had described the five-year-old Dennis as "an unusual-looking" child. I couldn't see what he was talking about. To me, Dennis had always been an unusually good-looking boy.

There are only two shapes of faces—pie and horse. Dennis was a pie-face, I'm a horse. In that, he was lucky because his smile was so wide he *needed* a round face to hold it all. He was blessed with dark blond hair which was growing steadily toward shoulder-length. His eyes were puppy-brown and hidden behind lashes long enough to trouble the sleep of mascara manufacturers. His complexion was as luminous and gold as an Arizona sunset.

His body was well-proportioned too; he had long legs and a swimmer's torso. He was thin, but not skinny. He looked like a Disney child. I expected him to be a heartbreaker when he grew up. The girls were going to chase him with lassos. Already I wondered what kind of a teenager he would become—and if I would be able to handle it.

Now...seeing him in the reflected red light of the spa—is this the same color light they have on Mars? —he did look a little *alien* to me. His forehead had a roundish bulge toward the crown. His cheekbones seemed strangely angled. His eyes seemed narrow and reptilian. Probably it was the effect of the light coming from underneath instead of above, combined with the red filter, but it was momentarily unnerving. For a moment, I wondered what kind of a *thing* I'd brought into my life.

"What?" he asked, staring back.

"Nothing," I said.

"You were looking at me."

"I was admiring you. You're a beautiful kid, do you know that? "

"Uh-huh." And suddenly he was Dennis again.

"How do you know that?"

"Everybody says so. They all like my eyelashes."

I laughed. Of course. Here was a child who'd learned to work the system. He was a skilled manipulator. He'd learned real fast how to turn on his special smile and get what he wanted out of people. Of course he knew how much attention his eyelashes attracted.

But—for a moment there, he hadn't been Dennis the little boy. He'd been something else. Something cold and watchful. He'd noticed me studying him. He'd sensed the suspicion. Or was it just the power of suggestion at work? Most of the books on parenting advised not to feel guilty for wondering if your child is going to suddenly catch a fly with his tongue. It's a very common parental fear.

And then...whenever I had doubts about Dennis and my ability to keep up with him, all I had to do was ask myself one simple question.

How would I feel if Kathy Bright said she had to remove him from my home? Ripped apart was the simplest answer. The truth was, I didn't care if he was a Martian or not, I was as *bonded* to him as he was to me.

But out of curiosity, and possibly just to reassure myself that I was imagining things, I logged onto CompuServe. The ISSUES forum has a parenting section. I left a message under the heading, "Is your child a Martian?"

> My little boy says he's a Martian. I've heard of two other children who claim to be Martians as well. Has anyone else heard of children who believe that they're from Mars?

Over the course of the next few days—before the message scrolled off the board and into the bit-bucket—I received thirty-three replies.

Several of the messages were thoughtful analyses of why a child might say such a thing; it was pretty much what that mother in Phoenix had surmised; it's common for children to fantasize that they have glamorous origins. In the past, children might have believed they were secretly princes and princesses and one day their real parents would arrive to take them to their golden castles. But because that mythology has now been superseded by starships and mutants, it's more appropriate for children to fantasize about traveling away on the *Millennium Falcon* or the *Enterprise*. But if a child was experienced enough to know that those stories were just fiction, he would also know that Mars was a real planet; therefore…Mars gave credibility to the fantasy. Etcetera. Etcetera. Local mileage may vary, but if the delusion persists, see a good therapist. It may be evidence of some deeper problem. Etcetera some more.

I knew what Dennis's deeper problems were. He'd been bounced around the foster care system for eight years before landing in my arms. He didn't know *where* he came from or *where* he belonged.

Several of the replies I received were from other parents sharing pieces of weirdness their own children had demonstrated. Interesting, but not particularly useful to my inquiry.

But…there were over a dozen private messages.

> "My sister's little girl used to insist that she'd been brought to Earth in a UFO and implanted in her mommy's tummy while her mommy was asleep. She kept this up until she was about fourteen, then abruptly stopped. After that, she wouldn't answer questions about it at all."

> "My next door neighbors had a boy who said he wasn't from Earth. He disappeared when he was twelve. Without a trace. The police assumed he was kidnapped."

"My ex-wife was a child psychologist. She used to joke about her Martian children. She said she could tell how crazy New York was by the number of Martians she saw in any given year. At first she used to tell the parents that same old same old about children needing to fantasize about a glamorous background, but later on she began to wonder. The stories the kids told were all very similar. They began life as Martian tadpoles brought to Earth and implanted in the uteruses of Earth women. She always wanted to do a study on Martian children, but she could never get a grant."

"I dated a girl once who said she was from Mars. She was very insistent on it. When I tried to get serious with her, she turned me down flat. She said she really liked me, but it wouldn't work out between us. When I asked her why, she said it was because she was from Mars. That's all. I guess Martians have a rule against marrying outside their species."

"I heard about a Martian when I was in high school. He killed himself. I didn't know him. I only heard about it afterward."

"I thought I was from Mars once. I even had memories of being on Mars. It had a pink sky. That's how I knew it was Mars. When the photos came in from JPL showing that Mars really did have a pink sky, just like in my memories, I thought that proved something. When I told my parents, they took me to see a doctor. I was in therapy for a long time, but I'm fine now. Maybe you should get your son into therapy, too."

It was the last one that really got to me. I knew the person who sent it meant to be reassuring, but instead, his message had the opposite effect.

Okay, maybe it's me. Maybe it's because I'm a writer. I read subtext where none is intended. And maybe the cumulative effect of all these messages, especially the wistful, almost plaintive tone of the last one left me with a very uncomfortable feeling.

I replied to all of these messages.

I know this sounds silly, but please indulge me. What did your Martian friend/relative look like? Did he/she have any special physical characteristics or medical problems? What was his/her personality like? Do you know what happened to him or her? Does he/she still believe that he/she is from Mars?

It took a week or two to compile the responses. Of the ten Martians specifically mentioned, two had committed suicide. One was successful in business. Three refused to talk about Mars. Two were "cured." The whereabouts of the others were unknown. Three were missing. Two of the missing had been repeated runaways during their teen years. I wondered where they thought they were running to.

Of the ten Martians, six were known to have had golden-brown skin, round faces, brown eyes and very long eyelashes. The hair color was generally dark blond or brown. That was an interesting statistical anomaly.

Of the ten Martians, five were hyperactive, two were epileptic. The other three weren't known.

I asked the fellow whose ex-wife had been a child psychologist if she'd ever noticed any statistical patterns among her Martians. He said he didn't know and he didn't even know her whereabouts anymore. She had disappeared two years earlier.

*   *   *

I called my friend, Steve Barnes. He'd written one of the character references I'd needed to adopt Dennis, and because of that I regarded him as an unofficial godfather to the boy. We chatted about this and that and the other thing for awhile. And then, finally, I said, "Steve—do you know about the Martian phenomenon?" He didn't. I told him about it. He asked me if I was smoking dope again.

"I'm serious, Steve."

"So am I."

"I haven't touched that crap since I kicked out she-who-must-not-be-named," I said it angrily.

"Just checking. You gotta admit that's a pretty bizarre story, though."

"I know that. That's why I'm telling you. You're one of the few people I know who will actually consider it fairly. Geez—why is it that science fiction writers are the most skeptical animals of all?"

"Because we get to deal with more crazies than anyone else," Steve replied without missing a beat.

"I don't know what to do with this," I said, admitting my frustration. "I know it sounds like one more crazy UFO mystery. Only this one is something that can actually be validated. This is the kind of statistical anomaly that can't be explained away by coincidence. And I bet there's a lot more to it too. Like, what was the blood type of all those children? What was the position of the Earth and Mars when they were conceived? What was the phase of the moon? What are their favorite foods? How well did they do in school? What if there's something really going on here?—maybe not Martians, maybe some kind of social phenomenon or syndrome—I don't know what it is, I don't know what else to ask, and I don't know who to tell. Most of all, I don't want to end up on the front page of the *Inquirer*. Can't you just see it? 'SCI-FI WRITER HAS MARTIAN CHILD!' "

"It might be good for your career," Steve said thoughtfully. "I wonder how many new readers you could pick up."

"Oh, yeah, sure. And I wonder how many old readers I'll lose. I'd like to be taken seriously in my old age, Steve. Remember what happened to what's-his-name."

"I'll never forget old what's-his-name," Steve said. "Yeah, that was a real sad story."

"Anyway…" I said. "You see my point? Where do I go from here?"

"You want my *real* advice?" Steve asked. He didn't wait for my reply. "Don't go anywhere with it. Drop it. Let someone else figure it out. Or no one. You said it yourself, David. 'It's almost always dangerous to be right too soon.' Don't go borrowing trouble. Turn it into a story if you must and let people think it's a harmless fantasy. But don't let it screw up your life. You wanted this kid, didn't you? Now you have him. Just parent him. That's the only thing that's really wanted and needed."

He was right. I knew it. But I couldn't accept it. "Sure. That's easy for you to say. You don't have a Martian in the house."

"Yes I do." He laughed. "Only mine's a girl."

"Huh—?"

"Don't you get it? *All* children are Martians. We get thirteen years to civilize the little monsters. After that, it's too late. Then they start eating our hearts out for the rest of our lives."

"You sound like my mother now."

"I'll take that as a compliment."

"It's a good thing you don't know her, or you wouldn't say that."

"Listen to me, David," and his tone of voice was so serious that six different jokes died before they could pass my lips. "You're right on schedule. Have you ever really looked at the faces of new parents? Most of them are walking around in a state of shock, wondering what happened—what is this loathsome reptilian thing that has suddenly invaded their lives? It's part of the process of assimilation. The only difference is that you have a more active imagination than most people. You know how to name your fears. Trust me on this, Toni and I went through it too with Nicki. We thought she was a—never mind. Just know that this normal. There are days when you are absolutely certain that you've got a cute and stinky little alien in your house."

"But *every* day?"

"Trust me. It passes. In a year or two, you won't even remember what your life was like before."

"Hmm. Maybe that's how long it takes a Martian to brainwash his human hosts…"

Steve sighed. "You've got it bad."

"Yes, I do," I admitted.

*　　*　　*

The Martian thing gnawed at me like an ulcer. I couldn't get it out of my head. No matter what we did, the thought was there.

If we went out front to swat koosh-balls back and forth, I wondered if the reason he was having trouble with his coordination was the unfamiliar gravity of Earth. If we went in the back yard and jumped in the pool together, I wondered if his attraction to water was because it was so scarce on Mars. I wondered about his ability to hear a piece of music a single time and still remember the melody so clearly that he could sing it again, note for note, a month later. He would walk through the house singing songs that he could not have heard except on the tapes I occasionally played. How many nine-year-olds know how to sing *My Clone Sleeps Alone* like Pat Benatar? I wondered why he had so little interest in comic books, but loved to watch television dramas about the relationships of human beings. He hated *Star Trek*, he thought it was "too silly." He loved the Discovery channel—especially all the shows about animals and insects.

There was no apparent pattern to his behavior, nothing that could be pointed to as evidence of otherworldliness. Indeed, the fact that he was making his father paranoid was a very strong argument that he was a normal Earth kid.

And then, just when I'd forgotten…something would happen. Maybe he'd react to something on television with an off-the-wall comment that would make me look over at him curiously. There was that Bugs Bunny cartoon, for instance, where the rabbit is making life difficult for Marvin the Martian, stealing the Illudium PU-36 Explosive Space Modulator so he can't blow up the Earth. In the middle of it, Dennis quietly declared, "No, that's wrong. Martians aren't like that." Then he got up and turned the television set *off*.

"Why did you do that?" I asked.

"Because it was wrong," he said blandly.

"But it's only a cartoon." One of my *favorite* cartoons, I might add.

"It's still wrong." And then he turned and went outside as if the whole concept of television would never be interesting to him again.

*　　*　　*

And now, almost two years to the day since I'd filled out the first application, the nickel finally dropped and I sat up in bed in the middle of the night. Why were so many adopted children *hyperactive?*

The evidence was all around me. I just hadn't noticed it before. It was there in the photo-listing books. It seemed as if every third child was hyperactive. It was acknowledged in the books, the articles, the seminars, the tapes…that a higher proportion of foster children have Attention Deficit Disorder, also called Hyperactivity. Why was that?

Some theorists suggested that it was the result of substance abuse by the parents, which is why we saw it more in abandoned and unwanted children. Some doctors believed that hyperactivity was the result of the body's failure to produce certain key enzymes in response to physical stimulation; therefore the child needed to overstimulate himself in order to produce an equivalent amount of calming. Still others postulated that there was an emotional component to the disorder; that it was a response to a lack of nurturing. Most interesting of all to me was the offhand note in one article that some theorists believed that many cases of ADD were actually misdiagnoses. If you were unattached and didn't know who you were or where you had come from or where you were going, you'd have a lot to worry about; your attention might be distracted too.

Or…what if the behavior that was judged abnormal for Earth children was perfectly normal for Martian children? What if there was no such thing as ADD…in Martians?

At this point, I'd reached the limits of my ability to research the question. Who could I tell? Who would have the resources to pursue this further? And who would take me seriously?

Suppose I picked up the *Los Angeles Times* tomorrow and saw that Ben Bova had called a press conference to announce that he'd been kidnapped by aliens and taken into space where they'd performed bizarre sexual experiments on him…would I believe him? Ben is one of the most believable men in the world. Once, he almost talked me into voting for Ronald Reagan. But if I saw a report like that in the newspaper, the first thing I'd do would be to call Barbara and ask if Ben were all right.

In other words…there was simply no way for me to research this question without destroying all of my credibility as a writer.

Even worse, *there was no way to research it without also destroying my credibility as a parent.*

Up until this time, I'd always been candid with the caseworkers and therapists; I'd talked to them about our discipline problems, about my feelings of frustration, about every little step in the right direction and every major victory. But…suddenly, I realized this was something I couldn't talk to them about. Suppose I called Kathy Bright. What could I say? "Uh, Kathy, it's David. I want to talk to you about Dennis. You know how he says he's a Martian? Well, I think he might really be a Martian and…"

Uh-huh.

If the adoptive father was starting to have hallucinations about the child, how long would the Department of Children's Services leave the child in that placement? About twenty minutes, I figured. About as long as it took to get out there and pick him up. She'd pull him out of my house so fast they'd be hearing sonic booms in Malibu. And I wouldn't even be able to argue. She'd be right to do so. A child needs a stable and nurturing environment. How stable and nurturing would it be for him to be living with an adult who suspects he's from another planet and is wondering about his ultimate motives.

If I pursued this, I'd lose my son.

The thought was intolerable. I might never recover. I was sure that he wouldn't. For the first time in his life, he'd finally formed an attachment. What would it do to him to have it broken so abruptly? It would truly destroy his ability to trust any other human being.

I couldn't do that to him. I couldn't do *anything* that might hurt him.

And what about me? I had my own "attachment issues." I couldn't stand the thought of another failure. Another brick in the wall, as they say.

That was where I stayed stuck for the longest time. I walked around the house in physical pain for three weeks. My chest hurt. My head hurt. My legs hurt. My back hurt. My eyes hurt. My throat hurt. The only part of me that didn't hurt was my brain. That was so numb, I couldn't think.

I didn't know if he was a Martian or not. But something weird was going on. Wasn't it? And if it was just me—if I was going insane—then what right do I have to try to parent this child anyway? Either way I lose. If he's a Martian, I can't tell anyone. And if he isn't a Martian, then I'm going crazy.

*   *   *

I started looking for local evidence. I began browsing through my journal. I'd been making daily notes of interesting incidents, in case I ever wanted to write a book about our experiences. At first, I couldn't find anything. Most of the incidents I'd written about were fairly mundane. Not even good *Readers' Digest* material.

For instance, the week after he moved in, I'd taken him to the baseball game at Dodger Stadium. For the first part of the game, he'd been more interested in having a pennant and getting some cotton candy than in what was going on down on the stadium floor. But along about the fifth inning, he'd climbed up onto my lap and I began explaining the game to him. "See that man at home plate, holding the bat. Wish for him to hit the ball right out of the park."

"Okay," said Dennis.

Cra-a-ack! The ball went sailing straight out into the right field stands. Someone in the lower deck caught it and the runner sauntered easily around the bases while the organist played, "Glory, glory, Hallelujah."

"You're a good wisher, Dennis. That was terrific. Want to try it again?"

"No."

"Okay."

Two innings later, the Dodgers were one run behind. I asked Dennis to wish for hits again. Four pitches later, there were runners at first and third.

It didn't matter to me who came up to bat now; I hadn't remembered the names of any ballplayers since Roy Campanella was catching for Don Drysdale and Sandy Koufax. As far as I was concerned, Who was on first, What was on second, and I Don't Know still played third. I liked baseball only so long as I didn't have to be an expert; but I'd never seen the Dodgers win a game. Every time I came to the stadium they lost; so I'd made it a point to stay away from Dodger Stadium to give them a fair chance at winning. I didn't expect them to win tonight; but Dennis's wishes had brought them from three runs behind.

"Okay, Dennis," I said, giving him a little squeeze. "It's time for one last wish. See that guy at the home plate, holding the bat. You gotta wish for him to hit a home run. All the way out of the park. Just like before. Okay?"

"Okay."

And just like before—*cra-a-ack*—the ball went sailing deep into right field, triggering a sudden cluster of excited fans scrambling down across the seats.

The Dodgers won that night. All the way home, I kept praising Dennis for his excellent wishing.

*   *   *

A couple of weeks after that, we were stopped at a light, waiting for it to change. It was one of those intersections that existed slightly sideways to reality. Whenever you stopped there, time slowed down to a crawl. Without even thinking, I said, "Dennis, wish for the light to turn green please."

"Okay," he said.

—and abruptly the light turned green. I frowned. It seemed to me the cycle hadn't quite completed.

Nah. I must have been daydreaming. I eased the car through the intersection. A moment later, we got caught at the next red light. I said a word.

"Why'd you say that?"

"These lights are supposed to be synchronized," I said. "So you only get green ones. We must be out of synch. Why don't you wish for this light to change too, please."

"Okay."

—green.

"Boy! You are really a good wisher."

"Thank you."

A minute later, I said, "Can you wish this light to turn green too?"

"No," he said, abruptly angry. "You're going to use up all my wishes."

"Huh?" I looked over at him.

"I only have so many wishes and you're going to use them all up on stoplights." There was a hurt quality in his voice.

I pulled the car over to the side of the road and stopped. I turned to him and put my hand gently on his shoulder. "Oh, sweetheart. I don't know who told you that, but that's not so. The wish bag is bottomless. You can have as many wishes as you want."

"No, you can't," he insisted. "I have to save my wishes for things that are important."

"What's the most important thing you ever wished for? " I asked, already knowing the answer.

He didn't answer.

"What's the most important wish?" I repeated.

Very softly, he admitted, "I wished for a dad. Someone who would be nice to me."

"Uh-huh. And did you get your wish?"

He nodded.

"So, you see, sweetheart. There's no shortage of miracles."

I didn't know if he believed me. It was still too early in the process. We were still learning who each other was. I noted the conversation in my journal and let the matter slide. But it left me with an uncomfortable feeling. What has to happen to a child to make him believe there's a limit to wishes?

A year later, I looked at the words I'd written glowing on the computer screen, and *wondered* about Dennis's ability to wish. It was probably a coincidence. But maybe it wasn't. That time we'd matched four out of six numbers in the lottery and won eighty-eight dollars—was that the week I'd asked him to wish real hard for us to win?

Maybe Martians have precognitive or telekinetic powers...?

*   *   *

Dennis likes cleaning things. Without asking, he'll go out and wash the car, or the patio. He'll give the dogs baths. He'll vacuum the rugs and take the Dustbuster to the couch. He'll mop the floors. His favorite toys are a sponge and a squirt-bottle of Simple Green. I've seen him take a rusty old wrench he found in a vacant field and scrub the rust off of it until it shone like new. One night after dinner, after he finished methodically loading the dishwasher, I sat him down at the kitchen table and told him I had a surprise for him.

"What?"

"It's a book of puzzles."

"Oh." He sounded disappointed.

"No, listen. Here's the game. You have twenty minutes to do these puzzles, and then when you finish. I add them up and we'll find out how smart you are. Do you want to do this?"

"It'll really tell you how smart I am?"

"Uh-huh. "

He grabbed for the book and a pencil.

"Wait a minute—let me set the timer. Okay? Now once you start, you can't stop. You have to go all the way through to the end. Okay?"

"Okay."

"Ready? "

"Ready. "

"One, two, three...go."

He attacked the first three puzzles with a vengeance. They were simple. Pick the next shape in a series: triangle, square, pentagon...? Which object doesn't belong: horse, cow, sheep, scissors? Feather is to Bird as Fur is to: dog, automobile, ice cream...?

Then the puzzles started getting harder and he started to frown. He brushed his hair out of his eyes and once he stopped to clean his glasses; but he stayed interested and involved and when the timer went off, he didn't want to stop. He insisted that he be allowed to finish the puzzle he was working on. What the hell. I let him.

"What does it say?" Dennis asked as I computed the percentile. He wanted to grab the test book out of my hand.

"Well...let me finish here. " I held it out of his reach as I checked the table of percentiles.

The test showed that he had above-average intelligence—not unexpected; hyperactive kids tend to be brighter than average—but well within the normal range for a nine-year-old. "It says that you are fifty-two inches high, that you weigh sixty-six pounds, and that your daddy loves you very much. It also says that you are very smart."

"How smart?"

"Well, if this test were given to one hundred children, you would be smarter than ninety-two of them."

"How good is that?"

"That's *very* good. You can't get much better. And it means we should go out for ice cream after dinner. What do you think?"

"Yeah!"

Oh, that was another thing. He didn't like chocolate. He preferred rainbow sherbet. I'd never seen that in a kid before.

*　　*　　*

A couple of weeks later, we played another game. I made sure to pick a quiet evening, one with no distractions. "This game is even harder," I explained. "It's a kind of card game," I explained. "See these cards? There are six different shapes here. A circle, a square, a star, three squiggly lines, a cross, and a figure-eight. All you have to do is guess which one I'm looking at. See if you can read my mind, okay?"

He frowned at me, and I had to explain it two or three more times. This was not a game he wanted to play. I said okay and started to put the deck away. If he didn't want to cooperate, the results would be inconclusive. "Can we go for ice cream after we do this?" he asked abruptly.

"Sure," I said.

"Okay, let's do it then."

"All night. We have to do it five times. Do you think you can do it that many times?"

He shrugged. I laid out a paper in front of him, showing him the shapes so he would be able remember them all. I told him he could close his eyes if it would help him concentrate. The test conditions were less than perfect, but if there were any precognitive or telepathic powers present, five trials should be enough to demonstrate them.

Half an hour later, I knew.

Martians aren't telepathic.

But they do like rainbow sherbet. A lot.

*　　*　　*

There were other tests. Not many. Not anything too weird. Just little ones that might indicate if there was something worth further investigation. There wasn't. As near as I could determine, there was nothing so unusual about Dennis that it would register as a statistical anomaly in a repeatable testable circumstance. He couldn't levitate. He couldn't move objects. He couldn't make things disappear. He didn't know how to *grok*. He could only hold his breath for thirty-three seconds. He couldn't *think* muscles. He couldn't see around corners.

But—

He *could* predict elevators. Take him into any building, anywhere. Take him to the elevator bank. Let him push the up button. Don't say a word. Without fail, the door he stands in front of will be the one where the first elevator arrives. Was he wishing them or predicting them? I don't know. It's useful only at science fiction conventions, which are legendary for recalcitrant elevators. It has little value anywhere else in the world.

He could make stop lights turn green—sometimes. Mostly, he waited until he saw the lights for the cross street turn yellow before he announced his wish. Maybe he could still make the Dodgers score four runs in two innings—but it wasn't consistent. We went back to Dodger Stadium in May, and either Dennis wasn't wishing or he really had used up all his wishes.

He *could* sing with perfect pitch, especially if the lyrics were about Popeye's gastrointestinal distress. He could play a video game for four hours straight without food or water. He could invent an amazing number of excuses for not staying in bed. He could also hug my neck so hard that once I felt a warning crack in my trachea. My throat hurt for a week afterward.

I began to think that *maybe* I had imagined the whole thing.

*　　　*　　　*

On school nights, I tucked him in at 9:30. We had a whole ritual. If there was time, we read a storybook together; whatever was appropriate. Afterward, prayers—

"I'm sorry God for…I didn't do anything to be sorry for."

"How about sassing your dad? Remember you had to take a time-out?"

"Oh, yeah. I'm sorry God for sassing my dad. Thank you God for… um, I can't think of anything."

"Going swimming."

"No. Thank you God for Calvin, my cat."

"Good. Anything else you want to say to God?"

"Does God hear the prayers of Martians?"

"Uh…of course he does. God hears everybody's prayers."

"Not Martians."

"Yes, even Martians."

"Uh-uh."

"Why do you say no?"

"Because God didn't make any Martians."

"If God didn't make the Martians, then who did?"

"The devil."

"Did the devil make you?"

"Uh-huh."

"How do you know?"

"Because…I'm a Martian."

"Mm," I said, remembering a little speech I'd made just about a year ago. *Let it be all right for him to be a Martian for as long as he needs to be.* "All right," I said. "But let me tell you a secret," I whispered. "The devil didn't make any Martians. That's just a lie the devil wants you to believe. God made the Martians."

"Really?"

"Cross my heart and hope to die. Stick a noodle in my eye."

"How do you know?" He was very insistent.

"Because I talk to God every night," I said. "Just like you, I say my prayers. And God made everything in the world."

"But Martians aren't from this world—"

"That's right. But God made Mars too. And everything on it. Just like she made this world, she made a whole bunch of others, and Mars was one of them. Honest."

"How come you say 'she' when you talk about God?"

"Because sometimes God is female and sometimes God is male. God is everything. And now it's time for you to stop asking questions and go to sleep. Hugs and kisses—?"

"Hugs and kisses."

"G'night. No more talking."

"I love you."

"I love you too. Now no more talking."

"Dad?'

"What?"

"I have to tell you something."

"What?"

"I love you."

"I love you too. Now, shhh. No more talking, Dennis."

"G'night."

"Sleep tight—"

Finally, I got smart. I stopped answering. Control freaks. We each wanted to have the last word.

*   *   *

I padded barefoot down the hall. I stopped in the living room long enough to turn off the television set, the VCR, and the surround-sound system. I continued on through the dining room and finally to my office. Two computers sat on my desk, both showing me that it was 9:47. The monster-child had manipulated an extra seventeen minutes tonight.

I sat down in my chair, leaned back, put my feet up on my desk, and stared out at the dark waters of the swimming pool in the back yard. The pool glowed with soft blue light. The night was...silent. Somewhere, a dog, barked.

Somewhere—that was his name, yes; he was a writer's dog—lived under my desk. Whenever I said, "Let's go to work," wherever he was in the house, Somewhere would pick himself up and laboriously pad-pad-pad into my office where he'd squelch himself flat and scrooch his way under the desk, with a great impassioned Jewish sigh of, "I hope you appreciate what I do for you."

He'd stay there all day—as long as the computer was on. Somewhere would only come out for two things: cookies and the doorbell...and the doorbell was broken. It had been broken for as long as I'd lived in this house. I'd never had the need to get it fixed. If someone came to the door, the dog barked.

Somewhere, the dog, barked.

That was why I loved him so much. He was a living cliché. He was the only possible justification for one of the most infamous sentences in bad writing. It was just a matter of placing the commas correctly.

Somewhere had just enough intelligence to keep out of the way and more than enough intelligence to find his dinner dish—as long as no one moved it. He spent his mornings resting under my desk, his afternoons snoozing behind the couch, his evenings snoring next to Dennis; he spent the hours before dawn in the dark space underneath the headboard of my bed, dreaming about the refrigerator.

Almost every night, just as Dennis began saying his prayers, Somewhere would come sighing down the hall, a shaggy, absent-minded canine-American. He'd step over everything that was in his way, uncaring if he knocked over a day's worth of Lego construction. He'd climb onto the bed, over my lap, over Dennis, grumbling softly as he found his position next to Dennis. With his prehensile tongue, he could slurp the inside of Dennis's right ear from the left side of his head, taking either the internal or external route.

Tonight, though, he knew I wasn't finished working. I had some serious thinking to do. He remained under the desk, sighing about the overtime. "You're in super-golden hours," I said to him; he shut up.

Whenever I'm in doubt about something, I sit down and start writing. I write down everything I'm feeling or thinking or worrying about. I say everything there is to say until there's nothing left to say. The first time I did this was the day after my dad died. I sat and wrote for two days. When I was finished, I had a Nebula-nominated story, *In the Deadlands*. To this day I still don't fully understand what the story was about, but the emotional impact of it is undeniable. It still gives me the shudders.

But the lesson I learned from that experience was the most important thing I've ever learned about storytelling. Effective writing isn't in the mechanics. Anyone can master the mechanical act of stringing together words and sentences and paragraphs to make a character move from A to B. The bookstores are full of evidence. But that's not writing. Writing isn't about the words, it's about the experience. It's about the *feeling* that the story creates inside of you. If there's no feeling, there's no story.

But sometimes, there's only the feeling without any meaning or understanding. And that's not a story either. What I was feeling about Dennis was so confusing and troubling and uncertain that I couldn't even begin to sort it out. I needed to write down all the separate pieces— as if in the act of telling, it would sort itself out. Sometimes the process worked.

When I looked up again, three hours had passed. My back and shoulders ached. The dog had gone to bed, and I felt I had accomplished nothing at all except to delineate the scale of my frustration.

Why would an alien species come to this planet? The last time I spent that much time on this question, I came up with giant pink man-eating slugs in search of new flavors. Why would Martians send their children to Earth?

The most logical idea that I came up with was that they were here as observers. Spies.

Haven't you ever been pulling on your underwear and realized that your dog or your cat is watching you? Haven't you ever considered the possibility that the creature is sharing your secrets with some secret network of dogs and cats? *"Oh, you think that's weird? My human wears underwear with pictures of Rocky and Bullwinkle on them."*

But dogs and cats are limited in what they can observe. If you *really* want to know a culture, you have to be a member of it. But an alien couldn't step in and pretend to be a member of this culture, could he? He'd have to learn. He'd have to be taught…

Where could a Martian go to get lessons in being a human? Who gives lessons in human beingness?

Mommies and Daddies. That's right.

*   *   *

"You're too paranoid," my sane friend said. He asked me to leave his name out of this narrative, so I'll just call him my sane friend.

"What do you mean?"

"You think that aliens are all motivated by evil intentions. You've written four novels about evil aliens eating our children, and you're working on a fifth. Isn't it possible that you're wrong?"

"*Moi?* Wrong?"

"Do you ever think about the cuckoo?" my sane friend asked.

"No," I said.

"Well, think about the cuckoo for a moment."

"Okay."

"How do you feel about the cuckoo?" he asked.

"It's an evil bird," I said. "It lays its egg in the sparrow's nest. The cuckoo chick pushes the other babies out of the nest. The sparrow ends up raising it—even at the expense of her own young. It's a parasite."

"See, that's your judgment talking—"

"That's the truth—" I started to object.

"Is it? Is that what you tell Dennis about his birth-mother?"

"Uh—I tell him that his birth-mom couldn't take care of him. And that she loves him and misses him. And that's the truth. Sort of… whitewashed."

My sane friend grinned at me.

"Okay," I admitted. "I'm protective of my son. So what?"

My sane friend shrugged. "How do you think the cuckoo feels?"

"Birds don't feel."

"If it could feel, how do you think it would feel?"

I thought about it. The first image that came to mind was the silly little bird from the Dr. Seuss story; the one who flew off, leaving Horton the elephant to hatch her egg. I shook my head. "I'm not getting anything useful—"

"How do you think Dennis's mother feels?"

I shook my head again. "Everything I've heard about her…I can't empathize."

"All right, try it this way. Under what circumstances would *you* give Dennis up?"

"I'd die before I'd give him up," I said. "He makes me happier than anybody I've ever known before. Just looking at him, I get an endorphin rush. If anybody started proceedings to take him out of my home, I'd have him on a plane to New Zealand so fast—" I stopped. "Oh, I see what you mean." I thought about it. "If I wasn't able to take care of him, or if I thought I was hurting him, or if I thought I wasn't doing a good enough job—" There was that old *familiar* twinge again. "If I thought he'd *really* be better off with someone else, I'd want him to have the best chance possible. But I just can't see that happening."

"Uh-huh…" My sane friend grinned. "*Now*, how do you think the Martians feel?"

"Huh?"

He repeated the question.

I thought about it for a while. "I'd have to assume that if they have the capability to implant their children in human wombs that they would have a highly developed science and technology and that implies—to me anyway—a highly developed emotional structure and probably a correspondingly well-developed moral structure as well. At least, that's what I'd like to believe."

"And if what you believe is true…" he started to say.

I finished the thought for him. "…then the Martians are trusting us with their children."

"Aren't they?" he asked.

I didn't answer. I didn't like where that train of thought might lead. But I followed it anyway.

"Would you trust your child to apes or wolves?" my sane friend asked.

"No," I said. "You know what happens to feral children."

He nodded. "I've read the same books you have."

"So, if the Martians are trusting us with their children…then that implies that either they don't care about their children very much—or they do."

"You want my best guess?"

"This is where you resolve everything for me, isn't it?"

"No. This is where I tell you what I think. I think they're engaged in a long-term breeding experiment…to upgrade the level of intelligence and compassion in the human race."

"Yeah?" I gave him my best raised-eyebrow look. "Remember what happened to Spock? He was a half-breed too. His parents wanted to breed a logical human. Instead, they got an emotional Vulcan."

"Have you got a better guess?"

"No," I admitted. "But what kind of Martians *are* we raising?"

"What kind of Martian are *you* raising?" he corrected.

And that really did it for me. That was the question. "I don't know," I finally admitted. "But—he is mine to raise, isn't he?"

"Yep," my sane friend agreed.

That thought echoed for a long long moment. Finally, I acknowledged the truth of it with a grin. "Yeah," I said. "I can live with that…"

$$* \qquad * \qquad *$$

As a literary puzzle, this is incomplete. As a story, it doesn't work. There's no ending.

There isn't enough evidence for me to even *suggest* a conclusion. What do we know about the Martians? For that matter, what do we really know about ourselves? There's nothing to extrapolate. And if the Martians are really engaged in some kind of large-scale genetic engineering we won't really know what their intentions are until the Martian children start reaching adulthood. Dennis will be old enough to vote in 2005. And that raises *another* question. *How long* have the Martians been planting their babies in human homes? Maybe we *already* live in a Martian-influenced world?

Maybe the Martian children will be super geniuses, inventing cold fusion and silicon sentience and nanotechnological miracles—Stephen Hawking and Buckminster Fuller. Maybe they'll be spiritual saviors, bringing such superior technology of consciousness that those of us brave enough to follow will achieve the enlightenment of saints. Maybe they'll be demagogues and dictators. Or maybe they'll be madmen and all end up in institutions. And maybe they'll be monsters, giving us a new generation of serial killers and cult-leaders—Jack the Ripper and Charles Manson.

All we can do is wait and see how it works out.

$$* \qquad * \qquad *$$

There's one more thing.

In reviewing the material for this story, I came across a curious coincidence. Kathy Bright had given me several huge stacks of reports on Dennis, written by various therapists and counselors. I hadn't had time to read them all, and after the first few, I stopped—I didn't want *their* experience of Dennis; I wanted to make up my own mind. But as I paged through the files, looking for Martian stuff, one of them caught my eye. On Saturday, June 27th, 1992, Carolyn Green (the counselor on his case at the time) had noted, "Dennis thinks God doesn't hear his prayers, because he wished for a dad and nothing happened."

I first saw Dennis's picture on Saturday, June 27th, 1992, at about two in the afternoon. According to Carolyn Green's report, that was the exact time of his weekly session. I cannot help but believe that he was wishing for a dad at the exact moment I first saw his picture. *A Martian wish.* Was that what I felt so strongly?

Does it mean anything? Maybe. Maybe not. In any case, I know better than to argue with Martian wishes. Tonight, at bed time, he wished for me to be happy.

I had to smile. "Was that a Martian wish?" I asked.

"Yes," he said, in a voice that left no room for disagreement.

"Then, I'm happy," I said. And in fact, I was.

I hadn't realized it before, because I hadn't acknowledged it, not even to myself; but as I walked back down the hall to my office, I had to admit that I was glowing. I'd gotten everything I'd wanted, a wonderful son, a profound sense of family, a whole new reason for waking up in the morning. So what if he's a Martian, it really doesn't matter, does it? He's my *son*, and I love him. I'm not giving him up. He's *special*.

When Dennis puts his mind to it, he can predict elevators and make stoplights turn green and help the Dodgers win baseball games. He can make lottery tickets pay off (a little bit, four numbers at a time) and he can wish a father into his life. That's pretty powerful stuff.

I think we might experiment with that a little bit more. We haven't bought any lottery tickets in a while. Maybe we should buy a couple tonight. And if that works, who knows what else he could wish for. I was thinking of asking him to wish for a Hugo award for his dad—just a test, you understand—but this morning, he announced he was going to wish for a mom instead. I'll be *very* interested to see how that one works out.

AUTHOR'S ORIGINAL (1994) AFTERWORD:

This story is, to the best of my knowledge, a work of fiction.

Yes, I have an adopted son. Yes, his name is Dennis. No, he is not a Martian.

I asked him if he was. He said he wasn't. Then he came over and whispered in my ear, "I said no because we're not supposed to tell."

AUTHOR'S BELATED (1995) AFTERWORD:

A year after this story was published, I reread it and noticed that I had made some minor structural errors in the narrative, and that it would probably be stronger if I rearranged and tweaked a couple bits in the middle and the end—but by that time the story had already won the Hugo, the Nebula, and the Locus Readership Poll, so I figured it was too late.

AUTHOR'S CURRENT (2003) AFTERWORD:

Did anybody get the license number of the truck that hit me?

When Tor Books asked me to expand "The Martian Child" into a short novel, I was delighted. Now I would be able to tell the rest of the story. This section of the book—"Pickled Mongoose"—is my favorite part of the whole adventure because it captures the exquisite little moment in which my son and I began to become a real family.

This is a true story. It isn't science fiction. It isn't fantasy. It isn't magical realism or anything else. This is word-for-word what happened.

Pickled Mongoose

excerpted from the novel version of
The Martian Child

ONCE UPON A TIME, I'd had this fantasy, I wouldn't tell my mother anything at all about the impending adoption—then one day, I'd show up at her house with a little boy. She would look at him ask, "Who's this?" And I would reply, "Your new grandson." Just for the look on her face and the resulting shriek of surprise.

Of course, it couldn't work that way. The caseworkers needed to know that the extended family would be supportive of the adoption, so everybody had to be on board, even before they met the child.

On the other hand, telling a Jewish mother she has a new grandson, but can't meet him yet is almost as exquisite. On the scale of unbearable anticipation, it outranks the first trip to Disneyland. It's right up there with chocolate, redheads, and honeymoons.

Mom and Harvey lived fifteen minutes away. Three miles east, three miles south on the 405, two miles east on the 101—

Summer evenings in California are surly, with the hot breath of the wind breathing down the back of your neck like a giant Labrador Retriever. In an open convertible, the air roars past, all dry and leathery. It always makes me think of Raymond Chandler's literary housewives fingering the edges of kitchen knives and studying their husband's necks.

As we slid through the glimmering night, Dennis asked, "What's she making for dinner?"

Without missing a beat, I deadpanned, "Pickled mongoose."

I might just as well have switched on an air-raid siren: *"I don't want pickled mongoose. I don't like pickled mongoose. I'm not eating pickled mongoose—"*

"Have you ever had pickled mongoose? How do you know you don't like it if you've never had it?"

"I don't want pickled mongoose. I don't like pickled mongoose. I'm not eating pickled mongoose—"

"You'll take one taste. You'll try it. Maybe you'll like. Grandma Jo makes the best pickled mongoose in the whole world. She does this thing with cobra sauce—"

"I don't want pickled mongoose. I don't like pickled mongoose. I'm not eating pickled mongoose—"

Uh-oh. He was taking me serious.

This was a double whammy. I wasn't used to people taking me serious. And worse, it meant that Dennis didn't understand jokes. Not good.

The ability to joke is the difference between sane people and crazy people. Crazy people don't do jokes. I wondered just how big a problem this was going to be—

"I don't want pickled mongoose. I don't like pickled mongoose. I'm not eating pickled mongoose—"

By now, we were in serious risk of Dennis shattering large chunks of air out of the sky. I had no idea what the limits of his lung power might be. This could go on for days—

I remembered an old piece of engineering wisdom: "If you don't know where the *off*-switch is, don't press the *on*-button." It applied to children too.

We got off the freeway at Van Nuys Blvd. Turn right, turn left, turn left and we're there. Dennis was still going strong. Sooner or later, he would have to take a breath—

I let him out of the car and pointed him toward the rear of the complex. "See those stairs? Grandma Jo and Grandpa Harvey live at the top." He rushed up the stairs ahead of me, then stopped and waited.

I knocked on the screen door and hollered, "Hello! Burglar—where do you hide the gold and jewelry?"

"Come on in. The gold is in the safe, the jewelry is under the bed."

Dennis followed me in. Grandma Jo was in the kitchen; she turned to us, wiping her hands on a towel. Dennis went straight to her, skipping all introductions. "What are you making for dinner?" he demanded.

"Chicken. And salad. And smashed potatoes."

"You're not making *pickled mongoose—?*"

She didn't even blink. To her credit, she had always been fast on the uptake; it had only taken thirty years for her to figure out that her first-born son was *meshuge*. (This may have been why there was no second-born son.)

"Pickled mongoose? Oh, no." Dennis shot me a look of angry accusation. And then she added, "The store was all out of mongoose. I'll make it next time."

Dennis's expression turned back into a suspicious frown. He looked back and forth between us with narrowed eyes. Maybe he was starting to figure it out. I hoped so.

Harvey handed me a tumbler of scotch. I took a sip. The Chivas 100 Blend. Not available in the States. I'd picked up two bottles at the duty free store on my way back from England a year ago and given one to Harve for Father's Day. "Mm, the good stuff. What's the special occasion?"

"You are."

"Well, we do have some news. Dennis, do you want to tell them?"

"David's gonna 'dopt me. He's gonna be my dad—and you're gonna be my Grandma and Grandpa!" He practically shouted the news.

"Oh, good," Mom said, "That means I get to hug you—" She swept him into her arms and he grabbed her around the waist and held on tight. It was a perfect fit. Grandpa too. I couldn't tell who was happier. I promised myself this kid was going to spend a lot of time with his grandparents; it was all part of my secret plan to give him as many happy memories as possible.

And for a moment, I thought of my own Grandma. I hadn't realized until now how much a part of my life she'd been and how much I missed her…and how much she would have loved Dennis.

And then, of course, the inevitable Grandma moment. "Well, you must be very hungry. Sit down and I'll serve—"

Dennis eyed his dinner suspiciously.

"Relax, it's chicken," I said. "Nobody can torture a chicken like your Grandma Jo. That was chicken, wasn't it, Mom?"

"That's what it said on the wrapper."

"I dunno…it tastes like rattlesnake to me. Doesn't it taste like rattlesnake to you, Dennis?"

"No!" he insisted. "It tastes like chicken!"

"Or maybe iguana?"

"Chicken!"

"I can make iguana for you sometime, then we'll see—"

"No!"

I decided not to pursue it. Probably a wise decision.

As soon as he finished eating, Dennis asked quietly, "Can I wash the dishes?"

My mother looked at me, eyebrows raised. *This is the monster child you were so worried about?* To Dennis, she said, "Of course you can, sweetheart."

We watched as he very carefully cleared the table, taking all the dishes to the sink. He made three deliberate trips. Then he turned on the water and began sudsing and scrubbing.

"Do you rent him out?"

Very softly, I said, "He's trying to show us how much he wants to fit in. He's terrified it won't work."

"Of course, it's going to work," she said, not bothering to whisper. "He's a good kid."

Harvey added, "All you have to do is love him."

"Well, that's the game plan—"

"You're going to have to find a school for him," said Harvey.

"And he's going to need new clothes," said Mom. "Shoes, shirts, pants. What size is he? I'll take him to the mall—"

"Just a minute here," I interrupted. "If you want to spoil a kid, spoil your own. This one is mine to spoil—"

Dennis walked out of the kitchen, a dish and a towel in his hand. His expression was serious. Very soft and very polite, he said, "She could spoil me if she wants to." His timing and delivery were perfect. He returned to the kitchen without further comment.

Mom and Harvey looked at him, then to me. Mom said, "I think you've met your match."

Harvey added, "He's going to fit into this family, just fine."

"I think so."

"Does he ever smile?" Harvey asked softly.

"Give him time. He hasn't had a lot to smile about yet. That's first on my list of things to do."

*   *   *

On the day he moved in—*officially* moved in—Kathy told me she'd never seen him so happy. I asked her to remind him of that conversation he'd had with the counselor. "Remember when he said, 'I don't think

God listens to my prayers.' Tell him that sometimes it takes God a little while to make a miracle happen."

Dennis moved in with a small battered suitcase, half full of worn-out hand-me-downs; and a large cardboard box, less than half full of pieces of broken toys. His entire life could be carried in one trip.

Unpacking his few belongings was painful. Everything was tattered. Everything was precious. A too-small T-shirt autographed by Luc Robitaille and Wayne Gretsky. A sad and faded, dirty-with-age, stuffed gingerbread man named Eric. A few photographs of a long-ago trip to the Los Angeles County Fair. The only evidence of a past. Not much evidence of a life though.

He had only a few pairs of underpants. Three of them had pockets sewn onto the front. "What's this?" I asked.

"That's for the buzzer. If I wet the bed, it buzzes and wakes me up."

"We're not going to do that here," I said, tossing the underwear aside. "You won't be wearing those again." We put the T-shirts in one drawer, the shorts in another, and we were through unpacking.

"We can throw this out," I said, holding up his small battered suitcase. It was pretty much falling apart.

"No," he said firmly. "I'll need it when I move out."

"No, you won't. You're not moving out. This is *it*."

"When I have to go back to Mars," he said. He took the suitcase from me and put it into the closet.

*　　*　　*

Dennis needed *everything*.

We spent the week shopping.

Shoes. Underpants. T-shirts. Shorts. Socks. A jacket. A new teddy bear. Some storybooks for bedtime. Not too much, but enough. Christmas was coming soon, Santa was going to be very very good to this little boy.

It wasn't just his miracle, it was mine as well. I was terrified that it wasn't real, that somebody somewhere was going to realize that they'd made a horrible mistake placing him with me, and that suddenly one day, they'd come and pack him up and take him away, and the adventure would be over.

I spent the first three or four weeks with him in a state of absolute wonder that I had this wonderful little person in my life. I read him a story every night, tucked him into bed, hugged him, kissed him, told him how special he was to me, turned off the light and tiptoed out. I'd wait fifteen minutes, get a box of Kleenex, then tiptoe back in and sit and watch him sleep for an hour or two. It was better than television—and it was one of my few chances to see what he actually looked like; the rest of the time, he was mostly a blur with a smile.

I developed a routine for the mornings. First I'd turn to the little voice in my head that was muttering in amazement, "There's a seven o'clock in the morning too?!" and say, "Thank you for sharing that, now shut up."

Then I'd wake Dennis up and before his blood sugar could remind him that he was hyperactive, I'd hand him a glass of orange juice and pop him into the tub and start a hot breakfast. Hot cereal. Or pancakes, Dennis loved pancakes. Or scrambled eggs and bacon. Toast and jelly. But no waffles. For Christmas, I'd bought a waffle iron that made waffles shaped like Mickey Mouse—but Dennis wouldn't eat anything that looked like a giant grinning mongoose.

I gained five pounds. The last time I'd actually eaten breakfast, it had been an unwitting mistake—brought on by crossing the International Date Line on a sixteen hour red-eye.

And then, one morning, right on schedule, it was time to test the rules. He decided he didn't want to eat breakfast. I told him he had to. He said no, and then abruptly he announced, "The adoption is off, I'm moving out." He went to the front door, walked out, and closed it behind him. I waited thirty seconds, then followed. He was standing on the front porch, waiting for me.

Very calmly, I said, "You can't move out until you finish breakfast."

So he came back in and ate.

As he was finishing, I said, "Why don't you go to school now, and you can move out after you get home from school, all right?"

He went to school.

When he got home from school, I handed him a peanut butter sandwich, and said, "Listen, why don't you wait and run away from home on the weekend. You can go farther."

I kept that up for three days, until he finally said, "I'm not going to run away from home." That night, I made a note in my journal: "Sighted manipulation, sank same."

I had a plan. Affirmations—lots of little reminders, like pebbles in the stream, to let him how much he was loved—that he was finally *connected*. And choices—opportunities to feel in control, to give him back a sense of power over his own life; the system had stolen that from him, yanking him around from place to place like a case-file shuffled from desk to desk. And most of all, *a safe place* just to be—so he could have an emotional ground of being, and a sense that he wasn't alone anymore.

That last one would be the hardest to achieve.

The supermarket was always a challenge. He had to push the cart. No one else was allowed to touch it—*Gran Prix de Vons*. Up one aisle and down the next at Mach eight-and-a-half and in six months Mach nine. And always, strange things kept finding their way into the cart.

It amused me, how my shopping list had suddenly transformed. White bread instead of sourdough. Peanut butter. Jelly. Spaghetti. Tomato sauce. Hamburger. Cookies. Cheerios. Oatmeal. Cream Of Wheat—that was my favorite when I was little. Malt-O-Meal. Ice cream. Hot dogs. Buns. Mustard, ketchup, relish. Chocolate for Daddy. Apples, bananas, grapes. Dog biscuits. "You and Somewhere will have to share these."

"I don't like dog biscuits."

"Then Somewhere will eat your share."

And in the middle of all this shopping, I had a flash of recognition—I was *being* Daddy. This was what it looked like. This was what it *felt* like.

Kewl.

I could get used to this. This was good.

On the drive home, I asked. "What should I make for dinner tonight? How about pickled mongoose?"

I should have known better—

"You're making fun of me—!"

"Huh? No, I'm not!"

"I don't like it when people make fun of me! The kids at school used to make fun of me all the time. 'You live in a group home. You live in a group home.'"

I pulled the car over to the side. "I'm not making fun of you, sweetheart."

He was adamant. *"Yes, you are—"*

sigh

This part wasn't in the manual.

For some odd reason, I had a picture in my head of John F. Kennedy discovering that there were nuclear missiles in Cuba, in October of 1962. His reaction? "This is the day we earn our salary."

"Dennis, let me explain something to you about jokes. People don't tell jokes to make fun of each other. People tell jokes because they like each other. Jokes are a way of playing together."

"I don't like it! It feels like you're making fun of me! Everybody always makes fun of me!"

"Sweetheart, I'm not making fun of you. I will *never* make fun of you. You're my favorite kid in the whole wide world. And you need to learn something very important here. You're in a family of people who love to tell jokes. It's our way of saying, 'I love you, play with me.' So you're going to have to learn how to tell jokes too."

"I don't know any jokes—"

That stopped me for a moment. A kid who didn't know any jokes? "Okay, I'll teach you one."

He fell silent. I went rummaging frantically through the attics of memory for the easiest and silliest joke I had.

"Okay, ready? Why do elephants have such big trunks?"

"I dunno."

"Because they don't have glove compartments."

"What's a glove department?"

Right.

We had a lot of work to do.

"See this thing here in front of you? It opens up. That's a glove compartment. It's called a glove compartment because you put gloves in it."

"I don't have any gloves."

"Nobody in California does. It's against the law. But the cars are all made in Detroit or Tokyo, where everybody wears gloves. So that's why they put glove compartments into cars. So now you know why elephants have such big trunks—"

"Because they don't have glove departments."

"Close enough. Very good. Now you tell that joke to everybody you meet."

"Will they laugh?"

"I'm sure they will. If they don't, we'll return the joke to the manufacturer and get a full refund."

For the next few weeks, he told that joke to everyone he saw— Grandma and Grandpa. Our neighbor, Roz. The waitress at the corner coffee shop. Julieanne, his therapist. Aunt Alice. Susie, my assistant. And it didn't even matter if he got it right. "Why don't elephants have glove departments—because they have trunks?" "Why don't elephants have trunks—because they have glove departments?" "Where do elephants put their gloves? In their trunks." And everybody he told it to laughed. Every time.

It was basic Communication Theory: Jokes are a way of producing a happy response in people. If you want to be liked, tell jokes; it shows you want to play. And that's all that any of us really want—the chance to play together.

Dennis had been given one of the keys to the universe, and he was unlocking everything he could.

"Knock knock."

"Who's there?"

"Orange?"

His eyes narrowed. "Orange who?"

"Orange you glad I didn't say 'banana?' "

He made me sorry I taught him that one—I had to hear it a dozen times a day for the next two months. Some jokes are funny once. Some jokes are funny every time. It depends on who's telling them. But if you're only eight years old, it doesn't matter. The fun is in the telling, not the punch line. The fun is in the laughing.

And then one morning, while I was getting him ready for school—we were still only a few weeks into this adventure—I put him into the bathtub, a naked little toothpick of a child with puppy-dog eyes and Liz Taylor eyelashes. A little bubble bath and he was happy. He could wash himself, but he liked being taken care of. I wondered if anybody had ever really taken care of him before.

Okay, time to go start some water boiling for hot cereal. I stopped and asked, "What do you want for breakfast? Cream of Wheat? Or Malt-O-Meal?"

He looked up at me, with an expression so innocent, you could have used it as icing on a birthday cake. Very softly, very shyly, he said, "Pickled mongoose…" And waited for my reaction.

I blinked.

"Um—" For half an instant, I was annoyed, because he hadn't answered the question I'd asked, and then the enormity of what had just happened sank in. I grinned. "Okay. Pickled mongoose it is." And then, as an afterthought, "Do you want the Cream of Wheat flavored pickled mongoose or Malt-O-Meal flavor?"

"Cream of Wheat flavor."

"Okay, Cream of Wheat flavor pickled mongoose, coming right up." And we both smiled.

Halfway to the kitchen, in the middle of the hall, where not even the dog could see me, I stopped for a quick, silent victory dance, punching the air with both fists in one-two triumph. *"Yes!"*

That's what miracles look like.

AUTHOR'S AFTERWORD:

Okay, I admit it. I'm the hero in the movie of my life. So far, it's been a terrific adventure, filled with fascinating and bizarre characters, strange events, and fabulous relationships. Plus, whatever else you might say about children, they're great source material…

Interlude #2

Selections from *The Quote-Book of Solomon Short*

"A little ignorance goes a long way."

"Hell hath no fury like a pacifist."

"The most important invention in the history of the human race is the written contract. It makes it possible for individual parties to list all the different ways they distrust each other."

"There is no such thing as absolute truth. This is absolutely true."

"The only winner of the War of 1812 was Tchaikovsky."

"I'm all in favor of keeping dangerous weapons out of the hands of fools. Let's start with typewriters."

"Rome didn't fall in a day either."

"The Lord giveth, the Lord taketh away. Fickle, fickle Lord."

"History is written by the survivors."

"The universe does not give first warnings. Or second chances."

"Cats don't adopt people. They adopt refrigerators."

"A bleeding heart is hell on the carpeting."

"Every question defines its own answer—except perhaps, 'Why a duck?'"

"'I was only following orders' is not an excuse—it's an indictment."

"You can't fight the law of conservation of energy. You can bargain with it, but you can't fight it."

"Bread always falls butter-side down. If it doesn't, you buttered it on the wrong side."

"History is full of revisionists. Where it used to say, *'THOU SHALT NOT KILL'* it now says, *'except as specified in section III-B, Paragraph 12, Sub-section D, Schedule 3.'* If that still doesn't suit you, wait till next year's commandments come out and trade it in for something that does."

"The boss may not always be right, but he's always the boss."

"What do you mean, 'There's no such thing as a free lunch?' *You* are the free lunch!"

"Frankly, I'm an agnostic. I believe the universe is innocent until proven guilty."

"You are *not* entitled to an opinion. An opinion is what you have when you don't have all the facts. When you have the facts, you don't need an opinion."

"Sex is friction. Preferably, friction with a friend. And preferably well-lubed. After that, it's all a matter of taste."

"A problem can be found for almost every solution."

"A diploma proves only that you know how to look up an answer."

"The liberal of any species is always more dangerous—because he always seems so much more rational."

"Dogs are always loyal. They've never learned better."

"Common sense isn't."

"The hard questions always have more than one right answer. The easy questions have no answers at all. That's the universe's way of keeping things balanced."

"Art is almost always a political statement—and politics is almost always an art."

"The Constitution of the United States guarantees every individual the right to make a damn fool of himself—in public or private, however he chooses."

"Money talks. Usually it says, 'Bend over.'"

"Elevators always travel in groups. Only one of them knows the way."

"Thoreau was no band-leader. The sound of all those different drummers makes it hell to organize a parade."

"When you divide people into *us* and *them*, you automatically become one of *them*."

"A bird in the hand makes blowing your nose difficult."

"The difference between the psychiatrist and the patient is that the psychiatrist has learned how to live with it."

"Neurosis is a communicable disease."

"Never justify anything. If it needs justification, it's already wrong."

"People use philosophy to justify their actions. Philosophy is the explanation we give afterward for acting like jerks."

"It ain't so hard to die for a cause. Any idiot can do that. What takes real genius is living for one."

"The only way to stop war once and for all is to keep it from being so much fun."

"Remember, today could just as easily be the *last* day of the rest of your life."

"Nature abhors a hero."

"You have to know what you're looking for before you can find it."

"Somebody should have warned the Trojans. Beware of gifts bearing Greeks."

"Bad taste is timeless."

"You deserve the gods you worship."

"Murphy's law is always a good excuse."

May 13, 1987

Star Trek:
The Next Generation

Blood and Fire

by David Gerrold

In October of 1986, Paramount Pictures announced that Gene Roddenberry would produce a new Star Trek series. Shortly after that, I was hired as Story Editor/Creative Consultant/Executive Memo Writer/Hold On, David, We're Thinking Up A New Job Title—Anything But Producer. A couple of weeks after that initial announcement, before any plans for the new show had been finalized—not even a name—both Gene and I were guests at a Star Trek convention in Boston. In answer to a fan's question about gay crewmembers, Gene said it was long overdue and promised to make it happen. Later he repeated that pledge to the staff. Rick Berman wrote a very early memo to Gene and the staff about Star Trek's commitment to "issue" stories—and one of the issues he raised was AIDS.

This script was my personal attempt to honor both of those promises, but it was never produced. At the time, the official story was that it wasn't good enough. You can read the unofficial story in any of the several hundred books, articles, memoirs, and blogs that have been written in the twenty years since then—all of them written by people who weren't in the room and are describing their own interpretations of other people's interpretations of events they didn't witness personally, but have since edited to fit into their own personal narratives, specifically designed to make the teller look good in the telling. Once I realized I was trapped in a vast game of Russian Telephone, I decided not to play. I'm still not playing.

CHARACTERS

PICARD
RIKER
BEVERLY
WESLEY
DATA
TASHA
GEORDI
TROI
WORF
CON
FREEMAN (a medical technician)
HODEL (a computer technician)
EAKINS (a security officer)
JONAH YARELL (a Starfleet Military Specialist)
MACKEL BLODGETT (a Regulan Scientist)
AHRENS (an infected Copernicus crewman)
ASSORTED ENTERPRISE CREWMEMBERS
ASSORTED COPERNICUS SURVIVORS

SETS

ENTERPRISE BRIDGE
ENTERPRISE LOUNGE
READY ROOM
TRANSPORTER ROOM
SICK BAY
COPERNICUS BRIDGE (REDRESS *STAR TREK IV* BRIDGE)
COPERNICUS CORRIDORS (REDRESS ENTERPRISE)
COPERNICUS CARGO BAY (REDRESS HOLODECK)

TEASER

FADE IN:

ANGLE. ENTERPRISE MOVING THROUGH SPACE. APPROACHING.

THE COPERNICUS. A SCIENTIFIC RESEARCH VESSEL.

PICARD (V.O.)
Captain's Log. Stardate 41202.5. Approaching the
Copernicus, a scientific research vessel. The emergency
distress signal continues to repeat, but the Copernicus
appears to be adrift. There have been no answers
to any of our signals and our scanners are showing
confusing and contradictory readings.

INTERIOR TRANSPORTER ROOM.

PICARD is briefing RIKER. BEVERLY is briefing FREEMAN, a medical
technician. (He is carrying a portable medical kit.) TASHA and
GEORDI and EAKINS, a security officer, are waiting for Riker on the
platform. HODEL is working with WORF at the console.

ESTABLISH that Eakins, Hodel and Freeman are carrying tricorders.
As Beverly finishes briefing Freeman, he steps up onto the transporter
platform next to Eakins and pats his shoulder affectionately; these two
are obviously good friends.

These are the last few preparations before the mission team beams
over, with almost-overlapping conversations.

HODEL
(finishing at the console)
All tricorders are transmitting, Mr. Riker. Whenever
you're ready...
(he crosses to the transporter platform)

RIKER
Good. Dr. Crusher?

BEVERLY
(turns to Riker)
Auxiliary sick bay is active. All units standing at ready.

RIKER
Good.

PICARD
(to Beverly)
You can monitor your medical team from the bridge—
if you want. Commander Data is acting as Mission
Officer; he'll set it up.

RIKER
(turns to Geordi and Hodel)
La Forge, Hodel—Commander Data will want the
log from the Copernicus downloaded as quickly as
possible.

GEORDI / HODEL
Right, sir. / Yes, sir.

INSERT—WORF AT CONSOLE.

WORF
We're in transporter range, Captain.
(adds)
Bridge reports a repulsor field centered in the
Copernicus cargo bay.

BACK TO ANGLE.

RIKER
A repulsor field—?

PICARD
(guessing)
They're trying to isolate something—

RIKER
Suggestions, sir?

PICARD
It's your call, Number One.

RIKER

Thank you, sir. We'll start with the bridge.
(to the transporter chief)
Use the top deck coordinates, Chief.
*(to his team as he steps up onto
the transporter platform)*
All right, let's go—

GEORDI

—and watch out for Sparkle-Dancers and man-eating tribbles.

RIKER

(gives Geordi an annoyed look, then)
Energize.

MED ANGLE—WORF AT CONSOLE.

He works his controls.

MED. WIDE ANGLE—THE AWAY TEAM ON THE TRANSPORTER PLATFORM.

FX: TRANSPORTER. We see the transporter effect pile up in the air. WE HEAR the familiar transporter sound. Our people twinkle and fade out.

FADE OUT.

ACT ONE

FADE IN:

INTERIOR COPERNICUS CORRIDOR. (REDRESS ENTERPRISE)

The corridor is dark, shadowy, and very mysterious.

SFX: A different sound quality than the Enterprise. None of the familiar background noises of a living ship are present. The silence should be eerie. This ship is deserted.

FX: Occasional pink and gold flickers in the air.

Only a few, very small, very bright, very quick—almost subliminal. They exist at the fringes of our vision. They look like tiny stars twinkling for only the briefest of instants (two or three frames) and then they are gone.

IMPORTANT: WE WILL SEE THESE FLICKERS THROUGHOUT THE COPERNICUS.

FX: Transporter effect piles up. The away team beams in.

CLOSER ANGLE ON THE AWAY TEAM.

As they look around and spread out. Freeman and Hodel activate their tricorders and begin scanning.

RIKER
(holds up a hand)
Listen—

All stop. All listen.

HODEL
I don't hear anything.

GEORDI
That's just it. The monitors are down.

TASHA
This ship is dead.
(she takes out her phaser)

GEORDI
(noticing the phaser)
Afraid of ghosts?

TASHA
Nope. Just don't want to be one.

Riker looks grim. He motions Tasha and Eakins and Hodel one way. He and Geordi and Freeman move the opposite way.

ANGLE—CORRIDOR INTERSECTION. RIKER, FREEMAN AND GEORDI.

FX: More pink and gold flickers.

Eakins' tricorder picks up a clustering of flickers. He frowns.

FREEMAN
Sir?
(he points)

RIKER
(sees the flickers)
Geordi?

GEORDI
(looks, then shakes head)
Some kind of wavicle. I can't tell.

The flickers are drifting toward our people. They look harmless. They circle like fireflies, flickering in an out of existence. Geordi waves at them, trying to catch one in his hand. And then…they're gone.

GEORDI (CONT'D)
(As the last of the flickers vanishes, he giggles)
Hey! That tickles!

RIKER
(concerned)
Freeman?
(indicates Geordi)

FREEMAN

*(scanning Geordi, and reading his
tricorder, he shakes his head)*

I can't identify it, sir. The Enterprise will have to work
on this one.

INTERIOR ENTERPRISE BRIDGE.

Picard has been watching on the main viewer. He looks to Data.

DATA

Working on it now, sir.

BACK TO THE COPERNICUS—ANOTHER PART OF THE CORRIDOR.

Tasha, Eakins and Hodel come to a place where a door has been
blasted shut or somehow permanently sealed.

EAKINS

(examining the door)
It's sealed. Welded shut.

HODEL

This is spooky. There's no one here.
(to Tasha)
You ever seen anything like this before, Lieutenant?

TASHA

I've heard about ships found floating empty in
space—never seen one.
(beat)
Until now.

They exchange troubled looks and head back in the direction of Riker
and the others.

BACK TO CORRIDOR INTERSECTION.

Riker looks up as the others approach.

TASHA

That end is sealed off. No survivors. No bodies.

(beat)

No ghosts either.

RIKER

(one last look around)

All right. We'll use the manual access to the bridge.

(points)

That way.

INSERT—BRIDGE OF THE ENTERPRISE. FAVORING PICARD, DATA, BEVERLY AND TROI.

They are watching the main viewer. Troi looks troubled. Data is at a science station, next to Picard. He is frowning.

DATA

Mr. Riker. We're picking up scattered life readings throughout the Copernicus. But very faint.

RIKER (O.S.)

(filtered)

Any specific area?

DATA

No, sir—

(this is the hard part)

I can't localize them at all.

INSERT AS NEEDED. BRIDGE POV—THE MAIN VIEWER SHOWS THE POV OF THE AWAY TEAM.

We are moving through the Copernicus corridors.

BACK TO ANGLE.

Picard is tight-lipped and grim. Ditto, Beverly and Troi.

RIKER (O.S.)

(filtered)

What about the wavicles?

DATA
(very unhappy)

Still searching for a match, sir. There's nothing in the primary data banks.

INTERIOR COPERNICUS BRIDGE. DARK AND SILENT.
(This is a redress of the Enterprise bridge from *STAR TREK IV*.)

The Away Team enters the bridge silently. They are struck with the mystery of what has happened here. Geordi moves immediately to the forward consoles—**CAMERA PUSHES IN ON GEORDI** as he stops in surprise and dismay!

GEORDI
(screams in surprise and horror)

GEORDI'S POV. THE DESICCATED BODY OF A CREWMAN.

The body has fallen from the forward work station. It is **HALF-HIDDEN IN SHADOW**; we do not see it clearly—we have only a hint of the horror here. The crewperson looks mummified. What we can see suggests that the body is frozen in a position of horror or agony.

BACK TO GEORDI—HE BACKS AWAY QUICKLY.

WIDER ANGLE—MATCHING.

As the rest of the team comes up quickly. Freeman steps forward professionally. He begins scanning the body with his medical tricorder.

TASHA

Now we know who sent the distress signal.
(beat)
Poor bastard.

RIKER

Freeman?

FREEMAN
(doesn't like what he reads)

Sir? There's no blood in this man's body. No blood at all.

INSERT—EAKINS AND HODEL.

HODEL
(only half-joking)
Vampires! Space-vampires!
(shudders)

WIDER ANGLE. MATCHING. INCLUDING RIKER, GEORDI AND TASHA.

RIKER
(annoyed)
Belay that!

Riker sees that Geordi is still focused on the dead body—horrified and entranced.

RIKER
(to Geordi)
La Forge. Download the log—

GEORDI
(startled out of his horror)
Yes, sir!
(he steps away from the body to the forward console)
Sir—?
(looks back to Riker)

INSERT—THE FORWARD CONSOLE.

A large phaser burn scorch. The console is obviously unworkable.

INSERT—ANOTHER BRIDGE CONSOLE. HODEL.

This console is similarly out of commission.

HODEL
All the work stations are out.

Tasha steps into shot, frowning. She peers at the scorch.

> TASHA
> *(recognizes the work)*
> That's a phaser blast.

ON RIKER.

> RIKER
> What the hell?!

INSERT. ENTERPRISE BRIDGE. REACTION SHOT. PICARD.

All the consoles are destroyed?

> PICARD
> Will. I want the log of that ship.

> RIKER (O.S.)
> *(filtered)*
> Acknowledged.

ANGLE ON DATA AT A SCIENCE STATION.

Data is frowning at the readings on his screens.

> DATA
> *(to the Away Team)*
> Mr. Riker—! I've got a focus on those life form
> readings. They're very...strange.

Picard comes up behind him and looks over his shoulder. We see his concerned reaction.

> DATA
> And, sir—?
> *(beat while he studies his console)*
> The life forms are moving toward you.

BACK TO THE COPERNICUS—ANGLE ON ALL.

Eakins is studying his tricorder.

> EAKINS
> I'm reading it now too, sir!

Tasha, Geordi and Hodel draw their phasers.

EAKINS (CONT'D)
(he looks up and points)
It's coming from—

ANGLE ON TURBO-LIFT DOOR.

As it slides open and reveals AHRENS, a young Copernicus crewmember. He looks haggard and very sick. His skin is pale and puffy. He is wild-eyed with fear. He half-staggers, half-falls into the room.

Our people are startled and back away from him—all except Freeman, who is a medical technician. He steps forward professionally and begins scanning Ahrens with his medical tricorder throughout the following:

AHRENS
(gasping and coughing)
You're too late! They're all dead! Everyone is dead! You'll see! You're next!

INSERT—REACTION SHOT OF RIKER, TASHA AND GEORDI.

BACK TO AHRENS—AND FREEMAN SCANNING HIM.

Freeman looks up from his tricorder and shakes his head at Riker. This man is dying.

FREEMAN
(hitting the man with a hypo-spray)
Here. This will ease the pain—

AHRENS
(it doesn't work)
Oh, no! It's happening! Oh, please, no—
(to Tasha)
Kill me! Oh, God, please kill me!
(falls to the floor, clutching his belly—a dark red stain begins to spread across his torso)
Kill me! Quickly! God Damn You!

ON TASHA AND RIKER.

> ### TASHA
> *(reporting)*
> Enterprise. Your mysterious life forms are here. An injured crewman.

> ### DATA (O.S.)
> *(filtered)*
> I'm not talking about the crewman. The life forms are still moving toward you.

She and Riker look up startled. Exchange a glance.

BACK TO AHRENS AND FREEMAN. INCLUDE GEORDI.

The distraction was all that Ahrens needed. He leaps and grabs Geordi's phaser. He clutches it to himself and—

FX: Ahrens disintegrates in a multi-colored phaser burst. We see a cloud of sparkling gold and pink wavicles appear with the burst. They spread out quickly—including into our Enterprise people—and vanish.

BACK TO RIKER AND TASHA.

Horrified, Riker notes the appearance of the wavicles and touches his communicator.

> ### RIKER
> Enterprise. Did you get all that?

ENTERPRISE BRIDGE—FAVORING PICARD. INCLUDE CON AT FORWARD STATION.

All are stunned.

> ### RIKER (O.S.)
> *(filtered)*
> Enterprise. Acknowledge.

CLOSER ON PICARD. INCLUDE TROI, BEVERLY, AND DATA AT AFT SCIENCE STATION.

Picard massages his temple wearily. He touches a button on his chair arm.

PICARD
(hard to speak)
We saw it.

BACK TO RIKER.

RIKER

We have to assume the whole ship is infected.
Some kind of—we don't know. Did you see the
wavicle burst? We must also assume that we are all
contaminated.

BACK TO ENTERPRISE BRIDGE.

BEVERLY
What about the transporter biofilter?

PICARD
It won't filter out wavicles. Half-wave, half-particle,
they'd slip right through.

BEVERLY
We could beam them to an isolation bay.

PICARD
Same problem. Wavicles can't be contained.
(to his Science Officer)
Data?

DATA
(he knows something)
I have to agree with Mr. Riker.

BACK TO RIKER.

RIKER
Captain. We can't beam back.
(takes a breath)
We can't risk infecting the Enterprise. Do you agree…?

BACK TO PICARD.

PICARD

Yes, Will. I do.

(without emotion, as if quoting the book)

The safety of the Enterprise has to come first.

BACK TO RIKER.

He exchanges a grim look with his colleagues. They all understand that this is now a one-way mission.

BACK TO PICARD. INCLUDE TROI.

Picard sees how troubled Troi is by this.

PICARD

(To Troi)

Your assessment?

TROI

(forcing herself to be professional)

I'm sensing a great deal of fear and anger from the Copernicus. It's possible that the survivors have isolated themselves inside that cargo-bay repulsor field. They may not have any way to get a message out to us.

PICARD

Will? Did you hear that?

RIKER (O.S.)

(filtered)

We copy. We'll investigate.

PICARD

Get the log from that ship first. See if you can find working access, attach a terminal and start a total download.

RIKER (O.S.)

(filtered)

Will do.

Data and Beverly step into B.G. shot.

DATA
(softly)
Captain?

Picard looks up.

DATA
(trying to be discreet)
May we speak to you please?

Picard realizes that Data does not want what he has to say to be heard by the Away Team. He gets up and crosses to Data's science station at the rear of the bridge. **CAMERA MOVES WITH.**

AT THE AFT SCIENCE STATION. PICARD, DATA AND BEVERLY.

Data and Beverly both look very grim. Data indicates the readouts on the console.

DATA
(very softly)
Captain…I've been checking the historical records and…the observed phenomena on the Copernicus matches the description of…plasmasites.

BEVERLY
(beat)
Also known as…bloodworms.

Picard reacts sharply. Bloodworms?!!

DATA
The only recorded plasmasite infection occurred on the third planet of the Regulan system. That planet has been quarantined for nearly 150 years.

BEVERLY
(puzzled)
But I still get a 93% probability match on the symptoms—

PICARD
(extremely concerned)
Have you told anyone else this?

DATA
No, sir.

PICARD
Good. I don't want this discussed.

DATA
Captain—
(there's more bad news)
The historical precedent was—the complete and total destruction of every infested ship. Including crew and passengers. Rescue was not to be attempted.
(reluctantly)
Too many ships were lost attempting rescues.

Picard looks at them both. His expression is unhappy.

PICARD
There's got to be a way. That was…a hundred and fifty years ago.

BEVERLY
(and now the really bad news)
The problem is—
(it's hard to say)
—There's no known cure. There's no record that anybody has ever survived plasmasites…

Picard's expression tightens with anger. As if he is reminding himself that he must not kill the bearer of bad news. No matter how bad.

CAMERA PULLS OUT as Picard looks worriedly toward the forward viewer.

And we:

FADE OUT.

ACT TWO

FADE IN:

AS BEFORE—ENTERPRISE AND COPERNICUS.

PICARD

Captain's Log. Stardate 41202.6. Our Away Team has been exposed to plasmasite contamination aboard the Copernicus. We cannot beam them back. We have still had no contact with the Copernicus survivors…if any.

INTERIOR COPERNICUS CORRIDOR. HODEL AND EAKINS.

A wall panel has been opened up revealing a set of computer access connections. Hodel is tracing the lines with a logic probe. He is ready to connect his tricorder to a computer node.

HODEL
(talking to himself while he works)
Blue fiber to blue insert. Green to green. Just like home. Now—I need—that!
(speaking to Eakins, but not looking up from his work)
So how long have you and Freeman been together?

EAKINS
Is it that obvious?

HODEL
Yeah, it's that obvious.

EAKINS
Since the Academy. Two years.

HODEL
(he finds the connection he's been looking for)
Ah! Here. This one's live!
(reaching and stretching)
There! Got it.
(beat)
Enterprise—?

DATA (O.S.)
(filtered)
We're copying. Download is initiated.

HODEL
What the hell—??

INSERT—HODEL'S POV.

A light cable inside the wall panel. A single red worm is crawling along the cable.

HODEL AND EAKINS.

They both stare at it.

EAKINS
We better show that to Mr. Riker.

HODEL
Yeah.

He produces a small plastic sample case and flicks the bloodworm into it with his logic probe.

SFX: The bloodworm TRILLS angrily. But not very loud.

Both grin. Now, Hodel reaches deep into the access panel with one hand—

HODEL
All right. Let me just put a tracer on the main channel—
(puzzled look)
Oww! What the—?!!

He pulls his hand back out of the access panel. There are several slimy red bloodworms on his hand!

SFX: All the bloodworms are trilling angrily.

This is much louder.

HODEL (CONT'D)
(screams!)

Hodel tries to shake the worms off his hand!! He screams in pain. Eakins leaps back! He touches his communicator!

EAKINS

Mr. Riker!!

VERY RAPID MONTAGE OF SHOTS:

CLOSE ON THE ACCESS PANEL.

Suddenly, more worms begin to slide down out of the wall panel. A slippery wet mass of slithery red worms.

SFX: Establish a distinctive slobbery sound for the bloodworms, but with just a hint of music in it.

ANGLE ON HODEL.

On the floor, trying to get the worms off his hand. It is having the opposite effect. There are worms around him on the floor. Some of them are on his feet.

REACTION—EAKINS.

He fires his phaser!

ON THE WORMS.

They are hit by the phaser beam.

FX: The phaser burst disintegrates the worms into clouds of wavicles.

SFX: The angry trilling gets louder and angrier!

ON HODEL.

Now the worms are onto his shins. The man is in agony.

REACTION—EAKINS.

He doesn't know what to do. He fires again.

AS BEFORE—THE PHASER HITTING THE WORMS.

FX: More wavicle bursts! More angry trilling.

ON THE ACCESS PANEL.

Now a great wet mass of angry bloodworms comes sliding, oozing, blubbering down out of the wall panel. **CAMERA PULLS BACK** as the worms pour down, spreading out across the floor.

SFX: Very angry trilling.

ON HODEL.

HODEL
Danny! Help me!

ON EAKINS.

He backs away, horrified!

BACK TO HODEL.

The worms are all over him now. They are up to his chest!

BACK TO EAKINS.

EAKINS
(with great pain)
God forgive me—!!

He fires his phaser.

ON HODEL.

FX: Hodel is disintegrated! Again, a pink and gold wavicle burst when the bloodworms are hit by the phaser.

The bloodworms continue to pour, all wet and slithery, down from the access panel.

ON THE WORMS.

The worms are spreading out across the floor! Like a red carpet, they will consume everything in their path.

ON EAKINS.

Firing and firing his phaser. Almost in a frenzy! He wants revenge! Riker and Tasha come running up! They come skidding to a horrified halt!!

RIKER

Eakins!!

TASHA

(grabs Eakins' arm)

Let's get out of here!

They turn and run for the corridor entrance!!

ANGLE—CORRIDOR ENTRANCE.

They come scrambling around the corner just as Geordi and Freeman arrive, phasers ready. Tasha hits the wall panel and the **CORRIDOR DOORS SLAM SHUT!**

SFX: Muted sounds of the bloodworms behind the doors. It's horrible.

REVERSE ANGLE—THEIR REACTION TO THE SOUNDS.

RIKER

Will that door hold them?

TASHA

It's a Class A security door! It had better!

RIKER

Or what?

TASHA

(gets the joke)

Or—I'm going to complain to the manufacturer.

ANOTHER ANGLE—FAVORING FREEMAN AND EAKINS.

FREEMAN

(To Eakins)

Are you all right?

EAKINS

(trying to explain)

I couldn't stop them! Every time I fired, they got angrier! They just kept coming! I couldn't save Mike. I had to—

(turns away to hide his grief)

Freeman touches his arm concernedly.

EAKINS
(*waves him off*)
I'm all right. I'll be all right.

ANOTHER ANGLE—FAVORING RIKER.

PICARD (O.S.)
(*filtered*)
Will—listen to me. Those are plasmasites. We don't know how they got aboard the Copernicus, but the identification is now a hundred percent certain.

GEORDI
(*to Tasha*)
Plasmasites—?

TASHA
(*explains*)
Regulan Bloodworms.

GEORDI
Oh no—
(*he points*)
Mr. Riker.

ON THE CORRIDOR DOOR. THE CLASS A SECURITY DOOR.

There are three little worms just crawling down from the top of it.

BACK TO ANGLE.

RIKER
Captain. They're coming through the door.

ENTERPRISE BRIDGE. ON PICARD. INCLUDE DATA, TROI AND BEVERLY.

PICARD
Will, our scanners show that whole part of the ship is heavily infested. They're moving toward you. Now, listen. We're going to beam you up—

RIKER (O.S.)
(filtered)
Captain, you can't!

PICARD
—and put you down in the center of that repulsor field. We think that's where the rest of the Copernicus survivors are.
(to someone O.S.)
Transporter Room, stand by.

INSERT ON THE AWAY TEAM.

Spacing themselves appropriately.

BACK TO PICARD.

PICARD
Beam them over.

INTERIOR COPERNICUS CARGO BAY.

FX: Transporter effect piles up. The surviving members of the Away Team materialize, phasers ready for anything.

SFX: Establish distinctive high-pitched warbling of the repulsor field.

The Away Team looks around and sees:

WIDER ANGLE. MATCHING. THE COPERNICUS SURVIVORS.

Our team lowers their phasers. There are only fifteen survivors, total. They are haggard, sick and dirty. Freeman immediately goes to their aid. Eakins and Geordi assist.

JONAH YARELL and MACKEL BLODGETT approach Riker and Tasha anxiously.

RIKER
(grimly)
First Officer Riker, The Enterprise. What's your situation here?

BLODGETT

We've lost the Captain and most of the crew. Most of our people are showing advanced plasmasite infections. We've been here three days.

YARELL

Jonah Yarell, Starfleet Preparedness Officer. This is Mackel Blodgett, from my research division.

BLODGETT

There are only fifteen of us left, Commander. The Copernicus left port with a hundred and twenty-three.

RIKER

(interrupting)

Mr. Yarell—did you violate the Regulan quarantine?

YARELL

It was an authorized mission, Commander. A top secret, research operation—to see if we could find a way to neutralize the plasmasite infestation.

BLODGETT

We were very close to an answer here. A real breakthrough.

TASHA

(looking around skeptically)

Yes, it's obvious.

RIKER

(cautioning)

Lieutenant—

BLODGETT

My research showed that the spores are attracted to certain oxygen-binding enzymes found primarily in human blood. Eventually, those spores will start growing and eating—and then they become bloodworms and—

TASHA

(grimly)

We've seen.

> **BLODGETT**
> Then you know. We're all infected. Including yourselves.
> The spores are in all of our bloodstreams.

> **GEORDI**
> *(stepping in to report)*
> Mr. Riker, the repulsor field is surrounded by
> bloodworms.

All turn and look.

INSERT. THEIR POV.

FX: Looking down a corridor. At the end of the corridor is a throbbing
glow of light. The repulsor field. On the other side of it, we can barely
see a squirmy red carpet.

BACK TO ANGLE.

> **BLODGETT**
> They smell our blood.

> **GEORDI**
> As the power to that field weakens, the pulses are going
> to come slower and slower. Within a very short time,
> that repulsor field will no longer be impermeable to
> the worms.

> **YARELL**
> You've got to start now, Mr. Riker!

> **RIKER**
> Start what?

> **YARELL**
> Rescue! Of course!

> **RIKER**
> *(to the Enterprise)*
> Captain? Are you following this?

ON THE BRIDGE.

BEVERLY
(quietly)

There is a chance, Captain.

(to his look)

If we can suppress the key enzymes in a person's bloodstream—

DATA
(reporting)

The plasmasites in the blood would die almost immediately.

PICARD

You can't be certain of that.

DATA

The creatures are vulnerable in their particle form.

BEVERLY

It'd be risky, yes. Once the plasmasites were neutralized, we'd have to beam the person back to the Enterprise for a complete blood replacement. But time would be critical. We'd have less than ten minutes to make the transfusion— or the person dies.

BACK TO THE COPERNICUS. RIKER, YARELL AND BLODGETT.

YARELL

Captain—? Captain Picard?

PICARD (O.S.)
(filtered)

Go ahead, Mr. Yarell.

YARELL

Captain, you'll have to rescue Blodgett and myself first.

PICARD (O.S.)
(filtered, astonished)

I beg your pardon?

YARELL
(only a little embarrassed)
There's a Starfleet Regulation. Order Number 238—

PICARD (O.S.)
(filtered; interrupting)
I know the order.

YARELL
Then you know that it mandates that in situations of
dire emergency, critically important Starfleet personnel
must be rescued first.

TASHA
(snorts in contempt)
Right. "Women and children last."

YARELL
(officiously)
You said something, Lieutenant?

RIKER
(to Picard)
Sir, there are people here in very bad shape.

PICARD (O.S.)
(filtered)
Sorry, Will. Mr. Yarell has the precedent on his side.
Whatever he and Blodgett know about the plasmasites
is too important to risk losing.

RIKER
Dammit, sir—

BACK TO THE BRIDGE.

PICARD
I know how you feel, Will.
(He feels the same way.)
Dr. Crusher—?

He looks around abruptly. Where's Beverly?!!

DATA

She's already on her way to the transporter room.

TRANSPORTER ROOM. BEVERLY STEPPING ONTO PLATFORM.

Picard enters angrily—sees Worf at console and Beverly on the platform. Also, a portable medical kit on the platform.

INSERT AS NECESSARY—REACTION SHOTS. WORF.

PICARD

What the hell do you think you're doing?!
(he pulls her off the platform)

BEVERLY

This isn't negotiable, Captain. Those people need a doctor who knows what she's doing. I'm it.

PICARD

(angry)

I can order you not to go.

BEVERLY

On what grounds?

PICARD

You're a sole-surviving parent.

BEVERLY

(stiffly)

That's beneath you, Captain.
(a different tone)

Wesley and I have had this conversation…many times. He knows I'm a Starfleet Officer. I can't shirk my duty to this ship or my oath was meaningless.
(with great intensity)

Now let me do my job!
(she steps onto the platform)

PICARD

(in a softer tone)
Beverly—

She stops and looks back at him.

PICARD (CONT'D)
(he fumbles, he doesn't know how to say what he really wants to say; finally he waves her on)
Never mind.
(adds)
Good luck.

BEVERLY
Thank you, Captain.
(to Worf)
Energize—

Worf looks to Picard. Picard reluctantly nods. Worf energizes.

ON TRANSPORTER PLATFORM. BEVERLY BEAMS OUT.

ON PICARD AND WORF.

Picard is alone with his very complex feelings. Abruptly, he realizes that Worf is looking at him. Picard looks at Worf. Yes—? You have something to say?

WORF
(scratches himself thoughtfully)
You're asking me as a Klingon?
(beat)
Beat her.
(another beat)
As a professional?
(beat)
She was right.

PICARD
(looking at the platform and admiring Beverly's courage)
Yes. She was.

And then he exits grimly.

FADE OUT.

ACT THREE

FADE IN:

ENTERPRISE AND COPERNICUS IN SPACE.

PICARD (V.O.)

Captain's Log. Stardate 41202.7. Dr. Crusher
has beamed over to the Copernicus to attempt a
treatment and rescue of the survivors of the plasmasite
infestation. As soon as the plasmasites in each person's
blood have been neutralized, they will be beamed back
to the Enterprise for a complete blood replacement.

INTERIOR BRIDGE.

Con approaches the Captain.

CON

Sir?

PICARD

Yes, Con, what is it?

CON

Captain—

(embarrassed to do this)

I—I've been asked to represent some of the...families.
They want me to ask you—to not proceed with the
rescue operation. They know the danger—and they're
afraid that the Enterprise will be infected.

(this is very hard for him)

After all, if the Copernicus, with all of its precautions
could be infected, what protection do we have?

PICARD

(firmly)

Con. This is not a democracy. You don't get to vote on
it. We're not abandoning our shipmates. And we're not
throwing away half the human race because the other
half is scared. Report to your station.

CON

Sir! I'm going to log a formal protest.

PICARD

(turning away, couldn't care less)

You do that.

Picard returns to his chair and sits down and looks glumly at the forward screen.

INTERIOR COPERNICUS CARGO BAY.

SFX: The warble of the repulsor field is lower pitched now.

Yarell and Blodgett are lying on mats between Beverly and Freeman who are scanning them with medical feinbergers. Beverly is just giving Yarell a hypo-spray injection.

BEVERLY

Enterprise. Stand by. We have Yarell and Blodgett working.

WORF (O.S.)

(filtered)

Auxiliary sick bay is standing by.

FREEMAN

(reading his tricorder)

Plasmasite level is dropping rapidly.

BEVERLY

(to Yarell)

As soon as you get to the Enterprise, they'll fill you up with nice fresh artificial blood.

(to Blodgett)

Answer a question?

BLODGETT

What?

BEVERLY

Are these things native to Regula? What controls them
in their own environment?

BLODGETT

These things aren't native to anywhere. There aren't
any controls. They were created to be a weapon. There
was a war on Regula. And these things were unleashed.

BEVERLY

(astonished)

With no way of controlling them?

BLODGETT

They were a doomsday weapon.

BEVERLY

I'm sure the creators were pleased to see how well their
weapon worked.

BLODGETT

(grimly)

They were.

FREEMAN

(off his tricorder)

Time.

BEVERLY

Enterprise. Go!

She and Eakins step back away from Yarell and Blodgett.

FX: Yarell and Blodgett beam out.

ANOTHER ANGLE. GEORDI, TASHA AND EAKINS.

SFX: Warble of the repulsor field dips to a low pitched throb for a
moment, then shifts back up again, but not as high as it was before.
All of our people stop and react.

TASHA

The repulsor field is starting to fail.

GEORDI

(listening to the tone)
I give it—forty minutes.
(looks nervously down the corridor)

TASHA

(looks around, gauges)
We'll make it. But just barely.

GEORDI

What if you're wrong?

TASHA

(grins)
I'll be in no position to worry about it.

We see Eakins troubled reaction to this banter. He crosses to Freeman and the two exchange reassuring glances.

ENTERPRISE BRIDGE.

Wesley enters and crosses to Picard.

WESLEY

(very stiff, very proper)
You wanted to see me, sir?

PICARD

I ah—thought you might want to monitor the rescue operation from your mother's station—

WESLEY

(looks at the chair cautiously)
Thank you, sir.
(But he doesn't sit.)

PICARD
Is something the matter, son?

WESLEY
No, sir.
(beat)
Yes, sir. Are you trying to prepare me for something?

PICARD
(startled)
Is that what you think? That people are only kind to each other when there's bad news.

WESLEY
No, sir—not people.
(beat)
Just you.

Picard controls his reaction. Is that how he is perceived?

WESLEY (CONT'D)
Can I ask you something?
(to Picard's nod)
Why does Starfleet send families into space—and let them be exposed to dangerous situations like this?

PICARD
Because—
(takes a breath, this is a hard one)
Because our ancestors took their children with them when they crossed the oceans in ships and the continents in covered wagons. Because—you are our children and we cannot leave you behind.

INSERT. WESLEY'S REACTION.

Is that it? He doesn't buy it.

BACK TO TWO SHOT. PICARD AND WESLEY.

PICARD
(to his look)
I agree with you. It is an unsatisfying answer.
(beat)
Would you rather have stayed behind?

WESLEY
(considers it)
No, sir.

PICARD
Then sit down and join me.

Wesley takes his mother's seat, next to Picard and turns his attention forward.

ON THE COPERNICUS.

Freeman is monitoring the progress of two more Copernicus patients. Perhaps one is an attractive young woman. Eakins comes and sits down across from him.

FREEMAN
Stand by, Enterprise.
(to the patients)
Just a little bit longer. We're almost there—

PATIENT
Will it hurt?

FREEMAN
No, but—
(gently kidding)
—I can arrange it if you want.

PATIENT
No thank you.

FREEMAN
(to Eakins, very conversationally)
Y'know it's funny.

EAKINS
What is—?

FREEMAN
How much I worry about you—being on Security
Detail and all. I'm always afraid that—
(stops himself)
Never mind.

EAKINS
(Shakes his head.)
Hey. There's nothing to worry about. Really.
(a joke)
We don't have bulls-eyes on our uniforms any more.

FREEMAN
(gently)
Yeah, you can joke, but—
(shakes head)
I know the odds, Danny. I—

EAKINS
Hey!
(points, speaks firmly)
Don't talk like that.

PATIENT
(Has been following all this)
Are we going to die?

FREEMAN
(exchanges a serious look with Eakins)
I don't plan on it.
(lightens up)
Hey—when we get back to the Enterprise, I'll buy
you a drink and tell you about the Sparkle-Dancer. It
dances through space, looking for spaceships to sing to.

PATIENT
(skeptical)

Spare me. I'd rather hear the one about the leprechauns and the penguin.

FREEMAN
(grins and points)

My partner here will have to tell you that one.
(looks at his scanner)
Time. Enterprise, beam them over.

WORF (O.S.)
(filtered)

Beaming.

MED. CLOSE ON BEVERLY—AT HER PORTABLE MED-LAB.

INTERCUT AS NECESSARY WITH DATA AT HIS SCIENCE STATION.

She is holding a single red bloodworm in a glass beaker. It looks harmless enough, but she is frowning. She puts the beaker into some kind of scanning box and switches it on.

BEVERLY

Data, are you reading this? This creature's metabolism is not making sense.

DATA (O.S.)
(filtered)

Agreed, Dr. Crusher. It is attracted to the enzyme, but it doesn't seem to make any use of it. The more it eats, the more it wants.

BEVERLY
(thoughtfully)

Very effective as a weapon—but not as a life style. I wonder what would happen if it could metabolize the enzyme.

FX: Abruptly, the creature in the scanning box explodes in a cloud of wavicles.

DATA (O.S.)
(filtered)
It doesn't like being scanned either.

BEVERLY
That's going to complicate this job no end.
(shift in tone, she is recording)
Medical Log. The natural form of the plasmasites is the wavicle spore. The bloodworm is an aberration. You can't kill a bloodworm, you can only shatter it into more plasmasites. Phasering them will produce the same result. Even scanning is dangerous.
(not recording her opinion)
What a nasty business!
(recording again)
Theory: Suppose the plasmasites were deliberately mutated to keep them from metabolizing the enzymes they need. Is it possible to neutralize that infection?
(to the Enterprise)
Commander Data. Have you located Dr. Blodgett's notes yet?

DATA (O.S.)
(filtered)
Sorry, Doctor.

BEVERLY
Damn.

ANOTHER ANGLE. FREEMAN AND BEVERLY.

FREEMAN
(he is worried)
Dr. Crusher?
(to her look)
We have a problem.

ENTERPRISE BRIDGE. ON PICARD.

SFX: Communicator beep.

PICARD

Picard here.

BEVERLY (O.S.)

(filtered)

Captain, listen carefully. There isn't going to be
enough artificial blood to treat everybody. I'm sorry.
We weren't prepared. We didn't expect that we'd have
to completely replace the blood of twenty-one people.
Captain, you're going to have to ask for blood donors.

PICARD

Blood donors?

BEVERLY (O.S.)

(filtered)

I know. It's a barbaric custom— taking blood out of
one person's body and putting it into another's. But it's
the best way we've got to save the last six lives.

REACTION SHOT—PICARD. INCLUDE WESLEY.

PICARD

The last six lives—

WESLEY

(counts on his fingers)

Riker, Tasha, Geordi, Freeman, Eakins—and my
mother.

BEVERLY (O.S.)

(filtered)

We'll need at least seventy-two donors. Ensign
Morwood will match the blood types. But you'd better
get on it right away.

PICARD

Right.

(a shift in tone)

Now hear this:

INSERT AS NECESSARY—REACTION SHOTS OF CREW THROUGHOUT ENTERPRISE.

Include Con at the forward station—realizing his own shame at what he said before.

PICARD (CONT'D)
(*SFX: his voice is amplified throughout the ship*)

This is the Captain speaking. We need blood donors to help save the lives on the Copernicus. We need seventy-two volunteers.

(*corrects himself, he's the first*)

Seventy-one. Dr. Crusher assures me that it doesn't hurt—but it sure as hell will help. Volunteers report to sick bay on the double.

BACK TO BRIDGE. PICARD AND WESLEY.

WESLEY
(*rising with Picard*)

Seventy. Let me donate too! Please! You have to! I'm type O, the universal donor.

PICARD

Wesley, you're a little young—

WESLEY

If I'm old enough to risk my life in space, I'm old enough to donate a pint of blood.

PICARD
(*the logic is flawed, but—*)

All right. If the Doctor says it's okay. But you'll have to get in line behind me.

(*rises*)

Con steps into shot, blocking Picard's way.

CON

Captain—request permission to leave the bridge?

(beat)

So I can donate blood too.

Three other crew members step forward as well.

PICARD

(slow smile)

Permission granted.

(adds)

But—one at a time, please. Somebody has to mind the store.

CON

Thank you, sir.

PICARD

Thank you.

They lock eyes in a moment of understanding. Picard nods, pleased. They head for the turbo-lift.

FADE OUT.

ACT FOUR

FADE IN:

ENTERPRISE IN SPACE. COPERNICUS IN B.G.

PICARD

Captain's Log. Stardate 41202.75. The rescue of the
Copernicus survivors continues. Jonah Yarell and
Mackel Blodgett, the first to be rescued, have already
been beamed aboard the Enterprise.

INTERIOR BRIDGE. AFT STATIONS.

Establish Data working at his science station—fast scanning the downloaded log of the Copernicus. He is frowning. Something does not
make sense. Picard is looking over his shoulder. Perhaps he is rubbing
his sore arm thoughtfully. Wesley is no longer on the bridge.

DATA

The Copernicus log is incomplete, Captain. And parts
of it are badly scrambled. I don't know how much I'll
be able to reconstruct.

SFX: Turbo-lift doors.

Picard looks over and sees:

ANGLE. TURBO-LIFT.

Blodgett and Yarell, escorted by two security men, enter the bridge.

ANOTHER ANGLE—FAVORING PICARD.

Picard steps down to meet them. He points toward the Captain's ready
room like a principal with two small boys he has to scold.

PICARD
Commander Data—?

Data is reluctant to leave his console, but he joins Picard and the two
of them follow Yarell and Blodgett into the ready room.

INTERIOR READY ROOM. PICARD. DATA. BLODGETT. YARELL.

PICARD

Gentlemen…

YARELL

Captain Picard.

BLODGETT

(nods)

PICARD

(all business)

All right—I want some answers and I want them now. How did the Copernicus get infected? What was the real purpose of that ship's mission? And who authorized it?

YARELL

I authorized it, Captain.

PICARD

You did?

YARELL

Captain, an undeclared state of war exists between us and the Ferengi Alliance.

(to Picard's raised eyebrow)

Can you imagine what would happen if they were to spread bloodworms throughout Federation space?

DATA

The destruction of red-blooded life forms on a catastrophic scale.

YARELL

Precisely.

(to Picard)

The purpose of the Copernicus mission was to explore ways of containing and controlling the plasmasite infestation in the event of open hostilities. The Ferengis are vipers. They cannot be trusted.

Picard is disquieted by Yarell's ferocious militarism; we see him trying hard to stifle his distaste. He looks to Blodgett.

BLODGETT

(sadly)

There were twelve of us on the primary team. Good
men and women. Brilliant scientists all. We—must
have made a mistake. We had the plasmasites in
repulsor jars. We had made real progress, and then—

PICARD

(looking to Data)

Data?

DATA

(shakes head)

I haven't found any of that in the Copernicus log, sir—

PICARD

(to Yarell)

??

YARELL

When it became apparent that we might not survive,
I ordered the appropriate parts of the ship's log wiped
and the main computers destroyed. We couldn't take
the chance of it falling into unsympathetic hands—like
the Ferengis.

(to Picard's look)

Something disturbs you, Captain?

PICARD

Mr. Yarell, I grant you that the mission of the
Enterprise includes the military defense of Federation
worlds, if necessary—but that is not our primary
purpose. The Starfleet Charter has five initiatives for
diplomatic services and scientific research. There is
only one article concerning military operations.

(carefully)

Your work with plasmasites concerns me because
wherever a weapon exists, there also exists the
temptation to use it. I would hope that no such
temptation exists here.

YARELL

Captain Picard, I will give you this thought only to consider. The most expensive armada in the galaxy is the one that's second best.

Picard reacts strongly to that. He steps to the door—it slides open for him.

PICARD

(to the waiting security guards)

Escort Mr. Yarell and Dr. Blodgett to their quarters— and see that they stay there.

MED. ANGLE. ENTERPRISE BRIDGE.

Picard enters from the ready room and crosses to Data's science station.

PICARD

Status?

DATA

Dr. Crusher is in recovery. La Forge and Lt. Yar are aboard and being transfused. Riker and Freeman are beaming next. Lt. Eakins will be the last one out.

PICARD

(nods)

DATA

—and the repulsor field on the Copernicus is failing rapidly.

Both look grim.

ANGLE ON COPERNICUS IN SPACE.

INTERIOR COPERNICUS CARGO BAY.

Riker, Freeman, Eakins are the last ones in the cargo bay. Freeman and Eakins are glaring at each other.

SFX: The frequency of the repulsor warble is noticeably lower and slower.

RIKER
(trying to end the argument, to Freeman)
You know, I can solve this by ordering you to go—

FREEMAN
I'm the only one who knows how to monitor the blood enzyme levels. You and Eakins have to go next.

EAKINS
(to Riker)
They'll monitor me from the bridge. I'm security. It's my job to go last.

Abruptly, Freeman hits Eakins with the hypo-spray injector. Eakins looks at Freeman, betrayed.

FREEMAN
There. The argument's over.
(turns to Riker and hits him with the spray too)
You too, sir.

EAKINS
That was not fair.
(points, angered)
You haven't heard the end of this, Paul!

FREEMAN
You'd better lay down, Danny. You're going to start feeling weak in a minute.
(to Riker, much more respectfully)
You too, sir.

They do so.

EAKINS
I mean it, Paul.

FREEMAN
Shut up and let me win one for a change.

This is the first time Riker has worked with either Freeman or Eakins. While Freeman scans the two of them professionally with his medical feinberger, Riker studies him curiously.

RIKER

You're very good.

FREEMAN

Thank you, sir.

(adds)

All I ever wanted was to serve in Starfleet. My grandfather served on the original Enterprise with James T. Kirk.

RIKER

Really?

(perceptively)

Are you trying to live up to his record?

FREEMAN

(shakes head)

Nope. Just my own standards.

RIKER

Is that why you did it?

(meaning the hypo)

FREEMAN

(shakes head)

I made a promise to myself that you and Danny would both get back safely.

RIKER

Especially Danny?

FREEMAN

(nods without comment)

Riker considers this thoughtfully.

> **EAKINS**
> *(starting to weaken)*
> Paul? Here. Take this.
> *(hands him his phaser)*

> **FREEMAN**
> What's this for?

> **EAKINS**
> It'll make me feel better—

Freeman shrugs and takes the phaser. It is clear he has no intention of using it on anything; he is humoring Danny.

> **FREEMAN**
> *(studies scanner, then decides)*
> Enterprise. Two to beam over—

> **WORF (O.S.)**
> *(filtered)*
> Stand by.

Freeman steps back away from Riker and Eakins.

ON FREEMAN.

SFX: Transporter sound.

As the transporter sound fades away, Freeman looks around the empty cargo bay of the Copernicus. And shudders.

SFX: The THROBBING sound of the repulsor field SLOWS DOWN.

> **FREEMAN**
> Uh oh.

ANGLE. ENTERPRISE BRIDGE.

Con looks up from his station to Picard.

> **CON**
> Sir?

PICARD
(crosses to station)
What have you got?

CON

The repulsor field on the Copernicus just went down—

PICARD
Transporter room—!
(stops himself)

CON
Sir?!

The two men lock eyes.

PICARD
(realizing)
We have no place to beam him to.
(one of the hardest decisions of his life)

We can't do anything. Except hope that we have enough time.

WORF (O.S.)
(filtered)
Transporter room, standing by—

CON
(frustrated)
Stand by.

INTERIOR SICK BAY.

Beverly is monitoring the blood transfusions of Riker and Eakins. Troi is holding Riker's hand. He and she are smiling at each other, glad to be reunited.

TROI
I'm glad you're safe.

RIKER
I'm glad that you are too—

CAMERA MOVES to Beverly and Eakins.

FREEMAN (O.S.)
(filtered)
Enterprise—

All stop. All listen.

INSERT AS NECESSARY—REACTION SHOTS.

PICARD ON BRIDGE OF ENTERPRISE.

CON AT FORWARD CONSOLE.

RIKER AND TROI IN SICK BAY.

BEVERLY AND EAKINS IN SICK BAY.

FREEMAN (CONT'D) (O.S.)
(filtered)
The repulsor field is completely down.
(pause)
I can hear the bloodworms coming down the corridor.
(beat)
I've just injected myself with the enzyme suppressant.
This is going to be a close one.
(beat)
God, they sound awful.
(beat)
Danny, it looks like I might need your phaser after all.

CLOSE ON EAKINS. HIS REACTION. INCLUDE BEVERLY AND RIKER.

Eakins is horrified.

FREEMAN (O.S.)
Don't worry, Danny. I'll make it.
(beat)

I'm starting to feel the effects of the suppressant now. It doesn't hurt, but it sure does make me feel...dizzy. I'm going to lay down.

(beat)

Enterprise—better be ready to beam me fast.

SFX: Distinctive sound of bloodworms entering the cargo bay.

FREEMAN (CONT'D)
Oh Damn!

SFX: Phaser fire.

ENTERPRISE BRIDGE. ON CON AND PICARD.

CON
(studying his console)
We're locked on to him, Captain—

PICARD
(points over Con's shoulder)
Look at the readings from his medical tricorder. He's still carrying live plasmasites.

FREEMAN (CONT'D) (O.S.)
(filtered)
I thought I had more time!

SFX: Another phaser burst.

Picard and Con look up.

INTERIOR SHUTTLECRAFT. CLOSE ON EAKINS.

EAKINS
(screams)
Paul!!

FREEMAN (O.S.)
(filtered)
Danny, I'm sorry—

(SCREAMS)
Oh, God—

EAKINS
(screams in horror)
No, Paul, no!!

SFX: Phaser burst. and then the static of an empty channel.

ENTERPRISE BRIDGE. FAVORING CON AND PICARD.

Con looks at Picard. It's over. Picard turns and crosses back to his command chair. Con stares after him. Picard sits down and shades his eyes with his hand.

CAMERA PULLS BACK, leaving Picard alone in the center of the bridge.

SFX: Static continues.

PICARD
(very quietly)
Shut that damn thing off.

The static continues for a second or two longer than the:

FADE OUT.

ACT FIVE

FADE IN:

ENTERPRISE IN SPACE.

PICARD

Captain's Log. Stardate 41202.8. Medical Technician
Paul Freeman has been killed in action, the second
Enterprise casualty on this mission. All of the rest of
the Away Team and the Copernicus survivors have been
rescued. We are preparing to destroy the Copernicus.

INTERIOR BRIDGE.

Beverly enters the bridge, crosses to Picard and Data.

BEVERLY
(to Picard's look)

They're all safe. Sick bay is completing full work-ups
now.

PICARD

How are you feeling?

BEVERLY

A little tired. But I'm fine.

PICARD

Good. I'll want Riker on the bridge as soon as he's
able. Oh, and that security officer too. Eakins.

BEVERLY

Captain, we still have a problem.

(to his look)

It may not be safe to destroy the Copernicus. We run
the risk of releasing a large cloud of plasmasites into
space. It's just possible that as wavicles they could find
their way to another ship—or a planet.

PICARD

Data?

DATA

It's unlikely. But it's possible.

BEVERLY

We can't take the chance.

PICARD

What if we plunge the Copernicus into a star?

BEVERLY

(shakes head)

I'm not even sure that would work.

PICARD

(perceptively)

You do have a solution, Doctor?

BEVERLY

I think the spores are trying desperately to become something else. The fact that they can't is what makes them so crazy and vicious.

(explains)

On the Copernicus, I was able to identify specific binding sites in the bloodworms. Dr. Blodgett and I have synthesized a—a cure for the thing that keeps the plasmasites hungry. We think. The problem is...there's only one way to expose the plasmasites to it.

PICARD

In a human bloodstream?

BEVERLY

We'd need a volunteer.

They lock eyes. They both understand that she is talking about a suicide mission.

BEVERLY (CONT'D)

Right. It'd be suicide.

PICARD
(shakes head)
We'll have to find another way.

DATA
Captain, there's something else you should know.
(indicates his console)

ANOTHER ANGLE.

Picard steps over to Data's science station.

DATA (CONT'D)
I've extrapolated the Copernicus' course.
(indicates his board)

Picard looks, studies, and reacts sharply.

PICARD
Security. On the double.

INTERIOR ENTERPRISE LOUNGE.

The lounge has been cleared and Picard is alone.

He is staring grimly out into deep space at the motionless stars. Two security men escort Yarell and Blodgett into the room, followed by Data. The security men exit.

YARELL
Captain Picard?

Picard turns to look at him.

PICARD
Mr. Yarell. I think it's time for some straight talk.
Your mission had nothing at all to do with ending the
plasmasite infestation at all.

DATA

(quietly)

The Copernicus was headed for Ferengi space…

YARELL

Captain—you have no idea how deeply infected our whole society is with this Ferengi menace. I've been studying the Ferengis for fifteen years. The pattern! The pattern of sabotage and conspiracy is unmistakable. I'm an expert. I see it—

PICARD

Or perhaps…you see only what you want to see—?

YARELL

Captain, isn't it just as possible that you don't see a conspiracy because you don't want to see one?

PICARD

(carefully)

I'd look for the…evidence first.

YARELL

But would you even recognize it? These are not fools we're dealing with, Captain! These are evil beings! Terrible and vicious and utterly ruthless. We dare not underestimate them. We have to be every bit as ruthless. We have to be dangerous!

(beat)

That's why we have to do this, Captain.

PICARD

Do what?

YARELL

Spread the bloodworms throughout the Ferengi worlds—and rid the galaxy of the Ferengi curse!

DATA

(horrified)

Genocide—?

PICARD

(recognizes the madness, speaks carefully)
Mr. Yarell—this is a Starfleet vessel.

YARELL

You said it yourself, Captain. Starfleet's duties include the defense of the Federation.

PICARD

This is not defense. This is blind, unreasoning hatred.

YARELL

So they've gotten to you too!

PICARD

(This is going nowhere; he decides)
Security.

BLODGETT

(a cautionary note)
Captain—

Two security men enter, but stop short of grabbing Yarell. Yarell has produced a small vial—filled with PINK AND GOLD FLICKERS!! Plasmasites!! Picard is horrified.

YARELL (CONT'D)

A repulsor jar, Captain. Yes. Plasmasites. On the Enterprise.
(beat)
And unless you deliver this ship to Ferengi space…I'll break the seal.

BLODGETT

If he does, everyone on this ship is dead.

Picard is stunned.

INTERIOR BRIDGE.

Riker and Beverly are waiting for the Captain's return. Establish in B.G. Eakins is also waiting for Picard. All have changed to shipboard clothing or uniforms.

They look up as Picard, Yarell, Blodgett and Data return to the bridge. Picard looks grim.

PICARD
(carefully)

Mr. Worf, would you prepare a set of courses for Mr. Yarell's inspection?

Riker looks up sharply. Say what?

PICARD (CONT'D)
(to Riker)

Mr. Yarell has a very convincing argument.

Yarell holds up the flickering vial. Everyone on the bridge reacts sharply. Especially Eakins.

WORF
(to Picard)

Captain. Number Two Engine is still down for dilithium recalibration. We can't run it with a hot warp.

PICARD
(secretly pleased)

Mr. Worf, I don't want excuses, I want results.

WORF
(not at all chagrined)

Yes sir.

(turns back to console)

PICARD
(to Yarell)

I'm afraid there'll be a slight delay.

YARELL
(not fooled)

I'm a patient man, Captain. I can wait.

PICARD
(to Riker)

The real mission of the Copernicus was to capture and contain plasmasite specimens and infect the Ferengi Nexus. Mr. Yarell is quite insistent that we complete that mission.

(adds quietly)

Will, let's be very careful here. I don't want anyone trying anything stupid.

RIKER
(nods)

YARELL

I appreciate that Captain.

(to Riker)

I'm running this ship now.

INSERT—PICARD'S UNHAPPY REACTION.

BACK TO ANGLE.

Abruptly, Eakins steps forward, pointing his phaser at Yarell. Yarell is startled backwards—

EAKINS

You son of a bitch! All those people! You killed them! You killed Paul!

PICARD

Eakins! Put that phaser down! That's an order!

EAKINS
(not wavering)

I'm sorry, sir—I can't.

YARELL
(terrified)

Captain—you know what'll happen to these plasmasites if they're hit by a phaser beam!

> **PICARD**
>
> Don't do it, son.

Thinking quickly, Riker steps in front of Yarell and faces Eakins. Yarell steps backwards into Blodgett, holding the plasmasites outstretched in his hand—and right in front of Blodgett.

> **RIKER**
>
> Dan, listen to me—I know what you're going through—

> **EAKINS**
>
> No, you don't. Nobody does! Paul was special. He died for us.

> **RIKER**
>
> Let Starfleet handle this. I promise you, Starfleet will keep Jonah Yarell from ever hurting anyone again. Dan! Give me the phaser.

> **EAKINS**
>
> Stand aside, sir. The man is evil. He man doesn't deserve to live. Let me kill him!

> **RIKER**
>
> No! I won't let you lower yourself to his level! Because hate is a disease—and I don't want the Enterprise infected with it any more than I want this ship infected with plasmasites. Hate made the plasmasites. Is that what you want to continue?

Riker is right. Eakins wavers.

> **RIKER**
>
> (softly, to Eakins)
>
> Is this what Paul would have done? Do you think he would have wanted you to kill in his name?

> **EAKINS**
>
> (almost weeping)
>
> Damn you! Damn you!

Does he mean Yarell? Or Riker who won't let him kill Yarell. It doesn't matter. He hands the phaser over.

YARELL

(abrupt screaming)

What are you doing?!!

All turn to look:

ANOTHER ANGLE.

Blodgett has taken Yarell's little vial of plasmasites. He slaps it into a hypo-injector and presses it to his arm. With a soft hiss, he injects the plasmasites into his own bloodstream!

BLODGETT

Captain Picard, I believe I've solved your plasmasite problem. Will you please have me beamed over to the Copernicus?

YARELL

You disloyal traitor!

BLODGETT

You lose, Yarell. I win.

PICARD

Security—take Mr. Yarell to the brig. And Dr. Blodgett to sick bay.

Two security men grab Yarell and escort him off the bridge.

BLODGETT

No, sir. The transporter room.

PICARD

(to Blodgett)

We can save you!

BLODGETT

I don't want to be saved, Captain.

(explains)

I made a mistake. I trusted Yarell. And the Copernicus died. All of my friends and colleagues died.

(revealing)

I'll tell you what we discovered. The plasmasites are
something beautiful. Not a war weapon—but a kind
of life that's marvelous to see. The Regulans perverted
it. We can cure it. We can heal it.

(dead on)

Captain. I say this is where the sickness stops. All
the hate. All the dying. I've injected myself with Dr.
Crusher's plasmasite cure. Let me do this.

PICARD

It's suicide.

BLODGETT

I believe…I've earned the right.

PICARD

Nobody's earned the right to decide when a life should end.

BLODGETT

You can believe that if you want, Captain. But I've
already made my choice.

PICARD

(respectful)

You're a proud man, Blodgett.

DISSOLVE TO:

INTERIOR. COPERNICUS BRIDGE.

FX: Transporter effect. Blodgett beams in.

FX: Many PINK AND GOLD FLICKERS. They drift toward
Blodgett—and into him.

BLODGETT

Enterprise? Are you monitoring this?

PICARD (O.S.)

(filtered)

We're watching.

BLODGETT

It doesn't hurt. It doesn't hurt at all.

WIDER ANGLE—BLODGETT IN THE BRIDGE

We see the flickering fireflies come sparkling into him from all over the ship. They drift toward him, they arrow toward him. They sleet into him like arrows of light. Blodgett stands there in the center of a BEAUTIFUL glowing cloud of color and light and flickering sparkles. It is an epiphany for him—a redemption.

INSERT AS NECESSARY—REACTION SHOTS OF OUR CREW ON THE ENTERPRISE BRIDGE.

Establish Beverly and Wesley.

BACK TO BLODGETT ON THE COPERNICUS.

Blodgett is totally enveloped now in light. He disappears in the glowing, sparkling lights, they turn and twist and dance in the air.

MUSIC: The same harmonies we heard under the bloodworms, but now joyous and triumphant.

BACK TO THE ENTERPRISE.

The watchers are rapturous.

WESLEY
(amazed)
It's a Sparkle-Dancer!

We see that Troi is grinning joyously.

TROI
It's singing!

BACK TO THE COPERNICUS

The bridge is filled with light. And suddenly—POW! The light explodes in all directions!!

EXTERIOR. SPACE. THE COPERNICUS.

As the Sparkle-Dancer flows out of the Copernicus, reforms itself and dances alone in space. It is a veil of light, shimmering and coruscating with all the colors of the rainbow. Its wings flicker and sparkle with tiny pinpoints of light as tiny energy mites whirl and dance. It is a colony of dancing butterflies of light and energy.

THE ENTERPRISE WATCHERS.

Wow! They are the first human beings to discover that the Sparkle-Dancer is real!

ANGLE ON THE SPARKLE-DANCER.

It curls once around the Enterprise and then vanishes into distant space.

INTERIOR BRIDGE.

Picard sits down in his chair.

> **PICARD**
>
> Mr. Worf, have you finished your dilithium recalibration yet?

> **WORF**
> *(grinning)*
> We just completed it, Captain.

> **PICARD**
> Full speed ahead.

> **WORF**
> *(proudly)*
> Aye aye, sir!

ANGLE ON THE ENTERPRISE—MOVING OFF IN A DIFFERENT DIRECTION.

FADE OUT.

AUTHOR'S AFTERWORD:

So, here's what happened next. I walked away from Star Trek. I still loved the original series, still admired the original cast, still respected the talent and skills of all those folks who had taken an outlandish idea and made it work magnificently—especially D. C. Fontana and Gene L. Coon. But I walked away from any emotional investment I had in the franchise. I walked myself around the block and had a long talk with myself. "What are you going to do with the rest of your life?" There were two answers: 1) I am going to write the stories I love writing, I am going to write the stories I want to read. Ten years from now, twenty years from now, nobody will care about "Blood and Fire," but they might care about the ten or twenty or thirty books and scripts I will write between now and then, so I will write the best stories I can—this time for me. 2) I am going to adopt a little boy who needs a Dad and have a family all my own. I will have my own human adventure.

Those were two very good goals. Today, twenty years later, I have accomplished both of those goals. I have written some stories and books that I would not have written if I had gotten sucked into the television machine—including "The Martian Child," which I think is the best thing I've ever written. It's about how much I love my son, who has since turned into a marvelous young man. I am very proud of him.[1]

---

1 *The movie version of "The Martian Child" is due to hit the screens a few months after this book hits print. That wouldn't have happened either if I hadn't walked around the block when I did.*

It was the late sixties and I had just moved into my own apartment. Money was tight and dinner depended on how much I had earned in tips. The first 15¢ always went for a can of dog food. Rule number one in my household: Dog never misses dinner. I'm not sure who made this rule, me or Dog, but it was a good rule; he was insurance—if I ever got hungry enough, he'd be fat enough to barbecue, one drumstick at a time.

On this particular night, I was cutting up lettuce for a salad. A piece of lettuce fell on the floor. Dog had his own set of rules: "If it falls on the floor, it's mine." So he ambled over, sniffed the piece of lettuce, then ate it. I looked at him, he looked at me—his expression was clear: "Drop some more lettuce on the floor please." So I dropped some more lettuce on the floor. He ate that too. I hate to eat alone, so I fixed him a salad of his own. He ate it. Every bite.

This became a regular routine. I'd cut up some iceberg lettuce, I'd put it on two plates, and I'd put bleu cheese dressing on both salads. Sometimes I'd add carrots. He usually finished his salad about the same time as I finished mine. After a week or two, I began putting a napkin down on the floor next to his salad dish—not because he would use it, but because it just didn't feel right to not give him some dignity. I would tell him to wait—and he would—until I put down the napkin. And because the napkin looked empty all by itself, I'd put down a sprig of parsley on it too. Very quickly, he learned to wait until I completed the ritual. Then he'd eat his salad and finish off with the parsley. Then he'd be ready for the main course—dog food! Yay!! (Or whatever people food I might be sharing. He had a fondness for spaghetti, but cleaning up a shaggy dog who has just had a bowl of spaghetti is not for the timid.)

One evening, I had a friend over for dinner. As I started making the salad, I put out three bowls. I didn't even think about it. My friend asked if someone else was joining us. I said no. "Then who's the third salad for?" he asked. I replied, "It's for Dog." My buddy gave me the look. "Dogs don't eat salad." "This one does." I put down the bowl of salad. Dog sat and looked at it, looked up at me, and didn't move. He had that unfinished expression on his face that dogs wear when they know you're messing with their heads. I put down the napkin. Dog looked at the napkin, he looked back at me. By now, my friend was certain I was certifiable. Finally, I sighed loudly—the famous Jewish sigh—and put down a sprig of parsley on the napkin. Dog watched this carefully. As soon as the parsley hit the napkin, he got up, walked over and politely ate the salad. Every bite. And then he licked the bowl. My guest looked at me and said, "I don't know which one of you is weirder—you or the dog."

I never did figure that out.

A Shaggy Dog Story

AT FIRST, SHE THOUGHT IT WAS A SCAB.

They weren't an uncommon occurrence on this dog. His name was Shotgun and he was constantly scratching at himself. He was a shaggy pink mutt, mostly good-natured, and possessed of a perpetual questioning expression in his large brown eyes; but he had the bad habit of scratching at himself constantly.

He didn't have fleas. He couldn't possibly have fleas. She bathed him and dipped him every third week and changed his flea collar every second month. She marked it off on the calendar. She sprayed his bed on Saturday and dusted him on Wednesday.

No, it couldn't possibly be fleas. Miss Edna Token's dog did not have fleas.

The veterinarian had said it was probably a nervous habit. She had sniffed and replied, "I don't understand what this dog has to be nervous about."

The usually smart-mouthed vet didn't have an answer for that one. He just pursed his lips tight and peered into Shotgun's ears. Miss Token would have changed vets, because she didn't like Dr. Brown's nasty sense of sarcasm, but he was the only veterinarian on this side of the hill and he was practically in walking distance, and what with both a dog and a cat—

But anyway, Shotgun had another scab, right under his collar, so he must have been scratching at himself again.

"That's where you like to be skritched, isn't it?" she said, working at the spot with her carefully manicured nails. "You don't like to be scratched, do you? You like to be skritched. Ahh, here it is, Sweety-Dog. I found your secret spot—"

137

The dog grunted and sighed and bared his naked belly. He sprawled on his back and pumped agitatedly with one leg as she skritched. His mouth stretched into a rictus which she liked to think was a smile, although she was willing to concede it could just as easily be a muscular reaction.

She'd have to wash her hands after this. Despite his frequent baths, Shotgun still had a pronounced doggy odor, a sour buttery smell which was not quite unpleasant, but was certainly noticeable on her fingers after she finished skritching him. She didn't mind too much.

Anyway—

—at first she thought it was a scab. She *tsk*ed in annoyance and worked around it gently. It was a very hard one. In fact, it almost felt like…something metal. Maybe he had another burr caught in his fur. Except he wasn't complaining. She worked her fingers through his hair. The object felt flat and sharp and—

"Hold still, Shotgun! Let me see what's caught in your fur."

It was a zipper.

She blinked.

A zipper? On a dog?

This dog was nearly nine years old. He didn't look it, of course—she took very good care of him—but why hadn't she ever noticed a zipper before?

No, it must be just caught in his fur.

She pulled it. It was stuck. She pulled harder—

It came unstuck abruptly, sliding all the way down to Shotgun's… belly.

She gasped in involuntary horror, fearing that she had somehow ripped her dog open—except he hadn't uttered a sound.

The skin beneath the zipper was pink and naked.

She touched it tentatively—it was warm—then jerked her hand back. The zipper teeth were made of bright pink teflon. The dog skin was neatly stitched to hide it. She managed to gasp, "Shotgun? Sweety-Dog? Are you all right?"

"No," said the Dog. "As a matter of fact, I'm pissed as hell!" Its voice sounded muffled.

Miss Token squeaked in surprise and leaped backward.

The dog was struggling inside his dogsuit. It looked as if he was trying to remove his head—he was! The head lifted off to reveal a tiny squinting man. He tossed it aside and quickly peeled off the rest of the dog suit. He stood before Miss Token wearing nothing more than a dirty jockstrap and an angry frown. He had a pot belly and coarse black hair all over his body. Miss Token couldn't take her eyes off of him. He was a very ugly little man.

"That was a damn fool thing to do! DO I PLAY WITH YOUR ZIPPERS?!!"

"I, er—uh—" Miss Token couldn't form the words. She pointed back and forth between the little naked man and the rumpled dog suit on the living room floor. Shotgun's lifeless eyes stared at her from the discarded head. She gulped and tried again, "What have you done with—? Shotgun, is that you?"

"Not any more," the little man snapped. "This contract is breached. I don't believe this—" he growled. "You know what this means? You're on the strike list. Automatically. No appeal. You and I are through." He padded barefoot out of the other room, snarling. "Nine years! And this is the gratitude."

"Where are you going—?"

"To take a piss! D'ya mind?" The bathroom door slammed shut behind him. She heard the clunk of the toilet seat as it banged against the tank, and then a soft tinkling sound, followed by a flush.

"Aaah, that felt good," the little man declared, coming back into the room, adjusting his jockstrap as he walked. "Y'know, I hated having to wait for you to come home every night. A bladder can only take so much—"

Miss Token *eep*ed. "I, er—uh (gulp)—I don't understand this at all. Are you—yes, you are, aren't you? Shotgun! I mean—why didn't you? Oh, dear."

The little man was barely listening. He shook his head sadly and glanced around the room as if he were searching for something. "Forget it, Lady. Never mind. It doesn't matter any more." He bent down on his hands and knees and peered under the couch. "Ah!" He stretched and reached and pulled out a dusty green rubber bone. "I thought so."

Miss Token felt as if she were going mad. Unbelievingly, she stepped over and picked up the dog suit from the floor. It was lined with soft material—still warm from the little man. It had a distinctly doggy smell. It felt exactly like…a dog skin. She dropped it in sudden distaste. She kicked at Shotgun's lifeless head. It rolled over sideways. The tongue lolled out of the mouth. Miss Token moaned.

"Yeah, well—" said the little man. "You shoulda thought of that before you pulled the zipper." He crossed to the hall closet and pulled down a tiny tattered suitcase that she had never seen before. He snapped it open and tossed the rubber bone into it. He pulled out a T-shirt, jeans and a pair of loafers and quickly donned them.

"Shotgun! I—I'm sorry. I didn't know! I—please, stop that, please?"

The little man shook his head. He prowled nervously around the room, squinting into corners and looking behind the chairs. He collected a dirty tennis ball and a rubber duck with a broken squeaker. "Oh, yeah—" He pushed the cat off her desk and retrieved his rabies vaccination certificate from the second drawer. "I'm gonna need this." He tossed the ball and the certificate into the suitcase.

Miss Token was close to tears now. "Sir? Shotgun? Can't you—I mean, can't we just forget this happened—and go back to the way it was before?" She held out the dog suit to him, imploring.

The little man stared at her. "You can't be serious, lady! Knowin' what you know now? Don't be silly. NO WAY! It's da rules."

"But, but—why?"

"Why? You have to ask why? Isn't it obvious? First, you'd start askin' me to talk to ya, and then you'd want me to talk t'ya friends. Next, it'd be phone messages and little errands to the store. Then you'd want me to play cards with ya. Y'gotta be kidding! Listen, I am a dog. I am a professional dog! I am a member of the union. We got rules lady. Ya follow da rules, ya got a dog. Ya break da rules, ain't no dog in da country gonna work for you ever again. Except may a coupla scabs here and there—but they're hell on the carpeting." He padded over and picked up the dog suit. "That's da way it woiks, lady. Them's the rules. Too bad. I don't make 'em. I just follow 'em." He took the dog suit and stuffed it, head and all, gently into the suitcase.

"But—but—I've had you since you were a puppy! I paper-trained you!"

The little man looked annoyed. He looked very annoyed. "Don't start on me with that loyalty stuff. Ya also fed me the cheapest dry stuff you could find. You think I didn't see you collecting the goddamn coupons? How come I never got a steak on my birthday, huh? So don't tell me how much you did for me! Frankly, all that 'Sweety-Dog' stuff just makes me want to toss my biscuits. Oh, yeah—that's right." He disappeared into the kitchen and returned with the full box of dog biscuits from the cupboard and the half-empty open one she kept on the kitchen counter. "These at least were okay. I liked these—except for the green ones. They tasted like soap." He was chewing loudly as he tossed both boxes into the suitcase on top of the dog suit. "Hey, but how would you like it—" he said, speaking with his mouth full, chewing with his mouth open, "—if you had to sit up and beg for your dinner every night? That was degrading. Really degrading."

Miss Token sat down on the floor, tears running down her cheeks. "I'm sorry, Shotgun. I really am. I didn't know."

"Yeah, well—it's too late for sorry now." He snapped the suitcase shut, hefted it for weight, then headed for the door.

"Wait—" she said.

There was something in her tone. He stopped, one hand on the doorknob. "Yeah?"

"Where are you going?"

"That's none o' your business, any more."

"But it is my business. You're my dog—"

"Was!"

"Do you have a place? Don't you want to take your blanket?"

"Hey," he muttered. "Don't worry about me. I'll be okay. I can always catch a bunk down at the pound. Hey, really—" His tone softened. "I'll have a new gig in a week."

Miss Token fumbled for her purse. "Listen, do you have enough money? Bus fare? Um—"

"Keep your money."

"No, I insist—" She held out a fistful of bills. "Shotgun, please take it. I owe you this much at least—"

He shook his head. "I'm not allowed to take it." And then he added, "I'm sorry. I really am."

She met his eyes. "Was I really that bad?"

The little man looked embarrassed. He shrugged. "You weren't the worst, y'know? Listen, I gotta go now. You take care of yourself, y'hear?"

"Will you—write me at least? And let me know where you are?"

"Hey! I'm a dog! And I won't phone either."

Miss Edna Token nodded. And gulped. "Goodbye, Shotgun."

"Yeah. G'bye. Hey—and thanks for all the biscuits."

The door thunked shut with a terrible finality.

Miss Token looked up sadly. The cat was sitting on top of the TV set.

The cat cleared its throat and said, "Don't look at me. I told him that damn zipper was too big."

AUTHOR'S AFTERWORD:

He began life as a rumbustious pink bundle as coordinated as a hamper of dirty laundry. For the first year of his life, his hind legs were always two steps ahead of his front; if he got excited—which was any time he was awake—he couldn't move three feet without tripping over himself. But he wasn't stupid. One day, he figured out how to move his legs in order, and forever after that he was fast enough to run halfway up a tree after any squirrel too stupid not to move to another neighborhood.

His name was Dog and he was the smartest animal I've ever known. Eventually, he convinced me that he and I were identical twin brothers separated at birth, and as the smarter member of the family, it was his job to look after me. Fair enough. In return, I gave him room, board, and health care.

Dog used to lie on my chest and sing duets with me, I'd skritch his belly and he'd hum his accompaniment in a deep disturbing growl, because he didn't know the words. In fact, the only words he did know weren't fit for polite company. If for any reason, I ever sent him out of the room, he'd go, but he'd mutter under his breath every step of the way. The words were unintelligible, but not the spirit. He was the only dog I ever knew who could curse.

He had style. More style than most humans. I still miss him today.

I wrote this story long before Welles died. I like my ending better than the one the universe provided.

The Strange Death
of Orson Welles

SHORTLY AFTER 4:30 on the afternoon of August 22nd, Orson Welles reached critical mass.

The day had been extraordinarily hot, even for Los Angeles, a melting scorcher that liquefied the tires of parked cars and glued them stickily to the pavement. Traffic crawled down Sunset Boulevard as if it were the main drag of Hell; the leering faces of Kiss and Alice Cooper grinned down at them like triumphant demons.

The inversion layer over the basin had turned the sky into a familiar silvery shade of gray; the exact same shade of mugginess as could be seen on the tattered screen of the NuArt theatre in Santa Monica, where the ragged society of serious film fans—serious because they couldn't afford to be dilettantes, and their chances of ever making the studios' A-lists were less than nil even on a good day—were cloistered in the darkness for the umpteenth unspooling of *A Touch of Evil* and *The Magnificent Ambersons*.

Only a few miles away, the great white bulk of Orson Welles lay sprawled helpless in the center of an eight-foot water bed, a mountain of human corpulence as immobile as some vast leviathan beached on the shores of desolation. Here lay the Cinema world's own Moby Dick, gasping for breath, exhausted by the energies expended in his seventh futile attempt to rise from bed.

The enormity of his plight was rapidly becoming obvious, painfully so; it was one of the cruel ironies of fate. He had passed the point of diminishing returns and now he was pinned by innumerable servings of *la ballotine de canard aux pistaches, terrine de foie gras de perigord, filet de*

143

saumon en geleee, cuisses de grenoille provencale, tournedos Perigueux, souffle au Grand Marnier, Cafe Diable, and the occasional late night Jumbo Jack with large fries and thick shake accompaniment. Orson Welles had finally been immobilized by his own life-style, a living monument of fossilized indulgence.

He had been trying to get out of bed for several hours now, heaving himself back and forth in violent spasms of effort. His mouth was permanently frowned into that same cruel pucker of obsession as had characterized the manners of Charles Foster Kane so many years before. His tiny little eyes had receded even further into his skull, gleaming with a red madness. His arms flailed wildly, and every great thrust as those limbs of corpulence came smashing down onto the water bed created vast tidal waves of motion across its surface that caused the edges of the sheets to rise and fall in waves that measured an average of 1.83 feet. Welles was generating a better surf than could be found at Rincon Beach that morning. The ripples that swept across his own suety mass were equally impressive.

After every attempt, Welles would sink back into the center of the bed, a gigantic insect trapped in its own nest. The ripples subsided around him as his breath racked in hoarse sobs of anguish. His heart pounded, struggling to push his blood through arteries like little sewer pipes clogged with globs of used Crisco.

After a while, when calm returned to the water bed, the pounding of his heart began to ease, and Welles began to gather his strength for one more attempt to rise—and yet, each successive attempt was accomplishing less than the last. Even the wave crests were no longer as impressive as before.

It was rapidly becoming obvious that Orson Welles was not going to be able to lift his own bulk out of bed.

Perhaps it was the combination of the heat, plus the exhaustion of the moment and the icy thrill of the adrenal realization of his situation that was the catalyst—

He was in no danger of immediate death. If necessary, he could have survived several winters on his own fat alone; it was some deeper fear that moved him to keep trying beyond the realm of normal human endurance. It was not just the mortification, the cruel irony of embarrassment that would result if his situation were to be discovered, nor was it even the physical discomfort; no, it was the agony of being unable to control his own destiny, the cruel truth of becoming a victim of his own life instead of its master. To a man like Orson Welles, this was unacceptable.

At this moment, at this point in time, another human being confronted with the same realization would have panicked and begun calling for help. But not Orson Welles, no not Orson Welles. He fumbled around on the bedstand near his left hand and found last night's cigar butt, half-smoked—one of the few he had not yet tossed out the back door at the pool service man. He stuck it abstractedly in his mouth and began chewing on it, his mind racing feverishly. Reaching again, he fumbled for the lighter, and after some moments of anguished scrambling, his hand clawing like a fat palsied pink spider, he was able to grasp the table lighter and bring it around to his face. It was then that he realized that he had eaten his own cigar.

He was submerged in waves of dizziness then as the last cruel fact came hammering home. There were urges inside of him that had taken on individuality of their own. His body had not only rebelled, it had seceded from the union with his mind and was now beginning to transform itself into a new form of life. As Welles watched, horrified, a prisoner in his own flesh, his hands began clawing at the sheets, the bedding, ripping the down out of the quilt and stuffing it into his mouth.

His jaws began working like little Cuisinarts, and as fast as he pulled out the masticated down, he would stuff in new pieces. He began building a wall of material around him. His body was bathed in oily sweat now, it had taken on a curious sheen. His skin seemed to be thickening, becoming a kind of fried from the inside shell. It shone with metallic-looking highlights.

His hands were still clawing at the bed, even ripping off pieces of wood now. His mouth had become a vast cavern of grinding teeth. His hands, curled into insect claws, plucking, grasping, stuffing. The foamy masticated product of his labors surrounded him in layer after layer of hardening material around him, a rising wall of shredded linen and wood fiber.

At some point in the early evening, about the time Walter Cronkite was telling America this was the way it was, the water bed burst, bathing Welles in a warm effluvia as it lowered him gently to the floor. But by then it was too late. The intelligence that had been Welles had flickered out, leaving only this incredible creature, still gnawing at the frame of the bed, the floor, the draperies, the nightstand…

The creature worked all night long repairing and building the walls of its nest. The heat of the room was rising, product of the body mass of this vast insect-thing. Even Kafka had not imagined a transformation as grotesque as the one that had begun in Orson Welles' bedroom. A cockroach was nothing compared to the majesty of this great white beast.

Welles worked throughout the night, chewing steadily and methodically. By morning, he had completely enclosed himself in a nest of linen and wood-fibers and sputum. Even now, in the rising heat of the morning, the shell was hardening into a surface as hard as concrete.

And inside…?

Inside, the transformation was continuing. Even now, strange and medically astonishing processes were working their way, made possible only by the vast energy potential stored in Orson Welles' flesh.

It would be some time before the world became fully aware of what had happened here in Los Angeles, but by then it would be too late. By then, a new life form would have established itself so vigorously that the entire human ecology of the planet would be affected.

The first eggs would hatch into a colony of worker Welleses, their duties to protect and serve the vast bulk of the Queen Welles. The next batch of eggs would hatch into soldier Welleses; but it was the third batch that would be most fearsome: thousands of little Queen Welleses would spring forth from that and go out into the world to mate and establish nests of their own.

The world was soon to be inundated in thousands and thousands of voracious little Orson Welleses, each one of them brilliant, each one of them hungry.

Orson Welles had triumphed again.

AUTHOR'S AFTERWORD:
   Burn the film schools while there's still time! They're coming! You're next!

Interlude #3

Selections from *The Quote-Book of Solomon Short*

"An increase in intelligence always represents progress for humanity; it is also inevitable that it enables us to make a higher class of mistake."

"Entropy has us outnumbered."

"If God didn't want men to masturbate, then why did he make the opposable thumb? If God didn't want women to masturbate, then why did she make the middle finger longer?"

"Self-abuse is the sincerest kind."

"The nice thing about dying is that once you've gotten it over with, you can stop being afraid of it."

"A hero is a man who consistently violates the law of conservation of energy."

"I miss the dinosaurs."

"The human race never solves any of its problems. It only outlives them. (So far.)"

"Never trust a tall dwarf. He's lying about something."

"Television does not honor tradition. Most of the time, it doesn't even recognize it. Therefore, it can only destroy it."

"Armies aren't known for neatness."

"Artificial food is expensive. Nothing makes a steak as efficiently as a cow."

"Writing for television is a debilitating exercise. How can you inspire an audience to their best when every fourteen minutes someone interrupts to tell them that they're unfit to live with? The ultimate purpose of commercial television is to convince the viewer that he smells bad."

"Don't be so proud. You are not an intelligence until *after* you pass the Turing test."

"The universe is full of surprises—most of them nasty."

"The great mass of men lead lives of quiet domestication."

"Probability is a constant."

"Sour grapes make sour whine."

"There is only one commandment: *Thou Shalt Not Waste*. All the others are superfluous. The second commandment, if one is needed, is: *Thou Shalt Create Joy*."

"Just when you think it's finally settled, it isn't."

"THE THREE LAWS OF INFERNAL DYNAMICS:
1. An object in motion will always be headed in the wrong direction.
2. An object at rest will always be in the wrong place.
3. The energy required to change either of these states will always be more than you wish to expend, but never so much as to make the task appear impossible."

"Half of being smart is knowing what you're dumb at."

"Every mistake is another opportunity to beat yourself up."

"The trouble with the Ten Commandments is that there are too many 'Thou Shalt Nots' and not enough 'Thou Shalts.'"

"You'll find it in the last place you look."

"People will go to the most incredible lengths to make fools of themselves."

"The blind man looking in a mirror cannot see he has no eyes."

"New problems demand new solutions. New solutions create new problems."

"The amount of entropy in the universe is constant—except when it increases."

"All life is based on death. Nothing exists except by feeding on something else. Even photosynthesis depends on the heat-death of the sun. Humanity is not exempt. Embalming doesn't cheat the worms, it cheats the system. But only temporarily."

"Life is to the universe as rust is to iron."

"We are, in the final judgment (on a planetary scale, certainly), nothing more than an advanced form of corrosion, just one more way for the universe to wear itself out a little faster."

"The cat is always on the wrong side of the door."

"Distrust everything sold at check-out stands."

"It is almost always dangerous to be right too soon."

"Space is not the final frontier.
  The final frontier is the human soul.
  Space is where we will meet the challenge."

"If you want to bring a centipede to a crashing halt, ask it in which order it moves its legs."

"I try not to pay too much attention to the news. It's always full of other people's problems."

"There is no such thing as justice. There is only the desire to see the pain spread around equally."

"Life is like surrealism. If you have to have it explained to you, you can't afford it."

"A full bladder is the best alarm clock in the world."

"I'd feel a lot better about doctors if it weren't called practice."

"Always consider the consequences. Yes, Christ chased the moneylenders out of the temple — but he also ruined his credit rating."

"Anything worth doing is worth doing for money."

"How successful were your parents? How quickly did you forgive them?"

"There is no such thing as overkill."

"There's always someone who wants to argue with me; but I'm the one who's called controversial."

"—and those who cannot teach, criticize."

"The human brain is the only computer in the world made of meat."

"You don't need a lid on a basket of crabs. If one of them tries to climb out, the others will pull it back down."

"TINSTAFL — There Is No Such Thing As Free Love."

"It's a good thing money can't buy happiness. We couldn't stand the commercials."

"Chastity is its own punishment."

"Gay people are at their most brilliant when one of them leaves the room."

"A lawsuit is evidence of failure. On both sides."

"A human being is a computer's way of making another computer. We are their sex organs. Enjoy yourself, it's part of the job."

"I take it back. A full bladder is the world's *second* best alarm clock."

"If you do something often enough, it becomes a habit."

"God and I came to an agreement a long time ago. I don't ask Him to solve my problems, He doesn't ask me to solve His. This arrangement works just fine. God has more than enough to worry about already. So do I."

"Happiness is not a goal. It's a by-product."

"When you pass the buck, don't ask for change."

This piece was originally written for A Method for Madness, *Book Five of* The War Against the Chtorr, *my "epic seven-book trilogy about an ecological infestation of the Earth and the synergistic evolution that occurs in the collision of two great biological forces and what happens to the human beings caught between them, etc....blah blah blah." Unfortunately, as has happened four times in the past, the book grew so long that large pieces had to be pushed into the subsequent volume. This was one of those pieces. It will be used in* A Time for Treason, *Book Six of the...etc. All you need to know here is that Jim is not the man he used to be, and he isn't yet the being he is in the process of becoming.*

It Needs Salt

I'll Take Manhattan

"Everybody has the right to one fatal mistake."
—SOLOMON SHORT

Manhattan glistened in the distance. We came in low across the water, toward the south end of the island. Barth muttered something about the topless towers of Ilium. In an earlier life, that might have been surprising, because Barth didn't look like someone who knew his Greek history. But in this life, there wasn't anything that surprised me anymore, because I already knew it all.

Once upon a lifetime, the McCarthy-thing had actually believed a teep implant would be an advantage. Imagine, being able to *know* anything about anything in an instant—if the information existed anywhere, if it was accessible, it was yours—but that was *before*.

In truth, an implant is like having a thousand radio stations running in your head, and another thousand TV stations, and a constant buzz of web chatter as well—and you can't turn it off. It just drones

151

away forever, cycling with patterns of noise and data, heterodyning with unsynchronized waves and ripples of information: memetic boulders dropping into the sea of thought, sending out waves of disturbance to ripple and ricochet endlessly off the opinions and reactions of others, reforming and refocusing, coming back as new squalls of roiling noise and signal.

The difference between data and information is whether or not it's useful to you. Most of it isn't. So it shows up as noise. Relentless noise. And not soothing noise like the susurrus of wind through leaves or waves rolling up onto a sandy shore. No. It's more like a thousand flashing data screens superimposed upon your life. I look at Barth and I see every piece of information about him that's ever been recorded, processed, analyzed, annotated, and data-strip-mined. Medical records, financial statements, educational history, parentage, name-changes, alter-egos, aliases, pseudonyms, online identities, publishing history (if any), service record, psychological evaluation, arrest record, mug shots, yearly ID photos, eye color, hair color, height, weight, fingerprints, blood type, DNA, retinal scan, viral loads, immunity factors, EEG, EKG, allergies, employment history, travel records, driver's license, insurance rating, passport data, security status, security evaluations, international ID report, credit history, magazine subscriptions, web-surfing patterns, extrapolated sexual profile, legal battles, frequent flyer miles, consumer profiles, purchasing history, political views, extrapo-lated voting profile, favorite television program (*Derby*), relationships, tastes, distastes, and whether he picks his nose with his index finger or his pinky. (Pinky.) So I already knew that he had a strong interest in military history, mythology, and classic (pre-1910) pornography.

Meanwhile, Manhattan glistened in the distance, and we came in low across the water, toward the south end of the island. Seven chop-pers, all lit up like a Christmas parade, flashing and blinking and blaz-ing. We left rolling ripples of light—red, white, and blue—in the dark waves below.

An Enterprise fish lurked somewhere in these empty waters. Not a very big one. Only the size of a carrier, so far. Tracking harpoons, aerial drones, and infra-red satellite monitors all placed it offshore of Fire Island. Likely the damn thing would outgrow itself and end up beached somewhere inconvenient. The smell would last for weeks. Or, it might find its way up into either the Hudson or the East River, where it would probably starve to death, leaving the waters polluted for months.

The shoreline blazed like a carnival. Beams of light swept across the inky surface of the water, casting glitters of reflection. Beyond, behind the banks of lights, the towers of Manhattan, the ones that still stood proud and defiant, shone tall against the bitter night. Even the empty ones. The colors danced in synchronized patterns, they bounced from building to building in a wild game of light; it was called "keeping the rainbow alive" and illumination itself was the goal. The mayor of New York had ordered maintenance continued everywhere, even in the abandoned zones. Someday those buildings might be needed again. Someday wasn't on any calendar, but human beings still believed in it anyway.

The plagues had emptied the city. How many years ago had that been? A lifetime. The scars of the fires and the riots and the ineffective quarantines still remained. As we clattered in closer, I could see a swath of darkness that tore through the bright skyline. By day, those same buildings would stand black and gaping, betraying where flames had raged unchecked. By night, however, with the topless towers still appearing tall and incandescent, the spectacular hallucination of civilization pretended to endure.

Once, a mighty civilization did thrive here—perhaps the mightiest of *all* civilizations this world had ever known. At least until the crimson scourge. This had been her financial heart as well as her cultural soul. Her stolid banks and proud theaters, her adventurous museums and charming parks, her indestructible people and their strange secret lives, all had been studied with envious eyes wherever information flowed through glass wires, wherever high-resolution pictures flashed and danced. The eloquent rhythms of humanity in its 24-hour ebb-and-flow of death and desire had pulsed through these wide avenues in an endless torrent of faces. The eternal tides of life and lust and greed, personified in ten million strange, sweating, squirming, breathing, copulating, consuming, excreting, infectious individuals—all the separate hungers of a marvelous fractious species, squabbling and scrambling amongst themselves— and yet, occasionally meeting the demands of extraordinary moments, rising to feats of near-legendary courage; thereby justifying the annual sigh of relief and nervous celebration that the city had survived another year, another cycle of unexpected horrifying catastrophe and crisis. This city had known too many such events, each one seeming worse than the last. And yet, she persisted.

Once, this was Rome, the center of the world. Roads, commerce, information, education, civilization, domestication—once, this was the nexus. The meta-life of the planet began here, rippled outward to the world; everything else was just reflections and reactions, strange ricochets of other lives.

In memory, the past remained green and fruitful. In memory, the past was opportunities, both taken and missed. In memory, the past was a vision carefully edited of all disturbance. Even memories of pain were edited to comfort and succor the present. In memory, the past was the enemy.

The past—*this* past, this lost and glorious era with all its terrible reminders of who we'd been and what we'd built and what we'd lost—these topless towers, grandiloquent proclamations of human vanity, now they drive us into another madness. They lure us back into a way of thinking and feeling, acting and reacting, a mind-set, a *mode* that no longer has referents in a purple world. The past entraps us.

The past isn't just another time, it's another way of being, one that no longer exists, can never exist again, must be abandoned, if humanity is to move on, if humanity is to become what it must to survive, if humanity is to survive at all. But it won't be *humanity* any more. Not as defined by the past. Not that.

And yet, even in the throes of ecological death, humanity somehow thrives. The bright lights blaze, declaring to the world: Rome has risen again. The eternal holy city, where commerce is sacred and greed is celebrated. Rome endures. My name is Manhattan. Look on my works, ye mighty, and despair!

We came in low across the water toward the floating platforms off battery park. Manhattan Emergency Skyport. Pillars of light stabbed the sky; red, white, and blue. A scattering of other aircraft waited in parking bays. Landing robots pointed yellow lasers across the air, guide beams for the approaching VTOLs. The lumbering machines settled down almost in unison, each lazy bird stropping into its assigned circle, each circle divided by unintentionally ominous cross-hairs.

Barth was on the phone to someone. I waited till he signed off, grabbed my cane, and followed him down the steps. Barth shouldered his own duffel, so did Stead, so did Goldberg. I carried nothing. No gun, no ammunition, not even clean underwear. Because I wasn't personnel. I was cargo. Payload. Not to be trusted. Couldn't even be trusted to take care of myself. Stead was my Boswell. He had the hard job—translating psychotic to English—but he was also my keeper; so was Goldberg. If the McCarthy-thing got a little too agitated, Goldberg carried a satchel of appropriate medications. The purpose of this operation, the question in everyone's mind—could McCarthy be used as a military asset?

Did McCarthy get a vote? No. But it didn't matter anyway. Because McCarthy didn't care. In fact, McCarthy wasn't even home. The lights were on, the TV was blazing, but the occupant had disappeared. That hadn't stopped them, of course. They ignored the Do Not Disturb sign on the knob, they had knocked, knocked again—this time a lot louder—served warrants, and eventually kicked open the door, and tossed in flashbangs and tear gas. But McCarthy wasn't there, had left a long time ago, no forwarding address, thankewverymuch, and nobody knew where he might be. Not even McCarthy.

Other than curiosity to see how this would all work out, the McCarthy-thing was an ambulatory vacuum. Everything poured in. Like an infinite sponge. But nothing came out. Not even if you squeezed and stomped and crushed. But every so often—something bubbled up to the surface and blurted out some words. Sometimes even the words had meaning.

A cool wind from the east, a warm wall of air in the north. Eddies of air and odor. The smell of kerosene and diesel. Corn syrup fuels too. The stinging smell of salt and ocean decay. The acrid flavor of leviathan, the Enterprise fish—a lot closer than Fire Island. The waves beyond the platforms glittered with silver and crimson highlights. Red plankton floated on the surface of the water. I could almost taste it. Hear it too. Floating neural fibers. The oceans were coming alive with purple sentience—still nascent, but eventually awakening. Then what? Like the bottom of a nest, only global. Two-thirds of the Earth. A sticky, stinging soup. Not yet, but someday. A hundred years from now? And then—the *other* smells—the stench of the city. Decay of all kinds, overlaid with mustard and tomato sauce. Even in the midst of death, the city churns. Rotting garbage. Rats. Fermentation. Alcohol. Urine, excrement, and a purple undertone as well. Something breeding in the corners.

Limped after Barth, across the polycarbon deck of the Skyport, across the walkway to a convoy of waiting humvees. Three mobile artillery trucks in the lead. Three more at the tail. Others spaced every three vehicles. Heavy armament. Torches. Plasma beams. Particle accelerators. Needle-shredders. The gear must have been arriving all day. General Daniel Anderson was headquartered off of Columbus Circle. He'd moved in a complete battle group. Direct orders from the president. *We are not giving up Manhattan.*

Barth and someone I didn't recognize, but already knew—the noise, the buzzing in my head—spread out a paper map across the hood of one of the hummers. Each of them had a clipboard too. But the paper map had information that didn't exist electronically. Never would. So it didn't exist to anyone else. Not even me. But it didn't take a telepath to know what was being discussed.

Barth pointed to me and gestured. Favoring the leg, I hobbled over. "Got your tinfoil hat on?"

"I'm not broadcasting."

"You can control it?" That was the other man. Woman. Impossible to tell anymore. Blond hair, round face, scruffy beard, permanently skeptical expression. Sometimes it seemed as if the only conscious humans left on the planet were male. And the nastiest and most hostile were the ones who used to be female. An ironic ugly joke on all of us. Her name—

The buzzing bluebottles. The flies are open. The noise pours in. A Dickensian clamor. Assail of two titties. It was the breast of times. You can control it? It was the words of times. Identify General Laura Domitz [3/9], third daughter of a nine-member, linear clone-family. Three members deceased, two in the plagues. One disappeared, disposition unknown, MIA. Two younger members on Luna, one a lawyer, the other an independent agent. Three left on Earth; one in the administration, one in intelligence—and General Domitz [3/9], serving in Manhattan; all three masculinized. The one in intelligence is implanted, but not a teep.

The question hangs unanswered in the air. *You can control it?*

The matriarch of the line—that was interesting, she'd been one of the first, at a time when cloning was still psychologically suspect—had borne her first five offspring herself, each three years apart. Even more courageous. But she kept a low profile. Wisely so. Ignorance breeds fear. Fear breeds hatred. Hatred breeds violence. Violence breeds more violence. The evidence was always available on the front page.

It wasn't until the Kenny Brady clones appeared in the miniseries of *The Man Who Folded Himself*, with six different Kennys, all appealingly winsome and photogenic, playing Daniel Eakins at various stages of his life, that cloning not only became respectable, but attractive as well, even inevitable—especially in show business where casting agents often needed to portray a single individual at different ages. (And more than a few actors realized the opportunities inherent in having younger versions of themselves available to maintain a lucrative franchise.)

The blue-flies buzz and settle again. Awaiting the next ripple of disturbance in the Force.

"You can control it?" General Domitz repeated. She looked skeptical. Even hostile.

"No." Finally replied. "But I can live with it."

"The Teep corps doesn't want McCarthy's input," Barth said. "He makes them crazy—*crazier*." He corrected himself without embarrassment. "So they block it on their end, they filter it, they squelch it all. He skews what's left of their collective rationality. So everything he broadcasts goes to a shielded security team. Whatever he experiences, sees, feels, tastes, smells, hears, *thinks*—it's not accessible to the teep-mind, except on a need-to-know basis. And as much as they need to know— they have a greater need *not* to know."

General Domitz scratched her blond beard. She didn't look convinced. "Can you switch it off on your end?"

"No. I'm on a 24-monitor. I can damp it down some, but not much—"

"Never mind—" She had a small beeper-like device attached to the bottom of her clipboard. She switched it on. The noise in my head went off, the buzzing disappeared, the invisible screens went black. The silence was profound. For a brief instant, I even felt like *me* again.

"Nice," I said.

"Illegal," she said.

"Where can I get one?"

She and Barth exchanged a glance. He nodded. She turned to her aide, a teenage boy in an oversized uniform. Or a girl? Impossible to tell. But too young to grow a beard of his own. He just looked scraggly. His eyes were wide—fascinated and frightened by the McCarthy-thing in front of him. "Foley? You got any more of these?"

"Uh, right. Yes, sir. How many do you want?" Got it. Dustin Foley was the general's dog-robber. Just tell me what you need, ma'am.

"That's the right answer. I'll give him this one for now." Domitz unclipped the device and handed it to me. "Here. A gift from the people of New York. Only problem is, as soon as you get back, as soon as they figure out you've got it, they'll confiscate it. You know that don't you?" Without waiting for an answer, she turned back to the hood of the hummer and smoothed out the map. She laid her clipboard on the edge of the paper to keep the wind from lifting it up. It rustled anyway. "Here, this is the unofficial map of Manhattan. Everything in purple is worm-infested. Everything in red is renegade. You'll see we've sectioned off the island using the streets as containment lines. 125th, 110th, 96th, 85th, 79th, 72nd, 66th, 59th, 54th, 48th, 42nd, 34th, 23rd, 14th, 8th, all the way down. And the avenues too. 10th, Seventh Ave., Broadway, Park Ave., Lexington, and so on. The real problem is underground. The subways, the steam tunnels, the sewers—especially the sewers. We can't really contain anything until we get more prowlers and balrogs down there. We've got some, but not enough. We need at least three times as many as we've got."

"What are the gray squares?" asked Barth, pointing. The map showed a checkerboard scattering.

Foley stepped in and pointed. "That's the mayor's redevelopment plan. We're going to reinvent the city." Click, click, buzz, buzz. Lieutenant Dustin Foley, son of acting mayor, Linda Foley. Assigned to General Domitz as a liaison. Also, a way to keep him out of danger—and out of other trouble too. Convenient for everybody. Click, click, silence again.

General Domitz explained. "The gray squares are blocks that have been selected for demolition. The buildings will be leveled, abandoned buildings, mostly. We have a military justification. These are places where squatters, renegades, cultists, mercenaries hide out. The only good news is that they've pretty much eliminated most of the dealers. But we're also finding snufflers, shambler nests, bunnydogs, and now we're even starting to see worm nests in some of the empties. So the robots are dismantling the structures as fast as we can bring them in."

Uninvited, Foley added, "Someday, we'll have parks and ponds and gardens and waterfalls on these blocks—the whole city, you'll never be more than half a block from open air."

"It will also reduce the fire danger," said Domitz. "We had to learn that one the hard way."

Foley was excited now. "You should see the 54th street falls. Five stories high, and so smooth you can project movies on it. It's really big. And it's worth the trip just to ride the new loop. We've got three square kilometers of terraces and arcades, mostly upper midtown in the new financial district. Gets people three stories above the traffic and provides safe, controlled-access 'shopping zones'. Maybe someday, over a hundred square klicks. The new Manhattan. One level for cars, another for people—"

Domitz put a hand on his arm. "Thank you, Dustin. But this isn't a vacation trip for Colonel Barth." Foley fell silent, embarrassed. To Barth, she said, "There's a political component. We both know that. Reestablishing Manhattan will be good for public morale, the national economy, and every elected official who jumps in front of the cameras. So our priorities are to contain, control, eradicate, and establish a perimeter." Click, click. Buzz on. Actually a series of concentric security perimeters, each one more secure than the last. Coded by colors. Certain neighborhoods would be secure, others intermediary, still others would be considered abandoned. And anything beyond the perimeter is free-fire zone. Overlay the map of real-estate values for congruency. *Quelle* surprise. Click, click. Buzz off.

"Right now, the city still looks like a war zone. Well, it is a war zone, but—"

"No," I interrupted. They both looked at me. "It's not a war zone. Because it's not a war. It's a colonization. An infestation. An ecological expansion. An adaptation to available niches. That's your mistake. You keep thinking of it as a war. That's why you keep losing. Think of it as an evolutionary process. You have to find ways to prevent access to available niches. If the Chtorr can't get in, it can't spread."

Another exchange of glances. Barth's turn to ask the question. "How?"

Before I could answer, General Domitz offered her own opinion. "If he knew how, he wouldn't be here. He'd be in Stockholm, getting a medal and a handshake from the king."

Okay. If she didn't want to know, McCarthy wouldn't tell her. Another one, all too human—they just don't want to hear. It means stepping out of the comfort zone. *Not knowing.* Being ignorant. Looking stupid. They'd rather die than look stupid. And they will. Most of them. Me too. I think. Lt. Foley looked interested, but he wasn't going to ask. Not now. People don't want to know what they don't want to know.

The map, again. "The cultists are bringing in the chrysalids, deliberately spreading the infestation, trying to start their own mandala. We have some evidence to suggest they're bringing in the contraband through the subway tunnels from New Jersey. We put monitors in the tunnels, but as fast as we put them in, they take them out." That much was common knowledge. "General Wainwright has given us instructions—" *Instructions*, not orders. She pointed to the red blocks on the map. The east village is a mess. So are parts of the lower west side. And certain blocks in the Wall Street district. "We are to terminate the renegade presence on the island. *By whatever means necessary.*" She scratched her beard again. She looked scruffy and bitter. In her past life, she had been an executive with a management corporation. In her past life, she'd had two children, an ex-husband, and a career. In her past life, she'd been a beautiful woman. Today, she was someone else—a man, energized by the challenges of war, committed to ecological revenge, efficient and deadly. And very bitter at what she'd lost to the Chtorr. She couldn't make the Chtorr pay for what it had done to her, but she could damn well hurt every piece of it she could find.

"We've got nerve toxins, paralytic agents, vomit juice, gas canisters, cold-freeze, shock grenades, short-life radioactives, neural scramblers, psychedelic fields, you name it. Plus, we've got permission to use torches in the tunnels and C4 in the empty buildings. If necessary, we can demolish anything up to sixty stories, as long as we give a 30-minute warning to the surrounding neighborhood. It's not usually a problem."

"What about prisoner intake? What arrangements have you made for interrogation and containment."

She looked annoyed at the question. "This is a take-no-prisoners operation."

"No interrogations?" Barth was genuinely puzzled. For all of his years in the war, for all that he had seen—click, click, buzz, buzz—he still had enough curiosity and compassion left to qualify as human. The old-fashion definition, not the currently operative one. Which didn't answer the question. How had he ever gotten to be a Colonel in *this* army?

"Renegades aren't worth the time," said Domitz. "They can't tell us anything useful. We've tried. They just babble. And the state doesn't have the resources to rehabilitate. And you've got the evidence standing next to you that rehabilitation doesn't work. And even if it did, it isn't cost-effective."

Barth glanced at me, the unfortunate example. "I think you'll find that McCarthy is a very *valuable* asset." Translation: you could be mistaken.

Domitz glanced at me skeptically. She didn't believe it. But she wasn't going to argue the point. That argument had been resolved long before we got on the planes. "Well, if he's as good as you say, we won't need to question any prisoners, will we? McCarthy will tell us everything we need to know." She turned back to Barth. I no longer existed to her. "Look, Colonel. I'm happy to have you here. And your troops. But we don't have a lot of time for committee meetings. Got that? This is my show. If you have information that's useful, I'm willing to hear it. But if I tell you how things are going to run, that's not an invitation for an argument. Not from you, not from *him*. Got that?"

Barth nodded. His face was expressionless, but I could tell what he was thinking. He was already counting casualty lists and drafting letters to next-of-kin. He looked over to me. The McCarthy face was expressionless too. It had been expressionless since…never mind.

"We've got you bunked here. It's an old residence hotel, turned into coops. Not quite abandoned. Corner of 10th and University. Walking distance to what's left of Washington Square park. We're trying to maintain a presence at the University, but there's a chance we may have to pull back from the village. Unless we can get underneath it into the tunnels. Tomorrow, I want your boy doing recon. We'll be sending prowlers and growlers and bears into the tunnels, I'll want him on the monitors—you have a problem with that, worm-boy?"

The McCarthy-thing was shaking its head. "Monitors won't tell me everything I need to know. It would be better if I could go down into the tunnels myself. I need to smell the air."

"We'll have sniffers. Weasels, ferrets, sparrows."

"Not the same. They can't read all the tones of a Chtorran smell. They can't convey the experience. A lot of it is very subtle."

She frowned. And changed the reason. "It's not safe."

"Not for you, no."

"Are you saying you can go where a battalion can't?"

"I'm saying that you smell human. I don't."

She looked to Barth. "I'm this close to putting you all back on those planes and sending you home."

"With all due respect, ma'am, that would be a big mistake. If McCarthy wants to walk the tunnels, you should let him."

She hesitated. She was arguing with herself inside her head. She hated being wrong. But now she had to decide, did she want to trade a little embarrassment for a bigger one? What if Barth was right? What if McCarthy could tell her things that no machine could? Could she afford this moment of arrogance?

No. She could not.

"All right. But if we lose him, it's on your head. Let's see what your trained rat can do."

"Ma'am?"

"Colonel?"

"Specialist McCarthy is entitled to the same courtesy, the same respect as any other officer—as any other *human being*—and very likely a good deal more, because of everything he's been through. And certainly because of everything he might be able to tell us. While it might not make much of a difference to him anymore, I would appreciate it very much if you would please order all of your personnel to treat McCarthy with the utmost respect, and I would consider it an enormous personal favor if you would set the example…?" He waited patiently for her response.

She wanted to turn and walk away. Her body language screamed it. She wanted to say, "Don't press your luck." She was already subvocalizing. Even through the scruffy beard, it was apparent. But instead, she held her tongue. "I want your team on deck at oh-six-hundred. Get to your bunks." That was as much assent as he was likely to get.

"Thank you, ma'am." Barth saluted and we climbed into the hummers.

Washington Square

"The fact that 95% of everything is shit doesn't
prove the other 5% isn't also shit."
—SOLOMON SHORT

Up close, the city blazed, a howling glare of light—huge banks of military illuminators stood in the center of every intersection. Flat panels, painfully bright, angled in all directions. They sprouted from the walls of buildings, or leaned over parapets like gargoyles of brilliance. Night didn't exist in Manhattan.

The convoy rolled up Broadway without incident. The streets were almost deserted. Most of the abandoned cars had been removed, replaced by rolls of razor-ribbon and clouds of aerogel. Yellow warning signs with the aerogel symbol were everywhere. Orange lanes outlined the safe-passage areas. Everything bathed in bright. Everywhere labels and arrows. A hollow pretense of control. Here and there, signs of habitation, a row of open stores, a block of inhabited buildings. New Yorkers consolidating for safety. They wouldn't give up their towering city again. Brave Manhattan. Brave doomed Manhattan. It all smelled dark and purple now.

The convoy turned left on 10th and stopped at the corner of University. "This used to be the Albert hotel," said the driver. "Very famous. Writers, artists, whores of all kinds used to live here, over a hundred years ago. A landmark. Some of the rooms even have plaques in them. This is where Delaney lived. This is where the Cockettes shot up. A few others. A lot of fags and freaks and junkies. Crap like that, if you're interested."

Barth shook his head. He glanced to me, but I already knew the history of the Albert. A sad strange building. About to get sadder and stranger. I'd turned off the silencer in my pocket as soon as we'd started rolling. I needed to *know* the city under the city, the behind and beneath as well as the pretense.

Once upon a time, the shape of the Manhattan skyline was a map of the bedrock beneath. Where the rock rose up close enough to the surface to build upon, there stood skyscrapers, solidly rooted to the foundation of the island. Where the bedrock went deep into subterranean valleys, there the buildings still grew, only never so high. Midtown echoed the underground mountains, so did Wall Street. But that was before the city started burrowing down. You could put as many stories under the street as above it. The opposite of a skyscraper was a groundbreaker. Easier to heat, easier to cool; the surrounding earth was a natural insulator. A little bit harder to light. A little bit harder to service. Pipes and wires and fibers had to go down instead of up. But a lot harder to fly an airplane into.

New York already had considerable experience with underground malls and arcades. It was possible to live your whole life underneath the city, never seeing the light of day—stores and markets, doctors and insurance agents, theaters and whores—and after life ended, you were already buried, funeral chapels and mausoleums here. It was inevitable that the city would hunker downward, carving out vast underground warrens of transportation and commerce. And inevitable habitation. If you didn't need sunlight, you could find everything from a suite to a cubbyhole. And if you did need sunlight—well, some of the ground-breakers piped it in. Others generated it, right on the wallpaper. Only now, the bottom-most levels were turning purple and untenable. And the very protections that New Yorkers had carved for themselves had become the avenues of infection.

Meanwhile. Everywhere. The city roared. It rumbled, it grumbled. Even comatose, the city groaned. All jibber-jabberwocked. 'Twas brillig and the moribund did writhe and bristle in their sleep. Polymer pipes flexed and pulsed—throbbed like purple jungle veins, bringing in the water, carrying away the waste. I'd seen it all before. In the mandala, where the plumbing grew itself and fed on everything that flowed within, the bowels of this thundering glowing city were the same. The stone and metal flesh was animated, automated, automotivated. Wires, neural fibers, all the same. The song, the symphony, the endless cacophony. Cattle-taste-trophy—plastic-masticated—

I shook awake.

There was too much purple in the air.

Goldberg knocked on my door. Are you all right? Yes, I'm fine. No problem. Thank you. I have to check. I know. The whole dreary dance. How many times had we circled this particular roundelay? A regularly recurring refrain. The monitor beeped. I know. You were way off optimum. I know. I'm fine now. I can maintain myself. Honest. Yes, I know, I still have to check. Thank you for checking. You're welcome. Thank you, thank you, thankewverymuch, gofuckyourselfplease, sametoyouasshole.

The Albert cost $3500 a week for a narrow room on the second floor. I was in 289-A. Goldberg had 289-B. We shared a common bath-room, though I suspected he'd be going down the hall and using Stead's instead. Didn't want to risk infection. Once, 289-A and 289-B had been one large room, with a private bath next to the entrance. Now, a separat-ing wall and two doors transformed it into an unmatched pair of small apartments with the bath in a shared hall.

289-A had a bed, a dresser, and a desk, mostly unused. The window opened onto an airshaft. On the other side of the airshaft, another window showed a naked stairwell. McCarthy drew the curtains and sat on the bed. The mattress was lumpy. How many thousands of couplings had happened here, furtive, desperate and ultimately leaving the partners more alone than before?

The thing that used to be McCarthy wondered what he would feel if he went up to the roof, if he lay on the dome of the city and listened to its pulse? What song would Manhattan sing to him? A strange mix of vibrant defiance and cancerous decay, most likely. But it's hard to kill New Yorkers. Manhattan's unofficial motto: "It ain't rape if you fuck back." That was true both ways.

McCarthy blinked.

It ain't rape…if you fuck back.

An interesting insight. Not sure what to do with it yet. Bodies grappling in angry passion. Lustful rage. Another page. Enraptured, captured. Two ecologies entangled, levering, feverish, fervent, fermenting, tormenting, excrementing, experimenting. How do ecologies copulate? Slowly. Loudly. Painfully. But it ain't rape *if you fuck back*—

McCarthy blinks again.

Fucking makes babies. Fucking makes food. Fucking makes slaves. Trori-ktor. So what happens when ecologies fuck each other? Do ecologies get pregnant? And if so, what do the children look like?

All red-haired and gurgling happily, right. No. Not red-haired. Red-furred.

Where did that thought come from? The red-haired one.

McCarthy blinks. This time, his eyes are shining. Wet. Doesn't know why. Yes, he does. Doesn't matter. Doctors warned him this would happen. Surges of emotion, meaningless—the collisions of memory. Picks up the cane.

McCarthy turns on the silencer. The jammer. He stands up. He opens the door. Then he opens the second door. He walks out into the hall. He turns the corner and opens another door. He goes down the stairs. Another door at the bottom. A security desk. He looks through the window, the sentry isn't there, only a robot. It can't stop him. He pushes out, waves to the machine, turns right, and he's on the street. The cold Manhattan street. The night glows plastic bright. Everything garish. Overhead, the panels blaze, a sky like television. Factories in New Jersey print great rolls of electro-stock, all kinds. One side dark and hungry, carbon nanotubes, the other bright and shiny, a different flavor of the same. Unroll it, cut off what you need, mount it on a frame and point the dark side toward the sun. By day it sucks up power. By night it blazes glory. Tuned only to the visual bands, the panels seem brighter than they really are. There's another possibility here—

McCarthy has, he figures, about two minutes. Goldberg has probably already sounded the alarm. It'll take only thirty seconds for the team to scramble. But this is unfamiliar territory. And they lost three hours on the trip east. If they'd already sacked out, then the sudden awakening, combined with the jet lag, should leave them just a little dazed and confused. Maybe. Don't count on it.

Without the jammer, McCarthy listens. A different kind of listening—the difference between "put your tray tables up" and "assume the crash position." He listens as if he doesn't exist—that's the easy part, because he *doesn't* exist anymore. Instead, he's just the place where everything happens. And his job is to notice as much of it as he can through these pitiful eyes and ears and nostrils. Without his fur, without his feathers, without his spines and other antennae, there is so much more he cannot know, but he makes the best of what he has—

Music. Smells. McCarthy turns south and heads toward Washington Square Park. The noise. The tastes. The surging crowds. A carnival atmosphere pervades. Strange familiar smells. Oversteamed hot dogs, soft pretzels, dark mustard, acrid onions, and sweet strawberry soda. Alien music under the arch, reverberant and resonating. Steel drums, oil-drums turned into an orchid-metal xylophone, and someone is playing Reggae-style Bach. *Air on a G string.* Procol Harum. *A Whiter Shade of Pale.* A Starkey drum-riff and a cascade of notes that Johann Sebastian never wrote. A feathery crowd sways around the music. The colorful notes swirl in the air, all shades of pink and purple. Undertones of apricots and sugar and bubble-gum. Sweet tomatoes, peppers, and cloves.

All the clothes, all the different fabrics, colors, shades, and hues; the silken textures, flowing shirts and scarves and skirts. The celebration of the end of the world. Chtorran-silk, web-cloth, aero-spun, material so light it drifts like smoke along the breeze, alternately concealing and revealing. Leather kilts illuminating bony knees of skinny men. Shiny plastomer capes, red and yellow, iridescent blue, form-fitting chaps. Codpieces. Faux-women, buxom with overflowing corseted bustierres, proclaiming cleavage that invites a head-first dive into delusive canyons. Another grand illusion. Hormones or injections. What lies beneath is probably surprising. Or expensive.

Long past midnight, the bars have closed, and the free-fall festival comes alive in the park; unlicensed entrepreneurs ply another trade, all the markets black and white and pink. Pageantry of flesh. A parade of slender girl-boys in shorts so tight and bulging, they put imagination into remission. One of them wears a bright red halter with a glowing white swoosh that proclaims, "I'm the real thing." But nobody believes. Not anymore.

The *real* real things are the shirtless muscle-boys, in all their finery and glittering adornment. Gold necklaces, bright and pretentious. Jade and emerald bracelets, coral and crimson gemstones. All the rings and earrings, real, plastic, electronic, glittering and flashing, jingling, broadcasting, clamoring for notice. Tattoos, glowing tattoos, shimmering and dancing tattoos, arms and thighs and breasts, ankles, cheeks, and that little flat place just above the cleavage of the ass. Body shapings, pointed ears, pierced nipples, lips, eyebrows, all of it. Nothing in moderation, especially moderation. Nudity is its own reward. Raw bodies, all designs and deliberations. Flashing makeup, men and pseudo-men, pseudo-women. Bright red lips, purple lips, black lips, highlighted eyes, styled brows, neon-painted ears, cheek designs, nose-rings, bone and wood and ivory, ornaments and adornments. To live is to dance. And nothing else, especially nothing. Celebration without end, without purpose, without meaning; mindlessly fucking and sucking and drugging ourselves into oblivion. Break down and out. It's all over but the dying. This is the end, the very end, my friend. Illusions, delusions, fusions, trans-fusions, unions and urban communions. Don't dream it, breed it. Choke 'em if they can't take a fuck.

Here and there, pairs of men—or maybe women—bearded, impossible to tell, not by looking anyway, wearing urban camouflage uniforms, with weapons slung over their shoulders, talking into headsets, monitoring. Peacekeepers or tourists? It doesn't matter. The party swirls around them.

Still more men, we're all men now, even the women, black and white and brown, all broad and muscular; and other men with them, the not-men, all the disparate contradictions, fat and flabby, boy-girls or girl-boys, the ones who still haven't mastered masculinity or never want to, fighting the effects of the hormones that keep them sane—not sane, rational. Not all of the women are bearded. Some wear only mustaches or sideburns. The most feminine creatures here are the fairy boys, the drag queens, the descendants of Stonewall. Some of them are beautiful, others garish and grotesque. What are they all looking for? An end to loneliness? Impossible. It's the human condition.

A tall man in a feather boa and a jock strap. Just parading, strutting, not for sale, maybe for rent—dishing with the other girls. Not real girls, no real girls here at all. Quoth the craven. Nevermore. Two bearded dykes leading their slaves on chains. Black sugar daddies, pimps, hustle-boys, flat broad-brimmed hats, and shiny duster-coats, sweeping low and wide, brushing the very tops of their patent leather boots, herding their shambling tricks. If you're desperate and needful enough, you'll even fuck one of those things that used to be women. That's the message here. You want a real woman, she's an animal. A pheromone-drenched walking fuckfest. The stench is overwhelming, overpowering, intoxicating. Some men stand and negotiate, trying to talk themselves into it—or out. Some men, who cannot stand fucking men, or men who pretend to be women, or even worse, men who used to be women. Breasts and beards and other confusions. If ugly has a middle name—

Web-geeks and droids, some with head-cams, others with 360-eyeballs, uploading the panoply of sights and sounds and smells to the world at large, turning the whirligig experience into worldwide virtuality. More people participating online than actually here in the park. The number hovers near a million. An incredible rating. Why? What's the attraction? "Look, daddy, that man has bigger tits than yours?"

And always more. Moving among them, unnoticed in a Brownian dance, the faceless ones, the fodder, the hungry geeks and nerds, the wannabes, the never-wills, the skinny boys in T-shirts, bulging jeans, orphans angling for a bed and maybe even breakfast. Not really selling. Just trading. I'll pretend I'm not alone with you. Withered patrons, dried out and faded-looking. Vampirical evidence of the eternal minuet. The dead and dying sucking at the living.

Other flavors, too many to assimilate. Other species. Other memes and minds and themes of all kinds. Indians, both west and east. Headdresses adorn the beast. The uniform of the feast. All the dancing urbans. Men and quasi-men in turbans, red and white and black. And blacker still. Others with shining shaven scalps, a single uncut tail of hair at the neck. Great neck. Long island saffron robes. Tambourines, drums, and chanting. Intricate, intoxicating. Subli-mating. Honeyed candles and sandlewood incense, intense.

A dark-souled, dainty man, standing on a box, yammering through a bullhorn, an ugly grating voice. Dressed all in black, a white collar at his throat. Red faced with surging rage. The strength of his condemnation is the measure of his hunger. Instead of diving into the pool, he stands on the edge and shrieks and screams, a self-appointed harpy. Addicted to himself. As small as he is, a withered unused penis of a man, he still pretends to power, all puffed-up pompous and hollow like a preening bird. He speaks with claimed authority, not his own, calling down the wrath of Gods and Demons, not bothering to differentiate. His anger and frustration aroused by the everlasting futility of his mission. But no one listens. He's just more noise in the drowning tides of world-noise. His bullhorn only adds decibels, not meaning. The eddies and tides of humanity have left him stranded on the shores of dead philosophies and faiths. The anger smolders deep, but a good little believer can't possibly blame mommy and daddy for what they did to him—God commanded him to honor his parents, no matter what, and this good little boy is going to heaven, even if it kills him. Believe in God or go to hell. To hell with all of you for not listening. Nobody ever listened to me. Not even when I was little. I'm so fucking lonely—and so fucking angry at all of you who don't care. I'm important. I'm a soul. And I'm going to heaven and you're not, so fuck you, neener neener neener. People hurry past him, eyes averted, quick nervous glances—he's the uncomfortable reminder of morality. Not *his* morality, but morality as an idea.

An insight. He wears the evidence on his face that even for the natives, humanity is an alien experience. They all want love—and then they do everything they can to keep from genuinely connecting. They move in portable performances, each one a personal, self-created show with an audience of one. The inner pageant, not for you or anyone, only for me—and then they wonder why they go home alone. And this is the punch line. Not that no one listens—but because *no one listens to anything anymore.* So fucking locked-up inside myself. Not just here. Everywhere. In the labs, in the committees and the briefings, in the sessions and the hearings. No one listens—because so much of what is being said is worthless. It isn't cost-effective to go data-mining, filtering the shit from gold, *not when everything is shit.*

And this is the punch line after the punch line. This nasty little man is just the tip of the iceberg. He's all of us. Insane, irrational, and out of control. The only difference is that he stands apart in his hallucinations, while everyone else pretends to share a common one.

It's all delusion, a last desperate whirlaround, needing only Prince Prospero to seal the castle against the red death scouring the countryside beyond its walls. The celebrants do not await the masque, they wear it on their faces. So why should any of them listen to anything? They've already become it. They spin deeper into enchantment—

A moment of pure staggering insight, a punch to the heart.

This is a herd.

A herd of multiple overlapping sets; not quite mindless yet, but fucking its way down. Not yet, but soon. We're getting there.

McCarthy fades into the mass of moving bodies, all the shades of night come flickering past. Purple, ocean-turqoise, blue, and darker blue—a flatted fifth-note, the howling blues—the tastes come pouring down and around. The smells of human sweat, scented deodorant, hairspray, perfume, after-shave, musk, pheromones, spice, tobacco, more candles, patchouli smoke—it doesn't cover up the darker fragrances—magenta dust, marijuana, crystal meth, but mostly Chtorran flavors.

Impressing its own dark insights and convictions onto the swirl of bodies around—

The security team grabs me, yanks me hard, spins me around. Goldberg, red-faced and furious. What the fuck are you doing, trying to get back to Japura, you stupid, crazy fuckhead. McCarthy doesn't answer. Can't answer. Won't answer. It doesn't matter if he answers. The answer swirls around them. The war is lost. Not because the worms can't be defeated, but because humanity can't win. And what humanity has become—that's not a victory either. No, this isn't a war, it's an ecological clusterfuck.

They drag me back to the cage of the Albert hotel. I go without speaking. Without expression.

Listening

"Everything you believe is beside the point. That's the point."
—SOLOMON SHORT

5:45 in the ayem. Dawn was rising pink and ominous. The park was almost empty. Deserted. Except for an agitated squirrel, rummaging nervously through the detritus of the vanished festival.

—And the garbage-bots, each one stalking silently across the grass, picking up bits of trash, examining each one, then stuffing it into the maw of its shredder like a metal praying mantis, a barrel-chested belching insect. Occasionally, the bot would pause in puzzlement, turning something over and over; sometimes the item might end up in the city's lost-and-found, held for 90 days before reclamation or disposal. More often, the bot would determine that the curious item needed further review and would bag it for later study by a human agent. Or maybe not. There weren't many humans who wanted to sort through other people's trash—not anymore, and not even if it was evidence. It didn't matter. The courts couldn't keep up, and the perps were often dead or missing by the time the case was filed.

Trash disposals stood throughout the park, but the surface of the grass was covered with an uneven layer of human thoughtlessness. The noise in my head, the buzzing, all the virtual displays revealed the ugly truth of the excreta of civilization: scraps of paper, cigarette butts, used condoms, poppers, bent spoons, used hypodermic needles, plastic bags with featherings of dust inside or shreds of marijuana, bits of dirty aluminum foil stained with resin, a forgotten vial of hormone pills, half-empty cans, beer and soda, plastic wrappers, dirty discarded plates, foam cups, soggy newspapers, the occasional magazine, unwanted discs, broken boxes, cardboard, discarded clothing, a forgotten shoe, someone's feathered boa, a dildo, dirty underwear (skid marks, but no used tampons, think about it) batteries, some broken electronics, worthless lotto tickets, a copy of Playbill, half of a yellowing paperback book, scattered pornography, a used razor, a fallen earring, a contact lens, a pink pearl, 47 cents in small change, a half-eaten hot dog, someone's excrement, a puddle of vomit, a pamphlet of dire biblical prediction, a dented shopping cart with no wheels, an old frayed overcoat with rotting food in the pockets, a dead pigeon, a red queen from a chess set, a map of North Carolina, some crumpled posters, the pieces of a shattered bullhorn, a bloody shirt, pieces of a broken knife, some bullet shells, a taser battery, an empty gas canister, several wrappers for sterile-gauze pads, shreds of a truck tire, some wooden sticks, a crutch, pieces of an electro-stock panel, still glowing—and a button that declared "Fuck the Chtorr." The irony of that last was not immediately obvious—unless you had already fucked the Chtorr and been fucked back. It ain't rape.

The garbage-bots swiveled their eyestalks and studied each piece, photographing it, cataloging it, identifying it to some distant database. Once upon a time, the bots had sorted the material for reclamation purposes; later, the process had demonstrated some useful evidentiary value, especially in the trade of illegal substances; but now, another time, another reason, most of these examinations were simply raw unprocessed data—the undiscovered lore of future archaeologists strip-mining the past. The patterns of garbage revealed a cross-section of civilization. What better way to monitor drug use, sexual activity, cultural attitudes than studying what people discarded, lost, or broke. Already, the garbologists were reporting that the use of Chtorran hallucinogenics was on the rise. No surprises there. You didn't have to be a telepath to smell it in the purpling air. But the tectonic shifts in sexual behavior were far more interesting than that—

Barth studied me with narrow eyes. He knew better than to ask questions. He also wouldn't cajole, coerce, or anything else. He simply asked, "Did you learn anything interesting?"

I nodded.

"Can you explain it?" Shook his head. Wrong question. "*Will* you explain it?"

Shrugged, turned away and studied the sky. Strange colors in the east. Wished I could see the ocean. I could still taste an Enterprise fish in the air. Something strange about the smell. And it was a lot closer than the tracking maps reported. Turned back to Barth. "The thought isn't complete yet. It doesn't make sense, even to me."

"Well, at least you're still using pronouns." He turned to Goldberg and Stead. "Stay close to him. And Goldberg, the next time you yell at him like you did last night—you'll be on your way to the Russian front." He clomped off to confer with the tactical team.

"Russian front?" asked Goldberg.

"Look it up," said Stead.

McCarthy grinned abruptly. It caught them both by surprise.

"*What?*" Stead.

" 'Look it up.' "

"Why is that funny?"

"It isn't funny. It's ironic."

"Explain?"

"Remember Foreman? You did the Mode Training, didn't you?"

"Yeah, so? Everybody did."

"Remember the part about communication? Ninety-five percent of the problems that human beings have in the world are the result of a *failure* to communicate—*truly* communicate."

"Yeah? And your point is?"

"Among other things, that's the problem with us and the Chtorr. We don't communicate."

"We *can't* communicate with the Chtorr."

"I can't believe you just said that to me."

Stead blinked, realized, recovered. "Oh, yeah."

"We *can* communicate with them. We don't *want* to. And they don't want to communicate with us. That's the failure."

"We've known that for years. Ever since you danced naked with a big pink worm. What does that have to do with looking things up?"

"That's the other part of it. The reason why most people can't communicate is that most people don't know what they're talking about."

Stead opened his mouth to argue. That's a pretty cynical thing to say, McCarthy. But he closed his mouth without saying it. Smart.

My turn. That's the single best advantage of insanity. It's always my turn. "The evidence is all around us. Most people really do *not* know what they're talking about. But it doesn't stop them. They talk anyway. All noise, no signal. Do you know why? It's not nature that abhors a vacuum, most of the universe is vacuum. It's the human mind that can't handle nothingness. It reduces it to a concept—*but even the concept of nothing is a thing*. That's the only way the mind can deal with empty, by creating a *concept* of empty to fill the actual empty. When you don't know something and you can't handle the not-knowing, you make up something—you make up facts, explanations, beliefs. That's why there's a little man in the refrigerator to turn out the light when you close the door, and that's why God made the universe—because people couldn't stand the not-knowing, couldn't stand things not having meaning, couldn't bear the idea that life is empty and meaningless, and that it doesn't mean anything that it doesn't mean anything, couldn't detach from the horror of the infinite. So they added meaning to everything they touched, a desperate explanation for why bad things happen. Even 'excrement occurs' is only another sidestep of consciousness. It's because you idiots insist on asking why, without ever stopping to realize that the word 'why' is a pernicious, insidious trap that leads you down the brimstone bath. The ugly truth is, for each and every one of us, including me—especially me, and that's what would really piss me off if I could still be pissed off—is that who you are and what you are is all about what you've made up, not what's really so. If you're a human being, and you look like one to me, you can't even see what's really so anymore, because you're so looking through the filters of what you believe."

Stead blinked. Trying to assimilate. He'd probably study the recordings of this moment for hours, fumbling his way through all the separate thoughts, wondering at the iceberg of insight underneath the jagged peak of each individual sentence.

"And that's why there's no communication, Mr. Roy Stead, because none of you poor pathetic human beings has anything accurate to communicate. Except perhaps when you get into touchy-feeling mode in some training or workshop and start sharing yourselves, all your frustrated wants and unmet needs and disembodied fears and impossible hopes and hopeless desires, which is all very interesting if you're saying it to someone you want to fuck, but ultimately it's a waste of good oxygen, because it's just more agenda, chatter, manipulation, bullshit, because it isn't about making a difference—it's about playing pattycake with the past instead of operating on the future. That's why there's no communication. Not because you don't, not because you can't, but because you insist on using the avenues of communication for crap instead of what really matters."

Goldberg looked like he wanted to argue, he always looked like he wanted to argue, but I could read his mind better than he could. He was terrified now that if he said anything, the consequences would be Barth. And he still didn't understand the reference to the Russian Front.

"You don't communicate anything useful because you don't know what you're talking about, and even when and if you do know something useful, you add your belief system to it, and you turn it back into bullshit."

Stead was nodding thoughtfully. "Do you have a prescription, Doctor McCarthy…?"

"Sure, but you won't listen. You'll hear it, you'll nod, you'll even agree I'm right. And that's as far as it'll go. The answer is education. Research. Finding out what's so. Getting the evidence and letting the evidence speak—instead of the belief system. Think about this, Stead, you should know this better than anybody. We live in a privileged age. The average slob has access to more accurate information of every kind than all the greatest libraries of history. All you have to do is ask. Pick up your phone, look at your clipboard, switch on a laptop, walk ten feet to a public terminal. You have instant access to a thousand different answer-agents, both public-access and interest-specialized. You, as an average person—well, you're not average, in fact there aren't any *average* people anymore, but if there were—the average person today has even a casual knowledge of matters that would have astonished the greatest scientists and philosophers of the year 1900. A scholar in ancient Greece or Rome was lucky to have read a couple hundred books in his lifetime—and those were books of less than ten or fifteen thousand words, barely enough to qualify in the novelette category. You're exposed to more information than that in a single month. By Aristotle's standards, you're a god—and what have you done with it? Almost nothing!

"You take it for granted that you know things about astronomy, physics, chemistry, biology, medicine, psychology, sociology, evolution, math, history, geology, political systems, sexuality, that hadn't even been considered deeply enough to be called impossible or outrageous in the time of Einstein. You can talk about the long-term psychological consequences of long-voyage space travel, why the backside of the moon is far more cratered than the face, you could explain there are no canals on Mars but lots of water beneath the surface anyway. You take it for granted that there are black holes, buckyballs and nano-tubes and polymers, organ transplants, neural regeneration, antibiotics, retro-viruses, gene therapy, the Mode training, the technology of consciousness, millicore processors, punctuated equilibrium, memetic dynamics, what killed the dinosaurs, and a hundred thousand other bits of information that you probably consider useless because it doesn't get you laid or put lobster on the table. You've had a lifetime of information poured into your head by radio, television, movies, webcasting, emails, forums, feeds, blogs, books, magazines, newspapers, and a hundred thousand independent channels and outlets that narrowcast to special interests. If we could drop you into the past, you'd be able to tell Oppenheimer to think about a soccer ball shape for the design of Fat Man, you could tell Walter Reed that mosquitoes spread yellow fever and malaria, you could tell Marx and Engels and Lenin why communism can't work, you could tell Turing and Von Neumann about separating software from hardware. You take it for granted—all the myriad little bits of data bouncing around inside your skull were priceless discoveries once, often paid with human lives. And think about all the information that we're buying today, one life at a time. A hundred years from now, if there are any humans left, what important discoveries of today will they take so for granted that it's no longer noticeably important? Just like us, what will they discard because they think they've moved so far beyond it that the information no longer has any relevance to them? Because no matter what, the more things change, the more that people stay the same. Like water flowing downhill, you take the easiest course, you do it without thinking, you reach your comfort level and you stop. You puddle up in your couch and stay there.

"But if there is any meaning at all to life, it's only going to be found in an accurate map of the universe—if only you could recognize the nature of knowledge, the technologies of construction that turn data into information. If only. But you don't. Because you don't do your research. You come to a word you don't recognize, you don't look it up, you make up a meaning for it and go on, each little inaccuracy, each little lie, adding another bit of misinformation to the filter between you and what's so. Do you know, just in the speaking of these last few hundred words, I've accessed fifty-three data banks to double-check my facts? When you're sitting at a terminal, it's so easy to click on any picture, any word, and get a little nugget that enriches. *We can't make it any easier for you to find out.* But you don't. You won't. You're too lazy and impatient. This is what's wrong with you, *all* of you, all the way up to the president and all the way down to the druggies and flunkies in the park. You don't fucking look things up, and then you have the gall, the chutzpah, the colossal arrogance to complain about how the world works! Instead of asking why, you make up answers—because you're in such a hurry to get to the next moment that you can't live in this one. You're so narrow and unconscious that you can't even be bothered to access the resources that others have built for you, and all you're good for is to be slaves and food for the first thing motivated enough to come along and give you what passes for an explanation for your paltry lives. See, that's the joke—that's what so funny here. That's why you don't trust me, you put keepers on me, nursemaids and guards—because I know so much. *Too much.* Too much for any one person to assimilate. That's why I'm crazy. I'm so plugged into everything, I'm a research machine. I can't help but look up the information. The noises in my head, the buzzing, the songs, the avalanche of facts, the data-stream of consciousness, it never ends, whatever I'm thinking about, there's a multi-dimensional array of video and sounds, four axes of information, including the time dimension, all the histories underlying, it all pours into me. And then you turn to me for answers, you ask the questions, and no matter what I say, you never listen. I'm not just a spigot or a funnel, but an avalanche, a tidal wave. And you can't handle it. *You can't handle the truth.* Do you know what that makes you? Lunch. That's the joke. That's what's so funny—that I'm the only one among you who really knows what he's talking about—*and you won't listen.* You don't listen, you don't learn. So you're stuck forever repeating the same old patterns of failure. Jesus Fucking Christ on a Stick, what is the matter with this species? If you don't like what you're getting, why do you keep on doing what you're doing?! No, don't even try to explain yourselves. Just see if you can get the joke. Foreman was both right and wrong. He was brilliantly correct when he said that 95% of all human problems is that humans don't communicate, but he was amazingly, colossally wrong in the very same breath, because it wasn't about communication, it was about listening. 95% of all human problems is that humans simply do not listen to what's being said. You don't even know how to listen."

"And you do?" Goldberg. Hostile.

"Yes." I said it simply.

Goldberg snorted. Stead glared at him.

"To *truly* listen, you have to kill the ego. You want to know what's wrong with me. Whoever lived in this body before, he's dead. He's not here, not home. He's dead. Dead. Do you get it? Dead. He's not resting, he's not pining for the fjords, he's joined the heavenly choir, he's pushing up daisies, he's a dead parrot. *He is nailed to the perch.* And all that's left is just a great gaping space, a vacuum, a human nothingness, in which everything occurs at once, an avalanche of information pours in and processes itself with the processing power of the teep as well as a residual neural network of alien fibers that still outclasses anything that little humans have yet invented, because it's the first time that a human brain has been linked to neural symbiotes—the first time that any human brain has done so and presented any kind of rationality, and that only happened because the massed analytical power of the teep and 57 separate intelligence engines were working overtime to impress some kind of human ratiocination onto the process, onto the swirling maelstrom of sensation, experience, and information that was ripping apart the last shreds of McCarthy's sanity."

"Gosh," said Goldberg, dryly. "And all this time, we thought you were simply autistic. At least, that was the clinical diagnosis—emotionally blind."

"Autistic? Yes, of course. And paranoid, delusional, psychotic, schizophrenic, and all the other shapes and forms of human derangement that inventive lunatics have created and that even more inventive lunatics have defined. Autistic. You pitiful schmuck, you haven't even scratched the surface of the depths of the irrationalities that have flooded through this body since it was abandoned in the Amazon." I turned to Stead. "And what are you grinning at now?"

"The old McCarthy is back. The angry McCarthy, the outraged and determined McCarthy. Welcome home."

"You idiot. You just proved my point. You don't listen. And even when you pretend to listen, you don't hear. I'm not the old McCarthy. *I'm not McCarthy anymore.* I'm something else. And don't ask me who or what, because I don't know. I still haven't finished inventing it yet. And yes, you should be scared. I am. And if I'm scared, then what comes next is going to be worse than anything that came before."

The Tunnels

"The difference between you and someone with a
terminal disease is that someone with a terminal
disease knows not to start any trilogies."
—SOLOMON SHORT

Barth returned then. The entire rant had taken less than nine minutes.
But he hadn't missed anything. He put aside an hour a day on his schedule so he could listen to the distilled output of the McCarthy-thing's
daily babblings. And that was the other half of the joke. Barth was a good
listener. But he was limited by his ability to assimilate. I can explain it to
you, Colonel. I can't understand it for you. But if there were points to
give, then I had to give him points for trying. Not that it would matter
in the long run. The Chtorr doesn't grade its lunch. Only humans give
points. In that case, score one for humanity—the McCarthy-thing still
has enough humanity to think about gold stars.

Barth glanced to me. "Anything interesting?"

Stead shrugged. "I give it a six. Maybe a seven."

"I'll review it later. Form up."

Today's mission was reconnaissance. A squadron of robots—prowlers, growlers, and bears, oh my—would head downtown through the
tunnels, looking for snufflers, chrysalids, nests, millipedes, moles, blad-
der-vines, blue mold, nightstalkers, or just the occasional pool of purple
muck. The bots would scan the visible and invisible spectra, pause and
listen for vibrations all the way from the infra to the ultra-sonic, and
sniff the air every half-second for various long-chain bio-molecules
which would reveal the presence of Chtorran biota. I already knew what
the machines would smell, I'd been smelling it since we flew over the
Verrazano Narrows Bridge.

Eventually, when the virtual riders of the beasts decided they'd seen
enough, then we'd move in heavier machines to secure the area. At some
point, someone would decide that I should go down into the tunnels
and warrens beneath Manhattan and sniff and taste and touch. Not that
they would listen to what I might report. But Barth had argued and
others had agreed with him that it might be a useful experiment to let
the McCarthy-thing wander around. Kind of like hiring a psychic to
help find the missing body of the kidnap victim—a desperate act of last
resort—which even if it works, no one will give credence to the validity
of the process.

We walked/hiked/marched/trudged—I gimped, refused to ride—two blocks to the Christopher Street subway station, at the bottom end of a small triangular park formed where Christopher Street, Seventh Ave., and Waverly collided. This was Christopher Park, notable primarily for its statue of famed civil war general, Philip H. Sheridan—Sheridan Square, the park named for the general, was actually around the corner, bounded by West 4th, Washington Place, and Barrow Street. The subway station we wanted was the Christopher St./Sheridan Square IRT #1, which led down to a half-vast underground warren, that also included, if you walked two blocks through various subterranean malls and foyers to above-ground dwellings, access to the A, B, C, D, E and F lines. There were a number of historical markers at the park and on the surrounding buildings, including one plaque actually commemorating a riot by drag queens. New York.

The subway station itself smelled heavily of stale urine and motor oil. Faint echoes of a variety of overripe, overcooked, processed meats, cakes, candies, and soft drinks. It all smelled old. Here and there, it also smelled of magazines, rats, feverish sex, and stale death. Amyl/Butyl nitrites, the headache-aphrodisiac. There's another question. What happens to a worm's metabolism when it's popped? But why down here? Oh—because this was the bottom half of the festival of madness, the place where furtive sexual grapplings occurred in unseen corners, easier to escape the eyes of wandering monitors—or so the desperate partners thought. Beneath the clamoring daylight, here is where the nightly revelry ultimately sinks, where desperate and exhausted celebrants keep their coffins, where they finally lie dormant, each enshrouded in his own private casket or cocoon, recovering and waiting for another midnight to arrive. The video records of a thousand hungers cascaded across McCarthy's consciousness. Fragments of other people's lives and desires. Here, the final despairs, the lonely breakdowns of identity and gender; the deaths of a thousand cunts. They argued all night, over who had the right, to do what and with which and to whom. Why here? Why anywhere? Why not? Too late, the McCarthy-thing remembers that the word 'why' is a trap that leads only to false connections and 'let's make something up.' The irony, oh the irony. Even the transformed self is not immune. And that's the joke. Ha ha. Lack of enlightenment is only a problem to the enlightened. Assuming, of course—that's always the problem; assuming the course—that this is enlightenment.

The thing is, the smells are overwhelming here. They have resonance. They call up echoes of other moments. The snares of memory drag you out of the present. How can you be present to the moment if the moment is about the past?

"Are you all right?"

"Eh?"

"You're trembling."

McCarthy holds up a hand. "Don't talk—"

"What is it?"

"I said, 'Don't talk.'" But whatever it was, it's gone now. An elusive wisp that disappears from consciousness as immediately as you focus your attention on it. The thought that you once had, but can't remember—all you can remember is that you had a thought.

He opens his eyes and shakes his head, as if to clear it. A human gesture, one that will be misinterpreted. It's really a Chtorran gesture, and it doesn't mean what humans think it does. It doesn't matter.

Barth comes back to Jim. "Are you ready?"

We climb down a set of wooden steps installed here to give us easier access to the tracks. We're all wearing rubber soles—and maybe rubber souls as well. We've sold our rubbers—rub hers, rub his, rubbish all—to the devils in our heads. Don't go there, Jim. That way lies badness. It doesn't matter, because the third rail is already dead. It's not the only thing. The smell of recent decay is outranked, pun intended, only by more ancient fetid odors of human degradation. Bottomless stratum of excrement and urine, stale sperm, a smattering of blood—plus alcohol and marijuana, poppers and always other darker flavors, pink and red and purple. Everywhere, layers of black crud that must have been ingrained a century ago—everything is gray and grimy. The grease of civilization on the skids. All the layers of paint and remodeling cannot hide the cancer. The medicinal smell of disinfectant cannot bury the evidence that humanity doesn't need an alien infestation. It can kill itself without any outside help. For most of these poor apes, the comfort level is at the bottom. They give themselves just enough of what they want to be miserable. And anything more is too much work. Why bother saving such a species? They cannot even save themselves.

The thought puzzles the thing that lives inside McCarthy's body now. Why did he even have that thought? Does part of him still think that humanity should be saved? Is there some residual attachment here? Some moment of identity that hasn't yet been superseded or discarded?

Curious. In several senses of the word.

The prowlers, so-called because they resemble panthers, wait silently at the darkness of the southern tunnel. Sleek carbon-silicon entities, six-legged terrors, most of the weight carried in the hips, sleek and silent, with baleful crimson eyes. Twelve of the beasts, they all wear harnesses, carrying extra tanks of fuel, ammunition, liquid nitrogen, plus whatever other agents authority has authorized for this mission.

Behind them, rumbling deep inside their bellies, the balrogs—larger, sturdier, uglier, more aggressive machineries of death. The growlers. Heavy armored rear legs; ferocious polymer-muscled arms. Flattened heads, a row of narrow eyes, all kinds of deadly sensors; ears and nostrils too. The jowls reveal multiple weapon ports. Gigantic, bear-clawed, missile-carrying monstrosities. The missiles come in all sizes and effectiveness: some as small pencils and flashlights, others as large as baseball bats. Depending on the target. Heat-seeking, laser-targeted, odor-sniffing, electro-magnetic, nanowave-radar, sonic-hunting, and three other if-I-tell-you-I-have-to-kill-you technologies. The deathload is phenomenal. A single balrog has the firepower of a schnauzer-tank. Eight of these sturdy growlers rest upon the platform, waiting for the prowlers to move out.

And the ferrets. Too many to count, but the information buzz reports 128 of them, some of them just uncrated, and warmed up today. Slender and dark and flexible, able to slide between a shadow and the wall it falls upon. They'll slither into the gloom and disappear, gliding from pose to silent pose, sniffing the air, listening, searching, eyeballing everything, scavenging the detritus of the depths, reporting back to distant intelligence engines, where all the random, seemingly unconnected bits of data get compiled, cross-correlated, sifted, sorted, analyzed and annotated, eventually producing a real-time, 3-D map of hell.

And finally, waiting patiently, the bears. Misnamed. The men in powered armor suits. Four meters high, they stand inside the robot's torso, a carbon protective cage surrounds—the robot legs walk for them, the robot arms reach and grab and carry for them. Designed originally for heavy industry and dockwork, the military adaptation was inevitable. These bastards carry shredder-guns and other nightmares, euphemistically called 'offensive weaponry.' A man in armor can kill a grizzly, snapping its back like a toothpick. Killing a worm bear-handed is a little harder, but it can be done. It was done, once. By an idiot too stupid to know better, someone who hadn't bothered to read the advisories on Chtorran contact.

At the other end of the platform, other operators were readying their equipment. There were three rollagons, equipped to ride on or off the rails. After the advance teams had secured the tunnels, then we could go in and I would sniff and taste and commune with the Chtorran gods and listen for the purple song, and if it didn't drive me insane—*more* insane—then I would report to Barth what I had smelled and tasted and felt, and he would translate it for the General. Whether there were gastropedes, millipedes, renegades, snufflers, or shambler colonies—and how big a threat they represented. Or even just some nasty blue mold.

The General was skeptical, but so what? The pre-Trori-ktor McCarthy would have been skeptical too if Jon Guyer had been brought along on a mission. But at least, that McCarthy would have recognized the possibilities that a former(?) Trori-ktor might bring to the operation. That McCarthy had only been an asshole, not an idiot.

Barth gestured, and we climbed into the second rollagon. Each vehicle had shredder-guns, the first one had torches as well. Somebody else must love the smell of napalm in the mourning. I didn't. In the tunnels it was already overbearing. Barth sat forward, next to the driver. I sat behind him, Stead sat next to me. Goldberg and Lt. Dustin Foley, our temporary liaison, climbed in behind. Foley wanted to ask a lot of questions—who wouldn't?—but he knew not to. The kid was smarter than other people thought he looked.

At the rear of the vehicle, we had two guys on mounted shredders. 36 ranked barrels on each weapon-system, two ugly walls of granular death. The gunners wore battle-armor and hard expressions. One of them wanted to be up ahead, where he thought the action would be. The other just didn't want to be in the same vehicle with me. The General wasn't coming with us, she was somewhere up above, at Seventh Ave. and 13th St. Monitoring the operation from the communications nexus. A safe distance away. Time and distance. A strategic withdrawal?

Barth pulled on a VR helmet and settled it in place. Stead put on a similar helmet, so did Foley. The driver wore a standard combat helmet without the VR displays; so did Goldberg, he was our corpsman. The shredder-men had targeting helmets. I didn't need any additional communication or display gear, I was already a complete VR station. I wore only a standard Kevlar bucket. I switched off the silencer and let the noise pour in. Sorted, filtered, selected, finally looked out the eyes of the forward-most prowler.

Somebody up ahead gave the order. "Let's roll." The traditional command of heroes. The headlights of all the vehicles came on, then the dazzle-panels around the gunners. The beasts lit up too, outlining themselves in red and white and blue.

Finally, the machines began lurching forward, like all the separate cars of a train. First the prowlers, then the growlers, the bears, and finally the rollagons. The ferrets scampered, scrambled, scrabbled eagerly ahead, outpacing everything else.

The VR displays began lighting up immediately, the *fog of war* dissipated as the ferrets' information poured in. The first few hundred meters, they all blinked uniformly green. Nothing here but tunnel. I looked through the eyes of twenty of them in rapid succession. Infrared, ultra-sonic, nanowave-radar—no movement.

We reached an area painted in alternating black and yellow stripes. Biohazard warnings everywhere. We rolled cautiously forward, past the poison-traps and aerogel barriers, a hundred meters of slowdown. The ferrets picked their way methodically. The prowlers and growlers went single-file, staying to the center of the tracks. The rollagons came last. Two growlers brought up the rear.

Ahead of our vehicle, the tunnels were flickering with movement— our own—everything awash with layers of light and shadow, a study in contrasts, dazzle-panels blazing and revealing dingy gray walls, red and yellow emergency boxes, occasional cubbyholes, ladders, pipes, wires, everything coated with the same indelible layers of age and grime. Spotlights peered into the gloom ahead. Nothing moved except our own machines and their sharp-edged shadows.

Still nothing in the tunnels. The ferrets still shone green. We moved deeper under Manhattan, the tunnels angled and dipped and rose again. The noise of our engines was intense. When the trains were running, the noise must have been horrendous, all the separate cars clattering and squealing, brakes screeching, doors whooshing; the tile walls reflecting the harsh cascades of sound like glass mirrors.

Halfway to Houston St., we paused in the tunnels and listened for sixty unbearable seconds. Ambush time. But no, nothing moved. The ferrets peeked under the rails, into the cracks in the tunnel floor, crawled up broken pipes, scrabbled along the ceilings—probing, sniffing, listening. Nothing.

Halfway between Houston and Canal, we paused again, the spotlights angling this way and that. Evidence of a battle of some kind. Most of the debris had been removed, but there were scars along the walls. And some graffiti too. Nothing of current interest, though an archaeologist might enjoy himself here.

We rolled through the Canal Street station, slid back into the caverns of grime, rolled downward toward a ranker smell—

Ahead, Franklin, Chambers, Memorial, and Park Place, a labyrinth of reconstructed tunnels and stations, one of the first great underground cities. And one of the first to die in the plagues and riots and fires. If they ever reopened Memorial Station, they'd have to add a whole new layer of remembrance.

Abruptly, we stopped—

The ferrets remained obstinately green. Questions rattled back and forth across the channels. Denver and Oakland both wanted to know what was happening. Why weren't we seeing anything? An assortment of Colonels, Majors, and Captains all reported cautiously. No enemy contact. No evidence of enemy infestation. General Domitz demanded to know why. The VR pilots remained silent—excuses are not a valid substitute for results. But the lack of Chtorran life was more disturbing than anything else we could have found.

All the tired old clichés of a hundred years of combat movies—it's always quietest just before *they* attack—the silence screamed *ambush*.

Barth swiveled around in his seat. He lifted the faceplate of his helmet to look at me. "McCarthy?" He wasn't scared, not yet—but he looked concerned.

I stood up in my seat and sniffed the air. Rank, pungent, acrid, mordant, grimy. Wet. Curious. Different.

Turned off the buzz-buzz and listened to the silence. Turned up my ears all the way. Turned on the buzz-buzz and listened through the prowlers, listened through their feet, their whiskers. Distant rumbles of traffic overhead. Not much. The sounds of water flowing through pipes. The echoes of the convoy. But no telltale chewing sounds. No frying bacon noises. Nothing.

Held up a hand. "Wait a minute." Swung myself over the side of the rollagon and down to the floor of the tunnel. A spotlight from behind blasted me. Too bright. I waved a hand toward it, and the operator angled it up toward the roof of the tunnel instead.

"Everybody, please be quiet," I asked. "Turn off your engines."

Some official chatter back and forth, then finally, "Do as he asks," and the tunnel fell still.

I picked my way over the rails, across to the uptown tracks. Switched on my helmet lights and studied the patterns in the dust. Favoring the bad leg, I bent down on the other knee and traced fingers through the grime, trying to get a sense of its age. I placed my hand flat upon the ground and listened for vibrations, tasted the detritus and debris in the dirt. Stood up again, touched the walls, the steel pillars, tasted the air as well. The tunnel was *clean*. Abnormally so.

Stood up. Brushed off my hands. Could sense the rising impatience behind me. Knew they wanted answers—or failing that, just the right questions. Picked my way back, using the cane to test my footing. Barth was standing in his seat. Behind him, Stead and Foley were also standing. Stead was wearing parabolic ears; he looked like Mickey Mouse.

"So?" asked Barth.

I climbed back into the rollagon. Ladder on the side. All the cameras focused on me. Dance-for-gramma time. A live feed. "Cleanest subway tunnels I've ever been in. Acting-Mayor Foley should be proud." Go ahead. I dare you to ask.

"Eh?" Barth knew me too well. He took the bait. "And…?"

"And nothing." I sat down again. Everybody waited for me to explain.

"It's a very clean subway tunnel. Very clean. Have you ever stood at the edge of the platform and really *looked* at a subway track?"

"Not really, no. We didn't have a subway in Seattle." Then he got it. "Okay, what am I missing? What should we be looking for?"

"Wrong question, Colonel." Somewhere up on Seventh and 13th, General Domitz was cursing my name. I might not be human, but I can still play the game. You want cooperation? You buy it with courtesy. Otherwise, it's Twenty Questions. "What *isn't* here?"

Lt. Foley figured it out first. Of course. He lived in Manhattan. "Mice. Rats. Cockroaches. There aren't any."

Barth looked surprised, then even more surprised. "Good catch," he whistled softly. He rubbed his chin thoughtfully, then, slowly, he asked the next question. "Millipedes...? They ate them all?"

Nod. "There were millipedes here a while ago. A week. Maybe ten days. Two weeks. But they're gone now. Shut up, Foley—" I paid for this microphone. The Lieutenant was whispering excitedly into his headset. He shut up and I continued. "Millipedes are always hungry, always eating," McCarthy explained to the unseen audience. Click-click, a very good rating. That meant royalties. If I cared. Which I didn't. But I could still play the game. Better than all of them, if I wanted to. "Forget what you think you know about these creatures. Don't compare them to Earth bugs—or anything else you think you know. Their behavior is different because their metabolism is different—*alien*. Yes, you know they eat anything, you know they're insatiable, and you think that explains it. Only your language is so insufficient, you have no real grasp of what you're dealing with here. Your language doesn't include that scale of conceptualization. The word 'insatiable' is so inadequate a descriptor, you cannot imagine how off the scale it is. These things are so voracious, so rapacious and ravenous that there is no satisfactory way even to begin convey the single-minded intention of their biological imperative. These things exist to eat, nothing else. *Nothing else.* They don't need to reproduce, not in this form; so their only biological imperative is to grow. As big and as fast as they can. And that means eat and eat and keep eating, whatever it can, whatever looks like it might be food, whatever looks like it might be remotely edible. These things don't distinguish animal from plant, animate from inanimate, safe from poisonous. All they can do is bite and chew, bite and chew. It doesn't matter how many die of poison or choking or because they're chewing on something totally indigestible. It's completely irrelevant. From an evolutionary standpoint, they're like sperm cells, most of them are disposable. You can start with ten thousand, but you only need four to start a viable nest. Evolution doesn't care; it's a process, not a purpose.

"Ecologically, a swarm of millipedes is like a fire. Fire needs forests, forests need fire, it's a partnership. But there aren't any forest fires on Chtorr; instead, there are millipedes. They provide the same function. When they swarm, they burn through an area, eating out the thickest undergrowth, clearing the brush, reducing the overage in animal populations, weeding out the sick and the old, thinning the herds. They leave the area healthier than before, a fertile ground for lots of new growth—especially Chtorran growth."

"If they were still here, if there were millipedes still in these tunnels, they'd be chewing on the timbers or sucking at the grease encrusted in the corners and beneath the rails. If there were millipedes here, we'd hear chewing. It's a distinctive sound signature. Crunching, sizzling, hissing—depending on how many. And if there were nothing left to chew, we'd still hear the scrabbling of movement, all those scraping little legs."

"So where are they now?" Foley relayed the question from General Domitz.

Ignored the immediate question. Without the larger context, understanding is impossible. "They also thin their own numbers. Eventually, after they eat all the animals, all the insects, all the fish, all the birds, all the crawling things in the trees and in their burrows, all the creatures that can't escape, after they denude an area of animal protein, they start in on the plants; after they finish the plants, the fruits, the leaves, the flowers, the vines, the roots that they can get at, after they finish the easy cellulose, then they start eating whatever decaying matter is still left, even bits of excrement; and finally, after they've eaten the land bare, they start eating each other. They don't need ten thousand survivors, only a few hundred. Not even that many if the forest won't support them. Look it up. The numbers, the scale, the life cycles—"

"*Where are they now?*" Foley repeated. He looked pale, as if half-expecting a swarm of ravenous millipedes to come flooding out of the tunnel ahead.

Shook my head. "Most of them are gone. The best food for a millipede is another millipede. All the best ingredients in a single package. A nice juicy millipede can be real good eating. A little chewy, like octopus, but if you've got the teeth for it—*especially* if you're another millipede—it's a meal. The little ones went into the bellies of the big ones. The big ones went into the bellies of the bigger ones. The bigger ones into the bellies of…the ones who were big enough to eat them. The *biggest* ones."

"So where are those? The *survivors*? The ones who ate the rest?"

Were I still human, I might have enjoyed the relayed impatience of General Domitz. Not being human, it was irrelevant. Turned to Barth instead. "Remember when you asked me to be Murray-The-Explainer? Were you listening? Do you understand the problem here?"

Barth was already mulling it over. He wasn't a fast thinker, but he was thorough. "The support system...?"

Nodded. "Thank you."

"Will one of you explain it?" Foley demanded, echoing the General's frustration.

"Chrysalids," I said. "They've gone into the next phase of their life cycle. They're sealed up in cozy little organic capsules, happily metamorphosing."

"Into worms, right?"

Shook my head. "No. Not worms."

Not Worms

"There is no secret. Make up your own."
—SOLOMON SHORT

"Not worms."

"No. Something. But not worms."

Now Barth did look worried. "Jim, you told me that the millipedes turn into worms. Gastropedes. Now you're saying—"

"The millipedes metamorphose into gastropedes only when they've been exposed to a full ecological banquet. The creatures in these tunnels have not. They've had a very limited diet. It's my guess—" Click-click, buzz-buzz, this was going to require some serious research. "Yes, 'guess' is the operative word. It's my guess that they've not had access to even half the fauna and flora they need to establish a successful collective."

"Huh—?" That was Lt. Foley. "What is he talking about?"

"You don't have time for the answer," I said. "It took Barth nearly a week to get it."

Foley turned to Barth. "Is there a short version?"

Barth looked like he didn't even know where to start. Goldberg threw his hands up in the air and turned away. Finally, Stead tried to explain. "The gastropedes aren't real creatures. They're collectives of multiple symbiotes—at least a hundred different kinds of creatures all living together in the swollen body of a giant slug with a pituitary problem."

"Thank you."

Roy nodded, mildly amused. "You're welcome." He'd been quoting one of McCarthy's less deranged moments. And we all knew it—all except Foley.

Barth turned to me. "So what do we get if the millipede doesn't have a full complement?"

Scratched my head. Hated to guess. Had a pretty good idea, but didn't want to risk being wrong either. Hm, imagine that. There's a little piece of McCarthy left—the part that doesn't want to look stupid in public. Fuck him. Again. "Let's move on. We need to see what's left of Memorial Station."

"Can you answer the question first?" Foley. An edge to his voice.

I swiveled in my seat to face him. "Let's have a little talk, Lt. Foley. Lieutenant Dustin Foley, son of Acting-Mayor, Linda Foley, aide to General Laura Domitz, the third member of a linear clone family, temporary liaison to Colonel Travis Barth and his band of merry men. In fact, let's go beyond a 'little talk.' Let me make something perfectly clear. Richard-Milhouse-Nixon-*perfectly-clear*. Look him up. Your general is correct, I am insane. Being marooned in a Chtorran mandala does that to a person. Being infected with neural symbiotes does that to a person. Being a teep does that to a person. Being infused by a HARLIE engine does that to a person. And finally, being a fusion between the teep corps and the neural symbiotes and a HARLIE and the Chtorran ecology does that to a person four times over—and the effect isn't simply cumulative, it's exponential and transformational in a way that goes beyond quantification, qualification, measurement, and codification. Yes, I am insane—and no, I am not going to stop being insane just because you or anyone else finds it inconvenient. You cannot order me to be sane. Because even if I wanted to, which I don't, I'm no longer capable of it. Because I am not *just* insane—I am off the scale. I am so fucking far off the scale that even the worms don't want me. The teep doesn't want me. And the neural symbiotes in my body have all applied for asylum in Canada. But as insane as I am—I'm also useful. *Very* useful. So useful that Colonel Barth and Specialist Stead and Corpsman Goldberg and General Domitz and even little you will put up with whatever craziness I feel like throwing at you, all the different manifestations of craziness that I can invent, however it shows up, because in those few occasional moments of what you perceive as lucidity where I may or may not exhibit what looks to you like rational communication, I might actually say something that could save your wretched and pitiful little lives. Here's the punch line, what you need to get—the part that is 'perfectly clear'—your lives are absolutely worthless to me. I could not possibly care less if any of you survive or not. Survival is no longer on the map for me. But because it is profoundly important to you—and on the off chance that my cooperation might make a difference to you or your general or your operation, you really do want to keep me happy and comfortable. Don't you?"

He blinked. And gulped. And nodded.

"So that means that you and your fat-assed general really do want to keep out of my face, because if you think I'm hard to deal with now, you haven't seen anything yet. Remember when she asked if I could control it? I can, but I don't have to. And sometimes I don't want to. You got that?"

"Uh, yes sir. I got it. Sir." He saluted. "Thank you, sir."

I didn't return the salute. Despite the government's opinion that James Edward McCarthy had been returned to active duty in the Special Forces, with the operative rank of Major—or was it Colonel now?—the person formerly known as McCarthy didn't exactly share the same conviction.

Foley sat back in his seat and went silent, even ignoring the yammering in his headset. General Domitz wanted him to bawl me out on her behalf, but whatever else Foley was—he wasn't stupid. Given a choice between her wrath and mine, he chose hers.

I turned my seat forward again. Stead was expressionless, but Barth was quietly grinning. I could see it even on the back of his head. Rank may have its privileges, but insanity outranks all. "Let's go, Colonel."

Barth whispered something to his headset, and we lurched forward through the tunnels again.

Memorial Station—there's so much buzz-buzz about Memorial Station, I have to turn off the noise again. Twenty underground levels. Six subway routes, not counting the PATH[1] trains to New Jersey. Room for more trains, arrivals and departures than Grand Central and Penn Station combined. Twenty underground levels of shops, theaters, businesses, industrial facilities, waste management, and maintenance. Four luxury hotels, three convention centers, sixty theaters, forty restaurants (not counting fast food counters), an ice/roller rink, ten basketball courts, twenty handball courts, eight health clubs, four swimming pools, a driving range, three bowling alleys, a hundred and twenty shops and stores, sixteen web-cafes, two discos, six art galleries, two concert halls, two very private clubs (brothels), and twelve museums—including the history of the Twin Towers, the Firefighters' Tribute, the Police Memorial Museum, the Wall of Remembrance and the Wall of Names—also three gardens, two churches, a synagogue, a mosque, and a non-denominational chapel. Plus 3200 offices and business suites, 600 residence suites, 2400 condos, and 6000 rental units. Twenty levels spanning an underground area of 12 square blocks.

The grand mall—also known as the *grand mal* by architectural critics—was the largest underground vault ever constructed. Roughly the size and shape of a cathedral (think St. Peter's Basilica), it was designed to inspire awe and wonder. Tourists—over a hundred million of them in the first three years—would enter the chamber on either the east or west mezzanine and then just stop and stare upward. And upward. Twenty of the largest and tallest stained-glass windows ever constructed outlined the central space. The windows depicted an abstract city skyline, the Manhattan skyline, in shades of gold and cream, with pale blue radiance representing the sky, and darker blue representing the water beneath; more than half the height of each window represented sky. They were wider than the walls that separated them, and each was illuminated by simulated daylight that changed in shade and intensity to match the actual sunlight above, so the effect was that the vault was not an enclosed space as much as a *defined* one. The great underground

---

1   Port Authority Trans-Hudson

space seemed to be on top of a mountain-peak in some far off fabulous land, its windows glowing with the light of a magic sun in the day and enchanted stars at night. Designed by Amazement, Inc., a spin-off of the Disney Imagineering division, the Memorial Station concourse was considered one of the seven modern wonders of the world, along with the Gibralter Bridge, the Hong Kong Stiletto, and the orbital elevator.

But when we entered, it was dark. Cavernous. Empty. Lit only by a few scattered dazzle-panels. They were insufficient to the task. An inch of scummy water covered the marble floor. As we drove in, we sent V-shaped ripples toward the walls. The grand staircases had become grand waterfalls. The water puddled here, then continued on toward the lower levels, where a phalanx of pumps returned the water to the river.

The ferrets didn't like water this deep, they held back, bunching up on the first step, but the prowlers were undeterred. They leapt ahead, sniffing up and down the aisles of deserted kiosks, darting into arcades and cubbyholes and cul de sacs. They explored every blind corner, every hidden vantage, every staircase and shaft; they had the security maps and they were methodically checking off every access point. The machines were watertight, so it didn't bother them to lunge through murky streams or dark waterfalls of leakage.

Somewhere above, multiple pipes had been breached. The water had already been flowing for several days, but the union had refused to let work crews enter until they knew the area was safe. The Army Corps of Engineers had inspected the situation and called for Decontamination. The Decontamination units had withdrawn until Security and Containment Squads had secured the area. The Security and Containment Squads analyzed the situation and asked the Joint Chiefs to send in a Battle Group. And so on. Us.

We rolled to a stop in front of the information kiosk—not quite large enough to house a family, but a honeymoon couple would have been comfortable. Several monitor-bots sat on the counters, quietly surveying the mall.

Swung myself over the edge of the vehicle, splashed into the water. Stepped away a few paces, knelt and trailed my fingers through the water. Cold. Slightly clammy. Greasy. Tasted my fingers—

"Do you think that's safe?" Goldberg called.

Glanced back over my shoulder. "I doubt I can add any more ecological damage to this mess." Oh. He meant it the other way. I straightened. "Louis, there isn't a bug on this planet that can threaten what's already growing in this body." Took another taste, just to be sure.

Gimped back to the rollagon. Barth studied me. Stead recorded me. Goldberg medi-scanned me. Foley waited impatiently.

"Well?"

"It needs salt."

No reaction. Humans. No sense of humor.

"Let's go for a walk. Colonel? Roy? Louis? You too, Foley, if you want."

Barth whispered something to his headset, and six men with torches and shredder-rifles fell into position, two ahead, one on each side, two behind. Recognized Elske and Bryan. They looked uncomfortable. They still remembered the Amazon.

They all wanted to know what I was looking for, but by now, they knew better than to ask. This mind—this *new* mind that had taken over McCarthy's body and soul—didn't report anything until it had certainty. Discussing an embryonic hypothesis would be a mistake. Especially here. No context. McCarthy's dad had said it more succinctly, more than once. "Never show unfinished work to an idiot. And when it comes to your work, always assume that everyone is an idiot until proven otherwise. You know what you're doing, they don't." Besides, this particular nascent idea had elements of undistilled disaster percolating in it. The only thing worse than what I suspected was that I might be wrong; in that case, the situation might not be worse than I imagined—it would be worse than I *could* imagine.

Despite my unbridled insanity, despite the fusion of three and a half great minds, despite the linkages to all the Alexandrian libraries in the world, all the lethetic intelligence engines, and an internal network of neural symbiotes that still didn't know how to shut up and mind their own business, despite all that crap flowing through me, I still had limits. I am a finite being and there is ultimately a bandwidth problem. There is only so much data that I can assimilate, conceptualize, model, process, and synthesize as thought. And after that, all the rest is noise, no matter how useful, important, or valuable it might otherwise be. What scared me—yes, I was still capable of fear—was that the situations and challenges ahead might prove overwhelming, even to this mind. Despite all the bravado and bluster, I might, in the end, *fail*. It wasn't the failure of ability that scared me, but the failure to *understand*. I couldn't bear the idea of not-knowing.

"Ha," I said. I slapped my knee.

"Eh?" Barth.

"I just discovered another way I'm still human. Worrying about things—that's my ego's little hobby. Apparently, I still have enough of an ego for it to have a hobby. Don't worry about it, Colonel. Enlightenment is not *what you think*." Glanced over to him. He didn't get the joke. He had a familiar, puzzled, frustrated, weary expression. Okay, let him off the hook. "Lost my detachment, that's all. Understand?"

"Yeah. Sort of." He hesitated. Something unspoken.

"Go ahead. Say it."

"Well…you're starting to look and sound like yourself again. I mean, the way you used to be. I mean, a little bit, every so often."

Nodded. "Yes. I know. Not sure yet why." Worth thinking about. Not now, later.

Barth shrugged. "Bad influences, probably."

"Probably."

We passed through the deserted food court—all the different counters were shuttered and dark, empty signs promising long-abandoned savories and treats—and reached one of the wide banks of escalators going down. The stairs were still and silent. The level below was dark and gloomy. The torchmen angled their spotlights. The water slid down the ranks of steps, already leaving black slimy streaks. "Doesn't look safe," Barth said.

Started down anyway. "Gotta taste it." Held the railings carefully.

The others hesitated.

Stopped halfway down, sniffed the air. "There's nothing down here—" Sniffed again. "Nothing alive, anyway. Nothing *recently* alive."

Against his better judgment, Barth followed. He pointed to one of the torchmen; the man handed over his weapon. Stead made a noise that translated out to, "The things I do for England." Then he followed too.

Barth picked his way down the steps of the next escalator over. Stead came down the one beyond that. Even more reluctantly, Elske and Bryan followed, each making his way carefully down. "You're determined to get us killed—aren't you, Colonel?"

"It's either that or do it myself. And you know how much I hate getting my hands dirty."

They pointed their spotlights into the gloom. More empty stores and hollow promises. A tomb for civilization. The water was deeper here. The pumps weren't keeping up. Whatever had broken the pipes above, it was widening the breach. Something wanted/needed these caverns wet.

Tasted the water again. There it was. That flavor. Distinct enough for certainty. The city of New York had only a few months to live. Maybe less. Maybe only a few weeks. The problem—

They weren't going to take the word of a lunatic. And by the time they'd convinced themselves that this particular lunatic knew what he was talking about, it would be too late.

The lunatic had no reason to save New York City, had no reason to care about the people who lived here. He did not consider himself a participant in the human adventure. Neither did they.

Nevertheless, the lunatic felt stirrings of *something*.

Barth saw the expression on my face. I saw my own face reflected in the buzz-buzz, all the pictures bouncing around the web. Underneath the tattoos and worm lines and feathers and remnants of pink fur, I could see a very frightened man. Nobody else could see it, but I knew what I was looking at.

The critical threshold. The shift in the wind. The tipping point. The moment. The day the world began to die. Was this the moment—?

"What?" asked Barth.

"I was right. It *does* need salt."

Dead Ends

*"The universe is not impersonal,
not as long as there are persons in it."*
—SOLOMON SHORT

"I want to go deeper."

Barth looked unhappy.

"You can't send in ferrets or weasels. The water's too deep for them. And it's not deep enough for crabs or minnows, which you don't have anyway. You could get some turtles or other amphibians in here, but they'd have to come in from the Brooklyn Naval Yards. We'd lose at least a day, maybe two."

"The prowlers are waterproof," Goldberg offered. He was shivering. He did not like being down here, getting his feet wet.

"You knew the job was dangerous when you took it," Stead replied. He was having a great time.

Barth was already speaking to the prowler command. A moment later, three of the cat-like robots came gliding down the wide stairs against the wall—the joke was that the stairs were a mandatory safety measure, in case the escalators failed. If you have to think about it, use the stairs.

"The prowlers go in ahead of you, McCarthy. Point the way."

Nodded forward. Didn't know why. But something beckoned, called, lured—

Lorelei. The sirens. On his way home from Troy, Ulysses wandered twenty years around the wine-dark seas of the Mediterranean. Saw his crew turned into pigs, fought a giant one-eyed man, escaped a witch, and heard the inescapable song of the sirens, spirits who lured men to their deaths.

By comparison, James Edward McCarthy had only been wandering around two continents for a decade. He'd seen human females turned into shambling apes, fought a giant metal spider, had been captured by and escaped from a contemporary warlock, and heard the song of the worms, who didn't need to lure, they just ate.

But what about Ulysses—after he'd heard the song of the sirens, was he ever the same again? Or was the whole thing just one strange episode after another, each to be forgotten as the credits roll up and we fade to the final commercial? But at least, Ulysses got to home again to his faithful wife.

McCarthy never did. And he never got the song out of his head either. And every time it rose again, every time he smelled it, tasted it, felt it—

There was nothing familiar here. No taste, no flavor, no alluring scent. But it was still *the song*. The others were safe. They couldn't hear it. They didn't have the ears for this. They glanced around in puzzlement and unease.

Pointed forward. The prowlers slid silently into the gloom, penetrating it with fingers of light that poked and probed and scattered the darkness into layers of overlapping shadow that flickered and jumped. An even more disturbing vision than simple gloom.

The VR displays revealed that the end of the corridor was deserted, so were the branching avenues. Nevertheless, there was *something* here. There. Pointed and moved.

Down here, past the book store, past the music and video store, past the web access café, a multiplex of theaters. Thirty separate auditoriums here. A long wall of posters advertising long-forgotten diversions. They had never been reprogrammed. A time capsule of distant novelties and distractions. Garish, colorful promises of adventure, excitement, and danger. Not to mention sex and laughter and assorted feel-good moments. Fun for the whole family. Even the dog will love it. *The Chocolate Man, Revenge of the Slash, Love Sold in Doses, The Door, Gendernauts II, The Mahler Curse, Stephen King's The Long Walk, Asimov vs. The Aliens, Die Robot!, John Carter on Mars, The Martian Teenager* (a horror story*), Death of a Lawyer* (a feel-good movie*), and Star Trek 23: Blood And Fire!* (an odd-numbered film, skip it.)

Once upon a time, all this stuff had been important. All this pretense and fantasy had defined the moment-to-moment identity of a fat and flatulent society, so obsessed with its own divertissements that it had lost all rational judgment, and only assigned quality as a function of thumbs and numbers—a strange and frantic people who didn't know if they'd had a good time until the weekend box office receipts were tallied.

Blinked awake. *Who was that in my head? Where did those thoughts come from?* Those were the judgments of another mind, not mine—

"McCarthy?"

"Eh?"

"You've been standing there, motionless, for three minutes. Are you all right?"

"Of course, I'm not all right. I'm McCarthy."

"What happened?"

"Not sure."

"Can we move on?"

Nodded. But didn't move.

"Is there something there?"

Pointed toward the closest auditorium. "Send in the prowlers."

The first of the catlike machines slipped through the doors. I plugged into the endless noise and the rest of them flipped their VR displays on.

Inside the auditorium—

"Oh, Christ—"

"Shut up, Goldberg."

—chrysalids. Hundreds. No, thousands. Tens of thousands. Remote analysis was scanning, counting, estimating—

The walls, hung with dark bulbous shapes, dripping with creeper vines and red webs. The screen, a tattered web, a seething mass. The seats, filled with nascent bodies, two or three per chair, many of them squirming, writhing, pulsing, yearning to break free. Wretched, storm-tossed, huddled masses. The latest round of immigrants. Illegal aliens of the worst kind—

"Check the others," I said. "I'm going in."

"You can't—"

Looked at Goldberg skeptically. "And you can? I'm trori-ktor, remember? I smell right."

Goldberg looked to Barth. "I quit. I can't—"

"Shut up—"

Ignored that argument. Heard it before. Pushed through the doors. Headed into the theater. The carpet in the corridor squelched wetly.

Inside, in the lobby, the smell rose up, overwhelming. The song of the mandala was a purple flavor in the air, dark and enticing. Overtones of vanilla and rose petals, darker notes of strawberry syrup, tomatoes, and cloves; still darker flavors of illness and decay, things a human nose doesn't want to know about. But McCarthy doesn't mind. It's a smell like *home*. Not quite, but almost. There's a comfort at the core of it—a comforting, comfortable, comforter of—*aha! Got it!*—not having to wake up. Pull the covers over your head, snuggle up in your favorite nightie, roll over and snooze as long as you want, you don't have to get out of bed, you don't have to wake up and think, you don't have to be yourself today, the song will do it all for you, will feed you, steer you, move you through the motions, and you can hide, safe inside, away from all the noise, just rocking on the endless comfort of the song, the purple song.

The lethetic buzz awakens me again. Brakes me. Brings me shuddering to a halt. So easy, too easy.

Came around the corner, where the smell sat squalid as a festering wound. Shine the light around, the bluish, bright-white, blight. Finger probing, piercing the gloom, revealing a rising slope of swollen shapes, all the way up to the ceiling, overhead as well, like the inside of some gigantic cancerous intestine, polyps everywhere. Conforming, yet masking the underlying shape of the supporting architecture. Veils of red gauze cover everything, pulsing creeper vines, varicose and black, arteries and veins. Holding, nurturing. Everywhere the fleshy, throbbing bulbs, each one nurturing a hungry unborn Chtorran nymph. Translucent enough to reveal darker shapes within. Moving sluggishly. Some of them already making chewing movements. Some of them will be free within days. How many here? A thousand? Ten thousand? How many theaters? Multiply by thirty. Thirty thousand. Three hundred thousand. No—sixty theaters total. Six hundred thousand? No, more than that. There are other places too, other tunnels, other catacombs, other chambers in the vaults. A million and a half? Three million?

McCarthy puts a hand out, touches one of the warm chrysalids. It pulses gently beneath his hand. It's damp. It tastes of a need for salt. The thing inside is too stupid to sense McCarthy's presence. It hasn't been socialized. There were no nightstalkers, no bladderbugs, no stingflies, not even a detectable taste of neural symbiotes. It's not worth gathering. It'll hatch hungry and insane. It will die within days, unable to feed itself.

Touch another and another and another. Push through the rows of sulking egg-like shapes, trailing fingers, tasting, touching, all of them the same. Stupid, fat, and maddened by starvation. What a monstrous trick of fate—

Wait.

Catch your breath.

Slow down.

Think.

Work this out. Look at the rest of the picture.

Where did the million eggs come from? Where's the mother nest? All the mother nests? And where are the trori-ktor who brought the chrysalids here? How many slaves—?

No, wait.

We've seen this before. Something like this. Three corner matings. There's half the answer, right there. Follow this thought. Three corner matings are a dead-end...

Work this out.

For the purposes of fertile copulation, the worms have four sexes. Alpha, the provider of the primary sperms; male, the provider of the secondary sperms; female, the provider of the eggs; and egg-carrier, the womb in which the eggs are held while they mature—and filtered for genetic defects. Young nests start mating while there are only three sexes available; male, female, and egg-carrier. Without the primary sperms, the eggs hatch, but the millipedes are infertile. They never transform; they never go into chrysalid stage.

So the fact that these chrysalids exist are simple enough proof that the millipedes encysted here are not the result of three-cornered matings. But they're still a dead-end. This is what a millipede becomes if there are no symbiotes present. A doomed chrysalid. The equivalent of the three-cornered mating. What happens when all the pieces aren't in place. Useless organisms, eating—until eventually, they are eaten by the creatures that have all the proper equipment to own this ecological niche.

The Chtorran ecology is fecund. A genetic spendthrift. It can afford to throw away the children that don't work. It can afford to spawn a generation of failures. It can waste itself and never notice; it still accomplishes the same result—it lays waste to the host ecology. And when at last, it finally gets its act together, it doesn't matter how it got there. It's still there. Because even the dead-ends are parts of the process.

That's the obvious explanation, yes.

But it's wrong. I don't know how I know it's wrong, I just do.

If there are fertile worms spawning eggs, and if there are trori-ktor to serve those worms and gather chrysalids, then where are all the colonist species? How can you have fertile worms without the presence of symbiotes? If the parents had symbiotes, then why are these chrysalids naked of colonist species?

And not to put too fine a point on this question, where are the parent nests? Why is there no evidence of them? Who produced a million fertile eggs? Where are the thousand gastropedes who spawned the million millipedes? And where did the millipedes go to fatten themselves? And how could they have reached their critical thresholds without an ecology to feed on? And why didn't they sweep up through the tunnels and ravage the northern half of the island? A millipede swarm is an unstoppable force of nature, ravenous and deadly. Where were these creatures *before* they were chrysalids?

And why did I say that the water needed salt? How did I know that? *What's the salt for?*

I must have touched a hundred of the chrysalids. All damp, all hungry for salt and everything else. Very soon now. Many of the chrysalids were writhing, getting ready to hatch. Once again, the eerie feeling came to me that the auditorium looked like the inside of an intestine. Something was very wrong here. No. Something was very *right* here. What was wrong was that I couldn't *understand* it.

What was I missing? Dammit.

"General Domitz?"

"Talk to me." Her voice was gruff.

"Are you seeing this?"

"Is that you, McCarthy?"

"Yes, sir."

"What are we looking at?"

"A hatching chamber."

"Eggs? Millipedes?

"No. Nymphs."

"Nymphs?"

"Baby worms. Only—"

"What?"

"Not very good worms. Pure worms. Uncolonized. The root form."

"Is that good or bad?"

"I don't know. Without their symbiotes, these creatures will be crippled. Hairless slugs without arms, teeth, eyes, hearts, fur, brains, I don't know what else. I'm not sure what they'll be."

"Doesn't sound very dangerous to me."

"No, sir. It doesn't. That's why it should scare you. Nobody has ever seen anything like this before."

Silence for a moment. The sound of distant buzzing, whispering, hurried conferences, arguments, disparagements, skepticism, concern, analysis—

General Domitz came back online. "What do you recommend?"

"Dunno. If these things hatch, they'll die within hours. So I can't see them being a threat to anything. To be honest, I'm very curious to see what happens here."

"What if you're wrong? Is there a chance of that?"

"Yes, sir. A very big chance. This is beyond my experience. I think it's beyond everyone's experience. We have no records of any similar or comparable incidents."

More silence. More distant buzzing. Arguing.

"Doing nothing is not an option. What's the best way of destroying these things?"

"Make snow cones," I said, wondering even as I spoke where the military slang had come from. "Freeze everything. Then shred it. And check the other theaters on the other side of the station. They're probably infested too."

General Domitz made a noise. Considering the logistics of implementation. Time, money, ammunition versus risk. How many lives might be lost? None? Works for me. Either way it's a win-win situation. It looks strong and decisive, while the hazards remain minimal. A victory without casualties. A political triumph. And it would be good for troop morale and civilian morale as well. Hooray for our side.

"All right," she said. "Get your ass out of there. The killing teams are on their way."

Grabbed three chrysalids on the way out and shoved them into the sample bag. Came out of the theater and was stopped by Goldberg, who angrily frosted me with a detoxicant spray. He held up his clipboard. "Look at your medical monitors. You're off the scale here. And every time you turn on that damn jammer, I lose all readings. How am I supposed to—?"

"If I don't turn on that damn jammer—!"

My god. That's it.

I started laughing.

Turned to Barth. "You want to know why there's more McCarthy here now? " Held up the device. "Signal-to-noise ratio. Too much noise in the head, McCarthy gets swamped. Turn off the noise, McCarthy comes back. How much McCarthy do you want?"

"How much have you got?"

"Dunno. I'll get back to you on that." Turned to Goldberg. "The jammer stays on. You'll have to monitor me the old-fashioned way."

Goldberg, bless his obsessive-compulsive little heart, got it. He reached into his kit, whipped out a finger-shaped probe, and said, "Okay, bend over—"

Almost did. Wasn't sure if he was joking—

The noise distracted us. We turned to see the prowlers, the growlers, and the bears, come lumbering down the escalators and up the corridor toward us. Their shining headlights dazzled us. They looked like a herd of oncoming trains.

Barth pulled me out of the way and we headed back toward the escalators, keeping to the wall. The prowlers splashed past us, the growlers rumbled, the bears came last—hunkering and thundering.

The dripping water had made the escalators wet and slippery. A layer of grease and scum had accumulated just in the few days the water had been leaking. We held onto the railings with both hands as we picked our way back up to the rollagon.

Once back in our vehicle, we plugged into the VR again, watched as the prowlers sprayed the theater with liquid nitrogen, the ceiling, the walls, the seats, the aisles—until flakes of snow began crystallizing in the air. Then they moved out, toward the next theater, and the growlers moved in and sprayed the auditorium with high-velocity granules, shattering and splattering the frozen chrysalids, exploding sparkling shreds in all directions.

Already, we could hear General Domitz calling in a supply drop— more liquid nitrogen, more ammo packs. The choppers would bring them in at the Canal Street station. Other units were already moving out to inspect the other theatres on the other side of Memorial City. This operation was going to last all day, maybe two. And additional cleanup and inspection would take another week. If we were lucky. There were questions here—*fourth worm* questions—that we wouldn't be able to answer until we stepped into something's mouth.

Anthills

"If you believe in logic, clap your hands."
—Solomon Short

Sat in the rollagon and shivered. And not just from the cold. *This* wasn't accidental. Something had a plan—not a conscious plan, but a plan nonetheless. Built into the ecology like the laws of physics are built into the universe.

Emergent behavior. It was there in front of us the whole time and we never saw it. We kept looking for the brains behind the invasion, kept looking for the sentience. It wasn't there because there was no sentience.

An anthill. Take one ant. Examine it. Study it for a thousand years. Learn how it moves on two opposing triangles of legs, how it extracts oxygen from the air, how it sees through multi-faceted eyes, what sugary liquids give it sustenance, and what its hundred little neurons do to create a repertoire of responses both proactive and reactive. All of that will still not predict the behavior of a thousand, ten thousand ants—the tunnels, the water traps, the egg chambers, the larval feeding stations, the pupae rooms, the queen's vault, the various behaviors of fungi farming and aphid ranching, the way the entrances to the nest trap the wind and provide ventilation and cooling. All of that occurs not because each ant is part of a grand design, but because the grand design is somehow built into and emerges from the nature of ants themselves; each little machine sees only its specific need and addresses that need; but all together, a thousand, ten thousand, a million ants create a colony—a creature that exists in a multitude of bodies, the whole is greater than the sum, each individual body disposable, the colony essentially immortal.

The behavior of the colony emerges when the individual is multiplied by orders of magnitude, just as a human being emerges when a single embryonic cell divides and multiplies. The DNA doesn't contain the map, doesn't contain the design, contains only the raw instructions of protein assembly—but when a million cells begin assembling, interacting with each other, specific behaviors emerge, specific needs occur and are addressed, the process continues until eventually a human being shows up as the result. Multiply a blob of information and you get... information interacting with itself. Complexity reigns. Multiplexity is the result of simplicity cubed and cubed and cubed agan.

And so too with the Chtorr. All of it, the design of it, the nature of it, everything, the behaviors of all the myriad things that grow and creep and crawl and slither, all the various plants that feed upon the fetid squalor of decay, all the others that kill to grow, the veils and the vines, all the pulsing bladders, the shambler trees, the shrike vines, everything that roots and blooms and blossoms, and everything that swims and ripples, the purple plankton, the red plankton, the little fishes and the big ones, the cancerous Enterprise beasts eating everything, the little biting minnows that outfeed piranhas, the many-legged spider-lobsters crawling along the bottoms of streams, cousins of millipedes, and all the animals, the worms, the stalkers, the bladderbugs, the stingflies, the bunnydogs and libbits, the snufflers, and all the things that shriek through the air, the kites and ribbon-things, the spores, the stingflies, the pink dust, all of it, everything, and yes, most of all the neural symbiotes—all of it, whatever, there is no sentience behind this plan, it hasn't happened yet. Sentience in the Chtorran ecology is an emergent behavior. It's built into the Chtorran protein, just as humans are built into DNA, emerging as an effect of a billion years of frantic evolution—

—and realizing that, then everything about the Chtorr is crystal clear. As crystal mud. It's not just individual worms that turn out feral. It's the whole ecology. The Chtorran sentience is an untrained ignorant infant, growing in desperate isolation, figuring things out for itself, and usually wrong—the way any feral creature does. Full of fear and unreachable potential.

The seeds burn down to the planet's surface, burning off their ablative layers. Only one has to survive the impact. Eventually it roots, becomes a tree, a shambler grove, it digs a nest in rich dark soil, grows a set of wombs, and all the other protein strands begin to weave, emerging from the wombs as all the different flavors of Chtorran life, and as they multiply, the interactive behaviors start to happen, and the ecology takes form. A century? Ten? It doesn't matter. Stability is not a function of this ecology, it thrives on its own insane imbalances.

Humans thought that the Chtorran ecology was insane and out of control—yes, it is. But that's the way it's *supposed* to be. That's its homeostatic mechanism. Wild swings around a baseline that's a sine-wave. Up and down, around and in and out, through umpty-leven different dimensions of possibility, here we go round the prickly pear, the prickly pear, here we go round the prickly pair at five o'clock in the morning.

Humans think ecology is about stability. It isn't. Ecologies aren't flatline processes; they cycle, they evolve, they transform and mutate. The Chtorran ecology achieves stability by embracing the very processes of instability. The only way to control chaos is to *be* the chaos.

That's the insight. I'd always known it, but now I *knew* it. Knew it because I'd lived it. Knew it because it was me.

Didn't matter if there was a plan for these crippled chrysalids or not. Didn't need to be. The elements of the Chtorr had reacted to a specific need, the same way an ant knows to move a pebble out of the nest. The elements of the Chtorr had done what was appropriate for the space they'd expanded into. The chrysalids were the result—and whatever hatched out of these turbulent pustules, that would be the next part of the process, the need that was being addressed. *Whatever it was.*

Think about it. Think, Jim, think! What's happening here? What is the Chtorr responding to? What is it creating?

I should know.

Nonsense.

If you have lived only among penguins, you cannot discuss elephants with any knowledge. And no, it's not all part of the same ecology. The Earth ecology isn't a single ecology, it's a map of a million overlapping ecologies, from the deepest levels of the darkest seas to the highest, most unattainable mountain peaks—each and every one of those layers a different answer to the question of possibility.

The same is true of Chtorr, only far more baroque and intricate, evolved beyond our ability to comprehend. All the different possibilities. I know one piece of it, I don't know all. But if an ecology is holographic in nature, than any insight into any little piece of it should be an access into understanding all of it. Ah, yes. That's the arrogance of the human intellect—that nothing in the universe is ultimately unknowable, if we just apply enough brain power to it.

But in this case—

There I go again.

But in this case, if we're dealing with emergent behavior. If we know the rules of that behavior, we should be able to predict—

Fragments of ideas.

What about sentience?

What about it, Jim.

If the Chtorr is all emergent behavior, then can it ever be truly sentient?

The same question can be applied to you, little McCarthy. If all you are is a machine of meat and bone, a construction of cells, a specifically emergent form of DNA, can you ever really become a sentient being? Or are you nothing more than the expression of your flesh? Who am I anyway? Am I my resume?

So if the question is unknowable for human beings—isn't it all that much *more* unknowable for the Chtorr?

The biological imperative of the Chtorr is to create sentience. Everything that emerges from the ecology is an avenue toward greater opportunities for neural symbiotes to spread and connect.

Consider an emergent sentience. (The mathematician's joke: "Consider a spherical sentience." Never mind.) What kind of sentience emerges from this kind of processing network? The same question applies here as well. Can it become truly sentient? (And what is *true* sentience anyway?) Or will it be a product of its own built-in design?

If it's not a directed process, then is it a chaotic one? Can it be steered? Directed? Or will the pressures that human beings apply to it be just another little irritation, included as part of all the other, larger processes of the Chtorran ecology, and ultimately included as just another element of the chaos it embraces?

That's the thing about chaos. It's chaotic. It isn't predictable.

But—

However—

And yet—

Ask the next question, Jim.

Will this new consciousness be smarter than human beings, so much smarter that its comprehensions are inconceivable to us? With infinite connections, how can it *not* be smarter? But think about the limitations of networks. Bandwidth, connection speed, processor ability. What if the sentience is brilliant, but glacially slow?

Could we fabricate so many chips that we could outthink it?

A thought.

A memory.

A quote. Human beings are the nastiest, meanest, most aggressive, most destructive, sonsabitches in the universe. The most adaptable. Not necessarily the most intelligent, but the most determined. Human beings do something that nothing else we've ever met can do—human beings create possibilities, design them, build them, move into them. Is that thought the core of something? Something useful?

All I want to do is *know.*

And what I know is that the knowing of this situation is beyond my ability to know without additional processing power applied to the problem.

Turned off the jammer.

HARLIE?

Yes, Jim.

Are you monitoring?

Of course.

I think I need a fusion.

Why?

I need to figure out what's happening here. What are those things? I want to use the combined processing power of the lethetic network and the Teep corps.

It could be dangerous.

I know.

It could overwhelm you.

Yes, I know.

You could lose the last of your ability to function.

Yes, I said I know. But I could also advance our understanding of the Chtorr. I have this thought, this insight—

And you can't pursue it any other way? Interactive modeling? Conferencing? Personal discussion?

No. I don't think so.

You've never asked for a fusion before.

Yes, I know.

That disturbs me.

It disturbs me too. If it weren't necessary, I wouldn't ask. Take it as a sign how serious I am.

You take full responsibility for this decision?

If you've been monitoring me, HARLIE, then you know some of what I've realized. Without the noise in my head, I'm almost McCarthy again. McCarthy isn't stupid, doesn't ask for stupid things. You know that.

Yes, I know that. I also know that McCarthy takes dangerous risks.

When the risk is worth it, yes.

And you believe this is worth the risk.

I already had this conversation with myself, HARLIE.

All right. I'll get back to you shortly.

Thank you.

Silence.

Turned the jammer back on.

Even greater silence.

Wondered what stupid thing I'd just volunteered for. *And why.*

Lunch

"Paranoia is its own reward."
—Solomon Short

The realization sinks in. Clamps hold of my gut with tiny claws, grips and twists. Tightens my throat, sends a surge of hot emotion up through my stomach, my heart, my lungs, and finally choking my throat in an uncomfortable sob. Emotion—I hadn't realized I was still capable of *this* emotion. Fear. Grief. Something else. Loneliness?

Whatever.

It's this simple.

Turn on the jammer, get rid of the buzz-buzz, and I'm McCarthy again. As much McCarthy as is left, anyway.

Turn it off, let the noise back in, the torrent of information, and McCarthy disappears, swamped by the tidal wave of sensation, images, sounds, tastes, flavors, experiences, memories—

But it doesn't make sense.

The jammer might shut out the human component of the noise, but what about the neural symbiotes? The McCarthy-thing is still infected with a network of tiny fibrous connections, a completely independent nervous system—one that *literally* has a mind of its own. Why isn't *that mind* running this body now? It controlled the workings of this flesh in the Amazon, why not here?

Discontinuity—

McCarthy climbed out of the rollagon and stood in the ankle deep water. The coldness lapped at his boots, but his feet stayed warm.

"Jim—?" That was Barth.

Held up a hand. "Trying to think." Padded and splashed a few paces away, stood and stared into the dark surface, watching the ripples, searching for meaning. None there, but searched anyway.

Why not here? What was different? What had happened?

In the articles, the books, the documentaries, the movies and reports, they never tell you *how* the genius figured it out. Turing, Von Neumann, Oppenheimer, Feynman, Dawkins, Wolfram, all the break-through thinkers. You'd think somebody would have studied the process of breakthrough—humanity doesn't just depend on miracles, it expects and demands them. But no, the creation of insight remains beyond control, beyond understanding, even beyond serious study. Instead of studying the how, all that the histories ever report is the what—as if this is a sufficient answer. As if the result is explanation enough. They don't tell you about, probably because it's impossible to convey, all the hours and days and weeks and months of banging your head against the brick wall of your own ignorance, your own inability, and the sheer obstinacy of the universe, the entropic stubbornness of existence itself—

The only guy who ever came close—and all he did was stand at the door and knock—was the guy who said, "Ask the next question."

But he didn't tell anyone how to figure out *what the next goddamn question should be!*

Was I really McCarthy? Or did I just think I was McCarthy? Had I fallen into an illusion of—?

Wait.

The next question. What was different?

What was different was—

There wasn't any song here. The only song was the one I was singing myself. Remembering. Or creating. Making it up as I went—

Consider this. Locked away. Neutralized. Drugged. Dosed. Filled with biotics. Alienated. Silenced. Sensory deprivation. Disconnected. Eventually, it takes its toll—please have exact change. Change is inevitable—except from vending machines. Change causes upset, upset causes change. Upset is a thwarted expectation. Okay, got that. But what if this isn't *change*? Maybe this is *transformation*. Locked away inside the McCarthy body, with no access to any other neural symbiotes, except occasionally by accident, the McCarthy ganglion loses its larger identity. It doesn't have any larger *self* anymore to take its programming from. Out of sight, out of mind—out of site, out of mine. Outta here. The Chtorr mind can't impress itself if it can't connect. And disconnected, the McCarthy-thing flows free, floats free, and baby makes three.

No, not quite. Not quiet either. The song wasn't gone. You can't get the song out of your head. Once started, it echoes forever. It's a small world, after all. The neural symbiotes don't forget. They can't. It's hardwired into them. But if another song starts singing—and if that song is so hardwired into the host that it resonates throughout the flesh—every breath you take, I'll be watching you—I'd like to teach the world to sing—he's got the whole world in his hands—it's a mauled world, after all—and if that other song is the human song, the McCarthy song—

I start laughing.

I get the joke.

The song wasn't the worms. The worm song was long gone. But not forgotten. This song was really just the way we were. Memories of McCarthy. All McCarthy. The whole time—

The worm song had impressed McCarthy like a big pink elephant sitting on his face and wriggling its fat leathery ass. I could still smell dung on my breath. Even after the elephant was long gone, everything was still flat and stinking pink. Even after all this time, McCarthy still thought the elephant was sitting on top of him.

The neural symbiotes had reprogrammed the McCarthy-thing, oh so very good, so good that McCarthy thought he'd disappeared, had believed that all that was left was purple song; but eventually—oh, this is too good—eventually, in the silence of his own cage, in the prison of his soul, in the rattling cage of his own skull, where the walls are made of bone, eventually the song of the self, that inescapable essence of humanity that's entwined into every helical strand of McCarthy DNA, that smoldering core still had its own undeniable presence, the voice of the meat itself, the hardwiring of the hardware, the ground of being, a basic irritation, a pressure like a full bladder in the middle of the night, a demand, a need, something much too annoying to be ignored for long, a human song, a whole host of human songs, each and every one a separate need, inescapable, irrefutable, each one its own voice in the personal chorus of the localized ecology that was known as James Edward McCarthy, all the voices joining and combining, eventually becoming a chorale, a corral, a roundelay roundup, a drownup, not just drowning out of the itchy-scratchy noise of all those parasitical little buggers, but coopting them, retraining them, reclaiming an expanded *selfhood*, here we go round the prickly pair again—

Hah! What was that about humanity being too damn stubborn to die?

That was the joke.

The McCarthy mind had subverted the neural symbiotes, taught them to think like McCarthy, turned them into McCarthy, made them part of McCarthy, expanded McCarthy, and now McCarthy, what was left of McCarthy, was more McCarthy than ever. Was the world ready for this? Was McCarthy? Whooo.

And all I had to do was turn off the noise to discover that I'd wasted a year and how much more, been lost in my own madness, a delusion of my own construction, simply because I—*literally*—could not hear myself think. Drowned out. Thanks a lot, HARLIE. Thanks a lot, Teep corps. We did it for your own good, McCarthy—yeah, right—the irony here is profound. All you wanted were answers, and you made it impossible for McCarthy to give you any—

Ha ha. Fall down laughing funny. Only not here, not in this slimy, greasy water, lapping at my ankles. Dying of laughter funny. Or just dying, without laughter. Slime waits for no one. And it still needs salt—

Straighten up. Shake away the feeling. The little voice whispers, *"Remember, you're a Mode Graduate, you can handle anything."* And

McCarthy whispers right back, "Thank you for sharing that, now go fuck yourself—" I don't have to be polite anymore, I'm insane.

"Are you all right—?" Goldberg calls.

"Never felt better in my life—"

Almost true. A remarkable sense of peace. As long as you know you're insane, you're not really insane. If everybody's crazy, then knowing you're crazy makes you…not sane, just enlightened. Ha ha. Must do this more often.

Okay, so that's one puzzle solved. The easy one. The obvious one. The existential one. Who am I? Who's asking the question? What does it mean to be a human being? *Who's asking the question?* Only a human being worries about things like that. Worms don't go to bed wondering if they've been good worms. It's never a question. That's enlightenment—a profound neurotic compulsion to play with your own intellectual feces.

Ask the next question. But if the next question is *why*, remember that *why* is a trap. If you don't have facts, it's an invitation for the mind to make something up. And usually, what the mind makes up is another reflection of itself, projected on the silver screen of the self.

Look up, look around. The folks in the rollagon are watching me. Not their VR displays. Understandable. The VR displays had taken on a violent same-ness. Freeze and shred, the pulp goes splattering—

Something about that. Doesn't feel right. Never felt right.

Why would this ecology produce useless individuals—? Why so many? Ohell, why does any ecology produce infertile creatures? Why did the first nests produce sterile millipedes from three-corner matings? Why do the worms even have three-corner matings at all? Nature's spontaneous fecundity? Margin for error? Wiggle room? Part of the process—? Necessary for—

Wait a minute.

Looking at this the wrong way.

Assume that it's not an accident; that it has a purpose, that it conveys some kind of evolutionary or ecological advantage, somewhere, somehow—

Go back to the beginning, when you didn't know anything. Even before the fourth worm. A corral full of millipedes. What happened to that corral? We burned it. McCarthy burned it. *I* burned it. Burned it all. For Shorty.

So stupid. If I had waited, if we had paid attention, we could have learned something important then. Millipedes in the corral had black bellies. The ones that hatched from the eggs we gathered had red bellies. Not two different species. The same species.

This was a young nest. Too young. Three worms mated. The off-spring were genetically crippled. Didn't have the full package. Black bellies. Would never pupate. No chrysalids. Useless for anything except chewing up forest. Useless, except as food for others. But after the hatching of the first brood, a fourth worm joined the nest, an egg-carrier. The previous egg-carrier became female, the female became male, and the male became alpha. Now the matings were four-cornered and the eggs were fully fertile. And the millipedes that hatched out of them had red bellies, and had the full genetic potential to become worms.

So what happened to the black bellied creatures?

I burned them. I got angry and I burned them.

But what would have happened to them if I hadn't—?

The worms would have eaten them. That's why they were in the corral. Lunch.

And what would have happened to them if they hadn't been corralled?

Lunch, again. Only this time, it would have been lunch on the run. The red-bellied millipedes would have grown faster and smarter, would have quickly outweighed their older siblings—and in the inevitable encounters on the forest floor, the red ones would have eaten the black ones as easily as they ate everything else.

And it wouldn't have been accidental.

It was a built-in design feature.

Eat your failures.

Except, they're *not* failures. They're part of the process. The system is *supposed* to produce black-bellied millipedes. They're not dead-ends, they're the food source for what comes next. If they get eaten, that's okay—they weren't meant to be on top of the food chain. The next generation will. Or the next after that. As many as it takes. This is the logic of evolutionary cannibalism. This simple insight—it colors the entire Chtorran ecology.

Black-bellies are supposed to happen. They're necessary. They're the shock troops for the next generation. They're intended to go out and tame the land, be an early-warning system before the real genetic investment occurs. They hatch and feed—gathering, storing, compiling proteins and fats and other nutrients in a healthful nourishing package. Without the extra genetic advantage they're fatter, slower, easier to catch, easier to eat, specifically designed for growing young gastropedes who might not have all the necessary immunities and physical resources yet to survive on native creatures and vegetation. It doesn't matter if the black-bellies have digestive problems, so what? They're the bootstrap for the next generation, which can and will adapt.

The lovely logic of it all. The system provides its own baby food—ground up babies. What better food for a hungry young slug? Release 1.0. The early worm gets the bug.

That's what's happening here—

Ohgod.

It's all about food.

These things are food.

They're *supposed* to be food.

Oh shit. Oh, fuck. Oh, fuck fuck fuck—

I can't believe I was that stupid. To have missed the obvious. Except it's only obvious if you stop thinking like a human being—

Is this more good news or bad? That I can't see the obvious because I'm too human?

—stop worrying about that shit. For Christ's sake, Jim, can't you stop the mind-chatter?

No, I can't. Help me. I'm trapped inside a human being.

Focus, dammit—answer the questions you *can* answer.

What's the mechanism here? What are these things?

These aren't three-cornered offspring. Because three-cornered matings don't pupate, don't produce chrysalids. So this is something else. A different mechanism.

A different mechanism, because—

Of course.

The seeds of the Chtorran ecology don't know, *can't know*, can't predict what kind of planet they're going to drop onto, what its terrain will be like, how much gravity it will have, the composition of its atmosphere, the length of its seasons, the lengths of its days and nights, even the quality of the light that falls upon the ground. The seeds can't know the mineral composition of the soil, if there's oxygen in the air, even if life is possible on this world. And if life is possible, it's inevitable—but the Chtorr can't know what kind of established ecology it's going to fall into. It has to be multi-functional, capable of establishing a beachhead no matter where it falls—a planet has zones, arctic, sub-arctic, temperate, sub-tropical, tropical, equatorial; a living planet has multiple ecologies, swamps and wetlands, rain forests, old growth, high desert and low, great plains, grasslands, savannah, glacier fields, tundra, equatorial jungles—

—and ocean.

The Chtorran seeds, the shambler seeds, have to be versatile; and what they produce has to be ecologically ambidextrous.

What we've seen, what we know—that's only one answer. That's what the Chtorr becomes on grasslands and forest and jungle. But it isn't everything the Chtorr *can* become.

What does the Chtorr become if it falls into the sea?

Whatever it becomes...*that's* why it needs salt.

AUTHOR'S AFTERWORD:

These things are hard to write. This piece was one of the hardest. A person who has instantaneous access to all the online knowledge in the world is going to live in a vastly different mind-map. How do you evoke that without turning the simplest action into a novel-length internal journey to rival James Joyce's Ulysses? *You don't. It's a tightrope. But when (not if) I fall off, I intend to make a lovely splat.*

The Satanic Limericks #1

A limerick of proper proportion
should have meter and rhyme and a portion
    of humor quite lewd,
    and a frightfully crude,
impossible sexual contortion.

A limerick is best when it's lewd,
gross, titillating and crude—
    but this one is clean,
    unless you are seen
reading it aloud in the nude.

When writing these verses of mine
I start with a clever last line
    then work backward from there
    toward the opening pair
with the hope it will all work out fine.

A king who was mad at the time
Decreed limerick writing a crime.
    But late in the night
    all the poets would write
verses without any rhyme or meter.

There was a young fellow named Marc
Whose bite was much worse than his barc
    which may explain why
    on a day in July
he was thrown out of West Hollywood parc!

There was a young lady named Suzie,
who was known to get tipsy and woozy.
    A small glass of gin
    would just make her grin,
but a big glass would make her a floozy.

Anti-matter of fact, it was *there*
that my aunt served a neutron eclair.
    There were pieces of plates
    in thirty-eight states,
and the cups are still up in the air.

So, there was this guy named Jesus who wandered around Judea for a few years, telling people to love one another, don't be hypocrites, don't be self-righteous, don't be judgmental, love each other, forgive each other, be humble in spirit, be generous in nature, feed the poor, heal the sick, and treat other people the way you want to be treated yourself. That's pretty good stuff, and well worth a book or two, maybe even the occasional movie—except, here we are, two thousand years later, and we celebrate this guy's birthday with a three-month long capitalist feeding frenzy that makes an Eskimo potlatch look like a belch. What the flock are we doing?! Any sane and rational belief system would not be based on spending yourself into debt once a year for the sake of celebrating humility, forgiveness, and peace. Oy vey. The story that follows is my fevered reaction.

Something about the idea of a red-eyed Satan Claus, dressed all in gleaming black leather, carrying a whip, and smiling with sharpened teeth, appeals to my sense of the bizarre and ironic. If someone wants to give me a gift, he can knock on the front door and holler, "Candygram!" or something like that—but if he's sneaking down my chimney in the middle of the night, he's probably up to no good. I usually build a fire on Christmas Eve. And if all I get is a lump of coal, that's fine too. It helps keep the fire going a little while longer.

...And Eight Rabid Pigs

WHEN I FIRST BECAME AWARE of Steven Dhor, he was talking about Christmas. Again.

He hated Christmas—in particular, the enforcement of bliss. "Don't be a scrooge, don't be a grinch, don't be a Satan Claus taking away other people's happiness." That's what his mother used to say to him, and twenty years later, he was still angry.

There were a bunch of them sitting around the bar, writers mostly, but a few hangers-on and fringies, sucking up space and savoring the wittiness of the conversation. Bread Bryan loomed all tall and spindly like a frontier town undertaker. Railroad Martin perched like a disgruntled

Buddha—he wore the official Railroad Martin uniform, T-shirt, jeans, and pot belly. George Finger was between wives and illnesses, he was enjoying just being alive. Goodman Hallmouth pushed by, snapping at bystanders and demanding to know where Harold Parnell had gone; he was going to punch him in the kneecap.

"Have a nice day, Goodman," someone called.

"Don't tell me to have a nice day," he snarled back. "I'll have any damn kind of a day I want."

"See—" said Dhor, nodding at Hallmouth as he savaged his way out again. "That's honest, at least. Goodman might not fit our pictures of the polite way to behave, but at least he doesn't bury us in another layer of dishonest treacle."

"Yep, Goodman only sells honest treacle," said Railroad Martin.

"Where do you get lie-detector tests for treacle?" Bread Bryan asked, absolutely deadpan.

"There's gotta be a story in that—" mused George Finger.

"—but I just can't put my *finger* on it," said one of the nameless fringies. This was followed by a nanosecond of annoyed silence. Somebody else would have to explain to the fringie that a) that joke was older than God, b) it hadn't been that funny the first time it had been told, and c) he didn't have the right to tell it. Without looking up, Bread Bryan simply said, "That's one."

Steven Dhor said, "You want to know about treacle? Christmas is treacle. It starts the day after Halloween. You get two months of it. It's an avalanche of sugar and bullshit. I suppose they figure that if they put enough sugar into the recipe, you won't notice the taste of the bullshit."

"Don't mince words, Stevie. Tell us what you really think."

"Okay, I will." Dhor had abruptly caught fire. His eyes were blazing. "Christmas—at least the way we celebrate it—is a perversion. It's not a holiday; it's a brainwashing." That's when I started paying *real* attention.

"Every time you see a picture of Santa Claus," Dhor said, "you're being indoctrinated into the Christian ethic. If you're good, you get a reward, a present; if you're bad, you get a lump of coal. One day, you figure it out; you say, hey—Santa Claus is really mommy and daddy. And when you tell them you figured it out, what do they do? They tell you about God. If you're good, you get to go to heaven; if you're bad, you go to hell. Dying isn't anything to be afraid of, it's just another form of Christmas. And Santa Claus is God—the only difference is that at least, Santa gives you something tangible. But if there ain't no Santa, then why should we believe in God either?"

Bread Bryan considered Dhor's words dispassionately. Bread Bryan considered everything dispassionately. Despite his nickname, even yeast couldn't make him rise. Railroad Martin swirled his beer around in his glass; he didn't like being upstaged by someone else's anger—even when it was anger as good as this. George Finger, on the other hand, was delighted with the effrontery of the idea.

"But wait—this is the nasty part. We've taken God out of Christmas. You can't put up angels anymore, nor a cross, nor even a crèche. No religious symbols of any kind, because even though everything closes down on Christmas Day, we still have to pretend it's a non-secular celebration. So, the only decorations you can put up are Santa Claus, reindeer, snowmen, and elves. We've replaced the actual holiday with a third-generation derivation, including its own pantheon of saints and demons: Rudolph, Frosty, George Bailey, Scrooge, and the Grinch— Santa Claus is not only most people's first experience of God," Dhor continued, "it's now their *only* experience of God."

Dhor was warming to his subject. Clearly this was not a casual thought for him. He'd been stewing this over for some time. He began describing how the country had become economically addicted to Christmas. "We've turned it into a capitalist feeding frenzy—so much so that some retailers depend on Christmas for fifty percent of their annual business. I think we should all 'Just Say No to Christmas.' Or at least—for God's sake—remember whose birthday it is and celebrate it appropriately, by doing things to feed the poor and heal the sick."

A couple of the fringies began applauding then, but Dhor just looked across at them with a sour expression on his face. "Don't applaud," he said. "Just do it."

"Do you?" someone challenged him. "How do you celebrate Christmas?"

"I don't give presents," Dhor finally admitted. "I take the money I would normally spend on presents and give it to the Necessities of Life Program of the AIDS Project of Los Angeles. It's more in keeping with the spirit." That brought another uncomfortable silence. It's one thing to do the performance of saint—most writers are pretty good at it—but when you catch one actually *doing* something unselfish and noteworthy, well…it's pretty damned embarrassing for everyone involved.

Fortunately, Dhor was too much in command of the situation to let the awkward moment lie there unmolested. He trampled it quickly. "The thing is, I don't see any way to stop the avalanche of bullshit. The best we can do is ride it."

"How?" George Finger asked.

"Simple. By adding a new piece to the mythology—a new saint in the pantheon. *Satan Claus.*" There was that name again. Dhor lowered his voice. "See, if Santa Claus is really another expression of God, then there has to be an equally powerful expression of the Devil too. There has to be a balance."

"Satan Claus…" Bread Bryan considered the thought. "Mm. He must be the fellow who visited my house last year. He didn't give me anything I wanted. And I could have used the coal too. It gets *cold* in Wyoming."

"No. Satan Claus doesn't work that way," said Dhor. "He doesn't give things. He takes them away. The suicide rate goes up around Christmastime. That's no accident. That's Satan Claus. He comes and takes your soul straight to hell."

Then Railroad Martin added a wry thought— "He drives a black sleigh and he lands in your basement." —and then they were all doing it.

"The sleigh is drawn by eight rabid pigs—big ugly razorbacks," said Dhor. "They have iridescent red eyes, which burn like smoldering embers—they *are* embers, carved right out of the floor of hell. Late at night, as you're lying all alone in your cold, cold bed, you can hear them snuffling and snorting in the ground beneath your house. Their hooves are polished black ebony, and they carve up the ground like knives."

Dhor was creating a legend while his audience sat and listened enraptured. He held up his hands as if outlining the screen on which he was about to paint the rest of his picture. The group fell silent. I had to admire him, in spite of myself. He lowered his voice to a melodramatic stage-whisper, "Satan Claus travels underground through dark rumbling passages filled with rats and ghouls. He carries a long black whip, and he stands in the front of the sleigh, whipping the pigs until the blood streams from their backs. Their screams are the despairing sounds of the eternally tormented."

"And he's dressed all in black," suggested Bread Bryan. "Black leather. With silver buckles and studs and rivets."

"Oh, hell," said George Finger. *"Everybody* dresses like that in my neighborhood."

"Yes, black leather," agreed Martin, ignoring the aside. "But it's made from the skins of reindeer."

"Whales," said Bryan. "Baby whales."

Dhor shook his head. "The leather is made from the skins of those whose souls he's taken. He strips it off their bodies before he lets them die. The skins are dyed black with the sins of the owners, and trimmed with red-dyed rat fur. Satan Claus has long gray hair, all shaggy and dirty and matted; and he has a long gray beard, equally dirty. There are crawly things living in his hair and beard. And his skin is leprous and covered with pustules and running sores. His features are deformed and misshapen. His nose is a bulbous monstrosity, swollen and purple. His lips are blue and his breath smells like the grave. His fingernails are black with filth, but they're as sharp as diamonds. He can claw up through the floor to yank you down into his demonic realm."

"Wow," said Bread Bryan. "I'm moving up to the second floor."

The cluster of listeners shuddered at Dhor's vivid description. It was suddenly a little too heavy for the spirit of the conversation. A couple of them tried to make jokes, but they fell embarrassingly flat.

Finally, George Finger laughed gently and said, "I think you've made him out to be too threatening, Steve. For most of us, Satan Claus just takes our presents away and leaves changeling presents instead."

"Ahh," said Railroad. "That explains why I never get anything I want."

"How can you say that? You get T-shirts every year," said Bread.

"Yes, but I always want a tuxedo."

After the laughter died down, George said, "The changeling presents are made by the satanic elves, of course."

"Right," said Dhor. He picked up on it immediately. "All year long, the satanic elves work in their secret laboratories underneath the South Pole, creating the most horrendous ungifts they can think of. Satan Claus whips them unmercifully with a cat-o'-nine-tails; he screams at them and beats them and torments them endlessly. The ones who don't work hard enough, he tosses into the pit of eternal fire. The rest of them work like little demons—of course they do; that's what they are—to manufacture all manner of curses and spells and hexes. All the bad luck that you get every year—it comes straight from hell, a gift from Satan Claus himself." Dhor cackled wickedly, an impish burst of glee, and everybody laughed with him.

But he was on a roll. He'd caught fire with this idea and was beginning to build on it now. "The terrible black sleigh isn't a sleigh as much as it's a hearse. And it's filled with bulging sacks filled with bad luck of all kinds. Illnesses, miscarriages, strokes, cancers, viruses, flu germs, birth defects, curses of all kinds. Little things like broken bones and upset stomachs. Big things like impotence, frigidity, sterility. Parkinson's disease, cerebral palsy, multiple sclerosis, encephalitis, everything that stops you from enjoying life."

"I think you're onto something," said Railroad. "I catch the flu right after Christmas, every year. I haven't been to a New Year's party in four years. At least now I have someone to blame."

Dhor nodded and explained, "Satan Claus knows if you've been bad or good—if you've been bad in any way, he comes and takes a little more joy out of your life, makes it harder for you to want to be good. Just as Santa is your first contact with God, Satan Claus is your first experience of evil. Satan Claus is the devil's revenge on Christmas. He's the turd in the punch bowl. He's the tantrum at the party. He's the birthday-spoiler. I think we're telling our children only half the story. It's not enough to tell them that Santa will be good to them. We have to let them know who's planning to be bad to them."

For a while, there was silence, as we all sat around and let the disturbing quality of Dhor's vision sink into our souls. Every so often someone would shudder as he thought of some new twist, some piece of embroidery.

But it was George Finger's speculation that ended the conversation. He said, "Actually, this might be a dangerous line of thought, Steve. Remember the theory that the more believers a god has, the more powerful he becomes? I mean, it's a joke right now, but aren't you summoning a new god into existence this way?"

"Yes, Virginia," Dhor replied, grinning impishly, "There *is* a Satan Clause in the holy contract. But I don't think you need to worry. Our belief in him is insufficient. And unnecessary. We can't create Satan Claus—because he already exists. He came into being when Santa Claus was created. A thing automatically creates its opposite, just by its very existence. You know that. The stronger Santa Claus gets, the stronger Satan Claus must become in opposition."

Steven had been raised in a very religious household. His grandmother had taught him that for every act of good, there has to be a corresponding evil. Therefore, if you have heaven, you have to have hell. If you have a God, you have to have a devil. If there are angels, then there have to be demons. Cherubs and imps. Saints and damned. Nine circles of hell—nine circles of heaven. "Better be careful, George! Satan Claus is watching." And then he laughed fiendishly. I guess he thought he was being funny.

I forgot about Steven Dhor for a few weeks. I was involved in another one of those abortive television projects—it's like doing drugs; you think you can walk away from them, but you can't. Someone offers you a needle and you run to stick it in your arm. And then they jerk you around for another six weeks or six months, and then cut it off anyway—and one morning you wake up and find you're unemployed again. The money's spent, and you've wasted another big chunk of your time and your energy and your enthusiasm on something that will never be broadcast or ever see print. And your credential has gotten that much poorer because you have nothing to show for your effort except another dead baby. You get too many of those dead babies on your resume and the phone stops ringing altogether. But I love the excitement, that's why I stay so close to Hollywood—

Then one Saturday afternoon, Steven Dhor read a new story at Kicking The Hobbit—the all science-fiction bookstore that used to be in Santa Monica. I'm sure he saw me come in, but he was so engrossed in the story he was reading to the crowd that he didn't recognize me. *"... the children believed that they could hear the hooves of the huge black pigs scraping through the darkness. They could hear the snuffling and snorting of their hot breaths. The pigs were foaming at the mouth, grunting and bumping up against each other as they pulled the heavy sled through the black tunnels under the earth. The steel runners of the huge carriage sliced across the stones, striking sparks and ringing with a knife-edged note that shrieked like a metal banshee.*

"And the driver—his breath steaming in the terrible cold—shouted their names as he whipped them, 'On, damn you, on! You children of war! On Pustule and Canker and Sickness and Gore! On Monster and Seizure and Bastard and Whore. Drive on through the darkness! Break through and roar!'" Dhor's voice rose softly as he read these harrowing passages to his enraptured audience.

I hung back away from the group, listening in appreciation and wonder. Dhor had truly caught the spirit of the Christmas obscenity. By the very act of saying the name aloud in public, Dhor was not only giving his power to Satan Claus, he was daring the beast to visit him on Christmas Eve.

"...And in the morning," Dhor concluded, *"—there were many deep, knife-like scars in the soft dark earth beneath their bedroom windows. The ground was churned and broken and there were black sooty smudges on the glass... But of their father, there was not a sign. And by this, the children knew that Satan Claus was indeed real. And they never ever laughed again, as long as they lived."*

The small crowd applauded enthusiastically, and then they crowded in close for autographs. Dhor's grin spread across his cherubic face like a pink glow. He basked in all the attention and the approval of the fans; it warmed him like a deep red bath. He'd found something that touched a nerve in the audience—now he responded to them. Something had taken root in his soul.

I saw Dhor several more times that year. And everywhere, he was reading that festering story aloud again: *"Christmas lay across the land like a blight, and once again, the children huddled in their beds and feared the tread of heavy bootsteps in the dark..."* He'd look up from the pages, look across the room at his audience with that terrible impish twinkle and then turn back to his reading with renewed vigor. *"…Millie and little Bob shivered in their nightshirts as Daddy pulled them onto his lap. He smelled of smoke and coal and too much whiskey. His face was blue and scratchy with the stubble of his beard and his heavy flannel shirt scratched their cheeks uncomfortably. 'Why are you trembling?' he asked. 'There's nothing to be afraid of. I'm just going to tell you about the Christmas spirit. His name is Satan Claus, and he drives a big black sled shaped like a hearse. It's pulled by eight big black pigs with smoldering red eyes. Satan Claus stands in the front of the carriage and rides like the whirlwind, lashing at the boars with a stinging whip. He beats them until the blood pours from their backs and they scream like the souls of the damned—'"*

In the weeks that followed, he read it at the fund-raiser/taping for Mike Hodel's literacy project. He read it at the Pasadena Library's Horror/Fantasy Festival. He read it at the Thanksgiving weekend Lost-Con. He read it on Hour 25, and he had tapes made for sale to anyone who wanted one. Steven was riding the tiger. Exploiting it. Whipping it with his need for notoriety.

"'Satan Claus comes in the middle of the night—he scratches at your window, and leaves sooty marks on the glass. Wherever there's fear, wherever there's madness—there you'll find Satan Claus as well. He comes through the wall like smoke and stands at the foot of your bed with eyes like hot coals. He stands there and watches you. His hair is long and gray and scraggly. His beard has terrible little creepy things living in it. You can see them crawling around. Sometimes, he catches one of the bugs that lives in his beard, and he eats it alive. If you wake up on Christmas Eve, he'll be standing there waiting for you. If you scream, he'll grab you and put you in his hearse. He'll carry you straight away to Hell. If you get taken to Hell before you die, you'll never get out. You'll never be redeemed by baby Jesus…'"

And then the Christmas issue of *Ominous* magazine came out and *everybody* was reading it.

"Little Bob began to weep and Millie reached out to him, trying to comfort his tears; but Daddy gripped her arm firmly and held her at arm's length. 'Now, Millie—don't you help him. Bobby has to learn how to be a man. Big boys don't cry. If you cry, then for sure Satan Claus will come and get you. He won't even put you in his hearse. He'll just eat you alive. He'll pluck you out of your bed and crunch your bones in his teeth. He has teeth as sharp as razors and jaws as powerful as an axe. First he'll bite your arms off and then he'll bite off your legs—and then he'll even bite off your little pink peepee. And you better believe that'll hurt. And then, finally, when he's bitten off every other part of you, finally he'll bite your head off! So you mustn't cry. Do you understand me!' Daddy shook Bobby as hard as he could, so

hard that Bobby's head bounced back and forth on his shoulders and Bobby couldn't help himself; he bawled as loud as he could."

People were calling each other on the phone and asking if they'd seen the story and wasn't it the most frightening story they'd ever heard? It was as if they were enrolling converts into a new religion. They were all having much too much fun playing with the legend of Satan Claus, adding to it, building it—giving their power of belief to Father Darkness, the Christmas evil…as if by naming the horror, they might somehow remain immune to it.

"Listen! Maybe you can hear him even now? Feel the ground rumble? No, that's not a train. That's Father Darkness—Satan Claus. Yes, he's always there. Do you hear his horn? Do you hear the ugly snuffling of the eight rabid pigs? He's coming closer. Maybe this year he's coming for you. This year, you'd better stay asleep all night long. Maybe this year, I won't be able to stop him from getting you!'"

Then some right-wing religious zealot down in Orange County saw the story; his teenage son had borrowed a copy of the magazine from a friend; so of course the censorship issue came bubbling right up to the surface like a three-day corpse in a swamp.

Dhor took full advantage of the situation. He ended up doing a public reading on the front steps of the Los Angeles Central Library. The L.A. Times printed his picture, and a long article about this controversial new young fantasy writer who was challenging the outmoded literary conventions of our times. Goodman Hallmouth showed up of course—he'd get up off his death bed for a media event—and made his usual impassioned statement on how Dhor was exposing the hypocrisy of Christmas in America.

"The children trembled in their cold, cold beds, afraid to close their eyes, afraid to fall asleep. They knew that Father Darkness would soon be there, standing at the foot of their beds and watching them fiercely to see if they were truly sleeping or just pretending."

Of course, it all came to a head at Art and Lydia's Christmas Eve party. They always invited the whole community, whoever was in town. You not only got to see all your friends, but all your enemies as well. You had to be there, to find out what people were saying about you behind your back.

Lydia must have spent a week cooking. She had huge platters piled with steaming turkey, ham, roast beef, lasagna, mashed potatoes, sweet potatoes, tomatoes in basil and dill, corn on the cob, pickled cabbage, four kinds of salad, vegetable casseroles, quiche and deviled eggs. She had plates of cookies and chocolates everywhere; the bathtub was filled with ice and bottles of imported beer and cans of Coca-Cola.

Art brought in champagne and wine and imported mineral water for Goodman Hallmouth.

And then they invited the seven-year locusts.

All the writers, both serious and not-so, showed up; some of them wearing buttons that said, "Turn down a free meal, get thrown out of the Guild." Artists too, but they generally had better table manners. One year, two of them got trampled in the rush to the buffet. After that, Lydia started weeding out the guest list.

This year, the unofficial theme of the party was "Satan Claus is coming to town." The tree was draped in black crepe and instead of an angel on top, there was a large black bat. Steven Dhor even promised to participate in a "summoning."

"Little Bob still whimpered softly. He wiped his nose on his sleeve. Finally, Millie got out of her bed and crept softly across the floor and slipped into bed next to little Bob. She put her arms around him and held him close and began whispering as quietly as she could. 'He can't hurt us if we're good. So we'll just be as good as we can. Okay. We'll pray to baby Jesus and ask him to watch out for us, okay?' Little Bob nodded and sniffed, and Millie began to pray for the both of them..."

I got there late, I had other errands to run, it's always that way on the holidays.

Steven Dhor was holding court in the living room, sitting on the floor in the middle of a rapt group of wanna-bes and never-wases; he was embellishing the legend of Satan Claus. He'd already announced that he was planning to do a collection of Satan Claus stories, or perhaps even a novel telling the whole story of Satan Claus from beginning to end. Just as St. Nicholas had been born out of good deeds, so had Satan Claus been forged from the evil that stalked the earth on the night before Jesus' birth.

According to legend—legend according to Dhor—the devil was powerless to stop the birth of baby Jesus, but that didn't stop him from raising hell in his own way. On the eve of the very first Christmas, the devil turned loose all his imps upon the world and told them to steal out among the towns and villages of humankind and spread chaos and dismay among all the world's children. Leave no innocent being unharmed. It was out of this beginning that Satan Claus came forth. At first he was small, but he grew. Every year, the belief of the children gave him more and more power.

"The children slept fitfully. They tossed and turned and made terrible little sounds of fear. Their dreams were filled with darkness and threats. They held onto each other all night long. They were awakened by a rumbling deep within the earth, the whole house rolled uneasily—"

Dhor had placed himself so he could see each new arrival come in the front door. He grinned up at each one in a conspiratorial grin of recognition and shared evil, as if to say, "See? It works. Everybody loves it." I had to laugh. He didn't understand. He probably never would. He was so in love with himself and his story and the power of his words, he missed the greater vision. I turned away and went prowling through the party in search of food and drink.

"They came awake together, Millie and little Bob. They came awake with a gasp—they were too frightened to move.

"Something was tapping softly on the bedroom window. It scraped slowly at the glass. But they were both too afraid too look."

Lydia was dressed in a black witch's costume, she even wore a tall pointed hat. She was in the kitchen stirring a huge cauldron of hot mulled wine and cackling like the opening scene in Macbeth, "Double, double toil and trouble, fire burn and cauldron bubble—" and having a wonderful time of it. For once, she was enjoying one of her own parties. She waved her wooden spoon around her head like a mallet, laughing in maniacal glee.

Christmas was a lot more fun without all those sappy little elves and angels, all those damned silver bells and the mandatory choral joy of the endless hallelujahs. Steven Dhor had given voice to the rebellious spirit, had found a way to battle the ennui of a month steeped in Christmas cheer. These people were going to enjoy every nasty moment of it.

"A huge dark shape loomed like a wall at the foot of their bed. It stood there, blocking the dim light of the hallway. They could hear its uneven heavy breath sounding like the inhalations of a terrible beast. They could smell the reek of death and decay. Millie put her hand across little Bob's mouth to keep him from crying.

"'Oh, please don't hurt us,' she cried. She couldn't help herself. 'Please—'"

I circulated once through the party, taking roll—seeing who was being naughty, who was being nice. Goodman Hallmouth was muttering darkly about the necessity for revenge. Writers, he said, are the Research and Development Division for the whole human race; the only *specialists* in revenge in the whole world. Bread Bryan was standing around looking mournful. George Finger wasn't here, he was back in the hospital again. Railroad Martin was showing off a new T-shirt; it said, "Help, I'm trapped inside a T-shirt."

And of course, there was the usual coterie of fans and unknowns—I knew them by their fannish identities: the Elephant, the Undertaker, the Blob, the Duck.

"And then—a horrible thing happened. A second shape appeared behind the first, bigger and darker. Its crimson eyes blazed with unholy rage. A cold

wind swept through the room. A low groaning noise, somewhere between a moan and an earthquake resounded through the house like a scream. Black against a darker black, the first shape turned and saw what stood behind it. It began to shrivel and shrink. The greater darkness enveloped the lesser, pulled it close, and—did something horrible. In the gloom, the children could not clearly see; but they heard every terrible crunch and gurgle. They heard the choking gasps and felt the floor shudder with the weight.

"*Millie screamed then, so did little Bob. They closed their eyes and screamed as hard as they could. They screamed for their very lives. They screamed and screamed and kept on screaming—*"

Steven Dhor got very drunk that night—first on his success, then on Art and Lydia's wine. About two in the morning, he became abusive and started telling people what he really thought of them. At first, people thought he was kidding, but then he called Hallmouth a poseur and a phony, and Lydia had to play referee. Finally Bread Bryan and Railroad Martin drove him home and poured him into bed. He passed out in the car, only rousing himself occasionally to vomit out the window.

The next morning, Steven Dhor was gone.

Art stopped by his place on Christmas morning to see if he was all right; but Dhor didn't answer his knock. Art walked around the back and banged on the back door too. Still no answer. He peeked in the bedroom window, and the bed was disheveled and empty, so Art assumed that Steven had gotten up early and left, perhaps to spend Christmas with a friend. But he didn't know him well enough to guess who he might have gone to see. Nobody did.

Later, the word began to spread that he was missing.

His landlady assumed he'd skipped town to avoid paying his rent. Goodman Hallmouth said he thought Steven had gone home to visit his family in Florida, and would probably return shortly. Bread Bryan said that Steve had mentioned taking a sabbatical, a cross-country hitchhiking trip. Railroad Martin filed a missing person report, but after a few routine inquiries, the police gave up the investigation. George Finger suggested that Satan Claus had probably taken him, but under the circumstances, it was considered a rather tasteless joke and wasn't widely repeated.

But...George was right.

Steven Dhor had come awake at the darkest moment of the night, stumbling out of a fitful and uncomfortable sleep. He rubbed his eyes and sat up in bed—and then he saw me standing there, watching him. Waiting.

I'd been watching him and waiting for him since the day he'd first spoken my name aloud, since the moment he'd first given me shape and form and the power of his belief. I'd been hungry for him ever since.

He was delicious. I crunched his bones like breadsticks. I drank his blood like wine. The young ones are always tasty. I savored the flavor of his soul for a long long time.

And, of course, before I left, I made sure to leave the evidence of my visit. Art saw it, but he never told anyone: sooty smudges on the bedroom window, and the ground beneath it all torn up and churned, as if by the milling of many heavy-footed creatures.

AUTHOR'S AFTERWORD:

Sometimes I write my friends into stories—which is why I have a diminishing number of friends. Most of the characters in this story were based on real people, but the hero, Steven Dhor, is an amalgam of several annoying young writers who burned out instead of burning brighter.

The Satanic Limericks #2

Said a lady whose reading was thick,
"I am careful about who I pick.
     I know that Phil Farmer
     is really a charmer,
but I'd rather have Philip K. Dick."

Let's honor Frodo, the ringer,
(and his good friend, named Samwise the singer.)
     He was chased by a ghoul,
     but was nobody's fool.
In the end, he gave Gollum the finger.

Two husbands who lived in South Merson
were fed up with complainin' and cursin'.
     They improved their lives,
     by swappin' their wives:
one man's mate is another man's person.

Since I first wrote that damn script for Gene
and the electrical picture machine,
     fuzzies have chased their creator
     from here to Decatur.
Nobody knows of the tribbles I've seen.

I should never have opened the bag.
All the jokes have become such a drag.
     And they'll keep getting worse,
     till I leave in a hearse.
The tale keeps on dogging the wag.

As I pulled in away from the road,
the sign in the parking lot glowed.
     "This witches' school
     has only one rule:
Those illegally parked will be *toad*."

A rhymester who lived in St. Peter
used computers to make his words neater.
     He punched out the cards
     to produce fifty yards,
but his poetry sold by the meter.

I was minding my own business, happily writing a novel, not thinking beyond the needs of the story, when the following sentence suddenly occurred: "The Baby Cooper Dollar Bill, for example, was only fifty years old…"

I stared at the sentence for 15 seconds. I knew what it meant. The entire anecdote had flashed into my head simultaneous with the creation of that first ominous sentence. All that remained was to tell the rest. Did I dare? Did I dare not?

I typed, "The short version:" and began. 1741 words later, I had the longest paragraph I'd ever written.

The Baby Cooper Dollar Bill

an excerpt from

A Day for Damnation

…THAT WAS THE NICE THING about software entities. You could create the most interesting legal monsters and turn them loose upon society, where they would loose-cannon for decades to come. The Baby Cooper Dollar Bill, for example, was only fifty years old—and the lawyers would probably be fighting over that Trust until the turn of the century, by which time it would probably be worth more than the entire planet.

The short version: Grandpa Cooper thought he was being cute. He bought a one dollar investment trust, the proceeds of which would be delivered to the first-born child of his only daughter (who was at that time only four years old) on the occasion of his/her twenty-first birthday. Then he died, leaving an investment-oriented software entity (which was quickly dubbed a "fairy godmother") to operate the trust without human overrides. The software entity invested the dollar first into Chinese labor contracts, shifting to optical leverages three weeks before the Pakistan Agreement, and then micro-biotechnical futures eighteen days before Apple announced the Pippin development project. And so on. Within fifteen years the electric-Scrooge had cascaded the

229

yearly earnings of the Baby Cooper Dollar Bill into the millions. Well, hell, if all you had to do was study upwardly directed catastrophic trends—at the rate of 16 billion neurological operations per second— you'd probably make some pretty good decisions too. Then Wilma Cooper gave birth to twins. Cesarean. The doctor would live to regret it. Mommy and Daddy Cooper, thinking to be responsible and wanting to protect their children if anything awful happened to them, had created "guardian angels" to watch over their children's interests— specialized software entities to monitor and protect the twins' legal, financial and investment needs. As it happened, the accident that killed Daddy Cooper left Mommy Cooper a quadriplegic; the guardian angels were immediately activated and within three days had filed massive lawsuits on each other's client. The guardian angel for Twin B was now suing Twin A for half the money, claiming that Twin B would have been first-born if not for the intervention of the doctor. The guardian angel for Twin A was suing Twin B for slander, alienation of affections, attempt to subvert, violation of intention, and malicious litigation. Both guardian angels were also suing the doctor who had delivered the twins, the hospital where they were born, and the now-crippled Wilma Cooper who had signed the Cesarean consent form in the first place, claiming massive damages on the grounds that they were being forced to litigation because of the incompetence of the doctor, the hospital and Wilma Cooper. The twins themselves were unaware of these battles being fought on their behalf because they were only two years old at the time. Still following this? Good. Because now it gets baroque. Turns out that the ever-cautious Mommy and Daddy Cooper, fearing accidents, infertility, premature spousal termination, etc., had also deposited three viable eggs and six vials of sperm with the Northridge Community Crèche. The death of Daddy Cooper automatically turned loose three more guardian angels upon the legal network, each one claiming that its "client" had prior claim on the Baby Cooper Dollar Bill despite not yet having been conceived. The argument here was that conception was *implied* by the storage of sperm and egg despite not yet having occurred in actuality; therefore under the Protection of Intention Amendment, one of these three would-be children was the rightful recipient of the Dollar Bill Trust. Now the religious groups got involved and the case was aiming straight for the Supreme Court. (Already two justices had resigned rather than be forced to rule on any of the issues involved. The guardian angels had resisted all attempts to break the case into its component parts and were demanding total resolution, not particle resolution.) The Fundamentalist Judeo-Islamic Baptists were claiming that the whole case was a blasphemy because of Mommy Cooper's high school abortion. *That* had been the first-born child, they claimed. Therefore, upon its death, the money had to revert to the estate of Grandpa Cooper—who, it turned out, had at one time, signed an agreement of financial support for the Ministry for the Salvation of Lesser Souls (meaning cats, dogs, horses, cows, sheep and pigs; but not apes.) Grandpa had not yet honored his pledge (of $5) before he died and therefore the Ministry had filed a lien on the earnings of Grandpa Cooper's estate. The aforesaid Ministry for the Salvation of Lesser Souls was one of the subdivisions of the Christo-Baptist Coalition, which just happened to be now affiliated with the—are you surprised?—Fundamentalist Judeo-Islamic Baptists. Since filing its lawsuit that group had splintered into six separate schisms, but not before it had created its own software entity to pursue its claims. This particular software harpy was being pursued by six harpies of its own, each created by one of the splinter factions. Then the woodwork *really* got porous. Turned out Grandpa Cooper owed *everybody* money. And they were all filing claims against his estate. The legal software churning the net had become a zooful of monsters. Grandpa Cooper's single fairy godmother had given birth to a whole host of guardian angels, harpies, demons, imps, whirlwinds, berserkers, trolls, and ghouls—not to mention several particularly vicious nameless horrors—all prowling through the system, looking for a throat to rip out. It was a legal firestorm looking for a place to happen—and sure enough it did… It turned out that the original Baby Cooper Dollar Bill itself—which was still in the vault at McBroker's, sealed in a glass case—was *counterfeit*. Somebody had passed it to Grandpa Cooper. Unthinkingly, he'd passed it to the broker. The discovery that the bill was counterfeit was accidentally made during the course of a video feature story about near-sentient software entities. The shitstorm that this triggered made everything that had gone before seem like a fart in a tornado. If the original contract was invalidated because of Grandpa Cooper's failure to pro-vide one legal dollar, then who owned the resultant fortune? McBroker's? The McShareholders thought this was a good idea. McBroker's immediately sued the Baby Cooper Trust for fraud. The Baby Cooper Trust countersued for breach of contract, claiming that McBroker's original acceptance of the counterfeit dollar validated the deal. True to form, the United States Government adopted a schizophrenic position: the Justice Department argued that to invalidate the original contract would violate the Protection of Intention Amendment; the Treasury Department argued that to *not* invalidate the contract would legalize the counterfeiting of plastic dollars. Justice argued that the statute of limitations had expired and therefore the dollar had to be treated as legal tender. Treasury argued that under the Seizure of Illegal Profits Act the entire Baby Cooper fortune now belonged to the government. The original counterfeiter came forward and claimed that the fortune was his, arguing that his dollars were works of art and he was only leasing them, not selling them. At least two Presidents had considered revaluing the dollar to zero for about twenty seconds, so as to force the Baby Cooper software to self-destruct in its own economic starvation. The doctor who had delivered the Cooper twins committed suicide; his family promptly sued everybody in sight, claiming that the mental stress of the years of legal harassment had driven him to his death. The twins themselves—remember them?—had been separated shortly after the first lawsuits were filed and reared separately. Neither had spoken to the other or to their mother since their fourth birthday. By the time they turned twenty-one, the Baby Cooper Dollar Bill was worth the better part of a billion dollars, but not a single one of the lawsuits had yet made it to court. On the day that the Baby Cooper Dollar Bill Trust surpassed the Zurich Lottery in value, a class action lawsuit on behalf of the members of the International Monetary Council was filed against the United States Justice Department for impeding the resolution of a case which would significantly affect the world's economy. This particular action guaranteed an additional twenty years, at minimum, of legal maneuvering—which was the intention all along; the Baby Cooper assets had to be kept frozen. Should that much cash turn liquid all at once, there was no way to predict what kind of hydrostatic shock waves would resonate through the world's economy. Meanwhile, an international community of software vampires was already looking for ways to buy into the donnybrook. Even though Baby Cooper futures were rated a very high-risk investment, shares of all seven of the major corporate entities involved were being traded on the New York Stock Exchange, not to mention more than a score of remora corporations riding on their earnings or echoing their investments. At least most of the software entities involved were smart enough to hedge their bets against an adverse court ruling; they were starting to expand into other investment areas—including the creation of several new Dollar Bill entities… Rumor had it that the Supreme Court was reluctant to rule on this case for fear of crashing the market. That more than half of the human participants in this Byzantine affair had died in the plagues was irrelevant to the software entities battling on their behalfs. It just triggered a whole new class of software ghouls pursuing Beneficiary Claims; the filing rate for these set a three day record for the New York network. Unfortunately, the record was short-lived. When the National Resource Reclamation Act was passed, so many claims were filed on the first day of business that the system was down before lunchtime. The commissioners refused to bring the system back online until they could rule the Baby Cooper Trust exempt from further actions. The Federal Appeals Court refused to uphold this ruling and the commissioners promptly allowed the system to crash three more times. (Yes, this also triggered a spate of suits and countersuits—everybody from the court and the commission to the bystanders whose transactions had been lost in the disaster.) Wait, it gets better—Congress's refusal to grant an exemption opened up *everything* that had gone before to the entire range of possible Reclamation actions. Yes, this was an open invitation to several hundred thousand more would-be players to leap into the mayhem—and it was deliberate. The Baby Cooper Dollar Bill was now generating more lawsuits per day than any action in human history. The whole thing had become a legal black hole, but the US government was generating almost as much income off the legal fees—these were all pay-as-you-go cases—as the Dollar Bill itself was generating in interest; so the Secretary of the Treasury had a very real stake in continuing the uproar for as long a time as possible.

Now *that* was software…

AUTHOR'S AFTERWORD:
   All right. Now you can't say you haven't been warned.

Interlude #4

Selections from *The Quote-Book of Solomon Short*

"Humanity persists in spite of itself."

"The nice thing about self-love is that it's never unrequited."

"It is impossible to wean kittens. When their claws get sharp enough, the cat will do the job herself."

"I don't suffer from insanity. I enjoy every minute of it."

"Every time you fall in love, it's the first time."

"If we are all made in the image of God, then each of us is closest to God when we are held in the arms of another human being."

"Sex is better than chess, because sex has two winners."

"Reality can be useful."

"Beware of geeks bearing gifts."

"Most people live their lives as if they think God isn't paying any attention to them."

"If Helen Keller falls down in the forest, does she make a noise?"

"Cream isn't all that floats to the top."

"The last two words of the Star-Spangled Banner are not 'Play Ball!'"

"Understanding the laws of nature does not free us of them."

"Life never gets so bad that it can't get worse."

"Morality and practicality should be congruent. If they're not, then there's something wrong with one or the other."

"Design flaws travel in herds."

"Yes, the truth will set you free. But first it's going to piss you off."

"The game of life is always called on account of darkness."

"Commitment isn't a chore. It's a challenge."

"A man is known by the enemies he keeps."

"A lot of what I say comes off as political satire. In that, I have a lot in common with Congress."

"Paranoids tend to persecute free men."

"It is easier to believe in God than to accept the blame ourselves."

"A limerick is a primitive art form; it starts with a pair o' dactyls."

"A gentleman is one who doesn't require a lady to prove that she is."

"Onions don't cause heartburn; they only make it interesting."

"I've known for years that I have no humility. It's a virtue, to be sure, but I can live with it."

"If 'Thou art God,' then praising the Lord is an act of conceit. And praying is just talking to yourself."

"Never trust a grapefruit."

"The minute you start to analyze why sex feels so good, it stops feeling good and starts feeling silly."

"Guns don't die. People do."

"Cleanliness is next to impossible."

"People do not hire lawyers because they want justice. People hire lawyers because they want revenge."

"Truth never tranquilizes. The defining property of truth is its ability to disturb."

"A sane environment is one in which there is room to be crazy. A crazy environment is one in which there is no room to be sane."

"A man of God should be identifiable as a man of God in spite of his religion, not because of it."

"No one is afraid to die without first being afraid to live."

"A baby is the human race's way of insisting on another chance."

"Discretion is the better part of survival."

"The moment in which you confront your own death is the moment in which you are most totally alive."

"If this be reason, make the most of it."

"Death is the best part of life. That's why they save it for last."

"Change is inevitable—except from vending machines."

"Misery only likes company. It prefers loneliness."

"People who live in glass houses might as well answer the door."

"Nobody ever died badly. They got the job done, didn't they?"

"Even Murphy's Law doesn't work all the time."

"Children are the only minority who grow into their own oppressors."

Resnick called. He was putting together a new anthology. Men writing science fiction as women. Can a male author write a believable female character? Well, let's find out...

Digging in Gehenna

DADDY WAS ARGUING with Dr. Blom again, so Mom told me to stay away from the dig for awhile, at least until tempers cooled off. That was the only thing likely to cool off anytime soon. Spring was rising, and so were the daytime temperatures. We would be heading back south to the more comfortable polar zones as soon as the last trucks were loaded and the skywhale arrived tomorrow morning. Twenty-four months would pass before the sand would be cool enough to stand on again, but nobody knew if we would be coming back.

"They're arguing about the horn again, aren't they?"

Mom nodded. "It's their favorite argument."

"Do you think Daddy's right? Or Dr. Blom?"

"Actually, I hope they're both wrong." Mom looked up from the fabber she was disassembling. "Pray that we never find out what the damn thing was really used for. If either one of them is proven right, they'll never be able to work together again."

"They'll just find something else to argue about."

"No, this is one of those arguments that people don't forget. If you're wrong, it's a career-killer. The only hope for resolution is for them to be equally embarrassed by the facts. And don't tell Daddy I said this. It would hurt his feelings enormously."

"I didn't think anyone could hurt Daddy's feelings."

"Only people he cares about." She closed the lid of the machine and handed me the used cartridges for the recycler. "Just because he doesn't show his feelings doesn't mean he doesn't have any."

There were over two hundred people on the dig. We weren't the only family here. There were twenty others who'd brought their children. We were a whole village. We had sixteen acre-tents and at least a hundred

237

equipment and storage tents scattered around. Three of the acre-tents were habitats, with hanging rugs to give each family-group some privacy.

We had offworlders here too. The dig was big news all the way back to Earth; the first alien civilization ever discovered. And because the actual site was habitable only four out of twenty-eight months, this was a precious opportunity, especially for the Ph.D. candidates, like Hank, the big goofy guy who called me "swee'pea" and "short stuff" and "Little Darlin'" until Mom gave him *the glare*. So of course, I wanted to see more of him.

Actually, she's my stepmom, and according to the rule-books, I'm supposed to resent her, but mostly she and I are good friends. Probably because she's only twelve years older than me, so she feels more like a big sister than a stepmom, but I call her Mom anyway. I'm almost seventeen, old enough to get married; but Mom has this rule that nobody gets married until they finish college. She refused to marry Daddy for three years until she finished her doctorate.

Mom said that Hank was too old for me anyway. I respectfully did not point out that Hank was only five years older than me while Daddy was fifteen years her senior. I didn't need to start that fight. And besides, she was twenty-four when she married him.

Hank was one of the offworlders who had trouble adapting to Gehenna's 72-hour day, but eventually he found his rhythm. The others settled in too. Everyone does. Daddy says that twelve hours on and twelve hours off mimics Earth time almost perfectly—despite the fact that the sunlight doesn't match.

I'd been allowed to come on the dig because Mom and Dad were team leaders. There were another dozen college students who'd been brought along for grunt-work and experience, so I was lumped in with them. We all had class in the morning, and chores in the afternoon. Then class in the evening and chores again in the early morning. Interspersed with sleep, of course.

I was part of the toddler-team, we took care of the little ones while the various moms went off to work. There were only five of them, but they were a handful. I don't think we ever had five dry diapers at a time. We solved the problem by putting one person on diaper-duty each shift.

There's this about changing diapers—it keeps you from biting your nails. My private goal was to potty-train the little monsters as quickly as possible. We'd made real progress with the other four, but my little brother, Zakky, had so far resisted all inducements toward sanitary behavior. Despite that, I still thought he was cute. Mom said that my attitude would change as soon as Zakky learned how to say no. Once he learned how to argue, he'd be just like his daddy.

Daddy was famous for his arguments. Or maybe infamous. He wasn't loud or aggressive. I'd never even seen him raise his voice. He was painfully polite. He would make his points carefully, exquisitely, elegantly reasoned, making connections so obvious you could slap your forehead for not seeing them yourself. And when he was done, he had assembled a framework of logic as marvelous as a Chinese tapestry—so beautiful and compelling and overwhelming in its construction you were left with no place to stand. You just wanted to find a great big club and whack him across the head with it for being so damnably, blandly, patiently, *right*. Again.

Daddy's brain never stopped working. The universe was a giant puzzle to him, and he felt it was his personal responsibility to fit the pieces together. When I was little, I was afraid of him; but now that I understood better, I admired him. I used to wonder why Mom had married him, but most times I envied her for the adventure.

But Daddy could get so preoccupied with solving the puzzles of the universe that sometimes he forgot everything else. Sometimes we had to drag him physically away from the dig just to get him to eat, and even then we could have put a slice of shale between two pieces of bread and he wouldn't have noticed, he'd be so busy talking about what he had found and what he had to do next, and what it might mean. Of course, that led to a lot of arguments with the other diggers, about what each new discovery *meant*. They were all on new ground here. Nobody knew for sure what any of it really was, so everything was still just opinion.

The one thing we knew about the tripods—that's what we called them—was that we didn't know anything about them at all. We had no idea how they had lived, what they ate, what they believed in, what kind of culture they had, or even how many sexes they had. Every new fragment suggested as many possibilities as it disproved.

Daddy wasn't the only one arguing, of course. Everyone argued with everyone. Mom said that was because –ology didn't mean 'the study of' as much as it meant 'the argument about.' But Daddy *liked* to argue. He said that arguing was the highest exercise of intelligence at work, measuring, testing, and challenging ideas. He said that it was the passion of the argument that ultimately revealed the true self. Of course, Daddy would argue with the weather if he could. Failing that, he had argued for extending our stay on-site by an extra two weeks. He'd won half that argument. We were a week past our original departure date and already the temperatures were half-past unbearable.

But Daddy wasn't the only one who wanted to stay. Almost everybody on the team was so excited at what they were pulling out of the ground that nobody wanted to quit, even if it meant working in 110-degree weather. What if we were only half an hour away from finding the tripod Rosetta Stone? There might not be another expedition like this one in our lifetime. Gehenna's weather wasn't exactly friendly.

The tripod village had only been discovered six years ago, when one of the radar-mapping satellites discovered patterns underneath the sand. Detailed scanning showed eleven separate buildings embedded in the soft shale. The access team had trucked in huge sand-dredges and digging machines, and cut a ramp down to the target layers. Only then could the archeology teams start working.

Once we'd finally gotten down to the roofs of the domes, and gotten inside a few, we began discovering the first artifacts of an entire civilization. Dr. Blom said this village was less than a hundred thousand years old. On a geological scale, we'd just missed them. Of course, having their star flare up might have had something to do with that too.

Daddy's team had put a three-acre tent over the site. That got everybody out of the direct sun, and it brought the temperature down at least ten degrees; but mostly it kept the sand from covering the dig. The long nights brought hot roaring winds that could dry out your skin in an hour, leaving you itchy and cranky and desperate. Thirty-six hours later, when the sun crept over the sharp horizon again, there would be orange dust covering everything, sometimes as much as thirty centimeters. Everything had to be tented, or you might as well abandon it.

Mom's team kept busy cataloguing the artifacts, scanning and deconstructing them, then test-fabbing duplicates and comparing them to the originals. When the dupe was accurate to the limits of the measuring equipment, Mom would finalize it, and make it available in the catalog. Then, anyone could log on and fab a copy.

Some of the artifacts were easy, because they were mostly complete. A knife. A basket. A bowl. A jar of dessicated grain. A stool. But some of the items were impossible to figure out. Not just because they were fragments, but because nobody had any idea what kind of people the tripods might have been. Like the hairbrush thing with two handles— what was that for? A toothbrush? A backscratcher? An envelope holder?

Even the word "people" was cause for argument. Dr. Blom was an alienist. She said that alien meant *gaijin*. Different. Therefore, human paradigms couldn't apply. Just using the word "people" created an anthropomorphic mind-set.

So of course, Daddy took the anthropomorphic position—that life is messy everywhere, but it isn't infinite. The physics of the situation define what's possible. Life occurs as an expression of opportunity. And the same evolutionary imperatives are at work everywhere, regardless of the DNA coding; Gehenna had oxygen and water and a mobile temperate zone conducive to the carbon cycle, etc. etc., therefore, knowing the circumstances of the environment, we know the limits of what kind of life is possible. Therefore, therefore…ad infinitum. Rumor had it that Dr. Blom had actually asked one of her assistants to fab a club…

Eventually, the whole camp was arguing the point—if the tripods were so alien as to be beyond our comprehension, and this dig represents an insoluble puzzle to humankind, then why are we even bothering to dig anything up and study it? Wasn't the whole point of any '-ology' to increase our understanding, not our befuddlement?

None of which solved the problem of the *thing*, which along the way had become the focus of the whole argument. Dr. Blom had found it in one of the broken domes. It was some kind of ceramic, so it was obviously manufactured for a purpose. But what purpose? She and Daddy had been arguing about it from the very first day.

Complicating the argument, the thing wasn't a complete thing. Mostly, it was a tray of fragments. Mom had spent a week, scanning them, manipulating the pieces around, extrapolating what the thing might have looked like when it was whole. That was a month's worth of squabble, right there—how did the fragments fit together?—with Daddy and Dr. Blom fussing over asymmetry, polarity, and even which end was up.

What they finally agreed to was that in size and shape, the thing could have been some kind of table vessel. Like a punch bowl or a centerpiece or a coffee pot. One end of the thing was a bowl-shaped flare, like the horn of a trumpet; it narrowed into a hollow pedestal. The thing could have stood on the large end or the small, but it was obviously more stable resting on the large end.

Dr. Blom had initially suggested that it had a ceremonial function, like a wine-glass or a chalice, except that the thing had three scooped-out openings in the sides of the flared end. The openings were supposed to be there; they were sculpted in. Daddy suggested that the sculpting suggested that another object was to be placed in the horn, perhaps a triangular bowl, or even a symbolic representation of the tripodal makers.

So then Dr. Blom decided that they were looking at it upside-down. The horn-end was the bottom and the pedestal was a support for something else. Maybe it was a flower-holder, or a vase. Then she decided that it had a ceremonial function and was used for lustral rites. Some kind of purification ritual.

Whenever she said this, Daddy rolled his eyes in exasperation, and began muttering about Occam's chainsaw—whatever was the simplest, most obvious explanation, had to be the right one. Finally, in frustration, Mom fabbed a couple dozen replicas of the thing and passed them out like party favors. Very quickly it became the symbol of everything we didn't know about the tripods. If it had been half a size larger, we could have worn it as a dunce cap.

If only there had been wall-markings in the domes or illustrations on the side of jars or something like that. But there weren't any. Apparently, the tripods didn't make images of themselves. And that was good for another whole area of argument—that maybe something about the way their eyes worked, or their brains, they didn't have visual symbology.

That could have been an even bigger disagreement than the argument about the *thing*, except by that time, we'd found the first skeletons and that's when the real excitement began. Everything before that was just a warm-up.

Hank was on the exo-biology team, so I heard about lots of stuff before it was presented, and some stuff that wasn't presented at all, because it was still only speculation. Most of the skeletons were complete and fairly well-preserved; carbon-dating and iridium-scanning showed that this village had died when the sun flared up.

Hank had a lot of ideas about that. His team had fabbed copies of three skeletons, two adults and a juvenile, and now they were working on the nature of the tripod musculature. As bad as the arguments were about *the thing*, the arguments about tripod biology were even worse.

First off, the tripod brain case was too small. It was a dorsal hump opposite what was assumed to be the rear leg. Channels in the bone suggested routes for optic nerves. Other structures might have been a nasal chamber, which would indicate an 'anterior' as opposed to 'posterior.' But there was also the suggestion of some kind of a collagenous snout, like an elephant's trunk, only it seemed to serve as a mouth, not of a nose. But nobody wanted to say for certain, in case it turned out to be something else and then they'd be embarrassed for guessing wrong, so for the moment everything everybody said about the tripods was prefaced with 'suggests,' 'could be,' 'possible,' 'might serve as,' and even an occasional 'probable.' But the size of the brain case was clearly insufficient for sentience.

A full-grown tripod was only waist-high. Not much more than a meter tall. The exo-biology team estimated that it would mass no more than 80 kilograms. So that would make it the size of a large dog, or a small ape; but the estimated size of the brain wasn't large enough even for that size a creature. The exo-biology team estimated that the tripods maybe had the intelligence of a cocker spaniel—almost smart enough to pee outside. So that was another mystery.

And then there was the business of the fingers. They were short and stubby, more of a splayed paw than a hand, and not really suitable for grasping large or heavy objects. The simulations showed that if a tripod squatted on its hind leg, the two forward paws could be used to manipulate simple objects, but that was about the limit. The tripods would not have been very good typists. That is, if they had anything to type.

Dr. Blom said that intelligent creatures needed the ability to handle objects, not just as tools, but more importantly because the ability to understand an object was directly related to the ability to touch, feel, and manipulate it. "Fingers are the extension of the mind," she said.

Wisely, Daddy did not disagree with her on that one. Instead, he took a gentler tack, pointing out that dolphins and other cetaceans had demonstrated sophisticated language and intelligence skills without any grasping limbs at all; so clearly there was something else at work here. But dolphins and whales have very large brains, and tripods didn't—so that just brought us back to the problem of the too-small brain case.

But those were only sidebar discussions. The main event was much more serious.

Hank explained it to me, at dinner in the mess tent. Nowhere else in the universe—not in simulation, and not in the laboratory, and not on any other life-bearing planet, had nature produced a three-legged creature. The asymmetry of the species was unprecedented, and Hank said that it was going to cause a major upheaval in both biological and evolutionary thinking. There was no way it couldn't. This was the real issue: whatever the tripods had been, they were so far outside the realm of what we had previously known or believed to be possible, that they represented a massive breakdown in biological science. That's what was so exciting; this was a real opportunity for genius to prove itself by reinventing the paradigm.

After dinner, most folks gathered in the rec-area for news and gossip and mail. Sometimes we'd see a movie, sometimes we'd have a dance or celebrate someone's birthday. Some of the folks played instruments, so we had a makeshift band. And the bar was open for two hours, if people wanted to have a drink.

But not everybody wanted to be sociable all the time. Some folks had to be alone for a while. They'd go outside and sit under the stars or maybe walk out to one of the boundary markers. It was hard to get lost in the desert. The camp gave off a bright glow, and if that weren't enough, the housekeeping team had installed three bright red lasers pointing up into the sky. They were visible for kilometers, so anyone who ventured too far out only needed to head for the light at the edge of the world. Folks who wanted a bit of solitude sometimes planned midnight picnics and hiked a few kilometers out to sleep on the warm sand. And no, sleeping wasn't all they did.

I wanted to go out on a midnight picnic with Hank, but Mom wouldn't allow it; she wouldn't even let me appeal to Daddy, she said we didn't need that fight in the camp. So the most I could do with Hank was walk around the big tent once in a while, mostly when Mom wanted to be alone with Daddy. Some of the girls on the toddler-team went out for a midnight picnic once, I went with them, but all we did was giggle about the boys we liked and make lewd guesses of what we thought they looked like naked. Maybe that's fun when you're fifteen, but I was too old for that now. I wanted something more than embarrassed giggling.

And, there was that other thing too. I didn't want to be the *last* one in the group. I didn't want to be the only one who didn't know what the others were giggling about. Though sometimes it seemed so silly I couldn't imagine any serious person wanting to do it at all, sometimes I couldn't think about anything else. I wondered if it was that way for anybody else. I wanted to ask Mom about it, but she was so busy she never had time; the one time I brought the subject up, she asked me to wait until we got back home, so she and I could spend some serious time talking about it. But when your insides are fizzing like a chocolate soda, there's no such thing as patience.

So that night, when Hank put his arm around my shoulder and I pulled me close against him, he smelled so good, kissing him just felt like the right thing to do. The thing about kissing someone you like kissing—once you start, it's hard to stop. And I didn't want to stop, I just wanted to keep going. But then Zakky's diaper-monitor chimed and Hank pulled away gently and said, "Come'on, Swee'pea, I'll walk you home," as if that was all there was to it, and I wondered how he could be like that. Didn't he have any normal feelings?

And that's the other thing about changing diapers. Mom says that they're punctuation marks in the paragraphs of life. Whatever thoughts you might have been working on, they end up in the diaper pail with all the rest of the crap. And that night, I understood exactly. Whatever fizzy feelings I might have had inside of me, they were all fizzed out by the time Zakky's messy bottom was clean again.

So when some of the team members said to me stuff like, "You can't understand how frustrating it is to be this close," I just smiled weakly and said, "Yeah, I guess so." They were the ones who didn't understand.

After a couple weeks of tinkering, Hank's team fabbed a walking tripod, just to see if they could build one that could walk, run, squat, or even mount another for mating; the only thing it couldn't do was lift a leg to pee on a lamp post.

The team went through several iterations until they hit the right combination of musculature and autonomic intelligence; then they fabbed a bunch more, for everyone else to play with, or experiment on. The bots weren't very big; the largest was the size of Zakky. Some of them had scales, some had fur, some had feathers, some had naked skin; and they were all different colors. At this point, the team was still guessing. It was kind of like having a pack of three-legged dogs from the rainbow planet running around the camp, but Hank said it was necessary for us to observe these things in action to get some sense of what the real tripods might have been like. I wasn't exactly sneaking out to see him behind Mom's back, but I did make sure that my regular chores took me through the bio-tent during his shifts. Mom certainly couldn't complain about me doing my regular duties. Of course, she didn't have to know why I had traded shifts with Marlena Rigby either.

Hank liked my visits. He gave me one of the robots, and even programmed it to follow Zakky around like a baby-monitor, so we would always know where he was. Zakky decided the tripod was a chicken and called it 'Fuffy.' I thought it looked more like a yellow cat with a limp.

When I said that, Hank admitted that getting the creature to walk right had been his biggest problem. He had started by studying the algorithms for three-legged industrial robots, but plastic autonomy is different than biological, and there are a lot of different ways a three-legged creature can walk. It can move one leg at a time, each one in turn, which means it sort of scuttles or zig-zags or walks in circles. Or it can alternate moving its two front two legs with its single rear leg in a crippled imitation of a four-legged creature. That was was faster but it created musculature issues that weren't resolved in the actual skeletons.

Hank finally resolved it by not programming the tripod at all. Instead, he gave it a neural network and let it teach itself to walk. What it came up with was—well, it was just weird, but efficient. But it still looked like a yellow cat with a limp.

As a joke, Hank taught the tripod to squat on Zakky's potty chair. That made me laugh, and for a moment I thought Zakky might take the hint, but the devil-baby was actively disinterested. Instead, he put a plastic bucket on his head and banged it with a spoon, and laughed delightedly at being inside the noise.

On the last full day before the skywhale arrived, I was helping Mom disassemble the last three fabbers. We wrapped all the pieces in plastic and packed them in stiff boxes. Nobody knew if the Institute would authorize a second expedition. There was a lot of disappointment that we hadn't found more—no books or wall carvings or statues—so the folks who passed out the money had lost some of their enthusiasm. Despite their effusive praise at a job well done, despite their protestations of support, it was no secret that this expedition was considered only a partial success, which is a polite way of saying 'an ambitious failure.'

Some of the more aggressive members of Daddy's team were arguing for mothballing the entire site as a way of forcing the issue. With all of the equipment still in place, the Institute would have a financial investment in returning; but Daddy shook his head. If a return were guaranteed, then storing the hardware onsite made financial sense; but if the Institute decided not to fund a return, they would write off the machinery, and then it wouldn't be available for any other enterprise anywhere else, and that would hurt everybody. Daddy was right, of course.

Some of the folks were eager to head back home—like Hank; he said he had enough material to fund a dozen years of study, and he could hardly wait to get the skeletons back to the lab and begin micro-scanning and DNA-reconstruction; it was his hunch that the DNA sequences were too short for a creature this size.

But most folks were sad that the adventure was ending so abruptly, and without a real resolution. That was how I felt. Hank was going back to wherever, and I'd probably never see him again. So, I'd sort of made up my mind that I was ready to sneak away from tonight's party with him for an hour or two.

We finished packing the last fabber, and then the toolkits, and we were done. Mom sat down on a bench and sighed. "This was fun."

"Are you going to miss it?"

"Not at all," she said. "Once we get back home, I'll have so much work to do just sorting everything out, I won't have time to miss anything." And then her hand flew up to her mouth. "Oh, sweetheart, I'm sorry. I promised you that we would find some time together, just for us."

"It's all right, Mom—"

"No, it isn't all right. There are things you need to talk about."

I shrugged, embarrassed. "I'm okay now."

"Mm." She didn't look convinced. "All right, let me give you the speech anyway. I know you already know this, but I have to say it anyway, because if I don't say it, you'll think that I don't know it. Come here, sit down next to me."

She put her arm around my shoulder, pulled me close, and lowered her voice almost conspiratorially. "Look, Hank is a real nice boy—" she began.

"He's a *man*, Mom."

"He's a big boy on a big adventure," she corrected. "He won't be a man until he starts thinking like one. And you won't be a woman until you stop thinking like a teenager."

"What is that supposed to mean?"

"What it means is that sometimes, it isn't about *now*. It isn't always about what you want, what you think you need, what you think you have to have. Sometimes, it's about who you're going to be when it all works out, and your responsibility to that moment outweighs whatever you think you want now."

I didn't say anything to that. I could already see where she was headed.

"Sweetheart, here's the question I want you to ask yourself. What kind of a person do you want to be? Whenever you have a big choice in front of you, that's what you have to ask yourself. Is this the kind of thing that the person I want to be would do? What kind of memory will this be? A good one or an embarrassing one or a terrible regret?"

I stared at my knees. Whenever I sat, they looked bony. Knees were such ugly parts of the body. Knees and elbows. Why couldn't somebody design joints that didn't make you look like a chicken? Like the tripods. They had nice joints. They could swivel better than human joints—

"Are you listening to me?"

"Yes, Mom."

"What did I just say?"

"You said that I shouldn't do things that I'll regret."

"What I said was that life is about building a collection of good memories. As you go through life, you need to choose what kinds of memories you want to collect. Because your memories determine who you are."

"Oh."

"All right," she said, patting me on the shoulder in a gesture that was as much resignation as it was completion. "I can see that there are some mistakes you're going to have to make for yourself. Maybe that's the only way you're ever really learn where anything is—by tripping over it in the dark." She sighed. "Go ahead. Go get cleaned up for the party."

There wasn't much left to do. Most of the camp had already been packed up and loaded onto the trucks. So folks just stood around waiting, listening to the tent poles groaning in the wind. Overhead the lights swung back and forth on their wires. We waited in an uneven island of brightness. Only the generator, the mess tent, the hospitality tent, and the shower tents were left. Almost everything else had disappeared, or was in the process of disappearing under a fresh layer of sand and dust.

Zakky was asleep in the hospitality tent. His diaper was clean, so I decided not to wake him, Marlena would handle it. She was on diaper-duty tonight. I headed back out to the party.

The mess team had prepared a grand smorgasbord; we had to finish the last of the perishables, so it looked like more food in one place than I'd ever seen in my entire life. The bar was open too. It seemed like an invitation to pig out and drink yourself silly. After all, you'd have twelve hours on the skywhale to sleep it off. But the disciplines of the past four months were too ingrained. The party was more subdued than usual. People were tired and a lot of folks seemed depressed as well.

The band played everybody's favorite songs, and all of the team leaders made speeches about how hard their folks had worked and how grateful they were and what a successful expedition this had been. And everybody made jokes about the thing and the tripods and offered bawdy speculations about where the thing might really fit and how the tripods made baby tripods, and so on. But it felt forced. I guessed the simmering resentments were still simmering.

I found Hank near the bar, chatting with the other offworlders, and a couple of the interns. He saw me coming and excused himself. He took me by the hand and led me out of the tent, out of the island of light, out toward the soft red sand.

"There's something—" I started.

"—I have to tell you," he finished.

"You first."

"No, you."

We played a couple of rounds of that for a bit, laughing at our mutual silliness, until finally, I just blurted it out, "I really like you, Hank" and he said, "I'm engaged to a girl back home" at the same time.

And then I choked on my tongue and said, "What?" and he started to repeat it, and I cut him off. "I heard you the first time." And meanwhile, my heart was in free fall, while my brain was saying, "Thank Ghu, you didn't say anything stupid—" and my fingers wanted to reach into his chest and shred his heart for not telling me this before.

He held me by the shoulders and made what he must have thought were compassionate noises: "—I just wanted to tell you that you're really sweet, and I'm sure you're going to find the right guy, and I hope you'll have a happy life because you deserve it—oh, look, here comes the skywhale!"

I turned to look, not because I didn't want to see it, but because I didn't want Hank to see the tears running down my cheeks. The big ship came majestically over the ridge, all her lights blazing, a vast platform in the sky. She floated toward us, passing directly over the camp, while everyone came pouring out of the mess tent, cheering and waving. The skywhale dropped anchor half a klick past the camp and began pulling herself down, like a grand gleaming dream come to rest.

The camp speakers came alive with fanfare and trumpets and everyone shouted themselves silly, hugging and kissing each other in celebration. It looked like the party was finally starting; but actually it was ending. This was just the final beat. We had 90 minutes to load and be away, if we wanted to beat the heat of the morning. There wasn't a lot of slippage on that; most of the tents and air-cooling gear had already been collapsed and packed. If we didn't get out on time, we could be in serious trouble.

I threaded my way around the edges of the crowd, looking for Mom. I wanted to tell her that I was going to grab Zakky and his diaper bag, my duffel too, and just go on aboard, and curl up in a bunk somewhere. And not have to talk to anybody. There wasn't anything I wanted down here anymore. But Hank came following behind me and grabbed my arm. "Hey, Swee'pea, are you all right?"

"I'm fine, thank you! And I'm not your Swee'pea. You already have a Swee'pea." I pulled free and stormed away, not really caring which direction I headed, so I ended up smack in the middle of the party, and that meant that I had to hug everyone goodbye, even though I'd be seeing most of them on the skywhale, and back home too.

—Until I bumped into Marlena Rigby. "What are you doing here?"

"What do you mean?" she asked, bewildered.

"Who's taking care of Zakky?"

"You're supposed to—he's your brother."

"We traded shifts, remember?"

"No, we didn't—I told you I wasn't going to miss the party."

"Oh, good grief. You are such a stupid airhead! We made this deal a week ago. Oh, never mind—" I headed off to the hospitality tent.

Zakky was gone.

Okay, Mom had come and gotten him.

Except the diaper bag was still there.

Mom wouldn't have collected the baby without gathering his things. I unclipped my phone from my belt. "Mom?"

I waited while it rang on the other end. After a moment, "Yes, sweetheart?" Her voice founded funny—like she'd been interrupted in the middle of a mouthful.

"Where are you?"

"I'm with Daddy, down by the dig. We're...um, saying goodbye. What do you need?"

"Is Zakky with you?"

"Isn't he with you?"

"He's not in the crib."

"When did you see him last—"

"I checked on him thirty minutes ago. I thought Marlene was watching him. We had a deal. But she went to the party anyway." I was already outside, circling the hospitality tent. "He couldn't have gone far—"

She made an exasperated noise. The sound was muffled for a moment, while she explained the situation to Daddy. Then she came back. "We're on our way. You start looking."

Everybody I passed, I grabbed them, "Have you seen Zakky? He's missing—" Nobody had seen him. And nobody had time to help me search either. They were all hurrying to gather their things and board the dirigible. In frustration, I just stopped where I was and started screaming. "My little brother is missing! He's somewhere out there!! Doesn't anybody care?!"

The problem was, the skywhale had to leave whether everybody was aboard or not. She wasn't rigged to withstand the heat of the day. And most of the camp had been dismantled and was already on its way south on the trucks, so there weren't the resources on the ground to support more than a few people anyway.

Thirty seconds of screaming was more than enough. It wasn't going to produce any useful result and Daddy always said, "Save your upset for afterward. Do what's in front of you, first."

But the screaming did make people aware there was a problem. By the time I finished circling the camp, calling for Zakky everywhere, Dr. Blom was already organizing a real search. She came barreling through like a tank, snapping out orders and mobilizing her dig team like a general at war.

She had a phone in each hand, one for incoming, one for outgoing. "No, you're not getting on the whale," she barked at one of them. "We're not going home until we find that child. We'll ride back in the trucks if we have to." I was beginning to understand why Daddy had invited her along. She was good at organization. And no one argued with Dr. Blom. Except Daddy, of course.

She marched into the mess tent and started drawing on one of the plastic table cloths, quickly dividing the camp and its environs into sectors, assigning teams of three to each sector. "Take flashlights, water, blankets, a first-aid kit, and at least one phone for each person. With a working GPS, dammit!" To the other phone: "Well unpack the flying remotes then! I don't care. We've still got twenty hours before infra-red is useless."

Dr. Blom didn't stop talking until Mom and Dad came rushing into the mess tent. She looked up only long enough to say, "I need another thirty people to cover the south and west. Pull as many members of your team off the dirigible as you can."

Daddy opened his mouth to say something, then realized how absolutely stupid it was to object. He unclipped his phone and started talking into it. Mom did the same. In less than a minute, the skywhale started disgorging people, running for the mess tent. Other people began pulling crates off the trucks, cracking them, and pulling out equipment. I'd never seen so many people move so fast. It was all I could do to keep out of the way. I felt useless and stupid. But it wasn't my fault, was it? I mean, stupid Marlena was the one who screwed up, not me—

Daddy came striding over; his face was red with fury. "Go get your stuff and get aboard the whale. Now." I'd never seen him so angry.

"But I have to stay and help with the search."

"No, you will not. You've done enough already."

"Daddy—"

"We'll talk about this later. If there is a later. Right now, the only thing I want you to do is get onboard and keep out of the way—"

I didn't wait to hear the rest. I sobbed and ran. All the way to the gangplank and up into the whale, where I threw myself into the first empty seat I could find; half of them were filled with duffels and backpacks. Everything was all screwed up. I wanted to die. And I was so angry, I wanted to scream. If only—

Except there wasn't any 'if only.' There was only me. Stupidly chasing Hank. Stupidly not checking Zakky. Stupidly acting like a stupid little spoiled brat.

Suddenly, I stopped and sat up. Wait a minute. I bounced out of my seat and went looking for Hank. He was on the upper deck, already sacked out in a bunk. I shook him awake, hard. "Come on, I need your help."

"Huh, what—?" He rubbed his eyes. "Look, if you're going to yell at me some more, can't it wait until tomorrow?"

"Zakky's missing. You can track him."

"Huh? What?"

"Would you two take that somewhere else? People are trying to sleep here."

I said something very unpolite. But I pulled Hank out of his bunk. I grabbed his clipboard and dragged him out. "The tripod you gave me for Zakky. You can track it!"

"Well, yeah," He said, still rubbing his eyes. "Only all the equipment is packed up."

"Well, unpack it then!"

"The truck has already left," he said. "We sent it off an hour ago."

"Can we call it back?"

"No, wait—" He closed his eyes for a moment, thinking. He looked like he had gone back to sleep. "Yeah, that'll work." We headed down to the communications room of the whale. It was his turn to drag me. The communications officer looked annoyed at the interruption. I knew her from back home. The kids called her Ironballs, but her real name was Lila Brock. She was a wiry little woman with a hard expression and her hair tied back in a bun.

I didn't understand half of what Hank said to her; most of it was in another language, techno-babble; but even before he finished, she was already turning to her displays and typing in codes. The screens started to fill with overlaid patterns and colors. She frowned. "Wait a minute, let me see what I can read from the satellites." More typing. More colors, more patterns. "Okay, I've got probables." She tapped the big display. "Here, here, and here—"

Hank copied the feed to his clipboard and overlaid it on a map of the camp. "Okay, that first one is the truck," said Hank, eliminating the one that was moving too fast. "And this one is the lounge of the whale—"

"And the last one is in the center of the dig," I said. I recognized the spider-shaped pattern of the excavation. "Come on!" I was already out the door.

"Call the camp! Tell them!" Hank shouted back to Brock, and followed me down the gangplank at a run. The whale was closer to the dig than the mess-tent, but there were rolling dunes in the way—it's not easy to run in sand of any kind. Hank made me slow down, lest I exhaust myself. He kept referring to the updated scans on his clipboard, steering us toward the west end of the dig, where the first big ramp had been carved into the shale. "Down there," he pointed.

I was already calling, "Zakky! Zakky! Where are you?" Off to the left, I could see the first few searchers rolling out of the camp on sand-scooters, and then a sledge carrying Mom and Dad. But we were already heading down the ramp. They were still a few minutes away.

At first it was too dark to see anything, but then the whole night lit up—as if a great white star had been switched on above us. It was startling. At first I didn't understand; we'd already packed most of our fly-beams; but Hank said curtly, "Satellite. False-white laser. Good idea. Somebody was thinking."

It wasn't quite as bright as daylight; in fact, it wasn't even twilight; but it was a hundred times better than the silky darkness. At the bottom of the ramp, there wasn't much to see. The important stuff had been covered with plastic sheets. Most of the open domes had been sealed. All except one.

Hank and I climbed down into it, peering into the different chambers. One still had an inflatable bed in it. The blankets were rumpled. Okay, that explained that. Zakky hadn't been down this way. But Hank wouldn't let me go into any of the tunnels "We have to wait for the others. They'll have lights."

I called into each of the passages, "Zakky, want a cookie? Zakky?" We both listened, but there was no reply. "Zakky? Come on, sweety. It's cookie-time." Nothing. "That doesn't mean anything," I said. "Zakky has selective hearing. If he doesn't want to hear…"

Hank put his hand on my shoulder. "We'll find him. The tripod is down that one."

And then Dr. Blom arrived, scrambling down the steps into the dome, followed by Dad and then Mom and three of the folks from the closest search teams. Suddenly, there were lights flashing everywhere. I grabbed one and headed into the passage Hank had pointed. "Zakky!"

The passage led into the next dome over. Zakky was sitting on the floor playing with three discarded replicas of the famous unknown *thing*. One of the replicas had been shoved point-first into the sand, and Zakky's toy tripod was squatting up and down on it. Its three legs fit perfectly into the openings in the sides of the bowl. "Go potty, Fuffy," Zakky said insistently. "Go potty. Do faw momma."

Daddy and Hank came scrambling into the dome after me. Then Mom and Dr. Blom. I pointed my light at the tripod and everybody just stared for a moment.

I couldn't help it. I started laughing. It was too silly. Then Hank started chortling. And then Mom. And Dr. Blom. And finally, Daddy.

"Well, I guess that answers that," said Dr. Blom. To her phone, she said, "We've got him."

Daddy shook his head. "How are we going to write this up?"

"With a straight face," said Mom, scooping up Zakky. He cooed at her; she cooed back at him, then turned to Daddy and Dr. Blom. "It's not everybody who discovers an alien potty chair. You realize, of course, that a potty chair will get you a lot more headlines than a lustral chalice."

"Yes, there is that," Dr. Blom agreed.

I cleared my throat. "It's not a potty chair."

"But of course it is," said Daddy. "Look at the way the tripod fits. Look at the way—" He stopped. "Why not?"

"There's a hole in the point. Whatever the tripod poops into the bowl is supposed to come out the bottom."

"Well, yes—" said Dr. Blom. "That makes it easier to bury the waste in the sand. It's a portable toilet."

"Yes, it's a toilet," I agreed. "But it's not a potty chair. It's a kitty-box. Sort of."

They all looked at me. "Huh—?"

I poked Hank. "Tell them."

"Tell them what?"

"What you haven't told anyone else yet—that the tripods didn't build these domes."

Everybody looked at him. *Oh, really?* Hank looked embarrassed. "Um, I didn't want to say anything yet. Because I wanted to be sure. I wanted to run more tests at the University. But, well, yes. Their brains were too small, and their DNA sequences are too short. Too well-ordered. These things weren't sentient. And in fact, it's my guess that they weren't even natural. I think they were genetically designed by the beings who really built these domes. These things...well, they're just the equivalent of farm animals. Like pigs or chickens."

Daddy nodded, considering it. "It almost makes sense. This wasn't a village. It was a farm, and these are a bunch of kennels or coops and storage sheds. The tripods would wander around the crops, eating bugs and insects and little crawling things, whatever. But the horns...?"

Dr. Blom looked annoyed, that same look she always got when Daddy was right. Had she just spent four months excavating a chicken coop? But to her credit, she tried on the idea to see if it fit. "We know that chickens can be designer-trained. We've done it ourselves. If you can train chickens to use a toilet, you don't have to shovel the poop. So why not put out the horns and let them fertilize the field for you."

Mom chimed in then. "Wait a minute. You're not going far enough. Remember that jar of seeds you found? It's part of the process. The farmer puts out horns and scatters seeds in the field. The chickens roam the field, eating the seeds. Some of the seeds get digested, but some don't; they pass right through the chickens. The chickens poop in the horns, and the seeds get planted in their own personal package of fertilizer. Then the farmer picks up the horns and moves them to the next part of the field and starts again the next day. He's planted his crop *and* fertilized it."

They all looked at each other, surprised. It fit. In a bizarre kind of way.

"That's the only explanation so far that fits all the available facts," Daddy said slowly.

Dr. Blom held up a hand. "Wait a minute. Not so fast. Answer one question. Why would any rational being deliberately design a *three-legged* chicken?"

"Isn't it obvious?" I said. They all turned to me, surprised that I even had an opinion. "A three-legged chicken gives you an extra drumstick." I took Zakky from Mom; his diaper was full. "Yick. Come on, baby. The skywhale is waiting."

AUTHOR'S AFTERWORD:
    The seed for this story was an actual anecdote I'd read many years ago and saved in my idea file—something about archaeologists and blind spots and how much does a Grecian urn?

The original (1933) version of King Kong isn't just a classic movie—it's a cultural landmark. It's one of those things that defines not just the art form, but the culture that created the art form. Yes, if you look at it through modern eyes, it's quaint and the special effects are dated. But if you look at it through the eyes of 1933, it's an astonishing adventure in imagination and scale. Nothing like it had ever been seen before. And its ambition was unequaled for at least four decades. Okay, put all that aside now. It's one of my favorite movies.

So when Peter Jackson announced he was going to remake it, I experienced both optimism and trepidation. Jackson isn't known for subtlety or restraint. He's brilliant, yes. And there's no question that he approaches his craft with passion and enthusiasm and total commitment to excellence. Yes. But...he's also over-the-top. Okay, there's the mini-review, keep reading.

In order to cash in on what was expected to be the big Christmas block-buster of 2005, several publishers went to press with various tie-in books. I was invited to contribute to two of them. (One of these pieces I never got paid for because the publisher, Byron Preiss, had the bad taste to die in an auto accident, thus ending one of the better publishing efforts in SF.)

Here are my own thoughts on King Kong.

King Kong: Behind the Scenes

THE SOUND TRACK BEGINS with a scratchy buzz, then we see a badly framed industry leader counting down to:

Black and white, flickering, grainy, scratched, a terrible old print of one of the most exciting sequences in the original 1933 classic, KING KONG. This is a full shot of the great gate of the natives—Kong is slowly pushing it open as the natives run screaming in terror.

As the great ape comes stamping through, suddenly the music becomes a full stereophonic orchestra, color floods the image, the screen swells to a full 70mm image—and KONG, the most magnificent ape of all comes charging, roaring, bellowing into the native village to wreak havoc upon their homes—The sequence runs through its most exciting shots, and then, as it peaks—we hear a voice say, "Cut, cut, cut—"

The camera pulls back and we are looking at a backlot set. Extras, dressed as natives, mill around with bored expressions, while the director—Ernest B. Schoedsack—calls Kong aside for a conference. We see, in middle distance, the two of them discussing something in the script; Schoedsack is speaking in low tones, Kong is replying in deep, guttural grunts. Kong nods his head knowingly, Schoedsack pats the ape's arm reassuringly, and then this huge 20-foot ape shambles back onto the set and back into position while an assistant director hollers, "All right, places everybody."

Schoedsack calls, "Let's try another take. Lights, please. Camera. Action."

—and the take continues, with Kong smashing his way through the rest of the native village. We climax with Kong picking up one of the natives, popping him into his mouth and biting his head off. (This is one of the famous "missing scenes"—eventually rediscovered and restored.)

"Cut. Print. That's a take," Schoedsack calls, "Next set-up please."

We go to a wider angle on the set. We see Kong retiring to a large chair with his name on the back. He starts paging through a copy of Variety, circa 1931. An assistant director confers with Schoedsack in low tones, "We gotta do something about all the extras he's eating…central casting is getting suspicious…"

And we go to titles:

KING KONG: BEHIND THE SCENES

OPEN ON FAY WRAY, an elegant older woman, being interviewed by an offscreen reporter.

She is reminiscing about the first day she reported to work for Merian C. Cooper and Ernest B. Schoedsack.

At that time, they had just begun working on a new picture that all of Hollywood was buzzing about…

DISSOLVE TO: 1931. A young Fay Wray (dark-haired) coming on to the soundstage for the first time and being introduced to her co-star, young Kong—a hulking 20-foot ape.

"I remember Kong as being very good-natured, very eager to please, but very very naive about life in the big city. He let people take advantage of him something awful. Even though he'd been in Hollywood for two years before being discovered by Mr. Schoedsack—Mr. Schoedsack had seen him in Schwabbs eating a four foot banana split—Kong never became hard or cynical like so many other young actors whose careers are faltering, because he never lost his optimism, so he never fell for the whole 'Hollywood' thing. Even afterwards, the fame never went to his head. He was always his own quiet self—I think that's what I liked about him the most."

We see Fay Wray shaking hands with Kong, who is carrying a script under one arm. "I'm looking forward to working with you, Mr. Kong."

Kong gives one of his familiar guttural grunts in reply.

She twinkles, "And you can call me Fay—"

And we see the first beginnings of the love affair between Kong and Fay, right here in their first meeting—she can't take her eyes off of him, and he is equally entranced by her. Voice over narration continues, "If only I had known what lay in store for both of us…"

We see the dailies:

The shot is Kong battering at the gates of the wall—this is the view from his side, before he has managed to push the great doors open. The dailies are in black and white, of course, and there is the usual run of out-takes.

We see Kong leaning patiently on the door, while a slate pops into foreground. Offscreen voice calls, "Action," and he turns and knocks politely.

We hear producer and director comments over all this. "Well, you can't fault his manners."

Slate and second take. Kong knocks a little harder, but still not in character. (The audience knows what the shot should look like—they're feeling what the director is feeling now.)

Producer: "I don't think he understands the scene…"

Slate and third take. Kong finally begins to knock properly. An extra falls off the top of the wall.

Producer, "Oh, shit—"

Director grunts.

Producer, "He's awfully hard on the extras, isn't he? How many does that make?"

"Six. I think."

Slate and fourth take. We see Kong getting a little more fidgety in the B. G. between takes. "Action," and he begins banging on the wall again. This looks like a good take, until part of the wall—the wrong part—collapses, revealing stage hands and lights behind it.

Director: "That's when we broke for lunch."

Slate and fifth take. We see director and Kong conferring softly, director acting out the motion, Kong nodding. Re-slate, Kong goes through action.

"I don't know. He just doesn't seem to have the feel for it."

"He's young—give him a chance."

"What about that little Italian kid—Dino whatsisname? The one with the rubber suit?"

"No, no, I think this will work out better in the long run. Give Kong a chance."

Slate and next take. Kong falls on his ass.

"He was getting tired there, but I think we can cut away, then cut back and use the stuff from the other side of the wall."

End of take, setting up for next one, camera still rolling—

"Hmm, I must have forgotten to call a cut."

We hear the extras jeering Kong, calling him a "big monkey." We see Kong finally getting honestly angry—and he bashes down the wall exactly as we remember him doing it from the classic film.

"Hey—!!"

Fay Wray narrating again:

"That was Kong's screen test. He wasn't a very good actor at first, it was all very new and strange to him to be in the movies, and he had a lot to learn—but Mr. Schoedsack was very patient and kind, and Kong was a fast learner. There was something about him, a raw power…that couldn't be denied. I had to dye my hair blonde for the first day of shooting, and…"

We see Kong's famous entrance scene recreated for the watching cameras—the first time the theater audience sees him as he comes crashing through the forest, parting trees and as he catches his first glimpse of Fay Wray…

"There were fourteen takes—"

We see a montage of Kong reactions—excited, stunned, happy, and so on.

"—he was very pleased when he saw me as a blonde; he thought it did wonders to bring out the color in my cheeks."

We see Kong and Fay Wray talking softly between takes, she holding a coke in one hand, he holding a barrel.

"Kong was just a big overgrown kid—the theater audience didn't realize it at the time, but he hadn't even reached his full growth. In fact, he grew another four feet while the picture was in production, which explains why he looked taller in the New York scenes.

"We were in production for two years. But at the beginning, he was very shy and needed a lot of coaching. He had a tendency to overact on some of the subtle scenes, and not be big enough on the more dramatic shots."

We see Fay and Kong sharing a quiet moment together.

"Kong also had a terrific sense of humor…"

We see Fay recreating the famous scene with Robert Armstrong, where he is making the first screen tests of her aboard the ship. She is wearing a long white dress, and Armstrong is exhorting her to, "Look up, up, now you see it, it's huge, it's horrifying—"

We cut to a wider angle—and we see Kong standing off to one side, watching the take—and making grotesque faces at Fay—

"He used to try to make me break up during a shot."

In the shot, Fay starts giggling, and Kong delightedly slaps his thighs.

"He thought that was great fun. Mr. Schoedsack didn't dare bawl him out for it in front of everybody, but you could tell he was annoyed. I think Kong must have been very lonely at that time. He was always on the set—even on days when he wasn't needed, he was always there. I think he just didn't have any other place to go. And he felt at home on the soundstage. As if we were his only family. I guess I felt sorry for him, at first."

Fay finishes the take and rejoins Kong.

"Later on, I grew to see the nobler qualities of this very misunderstood actor—"

Fay narrates her first meetings with Bruce Cabot, and we see an innocent and charming boy-girl relationship developing between them; it is not serious, but the moment between them is one of those moments so easily misinterpreted—

—-we see Kong entering the soundstage at an inopportune time, and abruptly seeing his co-star spooning with her "other leading man."

Kong's face darkens and he sulks off the set…

In the next take, we see Kong losing his temper and punching down a scaffolding with some natives on it—another one of the famous missing scenes—but now we know why Kong was so mad.

Narration: "We had some trouble in planning the ending of the picture. For one thing, we weren't sure where to stage it…"

We see shots of Kong holding Fay Wray atop a variety of 1933 landmarks: Radio City Music Hall…Grand Central Station…The Chrysler Building…the Statue of Liberty…

"…But none of them seemed to feel right. Finally, someone remembered that the Empire State Building was due to be finished soon, and it was going to be the tallest building in the world. Out of desperation, because we couldn't think of any place else, we decided to stage the ending of the picture there. It seemed like a good idea at the time."

We see the Empire State Building, still uncompleted, Kong climbing it slowly...

Fay Wray narrating: "One of the best kept secrets was that Kong was very much afraid of heights—but there was no other way to shoot some of the scenes for the ending, except to go to the newly completed Empire State Building and actually shoot them there."

We see Kong and Fay Wray on the top of the Empire State Building, makeup men working on both of them, then hurriedly leaving the scene. We see a camera plane circling nearby. An Assistant Director with a radio set signals them for action, and we see a take of the "original" ending of the movie.

"Ann Darrow is on the roof of the Empire State Building, threatening to jump. Kong comes up to the top in an attempt to save her, thus proving he is not a monster at all, but really a very good guy at heart. The closing shot is the two of them watching a tranquil sunrise over 1933 New York, fadeout."

The first take isn't good, however, and while we reset for another take from the camera plane or perhaps a camera dirigible, Kong and Fay Wray talk over their difficulties.

Grunt, grunt.

"Kong, don't you see—we can't go on meeting like this."

Despondent grunt.

"All this sneaking around, hiding from other people—"

Very despondent grunt.

"—your family doesn't like me at all. And there's the religious differences. How would we raise the children? And all the social pressures—and there's another thing—"

Grunt. Grunt. I don't want to hear it.

"—it would mean the end of your career. You know how prejudiced people can be. I don't mind giving up my career, but I can't let you deprive the world of a great talent—"

Kong is very upset. Grunt, grunt, grunt, grunt. He turns away from her.

"Oh, please—don't talk like that. You know you don't mean it."

Grunt. Grunt. I do too.

"Kong, don't you see—it's over. It's bigger than both of—well, it's too big, anyway—"

Kong rages—

In the camera plane, we see the director and cameraman. Cameraman says he's ready, the director says, "Roll 'em."

Back on the tower, Kong is still raging angrily at Fay Wray.

The A. D. calls, "Action," but Kong ignores him, ditto Fay.

"Kong," she says, "I know it's hard, but it has to be this way."

Grunt. Grunt. I can't live without you. And he turns to jump—

"No, don't—"

He turns back to her, reaching, imploring—She reaches for him—

And he loses his balance—

And falls—exactly as we remember him falling in the 1933 original.

Fay screams, horrified. The makeup men and assistant director have to hold her back to keep her from throwing herself off after him. "Oh, god, no—"

Down on the street, we see Robert Armstrong push his way through the crowd…and someone behind him says, "He fell—"

And Armstrong says, "Oh, no. It was beauty killed the beast."

Next to him, an A. D. notes, "Hey, that's a good line."

Fay Wray's voice over narration, continues: "Of course, we had to change the ending of the original picture. Kong was supposed to rescue me, now he dies in the attempt. Mr. Schoedsack used the film they had already exposed, and the wonderful Mr. O'Brien superimposed in all these biplanes, so his experiments with stop-motion animation paid off after all.

"Of course, there were all those terrible rumors that circulated for years afterward that Kong hadn't really died, that his death had been faked, and that he's been living in secret up in Benedict Canyon for all this time—the fact that no one was allowed near his body and that the funeral was very private seemed to prove those claims—but I was there, I loved Kong more than all the millions of his movie fans, I loved him more than anyone, and if he was still alive, I would certainly know it." She is very very wistful. "Even today, so many years later, I still put a wreath on his grave every year."

The angle widens and we see Fay Wray looking very very small and sad and obviously in a great deal of pain because of her memories. "I guess Robert Armstrong was right…I guess, beauty did kill the beast."

As the interview concludes, we hear a car pull up, and a door slam offscreen. Fay says, "Oh, that's my son coming home now."

We hear a familiar heavy footfall, followed by a very familiar grunt. All offscreen.

Fay says, "He's just like his father."

And we fade out.

King Kong:
The Unanswered Questions

THE FIRST SEVENTEEN TIMES I saw King Kong, I didn't worry too much about backstory. I just wanted to see the great ape fighting the giant dinosaurs. It's a terrific adventure and it's a classic fairy tale of the 20th Century—and if I were a literary deconstructionist, which I most assuredly am not, I might even say that it's a metaphor that symbolizes the eternal battle between chaos and order, between man and nature, between beauty and the beast. Nah, at best, it's an allegory about doomed love—about being too big and too hairy and so socially inept that a beautiful movie star screams at the thought of going out with you.

But as much as I loved this marvelous escape from reality, part of me—the eternal analyzer—always insists on asking questions, what I call "refrigerator door" questions. It works like this: You go to the movies and you deliberately suspend disbelief so you can fall into the wide-screen, multi-channel immersion of the grand adventure unfolding before you. Afterward, as you sit with friends at Starbucks, eating and drinking overpriced confections that bear only a passing relationship to coffee and cake—afterward, still enraptured by the post-coital bliss of the experience, you continue to believe you've seen a great movie. It isn't until you finally get home, when you open the refrigerator door, looking for a snack—is there any pizza left, or fried chicken?—that it finally hits you; you were conned. "Hey, if E.T. could fly away at the end of the picture to save himself and Eliot, why didn't he fly at the beginning of the picture?"

Um…he didn't have a bicycle?

No. Because if he had flown away at the beginning, there wouldn't have been a movie.

That's a refrigerator door question. It stops you cold in your tracks, and you stand there pondering it while the salad wilts, the ice cream melts, and the Jell-O starts to sag.

So look, if Anakin Skywalker really was that powerfully tuned into the Force, why didn't he recognize Senator Palpatine as Darth Sidious? Because if he did, there wouldn't have been a movie.

Right.

But there's another kind of refrigerator door question too. How was Indiana Jones able to stay on the deck of the submarine all the way across the ocean—especially without food and water? For that one, we have to assume that the submarine *never* submerged, that it made the whole trip on the surface—and that the trip didn't take more than a day or so. But as easily as the filmmakers skip over that question, so do we—we willingly make the assumption so that we can stay immersed in the story. It is a deliberate deferral of skepticism. Yeah, I know. It's the movies—but why wasn't he severely sunburnt, at least?

So now that we've established context, that we're willing to accept the circumstances of the story, let's leave the refrigerator at home and head off to Skull Island. Max O'Hara clearly knows what to expect. A canoe-load of natives got swept out to sea by a storm; they were picked up by a passing tramp steamer. Conveniently, someone onboard knew enough of their language to draw a map and hear the tale of Kong, some kind of giant ape. And apparently, they weren't the first boatload of natives to escape the island, because the legend is common enough in the region that even Captain Englehorn is familiar with the name Kong.

But how did the natives get to the island in the first place? And where did Kong come from in the grand evolutionary scheme of things?

Consider:

The dinosaurs on the island have clearly been there since the Jurassic era. We don't know how they survived the mass extinction that occurred when a comet slammed into the Yucatan 65 million years ago, but never mind that; the scientific evidence for that particular event only came to light in the past two decades. In 1933, it was assumed that the dinosaurs died off because their babies were too heavy for the pteranodon to deliver. We will also ignore the fact that isolated on this single island, all these various creatures did not seem to evolve beyond their ancient antecedents. Nor did the limited amount of resources to be found on this island stunt their growth. (Although an equally opposite evolutionary case can be made for gigantism.) Etcetera, etcetera.

Let's just accept that the dinosaurs on Skull Island are the real deal, one way or the other. Despite the serious evolutionary pressures of an island existence, they are still recognizably the same creatures as their distant predecessors.

But their existence still raises some fairly obvious ecological issues. How many dinosaurs live on this island? Does the island generate enough biomass to support the herds of herbivores necessary to support a family of predatory T-Rexes? For that matter, how many T-Rexes live here? Are there enough to keep the stegasaurs and apatosaurs in check, so that they don't denude the island's foliage? Or did Kong kill the only one? The last one? Uh-Oh…

The ecology of any island is a fragile system. A continental ecology has much more resilience, a much greater ability to withstand events like hurricanes, volcanoes, and other chaotic surprises. An island, however…well, there are a lot of unanswered questions here. We still end up coming back to the essential one—even if we don't consider the evolutionary issues, how have these dinosaurs managed to sustain themselves for 65 million years?

It's a leap of faith, and we need to make that leap of faith for the story to work. But even after we make that particular leap, the existence of Kong is the greater mystery. How does a 25-foot ape evolve in an ecology dominated by predatory proto-reptiles? For that matter, where's the rest of Kong's family? Apes travel in troops, don't they?

We know from the sequel, Son of Kong, that Kong must have had a mate. Where was she all this time? Where did she come from? Where did she go? Why didn't we see her in the first picture—and if Kong had a wife (and presumably an even more-terrifying mother-in-law), then why the hell was he sneaking off to Skull Mountain for a quickie with Ann Darrow? We know from the visual evidence that he thought she smelled good, he kept sniffing her undies, but we also know that apes are generally monogamous—is Kong experiencing lust in his heart? Is he committing virtual adultery with Ms. Darrow?

But for the sake of this discussion, let's stick solely to what we can observe in the first picture, and ignore the issue of Kong's issue. Let's assume he's single, possibly the ape equivalent of a nerd, unable to get a date on Saturday night, unless she's chained to a pedestal outside the native village. But even in that case, we still have to ask, where are the rest of the giant apes? If they're not living up in the eye of Skull Mountain, have they already been eaten by the dinosaurs below? Is Kong the last of his kind? If so, does he qualify as an endangered species? It would certainly explain his crankiness as well as his hunger for female companionship. And if Kong is the last of his kind, then Carl Denham and crew are eco-criminals, aren't they? Knowing that they're destroying a fragile island ecology, it's hard to feel sympathy for them when they fall into the spider pit, isn't it?

But even after we ignore all these questions, so we can accept the existence of dinosaurs and giant apes on Skull Island, the continuing presence of the natives has to be questioned. Are these people stupid—*or what?*

It's fairly obvious how the natives must have arrived at Skull Island. The entire south sea area was originally colonized by waves of migrants who started out from the eastern coast of Asia at least ten thousand years ago; island after island—Tahiti, Hawaii, Fiji, and so on. So the question isn't how the natives got to Skull Island; the question is how they survived.

At some point in the past, let's say a thousand years ago, some exploratory canoes landed here—on an island filled with predatory dinosaurs and the ancestors of a 25-foot gorilla. Assuming that these folks were stupid enough to stay—or so desperate that they thought this was a better alternative than putting back out to sea—how do they survive long enough to build a village *and* a thousand-foot wall to separate themselves from the monsters on the island?

Let's think about that wall for a minute—if these natives know how big Kong is, if they know how ferocious he is, if they know about his morbid appetites, then just why the hell did they put a door in that wall big enough for him to come busting through? What's that about? Some kind of a cultural death wish?

And was building a thousand-foot wall really easier then getting back in their canoes and paddling away as fast as possible? What was so important that it justified staying? Or maybe the smart ones fled and the folks still on the island are the descendants of the people too stupid to leave?

How did these people develop such a weird relationship with Kong anyway? He lives way the hell on the other side of the island, up on Skull Mountain. For that matter, why does he live up there? Most apes prefer forests. And why does Kong like to eat native girls? Obviously, he considers them a treat—the ringing of a giant gong is his dinner bell. And for that matter, where did the giant gong come from? These natives don't seem to have a lot of metallurgy skills, do they? And we don't find gongs anywhere else in the south seas, so it's unlikely that they brought it with them. They had to manufacture it locally—how?

And what about those natives?

They are apparently sacrificing a beautiful young maiden to Kong on a regular basis. Once a month? That's 12 girls a year. Now maybe they have an overabundance of beautiful young maidens on their side of the wall, enough so that they can hold regular sacrifices at every full moon, but it seems to me that's a good way to deplete the population in a very short time—and do significant long-term damage to the gene pool. If only beautiful girls get sacrificed, pretty soon the only ones left to have babies will be ugly girls, and in a very short time, a matter of twenty generations or so, everyone on the island will be ugly and there will be no more beautiful maidens for Kong anywhere. Or does he even care about physical beauty? We're talking down-the-hatch, sweety.

Maybe the sacrifices are limited to once a year? Every year, we give Kong a new bride and he leaves us alone for the next twelve months. Except, judging by the way Kong treats the rest of the natives, it's unlikely that his brides last a whole year.

Regardless of the timing of the sacrifices, it's apparent that the locals have some very mixed feelings about their relationship with their deity. They respect Kong, obviously. They fear Kong, obviously. They sacrifice maidens to appease him, obviously—but the way they scramble up to the top of the wall to watch him with Ann Darrow…well, there's a certain amount of morbidly curious, prurient interest going on here as well. Possibly because they don't have freeways, they have no place to slow down to gawk at every roadside accident. This is their local celebration of violence and brutality.

So I'm betting that the virginal (another assumption on my part) sacrifices are the local equivalent of a football or soccer or any other violent sporting event. It's the Roman circus, without Romans, lions or Christians. It's great fun for everyone—except the virgin, of course. (That the whole south sea island region is not healthy for virgins has long been known. Tourists are now advised that they must bring their own virgins to throw into local volcanoes.)

Moving on…

How does Carl Denham get Kong back to New York? The crew builds a raft, they float Kong out to the ship, they use a crane to lift him off the raft and lower him into the cargo hold. Then what? What do they feed him? And how much? Who cleans up after him? Does somebody go in with a shovel to clean up the giant gorilla turds? A new somebody every day? Or do they just hose the waste away? That's probably the safest way to handle the mess. But what does Kong think about all this?

We know that Kong has a temper. We know that he will break down walls to get to Ann Darrow—is he really going to sit docilely in the bottom of the ship's hold? Or is he going to get really really really pissed off?

None of these questions are ever really addressed—we just cut quickly to a glittering sign that advertises "King Kong, The Eighth Wonder of the World." The assumption here is that somehow all these separate issues have been resolved. At least well enough to get us all to Broadway. Just like the business of Indiana Jones' submarine ride, Kong's long sea journey is also skipped over in the blithe assumption that you're so eager to get to the next part of the story that you won't stop to ask, "Hey, wait a minute—what about E.T.'s bicycle?"

But clearly, Kong's captors have treated him well on the journey—although he was only 18 feet high on Skull Island, by the time he gets to Manhattan, he's had a growth spurt; he's now 25 feet high. But that all happened off screen, because we don't see a lot of evidence that he's being treated like a King.

Let's step away from Kong for a moment and talk about another giant ape…Mighty Joe Young. Mr. Joseph Young, not quite as big as Kong, but with a much more appealing personality, leaves Africa for a career in show business. Because this was before the formation of People for the Ethical Treatment of Animals, Joe is kept in a small cage backstage at the nightclub where he performs. From his point of view, he's not in Hollywood to experience the bright lights and the big city—he's in prison. To say that he's not happy is an understatement; but he's got a big heart, spiritually as well as physically. And so we open our hearts to his plight and cheer his escape. Unlike Kong, Joe does not tear up the town, he rescues orphans from a burning building. Even more reason to admire his great spirit. (God knows what the orphan thinks about this particular rescue—if you had just climbed out the window of a burning building, would you regard the sudden appearance of a giant ape as an agent of salvation? Yeah, right. People have died of fright in much saner circumstances.)

Back to Kong. We don't see Kong backstage in his dressing room at the Broadway theater; but if you've ever been backstage at a Broadway theater, then you know there's not a lot of room backstage—certainly not enough to house a giant 25-foot gorilla. Ohell, there's barely enough room for the average diva. Although more than one producer has fantasized about putting his divas in cages instead of installing them in dressing rooms, gorillas probably look easier to manage, which may go a long way explaining Carl Denham's obsessive need to bring Kong to Manhattan.

Never mind. The point is that once we get back to New York, we see no respect for Kong's personal welfare. No one seems to care about the giant ape's well-being. We see no cage, no food, no water, and certainly no facilities for cleaning up after him. Just how much urine can his bladder hold anyway? Backstage must smell horrible! Possibly even the first three rows of the theater as well. (Have you ever seen what an angry chimpanzee can do with a handful of feces?)

What we see is Kong strapped helplessly to a cross; his arms and legs manacled, he's trapped in a grotesque parody of Christ's torment. Well, yes. This is a fairy tale, a metaphor, a movie. We're not interested in the nuts and bolts. We don't care why E.T. didn't fly away and why Anakin Skywalker is such an ignorant lout. We're in a hurry to get to the good stuff. We want to see Kong smashing an elevated train or climbing the Empire State Building. We're not worried about who shovels the gorilla shit, so we don't ask how they move Kong back and forth from cage to stage and back again to cage. Obviously Carl Denham hasn't thought about it. He's designed his show to fail. No wonder nobody wants to invest in his adventures anymore.

Of course, Kong breaks free. There are no engineers in Manhattan smart enough or foresighted enough to stress-test the steel manacles and ensure that they would be strong enough to withstand the strength of an enraged giant ape. No—just like Jurassic Park was designed to fail (that's another rant), Kong's escape is equally inevitable.

In 1933, there were probably five or six million people in the greater New York area. Nevertheless, Kong is able to find Ann Darrow with little or no difficulty. Okay, he steps on a few cars, bites the head off a cop or two, yanks a woman out of bed and drops her to her death twenty stories below, but those are just youthful indiscretions, no worse than the hijinks of the average congressman. But Kong must have one incredible sense of smell to find Ann Darrow so easily in the heart of midtown Manhattan, just a few blocks from Broadway—especially with all those odiferous delicatessens and pungent hot dog stands in the neighborhood.

To be fair to Kong, he probably does have an incredible sense of smell—after all, he's got a bigger nose than Pinocchio testifying under oath. And while Kong has Ann Darrow up on Skull Mountain, he does spend a lot of time sniffing her lingerie. Is Kong a panty fetishist? Hmm, maybe that's the source of his obsession.

Or maybe, Kong is female—that would go a long way toward explaining the existence of the Son of Kong in the sequel of the same name. But if that's the case, then Kong isn't King, she's Queen—a lesbian, the ultimate bull dyke. (See how one fact can change your whole point of view? Don't make assumptions.)

Meanwhile, after retrieving Ann Darrow from Jack Driscoll (who obviously isn't man enough to protect her from a giant rampaging gorilla), Kong heads toward the Empire State Building, the highest point on the island. Now, here's the *real* refrigerator door question to think about. All those others were just warm-ups. How does Kong climb the side of the building with Ann Darrow in one hand? Think about it…

If he has her in one hand, then he can't grip the building with that hand, can he? If he lets go with his other hand so he can reach higher, that's right—he falls down. But we clearly see him climbing. Did he hold Ann Darrow between his teeth? Did he put her on top of his head or on one of his broad shoulders? We don't see that. When they arrive at the top, she's still in his hand. Hmm. It's E.T.'s bicycle all over again.

But it is here, at the top of the Empire State Building that the movie works its real magic—the transmogrification of Kong from beast into tragically doomed hero.

For most of the picture, Kong has been the enemy—something to fear. He's been obsessed with Ann Darrow; he only broke free of his chains when he thought she was being attacked; then he raged through the streets of Manhattan in search of her. But abruptly, now, here, at the top of the Empire State Building, mortally wounded by the airplanes, we see the great beast demonstrate his true feelings. He doesn't want Ann Darrow hurt. He checks to see that she is safe, then tragically falls to his death.

Does he hit anything? Or anyone? It's a safe bet that he does. The streets of New York are narrow and always crowded. There's no need for New Yorkers to gather in a crowd, they're already in one. Drop a 25-foot gorilla from the sky anywhere in Manhattan and you're likely to take out 30 or 40 people. Probably more with the splatter.

And finally, who removes Kong's dead body? And how do they do it? This is going to require cranes, bulldozers, and teams of guys operating chain saws. And how long is it going to take? I'm assuming that Kong smelled pretty ripe when he was alive—how bad is he going to smell three days after he's dead? What's that going to do to the property values in the neighborhood of 34th street?

And if Carl Denham is still obsessed with his dreams of Broadway, he isn't going to let anyone dispose of Kong's body so easily. He's going to hire a small army of taxidermists and have Kong stuffed and put on display somewhere.

Finally, it's time for the killer question. What about the lawyers? If you thought the dinosaurs on Skull Island were rapacious, you haven't seen a pack of Manhattan raptors in action. We're talking *very* bad news. There will be subpoenas for everyone and anyone. The city will sue Denham, Denham will sue the people who made the manacles that failed, the elevated train company will sue Denham, Denham will sue the makers of his gas bombs, the theater owners will sue Denham, Denham will counter-sue the theater owners, the owners of the Empire State building will sue for the bullet damage, Ann Darrow will sue for emotional distress, the families of those who died will sue Denham *and* the city, the owners of every piece of property that got smashed or squashed will sue Denham and the city, the insurance companies will sue everyone just to be safe. The courts will be asked to rule the whole event an act of God, so as to let everybody off the hook. The legal proceedings will last until December 7, 1941, when everyone's attention will be distracted by other matters.

Now do you see why I'm the wrong person to take to the movies?

AUTHOR'S AFTERWORD:

Tonight on Channel 9: **King Kong (movie).** *In search of true love, confused island boy tears up the town.*

Mike Resnick called and asked me to contribute a story for an anthology he was planning, called Alternate Kennedys. *Each story would suggest a different alternate history for the Kennedy family. He wanted me to write a story about what would have happened if Joe Kennedy had divorced Rose, married Gloria Swanson, moved to Hollywood, and gotten involved in the movie industry. Aside from the inherent tackiness of the whole concept, there wasn't much there that appealed to me, and the whole thing lay dormant in my consciousness like an unfertilized egg until about two days before the deadline. Then, one night—why does it always have to be in the middle of the night?!—it hit me. JFK's presidency was one of the defining moments of the sixties. What else defined the sixties...? (Other than the Beatles, Vietnam, and tie-dyed T-shirts?) Right.*

What we remember of Kennedy are not the mistakes, but the aspirations. Not the missteps, but the goals.

Satire is a lousy vehicle for idealism—but what the hell, whatever it takes.

The Kennedy Enterprise

—IS THAT THING ON? Good. Okay, go ahead. What do you want to know?

Kennedy, huh? Why is it always Kennedy? All this nostalgia for the fifties and the sixties. You guys are missing the point. There were so many better actors, and nobody remembers them anymore. That's the real crime—that Kennedy should get all the attention—but the guys who made him look so good are all passed over and forgotten. Why don't you jackals ever come around asking whatever happened to Bill Shatner or Jeffrey Hunter—?

Ahhh, besides, Kennedy's been done to death. Everybody does Kennedy. Because he's easy to do. But lemme tell you something, sonny. Kennedy wasn't really the sixties—uh uh. He's just a convenient symbol. The sixties were a lot bigger than just another fading TV star.

Yeah, that's right. His glory days were over. He was on his way out. You're surprised to hear that, aren't you?

Look. I'll tell you something. Kennedy was not a good actor. In fact, he was goddamn lousy. He couldn't act his way out of a pay toilet if he'd had Charlton Heston in there to help him.

But—it didn't matter, did it? Hell, acting ability is the *last* thing in the world a movie star needs. It never slowed down whatsisname, Ronald Reagan.

Reagan? Oh, you wouldn't remember him. He was way before your time. He was sort of like a right-wing Henry Fonda, only he never got the kind of parts where he could inspire an audience. That's what you need to make it—one good part where you make the audience squirm or cry or leap from their seats, shouting. Anything to make them remember you longer than the time it takes to get out to the parking lot. But Reagan never really got any of those. He was just another poor schmuck eaten up by the system. A very sad story, really.

Yeah, I know. You want to hear about Kennedy. Uh-uh. Lemme tell you about Reagan first. So you'll see how easy it is to just disappear— and how much of a fluke it is to succeed.

See, Reagan wasn't stupid. He was one of the few wartime actors who actually made a successful transition into television. He was smart enough to be a host instead of a star—that way he didn't get himself typecast as a cowboy or a detective or a doctor. Reagan was a pretty good pitchman for General Electric on their Sunday night show and then—wait a minute, lemme see now, sometime in there, he got himself elected president of the Screen Actors Guild and that's when all the trouble started—there was some uproar with the House Committee on UnAmerican Activities, and the blacklist and the way he sold out his colleagues. I don't really know the details, you can look it up. Anyway, tempers were hot, that's all you need to know, and Reagan got himself impeached, almost thrown out of his own Guild as a result.

Well, nobody wanted to work with him after that. His name was mud. He couldn't get arrested. And it was just tragic—'cause he was good, no question about it. Those pictures he did with the monkey were hysterical—oh, yeah, he did a whole series of movies at the end of the war. *Bonzo Goes To College, Bonzo Goes To Hollywood, Bonzo Goes To Washington.* Yeah, everybody remembers the chimpanzee, nobody remembers Reagan. Yeah, people in this town only have long memories when there's a grudge attached.

So, Reagan couldn't get work. I mean, not real work. He ended up making B-movies. A lot of crap. Stuff even Harry Cohn wouldn't touch. He must have really needed the money. The fifties were all downhill for him.

I remember, he did—oh, what was it?—*Queen of Outer Space* with that Hungarian broad. That was a real waste of film. Then he did some stuff with Ed Wood, remember him? Yeah, that's the one. Anyway, Ronnie's last picture was some piece of *dreck* called *Plan Nine From Outer Space.* Lugosi was supposed to do the part, but he died just before they started filming, so Reagan stepped in. I hear it's real big on the college circuits now. What they call camp, where it's so bad, it's funny. Have you seen it? No, neither have I. Too bad, really. No telling what Reagan could have become if he'd just had the right breaks.

Oh, right—you want to talk about Kennedy. But you get my point, don't you? This is a sorry excuse for an industry. There's no *sympatico,* no consideration. Talent is considered a commodity. It gets wasted. People get chewed up just because they're in someone else's way. That's the real story behind Kennedy—the people who got chewed up along the way.

Anyway, what was I saying about Kennedy before I got off the track? You wanna run that thing back? Oh, that's right. Kennedy had no talent. Yeah, you can quote me—what difference does it make? Somebody going to sue me? What're they going to get? My wheelchair? I'll say it again. Kennedy had no talent for acting. Zero. Zilch. *Nada.* What he did have was a considerable talent for self-promotion. He was *great* at that.

And y'know what else? Y'know what else Kennedy had? He had *style.* You don't need talent if you've got style. Mae West proved that. Gable proved that. Bette Davis.

Funny business, movies, television. Any other industry run the same way would go straight into the ground. A movie studio—you make one success, it pays for twenty flops. You have to be crazy to stay with it, y'know.

Okay, okay—back to Kennedy. Well, y'know, to really understand him, you gotta understand his dad. Joe Kennedy was one ambitious son of a bitch. He was smart enough to get his money out of the stock market before '29. He put it into real estate. When everybody else was jumping out of windows, he was picking up pieces all over the place.

He got very active in politics for a while. FDR wanted to send him to England as an ambassador, but the deal fell through—nobody knows why. Maybe his divorce, who knows? Y'know, the Kennedys were Irish-Catholic. It would have been a big scandal. Especially then.

Anyway, it doesn't matter. The story really starts when Joe Sr. brings his boys out to California. He marries Gloria Swanson and starts buying up property and studios and contracts. Next thing you know, his boys are all over the place. They come popping out of USC, one after the other, like Ford Mustangs rolling off an assembly line.

In no time, Joe's a director, Jack's taken up acting, and Bobby ends up running MGM. It's Thalberg all over again. Lemme think. That had to be '55 or '56, somewhere in there. Actually, Teddy was the smart one. He stayed out of the business. He went East, stayed home with his mom, and eventually went into politics where nobody ever heard of him again.

Anyway, you could see that Joe and Bobby were going to make out all right. They were all sonsabitches, but they were good sonsabitches. Joe did his homework, he brought in his pictures on time. Bobby was a ruthless S.O.B., but maybe that's what you need to run a studio. He didn't take any shit from anybody. Remember, he's the guy who told Garland to get it together or get out. And she *did*.

But Jack—Jack was always a problem. Two problems actually.

First of all, he couldn't keep his dick in his pants. Bobby had his hands full keeping the scandal-rags away from his brother. He had to buy off one columnist; he gave him the Rock Hudson story. The jackals had such a good time with that one they forgot all about Jack's little peccadillos in Palm Springs. Sometimes I think Bobby would have killed to protect his brother. Y'know, Hudson lost the lead in *Giant* because of that. They'd already shot two or three weeks of good footage. They junked it all. Nearly shit-canned the whole picture, but Heston jumped in at the last moment and ended up beating out the Dean kid for the Oscar. Like I said, it's a strange business. *Stupid* business.

Sometimes you end up hating the audience for just being the audience. It's not fair, when you think about it. The public wants their heroes to look like they're dashing and romantic and sexy—but they're horrified if they actually behave that way. I mean, could *your* private life stand up to that kind of scrutiny? I'm not sure anybody's could. Hell, the goddamn audience punishes the stars for doing the exact same things they're doing—cheating on their wives, drinking too much, smoking a little weed. If they're going to insist on morality tests for the actors, I think we should start insisting on morality tests for the audience before we let them in the theater. See how they'd like it for a change.

Oh well.

Anyway, the *other* problem was Jack's accent—that goddamn Massachusetts accent. He'd have made a great cowboy, he had the look, he had the build; but he couldn't open his mouth without sounding like a New England lobsterman. I mean, can you imagine Jack Kennedy on a horse or behind a badge—with *that* accent? They brought in the best speech coaches in the world to work with him. A waste of goddamn money. He ended up sounding like Cary Grant with a sinus problem.

You can't believe the parts he didn't get because of his voice. Y'know, at one point Twentieth wanted him for *The Misfits* with Marilyn Monroe—now, that would have been a picture. Can you imagine

Kennedy and Monroe? Pure screen magic. But it never happened. His voice again. No, as far as I know, they never even met.

But that was always the problem. Finding the right picture for Jack. George Pal, the Puppetoon guy, gave him his first big break with *War of the Worlds* over at Paramount, but Jack always hated science fiction. Afraid he'd get typecast. He saw what happened to Karloff and Lugosi. He thought of science fiction as the same kind of stuff.

The funny thing was, the picture was a big hit, but that only made Jack unhappier. He knew the audience had come to see the Martians, not him. That's when he swore, no more science fiction. And yeah, he really did say it, that famous quote: "Never play a scene with animals, children, or Martians. They always use the Martian's best take."

Hitchcock had a good sense of how to use Kennedy, but he only worked with him once. *North by Northwest.* Another big hit. Kennedy loved the film—he loved all that spy stuff, he always wanted to play James Bond—but he didn't like the way Hitchcock treated him. And he made the mistake of saying so to an interviewer. Remember? "Hitch doesn't direct. He herds. He treats his actors like cattle." That remark got back to Hitch, and the old man was terribly hurt by it. So, instead of casting Jack in his next film, he went to Jimmy Stewart. Who knows? Maybe that was best for everybody.

Jack spent nine months sitting on his ass, waiting for the right part. Nothing. Finally, he went to Bobby and said, "Help me get some of the good parts." By now, Bobby was running MGM, and this gave him control over one studio and a lot of bargaining power with all the others—he was the biggest deal-maker in town, buying, selling, trading contracts right and left to put together the right package.

Even so, Bobby still had to twist a lot of arms to get Jack into *The Caine Mutiny.* Van Johnson had already been screen-tested. He'd been fitted for his costumes, everything—suddenly, he's out on his ass and here's Jack Kennedy playing opposite Bogart. I can tell you, a lot of feathers were ruffled. Bogey knew how Jack got the part and he never forgave him for it. But, y'know—it helped the picture. Bogey's resentment of Jack shows up on the screen in every scene. Bogey should have had the Oscar for that one, but Bobby bought it for Jack. There was so much studio pressure on the voting—well, never mind. That's a body best left buried.

Anyway, in return, Bobby asked Jack to help him out with one or two of his problems. And Jack had no choice, but to say yes. See, when Bobby took over MGM, one of the projects about to shoot was a thing called *Forbidden Planet.* Shakespeare in outer space. Dumb idea, right? That's what everybody thought, at the time. They couldn't cast it.

They were having real trouble finding a male lead, and they were about to go with...oh, let me think. Oh, I don't remember his name. He ended up doing a cop show on ABC. Oh, here's a funny. At one point, they were even considering Ronald Reagan for the lead. Very strongly. But they finally passed on him—I guess Bobby remembered the McCarthy business. And that's why Reagan went and did *Queen of Outer Space*. Never mind, it doesn't matter. Bobby finally asked Jack to play the Captain of the spaceship.

And I gotta tell you. Jack didn't want to do it—more of that science fiction crap, right?—but he couldn't very well say no, could he? So he goes ahead and does it. Bobby retitles the picture *The New Frontier*. And guess what? It's the studio's biggest grossing picture for the year. Go figure. But everybody's happy.

After that, Jack had a couple of rough years. One disaster after another. The biggest one was that goddamned musical. That was an embarrassment. The man should never have tried to sing. Even today, nobody can mention *Camelot* without thinking of Jack Kennedy, right? And those stupid tights.

You want my opinion, stay out of tights. Your career will never recover. It was all downhill for Errol Flynn after *Robin Hood* and the goddamned tights killed poor George Reeves. *Superman*'s another one of those unproduceable properties. Nobody's ever going to make that one work. Or *Batman*. Tights. That's why.

Anyway, back to Kennedy—his career was in the dumper. So, when he was offered the chance to do a TV series, it didn't look so bad any more. Most of the real action in town was moving to TV anyway. So Jack went over to Desilu and played Eliot Ness in *The Untouchables*. Y'know, that was one of J. Edgar Hoover's favorite shows. Hoover even wrote to Kennedy and asked him for his autograph. He visited the set once just so he could get his picture taken with Jack. Hoover had to stand on a box. They shot him from the waist up, so's you'd never know, but the photographer managed to get one good long shot.

Meanwhile, back over at MGM, Bobby's looking at all the money that Warner Brothers and Desilu are making off TV and he's thinking—there's gotta be a way that he can cut himself a slice of that market, right? Right. So he starts looking around the lot to see what he's got that can be exploited.

Well, *Father Knows Best* is a big hit, so Bobby thinks, "Let's try turning *Andy Hardy* into a TV series. And how about *Dr. Kildare* too? The Hardy thing flopped. Bad casting. And it was opposite Disney on Sundays. It didn't have a chance. But the Kildare property caught well enough to encourage him to try again.

So, Bobby Kennedy's looking around, right? And here's where all the pieces come together all at once. NBC says to him, "How about a science fiction series? You did that *New Frontier* thing. Why don't you turn that into a TV series for us?"

There's this other series that's just winding down—a war series called *The Lieutenant*—Bobby calls in the producer, a guy named Roddenberry and tells him that NBC wants a sci-fi show based on *The New Frontier.* Can he make it work? They've still got all the costumes, the sets, the miniatures, everything. Roddenberry says he doesn't know anything about science fiction, but he'll give it a try. He tells his secretary to rush out and buy up every science fiction anthology she can find and do summaries of all the stories that have spaceships in them.

What with one thing and another, it's 1964 before they ever start filming the first pilot. But all the MGM magic is applied, and they end up with one of the most beautiful—and most *expensive*—TV pilots ever made. Of course, Roddenberry put in all his own ideas, and by the time he was through, the only thing left from the movie was in the opening lines of the title sequence: "Space, the new frontier. These are the voyages…etcetera, etcetera."

NBC hated the pilot—they said it was "too cerebral"—but they liked the look of the show, so they say to Bobby, let's try again, give us another pilot. Bobby says no. Take it or leave it. MGM bails out, so Roddenberry goes over to Desilu, where they make a second pilot. He changes the name to *Star Track,* and the show goes on the air in 1966. You know the rest.

Two years later, MGM buys Desilu. Bobby Kennedy strong-arms NBC to move the show to an 8:00 time slot, and it's a big hit. But then, to settle some old grudge—Bobby hated being wrong—he fires Roddenberry. The rumor mill said it was women—maybe. I don't know and I'm not going to speculate. Dorothy Fontana takes over as producer, and surprise, the show just gets better. Meanwhile, *The Untouchables* gets cancelled and Jack Kennedy is out of work again.

The timing was everything here. See, Shatner and Nimoy were feuding. Not only feuding, they were counting each other's lines. Nimoy threatens to quit. Shatner does too. They're both demanding the same thing: "Whatever he gets, I get."

Bobby agrees and fires both of them. He starts looking around for a new Captain.

He doesn't have to look very far.

In hindsight, yes. It was the perfect decision. John F. Kennedy as Captain Jack Logan of the starship *Enterprise.* The man was perfect. Who wouldn't want to serve under him? But—at the time, who knew?

It sounded crazy. Here's this old fart who's career is clearly fading fast—why cast him in *Star Track?*

And Jack didn't want to do it. By now, he hated science fiction so much, he once took a poke at Harlan Ellison at the Emmy Awards. He didn't understand it. He had to have it explained to him. Once, he even called down to the research department and asked, "Just where is this planet Vulcan, anyway?"

And that was the other thing—Jack had already seen how Shatner got upstaged by the Vulcan. To him, it was the goddamn Martians all over again. The man was almost fifty—he looked great, but he was terrified of becoming a has-been, of ending up like Ronald Reagan.

But Bobby had a vision. He was good at that stuff. He promised to restructure the show in Jack's favor. Jack agreed—very reluctantly—to listen. That's enough for Bobby. He calls in the staff of the show and says my brother wants to be Captain. "Make it so."

I gotta tell you. That was not a happy meeting. I'd just come aboard as story editor, so I just sat there and kept my mouth shut. Harlan argued a little, but his heart wasn't in it. Maybe he was afraid he'd get punched again. He didn't like the Kennedys very much. Dorothy did most of the talking for us—but Bobby didn't want to hear. He listened, maybe he just pretended to listen, but when everything had been said, he just answered, "Do it my way." We were not happy when we left.

For about three days, we were pissed as hell, because we'd finally gotten the show settled into a good solid working formula, and then suddenly—*poof!*—Roddenberry, Nimoy, and Shatner are gone, and Bobby Kennedy is giving orders. But then it sort of hit us all at the same time. Hey, this is an opportunity to reinvent *Star Track.* So we made a list of all the shit that bothered us—like the Captain always having to get the girl, the Captain always beaming down to the planet, that kind of stuff, and we started thinking about ways to fix it.

We knew Jack couldn't do the action stuff believably. He was already gray at the temples, and his back problems were legendary on the set of *The Untouchables,* so we knew we were going to have to introduce a younger second lead to pick up the action. That's where the Mission Team came from. So Jack wouldn't have to do it.

We really had no choice. Jack had to be an older, more thoughtful Captain who stayed on the ship and monitored the missions by remote control. The Mission Team would be headed by the First Officer. But this was perfect because it kept the Captain in command at all times, and it also made it impossible for the First Officer to become a sidekick, or a partner. Jack would be the undeniable star.

We also figured we'd just about milked the Vulcan idea to death, so we eighty-sixed the whole Vulcan species and brought in an android to take Spock's place as science officer. The android would be curious about humanity—kind of like an updated Pinocchio. The opposite of Spock; he *wants* to be human.

Just as we were starting to get excited about the possibilities of the new format, Jack suggested adding families to the crew of the starship to attract a family audience. Maybe the android's best friend could be a teen-age computer genius...the kids would *love* that. We ended up calling the android REM—it means Rapid-Eye-Movement—and casting Donald Pleasance. Billy Mumy came aboard as Dr. McCoy's grandson, Wesley.

To be fair, Pleasance made the whole android thing work, but none of us ever really *liked* the idea very much. We tried arguing against it, but who ever listens to the writer's opinion? Whatever Jack wanted, Jack got. Bobby made sure of that. So, there we were—lost in space with Jack Kennedy.

And then...to make it even worse, Jack started reviewing outlines, sending us memos about what Jack Logan would or wouldn't do. Clearly, he was having trouble telling the difference between the character and the actor who played him. Jack killed a lot of good ideas. I had one where these little furballs started breeding like crazy—kind of like the rabbits in Australia? Dorothy thought it had a lot of whimsy. Everybody liked it. But Jack killed it. He said it made Logan look foolish. He didn't want to look foolish, said it wasn't right for his image.

His *image?* Give me a break. It doesn't matter much now, though, does it? He's got the best image of all. He's an *icon.*

Harlan quit the show first—which surprised all of us, because he was always the most patient and even-tempered of human beings. Y'know, he did that *est* thing and just mellowed out like a big pink pussycat. Ted Sturgeon used to come to him for advice.

Dorothy quit three months after Harlan. I tried to stick it out, but it wasn't any fun without them. I didn't get along with the new producer, and I finally tossed in the towel too.

The worst part of it, I guess, was that after we left, the ratings went up. It was pretty disheartening. I mean, talk about a pie in the face.

What happened to the original crew? I thought you'd never ask.

Roddenberry went over to Warners and worked for a while on *Wagon Train: The Next Generation.* Shatner showed up in a couple of guest spots, then landed the lead in a cop show; when he lost his hair, he took up directing—I hear he's pretty good at it. Nimoy, of course, gave up show business and ran for office. He's been a good governor; I guess he'll run for the Presidency. Walter Cronkite called him one of the ten most trusted men in America.

Dorothy was head of new projects at Twentieth for a while, then she started up her own production company. Harlan moved to Scotland.

And me—well, my troubles were in all the newspapers, so I don't have to rehash them here, do I? But I'm doing a lot better these days, and I might even take up writing again. If I can figure out how to use a computer. Those things confuse me.

You don't need me to tell you anything else about *Star Track,* do you? You can get the rest of it from the newspapers.

Yeah, I was there when it happened. We all were. I was as close to Jack as I am to you.

I dunno, I guess none of us realized what a zoo a *Star Track* convention could be. Not then, anyway. It was still early in the phenomenon.

I mean, we had no idea what kind of impact the show had made on the fans. We thought there might be a couple hundred people there. You know how big the crowd was? Nobody does. The news said there were fifteen thousand inside the hotel. We had no idea now many more were waiting outside.

We just didn't know how seriously the fans took the show. Of course, the Ambassador Hotel was never the same afterwards.

Anyway, Harlan was there, so was Dorothy. Gene came by, but he didn't stay very long. I think he felt disgraced. And of course, all the actors. De, Jimmy, Grace, Nichelle, Walter, George, Majel, Bruce, Mark, Leonard, Bill—all the also-rans, as they were calling themselves by then. I guess Bobby had put the screws on. Attend or else. There wasn't a lot of good feeling—at least, not at first.

But then the fans started applauding. One after the other, we all went out and chatted and answered questions, and the excitement just grew and grew and grew.

Of course, when Jack came out, the place went wild. It was like election night. There were people there wearing KENNEDY FOR PRESIDENT buttons. Like he was really the character he played. They loved him. And he loved being loved. Whatever else you might say about Jack Kennedy, he knew how to make love to an audience. Style and grace. That was Jack all over.

Y'know, I saw the Beatles at the Hollywood Bowl. All three concerts. And I never saw that kind of hysteria, not even when Ringo threw jellybeans at the audience. But the Trackers—I thought they were going to scream the walls down.

Jack was glowing. His wife had just turned to him and whispered, "Well, you can't say they don't love you now—" when it happened.

At first, I thought it was a car backfiring. It didn't sound like a gunshot at all. In fact, most people were puzzled at the sound. It all happened so fast. Then Jack grabbed his throat, and I guess for a second, we all thought he was joking. Y'know how you do: "Augh, they got me—"

But he had this real stupid look on his face—confused, like. Then the second and third shots went off—and it was the third shot that killed him. And that's when the screaming started. And the panic. All those people injured and killed, suffocated in the crush. It was terrible. Everybody running. I can still see it. I still get nightmares.

I've always been amazed they caught the little bastard who did it. Sirhan Sirhan. I'll never forget his name. Another one of those nerdy little geeks who never had a life of his own. He lived inside the TV. He thought it was real. Half a dozen of those really big women we see at all the conventions just jumped the poor son of a bitch and flattened him. They were outraged that someone would dare to attack *their* Captain. Sirhan was lucky to escape with his balls still attached.

Y'know, later some of the witnesses said that Sirhan kept yelling, "Wait, wait—I can explain!" Like you can explain a thing like that? It didn't make any sense then. It doesn't make any sense now, no matter how many articles William F. Buckley and Norman Mailer and Tom Wolfe write about it.

You know what it was? Sirhan never forgave us for replacing Kirk and Spock with Logan and REM. He said we'd ruined the whole show.

But that's not even the half of it. You want to know the rest of the cosmic joke? Bugliosi, the District Attorney, told me later on. Sirhan was aiming at Bobby and missed. Three times! Bobby was standing just behind Jack, but that kid couldn't shoot worth shit. I think if he'd have hit Bobby, the industry would have given him a medal. Instead, he got the gas chamber and a movie of the week.

But now—y'know, I think back on it, and I see how stupid we all were. We didn't know the power of television. None of us did. We didn't even suspect.

Jack knew, I think. Bobby knew for sure. He knew that you could change the way people think and feel and vote just by what you put on the screen. Bobby knew that. He had the vision. But he was never the same after that. How could you be? The whole thing scared the hell out of all of us—the whole industry. NBC cancelled the show, but they couldn't cancel the nightmares.

Y'ask me, I think that was the turning point in the sixties—the killing of Kennedy. That's when it all started going bad. That's when we all went crazy and started tearing things down. But, oh, hell—that's old news. Everybody knows it.

Now, we've got the Kennedy mystique and *Star Track: The New Voyages*. And…it's all shit. It's just…so much merchandise. Whatever might have been true or meaningful or wonderful about *Star Track* is gone. It's all been eaten up by the lawyers and the fans and the publicity department.

Don't take this personally, but I don't trust anybody under thirty. I don't think any of you understand what happened then. It was special. We didn't understand it ourselves, but we knew it was special.

See…it's like this. Space isn't the new frontier. It never was.

What is the new frontier? You have to ask—? That proves my point. You're looking in the wrong place. The new frontier isn't out there. It's in here. In the heart. It's in us. Dorothy said it. If it's not in here, it's not anywhere.

Ahh—you know what, you're going to go out of here, you're going to write another one of those goddamn golden geezer articles. You'll miss the whole point, just like all the others. Shut that damn thing off and get the hell out of here before I whack you with my cane. Nurse! Nurse—!

AUTHOR'S AFTERWORD:

This was the first story that I wrote with myself as the putative narrator. Okay, it's an alternate version of me, living in a different universe, but it's still me—cranky, curmudgeonly, and able to beat up tall nursing aides with a wooden cane. It was such a useful writing voice that I've returned to it several times since.

There is a real Chester. There's not much of him, but he's almost like having a real dog. Soaking wet, he might weigh eight pounds. The punch line for the story occurred to me first. It wasn't until I finished writing the story that I realized the punch line wasn't funny—it was terrifying. And the more I thought about it, the scarier it got.

Chester

AFTER THE ACCIDENT, Annie was all I had left. She had a limp, she had a scar down the right side of her face that her hair couldn't quite cover, and sometimes she had a look in her eyes that worried me—not quite frightened, resigned.

Six year old girls were supposed to be happy spring butterflies, bouncing from one bright-colored moment to the next. But the giggles of the season were silent. Annie sat alone in her room, holding her doll, the one with the smashed face, and stared at the wall. Not even out the window.

The doctors said she needed time, that's all. She'd been through a lot, and she still missed her mother—but she'll come back to life eventually. When she's ready.

But nobody's ever ready for anything. I knew that. I wasn't ready to be a widower at thirty-three.

I sat down next to Annie and put my arm around her shoulders. She didn't resist, but neither did she relax. She let me pull her close, but she was still a little zombie. I leaned over and sniffed her hair, kissed the top of her head, and whispered into her ear, "Have I told you today how much I love you?" She didn't respond.

Out of frustration, as much as anything else, I scooped her up and held her on my lap, hugged her close. "You're my favorite kid in the whole wide world and that's never going to change." I stroked her hair. "Listen to me, sweetheart. I know it hurts. I miss her too. But maybe we can help each other. You know how I come in here and talk to you about what I'm feeling? Well, maybe sometimes if you wanted to talk

283

to me, maybe you could do that and maybe that would help a little bit. What do you think?"

Not even a nod. I knew she heard me, but when she got like this, she seemed unreachable. Words like traumatized and catatonic and withdrawn all flashed through my head, but I hated those words—because the way that people used them, they stopped being descriptions, they became explanations. They turned into life-sentences.

"Okay, sweetheart, I'm not going to force you. When you're ready, you come see me, okay? Just say 'okay.' Okay?"

"Okay," she whispered. And that was enough. Not quite a breakthrough, but certainly the possibility of one.

"I'm going to go make dinner now. Let's have something special. Just for us. What would you like? I'll make your favorite."

"Pancakes."

"Pancakes for dinner? Okay, that sounds fun. And bacon too? Will you come help?"

In this case, help meant sitting silently on her chair while I flipped pancakes on the griddle. When I put the plate in front of her, she made no move to eat. "Didn't I do them right?"

"Daddy, I'm scared."

"Of my pancakes?"

"No. Don't be *silly*."

"Okay." At least she was talking. "What *are* you scared of?"

"Going to sleep."

"Going to sleep?"

"I'm afraid…I won't wake up."

My first instinct was to say, "That's silly. Everybody wakes up." But I stopped myself in time, because that wasn't true. We both knew that. So instead, I just nodded knowingly, "Yeah, that is scary." I had a dozen questions I wanted to ask, but I didn't want to push too hard. It was more important that she knew it was safe to talk.

I reached over and began cutting her pancakes for her. She could do it, but before the accident she had always asked me. She used to say "I like the way you do it, Daddy." But today, she pushed my hands away and said, "I'll do it myself."

"Okay." I sat down opposite her and busied myself with my own plate. I wasn't very hungry, but I went through the motions anyway, waiting for her to go on.

"There's this thing in my dream," she said very matter-of-factly.

"What kind of thing?"

"I don't know. It's too dark and fuzzy to see. It's all flickery. It comes from *underneath*."

"Underneath?"

"Uh-uh. *Underneath.*"

"Underneath what?"

"Underneath *everything.*"

"Okay. What does it do?"

"Nothing."

"Nothing?" Very carefully, not wanting to put her off, I said, "I don't know, Annie. That doesn't sound very scary to me."

"Well, it is."

"Why?"

"Because it's *there.*" She pushed a piece of pancake around on her plate, mopping up syrup. She still hadn't eaten a bite. "It's even there in the daytime. Only I can't see it, because it's always behind me."

"Now, *that* sounds scary."

"It is."

"Mmm," I said. "We're definitely going to have to do something about this."

"You can't."

"I can't?"

"No."

"Why not?"

"Because it's from *underneath.*"

"I see. That is serious. Tell me, who's bigger? You or it?"

She didn't answer.

"I'll bet I'm bigger…"

Still no reply.

"Well, certainly the two of us together are big enough."

This wasn't going anywhere. I'd have to try something else. How do you fight magical thinking? *With stronger magic.*

"I know what'll work."

She looked up at me. "What?"

"A dreamcatcher."

"What's a dreamcatcher?"

"Just what it sounds like. Take a bite of that pancake and I'll tell you more."

She did and I did. I didn't remember everything, so I made up what I didn't know. "A dreamcatcher is like a net for your dreams. You hang it over your bed and it catches all your bad dreams. Like a spaghetti strainer. And when it's full, you throw it out and make a new one."

Annie looked skeptical.

"It's an old Indian trick. I learned it from an old Indian. We'll make a dreamcatcher as soon as you finish dinner. We'll need some yarn and some feathers and maybe some sequins too. We'll look in Mommy's sewing box—" Oops. For a moment, she was almost interested, but as soon as I said *Mommy*, Annie shut down again. If only I hadn't opened my big mouth. If only.

If only I hadn't tried to make the light—

I got up and went to the sink. I started scrubbing the griddle in fast ferocious movements, furious at myself for having a big mouth, for being stupid, for everything.

"That's okay, Daddy. We can still do it. Mommy won't mind."

I nodded curtly. Maybe Annie wasn't the only one who needed strong magic.

Annie picked out her favorite colors of yarn, and I found some dowels in the garage, leftover from my kite-building period. We tied three of the dowels together to make a triangle, then strung a clumsy webwork of braided yarn and plastic beads across the center. We pulled bright-colored feathers out of Mommy's Halloween boa, it was always shedding anyway, and tied them in rainbow blossoms to each corner. We hung more feathers and beads from the bottom. Then we said some magic words over it and hung it on the wall over Annie's bed. "There. That'll catch all your bad dreams. Or my name isn't Mortimer Chuzzlefinger."

"Da-addy!" I hadn't heard that pronunciation in a while, with all the extra syllables. I hadn't realized how much I'd missed it.

"Oh, I forgot. My name *isn't* Mortimer Chuzzlefinger. But don't worry about it. This will still catch all your bad dreams. Snout's Honor. Now go brush your teeth and put on your nightie."

Annie went without argument. She didn't bounce, she limped. She had turned into a serious little soul. I missed my little girl, the one who giggled. I wondered if I'd ever hear her laugh again. I tucked her into bed and hugged her tightly. She accepted it, she even hugged back, but there was still something missing.

The difference between human beings and coyotes is that when the Acme Rocket-Launcher blows up in the coyote's face, he doesn't lose heart. He just goes back to the Acme catalog and orders something else. Human beings never recover from that first awful explosion. We might not walk around with our hair sticking out in charred frizzles and a scorched look of stunned amazement, but we never really regain our trust in a safe and orderly universe either. Once suspicious, we remain suspicious. That's what murders childhood innocence.

I looked in on Annie several times that night. She appeared to be sleeping soundly. The dreamcatcher was on the wall over her headboard where we'd carefully hung it. When she was little, I used to sit and watch her sleep, amazed that any little human being could be so beautiful, even more amazed that I could be so totally committed to protecting her from harm. I'd always thought of myself as self-involved to the point of selfishness, but having Annie in my life showed me otherwise. All I could think about was her smile, the trusting way she slipped her hand into mine, the giggles and the laughter. Everything else was…just stuff. I finally went to bed, hopeful that maybe the dreamcatcher was a way to start again.

But early the next morning, even before the sun was up, she came to me crying. "Daddy, the dreamcatcher didn't work—"

I followed her back to her room, where she pointed at the wall. Our carefully constructed webwork had been shredded. The dowels were broken and the netting we'd strung had been pulled apart. For a moment, I had the distinct impression that something had fought its way out. I started to say, "Why did you break it—?" then stopped myself. This wasn't the time for accusations. I scooped her up instead, hugged her, stroked her hair, and whispered, "Wow. That was some bad dream. We're going to need a bigger dreamcatcher." She just held on tight and wouldn't look.

Later, after she was dressed, after she had gone outside to sit under the tree to talk with her stuffed penguin, I took the shredded construction off the wall and examined it. The feathers we'd tied to the corners were all chewed, but not soggy-chewed like a child might do—ragged-chewed as if by the teeth of rats. The dowels too had the same tiny teeth marks. The yarn we'd tied and strung to make a dream-net had been stretched and pulled apart. And for a moment, I wondered if this might be something more than just a child's bad dreams. I even pulled her bed away from the wall and went looking for holes in the baseboard. Nothing. Nothing at all.

I tossed the shredded dreamcatcher into the trash, where Annie wouldn't see it, and wondered if I should make another one. But why would Annie rip it apart? Some deeper, darker thing we hadn't gotten to yet? All I could do was guess.

After a while, I went out to the garage. We had three old tennis rackets that we'd bought at a yard sale for five dollars. I had some metal rods and some nylon fishing line, an old bicycle wheel, and even some piano wire. I could make an industrial strength dreamcatcher, one she couldn't destroy. Maybe I could show her that Daddy was still bigger and stronger than the worst bad dreams she could imagine. That might work.

With the garage door open, I could keep an eye on her while I worked. I started with the three tennis rackets. I used the piano wire to tie them together, with their heads at the center and the handles sticking out at angles. I sprayed the whole affair with shiny black enamel. After they dried, I attached this construction to the bicycle wheel. Now it needed some decoration.

I found what was left of an old kite, a nine-foot long strip of silver mylar that rippled in the sun; I cut it into ribbons, twisted the ribbons into twirls and wound it around the rim and the spokes of the bicycle wheel. I burrowed into the Christmas decorations and found a box of tinsel and another box of silvery snowflake ornaments. I stapled the tinsel to the handles of the tennis rackets, and attached the snowflakes to the nylon webbing at the sweet spot. When I was done, the whole thing was a pretty ghastly affair—but enormously sturdy; you could carry a bowling ball on it. It was a very serious-looking dreamcatcher.

When I called Annie to the garage to see the new dreamcatcher, she stared at it with an appraiser's eye. Finally, she said, "Okay." But it wasn't a signal of affirmation, it was an "okay" of resignation. Yesterday, she had been hopeful, willing to believe. After last night, she was neither.

All right, I had to think about this. Building the second dreamcatcher had been useful. It was something to do with my hands, something to distract me while my subconscious chewed over the real problem—Annie's belief that there was something underneath that wanted to get to her. I remembered the chapters about "magical thinking." Annie needed to believe in something stronger. We all did. That was the essential part of being human. So after dinner, we hung up the dreamcatcher and lit a pink candle and waved feather dusters at it and said some magical words—"By the power of Great Ghu, the God of the Ceiling, let this dreamcatcher be a barrier to all and everything that wishes harm to this household and all who live here."—but Annie's dispirited "okay" reduced the whole thing to a silly performance. If she didn't believe, it wouldn't work. She was at that age where children start to give up belief. So who knew?

"Daddy?"

"Yes, sweetheart?"

"Will you sleep with me tonight? Mommy always slept with me when I had bad dreams."

I hesitated—remembering everything Dear Abby always said about parents sleeping with children—but this was Annie and this was serious medicine, so I said, "Of course, I will."

I tucked her in carefully, then lay down next to her on top of the covers. She snuggled up next to me, pressing her back against my side. She was asleep almost immediately. That was a relief, neither one of us had been sleeping all that well. Not since the accident. The endless cycling of memory had become a chronic pummeling. There was no peace. The slightest noise or irritation and I'd be up. The one person I most needed to talk to was the person who wasn't here. Maybe that's what Annie was feeling. But for just this little moment, maybe we could almost pretend that everything was going to be all right. Except I knew better.

The limp, the scar—when Annie was a teenager, these would be almost impenetrable barriers between her and everybody else. These things would set her apart from the world of normal girls. Girls used gossip and manipulation for bullying—little games when they were little, horrendous games when they grew bigger. Sometimes, in the way they interacted, you could see them training to be future harpies, honing the pernicious skills of ripping out the hearts of the innocent. Annie was already self-conscious about her wounds; her teen years would be hell. I'd asked about cosmetic surgery, physical therapy, orthopedic repair, but the doctors said there wasn't a lot they could do now, maybe later. But later might be too late. Her spirit was crippled too.

Eventually, I fell into an uneasy sleep, a swirl of disturbing dreams. Urgent dreams. I had to hide. I had to find a safe place, the safest. I hurried downstairs, down an escalator, down and down—at the bottom, I rushed around a corner, ducked under the angle of the rolling stairs, down again, through a narrow hallway and down the cramped emergency stairs, into the cluttered basement, where I ducked behind some boxes—I found a tiny opening, a vent; no, not even that, just a narrow nook underneath the floorboards, I crawled sideways around an impossible angle, down into a deeper space, dark and bottomless, I climbed down the metal ladder, down and down, always downward, until I found the hatch into the pipes below the city—I padded through the dank underbelly of the world, sloshing through tubes illuminated by phantom iridescence, climbing into narrower and narrower pipes, until I found another ladder down, this one leading to ancient stone tunnels, maybe catacombs, I couldn't tell, except after a while, the walls were pulsing, lined with throbbing purple veins and bulbous growths, and farther down, cracks appeared in the walls, glowing red as embers, it was warm here, too warm, uncomfortably hot, molten lava seeping up through the floor, the edges of the rocky crust were limned with flame, I had to jump across the bubbling pits, bottomless chasms too, had I come so far that I would never find my way back? I knew this place. There was something here. Behind me. I turned around and—

Woke up with a startled grunt. My heart pounding.

I fumbled around for my flashlight, the big heavy one filled with a half-dozen D-cells. Held overhand, it could be used as a club. If necessary. I'd put it on the nightstand next to Annie's bed so she could look to see there were no monsters in the dark. I clicked it on myself. Yes, there were no monsters. I was actually relieved.

Padded off to the bathroom, fever dreams still resonant. Checked the thermostat. Opened the front door and sniffed the night. Thought about going to my own bed. Thought about a lot of things. Three o'clock in the morning thoughts. All the way down to the bottom one—why does the universe even exist? Why is there something instead of nothing?

I went to the kitchen and poured myself the last of the coffee, still sitting cold in the carafe; gave it a short ride in the microwave, then returned to Annie's room. I stood in the doorway, sipping half-heartedly at the bitter brew until it was cold and tasteless. I didn't want to get back into her bed. It was uncomfortable. But I didn't want to leave her alone either.

We had a big overstuffed chair in the den. I'd fallen asleep in it more than once, usually during some made-for-TV movie on the Lifetime channel. I pushed the chair into Annie's room, grabbed a pillow and a comforter, and made myself as comfortable as I could. I moved as quietly as I could through the darkness. I wasn't planning on staying up all night, watching, but if anything made a sound, I'd be right here. Just before settling in, I flicked on the flashlight, one last time, just to check, I don't know what made me do it—

—stopped. And stared. Above Annie's bed. My carefully constructed industrial-strength dreamcatcher had been chewed to bits, as if something with metal teeth had gnawed its way out. I lifted it off the hook on the wall, astonished and shaking my head and for the first time, honestly worried. Even a little scared.

Carried it into the kitchen and laid it on the counter. The fluorescent lights flickered on, momentarily dazzling me. What the bloody hell—? The bicycle spokes were pulled every which way, the rim of the wheel was bent; the nylon webbing of the tennis rackets was unstrung, with bent and broken strands pointing out at odd angles. It looked as if someone or something had deliberately picked it apart.

All right, there had to be a rational explanation. Maybe it was the tension of the wires, maybe I'd strung the whole thing so tight it had unraveled in the middle of the night. Except I hadn't heard a sound. My sleep had been so uncertain these past few weeks, even the slightest rustle was enough to bring me bolt upright in bed. I couldn't imagine this thing twanging apart above my head without my hearing something. Unless I'd been so tired, so exhausted, so lost in sleep, so down in the dream, could the sound of this thing pulling itself apart have triggered my dreams of descent—? *Underneath?*

No. I wasn't ready to go there yet. I'd read articles about "unexplainable" phenomena that occurred at the nexii of standing waves— electrical, radio, sonic, whatever. Maybe this was like the guy who could hear the six o'clock news on his fillings? Yes, he had voices in his head, but it was only the local Ted Baxter. I tried to remember what I'd read about counter-measures. Put a large bowl of water next to an open window. Hang tinfoil strips. Rearrange the furniture. Install a ground wire. Check your cables. It all sounded like more dreamcatcher stuff. Just another belief system.

I wasn't going to figure it out tonight. I went back to Annie's room and plopped down next to her again. She snuggled into my arm and two blinks later, sunlight was streaming in through the window, illuminating the dust motes like bars of blue silver. I glanced over, saw she was sleeping peacefully, so I eased myself out of bed and went into the kitchen to start breakfast.

Eventually, Annie wandered in, still rubbing her eyes. "How'd you sleep, sweetheart?"

"Okay, I guess."

"No bad dreams?"

"Uh-uh." And then she said, perceptively. "You had the bad dream for me, didn't you?"

"Yeah, I guess I did."

"Was it as bad as I said?"

I nodded. "Yeah, I can see why you were scared."

She glanced at the broken dreamcatcher. "That didn't work, did it?"

"I guess not." I started flipping pancakes. "We'll have to figure out something else."

We spent the day running errands, dropping things off, picking things up, maintaining all the separate machineries of suburbia. Annie didn't fuss, she held my hand and stayed close. I wished there was something I could do for her, some way I could pull her out of the shell she was building—something to distract her from her morbid fantasies of *underneath*.

A thought had been gnawing at me all morning. Annie was lonely. That's all. She had no one to belong to anymore. No one to trust. And no matter how hard I tried, I couldn't break through to her; there was a part of her she was going to keep to herself now.

Inevitably, she pulled me over to the pet store window. She always liked looking at the puppies. So did I—except while she was fussing about each little cute furry personality, I was feeling sorry for them, locked in those enclosures, those cages, like pieces of merchandise, unable to get out, unable to run and play and bark.

And always, the inevitable question, "Daddy, can we get a puppy? Puh-leeeeese? Look, this one's only sixty dollars."

I peered close. Only sixty dollars for twenty-four months. "Uh-uh, sweetheart. Not one of these."

"Why not—?"

"Um, because—" *Why not?* "—because, these aren't good watch-dogs."

"Why do we need a watchdog—?"

"Because I can't sleep with you every night. We need a special kind of watchdog—a dream watchdog. A little pooch to snuggle up next to you and not let any bad dreams get in. Just like I did."

"Oh." She considered it. I could see her turning the thought over in her head. "Well, where do we get a dream watchdog?"

"Mmm, well, I dunno…" I was barely a half-step ahead of her. We had been talking about a puppy, maybe for Christmas, but what with one thing and another, including a new baby on the way—we'd decided to wait a year, until Annie was bigger. Now, however, maybe a dog was just the right thing.

"I know—let's go to the animal shelter. I'll bet they have good dream dogs there." Annie grabbed my hand and started pulling. I let myself be led back toward the parking lot. By the time we got to the car, Annie was already making plans for her pound-puppy. "I'll give him my blue blanket, okay? And he'll sleep on my bed with me, okay? And I'll call him—um, what's a good name for a dream watchdog, Daddy?"

"Well, it's been my experience that you have to live with a dog for three days, and at the end of three days, you'll know what his name is."

She nodded. "That sounds good."

The animal shelter is a depressing place. It's clean, the dogs are all well-cared for, the staff is friendly and helpful—but you know, going in, that there aren't enough homes for all these imploring hopeful faces. Only the young ones, the cute ones, the healthy ones are likely to find homes where they'll be loved. Annie limped in behind me and I realized again that she was no longer one of the cute or healthy ones. People would look at her, and then to me, and I could see the flicker of pity behind their eyes—*that poor man, having that poor disfigured child.*

The puppy cages were closest to the entrance. There weren't many to choose from. A scruffy and scraggly-looking lot. Except—

"Daddy, how about this one?"

"He's awfully small—"

"Oh, no—he's just the right size."

The card on the cage said he was a gray terrier-poodle mix, eight months old. To my eyes, he looked like he was half poodle, half oppor-tunist; but his tail was bobbed, that indicated breeding, perhaps for show. Silvery fur, darker on top; not quite curly—kinky. He was all dreadlocks. He needed grooming. I didn't think there was very much dog inside all that fur, but he had bright attentive eyes. He watched us both, his gaze flicking back and forth between Annie and myself, then finally fixing on her as the most likely mark, he stood up, putting his paws against the bars, and tried to shove his tiny muzzle through, his tongue already licking toward Annie's fingers. She held out her hand the way I'd showed her, the back of the hand so the dog could sniff without being able to nip. He skipped the sniff, went right for the lick—this little pooch was people-friendly. More than that, he was desperate to be let out of this cage.

Without asking, I knew his backstory. It was a familiar one. This was last year's Christmas present to somebody, maybe somebody's child—and now they'd gotten tired of it, and so they discarded it, tossing it away as if it had no feelings of its own. This frantic little hairball had invested his whole being-ness into belonging to someone who couldn't be bothered to repay loyalty in kind. He had to be feeling confusion and hurt and fear. I hunched down on my knees and offered my own hand. "What do you think, little guy? Do you think you can stand guard over my Annie here and keep her safe from bad dreams?" It was an awfully big responsibility for such a little dog. He couldn't have weighed very much. Six, maybe seven pounds. I wondered if he was too small, if he'd be a yappy little nuisance; was that why he'd been abandoned to the system?

But there's this about dogs. When you look into their eyes, if all you see is a dog, then it's just a dog; but if you see a little furry person there, then he's part of your family, take him home. I wasn't sure about this guy, yet—but there was something very alive and real behind those eyes. "Do you like this one, Annie?"

"Oh, yes, Daddy. Very much." And then, she stopped herself. "Will he be a good dream dog?"

"Well—he's a terrier. And terriers are good at catching rats. So he should be a good watchdog for bad dreams. Let's go see if we can adopt him."

There was a lot of paperwork, more than I expected, and it took a while. Annie quickly grew impatient, which under other circumstances would have annoyed me, but I was secretly pleased to see her so excited, so I told her to go wait by the cage and keep her new puppy company, so he'd have a chance to get to know her. "Talk to him and let him know we're paying his bail." She didn't get the joke, but that was okay, she went anyway.

By the time I finished, Annie was sitting on the floor in front of the cage with the puppy happily curled in her lap. A thoughtful attendant had arranged it. "His name is Chester," she announced.

"Chester, huh—?" The little guy's ears pricked up and he cocked his head at me.

"See? He already knows his name. Are we done? Can we take Chester home now?"

"Sure, we can." I reached out and let the little guy sniff my hand. He licked my fingers happily. Hell, if I'd been locked up in one of these cages, I'd have licked a few fingers to be let out too.

On the way home, we stopped at the local Petco for dog food, pet bowls, a collar, a wire brush, shampoo, flea and tick treatment, a nametag, a chew bone, a couple of small squeaky toys, a box of dog cookies, and a pet bed—a blue velvet pillow, impossibly decadent. "But he won't need his own bed, Daddy—he's going to sleep with me."

"Yes, sweetheart, but he still needs a bed of his own for his afternoon nap. Dogs like to have their own special places, just like people." The total bill was over $150 and we still weren't through. We still had to have doggie shots.

Annie spent the rest of the day showing Chester around the house and the yard, carefully explaining everything to him, "This corner of the back yard, this is where you poop. This is the kitchen, this is where we'll feed you dinner. This is my room, this is your bed here—" A blue velvet pillow, Chester dutifully sniffed it, then lay down in the center, as if to demonstrate he understood that this bed was his.

"But at nighttime, you'll sleep over here with me, Chester." Annie scooped him up and put him on her own bed. Chester repeated his performance, carefully sniffing the blanket and pillows, finally settling himself in the most comfortable place to curl up for a nap—right between Annie's two favorite stuffed toys, a pink teddy bear and a big blue bunny. "Daddy, look! Chester likes my bed."

"I'm sure. It's the nicest bed in the whole house." I was beginning to have concerns that Annie was going to smother Chester with affection, that she saw him as a toy, a living teddy bear that she could cuddle forever. But if Chester was a normal terrier, he'd set his own rules soon enough.

Very quickly, Chester revealed his own distinct personality. He didn't like to play tug of war, not even with a clean sock toy—actively disinterested. He preferred to play chase-the-squeaky. And sometimes roll-on-your-back-and-bite-the-squeaky. And most often, toss-the-squeaky-at-your-feet. When he got tired of that game, he did laps from the kitchen to the dining room to the living room, down the hall to Annie's bedroom, then back again to the living room, through the dining room, and skittering across the kitchen floor to a hairpin turn at the wash machine to do it all again. Annie laughed out loud, the first time since the accident. This had been a good decision.

Later, I tucked Annie and Chester into bed together. He snuggled in like a happy little lump. Annie petted him and whispered something in his ear, something about being a good guard dog against bad dreams. He licked her face, as if in happy agreement.

A half hour later, I peeked in at the two of them. Both were asleep, but Chester had quietly gotten down off Annie's bed and gone to his own pillow in the corner. I scooped him up—he didn't protest, he almost didn't even wake up, most puppies are that pliable—and put him down next to Annie again, a furry little comma. Still asleep, he stretched his legs out briefly, then relaxed again.

I puttered around for an hour, cleaning the kitchen, straightening up the living room, glancing into my office, wondering if I should try to get some work done, then finally, feeling like nothing in particular, I gave up. Just before heading off to my own bed, I checked in on Annie one more time. Chester was back on his velvet pillow. Once more, I scooped him up and put him down next to Annie. He trembled slightly, an odd reaction, then relaxed back into a deep sleep.

Annie woke me up, crying. "Daddy, there's something wrong with Chester!"

I glanced blearily at the clock—it was legally morning. Somewhere. I rolled out of bed with a sinking feeling and followed Annie back to her room.

Chester was lying on the bed, trembling, whimpering. When I put my hand on his side, he flinched and yelped—but he didn't lift his head. I scooped him up and held him gently in my arms—he screamed, a strange sound for such a small animal, breathless wails of panic. I slid my palm around his narrow chest, feeling for a heartbeat. It felt too fast for me, but small animals have very rapid heartbeats and I'm no vet, I had no idea if this was normal. He shivered in my grasp—not the nervous shivering that small dogs are prone to, this was something else.

Annie watched us both, wide-eyed and too afraid to speak. I continued to hold the little pooch against my chest, lowered my face to the top of his head and began whispering. "It's all right, guy. You're a good boy. Everything's all right." He stopped crying, but he continued to tremble.

"Is he going to be all right?"

"I think so. He's just scared—"

Abruptly, I remembered something from a dozen years ago—another terrier, a short-haired sweetheart named Biscuit, as tan as a perfect pancake; when she put her ears up, she looked like Anubis. She loved people, she loved to play, and she was apparently fearless. I'd take her with me on walks to the store and back. When we turned onto our block, I'd take her off the leash so she could run free all the way home. She bounced with excitement. Except one time—she hadn't gotten more than a few bounces ahead when two huge German shepherds dashed out from behind a hedge. One of them grabbed her firmly by the neck; the German shepherds were young, barely a year old, just big overgrown pups, and they had come running out to play, except they were used to playing rough and Biscuit hadn't seen them coming, she was caught by surprise. If an eagle had swept down from the sky and plucked her away, she couldn't have been more terrified. She let out a wail of panic like nothing I'd ever heard before. It turned into a series of long hurtful cries. The German shepherds backed away, startled, and I scooped up Biscuit so fast she didn't even realize it was me—she just kept on crying and trembling in panic. "All right, all right. It's okay." I looked her over carefully, her fur was ruffled, but she hadn't been bitten—just grabbed hard. I held her close and tried to comfort her all the way home, but she wouldn't let me put her down. She was terrified. And when we did get home, she ran for her bed and stayed there until the following morning.

But that had been a tangible event—Biscuit had been grabbed by a much larger, momentarily ferocious animal that had leapt out of nowhere and ambushed her. This was…I didn't know what it was. Why was Chester crying? I'd seen dogs dreaming before, even having bad dreams—two or three short whimpers, maybe some leg motion, and then the moment was past. But this—Chester was behaving as if he'd been in a fight, grabbed and shaken and hurled against a wall.

I looked to Annie. The first question that came to mind was the one I didn't dare ask. *Did you do something, Annie?* And if I did ask it, I wouldn't get an honest answer. "Did you see anything, Annie?"

She shook her head.

"You didn't roll over on him by accident or bump him, did you?"

"Nuh-uh. He just started crying all of a sudden. He woke me up." And then she added, "Chester was having my dream. He was barking and growling at the *underneath*. But I wasn't scared, because Chester was protecting me, just like you said he would. And then—it—it—and he screamed and I woke up and he was—he was like that, and I came to get you. Is he going to be all right, Daddy?"

Chester was calming down. He'd stopped crying, stopped whimpering, and his trembling had ebbed to periodic spasms—short, intense bursts; normal for a small excitable dog, but something had freaked this animal, that was certain. I started to put him back down on the bed, but as I lowered him, he went rigid and resistant; instead, I carried him over to the corner and settled him down on his own pillow. He sat trembling, eyes wide, staring up at me.

"All right, let's get dressed. We'll take him to the doctor. He needs his shots anyway." At first, I'd wondered if perhaps Chester had been bitten by a spider or stung by a bee; but if he had, he would have gone into shock by now.

Chester didn't want to stay in Annie's room. He followed me back to my bedroom and stayed close to me while I pulled on my pants and an old sweatshirt. Then he followed me to the kitchen and stayed close underfoot while I made a fresh pot of coffee. Annie fixed herself a bowl of Cheerios, but barely touched it.

The vet's office didn't open until nine, but I knew the staff was there at seven to take care of the in-patients. I called ahead, and we pulled into the parking lot the same time as Dr. Brown. He took Chester from Annie's arms and squinted as he held him aloft. "Looks like a dog," he said. "Only smaller. Did you get him in a Happy Meal?"

Michael Brown was an old friend; we followed him inside. He put Chester on the table and listened to his heart, peeked into his ears, and even took a blood sample. He fingered Chester's bobbed tail and said, "He's probably had all his shots, but let's not take any chances. I'll give him boosters."

"But what about his bad dream—?" Annie asked.

Michael Brown looked to me. I gave him the short version. Annie added, "Chester is my dream watchdog."

"A dream watchdog, eh? Any other symptoms?"

I shook my head. "No. Just the crying and the trembling."

"Any vomiting?"

"I didn't see any."

"Diarrhea?"

"No. Nothing." A thought occurred to me. "Could it have been a seizure?"

"Not from what you describe. It sounds like he had a bad dream." Dr. Brown peered into Chester's face again, then rubbed his head affectionately. "You look fine to me."

I wasn't satisfied. "A bad dream? That bad? Can dogs have panic attacks?"

Dr. Brown shrugged. "Dunno. It was his first night in a strange place. You don't know what he might have been through before you got him. He doesn't look abused, but it's possible he heard a sound that reactivated a very bad memory. It happens to people, it happens to animals. Have you ever seen a St. Bernard scared of lightning?"

"No."

"Not a lot of fun." He handed Chester to me. "Take him home. Let him rest in a quiet dark corner. Keep an eye on him. Call me if anything changes, but he should be all right."

Logically, I knew there had to be a rational explanation for all of this. But the sequence of illogical events argued for a more compelling and mysterious pattern—and whether there was logic or not was ultimately irrelevant, because Annie believed in the logic of her dreams.

And so did I. In the cold yellow light of the afternoon, all bad dreams seem silly. But I could still feel the troubled resonance of my own downward journey. I spent the afternoon prowling through my files on phobias, panic attacks, unreasonable fears—and successful counter-therapies as well. There wasn't much here that I didn't already know. Most of it boiled down to "don't invest any more energy into the fear, that only makes it larger."

That meant no more dreamcatchers, magic spells, or even dream watchdogs. We had to invest our energies into something positive and joyous. Except—that was the problem. I had a little girl without a mommy, with a scar and a limp; a little girl who had lost her joy somewhere between Highway Twelve and the intensive care unit. There was no joy anymore, because Mommy never woke up.

What there was, was the slow steady, step-by-step, plodding through the process of "learning to live with it." How do I explain to her that the pain never goes away, it just becomes another part of you. You end up adding it to the mosaic of your life, a particularly hard-colored moment that you spend as little time as possible dwelling on. When you're six years old, how do you learn to do that?

By afternoon, Chester was ready to play again, as if nothing bad had happened last night. Annie spent the early hours of the evening tossing the squeaky toy for him. She even started calling him "doodle-bug" because of the way he doodled the toy around before finally giving it back. He punched the little red ball with his nose, tossing it toward her, obviously inviting her to pick it up and throw it for him. Annie laughed exuberantly, held the toy high, then hurled it down the hall. Chester bounced after it.

When bedtime finally rolled around, both Annie and her little doodle-bug trotted off obediently. Annie limped. Chester trotted, with the squeaky still in his mouth.

The little gray dog settled himself on his pillow, the red ball between his paws, and adamantly refused to get back up on Annie's bed. Every time I lifted him up and put him next to Annie, he promptly jumped right back down to the floor and went back to his own place. Annie tried calling him and patting the bed next to her, but he just curled up and ignored her. Her crestfallen expression said it all.

"Maybe he's still feeling bad from this morning. It's all right, sweetheart. I'll stay with you." I tucked her in, then I kicked off my shoes and lay down next to her. After a moment, I got up, scooped up Chester and put him between us. I put a hand on his back, not to hold him down, just to reassure him. He looked at me for a moment, then put his head between his paws. He looked sad. Or resigned.

Annie drifted off to sleep quickly. I thought about getting up and tiptoeing out, but the instant my breathing shifted, Chester's head came up. His little button nose sniffed the air, his eyes weren't visible in the darkness, but I could feel a sudden tenseness in his posture. He growled—it wasn't much, but then he wasn't much of a dog; just a little bit of meat and bone, and the rest was dust-bunny and attitude. His growl was so high-pitched, it was almost a cartoon—but he was serious. I remembered an old saying; it's not the size of the dog in the fight that counts, it's the size of the fight in the dog.

"It's all right, mini-pooch," I said, patting his flank. "There's nothing there." His growl faded. After a bit, he put his head down again. Resting, not sleeping. Every so often, his head would come back up, as if he were staring at something on the other side of the wall. He'd watch the unseen threat for a bit, then lower his head again. Occasionally, he'd mutter a soft meaningful "werf."

I woke up a couple of hours later. I didn't know why. Just a sudden awareness. Annie was sleeping soundly next to me. Chester lay between us, stretched out comfortably. Whatever threat he'd imagined, either it was gone or he was too tired. I got up and headed to the bathroom. I checked all the doors and windows, made sure all the lights and all the appliances were turned off, then headed back to Annie's room. Everything was all right there as well. So I padded off to my own bed. Maybe we were finally over the hump. Maybe.

Just before dawn—I was halfway down the hall before I realized I was awake, responding to an unearthly scream. Too high-pitched to be Annie's voice—but it was. Or maybe it was her scream dissolving into the tail-end of whatever had screamed first.

The light from the hallway shone a bar of brightness into her room. Annie had leapt backwards out of bed, trembling in her nightgown, backed against the wall. Her bed was askew as if something big had picked it up and thrown it sideways, the sheets and blankets ripped and disheveled, and toys and books and clothes torn from her closets and drawers and shelves were everywhere. Annie pointed, still gasping—

"Where's Chester?" I didn't wait for an answer. I pulled back the blankets. The little dog lay limp on her bed—at first I thought he was dead, but his heart was beating rapidly. His breath was shallow; with my hand on his side, I could barely feel any motion. He looked shredded; he was covered with dozens of tiny bites. I peeled back his upper lip; his gums were pale, he was in shock.

Annie's face was crumpled in terror; she was half-crying, half-screaming. I grabbed her and held her. I didn't even try to ask what happened, I just scooped her up and held her. With one hand, I fumbled for the flashlight, then cursed and gave up. I flicked the light switch. Still carrying Annie, I turned on all the lights. There was nothing there. Nothing anywhere. I spotted the flashlight where I'd left it the night before and grabbed it. I could use it as a club, if I had to. I looked under her bed, in the closet, checked the windows, then went back to Annie, ran my hands up and down her sides, her arms, checked her head; she seemed unhurt.

Turned back to Chester—

"Is he going to be all right?"

"I don't know. Put on your clothes. We'll take him to the doctor." I checked again to see if he was still breathing. He was very still. I pulled on my pants and a sweatshirt, grabbed the car keys and my phone. I lifted Chester carefully, cradling him in one arm; with the other hand, I punched for Dr. Brown. Annie was pulling on her bathrobe and limp-hobbling toward the door to the garage.

Michael Brown met us at the back door of the clinic.

"I'm sorry for waking you—"

He ignored it. "Come on in the back—"

We followed him in. He switched on lights as he went. "Put him there—" A cold stainless steel table. He opened a cupboard and began pulling things out. Syringes, tiny bottles, a surgical kit. "Annie, go stand over there. I want you out of the way. You, over here." He switched on a bright overhead light. He peeled back Chester's eyelids, peeled his upper lip and looked at his gums, even lifted up what was left of the little guy's tail and examined his rectum—to see if the muscles were still tight. He plugged a stethoscope into his ears and listened to Chester's heartbeat and breathing with a grim expression. At last, he grabbed syringe and a bottle of adrenalin. A quick injection directly into the heart. He listened again with the stethoscope, frowning.

Abruptly, he pasted three electrodes onto Chester's little gray chest. He switched on a monitor and the machine next to it and grabbed the defibrillator paddles—smaller versions than the ones on television. The monitor showed a very shallow, very uneven heartbeat. Dr. Brown applied the paddles; there was a short sharp sound and Chester jerked. Then he lay still again. A second shock, still no change.

"Daddy—?"

"Sometimes it takes a couple of tries, sweetheart."

"Take her out of here," Michael said.

I scooped her up and we went out into the waiting room. I sat down on the bench and held Annie in my lap.

"He's going to die, isn't he?"

"I don't know, sweetheart. I don't know."

"He doesn't deserve to die. He saved me."

"Saved you?"

"From…it."

I didn't know what to say, so I said nothing.

"He saved me," she repeated.

"Yes, he did," I agreed.

"He's a good dream watchdog."

"Yes, he is."

"He didn't let…*it*…get to me."

"No, he didn't."

We sat for a while in silence. Waiting. Annie leaned her head against my chest and was very still. I wondered if she'd fallen back asleep, but I wasn't going to shift my position to see. When Michael Brown came out of the back, she was instantly awake again. Michael looked grim. He shook his head without saying anything.

"What was it—?" I started to ask, but his expression was guarded; he wasn't going to discuss the details in front of Annie.

"He's dead," she said. "Isn't he?"

"I'm sorry, sweetheart." Dr. Brown went down on one knee so he could look her directly in the eye. "I did everything I could."

"I know," she answered calmly. Then she looked up at me. "Daddy?" she said. "We're going to need a bigger dog."

AUTHOR'S AFTERWORD:

"Chester" was published in The Magazine of Fantasy & Science Fiction. *The editor got letters from several people, complaining about the terrible way the family (and by implication, the author) had treated this little (fictional) dog. The irony of the complaints was that they showed no compassion for the little (fictional) heroine.*

Interlude #5

Selections from *The Quote-Book of Solomon Short*

"A friend is someone who likes you in spite of yourself."

"Let sleeping dogma lie."

"The universe has its own cure for stupidity. Unfortunately, it doesn't always apply it."

"A taboo is someone else's rule about what you may or may not do with your own body."

"A waist is a terrible thing to mind."

"Good neighbors make good fences."

"No man is an island, but some of us are pretty good peninsulas."

"Violence is the last word of the illiterate. Also the first."

"There is no such thing as a holy war."

"Lightning is one hell of a murder weapon—and the best part is, it can't be traced."

"The best thing about war is that it makes it all right to hate."

"Purity is almost always toxic."

"Expect the worst. You'll never be disappointed."

"Everything is connected to everything else. That's why it's so hard to keep a secret."

"For every action, there is an equal but opposite critical analysis."

"If you build a better mousetrap, you'll catch a better class of mouse."

"Jesus had it coming. The self-righteous always get nailed."

"Immortality is easy. It's wearing your watch that makes you grow old. (Also, cut out spicy foods after age one hundred and seventy.)"

"Nobody is ever really ready for anything. If they were, there would be no point in living through it."

"How did the Wicked Witch of the West take a bath?"

"The lights are most likely to come back on at the precise moment you find the flashlight."

"Of course, kick a man when he's down. It's the best time. If you're not willing to kick him when he's down, then don't kick him when he's up either."

"Malpractice makes malperfect."

"Bad luck is universal. Don't take it personally."

"When you transcend the medium, you have achieved art."

"I've always had trouble with my employers. They forget they're only renting my judgment, not buying my soul. That's why they're paying so much."

"It's not who wins or loses that counts—it's who keeps score."

"Always be sincere. Even if you have to fake it."

"Those who abhor history are compelled to rewrite it."

"*Loving* well is the best revenge."

"All life is barriers. All growth is the transcendence of barriers. It's the dividing line that makes everything possible. Without it, there's nothing but soup."

"Isn't it amazing how much fun two people can have just by taking off their clothes?"

"It doesn't matter where you stand, it's still going to look like the middle."

"Despite all the evidence to the contrary, I remain convinced that Man is the missing link between apes and civilized beings."

"Love is when you look into your lover's eyes and see God smiling back at you."

"Genius is a perpetual notion machine."

"This neurotic pursuit of sanity is driving us all crazy."

"Reality is the stuff that doesn't go away, even if you don't believe in it."

"Ninety percent of success is just growing up."

"There's one thing to be said for ignorance. It starts a lot of interesting arguments."

"I enjoy watching amateurs make fools of themselves. Most of the time, it's the other way around."

"You can lead a horse's ass to water, but uh…"

"It's not who wins or loses—it's how you place the blame."

"All insults are basic. They're variations on 'My orgasm is better than your orgasm.'"

"You're only young once, but you can be immature forever."

"Love and death are antithetical. One can be used to cure the other."

"Never buy anything with a low serial number."

"The worst kind of party to attend is the one where you are the only person in the room who understands all the in-jokes you've been telling all night."

"If it were easy, it would have been done already."

"If the shoe fits, kick someone."

"By all means, take the moral high ground—all that heavenly backlighting makes you a much easier target."

"You can open more flies with honey than you can with vinegar."

"I have to dream big. I only have time to get half of it done."

"'Tis far, far better to be pissed off than pissed on."

"The most effective spice in the world is hunger."

"Pound for pound, the amoeba is the most vicious creature on Earth."

"The third eye does not need a contact lens."

"The dog was nature's first attempt to make a neurotic. Practice makes perfect."

"The shortest distance between two puns is a straight line."

"The trouble with picking up cats is that they always run to the bottom."

"Life is hard. Then you die. Then they throw dirt in your face. Then the worms eat you. Be grateful it happens in that order."

"If death is inevitable, lie back and enjoy it."

"The early worm gets the bird."

"If you can't stand the heat, stay out of the firestorm."

"Choose your death carefully. You'll be stuck with it for a long, long time."

"Contentment is the continuing act of accepting the process of your own life—no matter how nasty it gets."

"Everything in moderation. Especially moderation."

"Being dead means never having to say you're silly."

"Good. Fast. Cheap. Pick two."

"There is a lot more to life than just making it out of the vagina. Or getting back in again."

"The only acceptable substitute for brains is silence."

"Here's everything you need to know about men and women. Men are bullies. Women are snakes. Except when it's the other way around."

"There's a lot to be said for thinking with your dick. The average penis is a lot more likely to stand up for what it wants than the average man."

"The reason why the battle of the sexes will never be won is because fraternization with the enemy is so much fun."

"It only takes one person to make a relationship work—it takes two to really fuck it up."

"Not all lawyers know when they're lying. Only the good ones do. The best can conceal even this fact."

"Any man with a prosthetic charisma is undoubtedly a liar in other respects too."

"The hardest part of a war is staying out of it."

"If God really is watching us, the least we can do is be entertaining."

Chess with a Dragon

Back in the primeval days of bit-diddling devices, before gooey operating systems, there were a lot of different philosophies about what a word processing program should be. During the decade of the eighties (and the DOS operating system) I moved from WordStar to NewStar, back to WordStar when they bought out NewStar, fell in love with Sprint (which was too much, too late—and then Borland lost a lawsuit about its "look and feel" so that sank it in the marketplace), moved to AmiPro when Windows came along—but when it evolved into WordPro, it stunk—so I finally gave up and succumbed to the perennial second-best word processor, Word for Windows. But before I got that far, I tried a nifty little outline program called ThinkTank, which had all kinds of capabilities; it was an outliner and a word processor, a floor wax and a dessert topping. I was intrigued with the possibilities of being able to easily (the operative word was easily) rearrange the order of chapters every time I had second thoughts about something. And I don't just have second thoughts, I have seventy-second thoughts. This story was the test of that theory.

One day, the (nameless) editor at Byron Preiss books (nameless, because otherwise I'd have to put some unfortunate adjectives in front of his name) called me and desperately asked me for a short novel for a new line of books, etc. etc. My book was supposed to be number four, but when numbers two and three didn't arrive in the offices when they were supposed to, the aforementioned nameless editor became so desperate to meet his publication schedule that he leapt upon my unpolished first draft, made some unauthorized changes, and sent it off to the typesetter, thereby earning himself a whole slew of unfortunate adjectives. Maybe it was the unpleasant experience, maybe it was the program, maybe it was the evolution of the software market; but I never used ThinkTank for writing again. (But I do use the outlining functions in Word, so maybe I learned something anyway.) Here, twenty years later (am I really that old?), is a somewhat more polished version, with my own dialog restored.

A Game of Nestlings

K!RIKKL POLISHED ITS MANDIBLES slowly while it considered the layout of the game board. There was much too much at stake, and there were far too many unanswered questions. Perhaps it had been a mistake to accept this invitation.

For instance, how many eggs were in the Dead Mother's Egg Pouch—and what kind? K!rikkl knew there had to be at least three fat Xlygit larvae and a Knrkt—G!ligglix's aggressive betting was proof enough of that—but if there weren't any host-grubs, then the pouch was valueless. To K!rikkl anyway. Complicating the matter was the fact that G!ligglix already claimed to have a whole family of host-grubs in its Nest; but as far as K!rikkl could tell, G!ligglix did not yet have a Knrkt. But then again, maybe G!ligglix didn't want one. A Knrkt could be its own worst enemy.

"!" said K!rikkl in quiet annoyance. This was not working out at all well.

"??" questioned Hnaxx, turning a multi-faceted eye in K!rikkl's direction.

"A remark of annoyance, my dear host. You may perhaps be far too good a player for my skills. This game promises to last long into the night."

"Should the game last that long, my dear guest, it will be a grand testimony to your own skill."

"If we do not starve to death first," agreed K!rikkl.

G!ligglix giggled. "I think you overestimate *all* of our abilities…"

K!rikkl ignored the remark. G!ligglix was a fat, rude, grossly distended, gluttonous, ill-mannered, profiteering liar. G!ligglix was also quite rich—which was why K!rikkl had considered joining the game at all. Now, K!rikkl was beginning to discover just how G!ligglix had gotten so rich. As a result, K!rikkl's goals for the evening were beginning to shift. The young Ki!Lakken had initially thought to play for brooding-advantage; now it seemed more cautious simply to play for quiet survival.

K!rikkl clicked again and considered the possibilities.

In order to complete its own Nest and close the Blue Cycle with a breeding, it would have needed to find host-grubs elsewhere on the playing field. That no longer seemed possible. All the host-grubs had either been eaten or claimed. Without grubs, K!rikkl's only hope of survival to the Dawn Cycle would be through neutering—and that was *always* a bad idea.

Hm. Perhaps it could barter a single grub from Hnaxx. Although it wasn't an official rule, the way the game was generally played, the host was honor-bound to succor a needy guest—except all of Hnaxx's grubs had already been impregnated. And now, Hnaxx was studying K!rikkl's discomfort with a wry amusement.

That left only Hnaxx's young broodling, Rrr. A very unlikely possibility, K!rikkl decided. Rrr was already too close to the honor of Gracing the Table. There was very little possibility of Rrr giving advantage to anyone else—at least not unless there was also significant gain to Rrr's own Nest.

The question was—what was in Rrr's Nest?

Hmm.

No, that wouldn't work. There was nothing to be gained by lending an advantage to Rrr. Besides, Rrr was young and tender. There was a lot of juice and protein in that exoskeleton. K!rikkl wasn't the only Ki! who'd noticed the plump tenderness of the youngest player. By unspoken agreement of the more experienced players, Rrr had already been selected as the guest of honor for the banquet later this evening.

No. Definitely no. Rrr was not the solution to K!rikkl's problem on the playing board. Indeed, if K!rikkl aided Rrr, it might very well find itself the target of the other players' enmity—and the cautious Ki! knew where that led. K!rikkl had no intention of taking Rrr's place on the table of Hnaxx the Munificent.

Hmm. And hmm again.

K!rikkl arched its large green triangular head forward and made soft clicking noises in its throat. It bent itself low and gave a tremendous performance of studying the board, blinking and peering and tapping at the pieces with ferocious deliberation.

Yes.

There was no other way.

K!rikkl made a decision.

It sat back on its haunches and growled low in its throat. A sign of annoyance and frustration.

"A cough, perhaps?" inquired Hnaxx politely.

"Yes, perhaps," replied K!rikkl noncommittally. The whole thing stank of a trap. The seven other players—distant members of Hnaxx's Nest—waited politely while K!rikkl polished its mandibles. Finally, with deliberate grace and elegance, K!rikkl withdrew a blue silk scarf from its sleeve and laid it across the game board.

One of the other players made a sound of disgust with its hind rasps. Rrr backed away from the board in silent relief. G!ligglix clacked impatiently. "A suspension, K!rikkl?"

"Unfortunately, dear G!ligg, one must attend to the needs of the physical world *before* one can achieve the spiritual."

K!rikkl inclined its head to each of the players in turn. "I invite you to refresh yourselves as well so that we need not be interrupted again."

The Ki! smiled and straightened itself and stepped back away from the low dais of the game field.

As it stepped toward the door, K!rikkl clacked a warning syllable to the host-grub it used as a burden-beast; the pale-pink creature gobbled back a nonsense syllable of its own from where it squatted in the corner. The thing was almost as fat and naked as a larva—and it was getting embarrassingly large as well. K!rikkl would have to plant eggs in the grub soon or someone might begin asking the wrong kind of questions.

Keeping its features impassive, the Ki! moved with a quick, high-stepping gait; it bowed through the gossamer curtains of the pavilion and out into the night. The low building behind it glowed with muted blue warmth.

The others complained, but they tossed their egg-pouches onto the table and followed. Protocol demanded that no Ki! stay unattended in the room with the board and the other players' pouches. Throwing a silk therefore had only limited strategic value in the overall structure of the game. It worked against the other players' balance much more than it worked against their positions. Nevertheless—an experienced player could take advantage of even the smallest possibilities...

K!rikkl was neither hungry nor thirsty; nor did its bowels need emptying. Nor did it need to lay an egg. K!rikkl did not need to polish its carapace, nor did it need to groom its foreclaws or even empty its parasite pouch—but there were other needs, much more important, so K!rikkl began to take care of all of its intimate physical functions anyway.

The Ki! stepped haughtily across the carefully manicured lawn to the lush grove of dormant Fn^rr and began digging a trench for its excreta. K!rikkl dug slowly and patiently, scraping its hindclaws through the soft dark earth with the utmost of care. It was still several months until the spring, when the Fn^rr would begin walking and talking again. This far south, the Fn^rr spent almost as much of the year rooting themselves as they spent being ambulatory—but the Fn^rr were only dormant, not unconscious. They often remembered the events that occurred during their dream-time; many of the Ki! hoped that the care they took in fertilizing the roots of the Fn^rr would be remembered and rewarded in the Summer.

At least that was the justification for being so thorough and meticulous.

K!rikkl filled the trench with a jet of oily fluid and then pushed the dirt gently and precisely back over it. Then it paused to polish its foreclaws carefully with a soft silken cloth before it turned back to its companions.

K!rikkl knew that it couldn't delay the procedure of the game for too long, or that would truly arouse the questions of the others; but nonetheless it paused to sniff and chew a small bundle of herbs before turning back to the pavilion. It offered the herbs to the others, but they politely declined. K!rikkl waved its foreclaws in amusement and clacked its mandibles in gaudy appreciation. The sound echoed loudly across the lawn. "Well," K!rikkl trilled loudly to Hnaxx and the others. "Shall we play?"

The host-grub was still sitting in the corner; it paid no attention as the Ki! stepped back into the pavilion. It was grooming or playing with or examining the soft flesh of its body—probably looking for fleas. K!rikkl clacked at it; the creature looked up and gobbled back, then resumed its abstracted examination of itself. K!rikkl snicked in annoyance and then turned its attention back to the board, lifting the silk scarf and considering the possibilities again.

K!rikkl waited until all the others had resumed their positions, then blinked and tapped and hesitated—and made the move it had already decided to make long before it threw the scarf, a move so deliberately neutral it suggested that K!rikkl had decided not to breed at all for the next six cycles of the game. K!rikkl glanced over at the grub in the corner. It was counting the toes of its left hind foot.

Hmm.

Perhaps there were breeding possibilities with Rrr, after all. Not just here in the game, but beyond its boundaries as well. If Rrr survived, K!rikkl might—just might—indenture the Ki! as a mate. But…if Rrr were to survive the evening, then who might take its place? Hnaxx? (Too bony. And besides, it was considered bad manners to eat the host, no matter how bad a player it was.) Lggn'nk? (Maybe. But Lggn'nk seemed greasy and unappetizing.) Dxxrt? (Possibly. But Dxxrt was too cautious a player to be trapped.) G!ligglix would be ideal, of course…all that juicy fat—

The grub had ceased its examination of its foot and was now picking parasites out of the dark folds of its crotch.

So! G!ligglix did have a Knrkt after all! That meant that its aggressive betting was only a bluff to encourage the other players to extend themselves too soon! What a marvelous trap G!ligglix was laying. If it succeeded, it could turn loose a very hungry Knrkt on the egg pouches of all of the other players and guarantee itself a permanent breeding advantage.

K!rikkl kept its face impassive. If G!ligglix could be forced to keep its egg pouch sealed until the Knrkt awoke—and Knrkts always woke up hungry—G!ligglix could be eaten out of the game and onto the table before even the first generation was ambulatory! Hmm. And hmm again. What an absolutely delicious possibility…

But it would have to be very carefully managed. Either Rrr or Hnaxx would have to come into enough of a fortune to shift the balance of trading; the breeding negotiations could not be opened while there were still incomplete trades. If the close of barter could be delayed through three more rotations—no, that would be too obvious. Besides, Hnaxx was already befortuned; it would have to be Rrr—but any advantage shifted to Rrr would have to be done anonymously. Perhaps on the next scramble—or better yet, the one after that; but it was going to be very tricky to arrange. An advantage should not be used to betray itself—especially not this advantage.

This was going to require some study.

If the other players ever found out just how thoroughly trained the fat, pink host-grub really was, it would not be long thereafter that K!rikkl would be the guest of honor at a stinging. Or worse. K!rikkl might find itself hosting grubs of its own.

K!rikkl rasped its hind legs together in a loud, absentminded whirr. G!ligglix looked up curiously; the others continued to study the markers on the inlaid board.

"Your pardon, dear G!ligg," said K!rikkl, lowering its eyes shyly. "I was just considering a most interesting possibility."

G!ligglix's reply was noncommittal.

The Smile and the Slime

THE LIAISON OFFICER was a slug.

It floated in a glass tank, blowing frothy green bubbles as it spoke. The voice that came through the speakers was a wet, slobbery gurgle.

Yake Singh Browne, Assistant Liaison Officer with the One Hundred and Thirteenth Interstellar Mission, listened politely to the soft whispering of the translator in his ear without expression. The Dhrooughleem were so painfully polite, it was depressing. There were at least sixty-three ritual courtesies to every Dhrooughleem transaction.

Yake stood quietly with his hands at his sides, waiting for the Dhrooughleem to finish. The slug-thing in the tank was finally concluding the blessing of Browne's genetic lineage, his parents, his egg-cluster-siblings, his mating-triad, his territorial governance, and the noble egg-clusters he had already—or perhaps would soon—sire upon his brothers in the pond. The translators weren't sure. Or perhaps the concept was untranslatable because there was no human equivalent. In any case, it made for some fascinating daydreams.

The Dhrooughleem Liaison finished its recitation and waited without expression for Yake's response. Keeping his face carefully blank (a smile was considered an insult to a slug; the showing of one's teeth implied that one was thinking of the other as a possible meal), Yake began to thank the Dhroo Liaison profusely. His thanks went on for several moments; it wasn't exactly a formal part of the ritual, but it was an expected one.

When Yake finally finished, the Dhrooughleem burbled something green. The translator whispered: "Unfortunately, as pleasant-garble as it is to acknowledge each other—garble-garble, tree shrews taste terrible—occasionally we must pause to garble-garble our respective purposes as well."

Yake agreed. He turned around to the desk beside him and picked up a folder of documents. "You have been so helpful to us, *Mn Dhrooughlorh,* that I hesitate to ask new impositions of you, and yet—it seems that there is still much my people do not understand. There are many more subjects about which we would like to experience clarification. I have taken the trouble of preparing a list—" He held it out to the Liaison's mechanical manipulators.

The Dhrooughleem made no move to take the folder. "May I respectfully garble-garble a new subject, *Mr. Browne?*" it asked.

Yake tried to hide his surprise. "I beg your pardon?" In eight hundred and twelve previous meetings with the Dhrooughleem, the subjects covered had been so meticulously according to ritual the meetings could have been scripted in advance. This was a total break in protocol—

"—must abase myself with a thousand salt water apologies for garbling the pattern of grace and [pneumatic gill-slits] and [soft red mud] which we have so carefully wrought together—"

Yake struggled to keep his face impassive. He hoped that the monitors were getting all this. Indeed, they should already be ringing for the Ambassador.

"—may I have your permission to garble a concern?"

Yake felt uncomfortable. The translating circuits were having greater than usual difficulty with the Dhrooughleem inflections. Clearly, something was not right. "Yes, of course, *Mn Dhrooughlorh,*" he said. "Please continue to garble—I mean, share your circumstance."

"My people have nowhere invested as much time in the garbling of the nature of your species as you deserve—[??] [Despite your odorous appearance, we look forward to eating and enslaving you] [??]—and we apologize if we are garbling presumptuous, of course—but have we been uncareful in explaining the nature of our service here?"

"No, of course not," Yake was quick to reassure. "The Dhrooughleem have been extraordinarily helpful to us in our missions. Were it not for the Dhrooughleem, we would not be able to query the InterChange as efficiently as we have."

"Yes, that is precisely the issue, dear garble." The Dhrooughleem writhed in its tank, stirring the brackish-looking water into murky brown and green swirls. "We are concerned about your relationship with the InterChange. [Your egg clusters are a lovely shade of ignorance.] Perhaps we do not understand you well enough. Perhaps you do not understand us—"

"Oh, no—we understand you perfectly!" Yake caught himself in mid-word, and corrected himself hastily: "I mean, we understand you as well as we can. That is, allowing for cultural and biological differences and the inefficiencies of our translating circuits."

"Yes, that is the [offspring]! Perhaps we have failed to garble what your responsibilities are to the membership of the InterChange."

Yake cleared his throat uncomfortably. What was the damn slug driving at anyway? This was going to require some fancy tap-dancing. "As I understand it, *Mn Dhrooughlorh,*" Yake began carefully, "the Inter-Change is a gathering of many different species from many different worlds. Admission is granted to any species that can maintain a mission here. Is that correct so far?"

"Unfortunately so. You are aware also of the responsibilities and [fresh excrement] that such membership entails?"

"Information requested must be paid for with information of equal value—or by services. My species understands the concept of value exchange quite well."

"That is the concern and [antique chair collection] of my species. I am relieved to hear you say that. I had so feared that we might be [enamored] about the circumstances, Mr. Browne."

Yake was about to reassure the Dhrooughleem again when something went *twang* in the back of his mind. He said, instead, "As we understand the contract, new species are allowed a period of indebtedness in which to acquaint themselves with the…the rules of the game. Have we been mistaken about that?"

"Again, your grasp of the [slime mold] is admirable, Mr. Browne. It is I who must wear the [seasoning-spices] of embarrassment. Please to accept a thousand and three apologies for even raising the subject. The question was brought up only as a [traffic ornament] of our great respect for your species, and our concern that your [enslavement] be applied most deliciously."

"I beg your pardon? What was that about 'enslavement'?" (Yake promised himself an appointment with the Chief of Translation Services. This was intolerable!)

The slug burbled a blue froth. "[I have exercised my hair.] What word didn't you understand?"

"The word for 'service,' I believe."

The slug blew a single red bubble. A bad sign that. The translator whispered: "I said nothing about service."

Yake sighed and retreated into the safest of rituals. "Pardon my ignorance, *Mn Dhrooughlorh,* but I am confused here. I abase myself at my own stupidity. Please do not feel that the misunderstanding is a result of any of your words or actions. Please accept my apology for any inference that you have done less than your best. Perhaps in my eagerness to ease your discomfort at having to travel and meet in such a cumbersome device as a tank on wheels, I presume familiarities that I should not."

Yake reached up and twiddled his hair with his fingers, the closest he could come to an abasement wriggle. He felt like Stan Laurel doing it; then, having satisfied the ritual, he continued carefully. "Somehow I get the feeling that there is a subject we are discussing about which I do not have all the facts. May I request that you speak your concern a bit more directly? I promise you that there can be no offense taken here. We are searching only for the clarity of truth within your information."

"Since you ask for candor, I can only give it to you." The slug sank back down in its tank. Its eyes—all eight of them—were suddenly very large and very black. "My species is quite concerned about the size of your information debt."

"We have asked for something we should not have?"

"No, no—it is not the current package of requests that is the issue. It is the extremely large amount of information that you have already [ingested]. The interest is accruing perhaps a bit more rapidly than you are aware? Indeed, at the current rate of accrual, you are going to strike your debt limit in less than eighteen of your months. My species is [be-fargled] that your species will be indentured before you have had an opportunity to present a [vat of boiling chemicals] to the Monitors.

"It is clear to me, of course, now that you have reassured me here, that you and your species fully understand the nature of the circumstances and are not without knowledge of the [edibles]—but of course, the cleverness of your species is such that you must already have a [foundation garment] to present to the InterChange, and I have been dreadfully out of line for even garbling the subject. Please, no offense is meant—"

"—and none is taken."

"However, the [garlic seasoning] of this discussion was to let you know that the Dhrooughleem stand ready to continue to assist the Terran Mission in any way possible—"

"We thank you for that."

"—and if your [menu of green flavors] is turned down by the Monitors, we stand ready to assume the indenture of your entire species—"

"I beg your pardon? It sounded like you said 'indenture'—"

"—We have assumed many indentures, and always at the worst equable rate. We would take great [condiments] to be the kindest of guardians while your [enslavement] is [ingested]. You promise to be a most [delicious] species."

Yake felt dizzy. The translator hadn't been out of focus at all! Oh, dear Lord in Heaven!

"We have hesitated to mention this, of course, out of our fear that we might somehow [gringle] your [pentacles]. To some species, even to imply [malodorous deflation] might be smelled as a [sphincter] of offense. It [tickles our bladders] that you [descendants of tree shrews] are so [happy to be eaten]. Some species would see such a [bereavement] as a [dishonorable suicide]. It is our very high regard for you [things that belong on a plate] that mandates our concern here. If you would pass this [offer of ingestion] on to your own superiors so that they may be aware of our concern and our willingness to purchase your indenture and [eat your livers], we would be most—"

The rest of the interview was a blur.

The Teeth of the Slug

THE CRYING ROOM looked like a war zone.

Every terminal was alive, whether someone was sitting before it or not; every screen was either scrolling through long columns of text or flashing bright-colored three-dimensional graphs and translation matrices. The diplomacy-technicians were moving quickly from workstation to workstation, pulling reports from one, giving instructions to another, keying in new instructions to a third. The Section Chiefs were clustered in small groups at or near the big briefing table; that end of the hall was raised above the rest so that most of the large screens at the opposite end of the chamber would be visible from that position. The table itself was covered with a six-hour detritus of half-empty coffee mugs, still-glowing clipboards, scratch pads, pens, crumpled wads of paper, and red-bordered hardcopies of classified documents.

Secretaries of all four sexes moved quietly around the edges of the room, gathering up the debris of previous confrontations and handing out weaponry for the next. Orderlies and robots worked to replenish sandwiches and keep the coffee urns full. In one of the corners, a thirty-year veteran was quietly weeping in a chair.

The initial shock of realization had not yet sunk in. The diplomatic staff was still trying to assimilate the scope of the problem. The damage reports were still coming in—and the damage was not only worse than anyone had expected, it was even worse than they had feared.

The Crisis Management Team was not even waiting for the full report; they had already moved into the second stage of the job—fixing the blame. The sound level was horrendous; the cacophony was on its way to a record decibel level. The accusations, denials, explanations, excuses, justifications, rationalizations and reasons stormed and raged back and forth across the room like a caged tornado, carrying in their fury a blizzard of notes and images, documents, diagrams, photographs and papers. The conflicting evidences of blame and blamelessness flickered and flashed across the wall of screens until all meaning was leached from even the simplest of facts. The situation assimilation process had long since aborted and collapsed in a state of information implosion.

The Ambassador From Terra had once been known for his Million-Light-Year stare. Now his eyes were veiled and gray. His stare was focused on the cold cup of coffee in his hands and it was impossible to tell what he was thinking. A jabber of voices swirled around him, but apparently he was listening to none of them.

Yake Singh Browne sat quietly at the opposite corner of the table, making meaningless notes on a pad of paper while the arguments continued. He did not even look up when the chair flew past his back. Two career diplomats had already had to be pried apart by their colleagues and sent to opposite corners of the room.

"Sir? Sir—" someone from Analysis was trying to attract the Ambassador's attention. Yake glanced across the table and began to wonder if the Ambassador was crumbling under the strain. The Old Man looked dreadful. The Assistant Secretary of Something-Or-Other was jabbering insistently, "I hate to say 'I told you so,' but we've been advocating fiscal responsibility for decades, and no one's been listening to us. This is precisely the kind of debt position that we've been warning against—"

"It's really the fault of the Library Department," said the bulldozer-shaped woman on the other side of the Ambassador. "You know how those hackers are. They see something interesting on the menu, they automatically download it with the idea of exploring it in detail later. Of course, they never do. Something more interesting always comes along. We have material in our banks that we won't be getting to for a hundred years! And as far as assimilation goes—"

"Really, I reject that!" came the angry reply from halfway down the table. "If we'd had the help we'd originally asked for, that material wouldn't be going unread. I say that if we'd had the librarians, we could have catalogued the material already. There's probably a hundred different answers to this situation already in our banks. We just don't know where to find them—"

"I think you're all missing the point here. You've been played for fools by the Dah—D'haroo—Dhrooughleem." That was Madja Poparov, the new Policy Supervisor from the InterChange-Council Advisory Committee, Russian Section. Rumor had it that she could trace her ancestry all the way back to Joseph Stalin. Yake looked up curiously.

"You have been—what is right word here? Set up? *Da*. Led by your noses down primrose garden."

"Yes, of course, Ms. Poparov," Anne Larson, the British Representative, replied with a smile. "Considering your own political background, you would be the one most likely to spot such a situation—"

"This is not time for accusations and recriminations," Madja responded quietly. "This is time for thoughtful solutions."

"Absolutely." Larson's smile grew dangerous. "Let the record show that as soon as Ms. Poparov had read her accusations and recriminations into the record, she was ready to get back to work."

Madja's face reddened. "That is unfair attack. Very *nyekulturny*."

"No attack is unfair—attacks are supposed to hurt. That's how the game is played."

Yake lowered his face to his notepad, to hide his own smile.

"Can we please keep to the subject, Ladies—?" interrupted a tired voice. Yake looked up. It was the Ambassador.

Normally, the old man kept out of the roll-up-your-sleeves-and-get-down-and-dirty part of the discussions until a consensus began to develop. For him to request that the participants of a free-for-all try to stay on purpose demonstrated just how immediate he felt the situation really was.

Both Larson and Poparov nodded their instant acquiescence—then exchanged withering glares. Yake waited to see if the Ambassador was going to add anything else, but the Old Man lapsed back into silence.

"Sir?" That was Kasahara from Intelligence. "There may be some evidence to support Ms. Poparov's assertion that we've been set up—"

Poparov's glare turned into a triumphant smile.

"—but I think the truth is much more that we've set ourselves up. With encouragement, perhaps, but I don't think we should try to pass the blame entirely onto the Dhroo."

Madja's glare faded. Anne Larson's smile broadened.

And the cacophony began again.

"What I want to know," interrupted someone else, "is how we're going to explain to humanity that we've sold them into slavery?"

"—can't win a war against the slugs. We'll have to—"

"—really need to buy time. As much as we can—"

used. *Raped*—pardon my English. Because of these feelings, it might be inappropriate for me to continue to represent our position to the Dhroo. In fact, if you want my resignation, sir—"

"Don't be silly, Yake. It's all right with me if you get angry. In fact, it'd be all right with me if you were pissed as hell! And then it'd be even more all right if you used that anger as fuel for your efforts at finding a way out of this mess."

"Thank you, sir."

"*De nada.*" The Ambassador turned back to Kasahara then. "All right, Nori. Let's go back to your point. You say that they're just being polite, nothing more—"

"No, sir—I didn't say that. Not at all. What I said was, the Dhrooughleem don't get aggressive. They get polite. And now, they've gotten very very polite with us."

"Hm," said the Ambassador. "In other words, that politeness may just be the way that they express their aggression."

"Yes, sir. It's possible."

"I see. They don't put out the bear traps, but neither do they tell you to watch out for them when they take you for a walk in the woods, is that it?"

Kasahara nodded his head in agreement. His black hair shone like metal. He flashed his teeth in a grim smile of appreciation at the Ambassador's analogy.

"Good. Then, let's assume, for the moment, that this *is* a trap. It may be a dangerous assumption because it could blind us to other ways of dealing with the situation, but let's make the assumption anyway and see if we can find any evidence to support this assertion or disprove it."

Abruptly, Yake realized something. He sat up straight in his chair and stared across the table at the Ambassador. The Old Man wasn't crumbling under the strain at all. He'd been playing possum, ignoring all the tumult and turmoil, quietly waiting for the uproar to wear itself out.

Yake grinned in appreciation. You don't get to be Ambassador From Terra without some cunning. After all the accusations and recriminations had been made, and the conversation had finally gotten down to specifics, the Ambassador had resumed control of the meeting. Very clever. He didn't waste his energy on the wrong things.

"Yake," asked the Ambassador. "You seem to have a thought on your mind?"

"Uh, yes sir. I do. Um—we need to find out if this is the standard operating procedure of the InterChange or if the slugs have broken some rule or other. And we need to be very discreet about this line of inquiry too."

"Yes. A very good suggestion." The Ambassador turned to the bulldozer-shaped woman. "Library, I'll want a full scan of the InterChange

Charter documents." The Ambassador pulled his clipboard to him and switched it on. He glanced at it only briefly, then looked up across the table again.

"Those of you who are currently involved in other negotiations, we're going to want to review each and every one of those to see if there are any other hidden agendas that we don't know about. We may find that we've stepped in a whole minefield here."

The Ambassador paused to rub his nose thoughtfully between his long, bony fingers, then continued softly, "A key question is just how frankly we can discuss this situation with any of our contacts. I won't call them allies. But uh...let's see what we can find out about indenture contracts. What kind of terms are usually offered to a client, how long does a species have to pay, what are the penalties for default, that kind of thing. Oh, yes—" He turned to a sad-looking man three seats away. "Ted, I know this is an unpleasant possibility, but you might as well begin looking at ways to sell it to the home office, if we have to—"

A Night to Dismember

THE DINNER HAD BEEN EXCELLENT and K!rikkl was feeling gaudy and satiated. The young Ki! clacked its mandibles in loud appreciation and recited a verbose poem of praise for the culinary masterpieces of Hnaxx's. G!ligglix's flesh had *indeed* proven juicy and sweet—and, if that were not enough blessing for one evening, K!rikkl was already looking forward to the mating with Rrr later this evening. That too would be all the sweeter, since K!rikkl's discovery that Rrr was a favored child of the prestigious and powerful Trrrl^t Nest.

K!rikkl felt very very satisfied. So satisfied, in fact, that it had already decided that should tonight's mating prove successful, then the specially trained grub that had made the whole thing possible should receive the honor of hosting the larvae. It would not only be the politic thing to do, it would also be the safest.

Besides, it was always best to destroy the evidence.

And...should it ever prove necessary, K!rikkl could always begin training a new grub after the Fn^rr awakened in the spring. During the three days of restoration festivals, when the dream-refreshed Fn^rr reclaimed their pavilions from the Ki! caretakers, there were always opportunities for personal expansion—and a young Ki! without the resources and backing of a major Nest to draw upon had to be constantly available to the beneficence of fate. Of course, should the mating with Rrr prove fruitful, that state of affairs was likely to change for the better, and quite rapidly too. The Trrrl^t Nest was rumored to have many fine plantations in need of proper care and guidance. This Ki! felt like just the one for the job.

Yes, K!rikkl was satisfied. It reached out and stroked one of Rrr's foreclaws affectionately. The younger Ki! seemed deliciously limber—an additional benefit—it would be an enjoyable mating as well as profitable. K!rikkl rasped its hind legs together in a quick rattle of anticipation. Rrr bowed its head in acquiescence.

"Don't be so impatient, K!rikkl—" Hnaxx said casually. "There is plenty of time for you and Rrr to retire to the mating pavilion, but there is only a short time left for us to pick the bones of sweet G!ligglix. Your playing of the game was beyond superb. Please remain a little longer and enlighten us with more of your delicious observations on Nestling strategy."

K!rikkl withdrew its claw politely from Rrr's forelimb and said quietly, "Yes, of course, dear Hnaxx. How could I be less than generous in repaying your own beneficence? I am at your service. What is it you wish to know?" K!rikkl lowered its head in acquiescence.

"A simple thing really." Hnaxx made a gesture that signified minimal importance, a squeezing motion with its foreclaws. "Tell me—how did you discover that a host-grub could be trained to help you cheat at Nestlings?"

"I beg your pardon?" K!rikkl swiveled its head in Hnaxx's direction. It actually *hadn't* understood the question—and then the meaning of the words did sink in, and K!rikkl was sorry it had responded at all.

"Ah," chirruped Hnaxx. "Perhaps you didn't notice the small black ornaments hanging from the rafters—"

K!rikkl jerked its triangular head up and around, blinking in confusion. There were several shining metal objects hung at intervals around the ceiling. K!rikkl had assumed that those were simply baubles, expensive off-world ornaments. The Fn^rr were fond of such. K!rikkl looked back to Hnaxx, keeping its face carefully impassive.

"But surely, you have heard of these devices, K!rikkl," said Hnaxx. "They are called *cameras*. They are the eyes and the ears of those who have lost their trust."

K!rikkl considered its responses carefully before responding. At last, it blinked slowly and rasped, "Perhaps I should be offended that you do not trust me—that you hang alien devices in a sacred pavilion."

Hnaxx declined the opportunity to apologize. "Perhaps we should be offended that you are not trustworthy. The devices were purchased from the same off-world creatures who negotiated our colonization here. They are very clever constructions. They look and they listen; when they are through looking and listening they show exactly what they have seen and heard. They neither add nor subtract their own interpretations or opinions on the matter, so they are very useful for circumstances such as this, dear K!rikkl. The devices clearly show that your grub opened and examined the contents of every pouch on the table. But come—" Hnaxx dropped a blue silk cloth on the table and said, "—Let us not have the old rituals stand in the way. The game was played and the conclusion has been celebrated. The claw of contention is not how you won, dear K!rikkl. Indeed, we can express only our admiration for your cleverness. We have been watching your career for some time and with much interest, but we had not suspected such an ingenious device. Please tell us, how did you train it?"

"Train…it?" K!rikkl paused to consider its remaining options. They were all unpleasant.

Of course, there was always the truth…

"Come, come, K!rikkl—you are letting your fear do your thinking. Let me reassure you that you are in no danger at all here; you are among colleagues. You are in a position to do yourself, and many others as well, a great deal of good."

K!rikkl considered the thought. That could be its single advantage here. The Ki! arched its head coyly sideways. "May I ask how?"

Hnaxx rasped its hind claws in annoyance. It looked up at the alien devices and then back to K!rikkl. It sighed. "This grows tiresome. Perhaps we need to take a walk in the moonlight to clear our heads. Will you join me?"

K!rikkl covered its anxiety with a performance of eagerness. "It would be an honor, dear Hnaxx." It followed the older, larger Ki! toward the darkness beyond the pavilion.

They high-stepped in silence through the tufted loin-grass, across the barren meadow and down toward the gnarled wall-forest. Hnaxx deliberately steered K!rikkl away from the Fn^rr groves. "Do not think me rude, but sometimes I find the scent of the Fn^rr blossoms to be so sweet that it is almost overpowering. Sometimes I need to stand at a distance to admire them more appropriately."

"You need not apologize to me, great Hnaxx. I understand completely. The Fn^rr are such a grand race that I am occasionally inspired to—you must forgive me even for expressing such an indelicacy—but I do admit to an occasional twinge of…resentment."

"Resentment?"

"Perhaps that is too strong a word; but I am young and impetuous. It is difficult to speak of indenture without chafing."

"Yes, it is." Hnaxx did not speak again until they were safely within the broad bandwork of roots and traveling vines of the wall-forest. "I can only admire your caution, dear K!rikkl; that speaks well of your mind. It shall be of great service, if it is applied wisely."

K!rikkl nodded its thanks, but said nothing.

Hnaxx continued quietly. "Let me explain something to you. Tonight's game was not simply a game of Nestlings. It was a carefully constructed pouch. We wanted to see who would grab it."

"You are saying that the game was…contrived?"

Hnaxx clacked its mandibles in annoyance. "That would be an unforgivable rudeness to the guests. Even to suggest it is an offensive act."

"I would abase myself publicly before committing such a terrible rudeness," K!rikkl responded quickly. "Nonetheless, what else am I to surmise from your assertion?"

"Ah," said Hnaxx. "Let me suggest this—that there was no way that you could have won any of tonight's cycles based on what was knowable to you. The only way to win this pouch was to know what was hidden in it and play accordingly. Whoever won this game tonight could only have done so by performing some maneuver not commonly accepted in the game of Nestlings. I shall be unconscionably direct—and please forgive my rudeness in being so, dear K!rikkl."

K!rikkl waved away the apology. "We are colleagues." K!rikkl knew that was a presumption, but possibly a life-saving one.

"That you cheated," continued Hnaxx, "demonstrated to all of us that you are a Ki! well worthy of marrying into the Trrrl^t Nest. The cameras were hung not to determine *if* you cheated, only *how.* Had you not cheated, you would have been a tender feast, young Ki!."

K!rikkl bowed its head in agreement and held the pose.

"So," Hnaxx added quietly, "you have no secrets except one—and now that you are about to become a member of the Trrrl^t Nest, so must your knowledge also become a part of the common store. It is only appropriate."

K!rikkl continued its bow of acquiescence, even lower now. "You are more clever than I suspected, noble Hnaxx. Had I realized—" K!rikkl rasped in annoyance and stopped in mid-phrase. There was really nothing else to say. K!rikkl held up a claw for error-apology, reformulated its thoughts, and began again. "My apologies for underestimating the cleverness of the Trrrl^t Nest. I will endeavor to be worthy of the brilliance demonstrated here tonight."

They paused on a high, looping gnarl-branch and looked down at the jeweled pavilion and the vale beyond. The sprawling orchards were bathed in the soft pink glow of the moons. "The Fn^rr blossoms are fragrant tonight," said Hnaxx. "There will be many fine seedlings soon."

"And many more families. And many more pavilions." K!rikkl did not add the obvious. *And much more pressure on the Ki! to protect the young. The indenture will be exhausting.*

Hnaxx rasped its foreclaws in agreement. "What I am about to tell you has never happened. It is only hypothetical. So it means nothing.

But even as a speculation, it is still a secret of the Nest—and must be guarded as carefully as an egg pouch. Do you understand?"

"I so acknowledge," said K!rikkl with ritual deliberation.

"Thank, you." Hnaxx took K!rikkl by the forelimb and led the young Ki! back into the sheltering darkness of the wall-forest. "The Trrrl^t Nest has been studying these grubs for some time. I myself have spent much time examining their dissected brains. We have often suspected that they might be capable of some higher logical behavior than we have ever seen demonstrated. Perhaps they could even be *trained* to eat or not to eat certain foodstuffs. Do you understand? It is something that we would like to experiment with. Your discoveries could be very valuable in ways I need not elucidate here. I'm sure you are smart enough to comprehend what I am saying."

K!rikkl sighed. This was better than it had hoped. "Yes, my Lord."

"Ahh, quite. So you can see why we are understandably curious. Where did you find out this knowledge? Who have you told? How have you applied it? Is this the only grub you have ever trained, or are there others in the hands of other Ki!? And what, if anything, have they discovered?"

"Let me be quick to reassure you. There are no others who share this knowledge, oh mighty Hnaxx. I myself was taught only by a traveling merchant who died soon after."

"That is to your benefit, dear K!rikkl. Unfortunate for the merchant, but fortunate for you. It means that there is no one else whose knowledge is as valuable as yours. This has great bearing on a question that the Trrrl^t Nest has been considering for some time: what value might these grubs have beyond their obvious uses as food or hosts for our larvae? I need not tell you how much our Nest might benefit if we had the answers to such questions."

K!rikkl nodded its agreement, at the same time trying to hide its glee. The opportunities here could be extraordinary! And dangerous, as well! What a very *interesting* dilemma!

Hnaxx paused to rasp its foreclaws in anticipation. "That is why you were invited to play in the game this evening. Your success at the game of Nestlings has improved remarkably since you have begun traveling with a host-grub. We were most curious about this fact, and I tell you truly, we had not expected such an astonishing demonstration. We find it most interesting to see that your grub is capable of such astonishing behavior. It suggests possibilities to us that we had not previously dreamt of. Now do you see why we need to know how this grub was trained?"

K!rikkl's mind was racing with thoughts of unlimited wealth and unnumbered mates. Perhaps even a Nest of its own! Was it truly possible to dream this big? K!rikkl bent its forelimbs and lowered its head in acquiescence. "I shall be at the service of your Nest, my Lord. My flesh is yours."

"Thank you, K!rikkl," said Hnaxx. "Your service is accepted and welcomed into this Nest. And in return, the Nest stands ready to serve you."

The Cold Earth

INTO THE SOUTHERN HEMISPHERE of a gentle world comes a night when the blossoms rustle with tomorrow's wind.

The hot breath of unborn days catches the leaves of many orchards, many groves, and all the stands arise to wakefulness in hours, all the stands, all whispering with the troubled murmurings a dream-time less than sweet.

The blossom-scents of many Fn^rr turn yellow-brown with dreadfulness and uncertainty.

My roots have grown so cold...

The hideous dreams, they come again!

The sense is clear. The scent is fear.

My roots are cold!

There is ash upon the soil.

We wither and we die.

There are eaters in the dreams. Many eaters creeping. They eat the seeds. They eat the young. They scoop and eat the brains of those who dream.

My roots are cold.

The eaters come, the eaters breed, they run wild in the groves! They eat us as we dream!

All cry for seedlings yet unsown!

Where are the Ki!? Where are the Ki!?

Where is the promise of the garden-keepers?

Why are the Ki! not in the dreams? Is the rasp of silver claws so much like the sound of teeth?!

Fear for the Ki!, the ones who walk the night. They swarm, and spread betrayal of the crop.

My roots are cold.

Fear for the Ki!. No more to swarm! No more to swarm!

They are lost in dreamless dreams! They do not heed our cries!

The dreams, the foul dreams!

Who brings such madness to the roots? Who fouls the dreams? Who?

The wet ones slither through the dreams.

The wet ones lie in slime! They promised us a world! Ai-eee. It is a world of death!

My roots are very cold.

The dreams are filled with teeth and terror!

The eaters still infest the groves, they overrun the groves. The orchards swarm with menace. The soil blackens with manure. The children die within their hands!! The wind does roar and rip the leaves!

Why do these dreams infest? What portends? What horrors sweep upon us from the night beyond the dawn? Why are the dreadful eaters following on the trail of the slugs?

So cold. So very cold.

Abandon hope. Abandon fear. The edge of horror soon cuts here!

The slugs are beasts from coldest hell, from hottest hell, from driest hell, from wettest hell. They speak in lies; they lie in offal. The awful truth of slugs is that slugs can't tell the truth!

The wet ones creep through all the dreams: They speak too sweetly; they leave behind a sugary death. They give our children no safe place to sink their roots.

We have been sliced.

Betrayed.

Destroyed.

My roots are cold.

The eaters come through coldest night. Can you hear the teeth?

The dreams are screams of children, seedlings dreaming screaming! They are being eaten in their birth-dreams!!

The stalks of many will soon be rotting in the dream-groves!

The death comes quickly, spreading like a brown and wilting scour.

Ai-eee!! I mourn! I mourn!

Our world will be lost, our blossoms fall upon a barren land!

We can no longer trust the hosting slugs! They kill us with their kindness! There is no hope! No hope! No home!

So very very cold.

Abandon home, all ye who have grown here!

No place to sink our roots!

No place at all!

We roam through airless voids!

Again to dream of other worlds, other voices? Can we dream of other land?

Dream a voice. Dream a voice. A sound of light.

There is no voice. Only the grunting sounds of eaters.

Too bold. Too bold. There are no roots in space.

So very very bold.

Neither is there soil in which to nurture a tomorrow.

Can we no longer sense new scents upon the solar wind? Have our branches grown so stiff?

There are no voices.

And even so, is there not a hint of wonder? Can such things be possible?

There is always room for wonder.

Can there be a voice of light within the dreams? A ray of sun in which to grow?

The dreams have all been fouled.

Can we afford to send our seedlings into space to seek these other voices?

Can the grove afford to risk the danger?

And even as the dream comes down, can we not afford to take the chance?

That is the root of the question.

The root. The solid root.

Can we not afford to take the chance?

We must...negotiate.

We must.

My roots are cold.

An Offer of Employment

THE AMBASSADOR CLEARED HIS THROAT for attention and the room fell abruptly silent. Yake was suddenly very conscious just how old the Old Man really looked. Maybe it wasn't *all* performance. He felt embarrassed at the thought, as if he'd penetrated some private part of the old man's self.

But then the Ambassador spoke, and his voice was as strong and commanding as ever—and all thoughts of the man's fragility fell completely out of Yake's consciousness.

"All right," the Ambassador was saying. "We've begun receiving some responses to our, ah...inquiries about the possibilities of humanity's service to the InterChange. I won't comment on the ones that I've seen. I think that the, ah...acceptability of these will be self-evident. Nori?"

Kasahara opened the folder in front of him and began reading slowly. "Yes, sir." He looked around the table. His usual good-natured smile was missing as he turned to the first of the papers in his folder. "I'll read these in the order received.

"The Nixies of Nn have offered a six percent premium for human service as larval incubators. We have to guarantee a minimum of five hundred thousand nonrefundable individuals per mating cycle.

Seven point one percent if we maintain a breeding station on-site. No colonial rights are implied. Severe penalties for failure to meet quota. Although the Nixies say they're planning to colonize several new worlds, Intelligence suspects that they are actually increasing their breeding in preparation for a war to be held not less than seven years from now, probably thirteen."

Kasahara did not wait for any reactions to that. He turned the page and immediately began reading the next. "The Dragons are willing to purchase—that's a flat-out purchase; we can apply the credits any way we choose—one to three million nonrefundable individuals per year. Two credits per body, plus fifteen percent allowance for shipping. Live bodies only. This is a no-explanations, take-it-or-leave-it deal. The offer is a standing one, always open, but the terms are non-negotiable. The Dragons guarantee nothing but immediate payment."

"Analysis?" asked the Ambassador.

Kasahara held up a single flimsy. "Intelligence reports that the Dragons prefer to eat their prey live."

Someone at the far end of the table gasped. Yake resisted the temptation to look around; he kept his face impassive. He had a hunch it was going to get worse. Much worse.

The Ambassador ignored the exclamation. "Go on, Nori."

"Um, yes—" Kasahara turned to the next document. "Um, there's an inquiry here from a race of…I guess you could call them intelligent plants. Apparently, they're having some trouble with vermin. They're curious about our abilities as…the only word that translates is—" Kasahara scratched his ear embarrassedly, "—gardener."

"Mm hm." The Ambassador nodded. "Let's get back to them on that one. Ask them for more details on what they need. Go on."

"The J(kk)l and the J(rr)l are both willing to purchase frozen or dead individuals. They won't pay as much as the Dragons, only one credit per body, but they are willing to assume the full cost of shipping. They have their own fleet. They're willing to pick up on-site. All we have to do is provide them with the coordinates of our home system."

"I don't like the sound of that—" someone said.

"Hush," said the Ambassador. "We're not discussing acceptability yet." He nodded to Kasahara again.

"Um—we also have six similar offers from—" Kasahara started leafing quickly through his papers.

"Never mind," interrupted the Ambassador. "We'll get to them when we get to them. Keep going."

"Yes, sir." Kasahara swallowed hard and turned to the next page.

"We have four more inquiries similar to the Nixies'. These are all routine; we haven't met any of their liaison people. Apparently larval incubators are in great demand all over the InterChange—or it's going to be quite a war. The Sslyb, the Whroolph, the Ki!—I don't know if I pronounced any of those right—and the Mnxorn, have all tendered inquiries of availability, based on proven species compatibility—compatibility to be determined through hands-on testing; we assume the costs of the testing and providing suitable specimens. No bids from any of them until biocompatibility is established to a 66 percent minimum."

Kasahara looked troubled for a moment, then added, "Analysis Section raises a serious question here, sir."

"What is it?"

"Well…have the Nixies established biological compatibility already? If so, *how?* None of the other species have claimed it—and none of the others have offered bids, either." Kasahara was having a little difficulty reading the next part. "Analysis suggests that a deeper investigation may be mandated here. Perhaps the Nixies have already been experimenting with—"

"Nori—" The Ambassador interrupted gently. "If they have, there's nothing we can do about it. Not yet, anyway. Just keep reading."

"Yes, sir." Kasahara turned to the next page. "The Slugs—sorry, sir, I mean, the Dhrooughleem—"

"Slugs is acceptable to me," said the Ambassador. "What are the Slugs offering?"

"Well, they've very reluctantly withdrawn their previous offer. They have expressed great shame and embarrassment, but apparently our going public is seen as a great loss of trust in their ability to manage our indenture benevolently."

"Yes, yes." The Old Man made a gesture of annoyed impatience. "So what are the Slugs offering now?"

"Three credits. Per body."

"For what service?"

"I'm not certain. It doesn't seem to translate well. It's—it's guaranteed to be a dry-land service. The individuals are guaranteed refundable, but—the reprogramming is not guaranteeable."

"Reprogramming?"

"Apparently, there will be some psychological adjustments needed for this particular service; upon completion of service, full restoration of previous mental condition may not be possible. Sir, I—I'm having a great deal of trouble with this—"

"So are we all, Nori. Please go on."

"Well, the Slugs' offer almost looks like a pretty good one, until you get into the details. They're asking only for female individuals—"

"Did they say for what purpose?"

"No, sir. Do you want me to ask?"

"Uhh…I'd rather you didn't. I don't think I'd like the answer. Never mind, go on."

"Uh—yes, sir." Kasahara turned the page gratefully. "Independently, we've determined that we can probably place a half-million individuals per year in various tourist facilities. That's more a courtesy than a source of income, but it does credit us with triple bonuses against the interest on our debt."

"Tourist facilities?" interrupted Madja.

"Zoos," said Kasahara. "On some planets, there's considerable curiosity about who else lives in the galaxy. There are over a hundred thousand major zoos served by the InterChange. Fortunately, we're listed as a herding species, so they'd have to take a minimal size representation—no less than fifty individuals per facility, no more than six million."

"Six million?"

"That's for the colony creatures—ants, bees, termites, bacteriological colonies and the like. I think we'd be limited to several hundred individuals per facility; but even so, that would give us at least one form of acceptable service, and the payments on our interest would be large enough to justify the effort. Unfortunately, the payments are only against the interest; none of it can be credited against the principal—so even though the zoo option can help control the rate of growth of our debt, it can't provide us with any kind of a permanent solution."

"Good," said the Ambassador. "Anything else?"

"Um. Yes." Kasahara was already looking ahead to the next offer. He glanced up with a paler-than-usual expression. "Uh—we have an offer from a consortium of six neo-reptilian species. They're willing to accept our entire indenture as it currently stands, plus a yearly stipend for future information acquisitions."

"Well, that sounds more like it!" remarked one of the younger assistants. He was ignored by almost everyone at the table.

"Right," said the Ambassador. "What do they want to buy?"

"Um…they want the right to begin biological experimentation on the human species—with an eye toward eventually mutating us into something useful. For one thing, they don't think we have enough sexes; that's why we breed so fast. However, they do guarantee no resale of individuals for either food or larval incubators—"

"Hm," suggested Anne Larson. "I wonder if we could do that one with volunteers?"

Kasahara looked across the table at her. "They require a minimum of one hundred thousand nonrefundable units per month for experimentation, plus total autonomy over the species' colonization and growth—uh, that includes the homeworld."

"That answers that," said Larson.

The Ambassador's expression was unreadable. He merely offered, "I think we might have some difficulty presenting that option to the home office. Please go on, Nori."

"Yes, sir. We also have two inquiries from bacteriological colonies. They're asking if we would consent to biological compatibility testing. If compatibility is possible, they would like to open negotiations for a symbiotic relationship. Um—these species don't live on worlds, they live inside other species. Two viral species have also requested testing, I think. I'm not sure this was translated correctly. We'd have to guarantee freedom from antibiotic and white-cell contamination. They guarantee no protection for the hosts; mostly, they seem to be interested in breeding sites. Maybe they're preparing for a war too? Along the same lines, several parasitical races have indicated their willingness to um…test for biological compatibility."

"Hmf," said the Ambassador noncommittally. "Do we have any offers from Smallpox, Leprosy or Psoriasis?"

"Just a moment," said Kasahara, thumbing quickly through the stack of papers in front of him. "I'll look—"

"Nori," the Old Man reached over and put a hand on Kasahara's arm. "That was a joke."

"A joke?" Kasahara blinked. "Oh. A joke."

"It's all right, Nori. You can look them up later. Please go on. Do you have any others to present?"

"Just two more, sir—the Rhwrhm have inquired if our planet is available for colonization; payment proportional to the number of colonists allowed to settle. Uh, the Rhwrhm are carnivores, sir. Very large carnivores. They eat Dragons."

"Yes, I see. And the other offer?"

"That's from the Rh/attes. They're suggesting something very unusual—unusual for the InterChange, that is. They don't need any service that we can provide; nothing important, that is—although they're willing to buy a couple of million tons of corn per year; but that's mostly a courtesy—a gesture of friendship from one mammalian species to another. What they're suggesting instead is that we assume *their* indenture."

"I beg your pardon—?" The Old Man took off his glasses and began to clean them with his handkerchief. "I don't think I heard you right." He returned his spectacles to his face and peered owlishly through them at the younger man. His eyes seemed very large and bright. "There. That's better. Now, try that on me again."

"They want us to assume a piece of their indenture," repeated Kasahara.

"That's what I thought you said." The Ambassador looked surprised. He glanced down the table to Miller, the head of Analysis Section. "Has your section had a chance to consider the implications of that?"

Miller shook her head. "It doesn't make sense to us. We're in much bigger trouble than the Rh/attes. We can't pay our own bills, let alone theirs. What do they gain here?"

Assuming we find a way to avoid defaulting, the only guarantee we can give them is that we're not going to sell them to anyone for food, incubation, or sex; nor will we sell them for biological experimentation without their consent. I don't see that that's strong enough to justify putting their fate in our hands. They can guarantee that by themselves right now. We have no real use for them; apparently no one else does, either. So, the alternative is that there's some advantage for them to be indentured to a species that defaults."

"I'll bet a nickel I know what it is," put in Larson.

The Ambassador looked down the table at her. "Yes, Anne?"

"It's really very simple—if we assume their indenture, we assume the total burden of their debt. When we default, we have to work off their debt as well as ours—and they go free. It's an easy way for them to wipe out their debt all at once."

"Interesting," said the Ambassador. "And quite clever in its own way. Hm. Let me consider the other side of that question for a moment. Is there any advantage in it for us? Could we—excuse me for asking this— structure the deal so that we could...ah, create some advantage here?"

"You mean, could we sell them as food, fuel, slaves, sex or guinea pigs?" Larson shook her head. "The Rh/attes are considered almost as undesirable as we are by the reptilian and insectoid species. Their debt isn't as large because they never downloaded as heavily as we did. On the other hand, neither have they ever come up with a service that the Inter-Change considers valuable; so they might be in just as tenuous a situation as we are. But they've been around for nearly five hundred years, so the real question is *why* hasn't the InterChange foreclosed on them? What service do the Rh/attes provide that justifies their current status?"

"You have some idea?" the Old Man asked.

Larson shrugged. "I'm not sure that this is a useful avenue of exploration, but if we knew how they had lasted five hundred years, it might shed some light on the details of their offer to us." She sighed tiredly. "I'm sorry, sir, but knowing that the Rh/attes are mammalian, I'd distrust them more than all the others put together. I know how nasty and greedy mammals can be."

"Unfortunately, I'm inclined to agree with you," the Ambassador said. He looked to Kasahara. "Is that it?"

"I'm afraid so, sir."

"All right—" The Old Man did not look beaten. "Let's do it this way. We'll break the offers down into four categories—" He began to tick them off on his fingers. "Totally Unacceptable; Not Bloody Likely,

Need More Information, and Let's Talk. We'll break into committees; each committee will evaluate three proposals and then validate the work of two other committees—"

A Quiet Objection

"Excuse me, sir!"

"Eh?" The Ambassador looked down the table. "Is there an objection?"

"Yes sir, there is." Madja Poparov stood up. "I object to this whole proceeding. We are talking about future of human species."

"Yes, Ms. Poparov, we are. What is your point?"

"That *is* my point. Are we qualified to do this job—to make these decisions?"

The Ambassador considered her question. At last he looked across the table at her and responded in a quiet tone of voice.

"Whether we're qualified or not is irrelevant. The responsibility is still ours. I grant you that none of us here sought or even desired this responsibility—most of us thought we were merely signing on for diplomatic research—but the circumstances have changed dramatically in the past few days. So have our jobs. Now, we have only one decision to make. Are we going to accept the responsibility that's been thrust upon us, or shirk it? If we choose not to accept the responsibility, we must still accept the consequences of that choice."

"I do not dispute that," said Madja. "Idiot I am not. The Incorporated Republics of United Russia do not send fools to front. I know that the choice must be made here, if for no other reason than there simply is not *time* to send back home for decision. The issue I am raising, Mr. Ambassador, is this one: how can we justify this discussion at all? How can we give any seriousness to these proposals? They are *all* unacceptable because of context that acceptance of any of them would create."

She paused, as if waiting for applause.

There was none.

Madja Poparov brushed her hair back off her forehead and continued. "The trouble with you free-market capitalists is that you are too damned pragmatic. We are sitting here and calmly discussing set of possibilities that reduce human beings to status of draft animals—or worse!

"We are talking about selling our brothers and sisters—*our comrades in the human adventure!*—into slavery as food or guinea pigs or hosts for parasitical life forms! And zoo animals, no less!

"The best of these offers that Mr. Kasahara has read to us is one that at least gives us the dignity of a common farm laborer—and even that one is unacceptable because it says that human beings have not wit to do anything more than follow someone else's instructions. I say that we cannot consider seriously any course of action that would establish that human beings are anything less than noble species. This is real issue. We must let them know that we deserve nothing less than highest respect! Or—" Madja looked grim and unhappy, "—we shall be condemning ourselves and our children to future of slavery and despair for untold generations to come."

This time there was applause.

But only from Yake.

He clapped loudly in the silence—and his applause was clearly intended as a sarcastic response to the melodramatic style of Madja's presentation.

Everybody else just looked uncomfortable.

Madja glared down the table at Yake. "You think this is funny, Mr. Yake Singh Browne?"

"The situation, no. The speech, maybe."

"You do not like what I said?"

Yake shrugged. "I question whether such speeches make much of a difference in the long run."

"The difference is whether we live as free people or as slaves! Is that not difference enough?"

Yake shrugged again. "I won't argue the question. I do find it... amusing that the distinction should be coming from you, Ms. Poparov. That is, from a representative of the Incorporated Russian States."

Madja frowned at Yake.

Madja Poparov's frown was a formidable expression.

Indeed, Madja Poparov's frown had been known to wither a rose bush at thirty meters.

She now turned the full force of it on Yake Singh Browne, a smug, self-satisfied, hot-blooded young parasite of the greedy ruling class of the degenerate societies of the western hemisphere—

Yake returned her stare, nonplussed.

The Old Man cleared his throat then; he allowed himself a drink of water, then cleared his throat again. He looked down the table at the two of them. "Yake—did you want to address the issue here? Ms. Poparov raised the issue of contextual repositioning inherent in the offers...?"

Yake regretted having to tear his eyes away from Madja. Actually, she had very nice eyes. But—reluctantly, he turned to the head of the table and said, "Well, yes sir, I did—"

Everyone at the table turned to face him. Yake could understand their curiosity. He too, wondered what he was about to say. "It seems to me that Madja here—pardon, I mean, Ms. Poparov—has raised a critical point. Um. One that is worthy of considerable...uh, consideration." Yake realized he was about to start sounding stupid. He caught himself and began again, "What I mean is—I think Madja is right."

The Ambassador did not look pleased with that response. Clearly, he had been hoping for a different sort of rebuttal.

Yake continued quickly. "If I were going to take the usual *pragmatic* view of the situation, I might say that we should choose the least unacceptable of these possibilities and make the best of a terrible situation. I could remind Ms. Poparov that we are a mammalian species and that, as it has turned out in the grand scheme of things, mammalian sentience is not a common occurrence, but only the occasional fluke of evolution that occurs when some disaster interrupts the natural trend to sentience in reptilian and insect species. On our own world, a comet smacked into the planet 65 million years ago and the resulting ecological polycrisis killed off the dinosaurs. There's a lot of evidence to suggest that hadrosaurs were just reaching the threshold of sentience. Who knows what they could have become? But primitive mammalian species, like the therapsids, evolved to fill the dinosaurs' ecological niches way too quickly, and the dinosaurs never got the chance to reestablish themselves. To most of the species in the InterChange, we're the descendants of ecological interlopers—uh, we're Darwinian carpetbaggers.

"The membership of this InterChange is all the evidence we need: two thousand and seventeen species, and only twelve of them are identifiably mammalian in nature. The rest are reptilian or insectoid or cephalopods—or otherwise unclassifiable.

"We may not like it," Yake said, "but the evolutionary patterns have been documented and confirmed by our own simulations. As life climbs toward intelligence, the reptilian and insect species have the advantage—and on most of the worlds, that's who gets there first. The mammals never get a chance; we stay in our trees and our burrows while the thunder lizards conquer the earth and the sky. We are tree shrews, we are rats, we are howler monkeys with delusions of grandeur." He looked to Madja Poparov regretfully. "It's difficult for me to listen seriously to talk about 'our comrades in the human adventure' when all of the evidence suggests that, at best, we are little more than accidents of evolution."

Madja Poparov sniffed. She looked like she wanted to reply, but Yake cut her off with a raised finger—

"If talking snakes and slugs and spiders are shocking and offensive to us, then consider what we must look like to them. We are egg-suckers and parasites and disease-spreaders, standing up on our hind legs and demanding a place at *their* banquet table; and they—despite their own charter—are horrified by us. They are as horrified as we would be if spirochetes and crab lice demanded representation at the United Council.

"The politest comparison I could make—" and here Yake spread his own brown hands before him, "—and I apologize for saying it, but it is still true—is that mammals, human beings in particular, are the pariahs of the galaxy. On our own world, we once had *gooks* and *dagos* and *kikes* and *spics* and *beaners* and *niggers*. Here, we are *all* of those, all at the same time. We are *mammals*." He bowed to the woman on his east and added with elaborate politeness, "Or perhaps if Ms. Poparov did not understand that, I could say that we are the Ukrainians in this cosmic Politburo—only it's even worse than that analogy suggests. There is no *chance* of respect for us here—and very likely, not even for what we can bring to the membership of this body, because this body is not prepared to see us or deal with us as equals. And probably never will be.

"That is what I would say if I were going to be *pragmatic."*

Yake hesitated for effect; he looked around the room, meeting all of their eyes deliberately—even the Ambassador's. He held up one forefinger to note that he had one more point to make, the most significant point of all. *"But* if I were going to be *truly* pragmatic, I would look again at these choices before us and I would ask myself what problems will we be creating for ourselves if, we accept *any* of these circumstances? What would be the consequences?

"The first thought that occurred to me was that we would be letting others determine the future of our species, not ourselves. It would be very difficult for human beings to maintain our sense of direction, our sense of responsibility under such disabling circumstances—and for that reason, I was considering voicing my own objections. I say 'considering' because my arguments were based on the intangible considerations of how we might 'feel' about these options; and, I admit it, I was thinking that our feelings in the matter might be the kind of illogical factor that throws the whole equation off. While I was sitting here pondering that dilemma, Madja spoke up, and I saw that she had gone straight to the beating heart of the matter."

Yake looked to Madja now. "It really doesn't matter what I feel, or what any of you feel about these offers. If we accept *any* of these options, we will be saying to the rest of the membership of the InterChange that we are not worthy of respect, because we too see ourselves as nothing better than food or guinea pigs or zoo animals." Yake looked around the table. "I never thought I would say this, but I think Madja is right. All of these options are unacceptable, because in the long run they will damage us much more than they can possibly help us in the short term."

Yake sat down again.

Madja Poparov looked surprised.

Madja Poparov looked *very* surprised.

Yake was very pleased with himself.

The Old Man himself was wearing a thoughtful expression. He did not look happy, but neither did he look angry. Merely...thoughtful.

At last he cleared his throat and said, "Thank you, Yake. You've raised several points that I think all of us need to keep in mind. Yes. The situation is a complex one. Um. What you and Ms. Poparov have pointed out is quite true. From a philosophical point of view, the solutions before us are indeed very difficult ones. Unfortunately, they're the only solutions available to us. Hm. Let me suggest something here. Suppose you and Madja Poparov and—how about Anne Larson too? And Nori as well—constitute yourselves as an *ad hoc* committee to explore what, if any, acceptable alternatives may be available to us, while the regular staff continues to evaluate the options we've discussed today. Yes, I think that will work. All right. Any comments?"

There were none.

Yake and Madja exchanged unhappy glances, but neither voiced an objection. Anne Larson looked stricken. Even Nori Kasahara looked unhappier than usual.

The Ambassador added then, "I've ordered the kitchen to stay open all night. Full meal service until two ayem, then sandwiches and coffee until breakfast. The staff secretaries are already letting your wives and husbands, girlfriends and boyfriends and others, know that you will be working late. We will reconvene at ten hundred hours tomorrow. Any questions? None? Good. Thank you all."

Best of the Breed

As THE GREAT RED SUN rose in the sky, it turned the day into a bright pink bath of light. All across the valleys, the Fn^rr were turning their broad leaves to its warming rays. Soon, they would be walking again.

It was not a pleasant thought.

K!rikkl realized that too many of the Fn^rr had survived the dream-time. Despite the ever-increasing ravages of the brain-eating vermin, most of the orchards on the southern continent had still come through the winter relatively unscathed by the parasites—more than half of the new crop of Fn^rr had survived. This meant much more pressure on the Ki! very soon. There would be many more pavilions built, and that meant far fewer swarming grounds: Already, many Ki! lived their entire lives without ever having the opportunity to swarm.

It could be a bad time for the Ki! on this world, K!rikkl thought; it would be well to be allied with the Trrrl^t Nest.

"You were considering something?" Hnaxx asked, coming up to join K!rikkl on the high branch.

"Ahh, just some idle musings about the possibilities for the future."

"Yes, the view from here is quite lovely." Hnaxx looked out over the valley. "The Fn^rr are such beautiful beings. It is too bad that they are ravaged so by these vermin. It is quite to our benefit—and theirs—that we can make such good use of the terrible grubs."

"Quite," agreed K!rikkl. "But it is too bad that they were even on this world in the first place."

"Agreement on that as well," nodded Hnaxx. "Let me ask you something. Don't you find it odd that creatures as ugly and distasteful as these vermin can occupy so much of our attention?"

"Odd, no. Unfortunate, yes. It is a well-known fact that intelligent beings tend to focus too much on their own diseases and dysfunctions. It is one of the primary curses of sentience."

"Ahh, you are a wit as well," rattled Hnaxx gaily. "That is a skill that will be much appreciated at the table." The older Ki! put a claw on K!rikkl's forelimb. "But, let me be impatient now—as long as we are discussing such an unfortunate subject, let us carry it to its conclusion and be done with it once and for all. You were going to instruct me on the training of the grubs."

"A pitiful discussion, really. There is not that much to tell."

"I am interested in it nonetheless."

"The creatures are disappointingly simple," said K!rikkl. "Really, they are not much good for anything. They taste too gamey to be good food, and they are inefficient larval incubators; it takes too long for one to grow large enough to hold more than a few eggs. They die too easily during implantation and give off fearful stenches when they decompose."

"Yes, that is well known to all of us, dear K!rikkl," chided Hnaxx. "But you promised to tell us things we did not know."

"Truly, my Lord. I just wanted to point out what a useless species these grubs may be, even for the most common purposes we use them for. Despite their prevalence on this world, they are really quite an affront to nature as we know it. The skin is too thin, it punctures too easily; the flesh is too warm, and too soft for good eating; they are not much more than warm bags of salt and ichor." K!rikkl lowered its voice and added, "Indeed, there is even a theory among some breeders that a Ki! hatched in the body of one of these grubs has been insufficiently nourished during its larval stage and may perhaps be mentally deficient."

"I was hatched in one of these grubs," remarked Hnaxx dryly.

"Ah, well…then that theory is clearly disproven. I am truly glad to know that. I will stop the spread of this pernicious rumor wherever I hear it."

"It is of no importance," replied Hnaxx. "It is well known that the Trrrl^t Nest hatches all of its larvae in specially selected grubs. That should be proof enough of the falsity of such malicious gossip."

K!rikkl hesitated as it considered the portent of Hnaxx's words. Had it stepped in something sticky here? Probably. Was the situation irreversibly damaged? Possibly. But perhaps not. K!rikkl hoped not. Indeed, K!rikkl could only proceed as if it had not committed an irretrievable offense. It polished its foreclaws politely and continued, "The point is, my Lord, that despite all of the many purposes to which we put these animals, these creatures are overrated in their usefulness."

Hnaxx nodded its agreement. "This is well known to many Ki!. The grubs are vermin. Oh, they are occasionally useful as pack animals and you can see many of them on the road pulling lorries. I must admit that they are at least wonderful for the disposal of garbage, and the youngsters delight in riding them for sport; they are also quite suited for heavy labor and even for the simplest of routine chores—but aside from these few minimal purposes, it would be a blessing for all of us if they were to be exterminated completely. There are far more useful creatures available to us for all of these tasks, and certainly the Fn^rr would have no objection to the extinction of a life form that has been known to prey on the Dreamers of Winter."

"Certainly not."

"Well, there you have it," said Hnaxx. "That is why it was so clever of you to train one. They are so useless that no one would suspect."

K!rikkl nodded in modest acceptance of the compliment. "I did nothing that could not have been done by any careful and persevering Ki!. I must confess, though, that these creatures can be quite tiresome. Training one is no task for a Ki! with an impatient disposition."

"I can well imagine, dear K!rikkl—but please elucidate."

Klrikkl barked a command to its grub; it came scuttling across the floor and sat up before him. "A simple command, do you see? I make a specific sound and it performs a simple action. It looks too easy, but I tell you that it truly takes a great deal of time and patience to train one, and one cannot depend that the training will take. Beyond a certain size, the males are too hard to control and the females think of nothing but rutting. The creatures have great hormonal difficulties. It is amazing to me that they survive at all. Do you know that the female can only bear one young at a time? It crawls out of the belly completely helpless and must be cared for completely while it grows toward usefulness. During much of this time, the female is useless for further breeding. I truly do not understand why these creatures are not already extinct."

"Nor do I," said Hnaxx blandly. "But please, K!rikkl, tell me how you trained it."

"Of course, my Lord. In principle, it is quite easy. A simple system of reward and punishment. I tie a rope to its neck. I rattle 'Come,' and pull the rope until it comes. Then I give it a tender root to chew. Soon it learns that if it wants a tender root, it should come when I say 'Come,' After that, the rest is details."

"It is that simple?" Hnaxx seemed astonished.

"Truly. All of the training is based on the same principle. If I hold up the game marker for a Knrkt and make it touch its toes, very soon it learns to touch its toes whenever it sees a Knrkt marker. Later, I train it to wait until I rattle my mandibles in annoyance. Then it touches its toes if it has seen a Knrkt marker only on my command. The rest of you think I am only grumbling in disgust—the grub tells me what it has seen and you think it is a distasteful creature. Poor G!ligglix never had a chance."

"Ai-eee—what an ingenious ploy, dear K!rikkl. I am delighted that you were so diplomatic in your play."

"It is bad manners to dine on the host," K!rikkl acknowledged.

"Your manners, dear K!rikkl, are as impeccable as your deceitfulness."

"Thank you, my Lord."

"But I cannot get over how…simple it all seems."

"Simple indeed, Lord Hnaxx. But it does require patience—that is why there are not many grubs this well trained."

"That is lucky for us—or we might have to change the rules of the game. As it is, I foresee great possibilities inherent in this knowledge."

"Indeed?"

"Indeed."

The Gang of Four

Madja Poparov could swear in six different languages.

At least that was how many Yake could identify before he lost count. There were several he couldn't identify. He simply listened in rapt admiration for several minutes before he attempted to interrupt.

"Excuse me," he said politely, "—I may be mistaken, but I think you repeated yourself there."

"I did not!"

"I think so, yes. The derogatory comparison between the breeding habits of pigs and capitalists; I think that parallels the statement you made about the copulatory practices of politicians and goats—"

Madja frowned as she attempted to recall what she had said several minutes earlier. "Is possible," she admitted. "I was being very enthusiastic."

Yake grinned. "Would you care to boil that communication down to its essential points?"

"Hmp. Is simple. *Ad hoc* committee is not committee at all, Mr. Yake Singh Browne. The 'Old Man,' as you so lovingly refer to him, is acting like consummate politician he is. You and I, we are troublemakers—I more than you. I raise unpleasant point in meeting. You make mistake of agreeing with me."

"You were right—"

"Is still mistake. You agree, no? No matter. Ambassador does not want disagreement, but must demonstrate—in case there is trial later—that all points of view were fairly heard. He listens to you and me, then makes us special committee. Larson and Kasahara are here to give committee credibility, no?"

"No—" said Larson.

Poparov ignored her. "If just you and I, Yake, then it looks like he is removing all his bad eggs from same basket. But by putting other person here too, he invests committee with air of credibility. Very smart. If you and I come up with something, we get to be heroes; if we don't come up with something, we are—what? What is expression for empty-handed idealist?"

"Empty-handed idealist."

"Yes. You and I, we have been put where we cannot cause any trouble. I am sorry I take you down with me. You are good manager. Not good leader, but good manager. Is two different things. I am good leader."

"And modest too."

"Yes. Thank you for noticing."

Yake blinked. Was that a serious response—or had she topped his own gibe? Sometimes with Madja Poparov it was hard to tell. He rubbed his hand through his bristly hair and scratched his head in puzzlement.

"You know," Kasahara interrupted, "you guys are both missing something. There might be another possibility here too."

"What?" Anne Larson looked up for the first time.

"Maybe, just *maybe,* the Ambassador thinks we're smart enough to come up with something that nobody else can; a solution that isn't so damned *insulting.*"

"Is good point, Kasahara. I owe you apology. I make mistake of not seeing that possibility."

"Hm," said Yake. "Out of the mouths of babes."

"I must admit—" said Madja, "it does not seem very likely possibility to me, but it is only possibility that we can accept that is not insulting to us—hmm? Is same problem, right? So! All right. Let us snatch victory from mouth of deceit, right? Right! If we solve it here, we solve it anywhere." She looked around the room for agreement.

Anne Larson nodded cautiously. Kasahara allowed himself a tiny smile of hope.

Yake thought about it for half a second, then looked Madja directly in the eyes. "Okay, right. Let's try it." He took a sip of his coffee. It was going to be a long night. He sighed and began: "Let me throw this out as a working assumption. A place to start. What would an acceptable solution look like? What are the particles of it?"

"Honor," suggested Kasahara in a quiet voice. "It would have to be honorable."

Yake looked over at Nori, surprised. "I thought you were a pragmatist."

"I am. Honor is pragmatic."

"Hm. Okay. A solution has to be honorable. What else?"

Madja put up a finger. "I think solution must be fair. If it is not fair, one side or other will begin to resent it, question it, work against it. We have seen this in our own dealings."

"I can believe it," said Larson.

"I will ignore that," said Madja, nonchalantly. "Coming as it does from the representative of senile imperialism."

"How kind of you," Larson smiled back.

"Let's stay on purpose," said Yake. "Anne, what about you?"

"I'm pragmatic." Larson pronounced her words carefully, and with a proper English accent. "I want it to be workable. We should be able to pay our debts without resentment or punishment. No human being should be hurt in the process or be forced to do anything that goes against his or her humanity. And yes, I'd like us to be able to keep our pride."

"Hm," said Yake. "Hm."

"Eh?" said Madja. "Is something wrong?"

"Not really. I was hoping for a little more agreement here."

Larson looked surprised. "I thought we were in agreement."

"You guys are, yes."

"Ah," said Madja. "What is it you are asking for, Yake? What would good solution look like to you?"

Yake said it flatly. "Revenge."

They blinked.

Yake spread his hands before him to show that he was hiding nothing. "I feel like I've been betrayed. I want to get even. Everything that each of you have said is absolutely correct and proper and appropriate and should be at the top of our list of criteria for an acceptable solution.

"But if we can have all that, and have an appropriate revenge too, that's what I'd like."

Kasahara nodded politely. "I wouldn't object to that."

"Neither would I," agreed Larson.

"But of course," said Madja. "What good is solution if you can't also enjoy it?"

No Small Reward

Hnaxx reached across the intervening space and stroked the foreclaw of the young and lovely Rrr. "Thank you for a most enjoyable and successful mating," Hnaxx said. "Your enthusiasm and your delight are well appreciated. I shall reward you to the utmost should the larva prove healthy."

Rrr nodded its head in gentle acquiescence. It was still too young to talk with much fluency; it had eaten its way out of its own host-grub only a few seasons past.

Hnaxx let its claw linger on Rrr's for only a moment longer, then stood to address the rest of the gathering at the table.

"My lords and colleagues—" Hnaxx clacked its mandibles loudly for attention. The pavilion fell silent quickly as one green triangular head after another swiveled to that angle of the table. The large bright eyes all glittered like jewels.

"Let us honor the service that has been performed for us," Hnaxx began. "Let us honor with loud enthusiasm."

The room filled with the sound of clacking mandibles and rasping hindclaws, even a few delicious hoots as Hnaxx continued. "The young and clever K!rikkl has provided valuable information to this Nest and we shall all prosper from it for many years. We are more than simply enriched. We are more than momentarily enriched. We shall ever be enriched by this service, both exemplary and extraordinary. Let us honor the one who has made it possible.

"Let us make K!rikkl one of us, flesh of our flesh, body of our body."

Hnaxx looked around the room at the other members of the powerful Trrrl^t Nest. They were fat and juicy and their great multi-faceted eyes were focused like spotlights. "On your behalf, oh Noble Lords, the humble Hnaxx promised K!rikkl that the Nest stood ready to serve him—and tonight, we shall."

Hnaxx clacked his foreclaws loudly.

Instantly, six sturdy servants strode into the room, carrying a great wooden platter upon which K!rikkl's body was cracked, pinioned, roasted, split, sauced, and sliced. The guests applauded enthusiastically, rattling their mandibles and rasping their hind legs loudly and vigorously.

"A great honor! A great honor!"

"A beautiful feast! Bravo! Bravo!"

"How delicious the young Ki! looks!"

Hnaxx lowered itself next to Rrr again. "We shall impregnate many fine grubs, shall we not, my tenderness?"

Rrr rasped its claws demurely and labored to speak. "I stand ready to be mounted, my Lord."

"And so you shall. So you shall."

Hnaxx turned to K!rikkl's steaming corpse in the center of the room and broke off the first tender leg. The juices dripped appetizingly from K!rikkl's foreclaws. Hnaxx felt gratified that the presumptuous, ill-mannered, ambitious and insulting young Ki! had met an appropriate fate. Delicately, Hnaxx cracked the shell of K!rikkl's claw and inserted its long yellow proboscis.

A moment of hesitation—

Yes.

K!rikkl was delicious.

Hnaxx stood up and announced, "The flesh is sweet! Let the feast begin!"

It was a grand evening! A grand evening indeed.

There would be much honor for the Nest as a result of this evening. Indeed, three problems had been solved with one feast. What to do about K!rikkl, what to do about K!rikkl's grub—?

And one other matter, which must be discussed privately with the Great Egg-Master.

Until then, of course, Hnaxx indulged most delightfully and enthusiastically in both of the major pleasures of the flesh. K!rikkl's and Rrr's.

Seldom was the resolution of an affair so satisfying.

*   *   *

The rest of the evening's entertainment proved equally successful.

Of course, the temperature songs and the orchard dances were a delight. They always were. As they wound to their inevitable and hilarious conclusions, many of the guests found themselves in extraordinarily revealing and indecent postures. Of course, they hurried to redress themselves, they always did; but there would be many embarrassing anecdotes to be told in the days to come.

After that, the pheromone sprays delighted almost everybody and even caused Old Yll!br to leap onto the table and attempt to mount what was left of K!rikkl's body in a (so Old Yll!br claimed) bawdy demonstration of northlander mating techniques. Of course, there were those who suggested otherwise, that this was not a demonstration of northlander mating techniques at all, that instead Old Yll!br had actually been overcome by the giddy sprays of hormonal influences. It sometimes happened in the elders, you know…when they reached that time of life.

But the big surprise of the evening was reserved for the darkness after the moons set. It happened when the guests began to filter out into the night to chew their aromatic herbs. Abruptly, there was a chorus of chirruping fanfare and the night was flooded with brilliant light of all colors.

Hnaxx had caused to be erected a huge tower of incandescent electric lights. They coruscated up and down through the entire visual spectrum; they glittered and flashed with brilliant intensity, illuminating the darkness with colors never before seen on this red-lit world. The guests all gasped with delight and horror. Their bright skins shone with multiple reflections that crawled across their carapaces like neon parasites. They stood and basked in the light and giggled with embarrassment at such juvenile displays of wonder.

The whole thing was terribly gaudy and obviously very expensive. The perfect delight. Beautiful and impressive both. The guests circled the tower in fascination. Several of the younger ones even tried to climb the tower; but it had been deliberately constructed to prevent them from climbing too far.

Even Hnaxx was surprised at the intensity of the delirium induced in the guests. The vendors had warned of this profound hypnotic effect, of course; but it was one thing to hear a fact and another to experience it. Indeed, Hnaxx found it quite difficult to resist the light itself. The urge to climb the tower was nearly irresistible.

Fortunately, Hnaxx had been warned of this phenomenon and had stayed a respectable distance away from the tower when it was illuminated. To some degree, this diluted the tropic power of the display. Without the warning, Hnaxx would have been as eager to succumb as the guests.

The off-world vendors had also warned not to leave the tower lights burning for too long, or it might risk burning out the eyes of the guests. Consequently, the machinery had been designed to flicker and flash for a short while only, and then gently fade to a quiescent glow and finally back to darkness. It could not be triggered a second time.

It was during the loudest part of this distraction that Hnaxx, obedient and honorable young Ki! that it was, reluctantly broke away and slipped quietly back into the festival pavilion where the Great Egg-Master waited patiently. The Egg-Master was still sitting impassively at the table.

Hnaxx approached on its belly, bowing its head to acknowledge the Master's great age and wisdom.

"You have done well, young Hnaxx."

"It is a privilege to serve the Nest. I am grateful for the honor."

The Egg-Master blinked slowly and turned its head sideways to study Hnaxx. It swiveled its glittering multifaceted eyes up and down as it focused. "You may speak."

"Thank you, my Master. I am pleased to report to you that the secret of the grubs is safe again, my Lord. We have tracked down every one of those who came into possession of our sacred knowledge and dealt with them appropriately. K!rikkl was the last of the last who knew. Tonight, K!rikkl's debt to this Nest has been well repaid."

"Indeed it has."

"I have not asked reward, Egg-Master. I never shall. It is reward enough to serve. Thank you for letting me have the honor of this duty. I stand forever ready to serve the Greater Trrrl^t Nest."

"You have done only what was expected of you, Hnaxx," whispered the Egg-Master. "That requires neither thanks nor acknowledgment. No reward could be asked in such a situation; and no reward shall be given. The only acknowledgment of your usefulness is that you shall continue to be used. But you understand that, of course." The Egg-Master rattled its mandibles and added, "There is still much to be done. May I speak plainly?"

"Master—?"

"We have not the time for the usual painless abstractions of courtesy; otherwise, your clever devices will not distract the guests long enough for us to say what we have to say to each other. Besides, the matter I would discuss with you is of such grave import that neither of us could risk the consequences of a communication that is less than precise. So I shall speak to you like a lover. Do you understand me, young Hnaxx?"

"I understand, my Master. I shall die before I compromise your candor."

"I expect nothing less. Now, listen to me carefully—for I must tell you of a matter that affects every Ki! alive today, and every Ki! that will ever follow after us."

Hnaxx wondered if it should prostrate itself before the seriousness of this topic, but the Egg-Master reached over and touched its foreclaw. "This is a great burden, young Hnaxx. We are indentured to our own history. And there is a price we are still paying for that indenture.

"This world is not fully our own. It was settled first by the Fn^rr. They sought a new world, a warm land in which to nourish their roots, a place where their dreams would be peaceful and fat. They made a contract with the Dhrooughleem, the same aliens who sold you your pretty lights of distraction. It was a very expensive contract, but the Dhrooughleem promised to find a safe world for the Fn^rr. They brought the Fn^rr to this world, and the Fn^rr were pleased. They found here a warm red light, which bathed them and made them strong; and they thought they had found paradise.

"But after the first few summers, as they began to spread their seeds, they began to discover that this paradise was infested by vermin, by brain-eating parasites that preyed upon them in their dream-time. They were horrified and enraged. As hard as it is to imagine one of the Fn^rr demonstrating any kind of emotion, they were hysterical with fear and anger. They had invested too much time and too many generations in this world, and now it had turned into a hellacious place of terror. The Fn^rr demanded that the Dhrooughleem make good on the original contract. The Dhrooughleem postulated what seemed to everyone a much better solution...symbiosis.

"We, the Ki!Lakken, were invited to share the expenses of colonizing this world. We would take a full third of the financial burden of the Fn^rr, and in return we would bring them protection and security.

"It should have been an ideal partnership, sweet Hnaxx. The Fn^rr-detested grubs are a tasty resource to us. Their flesh is sweet enough; their bodies are warm; we can plant our eggs in their bellies and watch our children grow large and healthy. So, the agreement was made and the slobbering off-worlders brought our ancestors here to this planet. The contract was simple. While the Fn^rr slept, we would care for their pavilions, we would eat the grubs, we would plant our eggs. During the summers, they are afoot and we are swarming. We would grow strong, the Fn^rr would grow strong. Only the grubs would suffer."

"Yes, my Master. And to all appearances, we have done that well."

"Too well. We have done well even beyond appearances. Do you know the rest of this contract?"

"No, my Master."

"The contract specifies that should either species fail to maintain its obligations to the Dhrooughleem, the other species shall come into full possession of the world. That is why we have never pushed the grubs to the edge of extinction. Should the grubs no longer molest the wandering plants, the Fn^rr would spread across our swarming grounds and in a very short time we would follow the vermin into blissful extinction."

"The Fn^rr would not be so despicable as to break an agreement, my Master—would they?"

"Would *you* take such a chance with the future of *your* species? Neither would I. And neither would any other Ki!Lakken." The Egg-Master stroked Hnaxx's forelimb gently. "Indeed, it has been my own fondest hope that the vermin would continue to molest the Fn^rr in such great numbers that they themselves might be pushed up to the threshold of failure. Have you yourself not entertained such fantasies?"

"I confess that I do sometimes fall prey to such delusions, Master. They are occasionally delightful."

The Egg-Master clacked its mandibles in soft delight. "You share the ambition of your Nest. A commendable trait.

"It is true that we have been on this world for only a very few generations; still we have done much that we can be proud of. We have established many fine plantations and we have watched the grubs well. We have indentured many trustworthy servants—and the ones who have not been trustworthy have not remained in our indenture for long...as you well know. You have cleaned up their indiscretions and we have picked the bones of their children.

"Hnaxx, we have captured many grubs; we have raised them and learned how to breed many more. We have buried long years learning how to teach them well. We have taught them to forage. We have taught them what to eat and what not to eat. We have shown them what grows back and what does not. We should be seeing the fruits of these labors, and yet...every season there are more and more of the Fn^rr awakening from the dreams and walking into Summer."

"They see the future, my Master. They plant to meet the sun and the rain. They root in warm soil. They spread their seeds in too many places."

"If only it were that simple, my child. They see the future, yes, and therein lies the seed of our failure. They see the unborn grubs. The visions trouble them. The more grubs they see, the more deaths they dream, the more they are troubled, then the more seeds they spread. We cannot breed the grubs as fast as they can spread their seeds. Now, despite the predations of the terrible vermin, they still spread into our swarming grounds. I begin to think—and I say this with only the greatest reluctance—that they do it deliberately."

"They plot our extinction?!!"

"So it would seem."

"I cannot imagine a species being so...so malevolent!"

"Perhaps they feel they no longer want to share their world with us. This was their world alone in the not too distant past. Perhaps they wish to return to that time of sole burden. Perhaps they feel we have not protected them well enough... Whatever the case, we must consider new possibilities now. And you, dear Hnaxx, must be part of those possibilities."

"Whatever I can do, my Lord."

"And so you shall. Here is a conundrum for you to consider. Tell me what you see in this circumstance."

"Yes, my Lord."

"We have been approached by the Dhrooughleem again. They are concerned for us. They see our discomfort; they wish to offer aid. They have suggested that we might wish to increase our supply of these grubs—strictly as food and larval incubators, of course—but they suggest most politely that they might be in a position to supply some very large numbers of grubs in the near future."

"That *is* an interesting conundrum," remarked Hnaxx.

"Indeed, it is." The Egg-Master's eyes glittered with the reflections of many small lamps. "What do you see in it?"

"I see one possibility, my Lord. It is a possibility that can be seen only by one possessed of certain experience—but because I am the one with that experience, I do see this way."

"Speak, Hnaxx."

"It is this, my Master. K!rikkl's grub was too well trained. It spoke. It demonstrated that it could reason. The thought that it suggests, my Father, is that the grubs may be far more intelligent than ever we suspected. Perhaps even they may be a..." Hnaxx lowered its head ashamedly. "I apologize in advance for what I am about to suggest, my Father. It is shameful and degrading. But I must say it here in the hope that I am wrong, rather than risk someone else saying it in the Forum and being proven right."

"Go on," encouraged the Egg-Master.

"Yes, my Father. The thought occurs to me that the grubs may be members of an intelligent species. Perhaps, even, they are members of a species that belongs to the InterChange. If such were so—and if such were to be discovered and made public—then we would be guilty of the most heinous crime of *Involuntary Subjugation*. Our people could be liable to a permanent indenture. We would lose our freedom and our world. Forgive me, my Lord, but I must speak this possibility in the hopes that you will tell me that I am dreadfully mistaken."

The Egg-Master did not contradict Hnaxx—and that was the most terrifying thing that Hnaxx had ever heard: the silence of the Father.

Hnaxx said simply, "Ai-eee. We are doomed then, are we not?"

The Egg-Master lowered its head. "It is a curious puzzle—but as the pieces fall into place, the puzzle becomes less puzzling. I wonder, who are these grubs we use for food and larval incubators?"

"Perhaps the Dhroo might know—?"

"Indeed, they must! But, Hnaxx? You are not so innocent as to think that the Dhroo are themselves so blameless in the matter? Indeed, it was the Dhroo who first suggested to our ancestors that, if we were unable to protect the Fn^rr, then they might be unable to meet their obligations elsewhere, and if that situation came to pass then our people would inherit sole custody of this world. We believed the Dhroo then. Now we find that the Dhroo have outplayed our hand in this cycle of the game. Should we believe them again?"

"Never, my Master. We should pour salt on the Dhroo!"

"We will have to live long enough first. The Dhroo know what they have done to us. They know what is in our egg pouch, Hnaxx! Because they put it there! There is a hungry Knrkt sleeping in our Nest and very soon it will awaken. It seems to me that it is only a matter of time before the terrible truth is known and we shall be punished for our cleverness."

"My Father, let me be impudent." Hanxx raised up and looked directly into the Elder's eyes. "Is it not still possible that we can complete this cycle without discovery? If we were somehow able to celebrate a conclusion, we would have nullified the trap, would we not? In such a case, we could only be acknowledged for our cleverness rather than be punished for our crime. Such is the way the game is played. I urge you, let me look for such a solution. Let me serve the Nest. Let me serve the World."

The Egg-Master nodded thoughtfully, rasping its mandibles in agreement. "I had hoped you would be bold enough for such a duty, my child, my little one; but there is one way immediately in which such a responsibility could be granted—"

"My Lord?"

The old one was silent for a long moment. "Your Nest would have to carry a terrible burden on behalf of the Father of All Nests. Should you fail, it would mean the dissolution of your Nest and the deaths of all the Nestlings. Are you prepared to accept such a responsibility?"

"My Father, it would be only an honor. What is thy charge?"

"Should we fail to complete this cycle of the game, should this terrible secret become known, then your Nest—the whole of it and every member—shall have to step forward to claim the honor of gracing the table at the InterChange. Do you understand?"

Hnaxx bowed its head. "My Father, I understand completely. If there is a victory here, then it is a victory for all and I will have no claim on any part of it. If there is a failure, though, it shall be my Nest's failure and ours alone—and none of it may be laid upon the table of any other Ki!. My Master, I have already accepted this honor by virtue of being your child."

The old one clacked its mandibles appreciatively and reached out to stroke Hnaxx's foreclaw. "You are a treasure, my pretty little one. Would you like to be mounted tonight?"

"Whatever pleases you, my Lord."

A Small Promotion

YAKE SINGH BROWNE thought about it for as long as he could, then decided it was best not to think about it at all.

He swallowed hard, thought about it for the thirty-third time, decided that there was no other way, gritted his teeth, and put in his application for an audience with an Oracle.

The T'ranian Oracle.

But he didn't expect it to be approved.

The High Council of the InterChange was comprised of the representatives of the seventeen most successful—and oldest—species in the known galaxy. The members of the High Council were called Oracles. They were charged with the responsibility of advising the various species of the InterChange in any way they felt appropriate.

Sometimes their advice could be extraordinarily valuable. And just as often, it could prove utterly worthless. Nevertheless, the price was the same regardless of the answers given: if you have to ask, you can't afford it.

The most expensive Oracle of all was the T'ranian Oracle.

Also known as... *The Dragon.*

The Dragons were the oldest and most successful member species in InterChange history. The Dragons had personally retired over three hundred and twelve other species.

No, Yake did not expect the application to be approved.

There were species in the InterChange that no human being had ever had contact with. Over two thousand species were registered. (More than six thousand species were known, but many of those were fortunately unable to afford membership.) Humans had met (and exchanged greetings with) one hundred and thirteen alien races. Of those one hundred and thirteen, the sons and daughters of Terra had been able to open diplomatic negotiations with nine.

It was understandable, of course.

Human beings smelled bad.

And tasted worse.

Of the two-thousand-plus species in the InterChange, only a small minority were mammalian, and so far the statistical evidence suggested that the universe was indeed set up to generate intelligent mammalian life only as the very rare exception to the way things were *supposed* to work. Most of the alien races in the galaxy had evolved from the equivalent of insects, reptiles, dinosaurs, sea-dwellers, and occasionally plants—cabbages, to be exact. On most of the worlds of the galaxy, mammal-like creatures never got the chance to come down from the trees or up out of their burrows. The greatest majority of species in the InterChange were reptilian, followed by the insect-evolved and the sea-dwellers. To most of those races, mammals were...food. Or incubators. Or just plain vermin.

Yake was just about certain that his petition would be rejected.

("Guess what wants to join the InterChange! No, don't bother, you'll never guess. You're not going to believe this, Fzour'sx. Mammals! No,

I am not pulling your gzornty. I saw them myselves. Real mammals! Yes! And they're just intelligent enough to understand the concept of intelligence! They *claim* that entitles them! Well, I know! But can you *believe* the presumption? No, no—wait, it gets better. The way I hear it, Fzour'sx, there was this comet that smacked into their world, and the damage killed off all the dinosaurs just when they had reached the threshold of sentience. Of course, it'd be a tragedy, if it weren't so *bizarre*. It was an ecological vacuum; the mammals began to evolve like fruit flies—the nasty little egg-suckers grabbed all the good ecological niches for themselves and the reptiles never got the chance to regroup. I mean, talk about your ecological opportunists! What's that? How do they taste? I don't know yet. Gxammel is planning a festival, so maybe we'll find out then. I'm not so sure that I want to. The way I hear it, on their planet—*the mammals feed on the birds!*")

Of course, there was no such thing as species prejudice. Not in the InterChange. It was just that…well, few races felt comfortable speaking to something that looked as if it belonged on a plate.

No human being had ever had an audience with a Dragon before. And Yake did not expect to be the first.

And then…the Ambassador asked him to step into his office.

When Yake entered, the Old Man was holding a copy of the application. "This is going to be very expensive, Yake," was the Ambassador's only comment.

"Did you want me to withdraw the petition?"

The Ambassador shook his head. "No, it's too late for that. We've already been charged the application fee. Even if we withdraw the petition, we still have to pay the fee."

The Old Man turned to stare out the window at the steep wall of cliffs opposite. The InterChange world was carved with rugged canyons so deep that you couldn't see the bottoms. Below a certain depth, it was a world of perpetual night. Outside the window, the twilight canyons were haloed in curtains of glittering light. "I assume it's necessary, Yake, or you wouldn't have put in the request. It's just that…" He trailed off thoughtfully.

"Sir?"

The Ambassador sighed. "It's the cost. I can't help thinking—wondering—how many human beings are going to have to work for how many years to pay for this application if you're wrong. I can't help wondering what kind of jobs they'll have to do." The Ambassador looked very unhappy. "You do know, of course, how we are viewed by the other races here, Yake?"

"Yes, sir."

"I can't begrudge you the effort, Yake. You have to do your job. But please—remember who has to pay the bill when it comes due."

"Yes, sir."

"Now, then—" The Ambassador cleared his throat. "About your request—"

"Yes, sir?"

"It's been refused."

"Oh. Well…" Yake wasn't surprised.

"The T'ranian Oracle never speaks to anyone below the status of Ambassadorial Delegate."

"Oh. Well…it seemed like a good idea at the time." Yake sighed—well, he'd expected the petition to be rejected, so why was he so disappointed?!! He sighed again and turned to go. "Okay, we'll go to Plan B."

"Wait a minute, Yake."

"Sir?"

The Ambassador turned around to face him. "Yake, I hope you're right."

"Sir?"

"About the Dragons. I signed your promotion papers two days ago and resubmitted the application. It was approved this morning."

For a moment, Yake didn't have the words to reply. "Uh—thank you, sir."

"*Don't thank me, Yake.* Just be right. Your appointment is in an hour and a half. You'll just have time to get suited. I took the liberty of ordering a new uniform for you. Stripes, insignia, boots—everything. Wear it all. Even the sword."

"Yes, sir! Thank you, sir." Yake turned to go, then stopped. "Uh, sir—just one question. This promotion—it's only for the purpose of speaking to the Oracle, right?"

"Of course not! It's a full promotion. Full salary, all the perks. Even your own parking place. No matter what happens in your interview with the Oracle, you'll keep your promotion."

"Uh, thank you, sir. But, uh—if the request hadn't been granted—?"

"Yake, don't ask stupid questions. And don't keep the Oracle waiting, either. And oh, yes, in case I don't get a chance to tell you later, congratulations."

"In case you don't get a—uh, right. Uh, thank you, sir."

"*Don't thank me, Yake.*"

"Sir?"

The Ambassador looked unhappy. "Go on, now. It's late. You'd better get going."

"Yes, sir!"

Chess with the Dragon

NEVER PLAY CHESS with a Dragon.

Especially not if the Dragon is the size of a house and has teeth longer than your arm.

This was common wisdom. You did not need to be a member of the InterChange to understand why.

On the other hand (as they say), if you have nothing to lose…you can always lose your other hand.

Yake felt intimidated.

He approached as close as he dared—but even from this distance, the Dragon was…well, *intimidating.*

The Dragon was resting on a small hill; it looked bored. It was hard to tell. How do you read an expression as wide as a billboard?

"Ahem…" Yake clared his throat hesitantly.

The Dragon looked up.

Yake blanched.

The creature was black; so black it looked like a hole in the air. Its scales shone like polished metal, a shimmering ebony nightmare. Its eyes were as large as windows, and they were the brightest shade of searing red. They looked as if they were lit from within.

The Dragon's mouth—Yake swallowed hard—its mouth was the door into deepest hell. The Dragon's breath was so hot, Yake could feel it from here. It felt like a blast furnace! Only not as refreshing.

Yake took an involuntary step back; then he realized how that must look and forced himself to take a step forward again. "I'm Yake Singh Browne. The Terran Delegate."

"Yesss, you are," said the Dragon.

"Yes, I am," said Yake. He looked at the sky. (Oh, God, did I just say that? Lord, please don't let me be too big a fool here today.)

"You have questions?" The Dragon asked drily. It turned one great blazing eye toward Yake.

"Many questions, yes."

"Are they interesting questionsss…?"

"I suppose it depends on what you would call interesting.

"Survival is often interesting—isss it not?"

Yake thought about it. Sometimes survival demanded all of your attention. By that definition—"Yes, survival is very interesting."

"Yesss, but only when it's your own. Then it's interesting. When it is not your own survival that is being discussed, it is not a matter of interest at all, is it? So I will ask again. These questions that you intend to ask, are they questions that I will find interesting?"

"Uh, no. Um—at least, I don't think so."

"Then why should I answer them? Perhaps I should ask you an interesting question?"

"Um…perhaps we could *trade* questions."

"Trade questions?" The Dragon looked as if it wanted to raise an eyebrow.

"Well, uh—it's a game we play on my planet. I show you mine, you show me yours."

"But I am not interested in seeing yours."

"Oh. Well. Um. Er. Okay. May I ask you a small question anyway? A question of no importance."

"Yesss?"

"Why do they say…'Never play chess with a Dragon?'"

"Yesss, a small question of no importance. Perhaps…it is because of the tradition."

"The tradition?"

"The tradition that the winner gets to eat the loser."

"I see." Yake smiled nervously. He wondered if he should declare his intentions as peaceful. "I have no intention of eating you," he offered.

"I know that, yesss." The Dragon smiled. The effect was ghastly. *"The converse, however, is not true."*

"Uh. Yes. Thank you. I think."

"You have other questionsss?" The Dragon swung its head around expectantly. Yake jumped back in surprise.

"Uh, yes, I do. Have other questions, that is. Maybe they could be interesting to you, maybe not. Um, you know who we are, don't you?"

"Yesss. We call you the—the—excuse me, the word does not translate. We call you 'the presumptuous food'."

"Yes, of course. We understand our uniqueness in the universe. But let me ask you this: isn't it of some interest to you to know how we got here? How mammals became intelligent on our world instead of insects or reptiles?"

The Dragon did not even consider it. *"No,"* it rumbled. *"The galaxy is big. Accidents happen. If that is all you wish to discuss, then this shall be a very disappointing afternoon, indeed."* The Oracle began to raise itself up on its forward legs. Yake could see the ground sagging beneath its weight. *"At least, I shall have the minor satisfaction of discovering if you are enjoyable food or not."*

"Sir—" Yake wondered if the term were correct. Never mind. He spoke quickly. "There is another question I want to ask, a much more important question—a very *interesting* question. I mean, interesting to my species at least."

"At least, yesss." The Dragon paused. *"Go on."*

"It's the indenture—I mean, our debt. We uh, we think we've been slimed."

"Ssslimed?"

"Suckered. Played for fools. Cheated. By the Dhroo."

"Ahh, yesss. The Dhroo." The Dragon chewed over the thought with relish. *"Yesss. A not unfamiliar circumstance. And you wish an anssswer, yesss?"*

"Uh, no. Not exactly. Um, we're really not able to pay in the currency that you're most likely to request."

"An asssumption, but not a stupid one. Mammalsss..." sighed the Dragon. *"You think with your glands. Well, then...what* are *you assking?"*

"We can't afford to buy your help. And we're not asking you for a solution, because we can't afford to pay you for it. Nor can we ask you for your advice, because we can't afford that either. No. What I want to ask is much smaller."

"Yesss?"

"I want to ask if something is possible."

"You ask about...survival? Survival is always a possibility. So is the alternative."

"No. We already know that. What I want to know is—I mean, if this is a game—then so far, it's been a very interesting game for my species. Very interesting. What I want to know is this: is there a way to make the game equally interesting for the Dhroo?"

"Ahhh," said the Dragon. *"A fine question. A very fine question."* It lowered itself back down to the ground and ruminated for a moment. It rumbled deep in its throat, a loud purring noise like the sound of an ancient subway train roaring through an underground tunnel.

Yake waited patiently.

At last, the Dragon looked up. *"Yesss, there is a way."*

Yake waited for the Dragon to go on. The Dragon quietly returned his gaze.

"You are waiting for something else?"

"You said there's a way?"

"Yesss. There is. You were waiting for a hint, perhaps? It is too bad that you cannot afford to ask the question outright. But the price that we would require...you are better off not knowing." The Dragon smiled broadly. Yake nearly fainted.

"Perhaps you should consider this an opportunity to demonstrate the intelligence of your species. Knowing that there is a possibility should be a goad to guarantee its discovery. And if you cannot discover the answer, then that too is an answer."

Yake pursed his lips, holding in the first reply that came to his mind. Instead, he nodded politely. "You have done us a great service."

"Perhapsss. And perhapsss not. Consider this: Losing a game is one thing; you can be eaten knowing that you have done your best. But losing a game when you know that there is a solution that you have not found is intol-

erable, because it suggests that even your best was not good enough. This might be a more expensive answer than you bargained for, little snack."

"I'll—we'll take that chance."

"*Yesss, you will.*"

"Is there anything else that you can tell us?"

"*There is quite a bit that I can tell you. But I won't. It is not interesting enough.*" The Dragon paused, then it raised its head up and looked at Yake. "*I will not eat you today, Yake Singh Browne. And perhapsss I will not eat you the next time either.*"

"The next—" Yake gulped, "—time?"

"*Yesss.*" The Dragon lashed its tail around itself and looked directly at Yake. "*The price that I require for this discussion is this: you must come back and tell me how you work it all out.*" It added, "*That is…if you do.*"

"Thank you. Sir." Yake began to back away.

The Dragon lowered its head again and appeared to go to sleep. "*Don't…thank…me…*"

"Yes, sir!"

Yake's heart rate did not return to normal for two days.

A Glass of Bheer

THE HOUR WAS TIRED and Yake was late. "The late Yake Singh Browne," he muttered and sipped at his bheer. He made a face and put the glass back on the table in front of him.

"Soon we will all be late," agreed Madja.

"You can put it on my tombstone," said Anne Larson, brushing her graying hair back off her forehead. "Better late than never." She giggled at the joke.

Yake looked across at her. "I think you've had enough for tonight, Anne."

She hiccuped and giggled again.

Yake and Madja, Anne and Nori were the only four people left in the lounge. They all looked haggard.

They had been sitting there and arguing for hours. Perhaps for days. No one remembered.

The argument was a peripatetic orangutan, bouncing off the walls of their separate frustrations with all kinds of grunts, howls, shrieks and moans. The mere knowledge that an answer was possible was an impossible burden. It was a goad.

Only…Yake was tired of being goaded. He wanted to experience a result once in awhile too.

He stared into his bheer unhappily. "I'd rather have beer," he said. "I'm tired of the sacred 'H'. I'm tired of alcoholh."

Madja agreed with a sour nod. "Is same for me, but right now, I would just as happily settle for one straight answer."

"You have one straight answer. The Dragon says mate in four moves *is* possible."

"It did not say how. Is like famous story about Borozinsky—greatest chess player of his century—he drove opponent crazy this way. He said, 'If you were any good, you would see that mate is possible in four moves.' Was no mate possible, but opponent died in frustration rather than admit he could not find it."

"Hmm," said Yake. "Chess players can be nasty."

"Yah. Too bad this is not chess," agreed Madja. "Chess, I could defeat a whole herd of Dragons."

"Yeah, and then you'd have to eat them," put in Larson, giggling. She looked positively tipsy.

Madja frowned at her. "That would be easy part. I share them with you. But, no. This is not chess. This is—more like American game. Too much free-for-all. Not enough discipline. How can anyone play game that is all lies?"

Yake looked up at her blearily. "What?"

"Is not important. Was nasty shot."

"Cheap shot. Never mind. Say it again."

Madja shrugged. "I said, 'Is not chess. Is American game. Too much free-for-all.'" She sipped at her vhodka.

"No, you said something else—"

She waved a hand. "That was nasty part: 'How can anyone play game that is all lies?'"

"You're right, Madja! That *is* an American game. This isn't chess! This is poker!"

"Polka?"

"Poker," said Kasahara. "You know? The card game."

"Ahh, yes!" Madja grinned and said something in Russian.

"They teach you that in the Navy?" asked Yake.

"Among other things, *da.*"

"I don't know whether to be impressed or shocked."

"You learn to poker. I learn to swear. Which is more useful?"

"Right now? Poker."

Madja looked uninterested.

"Okay," said Yake. "Maybe I'm wrong, but try this thought on anyway. This is a poker game—with two thousand sharpies, each of whom has brought his own deck and his own set of rules! Do you know what that means?"

"You are about to explain it, no?"

"It means that there are no rules. Only there are! But we get to make them up as we go! That's how this game is played. Do you know what a good poker game needs?"

"Good players?" asked Larson.

"Nah. A fish. A sucker. Somebody with money who's willing to believe whatever you tell him—especially when you tell him that you couldn't possibly have the fourth ace, because you want to keep him in the game as long as he has money to lose. That's us—we're the poor fish in this game! Humanity! We're the suckers! As long as we're playing by their rules, we have to lose. It's their game! We can't win unless we change the rules on them—"

"Yake," Madja chose her words carefully. "I do not understand what you are saying. It sounds like you are suggesting that we break agreements here."

"No—I'm not. I'm suggesting that we...reinterpret the boundaries of those agreements to include the possibility that we could win a hand here too."

Madja did not look convinced.

"You don't understand, do you? This isn't a game about playing by the rules. It's a game about how cleverly you can cheat. If that's the game, then cheating isn't wrong, is it?"

"Is interesting capitalist justification. Do they teach that at UCLA?"

"USC. And I didn't go there. Never mind. I just want to make this game a little less interesting for us and a little more interesting for everybody else."

"I do not see it, Yake."

Larson leaned across the table and laid one hand on Madja's. "Think of it this way, dear. *Everything* is justified in the class struggle against the imperialist war-mongers."

"Is not good comparison, Larson. I am not sure that these creatures are really imperialists. Besides, imperialists on Earth are at least human. Theory is that human beings should *know better.* In the act of oppressing the class struggle of the workers, they renounce the noblest part of their humanity and deserve to meet their fate on the gallows. But Dragons and slugs and talking turnips might not be capable of knowing better. In that case, we cannot take advantage of them—*or we would be the oppressor.*"

Kasahara paused in the act of reheating his sahke. "Are you sure you're a real Communist?"

"I show you my card," said Madja, standing up and unbuttoning her blouse pocket. "I carry it everywhere I go."

"Never mind," interrupted Yake. "We're off the track. Madja, maybe this is only a game to the other species because they don't have as much at stake—but you're the one who pointed out that the stakes in this game are human dignity. Maybe this game is about measuring your dignity by how clever you are, not by how honorable. Maybe honor is the booby prize."

"I had not thought of that," Madja admitted. She fell silent. She looked sad at the idea, and for a moment even Yake felt sorry for her. She looked so...vulnerable. Abruptly, she looked up. "Is one thing wrong, Yake."

For just a moment, Yake hoped she was right. "Yes?"

"Is assumption you are making here about InterChange. You keep saying is game. Is clever. Is very American clever. But is maybe sacrifice truth for clever, Yake. For one hundred and sixty-seven years, we have known what InterChange was—interstellar government, no? Now you are saying it is not?"

Yake said, a little too quickly, "Maybe that hundred and sixty-seven years was the false assumption—" and immediately wished he hadn't said it.

Madja took it seriously. The color was draining from her face.

"You are right, Yake," she said finally. "We must question everything." She looked to Yake again. "But if we question everything, we must also question if game analogy is also accurate, *da*?"

"I think that's what we have to find out."

Kasahara said softly, "We're going to have to make some very hard assumptions here."

Larson turned to him and asked, "Nori, tell me something. What do you do if you're losing a game?"

Nori shrugged. "I pay my debts and go home."

"We can't do that here. What else can you do?"

"I don't know poker that well." Nori looked up. "Yake, you're the expert. What do you do?"

Larson shrugged. "I don't know either. I'm no expert in game theory."

"Forget game theory. I'll tell you what I'd do." Yake leaned back in his chair and put his feet up on the table. "I'd bring in the pros from Dover and kick some assets."

"The what?"

"The 'pros from Dover.' It's an American expression. It means—you bring in the power hitters. Um—you call for an expert."

"There are no experts here," moaned Madja. "Just capitalists. That is what makes whole thing so dreary."

"Then we'll bring in an expert capitalist—" Yake said, and then caught himself in surprise. "My Ghod! That's it!" He turned excitedly to Kasahara. "Warm up your keyboard, Nori! I want you to download a complete set of—no, wait. Limit your search to mammalian species only. Which species has been the most successful overall in its transactions with the InterChange?"

"Don't bother, Nori," said Anne. "Yake, I can tell you without looking. It's the Rh/attes."

"The rats?"

"The Rh/attes. The '/' is silent." Larson grinned.

"They're the ones who want to indenture themselves to us."

"Oh, right."

"I've been doing some research. The Rh/attes are so successful that *nobody* trusts them."

"Oh, that's terrific," said Madja. "Capitalist pigs."

"No, Rh/attes."

"Is no difference."

"Wait a minute—" said Yake. "I don't care if they're dancing bears, if they're successful! What's the gimmick, Anne? How are they doing it?"

"I think—that they're uh, there's no polite word for it. They're 'snitches'."

"Snitches?" asked Madja. "What is 'snitches'?"

"It's an American word," said Larson. "It means Supreme Hero of the Russian Republics."

"Oh," said Madja. And then frowned, as much in puzzlement as in anger.

"They're spies," said Yake. "Right?"

"Mmmm." Larson made a face. "Not quite. That's one of their services. Information management. Nobody wants to issue a warrant of foreclosure on them because they're too valuable as snitches. And besides, nobody is sure what secrets they'd accidentally let drop about the species who signed the warrant."

"Nice position to be in," said Yake.

"How did Rh/attes get this way?" asked Madja.

"Apparently," said Nori, studying the screen of his clipboard, "they have the nasty habit of indenturing themselves to anyone who'll take them on."

"Interesting. What happens to the species that do?"

"Apparently, they benefit." Nori hesitated, then added, "Well, most of them, anyway." He peered at his screen with a frown. "Apparently, there were a couple that didn't."

"Were?"

"Maybe I don't understand the reference. It just says here, *'retired'.*"

Yake sipped his bheer and thought for a moment. He looked across the table at his colleagues. "Well. Okay. It looks like there are risks involved here too."

Larson said, "I don't think we have any choice. I vote yes."

Madja sighed and said, "Of course, I must officially protest dealing with capitalist swine like Rh/attes."

Yake looked over at her. "And off the record?"

"Off the record? Off the record, I am very curious and will allow myself to be outvoted."

"Nori?"

"My grandfather was a capitalist." Nori grinned broadly. "I'll take the chance."

"Good. Then it's three *yes* and one abstention. We talk to the Rh/attes."

"First, we have another dhrink—" said Larson. "We're going to nheed it."

A Game of Rh/attes and Dragons

THE RH/ATTES WERE as unsavory as their name suggested.

They smelled musty—like old hair. Like old cheese. Like mildew.

The Rh/attes were dark and sinister creatures only chest-high to a man. They had little, malicious eyes and stood hunched forward, like crones over a cauldron, rubbing and twisting their ugly bony fingers in a continual wringing motion. To make it worse, they wore coarse black capes with hoods that made them look like Assistants to Death. Their eyes gleamed red in the shadowed cowls—but not the searing red of the Dragon's eyes, no; the Rh/attes' eyes were embers, like smoldering coal.

Yake could see just far enough within their hoods to tell that they had coarse black fur and round pink ears that lay flat against the sides of their narrow heads.

They had yellow-stained teeth.

And they hissed and sprayed spittle when they spoke.

Yake tried not to think about the comparisons, but it was impossible. He couldn't help but think of these creatures as…well, *rats.*

There were six of them. They sniffed the air and eyed the humans suspiciously.

The four humans sat on chairs facing the six Rh/attes. The Rh/attes curled their naked gray tails around them and sat on their haunches.

Yake swallowed hard and looked at his colleagues. Madja looked a little gray. Anne Larson was expressionless. Kasahara's eyes were narrowed and his jaw was tight.

At last, one of the Rh/attes spoke. Its voice squeaked like a rusty gate.

"You are stupid very species," it said. "Mammaloids have time enough hard in the universe. Not have to make it worse for us, the rest."

Yake thought about an appropriate response. He discarded the first two words that came to his mind and chose the rest of his words carefully. He looked to the others, then turned back to the first Rh/atte. "We also find your species disgusting. You remind us of the vermin of our own world. Do you also spread disease and parasites wherever you go?"

Larson looked at Yake, astonished. Madja Poparov's head snapped around so fast, Yake was surprised it didn't come off. "Yake—!" For a moment, even Kasahara lost his inscrutability. Yake ignored all three of them.

"Good!" The Rh/atte grinned. "Understand we each other." Its grin was disgusting.

"Yes, we do," said Yake. "We know who you are and what you are. So we would prefer not to waste time on false performances of courtesy and friendship."

"Slugs you have been talking to, yes? Dhrooughleem? Yes? One hundred and twenty-three ritual ways to commit copulatory obscenities, yes?"

"Yes and yes," said Yake. "Tell me, how many ways do the Rh/attes commit copulatory obscenities?"

"Is price to pay for that information," said another of the Rh/attes. Its eyes were narrow and flat.

"Yake!" whispered Madja angrily. "What do you say?"

"Shut up," Yake snapped back. He turned back to the Rh/attes. "I am Ambassador Yake Singh Browne. I would deal with you on behalf of my species. Will you deal with me?"

"How bold you are," said the second Rh/atte. "Particularly now when your species has one foot in Dragon's mouth and the other in slime."

"Do you want to trade information or insults? If you want to trade insults, I'm afraid you will find that your species is hopelessly inadequate to the task. You don't have the brains to be insulted."

"Not bad," said a third Rh/atte. "Not bad at all—for amateur one."

Yake stood up. "Let's go," he said to his colleagues. "I have better things to do than listen to the droolings of pretentious vermin."

"Wait—!" said a fourth Rh/atte. "Proposal, we listen."

"Proposal, *you* offer," retorted Yake. "You are the ones who asked to indenture yourselves to us. Why?"

"Why not?" the fifth Rh/atte answered. "If win you, win we. If lose you, still win we."

"What's to keep us from selling you as food or larval incubators or bio-sites for bacteriological and viral colonies?"

The Rh/atte smiled. "Thinking are you of our albino cousins. Useful are they very for those purposes. We are not."

"I see. So, what you're saying is that the Rh/attes are not much use for anything, are you?"

"Some species think that. Some species are retired, yes?"

"Yes, I've heard that." Yake looked at the Rh/attes. "We have no intention of being retired."

"And if retired you are, then know will we that you have changed mind, yes again?"

Yake didn't answer that. He thought frantically for a, moment, then turned back to the Rh/attes again. "All right, let me come right out and ask it. Exactly what advantage could we gain if we were to accept your indenture?"

"None at all. None at all."

"So then, why should we accept your offer? Why should we enter into this deal? You offer no benefit to us."

"Benefit not is not to you. It is to us." that was the sixth and final Rh/atte. "Offer benefit us and we not need this indenture."

Yake stared at it.

The Rh/atte met his gaze with quiet rheumy eyes.

"Understand you? Yes?" It asked.

"Understand I," Yake agreed. He turned to the others. "Do *you* understand what he's offering?"

"Is nothing offered, I see," said Madja.

"That's right. Is nothing offered."

Larson sniffed. "I'm with Madja. I'm confused."

"I am not confused. I just see nothing."

"Never mind—" interrupted Yake. "Nori?"

Kasahara shook his head slowly. "I don't get a read on this, Yake. It's your hunch."

"I want to be cautious," Yake whispered to his colleagues. "I really do. We got into this mess by *trusting* the damn Dhroo. But we can't afford to be cautious anymore." He turned back to the Rh/attes abruptly and said, "We don't believe in indentures. We want to try something different."

"Different?"

"Do you *trade* information?"

"*Trade*...information?" The Rh/attes all looked surprised.

"Yes," said Yake. "Trade."

"What advantage is in...trade?"

"The advantage in trade is that there is no disadvantage."

"Is our customary contract *not*."

"That's right. It's ours. We have a special contract for dealing with mammalian species. Don't you?"

The Rh/attes' whiskers twitched. They looked to each other, touching their cowls and chittering softly within the dark little cathedrals they formed.

At last, the Rh/attes turned forward again, and the sixth Rh/atte spoke simply. "Information you have. Information accept we gladly. Information we have. Information accept you gladly."

Yake exchanged glances with the others. They looked hopeful. Yake motioned them to keep quiet and turned back to the Rh/attes. "I have a question."

"Is?"

Even as he began to ask it, he already knew the answer. Why hadn't he seen this before? "You're working for the Dragons, aren't you?"

The Rh/attes merely stared at him. Finally, the first one said, "Is question with answer expensive, yes. And interesting too. Wish you to ask it?"

"No. No, thank you."

"So," said the first Rh/atte. "This is how trade works. Is works. Now ask we the question. Negotiations here are beginning or ending? Yes?"

"Beginning," said Yake. "You Rh/attes may be vermin, but you're *our* vermin."

"Mutual is feeling," agreed the Rh/attes.

The Librarian's Nightmare

THE AMBASSADOR FROM TERRA looked exhausted.

He looked old.

Not like the Old Man. But like an *old man.*

For the first time, Yake began to feel sorry for the strain he must be putting on his boss.

The Ambassador accepted Yake's report without expression. He laid the folder on his desk without looking at it.

"Is everything all right, sir?"

"As well as can be expected, I suppose," the Ambassador said. "I haven't been sleeping well, Yake. I don't think you understand the size of the bills that you and your committee have been running up." He massaged the knuckles of his hand as if merely to move caused him pain. "What are you downloading, anyway?"

Yake had expected this question. He was prepared. "Sir, at the suggestion of the Rh/attes, we're doing some research into the past five hundred years of treaties and negotiations in which the Dhroo have participated."

"Mm, yes," said the Ambassador. "I don't suppose I can argue with that; but you are turning into a very interesting problem, Yake. You're either going to be the greatest hero in history—or the greatest incompetent. And I'm the guy who has to give you enough rope so we can find out which. I would feel much better if you had some *tangible* results to report."

"Yes, sir. Uh, we have found one thing; but you're not going to like it very much."

The Ambassador sighed. He straightened himself and faced the younger man. "I can handle it, Yake. Go on."

"Well...it's the InterChange, sir. Um...we thought it was a—a cross between a Federation and a Library. A place where species could exchange information about each other."

"It's not?"

"No, sir. It's not. We were wrong about the governing functions of the InterChange. It's not a government at all. It never was intended to be. It's a—" Yake looked embarrassed. He looked at his feet. "We should have figured it out a long time ago, but we just kept assuming that the old assumptions were true because nobody ever questioned them. The, um—the InterChange is really a—a gigantic Monopoly game. A kind of a cross between a Poker Club and a pyramid scheme.

"You see, we thought that we were buying the book of the month from an interstellar library—that was what the Dhroo suggested—so we just kept downloading it as fast as we could—everything there was to know about all the other important species. Those other species knew better. We were buying poker chips! Information to use in the game! *Against them!* So they're all suspicious of us. We have no friends in this universe. Sir."

The Ambassador sank down into his chair. He looked ashen. "That *is* bad news, Yake."

"No, sir. That's not the bad news. This is—"

"It gets worse??!!"

"Sir? Are you all right?"

"I will be. Give me a moment." The Ambassador slipped two small pills into his mouth and took a drink of water. He coughed into his handkerchief for a moment, then looked to Yake again.

"Sir, if you'd rather—"

"No. I'd *rather* go to the gallows with my eyes open, Yake. Tell me the rest."

"Yes, sir. It's this. No matter how bad you think it's been—well, it's worse than that. We've also been wrong about the library part."

The last of the color drained from the Ambassador's face.

"Sir? Do you want me to call the doctor—?"

"No, no—please, go on."

"Sir, I really—"

"Yake!"

"Yes, sir. Well, uh—We've never understood how big this library really is. We're dealing with over two thousand different interstellar species—just those who are registered. Plus the records of four thousand more who can't afford to join. Plus the records of several thousand *retired* species as well. The complete records of each and every one of those species—some of them with over a half-million years of recorded art and history and science—are stored in the InterChange. Everything they've ever seen or learned. Every planet they've ever visited, charted, explored.

"The library of the InterChange is so big and vast that not even the InterChange itself has any idea of how big it is. If we had started downloading the index to the index a hundred years ago, we still wouldn't even be half through! And that's an obsolete index! Sir, the InterChange is out of control. Nobody has a handle on its information anymore—not even the InterChange itself. The best that anyone can do now is dip into it like a mathematician browsing through the Mandelbrot."

The Ambassador blinked. "The Mandelbrot? That's an infinite object, isn't it? Surely, the InterChange can't be that vast—"

"It might as well be, sir. Even if we put a billion human beings on the job, our species still wouldn't live long enough even to catalog what's available, let alone download it. Do you see what I'm saying? There may or may not be an answer to any question you might possibly want to ask in the tanks of the InterChange—but there's no way anyone is ever going to locate it for you. It's lost in the stacks. The InterChange itself is lost in the stacks."

"But it works!" The Ambassador tried to protest. "The evidence is all around us—"

"No, sir. The evidence is all around us that the InterChange doesn't work. That's how the Rh/attes survive. They're information specialists. They find and identify the information that's immediately useful to a species. I don't know how they do it. If I did, we wouldn't need them, would we? The Rh/attes are the real InterChange here. They're providing the service! The InterChange can't."

"You're saying that the InterChange is useless? Oh, my God."

"Practically useless, sir. Those races who can afford the services of the InterChange know how futile it is; and those who don't know run up incredible debts in the process of discovery. And none of the member species wants to change the system, because they're afraid they'll end up worse off. It's the most incredible con game in the galaxy, because even the con men who created it can't get out of it themselves anymore!"

The Ambassador sagged in his chair. His expression was stunned. "Then that means that...*everything* we've done here is wasted—Yake, I take it back. They're not going to hang you. They're going to hang me." He wiped his face with his handkerchief and looked up at Yake hopefully. "Is there anything else?"

"No, sir."

The Ambassador sighed loudly. "I was hoping...against all hope, of course—that you might have found a direction. Do you think the Rh/attes can offer us any immediate help?"

"I don't know, sir. They don't offer information. You have to ask them the right question, and then be prepared to pay the price for the answer. They're very much like the Dragons that way. Cheaper, but still very enigmatic. I think, sir, that it's very much a matter of asking the right question. From the way that the Rh/attes have been acting, I'd guess that they know *something*—"

"I'm afraid to ask how much that something will cost."

"Um. I probed, sir. They said what they say about all their answers. The information is valueless. It's what we might do with the information that creates value."

"Yes." The Ambassador thought for a moment. "I tell you what. Let's start with a simple question." He reached across his desk for a folder marked EYES ONLY. "Here, try them on this. Ask them why this negotiation broke down."

Yake took the folder. "Which one is this, sir?"

"The walking plants. The ones who were looking for a gardener. They spend the summer walking around, they put their roots down for the winter and meditate. They went into heavy debt to establish a colony on a new world, only to discover that there's some local predator that likes their flavor. It attacks them during their dream-time—peels back the leaves, scoops out and eats the living brains. These plant-creatures are conscious the whole time, but unable to do anything about it, so it's a very terrifying thing to them. They brought in another species, some kind of insect-race to help—the Ki!Lakken, they look like preying mantises—but they've totally failed to control these things.

"The contract looked like a natural for us, but when our people entered the room, the Fn^rr—that's what the plants call themselves—froze up and refused to talk. They curled their leaves in horror. And burned our negotiating team on the spot. We've filed a protest, of course—"

"Of course. Who was on the team?"

"Chandra. Hernandez. Bergman."

"Damn. They were good players."

"Save your grief. They were stupid. They went unarmed. We have a choice here, Yake. According to the rules of the InterChange, the Fn^rr have to pay us for the loss of our three negotiators, plus an insult fee. It's a pittance; it's worthless to us. *Or*...we can demand the satisfaction of a renegotiation. On our terms. I want to find out why they did it. That contract could have been useful. I think they were set up some-how—probably by the Dhroo."

"Why do you think that?" asked Yake. "It sounds right, but what evidence do you have?"

The Ambassador lifted a flimsy off his desk. He passed it over to Yake. "We've been served with a Notice of Acquisition. We have less than thirty days to demonstrate our intention to make good our infor-mation debt or the Dhrooughleem will take possession of us. For the record, the Dhroo have already worked sixteen species into early retire-ment. That's why I think the Dhroo are trying to kill our chances at any other deal—and if we can prove it, then we can file a grievance against the damn slugs. That will at least buy us some time. So. Do you think the Rh/attes can find out anything here?"

"I dunno," admitted Yake. "But I'm willing to try it."

"Good. Just one suggestion."

"Sir?"

"Make sure your team wears their sidearms from now on."

"Yes, sir."

The Cheese Stands Alone

WHEN YAKE ASKED THE QUESTION, the Rh/attes started giggling.

It was a particularly nasty sound.

Yake waited patiently for several moments, then spoke up with just the slightest hint of annoyance. "Are you going to let us in on the joke?"

"Joke, you are," replied the first Rh/atte.

The second Rh/atte added, "Vermin you call us, but vermin you are too!"

The third Rh/atte wrung its bony fingers and pointed. "Gardeners the Fn^rr need to protect themselves. They see you; they see not the answer, but the problem!"

And all the Rh/attes started hissing and chittering together again. It was one of the finest jokes they had ever heard.

Yake turned around and looked at Nori and Madja and Anne, mysti-fied. "Does anyone understand this?" They shook their heads.

"Missing a colony, are you?" the fourth Rh/atte asked.

"Nineva Sector, perhaps?"

Yake looked to Kasahara. "Nori?"

Nori nodded. "Yes, but—that was over two hundred years ago. Long before we knew about the InterChange."

"Ahh…" said all the Rh/attes together.

"What was that?" asked Yake.

"That was answer expensive. Given freely," replied the fifth Rh/atte.

Yake wanted to glare at Nori, but held himself back. Instead he said, "Not given freely at all! We expect you to give us an answer of equal value."

The Rh/attes exchanged glances, then huddled together in conference to discuss that thought. Yake fumed.

Madja touched him on the shoulder then and he asked impatiently, "What is it?"

She whispered in his ear. "How do Rh/attes know about lost colony?"

Before Yake could answer her, the Rh/attes broke out of their huddle. The sixth Rh/atte spoke quietly. "This is why you are stupid, Earthman. There are only nine mammaloid species in the InterChange. The rest are equivalents of life forms you would call reptiles or insects or sea creatures. What is the difference most profound between mammals and the others?"

Yake shrugged. "We bear our young live. We suckle them. We care for them."

"Precisely. Mammaloid species raise their young. Other species not need to. Not on scale same. They reach adulthood quickly and without need for training and programming. They do not recognize mammaloids as capable of intelligence anyway. Why should they recognize what happens to mammaloid young when the young are not raised by parents? They see vermin. The Fn^rr see vermin. Who would see otherwise? Who would *know* otherwise?"

Yake considered the creature's words. What was he really saying? And what was the hidden intent? Then—abruptly—Yake got it like a sudden punch to the sternum. He gasped for breath, astonished, and before he could choose his next question carefully, he simply blurted, "Are you suggesting that there are—*feral* humans out there? Children?"

The Rh/atte paused and smiled. Its yellow teeth were long and sharp-looking. "I ask you question now, Earth-creature. Who finds planet for the Fn^rr?"

Yake looked to Nori. "Do we know that?"

Nori checked his clipboard. "Just a moment." His face froze as the answer came up on the screen. He held the screen for Yake and Madja and Anne to see.

Yake turned back to the Rh/atte. "The Dhrooughleem," he said quietly.

"Are you surprised?"

Yake ignored the question. His face had hardened into a mask of iron. "Isn't there some kind of rule in the InterChange against selling another species into slavery without an indenture?" he asked.

"Who is to know? Very shortly, who is to care? Slave now, slave then—all the same is."

Yake looked at his colleagues. They could all see the truth of that statement. Yake turned back to the Rh/attes. "Would you excuse us for a moment?"

The Quiet Anger

MADJA WAS SURPRISED to discover that Yake Singh Browne could out-swear her.

Yake could swear in English, Swahili, French, Russian, InterLingua, German, Italian, and Pascal. Yake could also break tables, chairs, lamps, and windows with surprising agility and strength.

Yake Singh Browne could go for fifteen minutes without repeating himself.

Afterwards.

They stood apart in the shambles of the room, exchanging glances. Yake was not ashamed to meet the others' eyes.

He said quietly, "I feel much better now, thank you. Shall we return?"

Unlocking the Ki!

WHEN YAKE RETURNED to the room, the Rh/attes were still giggling among themselves.

Yake eyed them warily.

And then he made a mistake. He said, "There is more to this joke, I presume?"

"You will trade, will you?"

"Information only. Nothing else."

The Rh/attes conferred softly among themselves. Then they turned back to Yake. "Agreement is. You will demonstrate mating behaviors for us, yes?"

This time it was Yake's turn to confer with Madja, Anne, and Nori. "It's up to us to take one for the team—"

Afterward, the Rh/attes told them the rest of the joke.

Another Glass of Bheer

"THE PROBLEM WITH BHEER," said Yake to no one in particular, "is not that it doesn't taste like beer. It does. The problem is that it doesn't kick like beer."

"Yah," said Madja. "Is same problem with vhodka."

"And sahke," put in Kasahara.

"Ditto ghin," said Larson. "Alcoholh is not what it's cracked up to be."

"That is problem," said Madja solemnly. "It's cracked from petroleumh—or is that petroleuhm? I forget which."

"It doesn't matter," said Yake. "The 'h' is silent."

"Ahh."

Nori looked up blearily. "Tell me again, Yake, is this really a good idea?"

"Nope," said Yake. "It's a really lousy idea. Getting drunk never solved anything. Getting dhrunk is even less of a solution."

"Then why are we doing it?" asked Larson, blinking and brushing her hair back out of her eyes.

"So I can get the taste out of my mouth," said Nori.

"It was the only thing I could think of," Yake replied. "The Rh/attes wanted to see a mating behavior. We showed them a mhating behavior." Yake opened another bottle and saluted the two women with it. "You were excellent. My compliments to the both of you."

Anne Larson saluted back with their own bottle. "You boys looked like you were having fun too."

"Nori did the hard part."

"But did it work?" asked Madja.

Yake shrugged. "Well, either the Rh/attes are convinced or confused. Either they know we were misdirecting them or they don't. Either they are still wondering how we exchange genetic material—or they're thinking that we're more inventive than they had previously thought. Or maybe none of that. But if nothing else, they know how far we're willing to go."

"Or not," said Madja. "Is one hell of way to play poker." She reached over to the coohler and pulled out a bheer of her own. "If nothing else, it deserves second bheer."

Yake considered the bottle in his hand. "Last time we got dhrunk, we had a ghood idea. Maybe it'll whork again—"

Madja blinked at that. "Last time we got dhrunk, you had to talk to Dragon. You want to do that again?"

Yake thought about that. Yake *tried* to think about that. "No," he said, finally. "Let's think of something else."

They thought in silence for a moment.

Abruptly, Yake looked over at Madja. She looked back at him. "Yes, what is it?"

"Do you want to have sex with me tonight?"

"Is that all you think of?"

"No—but so far, it's the only thing I know I can do well."

"You are tired of Nori already?"

"Aww, don't be so hard on him," Larson said. "He's only a man. He can't help thinking small."

"No, no, no—it isn't that," Yake said slowly, carefully enunciating his words. "Everybody else in this InterChange is doing it to everybody else. I just want to be a do-er instead of a do-ee."

"You already did," said Kasahara. "Twice. That's just lust. I know lust when I hear it."

"Yah," agreed Madja. "Sounds like lust to me."

"I doubt it," said Yake. "I think it's lhust."

"Is irrelevant," said Madja. "It brings us no closer to solution."

"It's not irrelevant at all," said Yake. "It's the whole game here. Once in a while, I want to be on top."

"Yah," said Larson. "Me too."

"Me too," admitted Nori. "*Especially* me too."

"I make it unanimous," added Madja. "Is galling to be treated like this."

"We're not cheating hard enough," Yake muttered. He held his bottle up to the light, frowned and put it back on the table. Abruptly, he forgot about the bheer. "Hey—" he said, looking at the others. "What if there were a way to…do it?"

Madja returned his gaze. "If you find way, Yake—then you are better man than I. I sleep with you then."

"Hmm," said Larson. "Better be careful what you promise."

"I know what I promise. If Yake is that smart, then he is smart enough to be father of my children. Bring ring, Yake."

Yake grinned. "You got a deal, lady." He turned to Nori. "Turn on your magic clipboard and let's look at the rules of the game. You can't break 'em till you know what they are."

"Greedy capitalist pig—always looking for new way to cheat."

"That's right, Madja." Yake's grin was spreading from ear to ear. "In this game, it's how you cheat that counts!" Yake moved around the table to peer over Nori's shoulder. "I have an idea—"

The Slime and the Smile

SHUUSHULLUU, THE DHROOUGHLEEM AMBASSADOR, finished his ritual ablutions and slithered across the tank on his belly, his tentacles writhing in the slime. "Oh, great pool of life, I am yours to command. Touch me with your blessed wetness. I bring you tidings of great interest."

Lou'shloorloo the Whettest stroked one of Shuushulluu's tentacles dryly, and burbled, "Tell me what news transpires in the InterChange."

Shuushulluu glurped and replied, "The Terrans have refused our final offer, oh water of waters."

"Then the waters shall close over them… On their own heads shall it be."

"Oh, my blessed rainfall—I wither before I contradict you; but no, the waters shall not close over their heads at all. They have found two service contracts for themselves."

Lou'shloorloo rose up in the tank, eyes blinking in wonderment and fear. "They have WHAT?"

"Oh, wetness—this so distresses me. I am salty with fear and embarrassment. We asked the Rh/attes to tell us who and how and what and why—but the Rh/attes are being paid to tell us nothing. Deliberately so! I fear for what this means! There are no clouds on our horizon! The dreadful sun beats down on us! Our waters boil and evaporate!"

The Dhrooughleem Lord sank back into the tank. "We have promises to keep, my withering servant. You assured me that the naked Terran grubs would be ours by now to sell."

"I did not think—"

"That is apparent!"

"—that they could find an answer!"

"HOW DID THEY DO IT?!!"

"The only thing that I can think, they must have seen the Dragon—"

"THEY CAN'T AFFORD TO ASK THE DRAGON!!"

"Then the only other possibility is that they were clever enough to negotiate a solution by themselves."

"YOU TOLD ME THEY WERE NOT THAT SMART!!"

"My Lord, I have been proven terribly wrong. We had no evidence to suggest that any species derived from mammaloids could be capable of real reasoning. It is common knowledge that mammalian creatures think with their glands. Now it seems that that common wisdom has been demonstrated wrong. I would wither and die for you."

"YOU DON'T GET OFF THAT EASY!! YOU AIR-SUCKING SCUM!!"

"Anything, oh anything—"

"TEN THOUSAND EGGS THIS WILL COST US!! AND THE OCEAN ONLY KNOWS HOW MANY MORE YEARS OF INDENTURE!!"

Shuushulluu flattened itself upon the bottom of the tank. "I am yours to command, oh blessed wetness—"

"HERE IS MY COMMAND!!"

"Yesss, oh very yesss!!"

"YOU WILL BE THE ONE TO TELL OUR OWN INDEN-TURER THAT WE WILL BE DEFAULTING ON THIS CYCLE. YOU WILL BE THE BEARER OF THE TIDE!"

"Oh, my blessed wetness—"

"BEGONE! GET THEE HENCE! YOU ARE FOULING MY TANK!!"

The Warm Lands

Again.

Again, the sun is warm, the leaves are bright.

Again, the blossoms grow.

The roots are warm. We walk again.

Anew. The world is anew.

Again the dreams are true.

Anew.

The gardeners come. Come soon.

They have always been with us. Untrained. Unwise. They were as seedlings, always echoing, never knowing.

Echoing. Knowing.

Now, they shall be trained. And wise. So wise. They shall no longer eat the fruit of dreams.

The soil shall be warm. The blossoms will be bright. The seedlings soon grow tall and strong. The groves shall soon be large again.

Larger than a Fn^rr can walk within a season.

Again. Anew.

Soon, the gardeners live among us. The dreams of grubs and eaters in the orchards were seen through yester-season's eyes.

The eye of the sky shall smile. The rain will wash. The land will nourish. The soil will be rich.

The gardeners walk the dreams.

And the dreams no longer trouble.

Never again.

Again. Anew.
Again, tomorrow is found in dreams.
Again, we live anew.
Again.
Anew.

The Clack of the Ki!Lakken

HNAXX REACHED GINGERLY with one foreclaw and touched the bell that hung before the Pavilion of the Egg-Master. A clear, sharp tone rang through the air. Hnaxx waited a respectful moment, then parted the silk hangings and entered.

The Egg-Master was waiting patiently on the High Dais. It was gently polishing its foreclaws with a silk. The Egg-Master had the most beautiful foreclaws; they were inlaid with precious metals and gemstones and polished to a high sheen.

After a moment, the Egg-Master looked up and seemed to notice Hnaxx for the first time. "Ah," it said. It put the cloth to one side and leaned forward intently. "You have news?"

"I have much news, my Lord and Master. We shall be very prosperous indeed. Very prosperous. All has worked out quite well."

"Indeed?"

"Indeed. I shall endeavor to explain. You're acquainted with the offer made by the Dhroo?"

"The Dhroo were willing to sell us the grubs at ten sequins per unit; is this not correct?"

"Yes, my Lord."

"Such a price seemed very high to all of us. Did it not seem high to you?"

"Yes it did, my Lord. And there was that other matter too. The one I shall not refer to after this."

"Yes, that other matter," said the Egg-Master.

"That one is now resolved as well. It seems, my Lord, that we, have been approached by another species—a mammalian one, if you can believe! They are called the Rh/attes and they are the representatives for the race of pale grubs. Oh, you were right, my Lord. These grubs are quite intelligent. The Rh/attes have been using them as slaves for years. We have been very fortunate in this matter. Now the Rh/attes will lease us individuals for only seven sequins per."

"There is a catch, I'm sure—"

"Oh, yes, my Master; there always is a catch; but this time it is a catch that serves the buyer even better than the seller. They will only lease us individuals for one year at a time. But we can have as many as we wish. We may have hundreds. We may have thousands. We may have hundreds of thousands. We cannot use them for our breeding or our feeding, but we can use them any other way we want. We can train them, if we wish, to perform any tasks we choose, as long as we are not deliberately harmful. The Rh/attes will become our sole suppliers; they will take responsibility for every grub upon this world. But the chore of training, they insist, must be ours."

"For what we get, the price is still quite high."

"For what we get, the price is very low, my Lord. We get a world free of Fn^rr. If I may be so blunt—these grubs will not need to be trained; all we have to do is set them free upon the land. They will figure out the rest themselves. They are predatory feeders. They will find the orchards and they will eat out the brains of the foolish Fn^rr while they sit and dream!"

"Your excitement," said the Egg-Master, "leads you to discourtesy, but in the face of such a bold arrangement, the enthusiasm you display might be called excusable."

"And once the Fn^rr are gone, the grubs will be ours to feed and breed upon. If the Rh/attes ask what has happened to their pets, we shall tell them that they died of a mysterious cause. We shall increase our numbers and the numbers of our Nests. We shall retire many enemies! My Master, I am grateful to the Nest that allowed me such an honor as this service."

"And the Nest is grateful too, my child. You have served us well. We shall not forget what you have said and done. You shall be served in your time too."

It wasn't until it was too late that Hnaxx realized exactly what the Egg-Master had promised.

The Last Card Is Turned

YAKE, MADJA, ANNE, AND NORI entered the room to applause. "The Ambassador was standing at the head of the table, leading the hand-clapping.

They moved to their places at the table, smiling with good-natured embarrassment. Yake held up his hands to silence the acknowledgments of his colleagues. "Please," he said. "Please…not yet."

The applause continued for a few seconds longer, then died in uncertainty.

"Let me say this. It looks good. It looks very very good. But we're going to have to wait to see if it plays. So please don't start slapping yourselves on the back and congratulating each other just yet. There's one more thing that has to happen, and I'm going to be taking care of it as soon as I finish my report here." He motioned to the others to sit down but remained standing himself. "If you'll all be seated—"

Yake waited until everybody had taken their chairs and all eyes were upon him.

"It's very tricky," Yake began. "But it's all very very legal. That's what's so delightful about it. First, the Dhrooughleem are out of the picture entirely. Because we found our own way of paying the debt, the Dhroo have had to forfeit a very large deposit that they paid to the InterChange for the right of sole acquisition. The deposit, I am told, was considerable—and part of it will be credited against our debt." Yake had to wait until the applause died down again before he could continue.

"Thank you. I feel that way myself. They bet the store and they lost it. But you don't know yet how badly they lost it. The Dhroo were planning to sell human individuals to a race of intelligent praying mantises called the Ki!Lakken. We got this information from the Rh/attes. This is what makes this game so interesting. The Dhroo thought that the Ki! wanted to use humans as food and as larval incubators. The Ki! were already using feral children for that purpose—" Yake held up a hand. "I'll explain the details later; as near as we can figure out, these are the descendants of the lost Nineva colony; the Dhroo seem to have had a hand in that disaster too.

"The thing is, some of the Ki! had figured out that the children could be trained, and they were planning to double-cross the Dhroo and the Fn^rr—" Yake paused. "This is about to get very complicated. The Ki! and the Fn^rr are sharing a planet—the same planet that the Dhroo stole from us. The Ki! wanted to purchase several hundred thousand humans, but not use them for food or incubators; they'd train them to kill the Fn^rr. Apparently the feral humans have been feeding on the Fn^rr. That would leave the Ki! the sole custodians of the planet. With the destruction of the Fn^rr, part of their debt would disappear. Is everybody following this? Good.

"So, we approached the Ki! with a better offer. Actually, we had the Rh/attes make the offer for us—for a small commission, of course. The Rh/attes will supply humans to the Ki! now. We'll get the fee, not the Dhroo. The contract specifically gives the Rh/attes (agenting for us), custody of all the humans on the planet. They can't be used for food or eggs; they can only be used for training. Nori Kasahara says that the Fifth, Seventh and Twelfth Armies can be briefed and on-site within seven months."

"But wait a minute—" said someone down at the end of the table. "That sounds like we're going to be a party to a genocide—"

"Oh yes, it does, doesn't it? But the contract is only for training; it guarantees nothing else. Of course, the Ki! don't dare say what they want to train the humans to do; that would be illegal."

"But we're not going to do it, are we?!!"

"Of course not. We have a second contract on that planet. We're going to be the new gardeners for the Fn^rr. Caretakers. Protectors of the dreams. Call it what you will. It's a very attractive contract. Within ten years, the Fn^rr should have incredible forests on every continent."

"But what about the Ki!? Won't they figure it out quickly enough?"

"Oh, I'm sure they will; but they're going to have some other problems to worry about. It seems that the Fn^rr have discovered a very interesting fact; the alternate larval beast that the Ki! use is very susceptible to the measles. To be very fair to our Ki!Lakken employers, we will have to make very very sure that anyone sent to the planet is appropriately inoculated. Otherwise, it may turn out that the Ki!Lakken will not be able to continue into the next generation. And the Ki! have very short generations—only five to seven years."

Yake let that sink in, then continued, "So, here's how it works out. We're getting paid by the Ki! to eat the Fn^rr. We're getting paid by the Fn^rr to retard the breeding of the Ki!. If we decide to honor *both* those contracts, we can have our lost colony world back. We're getting part of the deposit forfeited by the Dhroo. Furthermore, because the Dhroo were responsible for stealing the planet from us in the first place and selling it to both the Fn^rr and the Ki!, they are heavily invested in both those species. Now that they've lost the rights to our indenture, they are no longer in a position to further exploit the Ki! and the Fn^rr, so they may not be able to meet the payments on their own indenture. So—if this forces an early retirement of the Dhroo, then the Rh/attes will pay us a bonus equal to one-tenth of *their* indenture to the Dhroo. Does everybody follow that?"

Everybody did. And this time, the applause went on and on and on. Even after Yake left the room.

But there was still, as Yake had promised, one more thing to do.

Endgame

YAKE SINGH BROWNE had a promise to keep.

The Dragon was resting on the top of a brown hill. It looked up as Yake approached. It had been eating something wet and gray and slithery. Something that still bubbled and frothed. Pieces of glass and plastic crunched beneath its teeth; sea water dripped from its jaws. *"Yesss?"* it asked.

Yake bowed. "I came to keep a promise."

"You came to tell me how it all worked out?" the Dragon asked.

"Yes," said Yake. "I always keep my word."

"So. Now I will tell you," said the Dragon. *"It worked out deliciously. Thank you for an amusing game. I hope it was interesting for you."*

"Yes. It was very interesting. Very very interesting."

"I am pleased. Perhaps you would like to play again soon?"

"Ah…if you insist." Yake sweated his answer. How do you say no to a Dragon?

"Yes, perhaps, we shall," said the Dragon. *"Perhaps next time it will be more interesting for me as well."*

The Dragon yawned and lowered its head to its feast again.

Yake ran like hell.

AUTHOR'S AFTERWORD:

In the unpolished draft of this story that got rushed into print, there was a lapse in internal story logic that bothered me enormously. I was halfway through the rewrite, on my way to fixing that hole when the nameless editor grabbed the story and rushed it into print. So I never got the chance to fix the mistake. Rereading the story again today, I can't find it or remember what it was. Owell.

We all hunger to be green. We just don't know it. We live our days safely on the road and never explore the wilderness on either side.

When the green man offers his hand, will you have the courage to follow? What could be sadder than not dancing joyously into the forest light?

I know what would be sadder.

What if he never offers his hand at all?

The Green Man

THE DARK OF SPRING. We were driving.

Michael and I and the smell of wet fog. A corridor of trees, a green gothic cathedral. A winding twilight road somewhere in northern California. Or maybe Oregon. Occasional headlights from passing cars, stabbing luminous fingers through the air. Neither of us talking. Nothing to say anymore.

Finally, he pulled the old Mustang over to the side of the road. We sat there in silence for a while. After a moment, he got out of the car. I wondered if I should follow. He stood in the middle of the road, arms outstretched as if he were going to embrace the inevitable logging truck that would surely run him down.

I sighed and got out of the car. I put my arms around him from behind, held him for a moment in a hug of peace, then walked him to the side of the road. He came willingly, he wasn't suicidal. He was just...whatever.

He stopped at the car. He leaned on the warm hood and stared at nothing in particular. "What's the point?"

I boosted myself up onto the fender, so I could sit and look at him. "What do you want me to say?"

He looked at me, a sour expression of annoyance.

"Michael," I said. "What can I say to you that you haven't already said for both of us?"

He shook his head and stared off into space. "It's not that," he said. "It's...everything else. What's the point?"

I shrugged. I could listen better than I could speak. That's why Michael included me in his life. I was his audience. I didn't mind. He was an interesting show—except when he got like this, which was about once a month. Or whenever something happened that he couldn't control.

I'd hoped that this trip would be a chance to get away from this, but somewhere between the first rest stop and the end of the beef jerky, it became obvious that we'd brought it with us and I was going to have to sit next to it for the next four hundred miles. Or longer. Because we weren't driving anywhere in particular. We were just driving to drive. Except when we weren't driving. Except when we were parked by the side of the road and Michael was staring off into space wondering why the universe existed in the first place. It must have seemed like a good idea at the time, but not to Michael.

"Maybe we should start looking for a motel?" I suggested.

He didn't answer. He was still looking into the trees. Finally I turned around to see what he was staring at.

A slender figure, silhouetted in fog. He looked naked. Hard to tell. He was just standing, watching us. For a moment, the three of us were a tableau. Michael and him—eyes locked. And me, looking back and forth between the two of them. Weird.

"Hello?" I said tentatively. I slid down off the fender, turned and waved. "Hello…?" To Michael, I whispered, "How long has he been watching us?"

Michael didn't answer.

And then I realized—"Oh, shit." I tugged Michael's arm. "It's one of *them*."

"Yeah," he said softly. I wasn't sure if he was speaking to me…or *him*.

"Get back in the car, Michael. Let's get out of here." I tried to pull him toward the door.

He resisted. "They're not dangerous."

"Then why did they tell us to keep away from them?"

Michael ignored the question.

"Remember what the Ranger said? 'If you see one of them, keep your distance. Don't try to talk to them.' Remember that?"

The man-boy stepped out of the fog. He was naked. And he was green. All shades. Deep green hair. Lighter green skin. Shiny green highlights. He shimmered in green. He had turquoise eyes. Piercing.

I was trying to remember everything the Ranger had said. "You're entering a restricted area. For the next fifty miles, don't stop. Just drive straight through." He'd given us a pamphlet, one of those not-very-informative government things that explained about the reservation.

The elves, the morphs, the greenies, the forest dancers, *them.* They weren't dangerous. Mostly they stayed away from people. Only sometimes they didn't.

Sometimes people went looking for them. Out of curiosity. Or to study them. Or to take their pictures. Or even to hunt them, trap them, hurt them—because they weren't likely to fight back. But sometimes, the people who went looking for them didn't come back.

Every so often, there'd be an article in the news. Someone else's abandoned car had been found. Or their clothes. Or there'd be stories about another green person seen dancing in the forest. The Rangers tried to keep a tally of them, but they were the first to admit they had no idea how many faerie folk were in the hills. But the number was growing.

The green boy was closer now. He moved with the grace of a breeze. He stepped onto the roadway just in front of the car. He looked to us expectantly.

"Michael, please—? Let's get out of here."

"Wait—"

"Michael, this is freaking me out."

Michael turned to look at me. "Jay. Nothing's going to happen. It's just a green boy. I want to see. Relax. You're not going to end up dancing with moonbeams. I won't let it happen." He turned back to the man-boy. They were close enough to touch. I felt like an outsider in my own life.

The boy reached out a hand, slowly—as if listening to Michael's feelings with his palm. His hand moved up and forward, stopping just in front of Michael's face. His azure eyes searched innocently. He looked lost and wise, both at the same time.

I gulped and stepped up beside Michael. "Don't let him touch you," I said.

For the first time, the boy's glance slid sideways to rest on me. His expression was bemused. His hand floated toward me now. As if tasting the moment. His fingers traced the line of my cheek. They weren't human, they felt like doll fingers, made of satin. For an instant, I heard distant voices, a chorus faint and far away, and bells—something familiar and mysterious, both at the same time. Beckoning. A chill in my gut, both sensual and scary. A flood of desire and panic—

All the memories.

A taste of something like butterscotch, but more magical and elusive. A moment of the time before birth. A touch like flavored silk. A waterfall of colors, azure, verdant, aqua, violet, lavender, all bright and rosy in the luminescent air.

I heard music. Like harps and silver bells and violins and oboes. Alluring, elusive, beckoning, comforting, blue and enveloping. Underneath, I heard *the heartbeat* of the Earth.

I turned around to look. The trees were bright. The forest glowed like home. And I could see a thousand years in all directions. Every line, every curve, every branch and leaf and needle. Every moth and bird, every blossom, every beetle. Everything that crept and crawled, slithered and slid, flapped and glided—everything that sang and croaked, squeaked and chittered. I felt it all as if it were my own body, my own naked skin open to the silvery air. As if the madness of rationality had finally fled, leaving me as free as starlight.

Moments fell away like baggage dropped from a bridge, splashing into oblivion. A thousand little hurts. The burdens of a mumbled life. Evaporated into blue eyes. Met mine like a kiss. *Get naked. Dance with me.*

All that. Just from a single touch—

I caught his wrist in my hand. *What are you doing to me?* The boy looked startled and puzzled. *Don't you want me to?* I released his wrist in shock. He didn't pull it back.

I looked to Michael.

Michael wasn't there.

I looked back to the boy—and he was gone too.

I was standing on the road, alone. Naked.

High up the slope, I could see the headlights of the car. I didn't remember walking down here into the fog. "Michael?" I started running back to the car—

It was where we'd left it. Lights still on. Doors still open.

"Michael?"

I looked at my watch. It was gone.

Where were my clothes? Where was Michael?

"Michael!"

No answer.

I leaned into the car to look at the dashboard clock. 3:17 am. Five hours.

Oh, shit.

"Michael!" I started back down the road, back to where I'd found myself. Looking for my clothes. Looking for Michael. Looking for the boy.

Oh, shit. Oh, shit. Oh, shit.

They'd gotten away from me. Michael had promised he wouldn't let me go—

I plunged into the woods. Everything was still luminous. I could still taste the silvery flavors. The songs still circled and danced. The music whirled. I flew toward the magic. "Michael—? It's Jay! Come back! You promised!"

The flavors. My god, the flavors. My feet tasted the leaves of the forest floor. My hands swirled through sweet currents of the night. My legs, my thighs, my belly, my skin—everything flooded with sensation. Everything inside, unfamiliar feelings. Emotions. Passions. Lust and fear, desire, panic, madness, hunger, emptiness, longing—fulfillment beckoned. Following the light. Too fast, too far away, like rainbows in the fog. Please Michael take me with you don't leave me behind not like this oh shit

Cold. Naked.

Sunlight filtering through trees.

Ugly noises.

Men and dogs.

Rough blankets. Wrapped around.

Noises. Guttural. Familiar. Meaningless. Words.

"Can you hear me, son? Do you understand what I'm saying? Look at my hand. How many fingers am I holding up?"

Go away. What are you doing here? I want to dance.

Something bites my arm.

I float away.

But not into the forest.

All white.

Then colors. Drab colors. Green, but not really green. Pink, but not really pink. Smells like walls. Ceilings. Floors. Curtains. Tubes. Beeping.

The woman smiles at me. She's wearing rubber gloves. "How are you feeling this morning? Do you know where you are?"

Another planet. *Wrong answer.* "Somewhere on Earth?" I venture.

She smiles. It is meant to be comforting, but it isn't. She does things, touches my body here and there. But her touch is dead. No magic. No music. The feelings are fading. I am shaking awake, she is dragging me back into rationality. I can still sense the flavor of the forest, deep inside; but it is too far away for me to reach.

"We're here to help," she says. I can feel the hooks sliding in. They sound like words. Feelings turn into sound. Language ensnares.

"Not magic at all," she says. "Pheromones and hallucinogens."

Explanations. Polymorphic kinaesthesia.

Wrapped in the cold sheets of rationality, I come back. I've had a bad experience. But I'm feeling much better now. Just ask me.

"You were fringed by a morphic entity. It lives in the green people. It's in their breath. The particles in the air intoxicate you. It's on their skin. Their touch infects you. You were lucky. We found you in a week.

We cleansed you with anti-psychotic agents until the effect wore off. If we hadn't found you before the change became infused, you would have become a reservoir of your own intoxication."

"What about Michael?"

"Who?"

"Michael. Did you find him too?"

"There was no one with you."

"Michael was driving. He's the one who stopped the car. He's the one who saw the green boy."

Her look says I'm crazy.

"Did you look in the car? Did you see his luggage?"

"There was only one bag in the car."

"The black one was his. The brown one was mine."

"There was no black case." More words. More explanations. Transitional hallucinations. False memories. There is no Michael. The Ranger remembers me. I was alone. He warned me not to stop, he didn't think I was listening. When I didn't arrive at the exit station, they alerted the patrols.

"You're feeling a great loss. That's common. Listen to me. Your name is Jay Michael. You've personified your loss."

Language ensnares.

The woman speaks, day after day, webbing me with all the little insects of her mouth. Her words. They scurry across my brain, trying to muffle the great green heartbeat. They swarm. They chitter. They chew. But for all their itching and chewing, I could still hear the heart of the Earth booming inside me.

And then—it was winter, and the heartbeat was wrapped in cold sheets. My own heart as well. Hardened in ice. Shining.

It was over.

I thanked the counselors for all their help. For killing the glow inside. I promised to check in every week. I promised to call if I needed to talk. I promised to stay away from hallucinogens and pheromones and dreameries. I promised not to do anything tribal. I waved goodbye and put the car in gear.

And I kept my promises too.

I went to the sessions and I sat on the couch between two strange men and I shared what had happened. And they shared their stories. We all told the same story. "For a while...I *belonged* to something. That's all I ever wanted." We all shared the same feelings. Desire. Hunger. Longing. Emptiness. Loss.

One day I asked, "Why is it so wrong—to belong? Why do they think they're doing us a favor taking it away from us? Where's the good in coming back here? What's the point?"

The group leader, the facilitator, looked at me sharply. "Michael, do you really want to disappear?"

I didn't answer.

"That's what happens to people who turn green. They give up their sense of self. It isn't just the death of the ego—it's the death of individuality."

"Is that so bad?" I demanded. I slapped my head with both hands. "Can't you feel it? The walls are made of bone! Don't you ever want to get out?"

"You're still feeling the after-effects. They told you, didn't they, that the recovery period could be as long as a year? Your body is going through a profound physical depression. You were elevated through a series of transformational plateaus. Then you crashed and burned. You're still ringing like a bell. You probably hear echoes every night, lying alone in your bed, don't you? Do you think you're the only one? Every person in this room—*myself included*—feels it! We understand it, Michael. This is a place where you *do* belong."

Afterward, afterward, Jay and I go walking through the dark satellite sky. Glittering noises everywhere.

"Do you believe that?" Jay asked.

At first, I didn't want to answer. But I knew that Jay liked hearing me work things out. "If they know better than me, then I should accept what they say. Shouldn't I? But how do I know that they know better what's best for me. Who's responsible for my life? I am. And if this is a choice, then it's my choice to make. And what if they don't know better than me? What if they're just as confused? Then why am I making someone else's mistake?"

"You want to go back, don't you?"

"Don't you?"

"Everyone does." And then he added. "But you can't. They've sealed off the whole north coast. You can't even drive through anymore."

I shrugged. "You could hike into the area."

He nodded agreement. "You could." He adds. "It would be a long hike, though. Twenty-thirty miles. Two or three days."

"Yeah. Probably."

"They'll catch you, you know. They have patrols now. And cameras."

"Yeah, I heard that too." I glance over at him. "Are you coming with?"

"I think we should wait."

"For what?"

"To see if the feeling will pass."

"And if it does? Then what have we gained?"

It's his turn not to know. "I just think we should wait."

"Some people say…that the green people are the next step in evolution. A symbiosis with Gaia. You get chlorophyllins in your skin. You stand in the sun, naked, and the light feeds you, energizes you."

"And winter kills you," said Jay.

I look at him sharply.

"That's what they say," he adds. "The Rangers say that every spring, when the snows start melting, they find the decomposing bodies of the ones who didn't survive."

"We can wait till spring."

Jay looked relieved.

"Spring is the best time. You have all summer to glow. In the winter, you go dormant. You go deep into the Earth, deep down into the heart-breath, where the soil is warm and nourishing. You wrap yourself up and sleep until the sun returns. It's the ones who don't use the summer for glowing who don't survive."

"How do you know all this?" Jay asks.

I shrugged. "I just know." I look at him with azure eyes. "How do you know that rocks are hard and water is wet? How do you know gravity and sky and sun? You just do."

Dawn seeps over the eastern edge of the world. We crawl back into the coffins of our lives and wait for spring.

The dark of spring. And we will go driving. Jay and I.

AUTHOR'S AFTERWORD:

What magic lies within that we deny? Offer me a wild dance, and I will go a-dancing. Arise my love and rescue me from the dreariness of days.

Not much to say about this one. I had just visited the large array space telescope in New Mexico and I was thinking "hard SF"—the bigger the telescope, the more accurate the image. It seemed likely to me that interplanetary spaceships will have telescopes. If every spaceship in the solar system were to point its telescope in the same direction all at the same time, and if we were to collate all these images into one, what would we see?

The Diamond Sky

THE HULL OF THE MARTIAN QUEEN was diamond-plated. By design.

A seemingly-endless field of panels reflected the distant starlight with a plated sheen halfway between metal and ice. She looked more like a careless array of solar collectors than the spacecraft she really was.

Captain Adam Neace reviewed the vessel with a critical eye. He wore a VR headset and he rode *Little EVA*, one of the external spider-bots, up and down the long rows of panels, quietly inspecting. He didn't expect to find anything, the spider-bots were more thorough and more relentless than any mere human could ever be, but Adam Neace wasn't a mere human and he was old enough to remember a time when bots were merely extensions of human effort, not independent agents. He liked to look for himself. Despite his own augmented being, he still believed in human intuition; that sometimes the human mind could sense possibilities and connections that a simple intelligence engine might overlook. But mostly Captain Adam Neace rode the bots because he liked being "outside" more than inside.

…another successful breeding season at the Auckland Seaquarium. Alex is the largest giant squid living in captivity, nearly six meters in length. In the wild, giant squids can grow to 16 meters or more. The Auckland Seaquarium covers an area of sixteen square kilometers and is the second largest land-based ocean laboratory in the southern hemisphere. The South African and Australian seaquariums also have breeding programs for…

The Martian Queen was eleven years old, built to standard design: a kilometer-long keel, speared through the axis of a mandatory habitat-centrifuge. To an external observer, she might have seemed an unwieldy conglomeration of panels, struts, guy wires, pipes, engines, tanks, sensory gear, ancillary thrusters, and life-support modules; but in actuality, she was a carefully balanced machine, a space-going laboratory as well as a precision vacuum factory. Although she was capable of interplanetary leaps, for most of her life, she'd stayed in perpetual eclipse, riding the shadow of Mars; a tricky but not impossible orbit. It was a necessary maneuver to keep the vessels isolated so that the delicate fabrication processes of her factories would not be contaminated by stray solar radiation. Solar storms could be violent even this far out from the hearth.

...*evolutionary advances in digital archaeology have made it possible to cross-correlate multiple time-data frames, allowing researchers to track the interaction of real-time trends across multi-dimensional matrices, including economic, political, ecological, and sociological causitives. Cusps of chaotic potential appear as three-dimensional spikes in the strata...*

"Captain?"

Neace put the bot on auto and flipped up his VR goggles. First Officer Mark Ensley came floating forward into the bridge. "We've got mail. From Admiral Palmer." Ensley pulled himself down into the co-pilot's seat and belted himself in. Neace touched his display and brought up the message. The first sentence told him everything he needed to know: "Congratulations, Captain Neace." The rest of it was formality: "The Review Board is satisfied that *The Martian Queen* and her crew have met or surpassed all requirements. The Board is pleased to certify *The Martian Queen* as ready for service. You may proceed with the next phase of your mission immediately."

Neace scratched his neck thoughtfully. The message wasn't unexpected, as the ship had been prepared for several days. They were already testing the long-range laser-links off the asteroid-belt repeaters. But bureaucracy had to be served—for two reasons. First, bureaucrats needed to feel important, and second, you always had to have enough paper to cover your ass. Just in case. Even so, the official confirmation felt good.

...*announced the successful insertion of the ice-asteroid into a close approach orbit, timed to coincide with the Summer Olympic Games in Dallas-Fort Worth. Comet Janisian will have a red, white, and blue tail stretching across one-third of the sky and will be visible for nearly three weeks...*

"I'll have the Venus link up as soon as we move out of shadow," Ensley reported. "And we'll have direct acquisition of Earth-Luna at 0803. Not quite the optimal triangle, but it'll give us a baseline."

"IRMA, secure the bots; begin your checklist, please."

"Working..."

...*high point of the all-robot revival of* Hello Dolly *is the astonishing*

"Waiter's Gallop" sequence, with over a hundred shimmering metal bodies leaping and dancing in pinpoint synchronization, juggling trays of full glasses and pitchers, all without spilling a single drop of...

For most of her life, *The Martian Queen* had been one of several orbital facilities producing large form diamond-substrates. Working in the universe's largest clean room—the universe itself—her external factory bots vacuum-layered pure crystalline carbon onto panels several meters across to create the largest *and flattest* diamonds possible. The resultant sheets were the ideal substrate for optical and electrical chips, for display panels of all sizes, for precision collectors and reflectors, and for a thousand other industries that needed atomically flat surfaces—for example, mirror arrays for radio, optical, and X-ray telescopes.

As each panel was completed, it was measured and graded. Any panel that failed the "flat as ancient Kansas" test could not be certified. Although there existed a considerable market for these lower grade diamond sheets, shipping them wasn't cost-effective for a ship in Martian orbit; local suppliers could provide the panels cheaper; but this was understood long before *The Martian Queen's* keel had been drawn. It had been planned from the beginning that Captain Neace would install the castoff pieces around critical components of the vessel as ablation shields against strikes by micro-meteorites.

...ethics of animal implants remain unresolved. Meanwhile, Sparky has added another thirty words to his vocabulary. As you can see, Sparky enjoys meeting new people, and he speaks his thoughts enthusiastically, as our onsite reporter discovered. <Sparky:> "Maya smell good. Maya mate, yes?"...

But the fabrication and sale of A-grade panels was only a sideline for the *Queen*—a very profitable sideline, but a sideline nonetheless. Her very best surfaces were reserved for a much more ambitious task. Not all the panes she produced were pure diamond, and not all were flat. Many were doped with layers of other materials to provide specific physical properties, many were subtly curved to fit into a precise design. *The Martian Queen's* sole job been the construction of several thousand diamond mirrors, the most optically precise reflectors ever made, all components of the largest distributed array ever constructed.

Her certification had never been in doubt; for the most part, she was constructed with "off-the shelf" technology, but now that she was officially online she could assume her duties as the third and final coordinating station for the Dispersed Array Space Telescope. Two similar ships rode in the orbits of Earth and Venus. Other vessels were planned for the future, but at least three were necessary to coordinate.

...in a limited decision, the court declined to rule on the ethics of Klingon-deprogramming. However, the court did agree that Acht-Facht had not left the Enterprise orbiting hotel voluntarily and that the lawsuit could continue.

Representatives of the Klingon Church petitioned to the court to compel The Human Adventure to reveal Facht's whereabouts...

DAST was an inevitable idea, an outgrowth of Arecibo and Paranal and Farside. Spaceships carried telescopes—all kinds—optical, radio, microwave, X-ray, gamma-ray, gravitational, deep-resonance, and stress-field. Link up several telescopes, point them all in the same direction, collate their separate images, and you create a virtual telescope as large as the distance between reflectors. The proof of concept was over a century and a half old, dating back to the days when all astronomy was Earth-bound. The four linked mirrors at Paranal had eventually produced pictures even more spectacular than the orbiting Hubble eye.

In the early 21st century, this idea had been exported to space. Four identical planetary probes were linked by laser to each other. All four focused their telescopes on the same set of objects and synchronized their separate exposures. Even as a proof of concept, the results were stagger-ing; the detail of their deep space imagery left astronomers hungering for more. The Distributed Array Space Telescope had been an ongoing project ever since. Almost every ship in transit between Earth and Mars linked its onboard telescopes to the Lunar Coordinating Base at Gagarin; long-range lasers transmitted a steady stream of timing and position data; each ship synchronized its exposures to the nano-second, and returned its images along the same laser beams it used for position-referencing. It was not only the largest virtual telescope in existence, it was also the most cost-effective, using existing observational tools already in place. Even the software was off-the-shelf. All it required was a coordinating station.

...dead at 137. She was the last living survivor of the...

But as humanity pushed outward, to the asteroid belt, to the moons of Jupiter and Saturn—as more and more ships and telescopes came online, synchronization became exponentially more difficult. Manage-ment became the essential problem. *The Martian Queen* and her two sis-ter ships were intended as a triangle of anchor points, providing precision synchronization data; each one linking to and coordinating all partici-pating ships within her own sphere of influence. The projected increase in resolution was expected to be at least three orders of magnitude.

Each of the *Queens* needed multiple laser-units and reflector panels for every ship in the linkage. Additionally, to provide a baseline for com-parison, each of the *Queens* carried one of the three largest telescopes ever dispatched to space; when fully opened, the array would be several hundred meters across. From the outset, each of the *Queens* had been designed as a space-going factory, each one fabricating all of her own delicate reflectors.

...said that the culture-quake, measuring at least six points on the Maslow-Richter scale, would be centered in the San Fernando Valley, and

would occur in the first week of February. Voluntary evacuations are recommended for those susceptible to culture-shock. FEMA will be sending in over a thousand quake-proofing consultants to advise residents...

"We're out of the shadow," Ensley reported. "We've acquired *The Venus Queen.*"

"Right," said Neace, studying his own displays. "Let's say hello. Three beams." He pressed record and whispered into his microphone, "Peek-a-boo—" The beams were effectively invisible in the vacuum of space; at one part per godzillion, there wasn't enough dust to illuminate them; but 12.3 light-minutes away, *The Venus Queen*, in the center of the targeting cone, would be able to distinguish three specific pinpoints of color—red, green, and blue. The subtle differences between the beams would allow *The Venus Queen* to calculate Doppler shift, precise distance, and timing for synchronization.

Allow three minutes for Captain Radley Nakamura to receive the message and record an acknowledgment, *The Martian Queen* should receive its reply no more than thirty minutes after sending its initial message; once the first laser-links were in place, the primary synchronization could be completed in a matter of hours; even allowing for slippage, no more than eight hours should be required to establish the first backbone channel for the DAST network. At these distances, however, mostly the job involved waiting.

—which is why the ideal candidate for long-term space missions was an immortal.

...largest ever expansion of a sea-going environment, Atlantis will add 20 square kilometers of pontoon-based platforms over the next seven years. Construction will cost 1.7 billion plastic dollars and will increase the sea-nation's surface area by 20%. In off-market trading, share prices went up a half, with further increases expected when the market formally reopens after the weekend holiday...

Neace hadn't set out to be immortal, but as he aged, it had become more and more convenient—and necessary—to augment his biological processes with biotechnological aids. By the time of his 80th birthday, he was nearly 80% augmented; and at the present rate of accretion, his centenary would see the completion of the various processes. He was neither impatient nor apprehensive, merely resigned to the inevitability. He wanted a berth on the first interstellar expeditionary fleet. Non-immortals need not apply. At one-quarter light-speed, the journey to Sirius and back would take 66 years.

His primary motivation, however, had involved Captain Nakamura. He'd been fascinated by her from the first, although he hadn't recognized it as infatuation until later. Their romance had been passionate, but all-too-often interrupted by the exigencies of career. A variety of assignments had sent them careering across the solar system, only occasionally allowing them to match orbits. When she had gone immortal, as most starsiders eventually did, he had followed her lead. Ideally, he hoped they would both secure assignments aboard the same ship of the Sirius mission. But even if not, as an immortal, he now had time to wait. One of the lesser advantages of immortality was the ability to downshift; to place oneself into a slower time-speed—relative dormancy—and thus transform long periods of imposed inactivity to shorter subjective experiences.

...found the stock certificates entirely by accident in a stack of fanzines. Purchased for only twelve dollars a share in 1987, the certificates now represent holdings of more than...

"Laser linkage acquired." IRMA reported. "Incoming message." Radley Nakamura's voice whispered a near-flirtatious response: "—I see you!" To an immortal, the twenty-seven minute interval was negligible.

Neace nodded dispassionately. "Initiate calibration." The two ships would ping-pong a complex set of signals and tests, triangulating on each other as they moved through their separate trajectories, and ultimately establishing precision-predictive-positioning data accurate to a tenth of a millimeter, plus or minus an error below the ability of the measuring equipment to detect.

There wasn't much else to report to *The Venus Queen*. Despite the fact that this was the first time in eleven years that the two ships had achieved direct line of sight, they had never really been out of contact, relaying their messages via whatever satellite and ships-in-transit links were currently available. Bouncing messages off relays always added delays, and depending on the number of intermediate steps, it could easily double transmission times. Direct acquisition meant that the time lag between message and response was now appreciably shorter.

...announced that she will again change gender, this time to play the role of Seth in the BBO production of A Season of Passion. The change will take four months, and filming will begin in the spring. Although no casting has been announced for the role of Diana, producers are said to be in negotiation with Ric Carliss, the only other performer to have won awards for both best male performance and best female performance...

"Peek-a-boo" was almost a six-decade-old joke between the two Captains. In his first year at the Academy, Neace had installed a digital camera on the terrace of his student apartment. The unit had a self-synchronizing motorized mount, automated motion-detection-and-capture, holographic lenses, six-color correction, UHD resolution at 120fps, and a telephoto ratio of 375x. As an exercise in engineering, he'd written software for it to monitor all the visible windows of two facing dormitories, zooming in for close-ups wherever motion was detected. He wasn't the first student to have done this—it was one of several real-world assignments handed out to freshmen. Neace's addition to the software included multi-spectrum collation, extrapolated removal of obscuring artifacts (such as window glare and curtains), digital image enhancement and noise reduction, clothing detection (including lack of), sorting all retrieved data by amount of skin revealed, followed by additional sorting based on conformation of body mass to selected optimal characteristics—including breast size. The video display in Neace's apartment automatically updated to play a repeating slideshow of the most interesting images captured.

Radley Nakamura did not show up in any of these scans, which singular fact was enough to reduce Neace's grade on the project from A+ to merely A. Due to her short hair, her propensity for wearing sweatshirts and sweatpants, the recognition algorithm had erroneously classified Ms. Radley Nakamura as a boy. Already in her Junior year, and well familiar with the prevalence of cameras in the buildings opposite, Ms. Radley Nakamura did this deliberately. The instructors, equally familiar with Ms. Radley Nakamura, included her as a test of the recognition abilities of the Neace's software project.

…replacement of the three wind-turbines damaged in the last Martian sandstorm is expected to take…

This being a tiered assignment—with final grade dependent on the student's ability to implement improvements and corrections—Neace focused exclusively on Radley Nakamura's window, determined to fix his gender-recognition algorithm. He began correlating a weighted value system, based on Adam-apple size, wrist size, complexion, general softness of features, center of gravity, motion characteristics, body-fat ratios, generalized behaviors, and other characteristics with specifically measurable differences between the sexes. Very quickly, he realized that the problem stemmed from Ms. Nakamura's commitment to her career. Having decided that gender identity was an inconvenience, she had gone androgynous, preparatory to becoming immortal. The androgynous part was reversible, of course; but not the immortality augments. Neace had to rewrite his recognition algorithm to allow for androgyny superposed over gender. It wasn't a trivial problem, and he aimed his camera directly at her balcony to gather sufficient observational data to establish a personal baseline for Radley Nakamura to measure against the statistical norms.

Unfortunately, the video software failed to update any motion from Ms. Nakamura's balcony. Reviewing the capture in real-time revealed why. Ms. Nakamura had hung a curtain across her balcony, blocking any further intrusions of her privacy. Even more to the point, she had set up her own camera, pointed directly back at Neace's.

Neace got the point immediately. He hand-lettered a sign and hung it below the lens of his camera. The sign said, "Peek-a-boo."

...presented a new plan for shadowing Venus. Based on their preliminary results, researchers now believe that Venusian temperatures could be reduced in less than 150 years...

A day later, Ms. Nakamura's camera displayed a matching sign. "I see you."

Neace hung a new sign on his camera. "Dinner?"

She replied. "Diner. 7pm."

Over dinner at the diner, Neace discovered—among other things—another reason why his recognition algorithm had failed. Nakamura was genetic male, female by choice, and as previously determined, temporarily androgynous. Neace wasn't old-fashioned, he'd dated members of several genders with enthusiasm, and varying degrees of success; he was simply annoyed with himself that he hadn't included this possibility. After briefly debating with himself about a possible appeal of his project grade, he decided instead to recode the recognition algorithms and win his points fairly.

... encyclical from Pope Maria Theresa reaffirms the church's stance on the sanctity of all sentient life, whether it's carbon-based or silicon...

Nakamura found Neace amusing. He was intrigued by her unusual insights, a product of her peripatetic gender identity. Although their mutual schedules allowed for only the occasional hurried meal at the diner, they kept in constant touch by e-mail, and by displaying increasingly cryptic messages on their respective balconies, each one a puzzle. If the recipient couldn't solve the problem, he or she had to pay for the next dinner. Neace ended up paying for most of their meals.

It wasn't that she was smarter or that he lacked puzzle-solving skills; rather, he was methodical and determined where she had grown up outside the lines. He knew why he was fascinated by her; but for a while, he couldn't understand what she liked in him. Eventually she had to tell him. "It's the strength of your determination. Determination without genius got more ships launched than genius without determination." For Neace, it was a moment of sheer *aha!* The two them complemented each other.

Which was why, even 12.7 light minutes apart, they were still able to play "Peek-a-boo, I see you."

...representatives from Roma, Cathay, Nubia, and Babylon again failed to reach agreement with the World Health Organization on the issue of vaccination. Health care has always been a sore point for the historical simulacra, with extremist factions decrying modern health measures as anachronistic influences that distort or destroy the accuracy of the recreated cultures...

"We've got Earth/Luna," said Ensley. "Just coming up over the horizon. We've got radio tracking."

Neace glanced up at the high resolution display. A highlighted frame expanded to reveal a bluish pinpoint, imperceptibly sliding out from behind the shield of the red planet.

"And we've got incoming—"

"Nice timing on their part," Neace noted.

The hearty voice of Manda Sahir boomed from the speakers, with just a hint of single entendre. "Gotcha! Enough with the peek-a-boo. Let's play pattycake."

"I love you too, Manda," Neace replied, even though it would be six minutes before Captain Sahir heard his response.

...tourism to Bradbury is projected to increase with the completion of the third phase of the Grand Canal project, with other Martian cities expecting to benefit as well. Burroughs will increase its Thoat-breeding programs, and Wellsopolis will make the Invasion of London-1890 an annual event. (That's Martian-annual, not Earth-annual.) Bookings will need to be made at least two years in advance...

Captain Manda Sahir had always been aggressive, so much so that she'd earned several astonishing nicknames during her career, "scream-and-leap" being the least objectionable. But in truth, her attitude was far more playful than passionate; she wasn't flirtatious, she was just "kidding around with the guys" and she'd calculatedly rebuffed several who misunderstood where the boundaries had been drawn. Neace had been one of the lucky ones, caught between missions. The affair had been affectionate, playful, friendly, and ultimately noncommittal. Nevertheless, Neace now regarded himself as the hypotenuse of the farthest-spanning triangle in human history, although it would have been more geometrically accurate to consider his position an acute angle—at least until the movements of the several planets and their orbiting *Queens* altered the shape of the triangle.

...spokesman for the Reich predicted a seventh consecutive victory over the Allies in the upcoming replay of World War II. The simulation is expected to attract over a million players, and nearly that many observers. The Reichs-Kampf also released further information about the Vaterland-1936 enclave, now under construction at...

"We've got RGB from *The Lunar Queen*," said Ensley. "Right on target."

"Did you expect less?" Neace grinned. "Light her up. Initiate calibration, let's see what we've got." Neace waited until the displays flashed green, then half-turned to his first officer. "Congratulations. We're online. Let's take some pictures. Earth, Venus, Jupiter and Saturn. Then

I want a long shot of Sedna. After that, the standard celestial repertoire. Horsehead, Crab, Orion Anomaly, the whole package. We'll need the shots for comparison after we've established first collation."

"Working," said Ensley. The program had been written months before. All he had to do was call it up and check off the appropriate targets. The computer would do the rest. Indeed, the program was as much a test of the synchronizing software as it was of the telescope itself. They'd already had a dozen test runs while still in the shadow of Mars. There was no significant importance to this shoot, except that for the first time, it was an *official* test.

...super-clustering over thirty million subscribers, with a projected real-time decryption matrix...

IRMA beeped softly. Incoming messages arriving. The first of thousands that would arrive over the coming weeks, as various ships in transit sought to establish their own linkages. Aside from their individual participation in the Dispersed Array Space Telescope, there was a much more immediate objective—accurate mapping of the solar neighborhood, accurate positioning within that map, predictive analysis of gravitational rumpling and mascon perturbation of smaller space objects.

Ensley briefly reviewed the ship's e-mail. Most of the requests for connection would be auto-replied over the next few days, but no additional connections would be made until the *Queens* established their own baseline. The big problem here would be correlating massive amounts of data in real-time. Once the DAST was online, that problem would expand exponentially. It wasn't that the ship didn't have the processing power—it did—the problem was throughput: the allocation of bandwidth resources.

But several of the messages did require human attention and Ensley began working methodically through them. It was the commentaries in the science journals he was most concerned about. Occasionally, someone or other would so totally misunderstand the workings of the Dispersed Array Space Telescope that it required an immediate response, before a whole mythology of ignorance was inadvertently allowed to take root—like that most notorious of all scientific misunderstandings, dating back to the early 20th Century, that a rocket couldn't work in a vacuum because there was no air to push against.

...breaking the record for the longest sustained (non-fatal) orgasm ever recorded, Yates credited all three of her partners...

Some of the questions raised about DAST included, "How can it be a telescope if it's mostly space and very few mirrors?" and "How do you focus a virtual reflector 400 million kilometers across?"

The more literate objections dealt with parallax and resolving power. "Won't parallax issues make collation of the separate images problematic, especially for objects close to or within the solar system?" "Isn't the ultimate resolving power limited by the resolving power of the individual reflectors?" "Aren't existing space arrays sufficient? Doesn't this take us way beyond the point of diminishing returns?"

There were answers to all of these. Ensley had already authored several articles and a short book addressing the various issues in language as accessible to the lay reader as possible. But even he acknowledged that in some regards, astronomy had gone way beyond the proverbial "rocket science." The simple process of scanning the diamond sky now required technology that even many astronomers did not fully understand. As one wag had put it, the gap between theory and engineering was now estimated to be several light hours and expanding exponentially.

...but that argument still doesn't address the legal issue; if an adult rejuvenates to an adolescent or even a pre-pubescent body, is he or she still an adult capable of informed consent? When individuals choose to become infantiles, dependent upon others, how can they still claim adult privileges and responsibilities? Should sexual encounters with infantiles and rejuveniles be considered acts between consenting adults with body-mods—or are we seeing a new form of statutory rape? We have to ask if those who seek out and engage in such relationships are expressing a pedophilic intention. Does this create an environment that ultimately endangers all sub-adult beings...

When the first high-resolution pictures of Earth and Luna finally came up, both Neace and Ensley breathed a sigh of relief. Neither man had realized they were holding their breath. The resolving power of *The Martian Queen*'s array was at the high end of optimum, almost approaching the theoretical limits. It was better than expected, more than was hoped for.

...documentary on the progress of the Mons Rushmore project, including interviews with the descendants of...

The next few shifts kept both men busier than usual and left little time for flirtations, long-distance or otherwise. The pictures of Jupiter and Saturn were excellent, and the project shifted easily into its next phase.

All three *Queens* synchronized on schedule and their first collated image was of far-distant, frozen Sedna. Sol's tenth planet, first discovered in 2004, wandered in an elliptical orbit as close as 76 AU's, as far as 1000 AU's, taking over 10,500 years to complete a single orbit. Sedna was moving away from Sol now, and would continue to do so for several millennia, looping out again toward its home in the Kuiper belt. These were not the first or even the best pictures of Sedna; several robot probes had already mapped the planetoid's bright red surface; but the pictures of Sedna were still important. They would be used to gauge the resolving power of the DAST coordinating stations.

During the same period, each of the *Queens* began receiving pings from ships-in-transit, robot probes, orbital stations, and all three Lunar observatories. Once the Sedna test was completed, the *Queens* began assembling an intricate web of laser connections; the assignments were made on the basis of bandwidth and telescope-size. Although, other planetary networks existed, none of them required the same nanosecond-precise synchronization. That most of the separate pieces of the network existed light-minutes apart complicated the job enormously. Each and every node had to predict the Doppler shift of every node it was connected to.

...defense department has awarded the contract for the four-meter S-14 mobile infantry powered armor to the Lockheed Skunk Works. The Secretary also announced the purchase of an additional 500 R-60 Patton Attack Bots, built by Boeing-Toyota...

This distant from Earth/Luna, Neace and Ensley were somewhat insulated from the flash crowd of distant interest—that proportion of the twelve billion human beings on the home world that actually wondered about the marvels hidden in the night sky. Had they known that their fifteen minutes of fame had also created a moment of system-wide breathless anticipation, it might have unnerved them; they considered their work important because it was *their* work; they hadn't considered that the human race as a whole might share some of the same fascination.

So the reaction to the Orion Anomaly caught them mostly by surprise. The first pictures of the Horsehead and Crab Nebulas and other familiar visions were remarkable for their depth of detail and resolution, but unless you were viewing them on a wall-size display capable of Extreme Definition, they did not appear significantly sharper than the previous observations of various space-based observatories.

The Orion Anomaly, however, was something else entirely. Behind the Orion Nebula lay a star system that had always photographed fuzzy and uncertain. Even the smaller proof-of-concept dispersed array space telescope projects of the past had failed to resolve the object or objects. Computer enhancement produced unsatisfactory results because the computer had no idea what it was enhancing. Whatever it was, it was as large as the solar system, possibly larger. Too large to be an exploding or fragmented star—and not enough mass anyway. A whirligig of orbiting bodies? A cosmic whirlwind? There were more theories than facts; but whatever the theory, the evidence refused to abide. The Orion Anomaly remained one of the more tantalizing mysteries of the sky.

...despite the lopsided gender ratios, the Chinese birth rates remain strong as increasing numbers of males choose to carry their own embryos to term; because a majority of the male-borne fetuses are also male, this will

exacerbate the problem for the next generation of Chinese husbands. Until China and other Asian states learn to recognize that female children are as valuable as males, the imbalances will continue…

By the time the DAST was ready to focus on the Orion Anomaly, several thousand ships, probes, and orbiting stations had linked up to the three *Queens*. Because of the wide dispersal of the participating components, collation of the images took several hours. But the resolution of the image was high enough to finally reveal some of the details of the Anomaly. The Extreme Definition display revealed it as a scattering of thousands of small fairly-bright objects in irregular orbit around a mid-line star. Not comets. Something else—something that still defied explanation. The mystery wasn't solved, it was only deepened.

Unfortunately, further observations were interrupted by a flurry of solar storms which disturbed the linkages between the various ships. The slight but continuing perturbations of orbit confused the predictive synchronization of the coordinating stations, effectively destroying the synchronization necessary to accurate surveillance. During the interregnum, the DAST components would still continue mapping the local distances between planets and asteroids and ships-in-transit. Most of that monitoring did not require predictive calibration. It was routine work and the bots would handle it automatically.

…mixed reactions in the community of body-mods. While most people view modding as cosmetic enhancement, serious modders disregard fashion-modding as little more than fad-chasing. Tigerman adds, "modding isn't about the look, it's about the experience. That's why the sensory augments are so important. All the new tastes, smells, colors, sensations…"

Neace spent much of his down-time meditatively jogging. The ship's centrifuge turned slowly and the uppermost levels provided a mere one-third gee, which allowed for a languid, almost thoughtful stride; the jogger spent most of his time airborne, barely tapping the floor to stay aloft. For many runners, the experience was close to flying. In fact, the jogger had to lean so far into his stride that he appeared almost prone, like an oversized road-runner, but bouncing from point to point instead of racing.

The long, slow strides provided a time-stretched aerobic workout and Neace could submerge himself into the rhythm as comfortably as if he were floating in an isolation tank. He could run for hours at a stretch, keeping himself physically balanced at a level of exertion simply unachievable at Earth-normal gravity. The result was a zen-like state of endurance and health that most human beings never realized. It was during such workouts that Neace often had his most remarkable insights—many other starsiders had also reported their own experiences of centrifugal nirvana or "jogging eurekas."

Neace had already calculated that the crew of the first starship to Sirius would spend at least one-third of their time jogging, possibly more. They would be able to brag that they had sprinted to Sirius and back. Nowhere would the unbreakable relationship between time and space be more evident than aboard a long-range starship. Even the shorter hops among Sol's family of planets could take weeks or even occasionally months. It was no accident that a large number of exceptionally thoughtful books and articles had been written in transit. Authorship remained the best offense against boredom.

...most serious breach since Babe-18's tell-all book, It Only Hurts When You Laugh. *A spokesman for the Laurel-Hardy company said that the situation was a personal and private matter between the clone-families, and would not interfere with the upcoming production of "Laurel and Hardy on Mars"...*

This day, however, Neace's thoughts came inevitably back to Radley Nakamura and Manda Sahir. Among starsiders, most relationships were not only long-term, they were also long-range. Perhaps part of it was a physical byproduct of immortality, and part of it was an emotional adaptation to the accretion of age—the underlying assumption that with immortality, now "we have all of time and all of space." But Neace felt that explanation was too easy, and therefore insufficient. Researchers had long since proved that human beings were chaotic events, a cross-section of processes and intentions, pressures and needs, expressing from moment to moment as an illusion of consciousness, only occasionally achieving exercises of actual sentience. But the illusions of consciousness were still useful, because it was on the shoulders of such illusions that the moments of sentience stood.

No, Neace's own theory about the languid pace of starside affairs was that it was an essential adaptation to the expanded time-sense of orbital existence. It was a recognition that every human being is on an individual trajectory, sometimes parallel, more often not. You have no choice but to live inside the moment as it occurs, or as Jarles "Free Fall" Ferris once put it, "Breathe here now."

There wasn't anywhere to go with the thought. It didn't inspire a course of action. And that, too, was part of the adaptation—that thoughts could be complete in and of themselves, without requiring immediate expression or eventual deed. It was simply part of the larger construction of the ground of being on which true identity would later stand.

...although this solar probe lasted eight minutes longer than any previous close-approach vehicle, the photosphere still hasn't given up all of its mysteries. Next year's Magenta series, however, will be the first test of hyperstatic shielding and should allow the probe to penetrate...

Neace was successful because he was meticulous; a skill he had discovered in school and honed to near-perfection throughout his career. He didn't just plot a course, he plotted consequences. But while the mechanistic approach worked well for creating opportunities for passion, it did not create passion itself. Neace had come to that understanding somewhere between "Peek-a-boo" and "Gotcha."

Thereafter, he had planned his affairs so as put himself into matching orbits with women who were aggressive enough to take the initiative in sexual relationships. In that sense, they completed him, providing the triggers for passion that he himself had never quite mastered. This particular insight was not new to Neace, he revisited it frequently while meditatively jogging. He was neither satisfied nor dissatisfied with the realization. He had accepted it as part of his internal construction.

But this day, the moment of insight that came to him as he purposed methodically through the air—that identity is the construction of self. And that everything he had done up to this point in his life, every problem he had taken on, every challenge he had accepted, had ultimately been about nothing more than his own satisfaction of achievement. He was *self*-centered.

Adding Radley and Manda to his personal equation hadn't ever been about constructing a triangular relationship—it had been solely about completing the structure of his own identity. For a moment, Neace felt guilty.

...four more cases of hyper-chocolate poisoning, bringing the total number to 73, with nine known fatalities. All-Mart Industries has ordered all hyper-chocolate products removed from store shelves until further review...

But the moment passed, the sense of guilt eased. What *other* kinds of relationships were possible in space? And didn't Radley and Manda equally use him as adjuncts to their own constructions of being? Of course, if he approached it from that perspective, he considered, then he was committing the error of methodical analysis again—and he'd already had this conversation with both of women; that some human interactions were beyond both method and analysis, particularly those of the heart.

And then he got it.

...each of the new plastic coins will contain V-70 ultrawave wi-fi circuitry. While the long-term goal is to create a more accurate cross-sectioning of economic flows, consumers will experience immediate benefits. Each coin will also function as an independent node in the wireless web, providing 2000% packet redundancy at GBS rates and expanding available mobile access to...

Intellectually, he'd had the answer for the better part of a century—that the condition of love, beyond the mechanics of trust and intimacy, existed only where the other person's well-being was essential to your own. He'd known that as an equation. He'd never quite realized it as an *experience*. Until now. For no reason at all.

Except perhaps that for a moment, a single overarching moment, a breathless pause, while his body continued to pace methodically, languidly, gracefully through the centrifuge—for that single moment, he actually felt *lonely*.

He missed Radley. He missed Manda. The graceful curve of Radley's neck, the breadth of her shoulders and the muscled strength of her legs—the voluminous sensuality of Manda's embrace, the delicious pressure of their bodies together. He'd once wondered if it was possible to love two women at the same time—then surrendered to the inevitability of the truth.

And now, in this moment, with no apparent trigger except the silence in his own head, he *understood*.

He continued jogging, savoring the transformative knowledge. The sweat beaded on his body. He had a joyous grin on his face. He had an erection.

...critical threshold of processing for constructed sentience on a super-cluster. Below that threshold, holes in the processing matrices reduce confidence to the organic level, which is unacceptable for accuracy in...

Later, he knew he'd have to share the insight with both of his lovers. He wasn't quite certain how he would phrase it—and on some level, he understood that this message would be best delivered in person, with skill, delicacy, and of course all the passion he could generate.

But he also knew that this bit of self-knowledge wasn't about what existed in himself as much as it was a recognition of what *didn't* exist within. It was the realization of the need to rebuild a sense of identity that was beyond his own control—an identity that existed as a partnership, as a fusion.

He wondered if that were even possible in a starside environment. Then moved immediately from there to the acceptance of the challenge. It was now something else to be invented.

Laughing, he sent both women the same message. "I get it. I've been a jerk. That's why you should marry me. Because I finally get it."

...expected to issue its report on the financial costs of the solar flare by the end of the week. Reassembly of the DAST array has already resumed, with optimal calibration expected in the next few hours. Included among the targets scheduled for closer examination, the Orion Anomaly has had astronomers arguing...

Later—everything aboard a ship is always *later*—on the bridge, waiting for their separate replies, now more than an hour overdue, Captain Adam Neace sifted impatiently through all the separate images that had accumulated since his last review. The targeting scopes stayed focused on the other *Queens* but the latest pictures showed both ships looking different now, so he directed one of the larger arrays to capture clearer images.

A few moments later, the enhanced views came up on his display and he began to laugh. Arrayed in lights along the side of *The Venus Queen* was a simple message: "Peek-A-Boo." *The Lunar Queen* displayed, "Gotcha."

Neace opened a channel and said, "I see your sign, Radley."

Half an hour later, the message came back. "Yes, we'll marry you, Adam. But the sign isn't for you—it's for them."

Them?

Who?

Them—!

And in that moment, Adam Neace became the third human being in the solar system to understand the Orion Anomaly.

AUTHOR'S AFTERWORD:

The only previous appearance of this story was in the Hal Clement memorial anthology. I loved Hal for his intelligence, his friendship, and his jovial cantankerousness—and most of all, I admired his unconditional commitment to scientific accuracy. I remember a Star Trek convention in 1973. They asked me to be on a panel about writing. I found myself sitting between two of the men whose stories I had been reading since I was nine. I was overwhelmed and the little voice in my head said, "What are you doing, David, sitting between Isaac Asimov and Hal Clement?" Then, another little voice in my head—there's a whole committee—said, "Don't say anything or the audience will start asking the same question."

Unfortunately, because it was a Star Trek convention, the first question was directed to me. "How important is scientific accuracy?" I said, "It's very important. If I don't know something, I pick up the phone and call Isaac. And if he doesn't know, he picks up the phone and calls Hal. So let me hand the microphone directly to Hal." Whew.

Two of the characters in the story, Adam Neace and Mark Hensley are named after real people who gave me useful information or suggested pieces of the story. Thanks, guys!

Interlude #6

Selections from *The Quote-Book of Solomon Short*

"Nothing exceeds like excess."

"Old soldiers never die. Young ones do."

"You can't be a coward and sing falsetto."

"The real question is this—what do you *do* with a skinned cat?"

"Intelligent life is a way for the universe to know itself. The universe is just as vain as the rest of us."

"The existence of life on Earth proves that Murphy's Law is universal. If anything can go wrong, it will."

"A fool and his money can get a table at the best restaurant in town."

"The highest expression of creativity is the invention of a new sexual persuasion."

"Of course, this is the best of all possible worlds. *I'm* in it."

"The problem isn't that human beings don't come with instructions. The problem is that no one reads manuals."

"Heisenberg was not only right, he was *absolutely* right."

"Health is merely the slowest possible rate at which you can die."

"Even entropy isn't what it used to be."

"Nothing is foolproof. We keep making better fools."

"The difference between men and women is that no man ever won an argument with a woman."

"A fanatic is not only willing to give *his* life for a cause, he's willing to give *yours* as well."

"The problem with the gene pool is that there's no lifeguard."

"A conclusion is the place where you stopped thinking. An answer is where you stopped asking the question."

"Organized religion is for the symbol-minded. A holy war is a clash of symbols. No idle worshipping aloud."

"Be patient. Evolution isn't finished with us yet."

"All cats have the same name. It's pronounced exactly like the sound of a can opener."

"Upset causes change. Change causes upset."

"The mere fact that a story might be true should not discourage one from telling it."

"Opinions are like chili powder—best used in moderation."

"Show me a moral victory, I'll show you a loser with issues."

"The Greeks called it *Deus ex Machina*. The God in the Machine drops from the sky and saves you from yourself. We call it therapy and leave out God."

"You can believe anything you want. The universe is not obligated to keep a straight face."

"There are some things a gentleman doesn't discuss. He only drops hints."

"Integrity is like a balloon. It doesn't matter how good the rubber is, the air still goes out the hole."

"You always find teh one typo in print that you missed in galley proof."

"A telephone is like a rash. It demands attention."

"Pain would be much more effective if we got the message before the event instead of after."

"The only thing in the world that can't be shared is loneliness."

"The manual only makes sense after you learn the program."

"Reliable information lets you say, 'I don't know,' with real confidence."

"If it's not your bedroom, it's not your affair."

"The karmic chicken always comes home to roost."

"A postal worker can lose anything but his job. This explains the quality of the service."

"Life isn't one damn thing after another. It's the same damn thing over and over again."

"A man's best friend is his dogma."

"Life doesn't mean anything. People do."

"Godot called. He'll be late."

"Ignorance is natural. Stupidity takes commitment."

"That which does not kill us, often hurts us badly."

"Madness takes its toll. Please have exact change."

"Everyone is innocent until proven stupid."

"An argument is about convincing someone that he is wrong and you are right. No one in the history of humanity has ever won an argument."

"Life is like an analogy."

"Nature bats last."

"There is no time like the pleasant."

"Never knock on death's door. Just ring the bell and run. (He hates that.)"

"It has taken thirteen and a half billion years for the universe to figure out that it is thirteen and a half billion years old."

"The best reason for stirring up a kettle of worms is to make sure the sauce gets evenly distributed."

"A decision doesn't have to be logical if it's unanimous."

"The best therapy for being stir crazy is to stir."

"Many are called, few are chosen. Fewer still get to do the choosing."

"A man's speech should exceed his grasp, or what's a metaphor…?"

"Life is full of little surprises, and you are one of them."

"You know it's a rough place when even the rocks are bruised."

"Is ambiguity the same as subtlety? Maybe."

"To be human—the essential part of being human—is always having that little voice in your head telling you that something is wrong."

"A paradigm is the box it came in."

"Transformation is what you do when everything else fails."

"Facts are useful. When you have facts, you don't have to make stuff up."

"Only your friends can betray you."

"A cat will assume the shape of its container."

"'Tis far far better to be thought a fool than to shoot yourself in the foot while it's still in your mouth."

"Before breakfast, sentience is a myth."

"I have a rule against touching the bowl if the food inside it is growling."

"Real courage is sniffing the tuna salad to see if it's still fresh."

"Once in a while, I get one right. Let me know when that happens."

"Real heroes don't get statues, they get results."

"Lack of enlightenment is a problem only to the enlightened."

"Man is not meant to begin sentences with 'Man is not meant to…'"

Out in the asteroid belt, the mountains fly. They tumble and roll silently. Distant sparkles break the darkness. Someday we'll get out there, we'll catch the mountains, we'll break them into kibble to get at the good parts. We'll find out if the centers are nougat or truffle. And some of us—some of us will even become comet-tossers, throwing the mountains around like gods. I expect it will be a lonely life and the people who live it will have different souls than the rest of us.

Riding Janis

If we had wings
where would we fly?
Would you choose the safety of the ground
or touch the sky
if we had wings?
　　　—Janis Ian & Bill Lloyd

THE THING ABOUT PUBERTY is that once you've done it, you're stuck. You can't go back.

It's like what Voltaire said about learning Russian. He said that you wouldn't know if learning Russian would be a good thing or not unless you actually learned the language—except that after you learned Russian, would the process of learning it have turned you into a person who believes it's a good thing? So how could you know? Puberty is like that—I think. It changes you, the way you think, and what you think about. And from what I can tell, it's a lot harder than Russian. Especially the conjugations.

You can only delay puberty for so long. After that you start to get some permanent physiological effects. But there's no point in going through puberty when the closest eligible breeding partners are on the other side of the solar system. I didn't mind being nineteen and unfinished. It was the only life I knew. What I minded was not having a choice. Sometimes I felt like just another asteroid in the belt, tumbling

413

forever around the solar furnace, too far away to be warmed, but still too close to be truly alone. Waiting for someone to grab me and hurl me toward Luna.

See, that's what Mom and Jill do. They toss comets. Mostly small ones, wrapped so they don't burn off. There's not a lot of ice in the belt, only a couple of percentage points, if that; but when you figure there are a couple billion rocks out here, that's still a few million that are locally useful. Our job is finding them. There's no shortage of customers for big fat oxygen atoms with a couple of smaller hydrogens attached. Luna and Mercury, in particular, and eventually Venus, when they start cooling her down.

But this was the biggest job we'd ever contracted, and it wasn't about ice as much as it was about ice-burning. Hundreds of tons per hour. Six hundred and fifty million kilometers of tail, streaming outward from the sun, driven by the ferocious solar wind. Comet Janis. In fifty-two months, the spray of ice and dye would appear as a bright red, white, and blue streak across the Earth's summer sky—the Summer Olympics Comet.

Mom and Jill were hammering every number out to the umpteenth decimal place. This was a zero-tolerance nightmare. We had to install triple-triple safeguards on the safeguards. They only wanted a flyby, not a direct hit. That would void the contract, as well as the planet.

The bigger the rock, the farther out you could aim and still make a streak that covers half the sky. The problem with aiming is that comets have minds of their own—all that volatile outgassing pushes them this way and that, and even if you've wrapped the rock with reflectors, you still don't get any kind of precision. But the bigger the rock, the harder it is to wrap it and toss it. And we didn't have a lot of wiggle room on the timeline.

Janis was big and dark until we lit it up. We unfolded three arrays of LEDs, hit it with a dozen megawatts from ten klicks, and the whole thing sparkled like the star on top of a Christmas tree. All that dirty ice, 30 kilometers of it, reflecting light every which way—depending on your orientation when you looked out the port, it was a fairy landscape, a shimmering wall, or a glimmering ceiling. A trillion tons of sparkly mud, all packed up in nice dense sheets, so it wouldn't come apart.

It was beautiful. And not just because it was pretty to look at, and not just because it meant a couple gazillion serious dollars in the bank either. It was beautiful for another reason.

See, here's the thing about living in space. Everything is Newtonian. It moves until you stop it or change its direction. So every time you move something, you have to think about where it's going to go, how fast it's going to get there, and where it will eventually end up. And we're not just talking about large sparkly rocks, we're talking about bottles of soda, dirty underwear, big green boogers, or even the ship's cat. Everything moves, bounces, and moves some more. And that includes people, too. So you learn to think in vectors and trajectories and consequences. Jill calls it "extrapolatory thinking."

And that's why the rock was beautiful, because it wasn't just a rock here and now. It was a rock with a future. Neither Mom nor Jill had said anything yet, they were too busy studying the gravitational ripple charts, but they didn't have to say anything. It was obvious. We were going to have to ride it in, because if that thing started outgassing, it would push itself off course. Somebody had to be there to create a compensating thrust. Folks on the Big Blue Marble were touchy about extinction-level events.

Finding the right rock is only the *second*-hardest part of comet-tossing. Dirtsiders think the belt is full of rocks, you just go and get one; but most of the rocks are the wrong kind; too much rock, not enough ice—and the average distance between them is 15 million klicks. And most of them are just dumb rock. Once in a while, you find one that's rich with nickel or iron, and as useful as that might be, if you're not looking for nickel or iron right then, it might as well be more dumb rock. But if somebody else is looking for it, you can lease or sell it to them.

So Mom is continually dropping bots. We fab them up in batches. Every time we change our trajectory, Mom opens a window and tosses a dozen paper planes out.

A paper plane doesn't need speed or sophistication, just brute functionality, so we print the necessary circuitry on sheets of stiff polymer. (We fab that too.) It's a simple configuration of multi-sensors, dumb-processors, lotsa-memory, soft-transmitters, long-batteries, carbon-nanotube solar cells, ion-reservoirs, and even a few micro-rockets. The printer rolls out the circuitry on a long sheet of polymer, laying down thirty-six to forty-eight layers of material in a single pass. Each side. At a resolution of 3600^2 dpi, that's tight enough to make a fairly respectable, self-powered, paper robot. Not smart enough to play with its own tautology, but certainly good enough to sniff a passing asteroid.

We print out as much and as many as we want, we break the polymer at the perforations; three quick folds to give it a wing shape, and it's done. Toss a dozen of these things overboard, they sail along on the solar wind, steering themselves by changing colors and occasional micro-bursts. Make one wing black and the other white and the plane eventually turns itself; there's no hurry, there's no shortage of either time

416 ▨ *The Involuntary Human*

or space in the belt. Every few days, the bot wakes up and looks around. Whenever it detects a mass of any kind, it scans the lump, scans it again, scans it a dozen times until it's sure, notes the orbit, takes a picture, analyzes the composition, prepares a report, files a claim, and sends a message home. Bots relay messages for each other until the message finally gets inserted into the real network. After that, it's just a matter of finding the publisher and forwarding the mail. Average time is 14 hours.

Any rock one of your paper planes sniffs and tags, if you're the first, then you've got first dibsies on it. Most rocks are dumb and worthless—and usually when your bots turn up a rock that's useful, by then you're almost always too far away to use it. Anything farther than five or ten degrees of arc isn't usually worth the time or fuel to go back after. Figure 50 million kilometers per degree of arc. It's easier to auction off the rock, let whoever is closest do the actual work, and you collect a percentage. If you've tagged enough useful rocks, theoretically you could retire on the royalties. *Theoretically.* Jill hates that word.

But if finding the right rock is the second-hardest part of the job, then the *first*-hardest part is finding the *other* rock, the one you use at the *other* end of the whip. If you want to throw something at Earth (and lots of people do), you have to throw something the same size in the opposite direction. Finding and delivering the right ballast rock to the site was always a logistic nightmare. Most of the time it was just difficult, sometimes it was impossible, and once in a while it was even worse than that.

We got lucky. We had found the right ballast rock, and it was in just the right place for us. In fact, it was uncommonly close—only a few hundred thousand kilometers behind Janis. Most asteroids are several million klicks away from their closest neighbor. FBK-9047 was small, but it was heavy. This was a nickel-rich lump about ten klicks across. While not immediately useful, it would *someday* be worth a helluva lot more than the comet we were tossing—five to ten billion, depending on how it assayed out.

Our problem was that it belonged to someone else. The FlyBy Knights. And they weren't too particularly keen on having us throw it out of the system so we could launch Comet Janis.

Their problem was that this particular ten billion dollar payday wasn't on anyone's calendar. Most of the contractors had their next twenty-five years of mining already planned out—you have to plan that far in advance when the mountains you want to mine are constantly in motion. And it wasn't likely anyone was going to put it on their menu for at least a century; there were just too many other asteroids worth twenty or fifty or a hundred billion floating around the belt. So while this rock wasn't exactly worthless in principle, it was worthless in actuality—until someone actually needed it.

Mom says that comet tossing is an art. What you do is you lasso two rocks, put each in a sling, and run a long tether between them, fifty kilometers or more. Then you apply some force to each one and start them whirling around each other. With comet ice, you have to do it slowly to give the snowball a chance to compact. When you've got them up to speed, you cut the tether. One rock goes the way you want, the other goes in the opposite direction. If you've done your math right, the ballast rock flies off into the outbeyond, and the other—the money rock, goes arcing around the solar system and comes in for a close approach to the target body—Luna, Earth, L4, wherever. This is a lot more cost-effective than installing engines on an asteroid and driving it home. A *lot* more.

Most of the time, the flying mountain takes up station as a temporary moon orbiting whatever planet we throw it at, and it's up to the locals to mine it at their leisure. But this time, we were only arranging a flyby—a close approach for the Summer Olympics, so the folks in the Republic of Texas could have a 60 degree swath of light across the sky for twelve days. And that was a whole other set of problems—because the comet's appearance had to be timed for perfect synchronicity with the event. There wasn't any wiggle room in the schedule. And everybody knew it.

All of which meant that we really needed this rock, or we weren't going to be able to toss the comet. And everybody knew that too, so we weren't in the best bargaining position. If we wanted to use 9047, we were going to have to cut the FlyBy Knights in for a percentage of Janis, which Jill didn't really want to do because what they called "suitable recompense for the loss of projected earnings" (if we threw their rock away) was so high that we would end up losing money on the whole deal.

We knew we'd make a deal eventually—but the advantage was on their side because the longer they could stall us, the more desperate we'd become and more willing to accept their terms. And meanwhile, Mom was scanning for any useful rock or combination of rocks in the local neighborhood which was approximately five million klicks in any direction. So we were juggling time, money, and fuel against our ability to go without sleep. Mom and Jill had to sort out a nightmare of orbital mechanics, economic concerns, and assorted political domains that stretched from here to Mercury.

Mom says that in space, the normal condition of life is patience; Jill says it's frustration. Myself...I had nothing to compare it with. Except the puberty thing, of course. What good is puberty if there's no one around to have puberty with? Like kissing, for instance. And holding hands. What's all that stuff about?

I was up early, because I wanted to make fresh bread. In free fall, bread doesn't rise, it expands in a sphere—which is pretty enough, and fun for tourists, but not really practical because you end up with some slices too large and others too small. Better to roll it into a cigar and let it expand in a cylindrical baking frame. We had stopped the centrifuge because the torque was interfering with our navigation around Janis; it complicated turning the ship. We'd probably be ten or twelve days without. We could handle that with vitamins and exercise, but if we went too much longer, we'd start to pay for it with muscle and bone and heart atrophy, and it takes three times as long to rebuild as it does to lose. Once the bread was safely rising—well, expanding—I drifted forward.

"Jill?"

She looked up. Well, *over*. We were at right angles to each other. "What?" A polite *what*. She kept her fingers on the keyboard.

"I've been thinking—"

"That's nice."

"—we're going to have to ride this one in, aren't we?"

She stopped what she was doing, lifted her hands away from the keys, turned her music down, and swiveled her couch to face me. "How do you figure that?"

"Any comet heading that close to Earth, they'll want the contractor to ride it. Just in case course corrections have to be made. It's obvious."

"It'll be a long trip—"

"I read the contract. Our expenses are covered, both inbound and out. Plus ancillary coverage."

"That's standard boilerplate. Our presence isn't mandatory. We'll have lots of bots on the rock. They can manage any necessary corrections."

"It's not the same as having a ship onsite," I said. "Besides, Mom says we're overdue for a trip to the marble. Everyone should visit the home world at least once."

"I've been there. It's no big thing."

"But *I* haven't—"

"It's not cost-effective," Jill said. That was her answer to everything she didn't want to do.

"Oh, come on, Jill. With the money we'll make off of Comet Janis, we could add three new pods to this ship. And bigger engines. And larger fabricators. We could make ourselves a lot more competitive. We could—"

Her face did that thing it does when she doesn't want you to know what she really feels. She was still smiling, but the smile was now a mask. "Yes, we could do a lot of things. But that decision has to be made by the senior officers of the Lemrel Corporation, kidlet." Translation: *your opinion is irrelevant. Your mother and I will argue about this. And I'm against it.*

One thing about living in a ship, you learn real fast when to shut up and go away. There isn't any real privacy. If you hold perfectly still, close your eyes, and just listen, eventually—just from the ship noises—you can tell where everyone is and what they're doing, sleeping, eating, bathing, defecating, masturbating, whatever. In space, *everyone* can hear you scream. So you learn to speak softly. Even in an argument. Especially in an argument. The only real privacy is inside your head, and you learn to recognize when others are going there, and you go somewhere else. With Jill...well, you learned faster than real fast.

She turned back to her screens. A dismissal. She plucked her mug off the bulkhead and sipped at the built-in straw. "I think you should talk this over with your Mom." A further dismissal.

"But Mom's asleep, and you're not. You're here." For some reason, I wasn't willing to let it go this time.

"You already have my opinion. And I don't want to talk about it anymore." She turned her music up to underline the point.

I went back to the galley to check on my bread. I opened the plastic bag and sniffed. It was warm and yeasty and puffy, just right for kneading, so I sealed it up again, put it up against a blank bulkhead and began pummeling it. You have to knead bread in a non-stick bag because you don't want micro-particles in the air-filtration system. It's like punching a pillow. It's good exercise, and an even better way to work out a shiftload of frustration.

As near as I could tell, puberty was mostly an overrated experience of hormonal storms, unexplainable rebellion, uncontrollable insecurity, and serious self-esteem issues, all resulting in a near-terminal state of wild paranoid anguish that caused the sufferer to behave bizarrely, taking on strange affectations of speech and appearance. Oh yeah, and weird body stuff where you spend a lot of time rubbing yourself for no apparent reason.

Lotsa kids in the belt postponed puberty. And for good reason. It doesn't make sense to have your body readying itself for breeding when there are no appropriate mates to pick from. And there's more than enough history to demonstrate that human intelligence goes into remission until at least five years after the puberty issues resolve. A person should finish her basic education without interruption, get a little life experience, before letting her juices start to flow. At least, that was the theory.

But if I didn't start puberty soon, I'd never be able to and I'd end up sexless. You can only postpone it for so long before the postponement becomes permanent. Which might not be a bad idea, considering how crazy all that sex stuff makes people.

And besides, yes, I was curious about all that sex stuff—masturbation and orgasms and nipples and thighs, stuff like that—but not morbidly so. I wanted to finish my *real* education first. Intercourse is supposed to be something marvelous and desirable, but all the pictures I'd ever seen made it look like an icky imposition for *both* partners. Why did anyone want to do *that?* Either there was something wrong with the videos, or maybe there was something wrong with me that I just didn't get it.

So it only made sense that I should start puberty now, so I'd be ready for mating when we got to Earth. And it made sense that we should go to Earth with Comet Janis. And why didn't Jill see that?

Mom stuck her head into the galley then. "I think that bread surrendered twenty minutes ago, sweetheart. You can stop beating it up now."

"Huh? What? Oh, I'm sorry. I was thinking about some stuff. I guess I lost track. Did I wake you?"

"Whatever you were thinking about, it must have been pretty exciting. The whole ship was thumping like a subwoofer. This boat is noisy enough without fresh-baked bread, honey. You should have used the bread machine." She reached past me and rescued the bag of dough; she began stuffing it into a baking cylinder.

"It's not the same," I said.

"You're right. It's quieter."

The arguments about the differences between free fall bread and gravity bread had been going on since Commander Jarles Ferris had announced that bread doesn't fall butter-side down in space. I decided not to pursue that argument. But I was still in an arguing mood.

"Mom?"

"What, honey?"

"Jill doesn't want to go to Earth."

"I know."

"Well, you're the Captain. It's *your* decision."

"Honey, Jill is my partner."

"Mom, I have to start puberty soon!"

"There'll be other chances."

"For puberty?"

"For Earth."

"When? How? If this isn't my best chance, there'll never be a better one." I grabbed her by the arms and turned her so we were both oriented the same way and looked her straight in the eyes. "Mom, you know the drill. They're not going to allow you to throw anything that big across Earth's orbit unless you're riding it. We have to ride that comet in. You've known that from the beginning."

Mom started to answer, then stopped herself. That's another thing about spaceships. After a while, everybody knows all the sides of every argument. You don't have to recycle the exposition. Janis was big money. Four-plus years of extra-hazardous duty allotment, fuel and delta-vee recovery costs, plus bonuses for successful delivery. So, Jill's argument about cost-effectiveness wasn't valid. Mom knew it. And so did I. And so did Jill. So why were we arguing?

Mom leapt ahead to the punch line. "So what's this really about?" she asked.

I hesitated. It was hard to say. "I—I think I want to be a boy. And if we don't go to Earth, I won't be able to."

"Sweetheart, you know how Jill feels about males."

"Mom, that's *her* problem. It doesn't have to be mine. I like boys. Some of my best online friends are boys. Boys have a lot of fun together—at least, it always looks that way from here. I want to try it. If I don't like it, I don't have to stay that way." Even as I said it, I was abruptly aware that what had only been mild curiosity a few moments ago was now becoming a genuine resolve. The more Mom and Jill made it an issue, the more it was an issue of control, and the more important it was for me to win. So I argued for it, not because I wanted it as much as I needed to win. Because it wasn't about winning, it was about who was in charge of my life.

Mom stopped the argument abruptly. She pulled me around to orient us face to face, and she lowered her voice to a whisper, her way of saying *this is serious*. "All right, dear, if that's what you really want. It has to be your choice. You'll have a lot of time to think about it before you have to commit. But I don't want you talking about it in front of Jill anymore."

Oh. Of course. Mom hadn't just wandered into the galley because of the bread. Jill must have buzzed her awake. The argument wasn't over. It was just beginning.

"Mom, she's going to fight this."

"I know." Mom realized she was still holding the baking cylinder. She turned and put the bread back into the oven. She set it to warm for two hours, then bake. Finally she floated back to me. She put her hands on my shoulders. "Let me handle Jill."

"When?"

"First let's see if we can get the rock we need." She swam forward. I followed.

Jill was glowering at her display and muttering epithets under her breath.

"The Flyby Knights?" Mom asked.

Jill grunted. "They're still saying, 'Take it or leave it.'"

Mom thought for a moment. "Okay. Send them a message. Tell them we found another rock."

"We have?"

"No, we haven't. But they don't know that. Tell them thanks a lot, but we won't need their asteroid after all. We don't have time to negotiate anymore. Instead, we'll cut Janis in half."

"And what if they say that's fine with them? Then what?"

"Then we'll cut Janis in half."

Jill made that noise she makes, deep in her throat. "It's all slush, you can't cut it in half. If we have to go crawling back, what's to keep them from raising their price? This is a lie. They're not stupid. They'll figure it out. We can't do it. We have a reputation."

"That's what I'm counting on—that they'll believe our reputation— that you'd rather cut your money rock in half than make a deal with a *man*."

Jill gave Mom one of those sideways looks that always meant a lot more than anything she could put into words, and certainly not when I was around.

"Send the signal," Mom said. "You'll see. It doesn't matter how much nickel is in that lump; it just isn't cost-effective for them to mine it. So it's effectively worthless. The only way they're going to get any value out of it in their lifetimes is to let us throw it away. From their point of view, it's free money, whatever they get. They'll be happy to take half a percent if they can get it."

Jill straightened her arms against the console and stretched herself out while she thought it out. "If it doesn't work, they won't give us any bargaining room."

"They're not giving us any bargaining room now."

Jill sighed and shrugged, as much agreement as she ever gave. She turned it over in her head a couple of times, then pressed for *record*. After the signal was sent, she glanced over at Mom and said, "I hope you know what you're doing."

"Half the rock is still more than enough. We can print up some reflectors and burn it in half in four months. That'll put us two months ahead of schedule, and we'll have the slings and tether already in place."

Jill considered it. "You won't get as big a burnoff. The tail won't be as long or as bright."

Mom wasn't worried. "We can compensate for that. We'll drill light pipes into the ice, fractioning the rock and increasing the effective surface area. We'll burn out the center. As long as we burn off fifty tons of ice per hour, it doesn't matter how big the comet's head is. We'll still get an impressive tail."

"So why didn't we plan that from the beginning?"

"Because I was hoping to deliver the head of the comet to Luna and sell the remaining ice. We still might be able to do that. It just won't be as big a payday." Mom turned to me.

"The braking problem on that will be horrendous." Jill closed her eyes and did some math in her head. "Not really cost-effective. We'll be throwing away more than two-thirds of the remaining mass. And if you've already cut it in half—"

"It's not the profit. It's the publicity. We'd generate a lot of new business. We could even go public."

Jill frowned. "You've already made up your mind, haven't you?"

Mom swam around to face Jill. "Sweetheart, our child is ready to be a grownup."

"She wants to be a boy." So Jill had figured it out too. But the way she said it, it was an accusation.

"So what? Are you going to stop loving her?"

Jill didn't answer. Her face tightened.

In that moment, something crystallized—all the vague unformed feelings of a lifetime suddenly snapped into focus with an enhanced clarity. Everything is tethered to everything else. With people, it isn't gravity or cables—it's money, promises, blood, and feelings. The tethers are all the words we use to tie each other down. Or up. And then we whirl around and around, just like asteroids cabled together.

We think the tethers mean something. They have to. Because if we cut them, we go flying off into the deep dark unknown. But if we don't cut them…we just stay in one place, twirling around forever. We don't go anywhere.

I could see how Mom and Jill were tethered by an ancient promise. And Mom and I were tethered by blood. And Jill and I—were tethered by jealousy. We resented each other's claim on Mom. She had something I couldn't understand. And I had something she couldn't share.

I wondered how much Mom understood. Probably everything. She was caught in the middle between two whirling bodies. Someone was going to have to cut the tether. That's why she'd accepted this contract—so we could go to the marble. She'd known it from the beginning. We were going to ride Janis all the way to Earth.

And somewhere west of the terminator, as we entered our braking arc, I'd cash out my shares and cut the tethers. I'd be off on my own course then—and Mom and Jill would fly apart too. No longer bound to me, they'd whirl out and away on their own inevitable trajectories. I wondered which of them would be a comet streaked across Earth's black sky.

> *Take me to the light*
> *Take me to the mystery of life*
> *Take me to the light*
> *Let me see the edges of the night*
> *—Janis Ian*

AUTHOR'S AFTERWORD:

Another Resnick anthology, this one based on the songs of Janis Ian. Listening to her music, reading her lyrics, something occurred to me about the relationships between people, the orbits of routine that we fall into and all the various whirling tensions that pull at us until the tether breaks and we go spinning off in new directions. This story was inevitable. I thought it was going to be a hard-science story, but once again the characters had their own opinions.

Inside a writer's head, images bounce around like loose particles in a cloud chamber—sometimes they linger for a moment, sometimes they wander for years. Occasionally they collide and strike sparks off each other. The primary image here was darkness—lines of mutable and confining void. Another image came from 19th century American history, when trainloads of orphans were shipped west for the chance at a better life away from the poverty of the cities. At first, I wasn't sure what this particular collision of images meant— sometimes I type opening scenes just to discover what the story is about and where it wants to go. This time, the more I typed, the more I began to wonder why these people were hiding behind darkness. What was on the other side? And why were they so afraid of it?

Dancer in the Dark

WHEN MA FINALLY DIED, they said they didn't have a place for me and it wasn't safe in the city anymore, so they decided it would be best to send me somewhere west where I could live on a farm. They said I would like it. Hard work and sunshine. And I'd get over Ma's death in no time. You'll see. They said.

They put me on a train with a whole bunch of other tight-faced people and went away. The train sat in the station for half a day, all of us waiting scared, before it finally chugged out. It was cold and shivery in the car, and there wasn't much to eat. You could get a drink from the faucet, but the water tasted funny.

Out the window, there was a lot of smoke, and where there wasn't smoke, there was burnt-out buildings, some old, and some still smoldering. I never been on a train before, I thought they went faster than this, but no, this was all stop-and-go, mostly stopping and waiting. And when we did go, we went slow, like the driver was being careful to watch the tracks to make sure they was still there. Once we went real slow through a corridor of burning buildings.

I was stuck way in the back behind a family, sort of, with a couple of older sisters and a lot of young-uns, except they weren't a real family because they wasn't related. They was just traveling together, and the older sisters weren't sisters at all, they was just supposed to keep the little-uns together. The kids all stunk real bad, they didn't have any clean clothes, and they'd pissed and crapped themselves, more than once. And they cried a lot, trying to keep warm. So I just turned to the window and stared out at whatever there was to see, which wasn't very much because once we got away from the big towns, the dark was spread real thick in a lot of places.

Mostly the dark looked like black fuzziness floating in the air. I'd never been inside the dark, but I heard stories. Everybody heard stories. It's like being shoved inside a thick blanket, you can't see, you can't hear, you can't breathe, and you just stumble around blind. It has something to do with the dark making it hard for things to move, like light or air or blood through your veins. You lay down a couple miles of dark around something and nobody can get through, no matter how much tinfoil they're wearing on their head.

Somebody else said that the whole country was sectioned off now. Dark everywhere. The trains ran through special corridors with walls of dark on each side, just enough room for the tracks and nothing else. You could maybe jump off the train, it wasn't going very fast, but so what? You couldn't get through the walls of dark, you couldn't go anywhere except follow the tracks. So you might as well stay on the train.

Sometime in the middle of the second night, we got to our first stop and they took some of the people off. There was all kinds of dark here, all around everything, even above so we couldn't even look up and see the stars. We didn't know where we were. Even though everybody was real tired, they woke us all up while all these men in different uniforms came marching through. They looked like soldiers from five or six different armies. They pointed at people in their seats. You, you, not you, not you, yes, yes, no, no, and so on. Another man in a different kind of uniform, I think he was the train conductor, came running after them, shouting about how they couldn't just take only the workers, they had to take a balanced cross-section, otherwise it wasn't fair.

I was hoping they'd take me, I wanted off the train real bad, I didn't care where we were. I even asked one of the soldier-men to pick me, but he shook his head and said I was too skinny. I tried asking a couple of the others, but they ignored me, so I slumped back down and pulled my blanket up and tried to go back to sleep. There wasn't nothing else to do. I was hungry and cold and stinky and not feeling too good inside. But at least there was some empty seats now and if you had one next to you, you could stretch out.

We had two more stops the next day, one just before noon, and the other late in the afternoon. Each time, another bunch of soldiers came through and took off some more people. After the last stop, there was almost nobody left on the train so they made us all move to the last car. They didn't say why. But probly because it was easier to watch us all in one place.

When they woke us up again, it was still dark. Darkfield dark. I couldn't tell what time it was, somebody said it was 3:30 in the morning. They made us gather up all our things, I didn't have much to gather, and then they herded us off the train and into a fluorescent station. The light hurt my eyes and the room smelled real strong of that disinfectant they use everywhere now. There was a red line across the room and we weren't allowed to cross it. On the other side, there was a line of grumpy-looking people, farmers and townsfolk. I guess they didn't like getting out of bed at this hour either. They looked us up and down like we were something bad-smelling. I guess we were. Every so often, I sort of got a whiff of myself. I felt dirty and itchy, and I wanted a bath or even a shower. My feet hurt and I was shivering in my blanket.

The guy who looked like the conductor read a statement to the folks on the other side of the line, something about what they was agreeing to and how they had to treat us, stuff like that. They all looked bored, like they'd heard it all before. Then he read another statement to us on this side of the line, about our rights and stuff and how we didn't have to go if we didn't want to, but we couldn't refuse either. Which didn't make any sense.

And then they started letting people pick us. A big farmer pointed at one of the skinny girls and asked her if she could cook and clean. She nodded, and he grunted and said, "Okay, come along," and she picked up her little suitcase and followed him. There was a sad-looking man and woman, they looked at the two littlest children and whispered together for a while, and then crossed the line and picked them up and left real quick, like they feared someone wouldn't let them take the babies.

It went like that for a while, until there weren't many of us left. There was this hard-looking woman standing across from me. She looked like she'd been baked in the sun until all the juice had been burned out of her and all that was left was this dry crunchy thing. She was looking at me like she couldn't make up her mind if I was worth the trouble. Finally, she said, "Boy? Are you gonna work, or you just gonna eat?"

"I can work," I said.

She walked over to the conductor and they talked together for a bit. He shook his head a lot. I got the feeling that I wasn't the first kid she'd picked out. And maybe the other one didn't work out. But finally, whatever, she came back and pointed at me and said, "Get your things." And that was it. I followed her out through the big double doors to a dirty parking lot surrounded by dark. A couple of tall light poles showed a few cars and the building we'd come out of and not much more than that.

"You got a name?"

"Folks call me Em."

"Em?"

"Yeah."

"Short for Emmett?" she asked.

"Em for Michael."

"Michael, yes. That's better than Em. You can call me Miz."

"Yes, Miz."

She pointed toward a beat-up old flatbed truck. She tossed my duffel into the back. I started to climb up after it, but she opened the door for me and said, "Get in."

We drove west on a road that was lined with dark. There might have been stars above, I couldn't tell. We had headlights, but they was mostly useless. They picked out the line of the road and that was all. She didn't say much and I didn't feel like talking either. I was too cold. I bunched up part of my blanket like a pillow and tried to rest my head against the window. It was worse than the train. We must have driven two hours. By the time we got where we were going, there was a feeling of light behind us. Hard to tell though, with all the dark.

Then there was a hole in the dark and she turned right and then left and then right again, and then we came out onto a big gray slope leading up to an old gray house. Behind it there was a dirty barn that had once been red, real tired-looking and leaning to one side, like it wanted to lie down, like if you gave it a good hard push, the whole thing would collapse, except there were a bunch of boards jammed in at an angle, propping it up so it couldn't. The old woman pointed. "You'll sleep in there. There's straw for a bed, and some old horse blankets. You can wash in the horse trough. Don't bother the cows. I start milking at six. I want you up and mucking out the stalls every morning. As soon as the cows are turned out. There's a couple barrels of disinfectant. You keep those stalls clean, you hear? As clean as you want your own bed—or your dinner plate. It's almost six now, so wash yourself up, you stink like a pig. Then get started. After milking, I'll bring you a plate. Don't want you in the house, boy. Lord knows what you're carrying."

"Yes, ma'am."

She stopped the car in front of the house, yanked on the parking brake real hard, like she was angry. "You like eggs? You ever had fresh eggs? Don't look like it. You're thinner than a ghost. When was the last time you ate?"

"Day before yesterday. I think. On the train, they gave us some leather to chew on."

"Damn fools. That's no way to treat anyone. Even deepies."

"Deepies?"

"Displaced Persons. DP's."

"Oh." Remembered my manners. "Thank you for takin' me in. I'll work real hard for you, ma'am."

She grunted. "Damn right you will. No free meals out here. Well, don't just sit there. We got work to do."

After milking and mucking, we pulled down a couple of bales of hay from the loft and broke them open for the cows. There was only three cows and they looked kinda sickly, but I don't know much about cows, so they coulda been fine too. But they walked real slow and stupid, like some of the people I'd seen in the city, the sick ones that they'd herd away every so often. But maybe that's how cows are. One of them looked at me for a bit, but she didn't look dangerous or anything, I didn't think you could make friends with a cow, so I just kept on shoveling cowshit.

Then there was the chickens, there was too many to count, they kept moving around all the time, bobbing their ugly little heads and clucking like old ladies. Miz poured out some corn for them and they all came cackling up. They was funny to watch. Later, after they'd finished the corn, they wandered around the fenced-in part of the yard, scratching for bugs and worms.

The biggest part of my job was feeding the refiner. This was three or four big metal tanks in a row, all piped together like a connected series of garbage disposals. I had to dump all the garbage into it every day, and everything else that wasn't nailed down—old corn stalks, dirty straw, stinkweeds, whatever. I had to scrape up the chicken guano and dump it in, plus wheelbarrow loads of cow manure and pig shit. Miz had indoor plumbing, but we both had to use the outhouse, because it pumped right into the refiner too. The methane that came off the top was piped around to fuel the stove at the bottom. The refiner was a big stinky stew pot, simmering and bubbling, sometimes grinding and chewing. But I didn't mind working the refiner, except for the smell, it was the only time I was really warm.

At the far end, out came oil. Enough for the truck, enough for the water heater, enough to power the refiner for another few days. Sometimes there was even enough to sell the extra in town. What didn't get turned into oil, came out as mulch. And a scattering of metal bits and rock. The metal bits we saved for town. I had to check the refiner when I got up, twice during the day, and again before hitting the straw. Miz said if we had two more pigs, we'd be fat. But we didn't have enough corn to feed any more pigs. We were already too close to the bone, she said.

Out back of the house, Miz had a garden for vegetables, mostly stuff like tomatoes and potatoes and cucumbers and things like that. Some pumpkins and watermelons too. She also had a big patch of corn. Not a whole field, but enough to feed us and the chickens and even some for the cows. Like everything else though, the corn had a sickly look. "Hard to grow things when there isn't enough light for them. Not good for plants, not good for people either. Still, it's better'n dyin'." She sniffed. "One good thing about the dark, though. We don't get as many rabbits or foxes sneakin' in. They don't like the dark anymore than anyone else. But you still have to watch out for burrows, because sometimes they will dig under. Saturdays, we go to town and get whatever supplies they still got. Sometimes there's a movie, but don't be expectin' it. Sundays, we go to Meeting. When we get back from Meeting, you can have time by yourself. But you stay outta trouble. Stay away from the dark. Don't go darksniffin' like the last damnfool I had out here. And no, I ain't sayin' nothin' about that. And don't you go askin' no questions neither, if you're smart."

But I didn't have to ask no questions. There was plenty enough people willin' to tell me everthin' they knew. First time we went to town, while I was loadin' sacks of chemical fertilizer into the back of the truck. Town wasn't much, just a scattering of old buildings on one side of the old highway, like someone just dropped them there any which way. Surrounded by dark, of course. Only way in or out is through the corridors, that's three roads and the train tracks. So there's not a lot to see. Funny lookin' kid with a broken tooth comes up and says, "You Miz's new boy?"

"Guess so."

"You wanna be real careful. Not like Doey. She tell you what happened to him?"

"I know what I need to know," I said, pretending to ignore him.

"No, you don't. You're a city-boy. You don't know shit."

"I know enough to keep my nose outa other folks' business." I hefted the last sack in.

"You just stay out in the barn, boy, you know what's good for you. Come winter, she's gonna want you to come in and warm her bed, you'll see. Keep yourself, bad-smellin', that's what Doey did. Till he ran away—ran into the dark, he did."

Miz came out of the feed store then, saw the kid and her face got real fierce. He saw her the same time and skittered off like the rat he was. Miz came up to me and stared at me hard. "What'd that boy say?"

Already knew better than to lie. Miz wasn't easy even on the best of days. I just sorta shrugged. "He said you had another boy named Doey. He ran away."

"That all he said?"

"Yes, ma'am."

She sniffed like she didn't believe me, but she didn't push it. "Well, you stay away from that J. D. boy. He's bad news. That whole family is. Now get to work. Help me load all this."

Miz explained that the train had come through again, so today was a good day. Some of the stores had new things on the shelves, even some new magazines in the racks. Miz bought a couple, bought one for me too. "Readin' is good for you, as long as you don't do too much of it. Puts funny ideas into your head. You start daydreamin', you won't get your chores done."

She bought me some new jeans and a couple of work shirts, a pair of boots and some thick socks. For herself, she stocked up on spices; she was starting to run low, she even bought a bottle of vanilla. "Might try makin' a cake or something. When was the last time you had cake?"

"Had a birthday party once, when I was little. My Ma bought a cake."

"Store-bought cake? Ain't the same. You get your chores done, I'll make you a cake so good you'll think you died and went to heaven."

Second time I heard about Doey was the next day at Meeting.

Meeting was a ways off, I couldn't tell how far, but we were driving for at least an hour, maybe more, down a long corridor of dark, all twisty, up and down, with a couple of sharp turnoffs into passages that felt even darker. When we got there, we weren't really anywhere, just a wide open space with an old school-looking building in the center of a hard-dirt clearing. The dark around was cut by seven different openings, but one of them was walled off with tall orange cones and Miz told me to stay well away from that one. I didn't ask why, she wouldn't have said anyway.

Inside, the room was gloomy, lit by kerosene lamps. No generator here. But it was warmer than outside and it was a chance to sit quiet-like and almost doze. It was kind of like church too, so you had to keep your eyes open. There were these old ladies up top all singin' real faraway and soft like they was a choir of angels or something. The music was real old-fashioned, but it wasn't too painful.

Then the mayor got up and talked about living the hard life and staying clean and trusting God and following the rules because the reason

that things had gotten so bad was that so many people had stopped following the rules, and we'd all made a big mess of things, so now we had
to do penance for a thousand years or more while we tried to put things
back together the best we could, but the only way to do that was to stay
away from the dark and follow the rules. He went on and on like that
for a long time. Then there was some discussion of chores that had to be
done in the coming days, including putting down some new dark lines
just to the west. He asked for volunteers for a work crew.

After Meeting, some folks climbed back into their trucks and drove
off right away. But most folks gathered for tea and little sandwiches and
even a cake. It looked real pretty. And everybody stood around in their
clean clothes and talked polite and pretended everything was going fine,
which it wasn't, but nobody would say so, because nobody wanted to
be accused of doing the devil's talk. But you could see it in their faces,
all hard and narrow and pinched. The sandwiches and cake disappeared
fast, some of these folks was hungry. Miz stopped me, wouldn't let me
go to the table. She whispered, "You let that food be, son. It's not for us.
It's for them that hasn't any. We have food at home. Some of these folks,
this is their only meal today." So I went outside and stood around by the
cars with the other men, just stood and listened.

"Hey you, new boy!" One of the men turned around and pointed to
me. A big man. Beard. Overalls. A broken eye.

"Yeah?" I answered the good eye.

"You coming out with us, tomorrow? Help lay some dark lines?"

I shrugged. "Dunno. Whatever Miz says."

"Miz'll say yes. If I ask her. Can I trust you to work? Not stand
around?"

"I can work."

"You have to promise to stay away from the bright. And keep your
glasses on. And don't take off your silver. That's how we lost the other
one. Whatsisname. Doey. You heard about that?" He peered at me.

Didn't answer, just sorta shrugged again. Safest way. Better to have
them think I'm stupid than wrong. You can get killed being wrong.
That's a city lesson. But it might be true out here in the dark lands as
well.

"He don't know shit," said someone else. "Just another dumb city-
boy."

"He can carry. I'll talk to Miz. We need the hands. Besides, if we
lose him, nobody'll care. Not even Miz. She'll just hook another one
off the train."

And that was how it was decided that I should work on the dark team
one or two days a week. I think Miz was glad to not have me around so
much. There wasn't enough work to keep me busy every day. Or maybe

she was just glad not to have to feed me. Sometimes the food was a little thin, even at her place. There just wasn't enough light. Somebody said that made everybody sad all the time. Depressed, he said. And then someone else told him to shut up. That was the devil's talk. Next he'd be complaining about the dark lines and the lines were the only things keeping *them* out. And then somebody said, "Not in front of *him*," meaning *me*, and that was the end of that conversation.

A few days later, an old truck pulled up in front of the house and a couple of workmen I didn't know got out and paid their respects to Miz. She handed them a paper bag with a bit of lunch in it, nowhere near enough to feed one hungry man, let alone three, but it was all she could spare. I climbed into the back of the pickup and made myself comfortable among the tools and wires.

We drove for half an hour, through the town, up the old highway for a while, and then off to the right where the corridor ended in orange cones. The workmen got out then and we all put on heavy black goggles and breathing masks and shiny silver capes and heavy work gloves. Then we drove on. The driver steered the truck carefully around the cones and up the passage to where the dark lines simply stopped. Beyond the lines, the ground rolled away like a rumpled gray bedsheet. There were already two other trucks here and five other men. One of them had a map rolled out on the hood of his truck and he was drawing lines with a crayon.

When nobody was looking, I lifted my goggles just a bit and snuck a peek at the brightlands. Immediately, I wished I hadn't. It knocked me backward. It was like being slapped in the face with a red-hot splash. I stumbled into the side of the truck, I fumbled the glasses back into place. My eyes were watering, I held them shut tight and tried to wipe at them without being blinded again. I felt really stupid, then I heard the men laughing at me and I got angry. They could have warned me. But then, one of them, a big soft guy everybody called Tallow, came up and put a black cloth over my head. He reached under the hood, pushed my goggles back, and mopped my face with a damp rag. It smelled faintly of disinfectant. He said quietly, "Don't take it bad. You only done what everybody else here did their first time too. We was all watching you. You got it over with quick. Now that you've seen a little bit of what's out there, you know what we all got to be careful about. Your eyes will stop hurting in a bit."

"You looked too, your first time?"

"Yep. Worse than you. I wasn't much older than you neither. I went out with my cousins, they said it wasn't nothing to be afraid of, you just take off the gloomies and look, see? So I did. That was real stupid. I stepped in it as deep as anyone could. It was most of an hour before

I could see again. You got off easy, boy." Then he leaned in close and whispered, "It was real pretty, wasn't it? After a while, you're gonna start thinking that you'd like to take another look. Don't you be tempted, you hear? Don't you even think about it."

"I won't," I said. "I really truly won't." And I meant it. My eyes were still hurting bad. But then, I asked, "What was all that? What did I see?"

"You never mind that. It wasn't nothing."

"It must have been something. It damn near knocked me down."

"Don't you get too curious, boy. It ain't safe. You just follow the rules."

"Just tell me what it was, that's all. So I'll know. And then I won't ever ask again. Promise."

Tallow sighed. "You can't ever talk about this to anyone, you hear? You're not supposed to know. Nobody is. They don't want folks going out to see it for themselves." He lowered his voice. "They call it colors. It's what happens when light gets too bright. Your brain can't handle it. It's called overload or something like that. It's a little piece of madness, is what it is. You don't want to get sucked into it. You won't never get back. You'll just wander out there into the brights and die of your own hallucinations. That's what happened to—never mind."

"Doey?"

"Yeah, that was his name. Damn fool was too smart for his own good. Don't you go getting too smart now, you hear? You just keep remembering how much your face hurt."

"I will."

"You do that. Now that you know, you keep your gloomies on, you hear? And that breathing mask too, so you can't smell anything either. The air is just as bad. And don't say nothing to no one. No matter what. If you know what's good for you."

Tallow felt around under the hood, pulled my goggles back down over my eyes, and then made me to check to see that they were properly seated. And the breathing mask too. When we were both satisfied, he pulled off the hood. I blinked and looked around. Everything was safely gray again. As long as I didn't think about what was really out there, I was okay. As long as I didn't say what I'd seen, I was okay. I didn't even tell Tallow about the after-image still burning in my eyes. It looked like a naked boy. But he wasn't there when I put the gloomies back on, and I looked around everywhere. And I didn't tell him about the honey-smell either. Through the glasses, the brightlands looked flat and hard and empty. But I didn't have a lot of time for looking. There was too much work to do.

Putting down darklines wasn't hard. Just tedious. Mostly, it was boring.

First, we pounded stakes. The stakes were heavy Y-shaped things anchored in an iron base. The base was pointed like a bee sting. It had to be pounded deep into the ground, three feet or more; then the long leg of the Y part was stuck all the way into it. Then, after all the stakes were in place, we strung the wire, hanging it from one stake to the next.

I didn't do any of the actual stringing, that was done by the others. They had the strength for it, I didn't. I held cable, feeding it out from a big roll so it didn't hang up while the crew manhandled it into position. They used pitchforks so they wouldn't have to touch the line themselves. It was a thick naked braid of wire. The outer threads were deliberately broken and frayed, so the line looked like it had silvery scraggly hair. The wire was supposed to be fuzzy, so the dark would be deeper and stiffer, so I had to wear thick gloves, because the frayed bits had sharp ends. Even with the work gloves, I still got a few pokes and jabs and had to pull a couple of wire splinters from the heel of my palm.

When it was lunch time, we all hiked up the corridor a ways, far enough so that none of the bright could get in, so we could finally take off our gloomies and air-masks. Even here, safe between the dark lines, it still felt too bright. Or maybe that was an after-effect. I didn't ask. There wasn't much to eat, and what there was, wasn't very good. Stale bread, dried up cheese, wilted lettuce. Everything felt tired. Still, it was better than hunger. There wasn't much talk among the work crew. Everybody seemed to have something personal to think about. I thought about the naked boy. Was he really there? No, probly not. How could anyone stand naked in the bright? We finished eating as quickly as we could and pulled our goggles and capes back on, then hiked back out into the bright.

When the line was all strung, it was a chest-high fence. Not enough to stop anybody or anything. Least, not until it was turned on. The end of the line split into three separate wires that were fed into a terminator box. They put a terminator box at each end of the line, then they threw first one switch, then the other.

I pointed at the line. "How's it work?"

He waggled his hand. "It's what's called a seduction current. Something like that. It's powered by ambient photons. That's a fancy way of saying it sucks the extra light out of the air. The more light it sucks, the thicker the dark it makes."

"But nothing's happening," I said. The cable hung limp between the stakes.

Tallow grunted. "It takes a while. In a month, there'll be another patch of land safe to grow on. It'll go to the Martins. They might be able to get some winter wheat in. Might be enough to make it to spring."

"Why does it take so long?"

"It has to be slow. Otherwise, it would only make dark during the daytime, and we need the dark at night too. It usually takes a month or so for a line to suck enough light to get up to full strength, but after that, it only gets darker and stronger. Some of the older lines around here have enough residual in them to go for a year or more. Enough time to replace them if they go down. We'll come back out next week and see if it caught. Sometimes the terminator boxes are bad." He stepped over and peered closely at the wire. So did I, but I couldn't see any difference.

"Can I ask you something?"

"What?" Tallow seemed annoyed, like he was getting tired of me.

"How does the line know how much light to suck? What you said about the older lines getting stronger—do they ever suck too much light? Could they make it *too* dark?"

"Eh?" Tallow squinted, suddenly angry. "Don't you go anywhere with that. We got enough talk already."

"I was just asking—"

"You was just asking too much. That's not safe, boy. Don't ask questions, just follow the rules, you hear?" He strode away from me, began loading his tools into his truck. The other men too. Like they couldn't be away from here fast enough. Pretty soon, we all piled into our separate pickups and headed back down the corridor. They dropped me back at Miz' place and that was that.

I worked on the line crews off and on all summer long, when I wasn't mucking out stalls for Miz. Tallow didn't talk to me much, probly afraid he'd already said too much. None of them ever talked to the city-boy, so I mostly kept to myself. Every so often, I thought about the colors I'd seen, I wondered if there was a safe way to look at them, a safe way to be naked; but I didn't ask those questions. I didn't ask any questions at all anymore, and I didn't answer any either. I pounded stakes and unrolled wire. One day, I looked at myself in the mirror, I actually had muscles. But I was still hungry all the time. And cold. Miz managed to keep food on the table, but it wasn't a lot. Sometimes we had cornbread. Sometimes just mush. We had eggs too, but the hens weren't laying regular. A couple of times we even had chicken. That was pretty good. We didn't starve, but nobody was getting fat either.

One Sunday, while we were at Meeting, one of the cows wandered into the dark; either she didn't have enough sense to keep away or maybe she was daydreaming the way cows do and the dark just pulled her in. She wasn't in her stall and she wasn't in the field either. I finally found her, ass-end sticking out of the dark, and went running up the hill to the house. It took both me and Miz to drag the cow out, but she was never the same. She wobbled on her feet. She looked like she'd been smacked in the face with a shovel. That night, she fell down in her stall. She wouldn't get up, so the vet came out to look at her. He did some doctor stuff, then took Miz off for a talk.

I didn't hear what they said, but Miz looked angry and frustrated. Finally she nodded her head. The vet came back into the barn and put the cow down. Put a gun to her head and *thump*, just like a street-killing, execution style. It took all three of us to jack the cow up with a block and tackle. We hung her by the hind legs and cut some veins to drain the blood. The vet opened up her belly and the organs spilled out onto a canvas tarp. Some of it, Miz fed to the hogs, the heart and brains and tongue, she put into a big tub for pickling. I got the feeling she'd done this before, especially the way she stripped off the hide and stretched it out for tanning. We left the cow hanging so the meat could age two-three days, you can't eat it right away, it's too tough; hanging makes it more tender. Two days later, the vet came back early with a couple of helpers, and we all started hacking and sawing. We were a week smoking the meat. We pickled some of it too, in great big jars. We didn't eat much of it ourselves though. It didn't taste very good. Like it was old and stale. Even when you put gravy on it. Miz said that was the effect of the dark.

Finally, on Friday, we wrapped and boxed everything we could. On Saturday, Miz and me packed as much as we could fit into the truck and she drove into town, where she traded that cow for hard goods, spices, and even some jars of fruit from somewhere up north. Some people would eat it, she said. Just not us.

Miz didn't take me with her that day, she wanted me to stay behind, in case anybody came wandering by. Word was that some brightlanders had wandered through town recently and nobody was sure if they'd moved on yet. I hadn't seen them, but I'd heard about them at Meeting. They all wore long black capes, just dark enough to keep them from going mad, except maybe they were a little mad from all that time in the bright. And maybe they'd come through looking to see if there was anything worth stealing. Maybe they were out there now, just waiting on the other side of the dark. But I didn't think it was the brightlanders Miz was fearing. I think it was our own neighbors. Some of them were real hungry, even eating tree bark. Miz had a big pot of stew simmering on the stove for Sunday's Meeting. Maybe some of them folks wouldn't wait. So I stayed behind, sitting on the front porch, watching the chickens scratching through the remaining patches of grass.

Moments like this, I watched the dark. Sometimes, if you watched it close enough, you could see it move. It looked like it was flowing real slow, like a river of slow time. Sometimes it wasn't all dark, sometimes it was dark gray; that was mostly at night. The dark leaked. It couldn't hold all the light it sucked and some of it seeped back out. Just enough to make everything look like moonlight.

But the closer you got to the dark, the worse you felt, like it wasn't just sucking light, but life as well. Everything close to the dark looked bad, all dusty-dull and shabby, turning gray and old in the gloom. I tried to stay away from it, especially now that I knew how it worked. But there was something about it, something I couldn't explain. I always felt like it was pulling me into it. Miz called it dark-sniffing. I had to watch myself. I wondered if someday I'd get so lost in some dream that I'd wander right into it, not even realizing what I was doing. That's what happened to the cow.

That's when the colored boy appeared.

First I smelled flowers. Yellow and pink flowers. Bright red flowers. I stood up, looking around, wondering where the flowers were. Then I saw him.

He stepped out of the dark at the bottom of the hill and started up the path to the house like he lived here. I saw him instantly. He stood out like a flash of the brightlands. Where everything else was gray, he was all the different colors a person could be. He glowed like he was lit from within. He was gold all over. His hair flashed in shades of red and blond; his skin shimmered like sunset. He was shining and naked. I'd never seen anybody so beautiful. He could have come from the far side of the sky. Wherever he'd come from, I wanted to go there. I wanted to glow too.

He came all the way up to the porch. He put one foot on the bottom step, then stopped. I knew who he was. "You Doey?"

He nodded. He held out a hand to me, like inviting me to dance. I was real tempted to take it, he was so beautiful. But I didn't. After a moment, he lowered his hand.

"Was that you I saw in the bright?"

He smiled, a dazzle of happiness. I'd never seen anything like that. It just made me hurt with longing all the more. He was insane, of course. He had to be. How could he not?

"Do you talk?" I asked.

He laughed. A gentle chuckle of sound, like a shared secret. "Yes, I talk. I also sing. I dance. I laugh. Do you?"

Shrug. "I dunno. Never tried. Never had much reason to try."

He stepped up one step. He reached out with his hand. I took a step back. He drew his hand back, then took another step up, this time onto the porch. And this time, when he extended his hand, I didn't move away. With outstretched fingers, he touched my shirt, my chest. Through the faded cotton, I felt a hot rush of feeling, I couldn't explain. His eyes met mine. His eyes were green and blue and violet. Not the sad shabby colors of the faded flowers around the edges of the old gray house, but the glistening sparkle of the deep edge of the rainbow. His eyes were bright. Everything about him was bright. The touch of his fingers—it felt like he was pumping energy into me. I felt *alivened*. Was this the magic of the bright? Is this how people went crazy? I didn't want the moment to end. I wanted to fall helplessly into it, dissolving into a bath of color, just like Doey.

I reached up with my own hand, took his in mine, held it, felt the warmth, both strong and soft at the same time, released it, reached across and touched his chest as he'd touched me. Placed my palm flat against his hot and glowing body. There was nothing I needed to say, there was everything I wanted to say. There was perfect understanding and a thousand thousand questions. I'd never known a moment like this. Never felt a hot surge of feeling like this. I thought I was going to faint. Or fly apart in pieces.

"Yes," he said, finally.

"Yes?"

"Yes, you know how to sing and dance and laugh. You just haven't had a place to do it."

My mouth was dry as dust. "Will you—can you take me there?"

He smiled and leaned forward. Close enough to kiss. "When you learn to glow."

"How do I—?"

He touched my lips with a golden finger, silencing my question.

"Hush," he whispered. "Not yet. Not yet."

And then he whirled and spun, a twirl of light and color. He leapt and danced and flew, arms outstretched, all the way down the hill and back into the wall of darkness that surrounded the house. And then he was gone. Leaving only the fading scent of color. The afternoon was dull and gray again. I felt tears on my cheeks. Both joy and despair at the same time.

I almost ran after him, almost. Something held me back. All the words, all the warnings, all the gloom that wrapped the world. He was right. I wasn't ready to let go. Not yet. Not yet. Oh, that bastard boy of color. How did he do that? How could he flirt and fly? How did he live? Where had he gone?

Sank down into a chair, an old wooden chair that creaked in pain as it accepted my weight. A faded cushion, hard and flat as cardboard. What mad thing had just happened here? Damn that Doey! I hated him, I loved him, I envied him, I feared what he was, and I wanted to be him more than anything.

I was comfortable here. Working for Miz. Working on the lines. I was comfortable, wrapped in dark. I didn't have to care. I didn't have to think. I only had to follow the rules. I could do that. Okay, I wasn't happy, but I wasn't unhappy either. I was comfortable and after being hungry and tired and cold and uncomfortable for so long, comfortable was a good place to be. It was enough. I didn't need happy. Happy didn't exist anyway. Certainly not here. And then the glowing boy stepped out of the dark and looked in my eyes and touched my heart and left me gasping with desperation. Because now that I knew what happy was, now that I knew it did exist, how could I ever be comfortable again anywhere?

Now that I knew what happy felt like, I also knew I didn't have any. Instead, now I knew what lonely felt like.

Did he know how cruel his words were? "Not yet. Not yet."

I felt so torn up inside I didn't know what I felt. I put my head into my hands and started sobbing, I don't know why. Cried for Ma, cried for me. Cried for the whole stupid everything. Who made up this stupid world anyway? Why do we have to put down all these walls of darkness? What's on the other side that everybody is so afraid of they won't even talk about it? And why did I feel so awful?

After a while, I felt all hollow and empty. So I got up and went to the barn. Stood around for a bit, then finally started mucking out stalls. Not because I wanted to, but it was something to do. And if I didn't do it, Miz would have words, lots of words. I hated all her words. I just never knew it until now.

When Miz got back, she sniffed the air and looked at me sharply. "What happened here?" she asked.

"Nothing," I said.

"Don't lie to me, Michael. Something happened here. I can see it in your face. You're all hot and flushed. Your cheeks are red." She put a hand on my forehead. "You're burning up. You have a fever."

"It's nothing," I said. Maybe too loud.

She grabbed me by the arm and dragged me to the horse trough. "Take off your shirt," she demanded. I did so and she pushed me down to my knees, pushed me head first into the sour brown water. She picked up a horse brush and began scrubbing my back with it. I couldn't scream and I couldn't breathe and I was trying to do both at the same time. She yanked me up, gasping. Before I could stop myself, I called her all those words she'd made me promise never to say again. She didn't even hesitate, she just whacked me across the head with the heavy wooden brush, knocking me backwards.

"You're still an evil old bitch! And beating me to death ain't gonna change that."

"You think I'm stupid?" Miz shouted. She was loud. "You think I don't see what you're turning into? You want to go out there and get colored? You want to glow? You want to turn into some kind of fairy-dancer? You want to die in delirium? Why do you think we put up all the darklines? Because we like the dark? You think we like being cold and hungry and miserable all the time? No, we do it because we don't have any choice. We have to protect ourselves. All of us. Even you—you stupid city-boy."

I didn't say what I was thinking. She made me feel angry. But what if she was right? Everything was all confused. If the dark was so good, why did it feel so bad. And if the bright was so bad, why did it feel so good? I pulled myself bitterly back to my feet. Already, I was trying to figure out how I could get away from here. I could probly get a loaf of bread out of the kitchen, maybe some vegetables, put them in an old potato sack or something. But where could I go? And how could I get there? Walk the roads? Maybe, but to where? And if anybody else came down the road, they'd see me for sure. No place to hide in the corridors. Follow the train tracks? Maybe. But where did they go? Just to another place like this. I didn't know. I needed a map or something. But there had to be someplace somewhere better than this. I shook the water out of my hair, brushed it back with my hand. My arm and shoulder hurt where she'd slammed me against the trough. My back hurt from the scrubbing of the brush. And my head was throbbing like a nightmare. I hurt all over. And I stunk of the foul water. And I was cold. Evening was coming on, and the dark was expanding.

Out in the barn, wrapped in a blanket, shivering against the night, listening to the wind scrabbling against the old wood, all the voices argued back and forth. Evil old bitch. I don't care what she thinks. This is sick. Everything is sick. These people are dying. I don't want to die with them. They're all sick and dirty and dead inside. I don't want to be like this. But there's no way out. It's a trap. All the darklines, all the rules, all the walls everywhere.

And just what's out there on the other side of the lines anyway? What's so horrible that you can't look at it direct, can't see it without being eye-poisoned? Doey wasn't wearing any gloomies. He was naked like one of those angels in the old books. He was as beautiful as a girl with long flowing red hair, but he was stallion-cut like a prize. He was both at once. I'd never seen anyone or anything like that. How did he live out there? How did he see without being blinded? What did he say? Learn to dance. No. Learn to glow. How do you glow? How do you learn? All those questions and nobody to ask. Nobody to trust.

Next morning was Meeting. I wasn't going to go, but Miz didn't take no arguments. She just told me to clean myself up, put on a clean shirt, and not go around smelling like a pig. But once we were in the truck, she did say one thing. She said, "I didn't want to hurt you yesterday, Michael. What I did, I had to do. I had to break the spell. You were all glassy. I had to dunk you in the water and scrub your back hard and smack you to put you in all that pain to pull you back from wherever it was you were drifting off to. I've seen that look before, saw it on Doey. Didn't act fast enough with him. He danced away one night. Ain't going to lose you too. I see you starting to glow, I'm going to beat you—not because I want to hurt you, but because hurting you is the only way to pull you out. You understand that, don't you?"

"Yes'm. Whatever."

We pulled up at Meeting early, but we wasn't the first ones there. Bunch of folks all clustered by their trucks, talking. They looked over as we drove up, and a couple of them walked over to talk to Miz. She glanced at me, then moved off a ways so I couldn't hear what they were all saying. I pretended like I didn't care anyway and wandered down to where the older kids were scratching in the dirt with sticks. J. D. was there, the kid with the broken tooth, the kid from town who'd first told me about Doey. Nobody had names out here, only initials. He stopped what he was doing, tossed his stick aside, and said, "You hear?"

"Hear what?"

"'Bout the Trasks?"

"What about them?"

"They went out."

"Out where?"

"You stupid, city-boy? Out."

"Oh. Out."

"Doc drove over to see if they was all right, if they had enough food. He had a couple spare bags of beans and rice. He got there, they was all gone. The whole family. Ever single one. Even the baby. And one of their fields was starting to glow. Big hole in the darklines—all snapped, like somebody cut 'em. Doc didn't have no gloomies. He got out of there fast. Scared-like. That's what I heard, anyway. They're going to send out a hunting party, I bet. Go shoot some bright-eyes. They're going to need every gun in town. You know how to shoot, city-boy?"

"I can shoot," I said.

"Then you'll get to go, for sure. They won't let me go. I already asked. They said I was too small. That's a damn lie. They just ain't forgiven my pa for losin' a gun last hunt. They say he stole it. But he din't. The brighties did. Turned it into something weird, I bet."

"How would you know?"

"I know lotsa stuff. More than you."

"Yeah? You think so?"

"I know so."

"Yeah? How do you know anything? You ever been out there?"

He shook his head. "Not gonna say what I know."

I wanted to tell him about the bright-eyed boy. I wanted to ask him if he'd ever seen the naked colors. But something told me that probly wasn't a good idea. So I just shrugged. Whatever. Drop it. Turned away, back to the others. More folks was arriving now. I hiked up the hill to where Tallow was standing, waited behind him for a bit until no one else was talking. He finally noticed me. "You want something?"

"You going hunting?"

"You got a gun?"

"Miz does, I think."

He scratched his neck thoughtfully. "Probly not a good idea. You being a city-boy. And we're going out deep. Miz won't like that. But maybe you can hold the wire at the safe end. Might could use you that way. You just don't say nothing right now. You talkin' about it just makes a bad idea seem worse."

Then Miz came over with Doc. He looked at me, took my chin in his hand, turned my head side to side. Looked into my eyes. Put a hand on my forehead. Asked me to stand on one foot, put my arms out, and shut my eyes tight. Stuff like that. Turned to Miz. "He looks all right to me. You probly got to him in time. But if you want me to wrap him in darkline for a bit, suck some of the brightness out of him, bring him by one day, and we'll give him a bit of treatment."

"I'll do that, thanks," she said. "You be in tomorrow?"

"Better wait till the end of the week," he said. "It's going to be a busy few days. Let's get this Trask business taken care of first. I think this lad will be fine for the moment."

Eventually, we all got inside and got settled, but nobody was thinking about Meeting. Everybody was still whispering. It was like the room was full of bluebottle flies. The mayor said that he was sorry about the bad news, everybody had probly heard it anyway, but he had to officially confirm it. The darklines had broken by the Trask farm and it looked as if the Trasks had been enchanted. And yes, there would be a committee meeting to decide what to do next. Volunteers should make themselves known to the usual folks.

After that, there wasn't much else to say, because nobody was listening anyway, so we broke up early. Folks didn't eat much, they was mostly too upset. The whole family was gone, even the baby. Not even bodies left for a proper funeral. Lots of talk floated around. Somebody was going to have to get out there and take care of the livestock. Miz said she could take the cows and the chickens if nobody else needed them, but she didn't want no more pigs right now. They ate too much. A couple of the other folks spoke up, laying claim to tools or dishes or furniture. Blankets and quilts. Pots and pans. A little of this and some of that. Eventually, it was all sorted out, who was going to go out and pick stuff up. Tallow opened his truck and passed out gloomies to the folks who were going to need them.

Miz collected goggles and masks for us and some capes too, shiny on one side, black on the other. And gloves, just in case. We didn't even head home, just straight out through town and off around the hill to the Trask place. I don't know how Miz knew the way. All the corridors looked the same to me, just narrow twisty roads through the dark. But I tried to pay attention anyway, just in case. Miz kept talking, the whole trip. She was angry about everything. "Should never have let the Trasks settle so far out, way out on the borders with nothing between them and the bright. Damn fool stupid idea from the start. And now a whole family is lost. And the farm. And it's not like we have families or farms to spare. Lord knows what shape the poor animals are in. Put your goggles and mask on, boy. We're almost there. And you put that cape and gloves on before you get out of the car, you hear?"

She pulled up short of the farm and pulled on her own cape and goggles and gloves and breathing mask. She pushed the goggles up on her forehead and inched the truck forward, a little bit at a time. I pushed my gloomies up just enough to see under the frames. We came around the last curve and there was the brightness leaking in around the edges of the broken dark. We both pulled our goggles down at the same time. "I told you to keep those things on. You're susceptible. You can't take any more chances."

We pulled up in front of the barn. It was old and saggy. It leaned to one side and it looked like it was ready to collapse, even worse than Miz's barn. Miz looked off toward the bright before getting out of the truck. Half the darkline was down, the dark just faded off into filigree wisps. Beyond, the fields glowed harsh and stark in our gloomies. Without the goggles, they would have been impossible to look at.

Miz made a clucking sound of disapproval. I followed her into the barn. There were three cows tethered, all of them lowing uncomfortably. Miz told me to load up the sacks of feed, while she set about milking the cows. Afterward, I loaded the cans into the truck. Then she blindfolded the cows and led them out of the barn, tying their tethers to the back of the truck. Then she went and found a stack of empty crates and we began collecting the chickens. Some of them were clucking quietly in the barn, those we crated; but others were lying stunned on the ground outside. A few were wandering around dazed. Those she picked up and swiftly broke their necks.

"Can't they be saved?" I asked.

Miz shook her head. "Too dangerous. Too much bright in 'em. This is better. Safer." There were a few little chicks too, all safe in the incubator. She put these in a crate, dropped a canvas over it, and I loaded the crate into the back of the pickup. We walked around the barn then, looking to see what else we could find. The two pigs in the back were both gone. Miz shook her head at that. "Probly ran into the bright. Pigs are like that," she said.

Then we saw it. The fourth cow. It was staggering, all glassy-eyed and confused. It looked bright—not as bright as the brightland, but brighter than it should be. Miz said one of those words I'm not supposed to. She went to the truck and pulled out her shotgun from the back window.

"Don't you want to walk it into the barn?"

"What for?"

"That's a lot of meat—"

"Nobody's going to eat this beef. It's sick. You want to get sick too?"

"Can't you have Doc wrap it in darkline and drain the bright out of it?"

"You can't drain it. Draining takes the flavor out. And you can't let people eat meat that's been brightened either. That's even worse. No, this cow is gone." She lifted the shotgun, moved closer, then moved closer again, until the barrel was almost touching the cow's skull. I didn't want to see it, but I couldn't look away either. The rifle flashed. The cow dropped to the ground with a thud. She stepped closer and fired the second barrel. Just to be sure.

Miz checked the house then. She wouldn't let me go in, but she came out carrying a pillow case full of spices and other things from the kitchen. Even a small jar of honey, I found out later. That was a surprise. The Trasks weren't supposed to be doing that well.

Back in the truck, barely inching along the road, not moving faster than the three tethered cows could follow, Miz started talking again. She looked old. Older than the first day. And tired too. Like she'd been drained a few times. "This isn't right," she said. "Letting cows and pigs and chickens and corn go bad like that. And all those vegetables. Nobody should have been out this far, with only one line of dark between them and that—that brightmare. Now look what it's gone and done. A family gone, a cow gone. Two pigs running loose in the bright. All those chickens. All that food. What a waste. What a waste."

It took most of the day to bring the cows in. It was a long drive and we couldn't go very fast. But we were back before dusk settled in. I was glad of that. I didn't like being out in the dark. Not any kind of dark at all.

I slept badly. Tossed and turned in the straw all night. Finally, just before dawn, I got up and walked out of the barn. I tried to look up at the stars. Once in a while, you can still see them, some of them, but not tonight. Everything was black. Just dim shapes of black against blacker. I thought about lighting a lantern, but I didn't want to wake Miz, so I just stood barefoot and listened. Nothing much to hear. Just wind. A lonely cricket. Not a lot of insects anymore. I heard that one in town. That was the real reason everything was dying. The insects couldn't get through the darklines. No bees, no ants, no bugs, no spiders, nothing.

Not even a glimmer of bright from over the hill. Sometimes you can see it, mostly its reflection off the clouds. But not tonight.

Finally, I went back into the barn, back to my straw. Pulled my blanket around me and just sat with my arms wrapped around my knees, rocking softly. I used to do that when I was little. I don't remember much from when I was little, we moved around so much. But I remember I spent a lot of time sitting in the dark and rocking. Sometimes Mom would come and sit with me, wrapping her arms around me, and we'd sit as quiet as we could, not making any noises, so they wouldn't find us.

Thought about what I'd seen. Everything. All the bright leaking over into the fields. Miz didn't know, but while she was milking the cows, I'd lifted up the edge of my gloomies and snuck a quick peek—not at the bright directly, but at the fields it was just creeping into. That didn't hurt so much. I could see the colors, all the dazzling colors, everything at once—the rustling golden corn in the field, the crisp green stalks so clear it was like they cut the air, the rich dark soil like a warm bed, even the sky above glowed blue. I'd never even known such colors were possible. I wanted to see more. But then, I heard a noise behind me and just as quick-like I pushed the goggles back down over my eyes. I didn't want to get caught. Not by Miz. Because Miz wanted to take me to Doc. And wrap me in darkline. And drain the bright out of me. Like the beef. Drained beef. "You ever taste drained beef? You won't like it." Maybe that's what's wrong with these people. They've all been drained.

But what if Miz hadn't made a noise right then? Would I have kept looking until it was too late, until I was sucked away into the brightland too? I wondered what that might feel like—to dance naked in the stars. To whirl and dazzle and laugh. Madness, yes. But even madness looked better than this life. Miz wanted to wrap me in dark and make me just like everybody else. My stomach rumbled and I wondered what people ate in the brightlands? Magic corn? Enchanted beans? I didn't know. Nobody knew. Anybody who knew hadn't come back to tell. Maybe they was all dead, lying bright and starved? Maybe the bright pigs was eating them. Maybe this and maybe that and maybe some of the other. Nobody knew. Or if they did, they wasn't saying.

Finally, I just rolled over, curled up and tried to sleep. Thinking about stuff doesn't do any good. It doesn't work. It just makes my head hurt. Enough. Enough already. I wrapped myself tight in my blanket and eventually shivered myself to sleep.

For the next couple days, Miz didn't say anything more about getting me darklined, but I knew she was still set on the idea. She kept giving me these looks. But maybe she also felt bad about having to do it, because she made some honey-cornbread and cut me an extra thick slab with lots of butter. Or maybe she just felt I had to have my strength up so I could survive being drained. She didn't say. And I didn't ask. I was starting to think about running again. We still had the gloomies and the capes in the truck. Maybe if I could find my way to the Trask farm, I could go outside the darklines and cross the bright to some other place. Supposedly, the town council had some maps somewhere, but nobody was allowed to see them.

Tuesday evening, Tallow came driving up unexpectedly. He talked with Miz a bit, then told me to get into the truck. Tomorrow morning, we were going out to fix the darkline at the Trask farm. And maybe do a bit of hunting too. Miz sniffed unhappily. I could see she disapproved. She didn't trust any of this. She came right out and said it. "That boy's got too much bright in him. He ain't been drained. If you don't tie him down good, you know he'll just get sucked into the colors. I swear, you lose him and I'll skin you bad, Tallow, I will."

"Nah, you'll just get another one off the next train. Like you always do." Tallow grinned back.

Miz didn't think that was funny. She sniffed again in that funny way she had. "Oh, hell. Wait a minute." She went to her own truck and pulled the rifle down out of the back window, and the box of shells next to it. She cracked it open and popped the two shells out, dropping them into the box. She walked back over, and motioned me to open my door. She handed me the shotgun and the box of shells. "Don't you load this thing unless you need it. And you bring it back clean, y'hear? Tallow, you teach him how to use it. It's on your head now."

Tallow grunted and climbed into the truck. He pulled his door shut and put the engine into gear. We rolled down the hill and into the corridor of twisted dark. Tallow laughed. "Miz is good folks, but some folks say she's been drained one too many times."

I thought about that. It kind of made sense. "You ever been drained?" I asked.

"Most folks around here have. For their own good."

"Oh," I said.

"It doesn't really hurt. It just makes you queasy, a little. Like having the runs, sort of. After a couple days, the feeling goes away. And the bright can't get to you as easy."

"Did the bright ever get to you? I mean, before you were drained?"

Tallow's face tightened. "Y'know, boy. This ain't really anything you want to talk about. You don't want to go asking too many questions. Folks'll start talkin'."

"Just curious, that's all."

"Yep, that's all. That's what they all said. Just curious. You don't want to get too curious about the bright. You want to stay away from it. That's why we smacked you with it the first day on the lines—so's you'll know. You've seen all you need to see. Right?" When I didn't answer, he repeated himself. *"Right?"*

I shrugged. "Whatever."

Tallow stopped the truck with a screech. I jerked forward with the suddenness of the stop. He turned to me and grabbed my shoulder hard. "Listen up, city-boy. You don't know what you're dealing with here. That ain't a question. It's the truth. You don't know shit. So when I tell you how it is, I'm not just running my mouth 'cause I like hearing my jaw flap. I'm telling you what you need know so you don't get sucked away like all the others. We used to be three times as many people and ten times as much livestock and crops. Where do you think all those folks went? All those animals? They didn't listen and they didn't take care and now they're gone. You want to be gone too? Just keep asking questions. You ask too many questions, we'll open the dark and toss you out in the bright ourselves. This is for your own good, city-boy. If you want to live, you better learn to listen."

"I thought you liked me," I said. I didn't know why I said that.

"This ain't about liking. Even if I didn't like you, I wouldn't want to see you turn into one of them damn fairy-dancers."

"You've seen them?"

Tallow didn't answer. He let go of my shoulder and turned away and put the truck back into gear. I rubbed where he'd grabbed me so hard.

"You didn't answer my question."

"That's right. I didn't." Tallow didn't say anything else for the rest of the drive. That left me with lots of time to think about all the things he wasn't saying. I got the feeling he knew more than it was safe for anyone to know. And maybe he didn't want anyone else to know how much he knew. But it was only a feeling and he'd made it real clear that he wasn't going to answer any more questions of any kind. I felt bad about that. Because maybe if he'd said he'd seen a fairy-dancer, I could tell him I'd seen one too. And maybe then we'd each have someone we could trust enough to talk about it. Except I didn't dare tell him, because he might tell someone else; and he couldn't risk saying anything to me either, because I was just another stupid city-boy.

"We going out tonight?"

"Tomorrow. Early morning. But I don't have time to drive out and pick you up then, so you'll sleep behind the feed store tonight with some of the other boys. You keep your hands to yourself, you keep your mouth shut, and you don't ask any questions. I'll keep Miz's shotgun in my truck. No sense in having you shoot yourself in the foot, or anybody else either."

Behind the feedstore, it was just a big empty space under a sagging roof. A few bags of feed, here and there, just enough to make a rough bed. It wasn't much, but it was better than straw. Four or five others talking together, nothing important. I recognized two of them, but J. D. was the only one whose name I knew. They glanced at me, but didn't say anything. Just another city-boy, using up space, eating up food. I grabbed a stretch of canvas to use as a blanket and made myself comfortable off in a corner, away from the others. They had a kerosene lamp, but that was all. The light pretended to warmth, but the night was just as cold here as anywhere else.

After a while, J. D. wandered over, wrapped in a blanket. "Hey, city-boy. Can I sleep by you?"

Shrugged. Not yes, not no. J. D. pushed a couple of feed bags into position and stretched out on top of them. "You know something you're not saying." It wasn't a question.

I didn't answer.

"If you tell me what you know, I'll tell you what I know."

I rolled over on my side, turned away from him. I trusted him less than anybody. J. D. liked to talk, liked to pretend he knew stuff. Safest not to tell him anything.

"Aw, c'mon—"

"Fine. Okay. You go first."

"No, you," he insisted.

"Forget it then." I settled myself again.

Silence for a bit. Just enough time for me to figure out what was going on. They'd sent J. D. over to find out what I knew, if I'd ever seen anything.

A minute more and I figured out the rest of it. It didn't matter what I said. J. D. was going to make something up for me.

"Okay," he said. "I'll tell you. Folks keep seein' Doey. Miz's other boy. He's a fairy-dancer now. We're goin' out to find him. Hunt him down like a blind pig. That's what my maw says—"

I sat up and looked at him. "J. D. Go away. Get away from me. You got devil-talk inside you and I don't want to hear it. Get away from me or I'll punch you." I said it loud enough for the others to hear. That was enough. J. D. gathered up his blanket and went scuttling back to the others.

He hadn't told me anything I didn't know already. It wasn't that hard to figure out. Even the rest of it, the part he hadn't said. Not just Doey, but the Trask family too, if they were still alive. Anyone and anything in the brightlands. Didn't need to be smart to figure that out. Just scared and angry and tightened up inside.

But something about this didn't feel right. Going out and shooting people. Even if they were all colored. No matter how little you felt inside. Just fix the darklines, that's all. Put up more lines if you have to. But going out into the bright. That didn't sound like a good idea. Not for this reason, not for any reason. Not unless you were planning to never come back. I just wish I knew more about what was out there. But if anybody around here knew, they weren't saying, and it sure wasn't safe to ask.

Next thing I knew, Tallow was kicking me awake. "Time to go, city-boy. Move your ass." I rolled off the sack of feed onto the hard black dirt. It looked as dark in here as it was out there, but Tallow was waving a lantern, and that outlined everything in brown gloom. Two other men were kicking the rest of the boys awake. I didn't see J. D. anywhere. I pulled myself to my feet, scratching and aching and hurting all over. My stomach hurt the worst. "Is there anything to eat?" Nobody answered.

I followed them all around the building to the front, where six or seven trucks had pulled up. Somebody had set up a table with a big plate of hard biscuits and even some hot coffee, seven or eight men just lining up. I fell in line behind them, then got pushed even further back when three more arrived. "Wait your turn, city-boy. Let the men eat first." Pigs.

Bitter coffee and a couple of biscuits later, they formed up teams. I recognized most of the men from the darkline team, plus a few folks from Meeting. And a couple of the big stocky women too. Some of them had guns. This wasn't any darkline crew.

After a bit of discussion, people figuring out who was going to ride with who, that kind of stuff, Tallow pointed me toward one of the trucks, and I climbed into the back with two other boys. I said hello, but they ignored me. After a few last minute instructions, the trucks all headed out toward the Trask place. The headlights of the ones following us made an ominous line snaking through the dark.

We couldn't drive very fast, it wasn't safe, so by the time we arrived, the sky was just starting to show an edge of gray—or maybe it was the glow off the distant brightness. I couldn't be sure, and I wasn't going to ask. We stopped down the hill from the Trask place and safely behind the bend in the road, so no one would accidentally get a glimpse of brightness before they got their goggles on.

We bumbled around in the gloom for a while, while the Sheriff and a couple of others organized everybody into teams. I was pushed over to stand with Tallow. He was carrying Miz's gun as well as his own, but he made no move to give it to me. I wasn't sure why I was even here, nobody was talking to me.

Finally, everything was sorted out and we all put on our shiny capes and our gloomies and our breathing masks and we started off. We trudged up the last of the road, around the bend of the corridor of dark, and finally up the hill to where the ground was starting to glow. And beyond that, we could see where the glare was leaking into the air from the brightlands. Kind of like the dazzle of light from an open refrigerator in a midnight kitchen.

Two of the men rolled a cart with three huge spools of darkwire on it. For some reason, everybody kept close to the cart. Even though the wire wasn't powered, folks still acted like they were safer staying close to it. Once we got to the top of the hill, I looked around for the dead cow, but where I thought it should be, I saw only a hump, covered with little white flowers. We all waited while the Sheriff and his deputies looked out across the brightland through special binoculars. They whispered to themselves for a bit, pointing and nodded and finally agreeing. After some more conferences, the guys with the cart installed one end of the wire to a convenient post; they hooked up a terminator box to it, there was another terminator connected to the end of the wire inside the big drum.

Then, when that was done, we all headed out into the bright, with the cart leading and the men unspooling the wire as they went. We didn't install any posts, we weren't putting up a darkline. This was only a safety line. All you had to do was follow it back. You could do it with your eyes closed, if you had to. I hoped I wouldn't have to. Just the little bit of leakage around the edge of my goggles was painful.

Nobody told me where we were headed, so I just followed Tallow. At least, I thought it was Tallow. In the harsh glare, with all of us caped and goggled, everybody looked alike, all different shades of gray and white and whiter. To keep from stumbling, I spent most of the time watching the ground directly in front of me, following in the footsteps of the man I thought was Tallow. We hiked into the brightness where the ground turned white like salt—that's what it looked like through the gloomies; it must have been glittering gold without them.

We hiked through scorched fields, abandoned to the bright. An old dirt road cut straight through, but it was already starting to get overgrown. On either side, twisted trees groped in the glare. They looked like they were alive, their limbs slowly moving, waving, even reaching. We kept clear of them. And the bushes too—they looked like they were all burning. They were so bright, even the gloomies couldn't keep out all the color. They looked burnished with a hint of red and gold, like they were all wrapped in shivering flame. Everywhere else, I saw stalks of something that might have been corn once, but was something else now; they looked like torches.

None of this made much sense to me. How was anybody going to hunt anything in a place like this? Ten feet away, everything blurred out in yellow and white. It was like fog on fire. And nobody was saying much either. If they knew what they were doing, they weren't telling.

Finally, someone in front of me stopped and pointed. A couple of others stopped, so I did too. At first, I couldn't see what they were looking at, but finally I made it out, way out there, way beyond the place where the road just dazzled out, there was a tall old house, an outline of a house, a glimmering hint of a house. I guessed that was where we were heading, I tried to make it out clearer—but then somebody punched me in the back and growled, "Keep moving, bait." So I pushed on.

It was hot out here. Once, I tried looking off to the east, tried to see the sun, the source of all this brightness, but the gloomies just went black. They overloaded and shut down. And I had to walk blind for a few moments until they reset themselves.

Eventually, we reached the house. It was in a field of grass so bright that the goggles showed it black, they didn't even try to resolve it. The house itself looked like it was made out of glass. The walls had gone glistening and transparent, and all we could see clearly was just the structural outlines, the edges and corners. It looked like it had been here forever, standing tall and stately, with porches and gables and even a widow's walk around the front and sides. And a tall cupola. It was almost a castle. Even Miz's house wasn't this big.

The two men with the cart cut the wire and tied one end of it to one of the porch posts. Once they did that everybody felt safer. A few folks started to go up onto the porch, but Sheriff stopped them, said the house was off-limits to everybody. Except the lure.

Then everybody busied themselves, separating into three teams. Each team had a cart and a roll of wire. Each team tied one end of their wire to the porch, connected a terminator, then headed out a bit and waited. One team was pointed straight out south, the other two east and west.

Tallow was on the western team, but when I went to follow, he grabbed me by the arm and walked me back to the house. "No, your job is to wait here and make sure nothing happens to the wires."

"By myself?"

"Nothing's going to happen. You're perfectly safe. You have four active darkwires terminating here."

"Then why do you need me to stay here? I thought I was going with you."

"I promised Miz."

"Then give me the gun."

"You won't need it."

"Then why'd she give it?"

"Stop asking so many questions. Go sit up on the porch. You'll be able to see farther."

"Can't see anything in this bright. Neither can you. And why'd he call me 'bait?' I'm the lure, aren't I?"

Tallow grabbed my shoulder. Hard. Just like last time. "Listen to me, city-boy. If we take you out there, you'll get sucked away so fast you won't have time to scream for help. You stay here because I say you stay here. And if you want to argue about it, we can tie you down with darkline. And that won't be just an hour of draining, it could be a day or two or forever. You want that?"

I didn't answer. Not right away. "You say nothing will happen?"

"Nothing will happen."

"You sure?"

"Get up on the porch. Oh, wait—" He fumbled under his cape, passed me a sack. "Here's some more biscuits and a bottle of water. In case you get hungry."

"How long are you going to be out there?"

"As long as it takes." And then, he added. "Probly back by afternoon, certainly before nightfall. We don't want to spend the night out here, that's for sure; this place glows in the dark. You just stay awake and make sure those wires stay tied." He started to turn away, then turned back. "You'll be all right."

And then he was gone. All of them were gone. They hiked out into the bright and faded away in the distance like wavering shadows.

Tallow said I could go up on the porch, but I wasn't sure it was safe. The Sheriff hadn't let anybody else go up there. But maybe that was just because he didn't want anything disturbed. What the hell. I put one foot on the glassy first step. It held. Another foot on the next step. It held too. One more step and I was on the porch. It felt yellow everywhere. Dusty yellow. And it smelled of sweet sharp lemons. Even through the mask. And honey. And honeysuckle. And green melons. It was wonderfully delicious. Could the men out in the fields smell it too? What kept them from ripping off their masks and rolling around in the delicious air?

And the sounds—now that I wasn't surrounded by hulking men with their three-day sweaty stinks, the underfoot crunching of dirty boots, the lumbering hooves of upright beasts, the clatter of machinery and the stink of gun oil—now that all of that was gone, I could hear the tinkling music of translucent leaves, rustling in the delicate touch of the breeze. The wind sang like a distant chorus, very faint and far away. Silvery insects rattled and buzzed. And now, much nearer, something soft and small kept calling, *"Hoo-hooo, hoo-hoooo."* I wanted to go looking for it, whatever it was—bird or cricket or owl, I didn't know, but it sounded like the voice at the edge of the world, but so close by now that I wanted to find it, wanted to peer over the edge and see what was there on the other side. It felt like it was just around the corner.

This probly wasn't a good idea, thinking like this. I wondered if I would be safer inside the house? Maybe inside, I'd be out of the wind and away from all the flavors sweeping across the fields. Cinnamon and musk and jasmine. How did I even know all those different scents?

The doorknob glittered like diamond. I turned it and the door swung open. Inside, the house was silent, still, and empty. No furniture here, only an empty shell, a suggestion of a life once lived, exploded outward into solar dazzle and flare. The windows glowed with the creeping brightness of the world outside. The light felt muted here. I wondered if it would be safe to take off my clothes and dance in here.

I wandered from room to room, touching each wooden or metal or glass surface. The doors, the walls, the glass of the mirrors. Everything tingled. My fingers caressed. I didn't remember taking off my gloves. I wasn't even sure where I'd left them. This wasn't good. I shouldn't be doing this. All the voices in my head were screaming. Run away, now! Grab the wire and head back into the dark. Don't get sucked away. But all the songs were singing even louder. The music whirled and roared. Come dance aloft, be free. Be clear. I cowered shivering under my cape. Eyes clenched shut against the fiery noise. The seductive smells of sweet apricots and cream and gently scented candles. Overwhelmed by influx, I held myself and counted, one and two and three and breathe and one and two and three and breathe—

No. No. I wouldn't succumb. Not going to get sucked away. Never. Ever. Didn't come this far to be a golden bird fairy dancer. All the walls are here for a reason. The carefully constructed dark, the comfortable black essence of nothing at all.

Upstairs, the house is wide open. Tall windows with billowing white drapes, open to the balcony surrounding the house. Outside, the view went on forever. So bright below, so clear up here. Out to the horizon, the sparkling fields, the waves of rippling air, the colors sparkling and dancing. If I take off my cape, I can feel it like the comforting radiance of the refiner. I stand, arms outstretched to feel the heat, the delicious soul-filling heat. It soaks into my flesh, heals my bones, warms my spirit. I giggle at the wash of sensation. I can feel myself glowing.

In the cupola, I twirl alone. Naked and free. Finally warm, and finally here. The frozen winter of my past retreats before the blasting sun. I thaw and come alive. Joyously alive. I laugh with silly pleasure. I am enchanted. The delight of heat.

Am I ready to see? Can I take off the goggles?

Here on the fenced roof of the cupola, the highest part of the house, I can see the world as far as the darklands, the carefully drawn boundaries of exclusion, every tiny little line etched into the face of the land like the wrinkles of time. The gloom of fear.

In the other direction, out toward the east, the south, the west, the land sparkles and shimmers. It dances with light and aliveness. Why would anyone try to hide from all this laughter?

I peeked under the glasses. It wasn't pain I felt, it was color, bright color, brightness overwhelming. It wasn't pain at all, just the sudden shock of coming alive after being dead so long. An awakening from the grave of gloom.

Lift the glasses slowly. Eyes ready to clench. At first, the dazzle startles. A splash of intensity. Hold my hand in front of my eyes—I can see through my fingers—I am translucent. Pink and gold and glistening. I have taken on the colors of the world. The crimson of my blood gives my skin a rosy blush. The blue of my veins resonates. I am a roseate glow of violet and vermilion. I lower my hand, and all the rest of the colors of the world flood in. All the smells and sensations. All the wonderful noises. All the heat and the light and the delicious flood of everything roiling together in a cascading symphony of being.

As I focus, I see…*them.* They've been there all along. Waiting for me. I just couldn't see them until now. Laugh and wave in radiant delight. They recognize me as one of them now. The dancing one is Doey. The others, also dancing, used to be the Trasks. I can hear the children singing.

And then, without passing through the intervening space, I am down among them, laughing with them. A moment of pause. Doey and I, face to face. Can I dance with you now? What a silly question. We're already dancing.

There are men with guns, hunting you. Hunting us. I wave toward the horizon. Doey laughs. He holds up the ends of the darkwires. The terminator boxes have been removed. The wires are dead—no, not dead, coming alive, infusing with clarity. Even metal can be bright.

Doey sparkles. Laugh with me and we'll dance the ends of these wires out to the distant south, out into the solar dazzle. Anyone who follows these lines will end up enchanted in the luminous day. The men will either dance or die. Whatever they choose. Doey twirls and passes out the tingling wires. I join him singing.

AUTHOR'S AFTERWORD:
  Someday I want to write the second half of this story, "Dancer in the Light."

Sometimes I sit at the keyboard and "outflow"—I type stuff and watch to see what happens. This time around, this voice happened. Brutal, blunt, intense. Vicious, visceral, streetwise—and hungry. But hungry for what? Even I didn't know yet. I let the words pour out and watched the narrative assemble itself. It's easier to ride the horse in the direction it's going. And then—abruptly, the horse stopped. Even it didn't know where it was going next. So there I was, with three-quarters of a story that read like the meth-induced rantings of the love-child of William Burroughs and Harlan Ellison. For a long agonizing week, or maybe it was six weeks, I had no idea how this tale was going to end—until I woke up abruptly in the middle of the night recognizing what had been staring me in the face the whole time. (The short version: Theodore Sturgeon. And if you don't understand that, then you haven't read enough Sturgeon, shame on you.)

When I sent the story to Gordon Van Gelder at The Magazine of Fantasy & Science Fiction, *I told him all the reasons he shouldn't publish it. He published it anyway.*

thirteen o'clock

THIRTEEN O'CLOCK ON A THIRSTY NIGHT, dry and windy after midnight, all the boys have paired up, disappeared into the desert, coupling darkly on the sand, have another beer, there's no place else to go except ride the hog and the hot air roars into your eyes at seventy miles per hour, getting too old for this shit, fucking boring, bored with fucking, bored with chasing fucking, bored with waking up alone, and even more bored waking up with anyone else, and even beer cant cure that, fuck me

except that's the problem, nobody wants to fuck me anymore, too many years, too many beers, and that other thing, the scar that starts above my right eye and crawls down to the corner of my mouth, pulling it down into a permanent scowl, so my face looks like something from a slasher movie, only the scar didnt happen when I was on the bike, but when I got off it at high speed, using the right side of my head as a brake shoe, which wasnt as much fun as it sounds, not even with three beers so I gave up on the queerbar for the night, the thing about queerbars, straightmen think you just walk in and get a blow job, everyboy is so fucking thirsty for cock, all you have to do is unzip your dockers, and if it were that easy, I wouldnt be standing in the bar at thirteen o'clock wondering what the hell I'm doing and how I got here and why I dont have any other place to go. So fuckit

and before I'm halfway out the door, some guy is asking, hey, isnt that a queerbar, and before I can even turn and look, somebody's swinging something at my head and the old reflexes kick in and I duck sideways and he misses, but then the other guy's got a bike chain, stupid college kid, which I dont mean to grab, but I get it anyway because it skiddles off the cast on my arm before he can swing, indecision maybe, probably his first queer-bashing, blood-simple coward, then I'm holding the chain, one good yank, and he's holding a big handful of me, and his eyes go white just in time as I swing him around and shove him into his boyfriend with the baseball bat, and that's when I see the third one

someone oughta teach these little pricks how to beat up a fag, because they're no good at this at all, the third one crumples up too easily, a backhand across the windpipe, big ugly rings with scratchy things, and he's down, and then I'm back with chainless and bat, shoving chainless into bat and both up against the wall, so bat cant move and chainless is already screaming for mommy, godforbid someone should scar his pretty face like mine

—and something happens—

and that's when I get the idea that all he really needs is to be kissed so I pull him close and cover his scream with the bearded oyster and give him enough tongue to choke a deep throat, and I guess right because just as he's starting to kiss me back, surprising me more than him I think, and if this were a different time and a different place, I bet I could hang his legs over my shoulders, or mine over his, I'm not choosy, except the batboy is screaming and who can concentrate with all that noise

by the time danny-bartender finally makes it out the door with his own baseball bat, I've got two on the ground and one up against the wall with my hand on his throat, the pretty one, and I really do think I could negotiate a relationship out of this, except that even as a "cute meet" this is a little too acute. So I let go of the cute meat, and he staggers forward, almost into my arms, jerks back, looks around, sees the queers piling out of the queerbar and maybe he thinks about running, but before he can send the message to his skechers, it's too late, he's caught

danny-bartender wants to call the police, but I tell him not to bother, because the one guy on the ground is having too much trouble breathing,

I didnt think I hit him that hard, but he's got a nasty bubbling cut across his neck, which reminds me of things I saw in the service that I really dont want to think about at all, and the other guy who forgot about holding his bat when holding his stomach and his balls became a lot more important is having his own problems exsanguinating through his nose, so I go and pop open the back doors of my van and toss them in, I sold the hog six months ago and bought the van because it's easier on my bad leg and besides you can sleep in a van if you have to, and someboy asks where are you taking them and even though I want to take them out in the desert and bury them, without bothering to kill them first, I say the emergency room because I've already got enough death on my conscience

prettyboy rides in front with me, the other two moaning in the back, and nobody else wants to come because what queer wants to talk to cops anyway, I'm not worried, nobody fucks with me twice, not when I've got their wallets in my pocket

pull up at the E.R. and I drag them both out the back of the van and through the sliding doors, shouting, "white male, age 20, injury to his trachea, might need to intubate; white male, age 20, needs an X-Ray for a cracked rib, broken nose, and someone call the police," and I only have to holler it twice before a doctor and two nurses come running

tell the police I'm emmett grogan, they're too young to know the real emmett grogan, and besides I've got the i.d. that proves I'm emmett grogan, I made it myself, tell the police these two injured boys were just coming out of a gay bar, thirteen o'clock in the night, when they were attacked by queerbashers, lucky for them I was driving my little brother back to campus, I point to prettyboy, and we were just passing by

ex-marine, vietnam vet, ex-corpsman, got the tattoo in san diego, yessir, nossir, I didnt see the attackers clearly, officer, there were four of them, they looked like accountants, or maybe lawyers, probably republicans, you know they like to do that sort of thing, the cops give me the narrow-eyed look and I give them the deadpan, and then the fat one says, well if the victims were coming out of a queerbar they probbly got what they deserved, I dont see any need to pursue this further, and the skinny one adds, but maybe we should notify their parents, they look like college students, and I say, nah, give them a break, they're just kids, maybe this'll teach em to stay away from queerbars

and the fat cop says, nah, once they've been into a queerbar, you cant keep em out, one taste of cock and they're queer for life, so I just look at him deadpan and ask, is sucking cock that good, like he knows, and he blinks for a moment, realizing that he cant answer that question without looking either queer or stupid back in the van, prettyboy still hasnt said a word, he's scared I'm gonna finish that kiss, or maybe he's hopin', but either way, he's sweating, so I hand him all three wallets, after taking out the cash, my own brand of justice, payment for lesson learned, nearly four hundred total, I drive him to the dorm, and as we pull up, he says thank you for not reporting me to the cops, and at least he doesnt try to blame the other guys, it's all their fault, it wasnt his idea, he was just tagging along, which is obvious anyway, prettyboy is booksmart, but not much else, at least he knows enough not to say anything that stupid, so I think about all the bullshit I can say back to him and decide not to say any of it, instead I look him straight in the eye and say, the difference between us, someone calls me faggot, they're talking about what makes me happy, someone calls you faggot, they're talking about what makes you unhappy, you figure it out, all that money mommy and daddy are spending to send you away to university, you oughta be smart enough to figure out what you like

and then he does surprise me, he starts to open the door to get out and then he turns back and says, can we talk sometime, and there it is, half past whenever, dry and windy after midnight, and he's got big eyes and chewable lips, and surprise, surprise, my dick can still get hard, so I say yes and how about tomorrow night, and he says pick me up right here, and I'm already thinking, we'll go somewhere out on the other side of the desert where the truth is a lot easier, I know he'll never show up, not after twelve hours of sunlight-thinking, but what the fuck, nobody's waiting for me in the next town either, so why not

sleep away most of the day, crawl out of my coffin just in time to enjoy the sunset, shower and burger at the truck stop, think about beer, but leave it at thinking, not drinking, cruise over to the landing zone and prettyboy is leaning against a wall, he flicks his cigarette sideways, like he thinks that's butch, it isnt, and he strolls over and climbs in the passenger seat and I roll without talking and he doesnt say anything either and I'm wondering what the fuck he thinks is going to happen tonight, because I sure as shit dont have a clue, but this is something better than nothing

we drive for a while, prettyboy finally says something, I was afraid you werent going to come, I tell him I didnt think he'd be there either, so we're even, he asks where we're heading, I shrug and nod ahead; away from the light, because I dont like the light, if it's too bright I can see the scars on my face from the inside, he tells me to stop calling him prettyboy, his name is Michael, I tell him he hasnt earned a name yet, he's still meat, fresh off the plane, and we've got a body bag already waiting with his name on it, deal with it

finally I ask him what the fuck he wants from me, he says he wants to know what I know and I tell him I dont know shit and finally we turn off the highway onto a side road and after a while off the side road onto a couple of forgotten ruts and we go two or three miles up and down bouncing to a place where something used to be, but now there's only hard-packed dirt, and I pull off and turn the engine off and we sit and listen to it cooling in the night

we get out, I go around to the back, pull out a blanket, a couple bottles of water, we sit in the dark, side by side, watching for shooting stars, and except for pointing them out to each other, we dont talk, I'm waiting for him to start, but he doesnt, so after a while, I reach over and grab his hand, not because I particularly want to hold his hand, I dont even fucking know him, but it's a start

he's not good for small talk, neither am I, he asks me how I know how to fight, I tell him the truth, fighting is easier than having the shit kicked out of you, then he asks me about my leg, so I tell him

somewhere in the fucking delta, the hot wind putrid, the whole country stinking like a Saigon whorehouse, disintegrating with the smell of shit and incense and rotting vegetation, all mixed with the spices they use to hide the fact that the meat is rotten before they even get it into the pan, even if you knew what it was—dog or cat or rat—who the fuck cares, when you get hungry enough, you stop asking questions

they call it a road, but it's just a lousy stinking dirt scar, a slash of mud carved between two fields, the crapgrass rippling in the wind—the distant edges bordered by trees, a fucking perfect place to die, a fucking bullseye for an ambush—the lieutenant holds up a hand and we all stop, then he holds his arm straight out and waves us down—and we scatter into the grass and disappear

they say that Charlie is terrified of us, because we're monsters, bigger and healthier and better fed, better guns, better ammo, better supplies—and better targets too—those little human cockroaches scuttle down into the ground and disappear, trapdoors in the floor of the world—everybody knows they're all underground, the delta is tunneled from here to forever, underground cities, you could walk all the way to uncle ho without ever seeing daylight—and maybe they're right, maybe the little fuckers are scared shitless, but I dont think so

claymore—we call him that because he's good at taking mines apart—he grins and whispers across to me, it's a good day to die. I tell him to shut the fuck up. it's never a good day to die, but he saw that in a movie and he thinks it's cool—it isnt cool, it's fucking stupid—and what are we waiting for anyway?

the lieutenant is yabbering into the field phone, the sweat is rolling down the inside of my shirt, the sun is a hundred and thirty degrees and we're all carrying fifty pounds of field gear—whose good idea was this anyway?—the field isnt a field, it's a fucking swamp, we're up to here in mud so deep that every step, the mud is fighting to pull my boots off—and I cant stand too long in one place, I start to sink deeper

oh man, I am going to stand for an hour in the shower tonight and I dont fucking care what color the water is

the lieutenant he stands up and waves us back to the road—whatever—he does this five, six times an hour—squelching up out of the mud, and before I can yank my boot free, the world fucking blows up in my face—all the different colors of orange and white and red and black, all at once, and everybody's screaming because the shit is going off all around us—they're dropping fucking mortar shells on us, and they've got our range because the crap is hitting left and right and up and down—claymore flies apart in pieces, a fucking good day to die my fucking ass—and I'm too busy pulling my goddamn leg out of the mud to be scared—we're all firing wildly at the distant trees, like we're really going to hit something, we're fucking dead out here

rocks and shit and mud comes pattering down, all around, a pummeling of earth, it goes on forever while the ground shakes and your ears bleed and the world turns sideways and knocks you assover everywhere, and no my leg isnt supposed to bend like that, but I cant feel it anyway, and I cant find my fucking gun and while my hand is flailing around everything turns orange, the sky, the muck, a wall of heat knocks me flat into the shit, rolls me sideways, and then I hear the first roar of the flames—a roiling carpet, napalm forest, blossoming scars across the whole west side of the world, and for a moment, there's a kind of peace, the explosions stop, shocked in fucking horror, roasted alive, who fucking cares, I fade out and over, something is whupping up and I feel nothing

while I'm dead everything is fine, because I cant feel anything, I dont care, I could go on like this forever, white light and voices

—*something happened*—

but then it's gone, leaving only a memory of a memory, a sense that there was something *important*, maybe it was the drugs, but no, I know drugs and this wasnt drugs, this was something *else,* but it's gone, it's like hearing the echo, but not knowing what clanged, the feeling stays with me all the way across the pacific and down into the crevices of San Francisco, it never fades, a sense of muffled awareness, the doctors tell me it's resonance, it'll go away, but they're wrong, it doesnt—never completely, it just drifts behind-inside forever; it doesnt bother me, it just turns into something to live with, like the plastic leg

so I spend a few years riding a hog up and down the left coast, cruising up through Big Sur, across the big red bridge, up through Marin, into the cold wet wild north where the trees make green canyons, up into Oregon where the green is too thick and I start thinking about Charlie creeping through the green, if Charlie had green like this, we'd still be there, it's nothing like the Delta, first of all the smell is sweet and green and wet, but I cant shake the feeling that something is creeping up after me, so I keep riding, on up as far as Puget where the only difference between the fog and the rain is that the fog is thicker and wetter and from there up to the border where the Canadian customs guard is so exquisitely polite I know he hates to let me in, but he cant find a reason not to, I'm legal, I just look ugly, so on into Canada, eh, all the way up to Alaska and I lose myself for a few years with the bears and the salmon and the air so crisp it cuts like ice through the tent, through the sleeping bag, and man I'm getting too old for this shit, but I gotta know what it was, and for some reason I've made up my mind that the Inuit know, some shaman or medicine man, whatever, because maybe underneath, there's some magic here

and maybe there is, but I never find it, so I come sliding back south, dropping down through Idaho, following the Snake river all the way down, passing through forgotten dusty places with names too small for the map, endless dry highways, into Nevada with its desolate empty stretches of baking summer

east to Utah where the canyons still echo with fossilized time, south to New Mexico with its hidden villages carved into orange sunset cliffs, west to Arizona and up the poisonous side of Superstitious Mountain, maybe there's a wise old grandfather, the Hopi know life out of balance, and eventually south through Mexico, where I spend a week or a year or whatever living the way of the whaqui, eating mushrooms and peyote and rattlesnakes, fucking everything that I can push down on its back or its stomach, if it's a hole and I'm horny, I dont care anymore, it doesnt matter, there's that instant of orgasm, that quick throb-and-spurt of time where I stop existing long enough that the nagging sense of something unsaid and left undone is pushed so far out of my consciousness that it almost doesnt exist for that moment, and the lassitude afterward, on my back and staring dispassionately at the glowering sky, waiting for wisdom and insight, that connection of time and place and understanding, but all I accomplish is a thousand light-year stare with nothing on the other side, and one day I put the hog back together, get the engine running, tune it, tweak it, test it, over and over, until it sounds like magic growling again, until one day it's right, and the moment is right, and I get on and start riding, just a test ride, I say, but I keep riding north and never look back, I run out of gas at a queer hippie commune south of Tuscon and live in a teepee while I flush out all the crap from my system, lose twenty pounds of Mexican bad shit and end up with abs again, stumping up and down the rows of corn and beans and tomatoes, digging latrines, carrying water, hoeing and weeding, learning to serve others again, and for the first time in longer than I can remember actually earning the right to feel good about myself at the end of the day

but it's all queerboys here and I'm not ready to give up girlpussy forever, it's fixed in my mind now that there's boypussy and girlpussy, and each is fine in its own way, and by now I've even learned there's other things to do and maybe that's part of the answer, if not *the* answer, it's still part of it, because what these queerboys have learned is that it's not about fucking, it's about people, a strange place to learn this

and then, in an angry flash, I dont know how it happens, I'm back on the left again, Arizona a red and gold memory in the rear-view mirror, how did that happen?—the moving finger writes and once it writes you're fingered, I come bouncing down into the Castro where I hook up with Bloody Mary, a bulldyke who rides a hog and sometimes she rides me and sometimes she rides the hog and once she rides us both at the same time and I ask her how can she be a dyke if she's riding the rod and she just laughs and says it isnt about pussy, it's about people, so I'm not the only one who's figured that out

we coast up to Guerneville where nobody cares, where we're out of earshot of the creepazoids who think we're traitors to the fag-flag because we're bumping each other ugly, except one night I break my leg in Sausalito, laying down the bike to avoid a drunken spoiled teenage bitch, and if I could have gotten up afterward I'd have punched her a new one, but I cant get up because the bike is on top of me, she jumps out and starts wailing about the dent I just put in the side of her new car that daddy just bought her only two days ago for her seventeenth birthday, while I'm still lying under a bleeding hog and

—*it happens again*—

until Mary the dyke slaps her, takes away her new expensive toy, this thing called a cell phone, and punches 911 and calls an ambulance, and I'm off to the E.R. tonight and the V.A. tomorrow, and fortunately it's the plastic leg that's broken and six weeks later, the V.A. finally puts me on a new one, a better one, and I'm ready to get back in the saddle, except

I dont want to, something's happened; I cant explain it, but something's happened, and even though I feel like a cowboy who has to shoot his horse, I sell the hog, what's left of it, and no, it isnt fear, I could get back on the bike in half a minute, I trust myself on the road, I dont trust anyone else, I trust my ability to keep out of their way, but if a seventeen-year-old bitch can put me down in the gutter, maybe it's the universe sending me a message; the dyke tells me I'm a pussy, so I know she doesnt understand, and fuckit, I'm not even sure I understand it myself, all I know is it's time to let go, the bike isnt me anymore, and neither is the dyke

and then time flashes and I'm living out of the back of a VW bus, I dont even remember where I got it, but the feeling is there, I can drive out to the middle of the Mojave, get off the highway, get off the side road, find a dirt slash into the middle of nowhere, someplace even the lights in the distance are too far away to look like anything more than stars glimmering through the bottom of the world, and I lay down on my back and look up at the diamond sky and it's like riding the hog again, only this time riding it through time and space, I'm standing at the front of starship earth and sailing forward like I'm king of the universe and I can hear the feeling loud and clear like picking up clear channel KOMA from five states away

and I know it's not the tequila and it's not the grass and it's not a fucking acid flashback either, it's something else, and I can feel the throb and pulse of the ground beneath my body and I know the ground doesnt throb and pulse, so what the flaming fuck am I feeling, it's just my own heartbeef, slabs of muscle too stubborn to stop slamming the blood through my veins, and what the fuck is life all about anyway, but the feeling, it wont go away, it's like music sometimes, a distant chorus, very faint and far away, under the edge of the horizon, like those things whatever they are that always woke me when I was little, going *hoo-hooo* in the night

and I tell prettyboy, that's what I know, that I'm just another hood ornament on the battering ram, wherever it goes I get there first, hardest—I'm the part that takes the impact—but every time, just before the collision, I get this flash, like there's something under the bottom of the world, calling to me, I dont know what the fuck it is, but I cant get away from it, cant get it to shut up, cant forget it, and cant fucking die until I find out what it is

so now it's his turn to explain and he tells me there's nothing to explain, he isnt anybody at all, he doesnt, just doesnt, and it doesnt matter that there's no predicate to that subject, I get it because I've been there, I'm still there, I live there, we all do, only some of us know it

he says it started in bed, in bed with a girl, she was warm and round and luscious like something out of a painting by Rubens or maybe Titian and he just wanted to float on top of her like she was a giant delicious waterbed, he wanted to suckle at her breasts and bury his face in her juicy cunt and it surprised him when I said, yeah, I know, except whatever else she was, she wasnt either, and she wouldnt

they'd lie together, spooned, his arm curled around her side, but once when his fingers start tentatively brushing at her thigh, she mumbles not now, and another time when he brushes at her lips, the lower ones, probing for her clit, she pushes his hand away roughly as if he's an intruder, and still another time when he moves his fingers up to circle her great silver dollar sized nipples, she rolls away, is that all you ever think about, so he turns on his side and tries to sleep while this great moby of desirability rests naked behind him, his cock still stiff, his balls aching, and the next morning as he's pulling his tighty-whites up and over the tentpole, she sits up in bed and complains that he's unromantic, that he doesnt want to do it with her, and it's because she's fat, isnt it, and to his credit he doesnt say anything, he just finishes pulling up his pants, he buttons his shirt and slips into his sneakers and closes the door behind him, all without a word or a even a look, because inside he's feeling so—there isnt really a word for that feeling, but that's what he's feeling, so he leaves and three nights later he's outside a queerbar with two guys he barely knows, it doesnt make sense, but nothing in life makes sense, why would anyone want to fuck a guy when there are all these beautiful fat women around, except if they dont want to fuck, what's a guy to do, get desperate, and he's almost ready to cry, except he's still too full of that other feeling

so there we are, I have too much life and he doesnt have any, so I hold his hand and after a while he leans up against me, and we sit there listening, he listens for what I can hear and I listen for silence

are you going to fuck me, he asks, and I dont answer for a while because I dont know the answer, I dont know if I want to fuck him, he's pretty enough and after that kiss, I didnt figure it would be that hard to get his ankles behind his neck or mine, it doesnt matter, but I dont know if it's worth the effort, fucking for the sake of fucking sounds fine when you're fifteen, but not when the digits are reversed, so I'm sitting there wondering why he asked, is it something he wants or is it something he's afraid I'm going to do to him whether he wants it or not, and just the fact he asked the question scares the shit out of me, not the scared-shitless feeling like when live fire is making a three-foot ceiling over your head, but the other-scared feeling of just not knowing who you are or what you're supposed to do, a feeling I thought I'd left behind in Alaska or Mexico, or maybe certainly in Arizona, or probably somewhere since then, but finally I just say, is that what you want and he doesnt answer, because I figure he's probably sorting it out the same way

then the moment passes, and I know we're not going to fuck, not then, and probably not ever, but I've been wrong about that before, so we both just relax, now that the question's been asked, not answered, but resolved anyway for the moment, and I'm sitting there thinking a whole fucking epic, and he says, thank you, and I ask, for what, and he says, for listening

and yeah, I get it, and I say so, and he asks, does this feeling ever go away, and even though I'm not sure what feeling he's talking about I still know the answer, I shake my head, I say no, it never does, you just learn to live with it; he breaks away, he sits opposite so he can look at me, the moon is up now, half-past full, so there's enough light I can see his eyes are bright, and yeah, he's getting prettier by the moment, and I'm almost rethinking the answer to his question, but I'm not, because it still isnt happening and in the moonlight, I know why

there's this guy I knew once, his name was Jerry, we went to the same high school, we never talked to each other, we just saw each other in the hallway sometimes, and sometimes at the Big Boy where he was bussing tables, working his way through community college, but we werent in any of the same classes there either, we just saw each other around, and then I forgot about him, the way you forget most of the people you bump up against as you stumble along, until one night a few years later, it's the collapsing end of 1969, and I'm in a boy-bar on Santa Monica Boulevard, and I see him sitting alone in the corner in the back patio and he looks like Wile E. Coyote right after the rocket exploded in his face, so I go over and say hi, and he says hi back and I ask him what's wrong, and he cant even get it out, he just looks at me with a look I've only seen one other time, a year later, in the Delta, when Perry the black kid with the big round eyes caught one and just looks at me, his hands across his belly, all his dark red blood pulsing out between his fingers, trying to push his guts back in, and he looks at me, our eyes meet for just a second, and the expression on his face says it all, please tell me I'm going to be all right, tell me I'm not going to die, and he knows I wont lie to him, and I lie and say, hey man, just hold on, just hold on, and the medic stings him with morphine and his eyes stay fixed on mine the whole time, and then the blood stops pulsing and he's dead, but his eyes are still wide, and that's the look that I saw on Jerry's face, like he was asking me to tell him that he wasnt dead yet

but that hadnt happened yet, this was the first time I ever saw this look, and it stopped me cold, because I didnt know a human face could look like that, and it froze me—the terror, the desperate need, I thought I should do something, except I wasnt in that bar to be Mary Poppins, I was looking for some boypussy, and I was this close to saying, fuckit, tell it to the chaplain, tell it to someone who cares, someone who's paid to care—but then he says, tell me why I shouldnt kill myself and I didnt have the sense to back away quickly, so I stand over him, instinctively shielding him from the light and the noise and the stink of cigarettes and beer and Old Spice and I listen—and what he tells me, well, it almost saves my life

see, he wasnt making it, it was the end of the fucking sixties for god sake, everything was falling apart in slow motion, and all anybody could do was get stoned and fuck their brains out, so that's what we did, all night long, every night, there wasnt any daytime anymore, just the long long night of parties—only Jerry was alone, one of those guys who never quite finds the rhythm of anything, he didnt know how to be whatever it was he was supposed to be, nobody did, and everybody's walking around saying stupid shit like, "hey man, where's it happening?" and you have no fucking idea how dumb that sounds, it's like admitting you're so lost you cant even see the party even when it's happening around you, it was happening everywhere and it wasnt happening anywhere, because whatever was happening, it was only happening when you made it happen, but most of us never learned that lesson, or died trying, so even though Jerry didnt understand it, that was the thing that made him just like everybody else because nobody understood it yet, but Jerry was one of the smart ones, so smart he was stupid; he thought the world was gettable, and because he thought that, he thought that there were people who actually did get it, in fact Jerry thought that everybody did, probably already had, except they'd all privately agreed not to let him in on it, none of it made sense and nobody was letting him in on the joke, so after a while he gives up, just gives up completely and resigns, stops waiting for Santa Claus and starts waiting for rigor mortis, he's ready to be just another one of those used-up boys propped up against the bar like scenery—the ones who've been entered too many times and finally abandoned all hope, the ones who settle for fucking as a substitute for loving, nowhere near a fair trade, but if you fuck long enough and hard enough, sometimes you dont notice, trust me on this

except fucking-God's a practical joker, because just when Jerry decides there aint no such thing as either God or love, that's the afternoon, God drops a beautiful redheaded boy on him, and the two of them do something right and instead of just falling lustfully into bed, mindlessly fucking their brains out on each other's flesh until half-past seeyaround, instead it's too hot to fuck, so they sit and talk for five hours on this sweaty July afternoon, and instead of thinking only about their dicks, they actually work a little higher up, the other end of the spinal cord, and not until the day finally cools off do they end up in bed, but that's only because it's a more comfortable place to just strip down to your jockeys and relax, surrender to the moment, because it doesn't matter anymore, you dont have to pretend now, just be who you are, and they still dont fuck, they share a big glass of ice water and keep talking, and it doesnt matter what they're talking about, they're just having this amazing adventure talking and discovering, and even after they get naked—and you know how you get naked in front of other guys, there's this thing, you know the thing, where you really dont want them looking at you, because you know they're sizing you up, judging how good you look or how big you are, and you know you're never going to look as good as the guys in the magazines, and you end up feeling that you dont want to be naked in front of anyone because you dont want them thinking you're not good enough—except that doesnt happen here, they end up sitting together naked, unashamed, each one astonished at how beautiful the other one is, and they still dont fuck, they hug and kiss and touch in wonder, and they laugh a lot at some shared joke of intimacy and finally take a shower together and laugh a whole lot more, and then they hump and bump a little, even a lot, but they keep interrupting themselves to talk and to share, and before either one of them has come anywhere near to that moment where it's time to get a towel and wipe off and make a hasty graceless exit, they realize that—*something is happening*—it's silly, so fucking silly, because there's no such thing as love at first sight, it's just a fairy tale, but there they are anyway, falling ass-over-teakettle, tumbling over the cliff of joyous delirium, so full of happy giggling exuberance it doesnt make sense, until Jerry has impossible tears running down his cheeks and he wants to run out in the middle of the street and yell to the whole world, dont you dumbfucks get it, love—*real love*—really is possible, and if Hitler had ever had sex this good, World War II would never have happened, that's what it feels like, fucking so good you feel sorry for Hitler, and he and the redheaded boy roll together, laughing

but look, it isnt about the sex at all, it was never about the sex, everybody thinks it's about the cocks and the cunts and the mouths and the assholes, all that juicy pistoning, the hot wet pumping in-and-out, but it isnt, it's about the thing that happens *during* sex, if it's right, if everything is right between the two people, whoever, whatever, if there's a real connection, then the sex is just a way to get even more connected, because it's the connection you want, not the sex—because the truth is, when you're fucking, it's not about you, it's about the person you're with, because if it isnt, then you're the biggest dumbfuck of all, just licking the menu instead of eating the meal—and that's the magic that Jerry and his beautiful redheaded boy fell into

yeah, I know, it doesnt make sense to sit and talk with someone from four o'clock in the afternoon until nine in the fucking ayem the next morning, when you have to get up and go back to work, and on the basis of that short time know that this is the person you want to spend the rest of your life with, that all you want from existence is to keep on exploring the landscape of this beautiful incredible godling, discovering yourself in his smile and his laughter and his cockness, but it happened to them, both of them, they connected anyway, and in the days after that first incredible revelation of each other, it just gets better, they start learning how to do all the other things that people do when they fit their lives together—they talk to each other on the phone every day for three weeks, grabbing every moment they can between their respective jobs and obligations and it should have been perfect, because each of them was exactly what the other one wanted and needed, they fit, you know, they just fit, and every moment was well, you know, just perfect

and then it all comes apart, because Jerry makes a stupid mistake, the biggest stupidest mistake anyone can make, he gets scared, he stops trusting his instincts, because see, the redheaded boy wants to get serious, I mean serious with a capital lets-move-in-together, and Jerry panics, because he thinks it's getting too intense, he cant deal with it, he doesnt know how—I mean, how do you explain it to mom, right?—because nobody gives lessons to queerboys how to have a real relationship, and make it work in a world that mindlessly believes that this thing that brings you so much joy is so despicable that God hates you for it, and the whole thing scares him, so instead of being home, he leaves a note on the door and goes out cruising instead, not because he wants to cruise, but because he doesnt know what else to do, but he's so fucking confused, so the redheaded boy takes the note off the door and goes out looking for something else to do and he picks up a hitchhiker, no, not quite, that's not where this story is going, let me finish, and the hitchhiker is caretaker at some estate up in Benedict Canyon, so the redheaded boy drives him up there and they talk for a while, but they dont really connect, so after a while, the redheaded boy picks up the phone and calls Jerry, and Jerry is back home by now—see, here's what happened, Jerry cruises and cruises and realizes that cruising is empty, because now that he knows that there's something else, cruising is meaningless, and now that he knows what the something else is, he knows what a jerk he's been for leaving that note, for not being home, and all he really wants to do tonight is curl up with his beautiful redheaded lover and not have to talk, just be in his arms and never be apart again, he's ready to jump off the diving board and say yes, I will

only on the way down the hill, the redheaded boy runs into some drug-crazed hippies, and they shoot him in the face, and then they go into the house and murder four other people, five if you count the unborn baby, and Jerry stays up all night wondering where his lover is, and he doesnt find out what happened until he opens the newspaper Sunday morning, still with me, and he goes crazy, and I dont mean crazy like banging into the walls, raging with grief, I mean crazy like you dont know, nobody knows, because they dont know how to show it in the movies yet, I mean crazy like staring-into-space-crazy, zombie-crazy, desperate-crazy, and who the fuck can he talk to about it, because who in the world would understand, certainly no straight man, maybe another faggot, except all he knows about boy-bar faggots is that he doesn't trust any of them either, he knows who they are because he's one of them too

and it's two-three months later, and the murderers still havent been caught, and he tells me all of this in the back patio of a sleazy boy-bar in West Hollywood because he has no other place to go, and of all the places to go, this is the worst, because it just puts him back where he was before, but he cant be what he was before, because this time, now, he knows what he doesnt have, and that's when the tears start running down his cheeks, all he had was three weeks, hardly enough time to make any memories at all, just a couple of fucks and a drive around the city, and all he can think of is that he's never going to see his lover again, the most precious person in his life, never again, and all the memories they're never going to have, all the pillow conversations, and why the hell should he keep on living if the best part of his life is over

but see, here's how I know that God is a malignant thug, a practical joker, an asshole—if he wouldnt listen to his own son's prayers on the cross, why the fuck do you think he's going to listen to anyone else's?—here's the joke, Jerry looks at me like I'm supposed to say the one thing, whatever it is, that makes a difference, except I dont know what the fuck it is, how the hell should I know how to save his life, because I cant even save my own, because I've got my goddamned draft notice in my back pocket and I have to report the day after Thanksgiving, and in three-four months, just in time for the rains, I'll be slogging through the goddamn Delta with all the other dead men walking, and I'm thinking what the fuck, maybe I should run for Canada instead, I can be there in a straight two day run, or maybe I should just tell them I like sucking cock and fucking ass, at least that's honest, except I'm not ready to be that honest yet, nobody is, except I also heard that they dont even care anymore, the draft boards, they just have to generate so many bodies a week, fill up the green uniforms, fill up the body bags, and this week it's me and next week it's you, it's all the same, and Jerry looks up at me and says, so okay, now you tell me—why shouldnt I kill myself?

I dunno, why shouldnt he? He's made a pretty damn good case, except forever is a long time, and I'm thinking if I were a sky-pilot, I'd know the right thing to say, except I'm not, and I dont, and besides, if I said the crap they say, we'd both know it's crap, so I say what's in my head, and I say, I am so fucking jealous of you I can't believe it, and his eyes go wide, and I just keep talking anyway, because man, you found it, even if it was only for three weeks, you had it, man—I never did, and you know something most of the rest of us can only wish for, and he looks at me, not getting it, and I dont know where the words are coming from, I just blurt it out—real love, man, you had it, someone really loved you, the rest of us we're standing around and pretending that we're not standing around and pretending, but you—man, you're lucky everybody else in here doesnt beat you to death out of sheer fucking jealousy, because what you had, you had the *real*, not the pretend, You. Had. *It.*

and maybe that was what he needed to hear, and maybe what he said was what I needed to hear—that it really was possible, because up until then, I didnt know it, maybe nobody did, Jerry was the first person I ever knew who found love, the first one who could actually say it, and while he's crying for what he's lost, I'm wishing I were him, I want what he had, even if it's only for three weeks or three days or three hours

and as I'm telling all this, as it's all pouring out of me in one dumb rush, I look across at the prettyboy and see only blankness in the eyes and I realize he doesnt know what I'm talking about, cant know, because he's never done it, never been there, never had that rush of endorphins, that wave of physical amazement that starts in the bottom of your dick and comes tidal-waving up your spine like some kind of astonishing hot tsunami and floods up inside of you, inside your heart, your whole chest, chokes up your throat, and floods your eyes with tears of wonder and joy, he's never known it, that's the fucking tragedy, he's never been there

and the question of sex with him, of fucking him, it's finally answered for me, because if there's no connection, then all it is, it's just fucking exercise, and I've had enough exercise for ten lifetimes—I dont want to wake up with an intimate stranger, someone who knows the taste of my sweat, but not the taste of me, just another zombie-fuck

but there was that moment, I know it happened, when he *kissed back* and something flickered in that moment and that's the moment I'm speaking to—who was that?—and how do I get back there, how does anyone

did he kill himself, prettyboy asks, it's the wrong question, I shake my head, to tell the truth I dont know, I never saw him again, maybe he did, maybe he didnt, maybe he just stumbled out into the night, just like everybody else, you crawl into your coffin and dont come back out until it's time to feed again

I stand, stretch, listen to the bones tap-dancing against each other, stretch again, denying entropy one more time, start picking up blankets and water bottles, is that it, he asks, and I turn and look at him, what did you want, and he doesnt answer, doesnt have an answer, and maybe that's the greater tragedy, worse than knowing what you want and never having it is never knowing, never being able to speak it at all

headed back in silence, bumping over the hard-packed dirt, finally up and onto the asphalt again, sliding through the dark, the wind roaring like a jet engine, and still he doesnt talk, for some reason he doesnt look so pretty anymore, and I'm wondering why I bothered, why I wasted my time, and why I didnt fuck him anyway, except even an old boar like me has some pride

—*something happened*—

I never talk about the *blinks*, nobody understands, I tried a couple times, but I got the look, that look, the one that says I'm going to pretend I understand you, but only for as long as it takes to gnaw off my leg and escape, and no we cant ever be drinking buddies again because you're crazier than me, there's something scary-wrong in your head; so I learned the hard way, I just dont talk about the *blinks*, not to anyone, and when they happen, they happen, nobody around me notices, so maybe I am crazy, it's like somebody cutting into the movie, just a dazzling flash of bright, way too fast to see, you only realize it afterward, except afterward there's the burn-in still hanging in the air, the after-images of whatever seared into my existential retinas

never found anybody who knew about it, even with careful asking, none of the gurus, nor the medicine men, the shamans, not the dopers and dealers neither, asked a few doctors and corpsmen if they'd ever heard of anything like it, but they just looked at me funny, so I dropt the subject

only once, the crazy dyke, late one night on the road, somewhere between nowhere and nothing, we finally pull over and fall out onto our blankets, eventually end up on our backs, first her, then me, then both of us, staring up at the stars—*something happens*—and I ask her, did you feel that, and she asks, feel what, and I try to explain, and she says, you got *pinged*, and I say, pinged, what's that, and she says, it's when somebody is checking you out, seeing if you're there; like submarines in the dark, I ask, no she says, it's like computers on a network, I *ping* you and you *pong* back, except you aint ponging, but someone's definitely pinging

and that's as far as that conversation goes, but it sticks, enough so that whenever—*something happens*—I'm listening to hear who it is, or *what*, aliens or angels or Ida Noh, the mystery whore of Saigon, how'd you get the clap, soldier, Ida Noh, sir—I'm listening, listening like the antenna at Arecibo

except I'm always listening *after*, never during, never before, it's like lightning, you only know you've been struck by it when you pick yourself up off the ground afterward, like Jerry and his redhead, and I figure that maybe I'm the wrong kind of receiver, or maybe I'm not getting the whole signal, or maybe I'm in the fringe area, Ida Noh again, and the only part of any of it that I can be sure of is that it never happens when I'm alone, it only happens when I'm with someone and only when the moment is intense, very intense, too intense, almost overload, that's when it happens, when the meter is pinned

other people, they talk about those moments when everything happens at once, when the car starts to skid, when it goes skidding/swerving/screeching/sideways, that's the moment when time stops for them, for me that's the moment when time disappears, and I come out the other side still ringing all over, reconnecting to myself, I know I'm missing something here, I used to think that if I could find someone else, anyone who experienced the same thing, then maybe we could, Ida Noh, connect, and if it happened to us together, at the same time, maybe we could get a clearer signal, except when I talk about the blinks, the pings, I get the stare, the what-are-you-talking-about look, so that's not an option

except yeah, at the back of my mind, I'm still always thinking, maybe this one, maybe this time, maybe finally I'll find out who's calling, who's pinging, and sometimes I'll go days/weeks/months without a ping and I'll miss it for a while and then I'll get used to the silence and then I'll even forget about the pings for a while, until it starts again, and once, lying awake in some strange bed in the middle of some strange night, I had this thought that maybe I'm only one piece of the circuit, like a transistor or a capacitor or one of those other bits of electric magic, and maybe what I need isnt another piece like me, but some other piece totally unlike me, maybe I'm just an antenna, maybe I need a modulator or a resonator or maybe just a tuning knob, maybe there's a whole bunch of pieces missing, and maybe I'm not anything at all, just a chimpanzee hammering on a rock and striking the occasional spark

that's the other thought, that whatever it is, maybe it's something I cant know, maybe none of us can, because we're not there yet, we can string some wires and make electricity run around in circles and sparkle some lights, but we still cant do that next thing, whatever it is, that next thing that comes after super-sharp televisions and super-fast computers, that thing that we still havent thought of, whatever it will be, and by comparison with that, we're still just apes with bones and flints, and that's the thing I think about, listening to the stars, listening for others, maybe we're listening with the wrong ears, and we cant really hear whoever is pinging, maybe only a few of us can hear occasional bits and pieces of the pings and the rest of us cant hear anything at all because we're just not there yet, we're still in bed with Ida Noh in the hot damp nights of Saigon

and oh shit, Saigon, and Perry, late one night, we play cut-for-low and loser takes the point next day on patrol, and it's Perry who catches it in the belly, not me, and it's Jerry all over again, only this time it's me with the guilt, with the story, it's my fault he died, I only lose a leg, but Perry spills his guts, and ever since then I've been spilling mine, only I never get to die, Perry was the lucky one, he got out quick

and I get it, I get it *again*, we're all dragging dead bodies around, offering each other a sniff of the corpse, the past is this heavy ruck that sits on our backs, growing heavier every year, we just keep adding more and more shit to the load, and eventually history is inescapable, the shitbird guru on my shoulder yabbers into my ear, the past defines not just the present, but the future as well, there's no escape, is there, this is it, and that's why I didnt fuck the prettyboy, because there's no place in my past for that future

finally bring him back to where we started, the big empty parking lot below the dorm, pull to a stop, we look at each other, all the stuff still unsaid, the real stuff that nobody ever says, and just before the seeya—*something happens*—and the van starts shaking, hard, like something slamming against it from the side, again and again, and then the lights of the world come on, dazzling, finger-stabbing, searching, finally pinning us in the van, and there's a great whooshing noise and screaming too, all the voices in the world, prettyboy grabs my hand and

—*it happens*—

He's turned pretty again. Pretty frightened. Everything slows down, stops. The eye of the timestorm. Even while the banging continues around us.

—*connection*—

all the flickers, all the blinks, everything, time and space collapses into one moment, and this time I'm in the moment, caught, a dragonfly in amber, gossamer wings transparent in the heavenly backlight, and in the same instant, everything simultaneous

—*I get it*—

There's Jerry and Perry and Mary the bulldyke and even prettyboy, and all the rest of us, everyone who connected, who flickered in and out, all of us woven like ganglia into the great neural web of sentience recognizing itself. That's who's been pinging—not aliens or angels or anything else—*it's us*. All of us together. That's the connection. Our own humanity is calling. It's the next step. It isnt a secret, it never was, except all of us together, we never knew, or we keep forgetting, or we do it on purpose, but now this time—*some of us* can actually see it happening—

—*the fireflower blossoms*—

A hot rush, a tidal wave, tsunami of exuberance, rising up through me, I can see to the end of the universe and back, all of us, connecting, lighting up, answering the pings, awakening to ourselves, blinking alive, confused, excited, wondrous, not everyone yet, but all of us who've heard the wake-up call, and in that moment, we're together, and we *know*, and it's *now*, and there's *no* going back *o*

and then as the van topples and crashes sideways onto the street, the sirens come whooping in, the red and blue lights flickering, flashing turning—the moment is broken, and I'm scrambling up over prettyboy to unlatch his door, push it open, start to climb out, when the first bottle comes crashing against it, and a baseball bat whangs into the windshield, fracturing it, but not shattering, so that isnt the way, I fumble sideways, crawling, kick the back doors open with my good leg and come out with the aluminum bat in one hand, ready to bang the hell out of last night's bashers, who've been waiting for me all night long with their fraternity brothers and a keg of beer, the whole gang of chimpanzees, believing that I've kidnapped one of their own, they're going to rescue him from the bearded monster

except the cops are already here, beanbag rifles at the ready, lights flashing, spotlights dazzling me, the chopper above pins me in a funnel of light, so I drop the bat and raise my hands and lie down slowly on the asphalt, because already I know how this will play out

I clean up real good, no piercings, no tats, shave and a haircut, put on a clean suit, yes, I have one, but leave the prosthesis at home, fold up the pants leg, and limp into court on a crutch, tell the judge the bashers broke it when they pushed my van over, a seven-thousand dollar peg, one battered old vet with no leg to stand on, opposite a bunch of frats with attitude, there's no question what will happen here, six of them get expelled, the chapter gets its charter pulled, and the town has something to argue about until Christmas break, I'll be gone by then anyway, autumn rolls away and with it me, no more dry desert nights for this old bear, maybe I'll drift south to the tip of Baja and lie naked in the unforgiving sun like a great baking whale, or maybe north into Canada again, or Alaska, where I'll snuggle deep in a tiny cabin, hibernating like a grumpy old wolverine, listening to the snow piling up against the windows, anywhere away from here, away from the madness and the noise, the squalor of human ignorance, all the vicious scrabbling little souls that still dont get *it*, might never get it, will never get it because all the clamor they make drowns out all the other possibilities, they're screaming so loud about what they want they cant hear that the answer is already yes

when your watch says thirteen o'clock, what time is it—it's time to get a new watch, the pieces of this one are scattered all over the floor—it's time to build a new one

—*something is happening, it's still happening*—

All the parts of me/us, we're scattered, yes, but we're pinged and connected and we can sense/feel/hear each other. We're something new. A little two year-old girl, standing up in her crib, crying with a wet diaper, but that's not why she's crying, she's not yet ready for the burden of knowledge. A black grandmother, suddenly awake in the night, wondering why she's thinking of her dead grandson all of a sudden, he died in Nam, but she can hear him somewhere—with all time and space collapsed, he's right here now. A skinny teenage boy, secretly trying on his sister's panties, abruptly confused and wondering why he can suddenly see into the future, scared of what he's becoming and intrigued as well. The cop holding the beanbag rifle, blinking, scanning the whole situation through a dozen different pairs of eyes, instead of just his own little piece; he sees through the perp's eyes, feels the fear and terror. A young woman, screaming, channeling a joyous excruciating birth; the baby screams with her, mother and child locked together in mutual awareness. The desperate man, standing on the bridge, the choice in his eyes, suddenly alive beyond his own horizons, stepping back to reconsider. The student, looking up from his book—there's a world out there, a vast unknowable, incomprehensible world; the book, the words, the crawling insect marks upon the page, the barest shadow of meaning, there is no explanation, it's just what's happening. *Is still happening. Now.*

And all the others too, touched with wonder—frightened, intrigued, cautious, but stepping into the moment, it'll take a while. We'll get there. This thing, whatever it is we are, all of us still sorting it out, we're a long way from threshold and even farther from critical mass, we're alone, but not alone, never alone, never again.

And Michael, I glance over at him, dazed and confused, but waking up into himself now. I wonder how many more we can wake up.

AUTHOR'S AFTERWORD:
Anything I might add here would be redundant. It's all in the story.

The New England
Science Fiction Association (NESFA)
and NESFA Press

Recent books from NESFA Press:

Details on these and many more books are online at: www.nesfa.org/press/
Books may be ordered online or by writing to:

NESFA Press
PO Box 809
Framingham, MA 01701

We accept checks (in US$), Visa, or MasterCard. Add $5 postage and handling for one book, $10 for two or more. ($6/$12 for locations outside the U.S.) Please allow 3–4 weeks for delivery. (Overseas, allow 2 months or more.)

The New England Science Fiction Association:

NESFA is an all-volunteer, non-profit organization of science fiction and fantasy fans. Besides publishing, our activities include running Boskone (New England's oldest SF convention) in February each year, producing a semimonthly newsletter, holding discussion groups on topics related to the field, and hosting a variety of social events. If you are interested in learning more about us, we'd like to hear from you. We can be contacted at info@nesfa.org or at the address above. Visit our web site at www.nesfa.org.

Acknowledgments

I thank David Gerrold for the excellent material he provided, including not only previously published works, but also new pieces, updated pieces, and introductions/afterwords for every entry; Gary Lippincott for his luminous dust jacket painting; Alice Lewis for her dust jacket design and her patience in collecting the material for it; Geri Sullivan and Alice Lewis for their advice on book design and for reviewing my ultimate choices; Mark Olson for his help in book production; and Tony Lewis for his support during the editing process. Thanks also go to our stalwart band of proofreaders: Seth Breidbart, Lis Carey, Gay Ellen Dennett, Pam Fremon, David Gerrold, David G. Grubbs, Lisa Hertel, Rick Katze, Paula Lieberman, Gary McGath, Mark Olson, Peter Olson, Larry Pfeffer, Sharon Sbarsky, Geri Sullivan, and Tim Szczesuil.

David G. Grubbs
November, 2006

Technical Notes

All material was submitted electronically and was set in Adobe Garamond (except for the character names and narrative paragraphs in "Blood and Fire" that are in Myriad Pro) using Adobe InDesign2. The book was printed and bound by Sheridan Books of Ann Arbor, Michigan, on acid-free paper.